TriQuarterly

TriQuarterly is

an international

journal of

writing, art and

cultural inquiry

published at

Northwestern

University

TriQuarterly

issue 110|111 *fall 2001*

Editor
Susan Firestone Hahn

Associate Editor
Ian Morris

Assistant Editor
Francine Arenson

Editorial Assistants
Meghan Gordon
Cara Moultrup

Operations Coordinator
Kirstie Felland

Production Manager
Bruce Frausto

Production Editor/Design
Karen Keeley

Cover Design
Gini Kondziolka

Triquarterly Fellow
Eric LeMay

Contributing Editors
John Barth
Rita Dove
Stuart Dybek
Richard Ford
Sandra M. Gilbert
Robert Hass
Edward Hirsch
Li-Young Lee
Lorrie Moore
Alicia Ostriker
Carl Phillips
Robert Pinsky
Susan Stewart
Mark Strand
Alan Williamson

TriQuarterly congratulates and thanks the following authors and editors for honors and awards won for issue 107/108:

John Barth for his story "The Rest of Your Life," which appears in *New Stories from the South 2001*, edited by Shannon Ravenel.

Dan Chaon for his story "Seven Types of Ambiguity," which appears in the *Pushcart Prize, XXVI* anthology, edited by Bill Henderson.

Ha Jin for his story "After Cowboy Chicken Came to Town," which appears in *Best American Short Stories 2001*, edited by Katrina Kenison, guest editor Barbara Kingsolver.

Fred Leebron for his story "That Winter," which appears in the *O. Henry Prize Stories 2001*, edited by Larry Dark.

Susan Stewart for her poem "Apple," which appears in *Best American Poetry 2001*, edited by David Lehman, guest editor Robert Hass.

CONTENTS

Timothy Liu

Reading the Book of Odes Late at Night, I Turn Out the Light and Go On Reading

Though the ceiling looks down on you, be
free from shame in the confines of your own
home. It's not about what is seen but what is
known in the mind. Though the white fish die
and lie at bottom, they still are clearly seen.

Stuart Dybek

Blue Boy

1

CHESTER POSKOZIM'S YOUNGER BROTHER RALPHIE WAS BORN A blue baby, and though not expected to survive, Ralphie miraculously grew into a blue boy. The blue was plainly visible beneath his bluegreen eyes, smudges darker than shadows, as if he'd been in a fist fight or gotten into his mother's mascara. Even in summer, his lips looked cold. The first time I saw him, before I knew about his illness, I thought that he must have been sucking on a ballpoint pen. His fingers were smeared with the same blue ink.

On Sundays, the blueness seemed all the more prominent for the white shirt he wore to church. You could imagine that his body was covered with bruises, as if he was in far worse shape than Leon Szabo or Milton Piñero whose drunken fathers regularly beat them. Unlike Szabo, who'd become vicious, a cat torturer, or Milton, who hung his head to avoid meeting your eyes and hardly ever spoke in order to hide his stammer, Ralphie seemed delighted to be alive. His smile, blue against his white teeth, made you grin back even if you hardly knew him and say, "Hey, how's it going?"

"Going good," Ralphie would nod, giving the thumbs up.

When he made it to his eighth birthday, it was a big deal in our neighborhood, Little Village; it meant he'd get his wish, which was to make it to his First Holy Communion later that year, and whether Ralphie ever realized it or not, a lot of people celebrated with him. At corner taverns, like Juanita's and the Fox Head, men still wearing their factory steel toes hoisted boilermakers to the Blue Boy. At St. Roman church, women said an extra rosary or lit a vigil candle and prayed in English or Polish or Spanish to St. Jude, Patron of Impossible Causes.

And why not hope for the miracle to continue? In a way, Ralphie was what our parish had instead of a plaster statue of the Madonna that wept real tears or a crucified Christ who dripped blood on Good Friday.

For Ralphie's birthday, I stopped by Pedro's, the little candy store where we gathered on our way home from school whenever any of us had any money, and spent my allowance on a *Felix the Cat* comic, which I recalled had been my favorite comic book when I was eight, and gave it to his brother, Chester, to pass along.

Chester and I were in the same grade at St. Roman's. We'd never really hung out together, though. He was a quiet guy, dressed as if his mother still picked out his clothes. He didn't go in much for sports and wasn't a brain either, just an average student who behaved himself and got his school work done. If it wasn't for his brother, the Blue Boy, no one would have paid Chester much attention, and probably I wouldn't be remembering him now.

Looking back, I think Chester not only understood, but accepted that his normal life would always seem inconsequential beside his little brother's death sentence. He loved Ralphie and never tried to hide it. When Ralphie would have to enter the hospital, Chester would always ask our class to pray for his brother, and we'd stop whatever we were doing to kneel beside our desks and pray with a genuine, uncharacteristic earnestness. They were the same blood type, and sometimes Ralphie received Chester's blood. Chester would be absent on those mornings and return to school in the afternoon with a Band-Aid over a vein and a pint carton of orange juice, with permission to sip it at his desk.

Outside the classroom, the two of them were inseparable. I'd see them heading home from Sunday mass, talking softly as if sharing secrets, laughing at some private joke. Once, passing by their house on 22nd Place, a side street whose special drowsy light came from having more than its share of trees, I noticed them sitting together on the front steps: Ralphie, leaning against his brother's knees, his eyes closed, listening with what looked like rapture while Chester read aloud from a comic book. That was the reason I chose a comic as a gift instead of getting him something like bubble gum baseball cards. His bruised, shivery looking lips made me wonder if Ralphie was even allowed to chew gum.

2

The open affection between Chester and Ralphie wasn't typical of the rough and tumble relationship between brothers in the neighborhood. Not that guys didn't look out for their brothers, but there was often trouble between brothers, too. Across the street in the Projects, Junior Gomez had put out the eye of his brother Nestor, on Nestor's birthday, playing gunfight at OK Corral with Nestor's birthday present, a Daisy Red Ryder BB gun. In the apartment house just next door to ours, Terry Vandel's baby brother, JoJo, wrapped in a blanket, fell from the second story window to the pavement. Terry was supposed to have been baby-sitting for JoJo while their mother was at work. Mrs. Hobel, walking below, looked up to see the falling child. For weeks afterwards, while JoJo was in the hospital with a fractured skull, Mrs. Hobel would break into tears repeating to anyone who would listen, "I could have caught him but I thought the other boy was throwing down a sack of garbage."

As in the Bible, having a brother could be hazardous to your health.

For awhile, the mention of twins or jealously or even pizza, would trigger a recounting of how, just across Western Avenue, in St. Michael parish, the Folloni twins, Gino and Dino—identically handsome, people said, as matinee idols—dueled one afternoon over a girl. It was fungo bat against weed sickle, until Gino went down and never got up. Dino, his face permanently rearranged, was still in jail. Their father owned Stromboli's, a pizza parlor that was a mob hangout. Every time I'd ride my bike past the closed pizzeria on Oakley, and then past the sunken front yard where they'd fought, it would seem as if the street, the sidewalk, the light itself, had turned the maroon of an old blood stain. I'd wonder how anyone knew for sure which twin had killed the other, if maybe it was really Dino who was dead and Gino doing time, ashamed to admit he was the one still alive. If they ever let him out, he'd go to visit his own grave to beg for forgiveness. Shadows the shade of mourning draped the brick buildings along that street, and finally I avoided riding there altogether.

Out on the streets, I kept an eye out for my brother Mick, but at home there was constant kidding and practical jokes played on one another, and sometimes that would escalate into fights. I was older and responsible for things getting out of control.

Once, on an impulse, while riding my bike with my brother perched dangerously on the handlebars the way friends rode—in fact, we called the handlebars the buddy seat—I hit the brakes without warning, launching Mick into midair. One second he was cruising and the next he was on the pavement. It would have been a comical bit of slapstick if he'd landed in whipped cream or even mud, instead of on concrete. I wasn't laughing. I was horrified when I saw the way he hit—an impact like that would have killed Ralphie. Mick got up stunned, bloody, crying.

"Jeez, you okay?" I asked. "Sorry, it was an accident."

"You did that on purpose, you sonofabitch!" He was crying as much with outrage at my betrayal of the trust implicit in riding on the buddy seat, as with pain.

I denied the accusation so strongly that I almost convinced myself what happened was an accident. But it was my fault, even though I hadn't meant to hurt him. I'd done it out of the same wildness that made for an alliance between us—a bond that turned life comic, at the expense of anything gentle. An impulsiveness that permitted for a stupid, callous curiosity, the same dangerous lack of sense that had made me ride one day down Luther, a sunless side-street that only ran a block, and, peddling at full speed, attempt to jump off my J.C. Higgins bike and back on in a single bounce.

It was a daredevil stunt I'd seen in Westerns when, to avoid gunfire, the cowboy hero, at full gallop, grabs the saddle horn, swings from the stirrups, and in a fluid movement hits the ground boots first and immediately bounds back into the saddle. As soon as I touched one foot to the street the spinning pedal slammed into the back of my leg and I tumbled and skidded for what seemed half a block while the bike turned cartwheels over my body. Skin burned off my knees and palms. I'd purposely picked a street that was deserted, on which to practice. But a lady who could barely speak English poked her head out of a third floor window and yelled, "Kid, you ho-kay?" She'd just witnessed what must have looked like some maniac trying to kill himself. I waved to her, smiled, and forced myself up. Amazingly, nothing was broken, not even my teeth although I had a knot on my jaw from where the handlebars clipped me with an uppercut. I collected my twisted bike from where it had embedded itself under a parked car. Had it been a horse, as I'd been pretending, I'd have had to shoot it. If someone had done to me what I'd just done to myself, I would have got the bastard back one way or another. My brother let me off easy.

Although years later, when he was living in New York, studying acting with Brando's famous teacher, Stella Adler, Mick and I spent an evening together, drinking and watching a video of *On the Waterfront*. During the famous "I could have been a contender scene," in which Brando complains about his "one way ticket to Palookaville" and tells his older brother, "It was you, Charley. You was my brother. You should of looked out for me," Mick turned to me, nodded and smiled knowingly about what Brando had endured.

3

Chester was anything but a tough, yet despite his quiet way, you got the impression he'd lay his life on the line if anyone messed with Ralphie. You could see it in how he'd step out into a busy street, checking both directions for traffic before signaling Ralphie to cross. Or how, whenever a gang of guys playing keep-away with somebody's hat, or maybe having a rock fight, barreled down the sidewalk, Chester would instinctively step between them and Ralphie, shielding him.

That willingness to take a blow was an accepted measure of what the gangbangers called *amor*—a word usually accompanied by a thump on the chest to signify the feeling of connection from the heart—although in matters of *amor* as in everything else, the willingness to *give* a blow was preferred. There were guys in the neighborhood who'd lay their lives on the line over an argument about bumming a smoke; guys capable of killing someone over a parking space or whose turn it was to buy the next round. There was each gang's pursuit of Manifest Destiny: battles merciless and mindless as trench warfare over a block of turf. There was the casual way that mob goons across Western Avenue maimed and killed, a meanness both reflexive and studied—just so people didn't forget that in business, at least in capitalism on the street, brutality was still the lowest common denominator.

Not that there weren't ample illustrations of that principle at the edge of the daily round of life where bag ladies lived off alleys and the homeless, sleeping in junked cars, were found frozen to death in winter. Laid-off workmen became wife-beaters in their new found spare time; welfare mothers in the Projects turned tricks to supplement the family budget; and it seemed that almost every day someone lost teeth at one or another of the corner bars.

The shout would go up, "Fight!" and kids would flock in anticipation, especially if a couple of alkies were whaling at one another, because invariably loose change would fly from their pockets. The scramble for nickels and dimes would spawn secondary fights among ourselves. And if we weren't quick enough we'd be scattered by Sharky, a guy who'd lost his legs in Korea, or riding the rails to Alaska, or to sharks off Vera Cruz, depending on which of his stories you wanted to believe. He was a little nuts and people wondered if he remembered anymore himself where exactly his legs had been misplaced.

Sharky mopped up late at Juanita's bar, but his main source of income was scavenging. He'd rumble along alleys and curbs on a homemade contraption like a wide skateboard that he propelled with wooden blocks strapped over gloved hands, turning his hands into hooves. Late on summer nights, you could hear him clopping down the middle of deserted streets like a runaway stallion. Get in his way, and he'd threaten to crack your kneecap with one of those wooden hooves.

It wasn't an idle threat, he'd been in several brawls. They usually started with a question: "What the fuck you looking at, ostrich-ass?"

Anyone with legs was an ostrich to Sharky.

"Huh?" came the usual response.

But Sharky wouldn't let it go at that. "Admit it, you rude mother-fuck, you were staring at my bald spot weren't you?"

Sharky did have a bald spot. He'd roll slowly toward the con-fused ostrich who'd begin edging backwards as Sharky's pace increased.

"You never seen a bald spot on wheels before? That it? I'm very fucken sensitive about my bald spot. Or is it something else about me that attracted your attention? Like, maybe, that I'm at a con-venient height for giving head. You the kind of perv that wants a baldy bean doing wheelies while sucking your dick?"

By now, Sharky had gained momentum, and was aimed for a col-lision if the ostrich didn't take off running, which he usually did, with Sharky galloping after him, raging, "Run you perverted, chickenshit biped!"

Sharky obviously enjoyed the confrontations. What nobody sus-pected was that such spectacles were only a substitute for what he really craved: a parade.

There was no shortage of parades in Little Village. Most ethnic groups had one, and that must have figured into Sharky's thinking. St. Patrick's brought out the politicians, and St. Joseph's was also known locally as St. Polack Day since people wore red, the back-ground color for the white eagle on the Polish Flag. I never under-stood what was particularly Polish about St. Joseph, but I bought a pair of fluorescent red socks especially for the occasion.

The Mexicans had two big holidays: El Grito, a carnival at the end of summer, when, as part of the festivities, a wrestling ring was erected in the middle of 19th Street. There'd be pony rides, and Mick and I would try to time it so as to be in the saddle when the El roared overhead because the ponies would rear.

The Feast of Our Lady of Guadaloupe, the National Patron of Mexico, was more solemn. Each December twelfth, no matter the weather, a procession wound through the streets led by a plaster likeness of the Virgin who'd appeared, not to the Spanish conquerors, but to a poor Indian, Juan Diego. She'd imprinted her *mestiza* image on his cloak—a miracle still there for all to see at the basilica in Mexico City. She'd told Juan Diego to gather flowers for her in a place only cactus grew, but he did her biding and found a profusion of Castilian roses, and so all through Little Village people carried roses, and sang hymns in Spanish to the Virgin whose delicate sandal had crushed the head of Quetzalcoatl, the snake god ravenous for human sacrifice. Even the alderman and precinct captains marched holding roses. And each year there was the fantastic rumor that the great Tito Guizar, the Mexican movie star of *Rancho Grande*, a singing cowboy like Roy Rogers—would arrive on a palomino to lead the procession through the barrio. His movies played at the Milo theater on Blue Island where they showed films in Spanish. I'd study the posters I couldn't read and wonder if his rearing horse was a celebrity in Mexico, the way that Roy Roger's horse, Trigger, was a star in America.

Then, one year, Tito Guizar actually showed. Down Washtenaw, heading for 22nd, he came riding right behind the Virgin, not on a palomino, but on a prancing white horse whose mane blew in the feathery twirl of the early snowfall. The horse left pats of golden manure steaming in the street, while Tito Guizar, dressed in black leather chaps studded with silver, his guitar strapped across his back like a rifle, waved his sombrero, blessing the shivering crowd that lined the sidewalks to see him.

As the procession approached St. Roman's church, a motorcycle gunned to life spooking the white horse, and, while Tito Guizar whoaed at the reins, a Harley rumbled out of the alley beside the rectory. It was pulling Sharky, who was attached to the rear fender by a clothesline like a coachman commanding the reins of a carriage. The Harley was driven by Cyril Bombrowski, once known as Bombs. He'd been a motorcycle maniac until, doing seventy down an alley, he'd collided with a garbage truck. He had a metal plate in his head and didn't ride much anymore as, since the wipeout, he was prone to seizures. Now, people called him Spaz, and when he rode down the street, it was a tradition that whoever saw him first would yell a Paul Revere-like warning: "Spaz Attack!"

No one yelled anything this time. Behind Spaz and Sharky, a procession of the disabled from the parish emerged from the alley. A couple of WWII vets, mainstays from the bar at the VFW Club, one with a prosthetic hook and the other with no discernable wound other than the alcoholic staggers; and Trib, the blind newspaper vendor; and a guy who delivered pulp circulars, known only as—what else?—the Gimp, pushing his wheelchair for support; and Howdy, who'd been named after Howdy Doody because his palsy caused him to move like a marionette with tangled strings.

It was a parade of at most a dozen, but it seemed larger—enough of a showing so that onlookers could imagine the battalions of wounded soldiers who weren't there, and the victims of accidents, industrial and otherwise, the survivors of polio and strokes, all the exiles who avoided the streets, who avoided the baptism of being street-named after their afflictions, recluses who kept their suffering behind doors, women like Maria Savoy who'd been lighting a water heater when it exploded or Agnes Lutensky who remained cloistered years after her brother had blown off half her face with a shotgun during an argument over a will.

With their canes, crutches, and wheelchair it looked more like a pilgrimage to Lourdes than a parade. They'd been assembled by Sharky and now marched, although that's hardly an accurate description for their gait, beneath the banner of a White Sox pennant clamped in a mop stick that the Gimp kept mounted on his beat-up wheel chair. The Gimp never sat in his chair, but rather used it like a cart, piling it with bags of deposit bottles and other commodities he collected while delivering the circulars no one read. Today, the chair was empty of junk.

Their flag bore no symbol of allegiance, no slogan of their cause other than *Go Sox*, but what must have fueled Sharky's outrage all along became suddenly obvious: they were at once the most visible and invisible of minorities. Instead of bit players out of the Gospels, fodder for miracles, the Halt and the Lame were in for the long haul—which required surviving day to day.

As they passed the church, Sharky raised a wooden hoof, not in blessing or salute—more as if scoring the winning run—and on cue those parading behind him raised their fists. At that moment, Ralphie, wearing a cap and bundled in a checked scarf, stepped out of the crowd lining the curb, catching everyone by surprise, even Chester who couldn't do anything more than exclaim, "Hey, where you going?"

By then Ralphie had put on a burst of speed—the first time I'd ever seen him run—and caught up to the Gimp, climbed up on the wheel chair, and raised his fist, too.

4

A few weeks later, during Christmas break, Ralphie died on Gwiazdka. The word means Little Star in Polish and it's what Christmas Eve was sometimes called in the parish. At midnight mass on Christmas Eve, kids too young to be altar boys would file up the aisle to the manger carrying gold-painted stars on sticks. Had he been alive, Ralphie would have been among them. He was buried in the navy blue suit already purchased for the First Holy Communion he would have made that spring.

That was one of the observations invariably repeated at the wake, and afterwards, at the Friday night bingo games in the church basement, and at bakeries and butcher shops and pizzerias and taquerias and beauty parlors and barber shops and corner bars: "Poor little guy didn't make it to his Holy Communion," someone would say.

And someone would likely answer, "They should of made an exception and let him make it early."

"Nah, he didn't want to be no exception. That's how he was. He wanted to make it with his class."

"Yeah, he was a tough little hombre, never wanted special treatment, never complained."

"You know it. Always thumbs up with him."

"God should of let him make it."

"Hey! You start with that kind of talk and there's no stopping."

"Yeah, but just for this once, if I was God, that kid walks up there for his First Communion. Then, if it's his time, so be it."

"If you was God we'd all still be waiting for the Second Day of Creation while you slept off your hangover from the Big KA-BOOM. God knew he didn't want to be no exception. He made him that way."

"Yeah, he made him with blue fucking skin, too."

"Hey, maybe that was God's gift to us. Somebody too sweet for the long term in this world. Somebody to be an example—'A Little Child Shall Lead Them,' like Father Fernando said at the service."

"Talk about hungover, that priest was still shitfaced. The night before he was pounding tequila at Juanita's till they 86'd us out into the goddamn blizzard—snow piled so fucking deep we couldn't hardly get out the door. Me and Paulie have to help him back to the church, then Paulie falls in a snowbank and while I'm digging Paulie out, Father Kumbaya decides to take a leak. I look up and there's our new padre waving his peter in the middle of 26th."

"So, big deal, he's a human being. It was a beautiful service, he did a good job. I thought that older brother was a little weird though, guarding the casket like a Rottweiler. Somebody shoulda told him it was all right to cry. What's his name, anyway?"

"I don't remember."

"That little Ralphie was a saint. Don't be surprised if someday they don't canonize him."

"I think there's gotta be like miracles for that."

"Yo, that kid was a living miracle. Maybe that's it—why God put him here—what Little Village will be famous for: the Blue Boy. Mark my words, people will come from all over like they do to places in the Old Country . . . Our Lady of Fatima, the Little Infant of Prague, you know?"

"Yeah, somebody always figures out how to make a buck off it."

5

A year later there were yet to be miracles, at least none I'd heard about. But the Blue Boy wasn't forgotten. As we approached another Christmas vacation, and the first anniversary of Ralphie's death, Sister Lucidia, our 8th grade teacher, assigned a composition on the meaning of Christmas, dedicated to Ralphie's memory. Chester was in our 8th grade class and, at the mention of Ralphie, Sister Lucidia smiled gently in his direction, but he just stared at his hands. He'd been a loner since his brother's death, and all but mute in school. We'd heard the rumor that Chester periodically showed up, only to be repeatedly turned away, at the blood bank on Kedzie where the alkies went to trade their blood for wine money.

"Do your best," Sister Lucidia instructed our class, "This will be the last Christmas composition you will ever write."

The Christmas composition was an annual assignment at St. Roman, required from each class above third grade. The pieces judged best received prizes, and the top prize winner was read aloud at the Christmas pageant. Not that there really was any competition for top prize: it was reserved for Camille Estrada. She was the best writer in the school. Probably, before Camille, the concept of such a thing as a best writer didn't even exist at St. Roman. Camille was a prodigy. By 5th Grade she'd already written several novels in her graceful A+ cursive, and bound them in thread-stitched covers cut from the stays of laundered shirts. They were illustrated—she was a gifted artist, as well. And they were filed, complete with check-out cards, in the shelves beside *Black Beauty, Call of the Wild,* and the other real books in the school library.

Camille's early work, mostly about animals, had titles like *The Squirrel of Douglas Park* and *The Stallion and the Butterfly.* I never actually checked them out, but I read them on the sly one week when I was exiled to the library for detention. Camille loved horses, and they often suffered terribly in her stories. They were the subject of many of her illustrations: huge, muscular creatures with flared nostrils, often rearing, some winged, some unicorns.

By 6th grade she'd taught herself to type and then the writing really poured from her. Camille became founder, publisher, editor, and chief reporter on our first school newspaper, *Change the World*, as well as translator for an occasional Spanish edition. She represented St. Roman in the Archdiocese of Chicago Essay Contest, writing on why a Catholic Code of Censorship was needed for pop songs and movies like the Bridget Bardot film *And God Created Woman*. It was a foreign film that would never have played in our neighborhood anyway. Still, although none of us had ever seen Bardot on screen, the B.B. of her initials—which also conveniently stood for Big Boobs—mysteriously appeared as a cheer scribbled on the school walls: *BB zizboombah!* When Camille's censorship essay won, she got a mention in the Metro section of the *Tribune*.

At the annual school talent show, where "Lady of Spain" pumped from accordions, and virtuosos pounded "Heart and Soul" on the out of tune upright to the clatter of tap dancers, Camille would read an original poem written for the occasion. She wasn't a dramatic reader, but there was something inherently dramatic about her standing before the boomy mike, without a costume or an instrument to hide behind, her eyes glued to the page from which she read in a quiet, clear voice.

I liked it when she read aloud because I could watch her without seeming to stare. I'd always been fascinated by the way her myopic eyes illuminated her thin face. Her long lashes drew attention like those on a doll. Beneath them, her liquid, dark eyes gazed out unblinking, serious, enormous. Her voice was colored by a faint Spanish accent. She spoke in a formal way that sounded as if she was cautiously considering each word in English, a language in which she was so fluent on the page. Her reserve made her seem older, though not physically older like some of the boys who already had faint mustaches, guys like Brad Norky, who actually *was* older, having been held back. Once, at a talent show, I overheard two elderly women talking about the way Camille had read her poem about the ecstasy of St. Teresa.

"She has an old soul," one of the women observed and the other said, "I know what you mean."

Even back then, in a way, I knew what she meant, too.

From 7th grade on Camille wore rouge that looked artificial against the caramel shade of her skin and made her appear feverish. She got glasses that year: ivory sparkle cat frames that matched the barrettes clamping back the thick black hair she'd previously worn in braids. She was no longer quite flat-chested, though the rose-colored bra outlined beneath the white blouse of her school uniform hardly seemed necessary. She could have used braces.

In 7th grade, a gang of us proudly calling ourselves The Fuckups would sneak off at lunch to our boy's club—the doorway of an abandoned dry cleaners where we'd smoke Luckies, spit, and discuss things like the rumor that some of the girls were washing their school blouses over and over to make the fabric thin in order to show off their underclothes. I made the mistake of mentioning that even Camille Estrada's bra was showing, and, as if dumbfounded, Norky asked, "No shit? Estrada has titties! You think she might have a hairy pussy, too?" Then, he burst into mocking laughter.

Even my best friend, Rafael, couldn't resist breaking up.

"Instead of BB's she got bb's," he laughed, "bb-*ittas* . . . hey, maybe she'll publish the news in her paper."

"Headline!" Norky shouted, "Stop the presses!" and with the chalk he carried to graffiti up our doorway, he printed in huge letters on the sidewalk: ESTRADA HAS bbs.

He chalked it on the graffitied tunnel wall of the viaduct on Rockwell, and along the bricks of the buildings we passed, and on the asphalt of the street where the little girls drew hopscotch courts alongside the school. It was one of those phrases that inexplicably catch on, and for the next couple of weeks it was everywhere—in the boys' bathroom, at the Washtenaw playground, on the concrete basketball court at the center of the row Projects: ESTRADA HAS bbs.

In class, when I'd sneak a glance at her, it seemed her rouged cheeks burned, but perhaps that was only a projection of my secret shame.

Near the end of 7th grade, my desk was moved out into the corridor where I was banished after topping one hundred demerits in conduct. Then, our teacher that year, Sister Mary Donatille—the only nun who insisted we say the Mary in her name—introduced Partners in Christ. It was an experimental program, borrowing, perhaps, from AA in that it teamed habitual bad boys with sponsors—good girls—so as to give the boys a taste of the rewards of behaving. I can't say what it was for the girls, torture probably; for the boys it was a subtle form of humiliation. Camille was assigned to be my Partner in Christ.

At St. Roman, two kinds of kids stayed after school: those in detention, and the teacher's pets who were invited to help the nuns clean the classrooms. Detention time was spent copying chapters from the New Testament, but, thanks to Sister Mary Donatille's experiment, instead of rewriting the Apocalypse, I got to clean the erasers with Camille. It was an honorary task, only pets were entrusted to take the erasers out behind the school and beat them clean against the wall. Although I'd been reassigned a seat beside Camille in class, we still hadn't spoken. We stood together, engulfed in chalk dust and an uncomfortable silence relieved only by the muffled thud of felt against brick. In blocky chalk impressions I pounded out F-U-

"I really like your vocabulary," Camille said.

"Real funny."

"No, I mean it," she said, "You have a neat imagination."

I looked at her, too puzzled to respond. I didn't know if she was putting me down or putting me on or applying some kind of condescending psychology, or if she was just spacey.

"That story you wrote for Christmas. About the ant. It was so cool. I wanted to publish it in the paper but it was too long."

She was referring to "The Enormous Gift," a story I'd written for the Christmas competition. I frequently missed getting my homework in, but I'd found myself writing the story with an excited concentration I didn't associate with school work. The assignment that particular year had been to write a story about a gift brought to the baby Jesus in his stable at Bethlehem. In my story, the gift was a crumb of bread that weighed a thousand times more than my narrator, an ant, but he hoisted it nonetheless and, after narrow escapes involving spiders, sparrows, the hooves of oxen, and soles of sandals, finally crept into the manger to offer his gift.

"After you read it I kept thinking about it and saw what you meant," Camille said. "How it was like a little miracle for the ant to bring the first bread to Jesus who'd later make the big miracles of the loaves and fishes, and turn bread and wine into his body and blood."

I'd never thought about any of that, to me it was just the adventure of an ant.

"The Enormous Gift" was chosen to be read aloud in class, but it didn't win the school competition. Camille won with "O Little Star of Centaurus," a story in which the Christmas star was revealed to be a space ship in the shape of a winged horse. I couldn't help but visualize it as the fiery red Pegasus trademark for Mobile gasoline. It had traveled from the constellation Centaurus where light years ago Christ had appeared to redeem an advanced but brutal race of hoofed aliens. The Centaurians, now converted to brotherhood and peace, had learned that Christ was traveling through the universe, redeeming world after world, and so in homage they followed him through time and space, to witness each reappearance. The gleam of their ship was the star that guided the Wise Men who, in each new world, came bringing gifts on each new night of Christ's infinitely repeated birth.

"Your story knocked my socks off," I said, not adding that ever since I'd heard her read it, I'd wondered if the Christ on Centaurus had hooves like the other Centaurians. Her story didn't say, but it posed problems for his crucifixion.

"Thanks," she said, "but I thought yours should have won."

"No way. They should make yours into a movie. How'd you make that up?"

"How'd you think of the ant?"

"I don't know. I like to read about bugs and stuff." I said, not mentioning how during the summers I'd sneak off down the railroad tracks to the Sanitary Canal where I hid a homemade net for collecting butterflies.

"I never purposely try to make things up," Camille said, sounding suddenly proper, the way she did when she spoke aloud in class. "It just happens. It's not about made-up anyway, it's about feeling."

She looked at me for agreement but the transformation in her voice put me on guard.

"It's about feeling, you know?" she repeated. "That's what's important," she insisted, as if I'd disagreed.

She went back to cleaning the erasers, clapping them together like cymbals, the poofs of chalky smoke surrounding her bronzed by the same rays that shafted through the clouds massed over the convent. She stared at the two chalk-dust letters I'd pounded on the bricks, and back at me, then beat in a blocky C.

"Want to collaborate?" she asked.

I stood there, confused again, refusing to admit to myself that she intimidated me, but feeling hopelessly immature beside her all the same.

"So, come on," she said and beat out the slanted upper bar of the missing K. I beat an impression of the straight staff. She added the lower slanted bar. Not much chalk remained on the erasers and they left only the faded ghost of the word. I became conscious that my heart was beating.

She read our collaboration aloud as if it were composed of air flowing across her overbite, as if a whisper recreated its faintness on the bricks.

"Don't look so surprised. You don't know what I think," she said, then added, "I have stories I don't show anyone."

"Like what?"

"I don't think someone should be blamed for stories any more than they should have to confess their dreams. Boys don't have to confess their dreams. Do you?"

It was something I'd never thought about, and I wasn't sure what she was getting at. If she was referring to wet dreams, they were something I'd yet to experience. Later, in high school, I'd think back to the two of us behind the school and realize that's what she probably meant, but at the time all I did was shrug.

She hunched her skinny shoulders, mimicking me. "Maybe I'd tell you if I thought you could keep a secret," she said.

"Sure I can," I told her.

"It would have to be a trade. First you have to tell me something you want me to keep secret."

"What if I don't have a secret?"

"Everybody has. But if you're an exception then make one up."

28

I knew that telling her about collecting butterflies wasn't the kind of secret she was after. Even at the time, it seemed strange to me that we'd been in school together for years and hardly talked, and now suddenly we were having the kind of conversation I'd never had before with a girl or anyone, a conversation that, whether Camille knew it or not, was already a secret I would keep. I laughed as a way out of answering.

"What do you have to do penance for?" she asked.

"You mean the old five Our Fathers and five Hail Marys," I said. In my experience that was the penance no matter what you confessed. I didn't know if it was the same for girls or not.

Camille looked at me unamused. "Have you ever written a story that was a sin, one you had to do penance for?"

"Penance for a story?"

She gathered the erasers into an unbalanced stack and turned to go inside, leaving me to pick up the erasers that dropped behind her. "You're a big help," she said sarcastically, but added, "Honest. I knew you weren't a loser."

That night, I went to sleep thinking about her—another secret—and looking forward to the following day when we'd go out together to beat the erasers. I didn't know what I'd tell her, but I'd tell her something. But next morning, during the Pledge of Allegiance, before class even began, Diane Kunzel, Norky's Partner in Christ, let out a scream. Norky had magic-markered a smiley face on a white sausage-shaped balloon he'd worked through his open fly as if exposing himself. Sister Mary Donatella attacked him, slashing at his greasy DA haircut and stabbing at his balloon with the pointer she used during geography when she stood before the pulldown map that was green for Christian countries and pink for Communist ones. Partners in Christ came to a bitter end that morning.

"Don't cry girls, these boys would try the patience of an angel," Sister Mary Donatella said.

Camille wasn't crying. She showed her teeth in a quick, regretful, overbite smile and fluttered her fingers goodbye as I packed up. We boys were reassigned to seats at the perimeter of class, and for the remainder of 7th grade I never really spoke with Camille again.

But I still thought about her when in 8th grade we were asked to write our last Christmas composition and dedicate it to Ralphie. I wanted to write a story, not a composition, one that would be read aloud, so that Camille would hear it. I was dedicating it to Ralphie, but, in a way I couldn't have articulated then, it was secretly dedicated to Camille.

Unfortunately, I didn't have a story to write. I remembered the comic book I'd given Ralphie for his last birthday, but didn't get far trying to write a Christmas story with Felix the Cat as the hero. When I thought of Camille reading the few uninspired sentences I'd managed, the words seemed unworthy—lifeless enough to shred.

I wanted a story that came out of nowhere, one I could get excited about the way I had when I'd written from the viewpoint of an ant—although writing about an ant seemed wimpy now. Sister Lucidia had made it clear that dedicating our compositions to Ralphie didn't mean we were to write about him. Simply writing, as usual, about the true meaning of Christmas was all that was required. Yet, when I thought about Ralphie, already dead a year, tales about an ant or a red-nosed reindeer or a snowman come to life seemed the childish fantasies of a *day-dreamer*—a term my father equated with *fool*—and one he applied to me when he was feeling particularly contemptuous towards my behavior.

"You better wake up and smell the coffee," he'd warn.

Getting desperate, I tried to write a story my father had told once about the first Christmas he'd spent as a child after his father had been sent to the state mental hospital, and how on a bitterly cold Christmas Eve he'd met a boy named Teddy Kanik who would become his best friend for life. It wasn't the kind of story my father had ever told me before. He told it after I'd accused him of being a Scrooge because of his cheapskate way of shopping for a Christmas tree. Before I could get to the story as my father told it to me, it seemed necessary to explain that shopping with him for a Christmas tree had become an annual ordeal. Each Christmas season, Mick and I would trudge after him from one tree lot to another in the cold—he was a comparative shopper. He insisted we drag along a sled for hauling back the tree, the way we had when we were little kids. Mick and I would argue over who got stuck pulling the old red Flexible Flyer, its rusted runners rattling over the partially shoveled sidewalks. It had become our family tradition—a terribly embarrassing one. My father loved to bargain and everything, including the way he'd browse the rows of Christmas trees, shaking his head at their overpriced and undernourished condition, was part of a master strategy. His opening gambit on anything he bought, Christmas trees not excluded, was always the phrase, "So how much you soak for it . . ."

That phrase was as far as I got in writing my father's story. It suddenly occurred to me that, should the story be read aloud in class, it would be as embarrassing as shopping for a tree with my father. But there was more to it than that. Each sentence I wrote about shopping seemed to take me further away from the story as my father told it, and I knew why I was digressing, treating it as a joke: his story about meeting Teddy Kanik one Christmas Eve so long ago depressed me. It seemed to have happened in a different world— the Chicago in which my father had grown up an immigrant— only blocks away, but in an alternative universe, one forever sunk in a Great Depression. That wasn't a feeling I wanted to bring into a class in which I had a reputation as a clown to uphold. I thought about Camille confiding that she'd written stories she kept secret, and realized my father's story was better kept a secret, too.

By now it was late. I probably would have given up if all I'd wanted was to impress Camille, but writing a story was the only way I could imagine communicating with her. Despite what Sister Lucidia had said about simply writing about the meaning of Christmas, I didn't seem able to concentrate on a story dedicated to Ralphie if he wasn't in it, so this time I tried writing about the funeral.

I hadn't ridden in the line of cars that left for the cemetery after Ralphie's requiem mass, but I'd stood on the church steps and watched the confusion of spinning tires and men in dark topcoats rocking a hearse piled with snow and flowers out of a rut along the curb. Then, the taillights of the cortege slowly disappeared down Washtenaw into a whiteout. I envisioned their headlights burrowing through the blizzard as they followed the hearse up Milwaukee

Avenue, way out to the Northwest Side where I imagined the snow was even deeper. I'd heard how, when they finally reached St. Adalbert cemetery, they had trouble finding the grave site. In my story, the drifts were so deep that all but the crosses of the tallest monuments were buried. In that expanse of white, it was impossible to find Ralphie's plot, but as the procession of cars wound along a plowed road they came to a place I described as *"an oasis of green in a Sahara of snow."* There, gaping from exposed grass, was a freshly dug grave. At my grandfather Mike's funeral I'd noticed a robin with a worm in its beak fly from his open grave, so in my story birds—robins, doves, sea gulls—flew out of the hole as if a cage door had opened, and circled cawing overhead. When I reread that sentence, I scratched out *robins* and wrote in blue jays. Only after the graveside service did snow drift over Ralphie's plot which was marked—as I'd heard it actually was—with a simple gray stone that made no mention of his being a blue boy. But in my story, when the snow melted in spring, his gravestone had turned blue. I tried different shades: turquoise, cornflower, Prussian, all the blues in a giant 104 box of Crayolas. None seemed right.

It was long past my bedtime. Mick had gone to sleep in the room we shared, where I'd been writing cross-legged on my bed, so I'd relocated to the kitchen table. My father had looked in on me before he'd turned in, obviously amazed to see me slaving over homework.

"Don't burn that midnight oil too late, sonny boy," he cautioned.

Quiet in our flat was when the motor of the refrigerator grew audible. I could hear its hum, and the toilet trickling, the crinkle of cooling radiators, and, from down the hall a harmonica, maybe Shakey Horton or Junior Wells on the bedroom radio still faintly playing tuned to the black rhythm and blues station that Mick and I listened to on the sly before we went to sleep.

"I'm going down to the basement and put my blue light on," Sam Evans, the DJ would announce at midnight.

What blue was that gravestone emerging from the dirty snow in spring? As blue as the blue light in Sam Evans' basement? Or some daylight shade of sky, or blue as the lake, a cold blue that Norky once in an oral presentation described as "turn-your-balls-blue," and for a time after that we took to calling Lake Michigan, Lake Blueballs.

It actually offended Camille. "Sometimes people look but don't see what's beautiful all around us, like the lake," she wrote in *Change the World*. "It's a melted glacier, an Ice Age turned to sweet water. I love its taste."

I slipped my jacket on and went out the back way and walked down the alley that led to an Ice Age so fierce the air felt crystallized, as if the snow tailing off the roofs might be flecks of frozen oxygen. It took a conscious effort to inhale its sharpness, yet instead of cursing the cold, I had a thought that maybe the purpose of winter was to make you realize with every breath that you were alive and wanted to stay that way. I thought about Ralphie and the other kids I knew who already were dead, some from accidents, some, like Peanuts Bizzaro, murdered. Peanuts had seemed indestructible. He was a boxer who'd prided himself on not getting hit. He made boxing something daringly beautiful, like diving off a high board. In winter, we'd all go to watch him fight at the steamy Boy's Club gym, and I was one of an audience of guys outside the cyclone fence surrounding the warehouse lot on Rockwell—a lot with floodlights mounted too high to bust with rocks—watching Peanuts dancing, jabbing, throwing combinations, repeating, "I'm fast, I'm flashy," although those lights and the bluish shadows they threw made it seem slow-motion as he methodically beat the piss out of a much beefier kid from the Ambros. The kid, called Dropout by his gang buddies cheering him on, had wanted to box at the Boy's Club, but he was obviously heavier than Peanut's welterweight class, so when the boxing coach refused to let them put the gloves on, Peanuts offered to take it outside. Dropout wasn't even trying to box anymore. He was grabbing and kicking, and Peanuts was nicking him with his fists, calm and cool as a matador, asking, "Am I fast or what?" Then, from outside the fence, came a single pop that echoed off the stacks of oil drums. Guard still up, Peanuts went down to one knee, and Dropout kicked him over, then scaled the fence and took off with the rest of his buddies.

Peanuts tried to climb the fence, but slid back. Out of nowhere, his older brother, Tony, came running and nearly cleared the eight foot fence in a jump. He wrapped his Levi jacket around Peanuts who was shivering, turning blue under the lighting, and repeating, "No fair, no fucken fair."

Ralphie never had a fighting chance. I thought of him, and of Peanuts, of Gino Folloni, and the others all buried under earth frozen too hard to break with a spade. They couldn't feel the cold because they were the cold. Maybe they could hear the wind, but they couldn't see how even colder than earth the boulder of moon looked through the flocked branches of backyard trees. I stopped, made a snowball, hurled it, and for a moment the snow knocked from the branches maintained in midair the shape of branches, before disintegrating. I wasn't wearing gloves and my hands burned numb. Suddenly, I felt choked up and I started to run as if I could outrun the feeling, which, in fact, is what I did, sprinting down three blocks of alleys without stopping to check the cross streets for traffic, but there weren't any cars and finally, when my nostrils and lungs felt at once frost-bitten and on fire and I could no longer remember why I was running, or if there even was a reason, I stopped and turned around, jogging home under streetlights that looked as if they, too, should have been exhaling steam.

The kitchen was filled with a dizzying warmth. It would have felt warm if the only sources of heat were the overhead light and the humming refrigerator motor. There, on the gray Formica table, lay my smeary blue ballpoint pen and three-holed loose leaf papers, my story, and the scratch paper on which I'd listed various kinds of blue. I tried to reread the story and couldn't. The only thing left to make it feel right was to compress it in both hands like a snowball, before throwing it into the trash bag under the sink.

Everyone handed in compositions but Chester and me. Sister Lucidia didn't say anything to Chester, but she told me to sign my name on a blank sheet of paper, title it *Christmas Composition*, and below that to write dedicated to Ralphie.

On the last day of class before Christmas vacation, when she returned the compositions, she handed the blank paper to me marked with a red *F.* Written in red ink was the comment: *I see that your gift this Christmas was an ENORMOUS nothing.*

After returning the papers, Sister Lucidia placed a scratchy record of carols on the portable turntable and while it played, she announced what we all already knew, that Camille's essay would represent our class at the Christmas Pagent again that year. As customary, Sister Lucidia asked Camille to read her story aloud for our class. Camille rose to read at her desk, but Sister motioned her up before the class. Camille was to be our valedictorian, too, the first one ever at St. Roman, and Sister Lucidia had begun coaching Camille on her oral delivery in preparation for her speech at graduation.

"'A Christmas Carol for Ralphie: A True Story,'" Camille read, her quiet voice in competition with the *Ave Maria*. She enunciated carefully, eyes glued to the page, rouge burning on her cheeks. She appeared to be overheating and partially unbuttoned the navy blue cardigan she'd taken to wearing over her school uniform.

"Try looking up at your audience from time to time," Sister Lucidia suggested. "Eye contact, that's the secret."

Camille's composition opened with the sound of prancing hooves: not reindeer on a rooftop, she told us, but Tito Guizar on the white stallion following the Virgin down Washtenaw. Listening to her recreate the scene, I wondered if she'd been there. I didn't remember seeing her, but there had been a crowd of people on the sidewalk watching Tito Guizar. When she came to the part about Sharky leading his parade out of the alley, she looked up at us, her audience, and asked, "What if Charles Dickens, the author of *A Christmas Carol*—one of the greatest writers in the history of the world—was there in the crowd?"

She dropped her gaze back to her paper. "I think I saw him there that afternoon," she said, then, deliberately making eye contact, asked, "If Dickens can transport us in time back to London, why can't we transport him to Chicago?"

Maybe eye contact *was* the secret because it almost seemed as if she was asking me the question.

"You don't have to be transported to London on Christmas Eve a century ago to know that, as Dickens wrote, 'the business of Mankind is Man.' You don't have to be visited by the ghosts of Christmas Past, Present, and Future. But if you were, who would your ghost of Christmas Past be?" she asked, "Each of you has one. What would your spirit of Christmas Present look like?"

She paused as if waiting for an answer, and though I now realized her technique was to make eye contact whenever she asked a question, the question nonetheless seemed directed to me as if there was a secret connection between us.

Before I could think who my ghost might be, Norky turned in his seat a row over, and whispered, "Bridget Bardot," then shook his fist as if jerking off and made a demented face which confirmed the ill effects of masturbation. Otherwise, the class was quiet, everyone intent, but Chester who'd buried his head in his arms as if asleep at his desk.

"Maybe the ghost might be disguised as a blind man who sells newspapers, or, instead of dragging chains, come rattling on a little cart, with hooves strapped to his hands," Camille suggested.

However different our ghosts might be, Camille said, she guessed that everyone in our class had the same Tiny Tim—Ralphie—and that we needed to be inspired by his example to change the world. To change the world, we first had to change ourselves. We had to make Christmas in our hearts and love one another.

Norky turned, caught my attention, and raised a sheet of paper on which in big letters he'd scrawled ESTRADA HAS BBs.

I hated to admit he was right—maybe it was an optical illusion, but whenever Camille paused for breath, her white blouse beneath her blue sweater seemed to strain against the swell of her breasts as if she were developing before our eyes.

She took a deep, breast-heaving breath and said that a blue boy was not so different from Tiny Tim with his crutch. And that Tiny Tim with his crutch was not so different from Jesus with a Cross. She said that on that day last December when he ran to join the band of disabled marchers, Ralphie "mounted the wheelchair like a prince assuming his throne." She said he raised his blue fist not in triumph or, as some claimed after he died, to wave goodbye, but as if to cheer as Tiny Tim would, "God Bless Us Every One!"

"That's not what happened," Chester said quietly.

He'd lifted his head from his arms, and without asking permission, half rose at his desk which was in the front row.

"Chester, do you want to add something?" Sister Lucidia asked, giving him the floor, not that it was necessary since Camille had immediately stopped reading and now stood as if trapped before the class, more uneasy than I'd ever seen her.

Chester sat back down. "Lots of little kids chase parades," he said. His voice trembled. "How come for once in his life Ralphie couldn't just do what other kids do without somebody making it a big deal?"

"Of course he could," Sister Lucidia said, "What Camille meant was . . ."

"She shouldn't make stuff up about him," Chester interrupted, rising to his feet with a force that jarred his desk and sent the needle on the portable player on Sister's desk skipping across vinyl. "He wasn't joining anything!" he shouted at Camille. "He wasn't like them. His fist wasn't blue. That's bullshit. What do you know?" he demanded. "You don't know shit! And he hated being called a Blue Boy. That wasn't his goddamn name. He wasn't some fucking freak. He wasn't some crip in a story. He didn't want your fucking feeling sorry for him. We don't need it. What do you know? You don't know fucking dog shit! Go fuck your four-eyed self!" he yelled after her as Camille ran from the room.

6

"How much you soak for it," my father asked, studying the tree with a characteristic combination of suspicion and contempt.

His appraisal was accurate, it wasn't much of a tree. The lots were already picked over. Each year we'd shop later in December in order to get a better deal. I'd begun to suspect that, if he could, he might have bought a tree after Christmas the way he bought Christmas cards on sale.

"You don't unload these trees soon and you'll be stuck with them. You won't be able to give them away." As usual, he marshaled his arguments before getting down to talking turkey, applying what he called "psychology," even though the kid he was bargaining with didn't own the lot. He was a sullen-looking teenager in a hood who kept his eyes on his own stamping feet. The unclasped buckles of his galoshes jangled; I could smell the resin on the oversized canvas mittens he wore. He hadn't bothered to leave the flickering, illusory warmth of the garbage can where he stood smoking a cigarette and burning boughs while we'd wandered through what was left of the tiny pine forest. During summer, lots like this were eyesores, clotted with trash, ragweed thrusting from bricks and broken bottles. But each December they were transformed—strung with colored bulbs and plastic pennants like used car lots. A horn speaker, blaring maniacally as an ice cream truck in July, crackled "Here Comes Santa Claus."

"*Maybe* I'd go a fin on this one," my father grudgingly offered.

"I don't make the prices, mo'," the kid told him.

"Well, just between us, what do *you* think it's really worth?" my father asked, "If you were shopping for it."

"Whatever the tag says, mo'."

That second "mo" caught my attention. The first time, I'd thought maybe he'd mumbled "man," but it was "mo" as in "mo-fo" as in "motherfucker." I wondered if he was high. My father seemed not to have noticed. His general obliviousness to gang etiquette in the neighborhood had always alarmed me.

"Suppose the tag fell off," my father prodded, "trees don't grow in nature with price tags, you know."

The kid shrugged as if it wasn't worth talking about. "Look, mo', you buy it or you don't."

"I offered a fin . . . with an extra six bits in it for you if you saw the stump," my father said, conspiratorially.

"Why you come here and insult me for, mo'?"

"What? You want I go see what the competition has to offer? Maybe you haven't noticed, but they got a very nice selection of trees down the block, and another down the block from that," my father said, not adding that we'd already cased every lot in an eight block radius before determining that this lot had the cheapest trees—no doubt because they were the scruffiest. "There's more trees out there than customers," my father informed him, amused by the irrefutable laws of capitalism now working to his advantage.

"So go fucken waste their time."

Mick and I looked at each other and back at the guy.

"What you looking at? How you like I shove that sled up your ass, kid?" he asked me.

We walked off, me dragging the sled.

"I didn't like his attitude," my father said.

I didn't say anything. I was furious. All the times my father embarrassed me returned in a rush: the way he'd stop his beater in traffic to pick a piece of scrap he thought might be worth something off the street; how I'd unpack my lunch in school to find he'd made me what my friends called "a puke on white"—last night's chop suey on now dissolved slices of Wonder Bread; how at Maxwell Street, or Jewtown as it was called with typical Chicago ethnic sensitivity—an outdoor market my father haunted where endless haggling was the rule—while I tried on trousers behind the makeshift dressing room of a windblown sheet, he'd yell, "Do they fit in the crotch?" I was banging the sled over curbs as if yanking the leash on a dog I was trying to kill.

"Pa-rum-pa-pum-pum," Mick hummed to himself as he had the entire time we'd been out. "Me and my drum."

"Hey, take it easy on that sled," my father said. "If you can't make something, don't break it."

I gave the sled a jerk that slammed it along a building so that its metal runners sparked off the bricks, and my father stopped, challenging me to try it again. "Someone having a problem here?"

"You are really a Scrooge, mo'," I told him, and braced for an attack that, this time, didn't come.

Later that night, while Mick helped my mother bake gingerbread, my father and I strung the bubble lights on a Scotch pine to a burble of carols courtesy of the Lawrence Welk orchestra. It was the first long needled pine we'd ever had and seemed exotic—a pedigreed Persian cat of a tree. There were still pine cones on it. The bushy needles made stringing the lights trickier, my father observed, then we continued working in silence.

"Be a good night for some homemade eggnog," he offered. "The real thing made the old fashioned way." He prided himself on his eggnog; it was the best I've ever had. He began talking about his father, my grandfather, whom he'd never mentioned, and whom time his father would send him to a barrel house—a tavern where beer barrels served as a bar—with a pail to bring back a special holiday brew. Everybody at the tavern knew his father. There were local prize fights back then, one tavern's champ against another's, and his father, whose name was Michael, fought every Friday night. He fought as the Wild *Goral*, which sounded like an abbreviation for gorilla, but meant the wild man from the Tatra mountains—although my father added cryptically, rather than a hillbilly, his father might have been half-Jewish. He told me how once his father, Mike, came home late with his front teeth broken and how he sat groaning, drinking from a fifth of whiskey, and spitting blood into the beer pail as he worked at his teeth with a pair of pliers trying to pull the stubs out of his bloody gums, rather than pay a dentist. Finally, Mike tried to get my father to yank out what was left of his teeth, and when my father wouldn't, his father got furious and chased him, trying to brain him with the whiskey bottle, until my father escaped by running out of the house.

Long past midnight on one of those Friday nights, drunken men brought the *Goral* home, half-conscious, blood running from his nose, mouth, and ears, his paycheck gone. He lay moaning in bed for a day, then slept for two more, and when he regained consciousness he was dazed, speechless, nearly helpless, and finally, after weeks that way he was taken to Dunning, the state mental hospital, a Palookaville from which he never returned.

My grandmother, Victoria, barely spoke English. She worked at home as a seamstress during the day. After they took Mike away, she got a second job at night scrubbing floors in a downtown office building. My father was eleven at the time, the oldest of the six kids, so, as the man in the family, he had to work several jobs. He'd rise at five AM to deliver milk, then delivered newspapers, then attended grade school, and immediately after school he'd head for the flower shop on Coulter Street where he worked until suppertime. The shop was closing late on the Christmas Eve of the first year of Mike's incarceration, when the florist told my father there was a rush order on a wreath—not a Christmas wreath, but a funeral wreath. They made it from pine boughs anyway, stuffed with wet sphagnum moss, and tied with a black ribbon, and after my father helped work on it, the florist sent him to deliver it. The address was in a neighborhood my father wasn't familiar with. He went through the city in the dark, half lost on the snow-drifted streets, holding the wreath out before him. He didn't have gloves and when he finally found the address, on a street that has since been erased by an expressway, he couldn't knock because his hands were frozen to the wreath. He had to kick at the door.

A boy his own age answered, the son of the man who had died. The family couldn't afford a funeral home so the body was laid out dressed in a Sunday suit in a small living room, or parlor, as my father called it—he always referred to living rooms as parlors. When the kid who'd answered the door saw that my father couldn't let go of the wreath, he invited him in and sat him down beside the oil stove. There was a pan of water on top of the stove and the kid, Teddy Kanik, brought a wash cloth and towel and bathed my father's hands until they thawed. He made him a cup of tea. They were best friends from that day on.

It's a story I heard my father tell twice: once that evening as we strung the bubble lights on the Scotch pine, and then again, thirty years later, after he'd retired from his job at the foundry. He'd retired in Memphis, Tennessee, where he'd been transferred after his plant closed in Chicago. I was visiting after he'd had a stay in the hospital for the kidney ailment that would ultimately take his life. We were telling stories, laughing about all the crazy people from the old neighborhood, and I tried to get him to tell what he remembered about Poland. He was very young when, to use his phrase, "they came over on the boat." Instead, he told the story about his father again, and when he reached the part about kicking at Teddy Kanik's door, hands frozen to the funeral wreath, unable to knock, he broke into tears, something I'd never seen him do, excused himself, and rushed from the room.

At my father's funeral, when there might have been an opportunity to pay a few words of respect, that story set in the dead of winter returned to my mind. It was summer in Memphis—"a scorcher," my father would have called it—and his story seemed even more foreign there. Not the actual feeling itself, but the recollection of an old feeling from childhood, one for which I still don't have a name, returned: an inexpressible protectiveness towards my father—a concern that, despite his faith in hard work and practicality, he'd never wholly appraised the reality of the country in which we lived. We shared a home, we shared a life, but there was a dimension separating us. He inhabited another America, a place distant like Dicken's London or Gogol's Moscow. He feared that we, his sons, would go wanting, and that fear had set us at odds with him. I thought of telling his Teddy Kanik story at the wake, but wasn't sure what the point of telling it might be; the story wasn't a way he'd want to be remembered in public, nor a way of saying goodbye. And yet the story itself diminished anything else I could think of to say, and so, to my shame, I left my father unprotected and sat silently and listened to the priest mouth the usual cliches.

Mick had flown in from New York for the funeral toting a huge bulging soft-sided plaid suitcase. Before his flight, he'd rushed to the Lower East Side to buy containers of *pierogi* and borscht, jars of herring, garlic dills, horseradish, kraut, links of fresh and smoked *kielbasa*—sausages my father loved and wasn't able to eat in his last years because of his restricted diet. Mick knew that after the funeral a meal would be required. He stuffed in a bottle of *wisniowka*—a cherry brandy—and a bottle of 150 proof Demerara rum, then, at LaGuardia, checked the suitcase through to Memphis. Everything but the *wisniowka* and rum arrived broken and run together.

The rum was for Mick's private tribute. He'd been working as a bouncer at a strip club on 42nd Street, and living in Queens with one of the dancers, a striking Puerto Rican woman who'd introduced Mick to Santeria. He'd become an initiate and wanted to become a santero. He wore his *caracoles*—a shell necklace no one was allowed to touch—and brought a thick black candle inscribed with esoteric symbols that he erected before my father's tomato patch in the backyard. It was an offering made to Oya, patron of whirlwinds and cemeteries, to ease the entrance to the world of the dead. Oya's syncretic form, he explained, to ease our mother's misgivings, was Our Lady of Montserrat. Beside the candle, he set a shot of rum; Oya, fiercest of the female orishas, liked her drink strong. In the humid, bug-roaring darkness of Memphis, the orange candle flame flickered eerily off the tomato netting until our mother went out and drenched it with a blast from the garden hose.

The rum that Oya didn't require Mick and I killed driving around at night between BBQ places and country bars in my father's gold Chrysler. We ended up in a pool hall. My father had been a skilled pool player. Neither Mick nor I had inherited the gene. Maybe it was the similarity of our inept play, but people kept asking if we were twins. No, we told them, just brothers.

After the funeral we served a meal of Memphis BBQ and Lower East Side Polish sausage to my father's surviving brother and three of his sisters who'd all traveled from Chicago. We said a brief prayer and downed a *wisniowka* in a silent toast to my father's memory.

I sat beside my Aunt Olga, my father's youngest sister.

"When we were kids, your father kept us all going," she told me. "One year, when we barely had enough to eat, he somehow managed to show up with a tree on Christmas Eve, because, he said, our family shouldn't be without one. He was a good brother. He was a good guy."

"He never told me about that," I said.

She daubed her eyes. "There's a lot he didn't talk about."

That was the first of times to come when missing my father took the shape of being startled that he was no longer there to answer a question regarding a past I knew so little about and to which he'd been my only link. I wished, with an intensity that ambushed me, that I could have asked him for the details on how he'd come up with the tree. It sounded like another story that might have made Charles Dickens proud.

7

When, in her composition, Camille Estrada told how she'd seen Charles Dickens standing on Washtenaw, I imagined Dickens there, too, a familiar face in the crowd watching Tito Guizar ride by, the steam of his horse's droppings mingling with the smoke of incense. Camille might have argued that if Tito Guizar could actually appear parading through Little Village behind the miraculous

Virgin, then why not Charles Dickens? The appearance of the Mexican cowboy star complete with stallion, chaps, sombrero, a guitar strapped across his back like a carbine, was barely less remarkable than that of an old, British writer would have been. Dickens was the man in a starched collar with a blue cravat that matched his worn, serious eyes; his auburn hair was thinning, his flowing beard was the kind one saw on homeless hermits that lived by the railroad tracks. That was how Dickens was pictured on the cards with which our family played a game called *Authors*. Dickens shared the deck with Shakespeare, Sir Walter Scott, James Fenimore Cooper, Washington Irving, Longfellow, Tennyson, Alcott, Twain, Poe, Hawthorne. At bedtime, our mother would read from those authors to Mick and me.

"No wild stuff," she'd caution, "this is reading time."

It was the closest thing Mick and I had to sacred time.

She read Alcott's entire *Little Women* and we listened intently to every word. On the Dickens' card, beneath his likeness, four books were listed: *The Pickwick Papers, David Copperfield, Oliver Twist, A Christmas Carol*. From those, Mother read *Oliver Twist*. We owned a set of 78 rpm records of a dramatized reading of Christmas Carol, staring Basil Rathbone who was also Sherlock Holmes. My father had gotten a good deal on it at Maxwell Street.

Camille had tried to summon up the authority of Dickens' fiction to justify the true story of Ralphie she wanted to tell, a story destined to end with the hopelessly pathetic fact of a little boy dying on Christmas Eve. On some level she must have asked herself, who would read *A Christmas Carol* a second time if Tiny Tim died at the end? She needed a rebirth, a resurrection. A year had already passed without a single miracle. Although parishioners had prayed *for* the Blue Boy so long that it had become a habit, they were bound to give up praying *to* him. It would occur to them, as it had to me on the one shameful time I prayed to Ralphie and asked him to help me make the basketball team, that if Ralphie's wish to live long enough to make his First Holy Communion hadn't been granted, then why would he have the clout to intercede for anyone else? Gradually, but sooner than had ever seemed possible, he'd be forgotten.

Camille needed to summon the timeless power of Dickens' story in order to superimpose what remained of Ralphie's spirit on the streets of Little Village. Her borrowing of images from Dickens wasn't so different from the local spray can artists who painted murals on the crumbling walls, as if Diego Rivera-like visions might shore up what urban renewal had not. There was a permanence to Dickens' story that Camille aspired to. And in that, her tribute was not unlike the tributes of the gangbangers who sometimes tattooed an indelible blue tear at the outside corner of one eye in memory of a wasted homey. That's what Tony Bizzaro did after his brother, Peanuts, died.

It's about feeling, Camille had told me that one afternoon when we were partners in Christ.

She refused to settle for a tribute that took the shape of silence. She failed for want of accuracy; even, perhaps, for want of honesty, but not of feeling. Not for want of *amor*.

I don't know what became of her. After Christmas break that year in 8th grade, a rumor spread that beneath the blue cardigan buttoned to the top no matter what the weather, Camille was wearing falsies. Sister Lucidia didn't inquire about the matter directly. Instead, she asked Camille not to wear the sweater during class, it wasn't part of the school uniform. Camille correctly observed that by 8th grade the uniform code wasn't strictly enforced, and besides, she was cold. So, Sister Lucidia offered to move her to a desk next to the radiators. Camille thanked her politely and said that wouldn't be necessary, in the future she would leave her sweater at home.

But the following day, Camille still wore the blue sweater. After morning prayer, Sister Lucidia reminded Camille that she'd promised to leave her sweater at home, and asked her to hang it in the wardrobe—immediately. Camille remained seated, composed, silent, defiant. Sister Lucidia observed that such behavior was hardly what she expected from the class valedictorian. The class had gone quiet. There'd never been a hint of confrontation between Camille and any of the nuns before.

"I want you to remove your sweater now," Sister said, taking a step down the aisle towards Camille.

Camille replied softly in Spanish.

"What did you just say?" Sister Lucidia demanded. The previously inconceivable possibility that Camille might have just cursed her, stopped her in her tracks.

I wondered if Camille had cursed, too. But later, Rafael told me what she'd said was a proverb he'd heard his *abuela* use: *"el habito no hace al monje." The habit doesn't make the monk.*

Camille didn't repeat the words. Almost wearily, she began unbuttoning her sweater, but Sister Lucidia stopped her.

"Camille, I want to speak with you in private. Please go to the principal's office and wait there for me."

This time, Camille complied immediately. As she rose and left class without another word, the nearly unbuttoned sweater gave us a flash of a bosom worthy of Marilyn Monroe. It looked padded or, more accurately, it didn't look natural on her, but I remember thinking, what if those weren't falsies Camille was concealing?

"BB zizboombah!" Norky saluted, and Camille's lip retracted in what may have passed for a smile.

Afterwards, we learned that instead of the principal's office, Camille had gone to the small school library where a senile nun named Sister Angelica presided over the books. Camille didn't demand her old, illustrated novels back. She checked them out on library cards and left, never to return. That was the last time I saw her, but hardly the last time I thought about her.

By junior year in high school, my earlier fascination with stories from Greek mythology had evolved into an addiction to science fiction. I'd read on the bus to and from school, and sometimes late into the night, and each Saturday I'd stop for a new fix of sci-fi at the Gad's Hill Library, which had also been my father's neighborhood library. Sometimes, I'd imagine him going there when he was my age. He'd told me as a kid he'd read every Hardy Boys mystery on the shelves, but that, after reading a biography of Andrew Carnegie, he realized reading novels was impractical, the way a day-dreamer would waste his time. I decided to read every book in their science fiction section.

One sleeting, gray afternoon, sitting at a window table in Gad's Hill, reading Ray Bradbury's *The Illustrated Man*, I came upon a story called "The Man," about earth voyagers to a distant planet who just miss Christ's appearance there. The Captain vows to keep questing after the Man until he finds him. "I'll go on to another world," he says, "And another and another. I'll miss him by half a day on the next planet, maybe, and a quarter of a day on the third planet, and two hours on the next, and an hour on the next, and a minute on the next. But after that, one day I'll catch up with him."

There were no hoofed Centaurians, nor was the space ship a winged horse, but the idea of following Christ from world to world was so reminiscent of Camille's story that I couldn't help but wonder if she'd stolen it. Or if, by 7th grade, her imagination was already the equal of Bradbury's. I recalled the afternoon when the two of us stood beating erasers, and Camille confided that she'd done penance for stories—stories that I'll never know if she wrote or only imagined writing—and how she wanted me to tell her a secret from my dreams—a secret from dreams I hadn't had as yet, and so didn't quite understand what she was after.

"It's about feeling," Camille had insisted.

I didn't understand then that she was talking about risk.

8

There's a recurrent dream that visits me less and less frequently. I first had it after my father took ill. In the dream, I'm pulling the red sled, but not loaded with a Christmas tree. What I'm hauling is an automobile battery, just as we actually did once in winter when my father's Plymouth died at the factory lot. Rather than spend money to have a wrecker come out and jump it, he unbolted the Atlas battery and caught a ride home with a fellow employee. He left the battery at a gas station to be recharged and after supper we walked to the gas station, with the sled. The grease monkey— as my father called mechanics—said he couldn't guarantee the battery would hold a charge, and that in this subzero weather the safest thing was to buy a new one. My father didn't even bother to ask what he soaked for it.

The old sled creaked when my father set the battery on it. He cautioned that we had to be very careful not to tip out the battery acid, and told me to center the battery on the sled. I couldn't even budge it.

"You practice lifting that, sonny boy, and you'll become Charles Atlas," he laughed. "Nobody will kick sand in your face." Then he repositioned it and we began the long trek back to the factory lot.

A curfew of cold had emptied the streets. It was probably approaching my bedtime—unusual for my father to have kept me out late, but that's how it happened, as if something important was going on. We crossed Rockwell, a border between blocks of apartment buildings and blocks of factories. Past Rockwell, the total absence of trees gave the industrial strength streetlights a bluish glare that made the temperature seem to drop another few degrees. Even in summer the cracked, fissured sidewalks could be treacherous as if a localized quake had occurred along these miles of truck docks, warehouses, and abandoned factories. Snow piled up unshoveled all winter. We took turns tugging the sled through the drifts and over mounds of dirty ice, one of us pulling, the other steadying the battery. I secretly wouldn't have minded the sled tipping as it threatened to repeatedly, because I wanted to see the reaction between battery acid and snow. But as we continued, wind bored to bone, and my feet in rubber galoshes and fingers in rabbit fur-lined gloves went achingly numb. My face felt raw and chapped from the woolen scarf I'd raised like a mask, and I began worrying that the battery would be dead when we got to the car, that the engine wouldn't turn over, and we'd have to lug the battery all the way back. I don't remember a word of what we said as we walked, if we said anything at all, and yet there's not a time when I felt closer to my father.

In the dream, I'm tugging the sled alone, and, without my father along, the effort seems increasingly senseless. Knee deep in drifts, navigating mounded ice, I glance back to make sure the load hasn't tipped, and in the squint of streetlights realize that it's my father, blue with cold, and reduced to an ancient child the compressed weight of a battery, that I'm pulling.

Who knows why certain humble objects—a comic book, a bike, a sweater, a sled—are mysteriously salvaged by memory or dream to become emblems of childhood? Childhood, an alternative universe expanding into forgetfulness, where memory rather than matter is the stuff of creation.

At the end of each day at St. Roman, classes would be released in order of seniority, so Chester would always have to wait for Ralphie's class to let out. He'd wait for Ralphie on the corner by the church. If it was raining, he'd have an umbrella already opened. Usually, Chester the only boy at school with an umbrella. At least it was a black umbrella. Then, he and his brother Ralphie walked home down Washtenaw together, engaged in some secret conversation, laughing at some private joke.

Once, the spring after Ralphie died, I was released early from detention because the April afternoon was darkened by the total eclipse of a thunderstorm. The corridors were empty, all the classes had already fled home. Outside, I noticed from a half-block away that Chester stood on the corner waiting with an open umbrella. He must have stayed to watch the younger kids file out. And he was still there waiting after they'd gone. Although I saw Chester in school every day, I really hadn't talked to him since Ralphie died. We'd paid our condolences as a class, but I'd been feeling vaguely guilty around Chester for not having said something, though, of course, there seemed nothing to say. It was raining hard enough that when I held my history book over my head I could feel as well as hear the drumming rain. I didn't realize until I walked past him that Chester was crying. Maybe he thought no one would notice in the rain. Or maybe he didn't realize it himself, as he made no attempt to conceal his tears.

"You're getting soaked," he said and gave the umbrella a little lift meaning that he'd share it.

"I'm okay," I said. "I got my book, but thanks."

"All right," he said and gave me the thumbs up sign that probably he'd taught to Ralphie.

I gave it back. And for no good reason, as I walked away, I felt forgiven for having done something so phony as praying that one time to Ralphie as if death had turned him into something other than himself.

How many others back then pretended to pray when what they

were doing was crying in secret—in secret even from themselves? Or praying as an alternative to futile tears? Or perhaps, praying because they thought they should have cried, or should continue to cry for what they've forgotten or will forget. Praying because one grief connects with another, and feeling insists upon being expressed, even if only in secret as prayer. A prayer for the brother for whom one might have been a better keeper; a prayer for the father one might have loved more gently; a prayer prayed the way children do, as if making a wish, as if hot tears are streaking a wild, cold heart; a prayer for all of God's blue boys.

John Barth

from Coming Soon!!!: "Read Me"

C ALL ME DITSY, CALL ME WHATCHADURN PLEASE; JUST AN OLD-
fart Chesapeake *progger*'s what I am, with more orneriness than
good sense—else I wouldn't be sitting here a-hunting and a-peck-
ing on "Big Bitsy's" ergonomic keyboard whilst the black wind
roars and the black water rises and the power flickers and the cabin
shakes. I'd've hauled my bony butt across Backwater Strait to high
ground over in Crassfield whilst the hauling was still doable, before
the storm-surge from Zulu Two (stay tuned) puts Hick Fen Island*
eight fingerforking feet under Backwater Sound.

"Whoa ho there, Dits," my mind's ear hears the gentle reader
gently interpose: "Where's Hick Fen I.? Where're Backwater Sound
and ditto Strait and mainland Crassfield? Who's Zulu Two, an
whaddafug's a *progger*, and who's thissere EARL character, that you

---

*Avge year-round human population exactly 1 these days and holding. Median elevation
0 ft at mean high water, as we're 1/2 tidemarsh. *Max* elevation, just under Big Bitsy's
ergonomic chair. An acrophobogenic 6 ft and sinking. Predicted storm-surge? 12 to 14. . . .

haven't even mentioned yet?" All in good time, mon semblable et cet, which Yrs Truly don't happen to have a whole skiffload of just now. Anyhow, old Ditsy-Belle's a gal that likes her stories straight up, if you read me: Get things going, says I, then cut to the chase, or old Dits'll chase to the cut. *Once upon a time*'s about as far as we'll go in the way of wind-up for your pitch. You say *It was a dark and stormy night?* We copy, mate: now on with the story, ess vee pee.

Ditsy-Belle, Ditsy-Boy: I've done time in my time as mainly male and ditto feem; have attained the age where what's between my legs matters less to either of us than what's between my ears or just 'twixt you and me. Which is to say, a certain high-density disk-in-the-hand that I progged from the bush this morning after Zulu One (a dark and stormy night forsooth) in the westmost marshes of B.E.W.A.R.(E.), the Backwater Estuarine Wetlands Area Reserve (East): a double-sided disk triple-zipped in a Ziploc™ baggie inside another inside another and hence bone dry enough, as bones go hereabouts, that I could read its blot-free label through all three bags in the mucky marshgut whither it'd wended from wherethefuckever. To wit:

Coming Soon!!!

Not quite your classic message-in-a-bottle—of which, by the way, I have found none in seven decades of dedicated progging—but piquant, piquant, no? After Tropical Storm Zulu, however (now redubbed Zulu I), the marsh-pickings were uncommonly plump, and tempus was a-fugiting—the Weather Service warning all hands that Tee Ess Zee had made an unheard-of U-turn off the Jersey Shore, regrouped and refueled, and was chugging more or less back our way as full-blown *Hurricane* Zulu; first time they ever reached the end of the alphabet, and with autumn prime-time yet to go! Anyhow, a chap can't just kick back in the cordgrass and thumb through a computer disk with his/her bareassed eye, capisce? So I tossed *CS!!!* in the crab-basket with my other objets trouvés and carried on with my progging, I did, figuring I'd cull and triage and boot up and peruse at my fatherfreaking leisure.

But stay: ¿Qué quiere decir, Q'est-ce que ça veux dire, Was bedeutet ein *progger*, prithee?

A: One (of any gender, both/all/none, in good old low-inflected English) who progs. And that's a long Oh, mind, as in *programmer*, not a shorty as in, well, *long*.

Q: And to prog? Or, as some may spell it, progue?

Let us begin with the Chesapeake Estuarine System, kiddies, and cut thence to the chase. Formed in its current configuration 10K years back, it was, at and by the end of the latest glaciation, with a probable prompt 35,000,000 years earlier from a mile-wide meteorite-strike 140 miles SE of Our Nation's Capital. The drownèd mouth of your Susquehanna River, is your C-peake Bay, and your largest mothering estuarine system in your USFMA, maybe your ditto world. At 300-plus kilometers north/south but only an average dozen-plus east/west and a mere measly average *three Ditsy-depths* top/bottom, she's as tall and slim and shallow as the female lead in a dumb-blonde joke, is Ms CB. And she *is* a she, make no mistake as you could with me: Your Old Man River might just keep rolling with his one-track male no-mind, but our vagrant Chess not only ebbs and flows like the moonstruck mother she is— any old off-the-shelf ocean does *that*—but mixes salt and fresh till her average salinity just about matches that of the sack we all first swam in, or for that matter human tears. Add to which, her western shore's mainly high ground, her eastern mainly low, and her *lower* eastern mainly tidemarsh; add to *that* that her prevailing storm-winds are northwesterly, and in your southeast quadrant you've a proper progging ground: e.g., B.E.W.A.R.(E.).

Strike that, mate: A proper soggy prog-*bog* is what you've got. This brackish isle, this crab- and skeeter-rich wetland labyrinth: this . . . Hick Fen.

To prog, or progue ("origin and sense-history unknown," says my just-now-downloaded dictionary—but prog on, pal, and see below) = in general, to pick and poke about, to scavenge and to scrounge. More particularly, hereabouts, to beachcomb where no beach is, only the odd sandspit or low-tide mudflat 'mongst the marsh; to putt or pole or paddle one's shoal-draft john-boat, skiff, or own canoe* along the inches-deep but megamiles-long margins of the Bay's lee shore in leisurely but sharp-eyed search of . . .

Whatever. "Seek," saith Scripture, "and ye shall find," whereto your proper progger doth append "Amen—long's ye seek nothing in particular." Go ye forth a-progging for a certain length of half-inch braided nylon dockline or a spare red plastic fuel funnel, and you'll turn up a brace of used condoms like tired sea-nettles (but Day-Glo green, with ticklers), a snarl of fisherman's monofilament, a former spaniel, and the usual Big Mac boxes and Coors beer cans. Prog ye on the other hand for Whatever's Out There, and in addition to the routine assortment of usable lumber, salvageable gill-net, cork floats and other piscivorian accessories, doubler-crabs a-mating in the eel-grass, and yachtsfolks' hats sunspecs boathooks and personal flotation devices, you may turn up (to cite a few choice items from my own life-list) an entire summer tuxedo fetchingly entwined with a strapless ball gown, a former CIA clandestine services officer with forty pounds of scuba weights 'round his waist and a 9mm bullet hole abaft his left ear, a ship in a bottle (the latter uncorked and stranded one-quarter full of mucky Backwater; the former, a miniature square-rigger, storm-battered but still bravely afloat inside), a bottle in a ship (grounded and abandoned thirty-five-foot cruising sloop, both sails set, lunch half eaten on the dinette table, course plotted on the nav-station chart, and an unpopped liter of Dom Perignon in the wine-locker along with sundry inferior vintages, all which I liberated, finders keepers), and—different decade, different marsh, same old progger—a Ziploc™'d computer disk entitled

Coming Soon!!!

Yeah right yes well: not as soon as Zulu II, was Ditso's guess, so I progged on for a spell, netted me a clutch of peeler-crabs, an orange rubber oysterman's glove (lefthand, just right for RH shucking, and afloat fingers-up like a drowned waterman's last bye-bye),

*Hence Ditsy's non-Definitive Derivation: fr Fr *pirogue*, a dugout canoe, fr Sp *piragua*, ditto, corrupted fr Carib by Conquistadores and fr Fr by Br as once ruled the waves.

also the aforementioned brace of french-ticklered french letters (good as new once inside-outed, rinsed in Backwater Creek, air-dried, and recocked for firing; you never know who might turn up, and a girl can't be too careful these days with all them Ess Tee Dees floating 'round, d'accord?), and a pink glass fishnet-float, size of a canteloupe with net still rinding it, that must've blown either transatlantic from Portugal or transchesapeake from some gussied-up crabhouse across the way, as no waterperson hereabouts ever used such kitsch except for the odd decorative accent. Then I hustled home as the wind rerose and the sky redarkened over B.E.W.A.R.(E.); hauled my progging-skiff (*Nameless*, I call her) 'bout as high as high goes on H.F.I., which is atop of my dock-deck and slip-knotted to my porchposts, ready to be jumped aboard of with my Getthehelloutahere bag atop Big Bitsy's workstation when cometh push to shove. Tidy anal-retentive that I am, I next stashed my take here and there as appropriate, and only *then* hauled my arse and the Ziploc™s three to my cobbled-up workstation and peeled off those serial containers the way Sir Summertux and Lady Strapless must've peeled off theirs, to have at the Thing Contained: (((the pearl))) within ((the oyster)) within (the shell) within the shucker's bushel,

COMING SOON!!!

Which doth remind me, that trebled exclamation, of lusty EARL&me a-hollering the like as we went to it once upon a time in yonder saltmarsh ("Your skiff or mine, hon?") or up on my dock-deck or over to her/his lab, wherever the rut smote either of us and whoever was that day's humper & who humpee. Sometimes a question, sometimes a warning to them as'd rather spit than swallow, most often a hopeful ejaculation, pardon my English, as me&him both were of an age more prone to ooze like the marsh we mucked in than to hey-diddly-diddle cow the moon. EARL! EARL! EARL!: mainly male through our joint marsh-tenancy, he was, as I was chiefly fe-, although our having each burnt her/his candle at both ends helped bring us together, you might say. E.A.R.L. is what his billcap advertised: the Estuarine Aquacultural Research Laboratory over to B.E.W.A.R.(E.) till the Navy reclaimed Westmarsh Island for an aerial gunnery target during the Persian Gulf Set-To. And "EARL"'s all the handle on that chipper chap I ever had or wanted, just as he in turn made do with hailing me, as boatfolk will, by the name of my skiff—old *Nameless?*—leaving off its first syllable by way of *tutoyer* (Less is More) as we came to know each other better.

Which I trow in very sooth is *why* we came, dear EARL and I, each for and/or in/on the other, depending on who et cetera in our Hick Fen hump-du-soir: *to know each other better*, not via names and résumés but in the King-Jim-Hebrew sense, the all but word-free knowing of skin and eye and nose and tongue, of show-and-don't-tell, of scratch-and-sniff and lay-low-and-behold, of stroke and poke and squeal and sigh, of lick and split—of, in short and at length, the intercourse of Intercourse,

COMING SOON!!!

Not. But come it did and came, not so long ago, till it went with the wind of our Pentagon's latest, and the E.A.R.L. facility went with it, and pissed-off EARL with phased-out E.A.R.L.—not before, however, one glorious fuckitall joint progging of his half-disman-tled aquacultural establishment, wherefrom we liberated not only a banquetsworth of prime tilapia and home-grown *Ostreae virginicae* (two of his graduate students' dissertation-projects down our pipes, EARL grumbled, shaking a free fist at the F-16s violating our air-space from their base at Patuxent, 'cross the Bay) but a zip drive here, a modem there, here a keyboard, there a 17" color monitor and a laser printer and a CD-ROM gizmo and a hutch-topped workstation—all destined for recycling and replacement anyhow, so swore he. Thus came it to pass that before she could say Shucks or Shiver me timbers, old Dits was multigigabyte *wired*, man, and Big Bitsy (as we dubbed our only joint creation) was *online*—via what net-server, deponent saith not. Showed me how to up-and-run the sucker, dear EARL did, as I'd showed him a thing or three about snagging the odd out-of-season goose and rockfish, never mind how. Set me up proper for a different kind of progging, did the pearl of E.A.R.L.—that salty dog of B.E.W.A.R.(E.), that tongue-in-cheek namer (my tongue his cheek, then skiptomelou and all hands change partners all partners hands) of Hick Fen Isle, pop I and holding: I mean a-progging through the warpèd woofs of your World Wide Web, a high-tech dreck-catcher if ever there was and a not-bad second-best companion on a dark and stormy night when there's not squat to do on H.F.I. except pick one's nose and suck one's home-brew and watch sitcom reruns till the power goes, sometimes all three at once. Nowanights that menu's larger by one mighty item, with its own menus of menus of WWW menus. . . .

And here (some pages past) is where I came in: booted up Big Bitsy, unzipzip-zipped and slugged in its slot that proggèd program, then open-sesame'd with mouseclicks twain its triply exclamatoried icon. Found in the window thus 4squared upon my monitor one of those Start-Here mini-icons called READ ME; clicketyclick and what to my wandering eyes should appear but the text you've just read (if you've read it, my dear)—I mean READ ME, "Call me ditsy," et cet—followed by the option-buttons below, wherefromamong (skipping most of the text, as I'd read it this far already) I no sooner clicked O (for On with the story) than Z Two struck as if Z-squared: power down, storm-surge up, cabin shaking, lights out for the territory and that's all she wrote.*

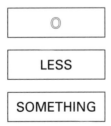

---

*Not. Zulu Two's a humdinger, all right, fit to fin this tempest-tossed siècle with. But there's those of us as've weathered the stormfraught alphabet before, and learned therefrom a few things the hard way, and survived thereby to tell the tale, so to click; anyhow to run enough versions thereof to catch its drift. Will therefore now rebag(bag[bag]) this disk, refloat it off on the surge To Whom It May Concern, catch me a few raftered z's till Z has zed, then set out a-progging mañana after washed-away *Nameless* in hopes of refinding her and the porch she's moored to and/or EARL or/and who knows, maybe my own ventriloquizing self. Let me however just leave you, TWIMC with this wrap-up sentiment, and then the option-buttons are all yours: It is one thing for an A-10 attack bomber to disappear into Colorado's wild blue yonder, or a multigigaton bulk carrier to break up in the Roaring Forties with nary a trace; you may invoke your Yew Eff Ohs and your Bermuda Triangles to your nutcase heart's content. But man & boy et al I've worked the Bay since Hector was a pup—a-oystering, a-crabbing, a-haulseining, a-rod&reeling, even a-bay-piloting and a-hydrographic-charting a once upon a time. I know this Chesapeake the way I once knew my EARL's sweet bod, is what I'm saying: every blessed freckle and lump and cranny-hair. Even know her bottom, durned if I don't, I mean my Chessie's, the way some seasoned Bay-sailors know her top. And you can't tell *me* that there is or lately was (as this here disk claims) a great mothering *showboat* stuck on a shoal with all hands somewhere out there, that nobody's yet caught sight and fetched the TVnewscopters athwart of: Nosirreebob! But if somehow there subjunctively were, after all, so improbable a beastie as *The Original Floating Opera II* aground out yonder on "Ararat Shoal" and floating SOSs off in Ziploc™s while *en attendant Zulu*, you can bet your bottom shekel she's history now.

But don't take Ditsy's word on't, mate, for I'm a coin as 2-sided as this disk: For more on TOFO II click LESS (you get the idea) or whateverthefug else you opt. Hop to't now 'n' click something, though, luv: Curtain-time's a-COMING SOON!!!

58

Tess Gallagher

Her Speaking, Her Silence

No one knew what had caused the sudden death of her mother's dog—not the veterinarian, his receptionist, nor the high school boy who'd last walked the dog. Gretta was told an autopsy could be performed by Dr. Milburn, but naturally, it would be an added expense.

"Did she run away?" her mother, Rose, asked. She had edged her chair back from the kitchen table. The tail of one gray braid from the bun at the back of her head rested limply over her shoulder. She was still in her robe.

Gretta said only, "Monet's dead, Momma," and continued to pry details from the receptionist. Their little holiday at her sister's seemed to be ruthlessly over.

Rose had been accompanied each day by the black cocker spaniel, Monet. Its spirit of eager attentiveness had accompanied her as she'd hauled leaves to the compost heap in her red wheelbarrow. When Gretta arrived at her mother's each evening, the spaniel would bound toward her in welcome as if shot from a cannon.

Gretta recalled how trustingly the dog had leapt onto the floorboard of the jeep that last morning at her mother's. Up it had scrambled onto the passenger seat, excited to be going anywhere, even to the vet's. It had been especially well behaved once they had arrived. This came back painfully now. Gretta had stroked her glossy coat and told her—"Good Monet! Very good girl!"—the dog's tongue splashing her hand as it gazed up as if to say, "What's next—you-to-whom-I-have-entrusted-myself?" Gretta had then handed the dog's leash to an assistant, bent down, caressed Monet once more, matter-of-factly, as if nothing out of the ordinary were happening, then left through the glass door without looking back. How differently she saw the scene now. Still, she was glad she hadn't turned. Nothing worse, she felt, could lodge in one's consciousness than the limpid eyes of an animal's unquestioning regard.

"Never a sick day in her life," Rose said—her silent mind suddenly eruptive.

"Dr. Milburn's receptionist says the dog was just fine," Gretta reported.

"Then the next thing, they found her dead." She intoned the practiced bad-news decorum of the receptionist: "Sometimes these things happen and you don't know the cause."

"It was a very hot day," Rose said aloud, but to herself. "They fed her dry food, but didn't give her water. Maybe all the windows were shut. She must have died like those dogs locked in cars for hours with the windows up. My poor Monet!" Then she was weeping. Having weathered the Great Depression, Rose habitually met adversity with resourcefulness and stoic self reliance.

But now she was really and truly crying. Gretta tried to think on what other occasions she'd seen her mother weep. There'd been the time their younger brother, Lyle, to whom her mother no longer spoke, had lost the end of his finger to a lawn mower when he was ten. She'd cried then. Lyle had played the piano and Rose had entertained visions of him as a musician. He was an only son and Rose now cried on most occasions when she spoke of him, as if he were dead, as indeed, Gretta thought, he might as well be, for it had now been eight years since Rose and Lyle had broken with each other over what Gretta considered matters of money and pride.

Gretta had also witnessed her mother shed tears once inexplicably while telling a dream about a boy killed by a fall from a tree. In her dream sheep grazing had moved forward to huddle protectively around the fallen child. But somehow Rose had known it was too late for protecting and that the boy would not survive. Gretta had mentally connected the dream to her brother, because he'd been a sleepwalker and she recalled following him through the sleeping house one night, trying not to wake him, but ready to stop him, should he endanger himself. How strange he had seemed, a feeling which had persisted beyond that long ago childhood night. She felt he was somehow different, even a little cursed, certainly more in need of vigilance than she or her sister. How had she gotten him back to bed? She couldn't recall.

The trouble between her mother and Lyle had persisted like an inaudible murmur over the years. Gretta could imagine other families carried worse, but she felt ashamed when people asked why, since he lived in the same town, she didn't ask him for help with her mother. She used a shorthand phrase: "They don't get along," and so exited conversations in which she might have confided how heartsick the situation truly made her. She'd tried, on several occasions, especially at holidays, to broach the possibility of the two healing their differences. But each held ground, would steam and fissure and gust complaints so vehemently when she mentioned the other, that she finally stopped trying. Still, she continued a silent witnessing not so far from those childhood nights when she'd followed her brother room to room, afraid to startle him awake, but ready to guide him back, should he try to leave the house.

As she and her mother began the drive toward home from her sister's the following day, children playing with dogs caused Gretta to recall glimpses of Monet dashing through the corn, the dog's mitt-like ears swinging to and fro as it ran.

"She never strayed off my place," Rose said, assuming a mutual ongoing current of concern with Gretta. "We'll never know. Maybe the boy who walked her couldn't handle her. Maybe she got loose and was killed."

Gretta couldn't really take in these alternative deaths. She only knew she didn't want to interrogate anyone at the clinic where the mater had been left swiftly behind. She too wanted the unexplained death to move into the past, but she saw her mother wouldn't allow this.

"They're not about to tell us," Rose said, as if some deeply accumulated suspicion about the way the world at large worked had now begun to attach itself to the dog's death. "Who's going to ask for an inquiry?" Rose said. "She's just a dog." Gretta knew she was right, that if there'd been neglect they would never know.

The salutary poinsettia Dr. Milburn had sent Gretta at Christmas, after her own cat's death, should have won him more favor that it had. The ritual of flowers was helpless to assuage such deaths. An embarrassed decorum prevailed instead, as if the unspoken and unacknowledged deaths of animals dared, unreasonably, to rival and even, at times, to outstrip the griefs of the human-to-human world. All of this, Gretta realized, was well protected by an off-limits designation of feelings for animals as "sentimental," an over-investment. How considerate language was, she thought, peremptorily fortifying its practitioners against otherwise legitimate pains.

Rose had discovered Monet, the painter, through a photograph and diagram of his lily pond in a garden book. She had talked now and then about having someone dig such a pond on her property, and had even made a list of the aquatic plants from Monet's pond. But the intention stayed a dream.

"Monet was on the shore painting," Rose suddenly began to recall, "but he was painting and forgot about the tide. There went his easel, out to sea." Her mother seemed to feel her own inattention might have caused her dog's death. After a silence she said, "She was only a pup."

"Nine years ago you got her, Mother," Gretta said quietly. They had, in fact, recently spoken of how Lyle, in the pre-silence days, had discovered the mud-spattered dog trotting along the roadside. When no one had claimed it after a few days, he'd brought it out to their mother. This was perhaps the last act of kindness that had passed between them.

"He thinks a dog's the only fit company for me since your father died," Rose had remarked at the time. The dog had worshiped her, clicking back and forth on the kitchen tiles, responsive as the tail of a kite to her every move. Yet when Gretta asked what she'd named it, she said, "Nuisance. It's always under my feet."

She spoke to it in an affectionate scold, and the more attention she gave the dog, the more constricted the animal's territory became. But a few weeks later the Nuisance was renamed "Monet," and Rose had placed a rug at the foot of her bed where the dog would sleep on the coldest nights. Her mother's quarrelsome tone persisted with the animal when anyone was within hearing, yet Gretta suspected there were reasons for the dog's affection, and that when her mother was alone she caressed it and spoke to it as if it possessed an understanding and sympathy the rest of the world lacked. All the pain she eventually locked up in her heart against Lyle had seemed to flow out again as love for her dog, the one living sign between them.

"I'll dig the hole," her mother said, as they took the familiar turn off the highway and came to her house. Gretta helped her to the entry with her cases.

As she drove toward town, she realized that at the vet's she would have to carry the box with the dead dog inside and place it into the back of the jeep. She dreaded the weight of the box. She hoped, when she got it home, her mother would not want to look inside.

When Gretta entered the clinic office Dr. Milburn was standing behind the counter. He raised and lowered his shoulders as their eyes met.

"Wish I knew what to say."

"Not easy," Gretta said.

Dr. Milburn was a freckled man whose blue eyes, marooned there in his broad face, always reminded Gretta of a male version of Little Orphan Annie. Before, when she'd taken her cat to the clinic, they would talk about local events. He'd joked once that he'd won five bags of steer manure for the smallest fish caught in the salmon derby. Despite past congeniality, she realized she now subscribed to her mother's accusative anguish which intimated that Dr. Milburn had somehow allowed things to come to this. Her mother, she knew, would have sunk her tongue into him like a buzz saw.

Gretta loved her mother's clear anger. How seldom one encountered truly righteous anger anymore, she realized. Oh, a person could meet theatrical, in-your-face, off-the-wall venting in public places often enough. But that purified river-of-gold, nail-on-the-head, truth-giving anger—no, that was rare. There was something almost epidemic, she felt, in how uniformly people eased things out these days, jettisoning righteous anger before it could take on its antiseptic flush. It was no wonder, she thought, that Lyle was afraid to come near her mother.

When Dr. Milburn said, "I'll carry the box for you," Gretta realized with a pang of sympathy for him that scenes with dead pets and bereft owners occurred regularly in his life. He disappeared into the back of the clinic, a mysterious place where customers were never allowed—with good reason she now supposed.

Moments later the veterinarian reappeared through a door opening onto the parking lot. Suddenly, against everything she'd intended, Gretta reached out and Dr. Milburn handed her the dead dog in the small brown cardboard box. It was surprisingly light. Maybe her mother's imaginings had been right and this was only whatever was left of the animal after an accident. Or maybe the dog was indeed lost or buried elsewhere and not in the box at all.

"She's taking it hard," Gretta said, trying to bridge the awkwardness as she stepped past the doctor toward the open jeep hatch.

"I'm really sorry," Dr. Milburn said. Gretta slid the box into the jeep and brought down the hatch with a mean little click. She didn't want to say the next thing, though she didn't clearly know

64

what it would be, so she opened the door and climbed in. Dr. Milburn backed off a few steps. Instead of waving as she backed out, she held up her right hand like someone testifying. In the rear view mirror she saw the veterinarian turn and walk, head down, through the back entrance and into the clinic. It was, she knew with an odd tug, the last time she would intentionally see Dr. Milburn.

When Gretta arrived she found her mother digging the hole near a giant cedar in the front yard. White hair puffed from the edges of her mother's red wool scarf and the loose end of her braid against her shoulder retained the arc it had held when coiled to her head.

Gretta gazed into the shallow hole. The dirt was rich and black—the sort of dirt in which things grow well. Her mother's foot came down with determination on the ridge of the shovel. She scooped out dirt, then turned it onto a cone-shaped pile at the side of the hole.

"Let me see the box," Rose said quietly. Gretta went back to the jeep, raised the hatch and reached inside. Whereas the live dog would have leaped from her arms, she again experienced the stillness and weightlessness of the cardboard carton. She bore it away from her body.

The dog, in its sudden, unexplained death, seemed strangely to represent a multitude of unexamined animal deaths for which human beings were, as a rule, not held accountable. But beyond that, it was also like some relic of her mother's and brother's reciprocal refusals, some culmination or silent last retort between them. "She's old. We won't have her long," she'd once appealed to him. "Make your peace with her." What Lyle said had silenced all pleas: "As far as I'm concerned, she's dead." After that, when she was with her mother, Lyle's words would occur to her and she would look across eternity at Rose as if she were alive and dead at once, which meant that Gretta also felt herself to be outside time. Gretta caught herself wanting to ask each of them: *What do you want of me?* She doubted they would know. Still the question persisted: What was her place in the matter?

"Did he say any more?" Rose asked, still thinking Dr. Milburn might have sent her some fresh clue.

"Only that he was sorry," Gretta said. But her mother was absorbed by the box in her hands. Gretta saw it was all she could do to imagine her dog inside. Rose bent and tried the box in the hole. Then she moved it to the side and began to widen the opening. There was a gloom under the low boughs of the tree. The wind ruffled fallen leaves from nearby maples.

Gretta thought that Lyle, if not for the unfathomable breach with their mother, might also be standing with her at this moment. How a mother could throw away a son, for whatever reason, she could not fathom. And likewise, Lyle's disavowal baffled her. She did know that no matter how badly her mother might treat her, there was no way Gretta could imagine turning her back on her. But she did not think herself better than Lyle. She thought only that love, whatever form it took, involved a quenching of one's will, a giving over for mysterious reasons, against the tide of one's own advantage or even wrongs. Lyle's heart had clanged shut and she had felt the horrible *forever*, the rueful, piteous finality of it. He had somehow galvanized his will to a fixity that abolished all that might be expected of a son toward his mother. Was he free then? And if so, what did such freedom mean between two people who had once held that bond—mother and child? It was an enigma Gretta revisited again and again, as if she might uncover some clue as to how people were bound together, and how their ties could be irretrievably broken.

"He should meet such as my Monet again," her mother said, speaking again of Dr. Milburn. But Gretta felt Rose was also speaking of her own slim chance of ever again finding such unstinting devotion.

Her mother tamped the loose dirt over the box with the back of her shovel. She passed the sleeve of her sweater across her face, then adjusted her scarf. The shovel was like a third presence between them as they walked to the house. Gretta had read somewhere that because of its use in gardens and graveyards, the shovel was one of the oldest implements on earth. She thought of her mother as a kind of human shovel, ancient, made for digging, for turning the earth, for getting to the bottom of things.

In the weeks that followed, as they went about their errands, Gretta more than once observed her mother in a close group talking with people neither of them knew. She recalled how Rose had often confided to strangers that her own son did not speak to her. But now she was telling the death of her dog, making known the actions of Dr. Milburn, the veterinarian who had reported the animal dead without a reason—a perfectly healthy dog. *Dead without a reason.* Rose told the story at the bookstore and at the supermarket. She told it when the winter tires were put on her car. She spoke of it from her garden, to people walking past. Several shook their heads and vowed, although she had not asked for this, that they would never again take their animals to Dr. Milburn's clinic.

A week after the dog's death Gretta had been intercepted in a hallway at the investment office by her investor's partner, a Mr. McNelly, whom she knew slightly. He was a white-haired, distinguished looking man—the sort you would trust with your money because he was tall, had good posture and wore a vest. He began to report an encounter with her mother.

"She told my wife, and she just stood at the roadside and cried," Mr. McNelly said.

"She's alone all day now," Gretta said to the broker.

"You're not a dog," Mr. McNelly said matter-of-factly. It was not something one ordinarily pointed out. His odd remark seemed to imply Gretta could not hope to console her mother, and that perhaps Gretta had even mistaken her own importance in her mother's life—not only in this matter, but altogether. Gretta moved past the man and entered her advisor's crisply sterile office and took a seat. *What, in the scheme of things, was a dog?* she wondered, as she looked around at the computer screens with lists of commodities jerking in columns off into wider, ungraspable space.

Mr. McNelly's pronouncement reverberated. The largeness of what the animal had given her mother impressed her freshly. What, after all, could absorb loneliness as animals did—without speech, without demanding anything in return, indeed taking whatever came? She again saw how much of her brother's defection from her mother's life this dog had unknowingly assuaged.

At last her financial advisor, Mr. Henry, came briskly into the office and began at once to talk animatedly about new tax laws and tax exempt bonds. How the market, though bullish, would hold a bit longer. Perhaps *we* might *venture in* after all. He always used *we* when he proposed a new investment. He had purchased some "strips" but *we* would "unload them" at a profit *at the right moment*. There'd been losses, he acknowledged, but only "on paper." Let them alone, he said. He always said this. Gretta watched as he ran options onto his computer screen. She felt soiled, unable for commerce—this vague manipulation of funds, dividends, losses in far places. Instead she began to tell Mr. Henry about her mother's dog.

"Monet," he said. "Wasn't he that French painter who went blind?"

Gretta felt half blind herself, yet plunged ahead with her account of the dog's sudden and unexplained death. It was as if her entire consciousness were submerged, awash in the sting and pull of something she could only follow to its farthest reach. She described picking the box up from the veterinarian, and her mother as she'd dug the hole, how painfully light the box had been. She told him what it was like to go to her mother's now, how she missed the dog racing at her with the unmindful lunge of ecstatic recognition, the impetuous devotion her mother had been bold enough to receive as love. And, as she spoke, an image came to her of some as-yet-unlived scene. She was standing at her mother's graveside and she knew somehow that, then and only then, Lyle would be there too. She realized she felt a mixture of things—regret, relief, joy. But most of all regret that it was too late—that she must now receive him in her mother's stead.

"Yes," Mr. Henry said. "There's nothing like the love of a dog. I'll never forget my childhood dog Tippy."

Gretta knew he had turned from matters of finance, of gain and loss, to say this, and that Mr. Henry meant his remark as a connection to what she'd just told him. But she felt, no matter what he might utter, the exact harm of what had befallen this dog, her mother, Lyle and even herself had eluded him.

As she gazed at the scrolling columns of figures on the computer screen she thought of the hourly affection given by her mother's dog. Let Mr. Henry figure percentages on that! She fixed her attention on the screen. Names and figures dissolved to ungraspable shapes that flickered, then rolled upward and away in the screen's icy glow.

Mr. Henry continued to reassure her that the market was strong and going to stay that way. His voice rose and fell at a distance, tidal and not in the least in need of her. It raised her mother's voice, relentlessly telling and retelling something she refused to forget. Like most voices on earth, Gretta realized, it was an unrecorded voice. Yet it was nonetheless etching itself onto the cosmos as only it could. If she were to tell anyone what she heard, what she loved in this voice, it would be like trying to find words to describe the raw pungency of seaweed to someone who'd never walked near the sea. Something ribbon-like and threaded through waves would still be utterly missing. The voice kept speaking, no matter what anyone received or understood, and this speaking made the world more present, more searching and alive. Gretta didn't know why this was so, but it was, and she was again touched with pity for Lyle, that he was never again to hear that voice. This aspect of his disaffection affected her own awareness, so now when she heard her mother speak she also heard her for Lyle.

Mr. Henry stood before her at the door leading into the corridor. They were both smiling as if, through mutual effort, something difficult had been accomplished, yet Gretta felt neither of them, had they been asked, could have said exactly what it was. Two sleepwalkers had simply chanced to collide in daylight and woken briefly to greet each other.

Then, like reaching into the next life, she pulled open the door and was carried forward into a hive of voices that clung to her and swept her along inside a wide cacophonous fervor—overlapping, insistent. Her own voice was there too, marooned inside her. Also present was a deep listening that included her brother, whether he knew it or not. And something else was alive for her—something of what it was to speak words, to utter unresolvable, unspeakable pain—or like an animal, to simply make the same noise, helplessly, again and again.

Largesse

CHRISTINA HAD A RICH AUNT SHE HAD NEVER MET, HER MOTH-
er's first cousin, actually. Aunt Demaris lived on a ranch in Alabama part of the year and on a ranch in Texas the other part. She
and her cattleman husband had not been blessed, as she put it,
with children. Her Christmas presents to Christina, which usually
arrived before Thanksgiving, were lavish and sometimes completely inappropriate. Christina was allowed to open them at once
because her mother and grandmother were just as curious as she
was to see what was inside.

One Christmas a sizeable box arrived from Maison Blanche in
New Orleans. Excavating through postal paper, store gift wrapping,
and tissue paper, all of which the grandmother folded and saved,
they confronted what at first appeared to be some flattened exotic
animal. But no, it was a child's coat of spotted fur with matching
hat and muff.

"She's out of her mind," said Christina's mother, "this is *leopard* skin. And it's her handwriting on the card, so it's not some hired shopper's folly this time."

"The child can't possibly wear this to school," said the grandmother. "And she certainly can't wear it to church."

"Perhaps they haven't heard at Maison Blanche or out at the ranches that there's a war on," remarked Christina's mother in the low deadpan voice she employed for her caustic mode.

They gave the coat, hat, and muff to the cleaning woman's little daughter. Christina's grandmother lied tactfully that the coat was too tight in the arms for Christina, and that of course the hat and muff must stay part of the ensemble. Christina never tried on the coat, nor did she remember wanting to. The thank-you note had to be written all the same, and she went to work on it on Christmas day, after the presents had all been opened and there was a sad lull in the living room. Her grandmother was doing a crossword puzzle. The Christmas day edition of the local newspaper rested on her mother's lap; she had been rereading the interviews she had done with the wounded servicemen at the local military hospital.

"So far I've got *Dear Aunt Demaris*," Christina said glumly.

"That's an opener," said Christina's mother. "Be thankful I didn't name you Demaris."

"You wouldn't have!"

"She hinted. But I said your father had his heart set on Christina."

"He did?" Christina's father had been out of the picture since her infancy and she was always interested in more information about him when her mother was willing to volunteer it.

"No. He wanted to name you Greta."

"*Why?*"

"Oh, after Garbo. I don't know."

"*Dear Aunt Demaris. Thank you so much for the*—WHAT? Help me!"

"You need an adjective," said her mother.

"I think I used wonderful last year."

"Let's see: remarkable, unusual, unprecedented . . ." Her mother uttered a snort and lost control. "Thank you so much for that unprecedented disaster of a coat." They both dissolved into wild laughter.

72

When they had finished, the grandmother, without looking up from her puzzle, suggested, "How about grand? Thank you so much for the grand coat."

"Mother, that's just inspired!" Christina's mother exclaimed in sincere admiration.

"I must get something out of my crosswords," replied the grandmother.

Liberalities from the unmet aunt in Texas marked successive Christmases: the filigree and pearl music box that played "Toora Loora Loora"; the gold mesh bracelet studded with heart-shaped diamond chips that Christina admired on her wrist until she lost it in mid-summer; the brocaded kimono-bathrobe with its big sleeves that caught on doorknobs; the rabbit fur jacket, worn once to a dance and then packed away. Christina's thank-you notes got easier, as did her command of adjectives most likely to impress and please. After Aunt Demaris requested it, she always enclosed a school picture of herself.

When Christina was fifteen, Aunt Demaris wrote, or rather her secretary wrote and Aunt Demaris signed the letter in her ornamented script, inviting Christina to spend Christmas with them at their Texas ranch. While the mother and grandmother were debating over what to do, a telegram arrived: ALL EXPENSES PAID OF COURSE STOP PHONE COLLECT STOP EAGER TO HEAR.

"Well, here it comes," said the grandmother.

"Pandora's box," Christina's mother enigmatically murmured. "What about it, Christina? It's your invitation. Would you like to go?"

"I don't know, I guess it would be an experience." Christina tried to picture how the older couple would go about entertaining her. She was pretty sure there would be shopping. She hoped her uncle would not expect her to ride a horse well.

The phone call was made, not collect, the mother and grandmother were too proud, but then they regretted it. First a maid who couldn't speak English answered and had to go and get another maid who could, and then Aunt Demaris was "detained" for a while longer. When at last her cousin came on the phone, Christina's mother's face crunched between the eyebrows and, looking strained, she started speaking in a funny way. At first it sounded like a parody of someone being gushy, but later she explained to Christina that Aunt Demaris brought that out in you. After Christina's mother finished the phone call, she declared herself exhausted and went to lie down.

The airplane ticket arrived, followed by a huge package from Neiman-Marcus. Inside was a white Samsonite suitcase and inside the suitcase were a black velvet skirt and top, a turquoise velvet cummerbund, a black taffeta slip, and dangling earrings of turquoise and hammered gold.

"I suppose she trusts us enough to supply the proper underclothes," the grandmother remarked as she carefully folded the tissue paper.

In the weeks preceding the trip, they crammed Christina with Demaris stories, some she heard before, but this time with an extra deliberateness, as though they were preparing her for some kind of test.

"She was always strong-willed," said the grandmother. "Even before her parents were killed. She was my husband's little niece. He and his brothers helped raise her in their mother's boarding house. This was when they were all struggling to make ends meet. The boys worked in the iron mines and came home every morning with rust-colored skin, and the mother cooked for the boarders and changed their sheets. But they treated Demaris like a princess, and I guess she just assumed that's what she was. When she was sixteen she made them all become Roman Catholics. All but my husband, he was in the Masons, you know, and had to refuse her. Then she met Karl, he was from a family of German immigrants, just a young assistant in a butcher shop. She made *him* become a Catholic and taught him math and good English and next thing you know they owned a meat market, and they branched out into cattle and before they knew it they were millionaires. Demaris credited their good fortune completely to the Lord, but she was always very appreciative of my husband's family. Though she never warmed to me. I was too reserved, I guess, the way mountain people are. And

I wouldn't play cards with them on Sunday when we visited down in Alabama."

"I think the math and good English ought to get some credit for the fortune, too," said Christina's mother.

"Good English? I'm not so sure. Look at me and all *my* English—where has it gotten me?"

Christina's mother drove her a hundred and fifty miles across the state so that she could fly to Texas without having to change airplanes. This was possible because the junior college where she taught English for not enough money was on Christmas break. Despite her brilliant feature stories (what other local reporter could have interviewed Bela Bartok in French?) she had been let go from the newspaper after the war so that the men could have their jobs back. In her low moods, she could be quite caustic about this.

Christina's mother had turned down the grandmother's offer to come along. This made it into an adventure, since the two had never traveled anywhere alone. Mother and daughter left before dawn, while the stars were winking in the black winter sky. Aromas from the bacon and egg sandwiches and the thermos of coffee, packed by the grandmother, wafted enticingly from the backseat of the old car, bought new in a more prosperous era, when the grandmother's husband was alive. As they wound down the steep curves of the mountain roads and the sky began to lighten beyond the ranges, Christina's mother suddenly began to talk with a strange urgency about the father who had been out or the picture since her infancy. "He was just so damned handsome and charming and equally unsuitable, but I wanted him, and I got him. By the time you were on the way, I knew it wasn't going to work. But I still wanted you. Daddy was still alive and he and mother wanted you, too."

"*Why* did you know it wasn't going to work?"

"He was unstable. Also he drank. When he was doing that he could be mighty cruel."

"You mean like *hit* you?"

"Oh, that, too, but the things he said hurt more."

"Like *what?*"

"I've forgotten. I really have. I need my self-esteem. And he was a sick person, so it wasn't entirely his fault. He was in a mental hospital for servicemen during the war."

"Is he . . . in one now?"

"No, the last I heard he was in Florida, teaching tennis in a hotel."

"Doesn't he ever want to see me?"

"I think he probably does, but, you know, Christina, everyone isn't as *resolute* as we are. Some people can want to do things, but then they don't follow through. Now your Aunt Demaris is the very opposite of your father. She follows through. Which is why I got onto this subject, which isn't my favorite. But I needed to fill you in some before you were exposed to . . . well, other points of view." She was being unusually careful in choosing her words. "When Daddy died suddenly, Demaris and Karl drove up for the funeral in their Cadillac and we'd hardly buried him before Demaris made me a proposition. She wanted me to bring you to live with them, she wanted to sort of adopt us both. The offer didn't include Mother. Demaris didn't like Mother very much. She considered her 'cold'—Mother didn't know how to gush—and also I think Demaris had Mother's role in mind for herself. I said I would need some time to consider it."

"Did you consider it?"

"Not really. Oh, I fantasized some. Obviously we would have been spoiled to death, but I would have sacrificed our independence. And how could I have just deserted my own mother like that at such a time? But Demaris is the type of person it's easier to turn down in a letter."

They were down the mountain curves. The morning sun grew stronger along the straight road until they could feel its heat inside the car. "Why, it's plain warm down here in the flatlands?" said Christina's mother. She pulled into a roadside picnic area and they ate their sandwiches in their coats at a table strewn with fallen leaves and acorn shells. Each time they unscrewed the top of the thermos, the hot coffee sent steam into their cold faces. "Well, isn't this just *grand*," declared her mother meaningfully, and they both recalled the leopard coat and hat and muff and burst into giggles. The mother breathed in the sharp, clean air and looked around with delight at the deserted picnic grounds and the bare trees. "You know, despite everything, I am glad to have kept my independence. I hope you will feel I did right."

The elderly man by the window offered to trade places with her when he learned that this was to be Christina's first flight. They changed seats and he laughed good-naturedly when he had to keep letting out the seatbelt straps to make ends meet over his portly middle. He sat back in complacent nonchalance as the plane roared and shuddered and raced down the runway past the point of no return and lifted into an emptiness tilting dangerously to one side and then the other. Christina was grateful to have the example of his calm masculine demeanor. By the time they reached cruising altitude, the most amazing fictions, replete with realistic details, were pouring out of her in response to his congenial inquiries. She was going to spend Christmas with her father, who owned ranches in Texas and Alabama. Yes, her mother and father were divorced, had been since she was a little baby. At first they had been crazy about each other, but it just didn't work out.

That happens, he said with an understanding nod.

Her father insisted on having her every other Christmas. They would ride around the ranch on horseback and then go into town and have lunch and go shopping. Her mother always worried he would spoil her with all his money, but she had hopes and dreams of her own, and besides, she valued her independence.

As they were landing, the man declared feelingly that he would have considered himself honored by the gods to have been granted a smart, lovely daughter like herself.

As they disembarked, an elegant, sharp-faced man in black tie and evening clothes stepped forward at the gate and pronounced her name. For an instant she was confused, it was like walking into her own fantasy. As the man was introducing himself as Clint, who worked for her uncle, she was aware that her traveling companion, a few passengers behind, would assume he was witnessing the father-daughter reunion. What if he should come up to them and say something to expose her? But he passed on discreetly, with a brief nod and a wistful smile.

Close up, Mr. Clint, as he told Christina everyone called him, was not as elegant as his first impression. His face was tough and large-pored, and after he had stored her suitcase in the trunk of the Cadillac and explained that her aunt and uncle were at a dinner party they could get out of and had sent him to meet her, settle her in at the house, and then go back to pick them up, she decided he must be some kind of upper-grade servant, between a butler and a chauffeur. But he was a smooth-enough talker without saying or asking much and glibly kept awkwardness at bay.

It was dark by the time they turned into the gates of the ranch, which was named "New Canaan" on Aunt Demaris's stationery, so she couldn't admire the approach, which Mr. Clint boasted was stunning. In daylight from this entrance road you could see a hundred miles in both directions. That would be farther than she and her mother had driven today. But it would be a hundred miles *less* than her mother would have driven on the round trip. For some reason this gave Christina satisfaction.

The house was lit as though the aunt and uncle were having a huge party themselves, but inside there was nobody at home but the maids in their black uniforms and white aprons, only one of whom spoke so-so English. They served Christina her lone supper in the chandeliered dining room: thin slices of steak in a tasty sauce, with yellow rice and some spicy compote and warm tortillas swaddled in white linen on a silver dish, with guacamole and sour cream and a pale-green relish heaped attractively in crystal side dishes. She would probably have eaten twice as much if they hadn't been taking turns peeking at her through the tiny hole in the kitchen door. She tried a bite of the mystery relish and choked: she had drunk all the water in her goblet. The maid who didn't speak English burst through the swinging door with a pitcher of water. "Too *caliente*," Christina apologized between gulps. "But it's *muy buena, gracias.* Everything is just *muy buena! LA COMIDA ES MUCHA BUENA.*"

The other maid rushed into the dining room. Standing on either side of her they began chattering eagerly at her in their language. Christina exhausted her meager supply of Spanish phrases convincing them she could not follow. For dessert there was *flan* with caramel sauce, and a small glass of a sweet pinkish wine.

Big and little clocks, distant and close, kept chiming the quartet hours and still they didn't come. Christina felt it would show poor manners to go to her room and lie down, so she chose a tolerably comfortable straight-backed brocade sofa, beneath a life-size oil painting of a platinum blonde Rubenesque lady in a low-cut red gown and red jewels. Feeling more relaxed from the sweet wine, she arranged herself into a portrait of a modest young woman awaiting, not at all resentfully, the return of two *grand* people she had been longing to meet. The Christmas tree in the corner of the living room was loaded with ornaments that had the look of all being bought at the same time. It was bigger and bushier than the one that now took up most of their living room back home, but this room was big enough to dwarf the larger tree. Beneath the tree were piled dozens of professionally-wrapped presents, an excessive number of them bearing cards with her name. She wished she had brought gifts, but nobody had been able to come up with any sure idea of what might please the millionaire relatives.

The Texas Christmas tree blinked its colored lights at her. On and off. On and off. They will be getting ready for bed now at home, Christina thought. My grandmother is switching off her last program; my mother reads a couple more paragraphs in her library novel, then sighs and turns down the page. Maybe they are speaking of me at this very moment. Then with a desolate jolt she remembered they were two time zones later than she and by now would be asleep. On and off blinked the lights.

Then there was a sudden brightness and energy, a burst of outdoor air and a fusillade of extravagant welcomes and endearments. The maids fluttered about like two nervous black birds, plucking at the sleek coats of the two large people who stood quite sumptuously still allowing themselves to be unwrapped for her delight.

Christina heard herself called blessed girl and darling one and *much* prettier than her pictures and a great deal more. She was praised exorbitantly for her courtesy in waiting up for them. Now she, too, was standing, offering herself to their hugs and compliments and perfumed kisses. Aunt Demaris was of course the platinum blonde lady in the oil-painting, only now she was wearing a black gown and different jewels and had grown much more Rubenesque in figure. But her face was still elegantly-planed and beautiful. "We had a *flat tire*, of all things! Would you believe it, darling?"

"Inexcusable is what I say," roared the big rosy uncle. "A brand new automobile just out of the showroom and there we are on the side of a dirt road, me and Mr. Clint, jacking up a blowout in our tuxedos," Despite the mishap he seemed elated.

"He was superb, Christina. Yes, you were, my darling. Mr. Clint wasn't too keen on spoiling *his* finery until your Uncle Karl here set the example. He gave me his cufflinks to hold and rolled up his sleeves and got right down to business in the dirt."

"I hope I haven't forgotten how to change a tire," said the uncle, whose clothes bore no sign of any contact with the dirt. "Well, well, well, Demmie," he exclaimed expansively, an arm around each of them. "We hit the jackpot, didn't we, with this pretty girl here!"

After another glass of the sweet wine for her and her aunt, and "something stronger" for the uncle, during which there were extensive inquiries about her airplane flight and her dinner and the well-being of her mother and grandmother, whom Aunt Demaris said they must remember to phone first thing in the morning, they sent Christina of to bed. Since she had been to her room last, the maids had unpacked her new suitcase and put everything away where they thought it should go and turned off some lamps and turned on others. Everything looked inviting and pretty, if a little stuffy and overdone. Her folded pajamas awaited her on the pillow, her cosmetics and brush and comb were laid out across the glass top of the vanity. She hung up her dress and got into her pajamas and went into the adjoining bathroom to rinse out her stockings and panties. She had just arranged them on the towel rack above the bathtub and was drying off her hands when there was a soft knock at the bedroom door.

"I simply had to see my girl one more time," said her aunt, sweeping in. "Ah, you're already in your dear pajamas. Are these flannel? We might want to get you something lighter while you're in Texas." Demaris had changed into a creamy satin kimono with braided gold loops down the bosom. Her face, cleaned of its makeup and lubricated for the night with an orange-smelling cream, made her seem simpler and more open.

"Come sit here by me on the bed and let me look at you." Which she proceeded to do in minuscule detail. Face, hair, nose, eyes, figure, were described and praised in turn. Then she stroked Christine's hands and pulled at the corners, proclaiming them to be exact replicas of her grandfather's. "Uncle Tommy had the same sweet hands, small for a man's, but strong—he worked in the iron mines when he was young, you know. He was the world's kindest man. I wish you could have known him!"

Christina said she wished she could have, too, adding that her mother and grandmother still spoke of him most every day.

"Not a *single* day goes by that *I* don't think of him," rejoined her aunt passionately, making Christina feel she had betrayed them at home by not exaggerating and saying every single day.

Aunt Demaris strolled into Christina's bathroom and stood gazing pensively down into the toilet bowl, as if hoping to read clues to her niece's character. Thank God she had flushed. Then she saw her aunt stiffen when she discovered the stockings and panties dripping on the towel rack above the tub. "Ah, darling," she scolded sadly. "We can't have you doing the *washing* here. We'll let it go this time, but from now on just put your little things in this net bag behind the bathroom door and Marta will take care of them for you."

Christina had not failed to notice the baby blue rosary draped invitingly across the small, framed wedding picture on her bedside table. A young, slim, rather fierce-looking bride clung proudly to the arm of her butcher boy husband. As it happened, Christina was acquainted with the mysteries of the rosary, as well as its soporific effects. But she had no desire to disturb it from its ornamental function tonight and presently consigned the whole room and its contents, as well as those of the adjoining bathroom into pitch darkness. She arranged her limbs straight as a mummy's between the soft Marta-laundered sheets and simply breathed in and out until she could feel the return of her own spirit come like a sudden rush of oxygen to her lungs. Scenes she had no control of, based on nothing she had seen during this eventful day, surged toward her on the inside of her eyelids, then rapidly gave way to other scenes. As she lay there calming down she rightly guessed that she would make many stupid mistakes before the end of her visit, and that she would be forgiven each time, perhaps even loved more for them. They would be discussed as touching and charming and a little sad after she was gone.

Already she knew deep down in a part or herself she had yet to meet, that these people were not for her. But there would be future opportunities for temptation, and one or two times just short of desperation, when she would do her level best to surrender herself into their captive embrace. But each time, by the grace of God, wherever he operates from, and thanks to the independence her mother had early ruined her with, she would sabotage herself and blight her chances, again and again, with these grand people so eager to make life easy for her.

Cris Mazza

Familiar Noise

DOWNTOWN IN A LITTLE OVER AN HOUR BY CITY BUS. RONNIE spreads a slice of bread with peanut butter, her father eats, dozes some, wakes to stare at people on the sidewalk whenever the bus slows at a light or stops to exchange passengers. Then Ronnie leaves her hunting-vested father in the library with a Zane Grey novel and some plastic-covered gardening and outdoor magazines she selects from the periodical rack. Signs in the library forbid its use for sleeping by the homeless. Not only the odor and snores, but the dufflebags or grocery sacks, layers of ragged coats or fatigues no matter the weather, and the use of newspapers as drapes to block fluorescent light, will alert librarians to route them out and send them away. Her father doesn't smell, his hair and scalp are clean, only the bulky, blood-stained, fatigue-colored, underwear-stuffed hunting vest suggests his transience. So she has to take the hand-cart with her, several blocks away, to the county administration building and the department of records, then must leave the handcart behind an empty security guard station because taking the gun through the metal detector would likely elicit too many questions.

Of birth records, she finds only one, hers, Veronica Tattori. Her father and mother weren't born in San Diego County, not even in California. In this category, births, their names only appear once, as her parents. Chad could've been adopted. Adoption records would be sealed, wouldn't be considered county business. But Ronnie remembers photographs of her pregnant mother, leaning over to put her distended belly into toddler Ronnie's arms like a beach ball. They might've used the gestation as a first home-schooling lesson on reproduction. Ronnie can't remember when she *didn't* know that you put the doe in with the buck, observe the mounting, the agitation, the fall, and a month later, almost exactly, the fertilized doe constructs a nest of straw and her own softest fur, then delivers the litter of finger-sized, blind, pink, hairless, practically-still-fetal offspring. Ronnie knows her imagination never ventured to draw a picture of her parents engaged in similar behavior. She can't recall any distinct shift from ignorance to procreative knowledge. It was like the history or mathematics or geography her mother taught her, mornings at home—human reproduction was information without personal participation. Never having set foot in a schoolyard bustling with the heated bodies of jostling children, half of them male; never having known a boy older than the four or five-year-old Chad, never having had daily contact with testosterone-impelled adolescent youth, she's known only her father, and old men, and now he's one and the same.

And what's the point in this particular strain of lament? Too many other things she's never done, and who can weigh one as more considerable than another? She never took a test, never wrote a term paper, never sent an application to any college, never joined scouts or soccer or band. Didn't ever have a part time job flipping hamburgers or scooping ice cream. Never danced under black lights or a disco glitter-ball, never waved a pom-pom, never lay on the floor with her feet against the wall twirling the phone cord around one finger and pressing the receiver to her face, never rode in a fast convertible. No softball teams, no summer camp, no cap-and-gown, no new workplace wardrobe, no first car nor first apartment, no girls' night out, no wedding showers, never a brides-maid.

No need to examine county marriage and divorce inventories, she turns her attention to deaths. Tattori, Alicia Elizabeth. b. 4/10/32 d. 6/15/73 Cause of death: accidental drowning. No news here. Ronnie was seventeen and, the day before, had been told her home schooling was complete.

But, again, no Chad in this category. No *Chadwick Keith*. Would've said *b.* 1962, maybe '61. He's not on microfiche nor microfilm here. No birth, no death, as though the tragedy has been erased. Her father is right, no one knows he ever existed.

On their way to the bus stop, she'd thought aloud: "Before we go traipsing all over the county, I should put our papers in a safe place."

"Too much stuff. Don't need it."

"I know, you always thought we brought too much." She'd thought the handcart might rattle itself to pieces rolling over the dirt roadside on Central Avenue. "But I'm only talking about some papers, birth certificates, your Army discharge papers, social security stuff. Maybe I'll get us a safe deposit box. I hope we got all the stuff out of the house. Did you know we don't have a birth certificate for Chad?"

"Can't prove he lived or died."

"What's that supposed to mean?"

No answer. So she'd taken the detour to the office of records before doing their banking business.

At a drug store between the county building and the library, she buys two maps, City of San Diego together with East County—which contains Dictionary Valley—and a map of North County which includes the fairgrounds, lagoons, coastal sloughs, and inland rolling hills and flatlands now burgeoning with housing developments and growing cities no longer small enough to call towns or suburbs.

After sliding the worn manila folder of papers into the safe drawer, she pins the key at the bottom of the game pouch on the back of the hunting vest. She'll need to restock their cash, although hesitates to carry more than twenty dollars, so she picks up a list of branch locations. The estate sale two years ago, auctioning the land and house and most of the contents, netted enough to eliminate the hospital debt from her father's treatment in an emergency room, three days in intensive care, and over two weeks on the ward. But she has been able to save some every month from her nurse-aide checks, after paying the part of her father's monthly bill not covered by Medicare.

Although Ronnie expects to find him sleeping where she left him, he's not asleep and not at the table where the magazines and Zane Gray novel are spread in a fan around where he'd been. He's not far away, though, on a vinyl bench in the video section watching a PBS *Nova* about the formation and drift of the continents. A tap on his shoulder and he follows her back to the table where she spreads both maps. She's also taken every individual bus schedule from the rack in the library foyer.

"Help me, Dad. Where did we used to hunt? And which is the one you want to go back to?"

In the chair beside her, elbows on the table, his face barely six inches above the map, leaning so far over the table his butt lifts off the seat, with one finger he traces interstate 805 down to the border. The freeway probably wasn't yet constructed when they hunted in the South Bay.

"Dad . . ."

His finger returns north on 805 then veers onto an even newer expressway, the South Bay freeway, which heads east before it curves gently to the north and slices through Dictionary Valley.

"No, Dad . . ."

But his finger jumps from the freeway, crosses the reservoir, stops, traces the name of a planned community. "What's this?"

"Something called Sunnyside. Looks like all houses now." The streets and tiny printed names entwine and circle each other like a thumbprint. "Did we hunt there?"

"Not anymore."

"Well we can't go back *there*, Dad, what're we gonna do, walk into someone's living room or bedroom and say I used to hunt—"

"Not there. Figs." He points to a thin black line crossing a white two-inch expanse of map, just above the border, Dairy Mart Road, no other roads, no names of communities, no little schoolhouse markers, no shopping centers, just the blue line of the Tijuana River. "In the river valley."

"I don't remember rivers when we hunted. Maybe little creeks."

"It floods, everyone has to be saved and they always go back. And their horses."

"You mean where they lifted the horses out with helicopters that time the Tijuana River flooded? We used to hunt there? Is that where you want to go first"

"It *floods*. No one should live there. Morons—keep going back."

"So you're saying that's not where you went with Mom's and . . . the . . . ashes?"

"Not where it floods."

"God, Dad, just tell me *where*."

"We hunted all over."

"Do we have to remember and find each one so you can say *not there?*"

"Maybe you can remember for me."

"I don't know where you took her ashes. You didn't take me with you."

Her father has yet to take his eyes from the map. His finger re-enters the interstate. "North."

Other than recognizing an approaching season—dove, rabbit, duck, shellfish, winter produce, spring buds needing protection, summer fruit to preserve, autumn pruning and mulching, trout season, the next high tide, the next forcasted rain or dry Santa Ana wind—Ronnie can't recall looking into the future with either anticipation or curiosity over what changes might await her there, nor with concern over how she would prepare for or build toward another life. Now looking ahead with design was a difficult custom to suddenly be capable of.

On another bus heading north, Ronnie tries but has trouble pushing her thoughts forward to next week or next month, let alone an eventual time when she'll be living in an apartment somewhere, hearing a phone ring through one wall, a stereo pulsate through another, planting her father in front of a television while she's out to work for whatever kind of employer will find her skilled enough. Isn't that the only feasible forecast, after they're done doing whatever it is they're doing? She clasps her hands in her lap to prevent herself from using nails and teeth to peel pieces of cuticle from her fingertips.

"Dad, we have to decide where to get off the bus."

"Okay." He lifts his head as though waking up.

"How about where Mom shot the hawk? Wasn't that a place we used a lot? It's the only place I even remember. Probably because of that hawk. I remember that."

"We never took a bus."

"I know but this time we had to."

"It's getting late. Best in the morning."

"We just need to find the place."

"Everything's changed."

"How did you get there? Can you remember?"

"Camino Real. Lots of good places. Go north as far as there's time for, then work your way south . . . toward home."

"We don't live south anymore. We don't live anywhere anymore."

Probably our most game-rich hunting area was just off the seaside freeway in North County where several lagoons carve into coastal lowlands, meeting small creeks, creating marshes and, slightly further inland, dry washes and small orange sandstone gorges. It was private property where the landowner ran cattle, so the small creek making its way toward the ocean had been blocked in several places with dirt dams, creating watering holes no more than 30 feet across. In an arid region, water attracts birds—especially dove who feed in grain fields and on the seeds left behind after cattle forage. It was lowland but not really flat— the stubby sandstone bluffs and gullies, slightly higher plateaus, partitioned by clusters of huge eucalyptus trees imported 50 to 75 years before. Dry, steppe bushes—anise, tumbleweed, buckwheat, wild oats, lemonaid berry, sage—and familiar sandy watersheds, bristly sand grass where grasshoppers flew in front of each footstep. We found snakeskin and weathered, bleached seashells. The whole tract was crisscrossed by cattle trails, dotted with parched cattle droppings. We never saw the cattle.

It was when our mother joined our father hunting, when we were 2 and 4, that they began bringing us along. Partly to expose us to the philosophy: Shooting was something you did with concern for safety as well as preservation of the terrain, including mindfulness of game limits and which birds were strictly off-limits; and was an activity you did as calmly and quietly as possible, except for the report of the shotguns. Partly to teach us the techniques: We padded softly in their footsteps, trained to stay behind them, to stop and squat down as soon as we heard the whistle of dove wings, so our parents could raise and aim their firearms and follow the flock in their sights, in a complete circle, over our heads, and pull off the four shots allowed them by two double-barrel shotguns.

The practical reason for taking us hunting was that we were the bird dogs. Dogs qualified to not only find the downed game, but to first locate and collect the spent shells which could be refilled at home. While still the only people on the face of this terrain, we did occasionally find other shells and picked them up too; sometimes our father could reload more shells than he'd spent. After gathering up the four shells, after tramping into the underbrush to where our conditioned eyes had marked the exact spot the game had fallen, we decapitated and drained blood from the bodies before the retrieve was completed and the headless bird slipped into the back flap of our father's hunting vest.

There's a grocery store and strip mall where the bus stops at the corner of El Camino and La Costa. But the stores are not at street level, they're part way up a hill—a sharply sloped landscaped embankment—with the backs of the buildings and their signs looking out over the street toward the ocean. It takes a while to get her father up and into the aisle, put her rucksack on her back and lift the handcart from the empty seat in front of them. A group of men waits, standing close behind her. Two kids with skateboards go out the side door.

From where the bus drops them, they can either walk to the corner, turn right, go uphill on the sidewalk half a block, turn right again and enter the strip mall. Or they can hike straight up the landscaped embankment on a narrow dirt path worn through the ground cover by many short-cutters. A small, low sign beside a sprinkler head in the landscaping groundcover says *Auga Impura, No Tomar*. The group of men who'd been crowding behind her in the aisle of the bus choose to go single file up the dirt path. Three Mexican men with a fourth who's head-and-shoulders taller, all are wearing worn jeans, T-shirts, and flannel jackets. The Mexicans wear Dodgers baseball caps, their thick black hair dented in back by the hats. The fourth man has long dirty-brownish hair in a ponytail and carries two plastic water jugs. The teenagers lounge on the bus stop bench and light cigarettes. Their pants are longer than shorts and shorter than jeans, huge barrel-wide leg holes with their bare shins sticking out and immense high-up sneakers on their feet.

Ronnie and her father use the sidewalk. It takes a while. Her father is clearly tired. Outside the grocery store, beside the phony fireplace logs and drinking water dispensers, there are two tables with umbrellas, as though the grocery store is also a French cafe. Her father, as if given an unspoken direction, sits and waits there while Ronnie goes in to get fried chicken and potato salad at the grocery's deli counter. They stay at the table to eat. It's around 3 in the afternoon. The teenage boys from the bus have attracted another one riding a tiny bicycle the size a clown might use, and the three are on the asphalt in front of the store using the concrete curbs and parking bumpers for skateboard tricks. Several cars, backing out of parking slots, have to jerk to a halt as a skateboarder or bicycle suddenly whizzes behind them. The parking lot echoes the crack of board against concrete, the shouts of the riders—*Dude! Dream on. Like hell. Fuckin awesome!*—now also car horns and the boy's surly curses in response.

The migrants come out of the store, each with two bulging sacks. It's easy to identify milk, juice, bread, bananas, a cantaloupe and head of lettuce, in addition to the bumps of miscellaneous cans and boxes. Ronnie's father bites the meat off a drumstick, his eye on the skateboarding boys.

The potato salad is so goopy, there's probably more mayonnaise than potatoes. "Hey, Dad? . . . Why didn't Chad have a birth certificate?"

"One thing and another."

"What does that mean?"

"Born at home. Just us there."

"But there's also no—"

The store's automatic door opens for a man in a red coat to come out. He cups his hands to his mouth and shouts, "Hey, fellows, no skateboarding allowed here, please leave the parking lot, it's dangerous, someone's going to get hurt." He's ignored, finally bellows, "Hey, you boys, *hey!*"

"Dude, it's a free country," one boy yells.

"Not on private property."

"Fuck you."

"You can say that to the cops." The red-coated man retreats into the store. As Ronnie stands to bundle the bones and trash from the table, the long-haired migrant comes over to use the drinking water machine, and the boys roll right past the table in the car exit lane, standing upright on their boards, the bicyclist following, insolently disregarding a car that's forced to inch slowly behind them. As they head out of the parking lot, their smirks are aimed at Ronnie, at her father, at the man filling his water jugs. The bicyclist sneers "get a job" over his shoulder.

The bank next door has its own parking lot, ringed by narrow ribbons of sparse landscaping—hard, raked dirt sustaining typical mock-orange shrubs and medium-sized heavily-pruned eucalyptus trees. On one side of the building, a wider bed of dirt with winter pansies and heavenly bamboo, backed-dropped by a waist-high hedge and the windowless, doorless side wall. The drive-through lane emerges on this side of the bank, the entrance is on the opposite side.

"We have wheels, so we'll drive through, okay Dad?"

"What for?"

"Money, for a motel tonight. Maybe three nights. Think two or three days will be enough?"

"Plenty for some things, not enough for others."

"For what you want to do. To find the place you want to find and do whatever you have to do there."

"I promised her I'd come back."

"Yes, I know."

Midway across the bank parking lot, she spots the three boys in a far corner sitting on a curb in the spotted, flickering shade of one of the larger trees, their feet on their skateboards in the gutter. The bicycle lying on its side, crushing a couple of shrubs.

Just before the drive-through lane makes a left turn toward the back of the building, a big convex mirror mounted high on the corner provides a darkly distorted, far-away view of what lies ahead. One car is idling in the narrow lane. An arm reaches from the window to touch buttons on the bank machine. The drive-through is almost a tunnel—asphalt lane, stucco bank wall, stucco overhang, and on the other side of the car, a shoulder-high stucco wall including pillars that support the overhang. The wall separates the drive-through corridor from the same landscaped embankment sliding downhill to the bus stop on El Camino Real.

After the car drives on, Ronnie moves forward, leaves the handcart in the middle of the lane. On some silent cue her father's hand replaces hers on the handle and he stays behind as she steps to the ATM machine. The wallet is three layers down, canvas pants on top, jeans under that, then spandex bicycle shorts with a hip pocket holding her billfold. Three nights in a transient motel, can't be more than $90 for two, plus food—she decides on $120. While the machine seems to count bills—humming and whining, like a discussion behind the wall regarding whether or not to give her that much cash—her father also makes a noise, a startled grunt. The handcart clattering to its side as he falls and cries out once more—and for a second, less than that, waiting mesmerized for the thick stack of bills to shoot from the machine, Ronnie's heart flies, a hot flash of freedom: another stroke? But he'd taken his medication that morning. Her short flight already over, a brick wall slams into her from the rear, the machine spits the money, a hand not hers grabs it, her arms pinned behind her back, another hot hand over her mouth, too many hands to count, the wallet pried from her fingers.

"Welcome to the neighborhood."

"Time to pay taxes, bitch."

"Dude, bring'er over here."

"How do we even know it's a girl?"

"Being ugly's no excuse, man."

"See if she has anything else." Knapsack ripped from her back.

"I'm not touching her stinking shit." The knapsack kicked into the lane where her father, on hands and knees, struggles to get up, one foot under the handcart as though the cart weighs enough to pin him down. Then she's seeing only a blur of concrete and bare moving legs and big athletic shoes and the hedge and the wall of the building down where it meets dirt. She's on the ground, half in the bushes, between the wall and the hedge's lowest branches, bushtits fleeing shrub-to-shrub in a twittering panic of tiny flickers and flutters.

"Fucking Christ she's fucking biting me."

"Stuff something in her mouth."

"What, man?"

"Shit, your dick, asshole."

"With those teeth?"

"Christ, look where we are, someone's gonna come."

"Yeah, like *you*, dude."

"*Me*—why not you?"

"Sonofabitch she's strong, *hold* her, dude, I can't get my pen out."

"Maybe it ain't even a *she*."

"Like, then, find *out*."

"How?"

"Dude, didn't you take sex ed 101?"

"She's like, wearing fifty-million fucking pairs of pants."

"There—*tits*, it's a bitch all right."

"Call those tits?"

"Like I said, ugly's no excuse."

"Suck it, dude."

"Get outta the fucking way, man, she's getting her passport."

Her two sweatshirts and two T-shirts bunched over her face, twisted elastic bra strap across her eyes and nose, a pair of hard knees on either side of her head, something cool touches her chest, sharp scent of ink, between collarbone and breasts a line crosses her sternum, then two circles dip around and back up, circling each breast like wire rims of a bra, below that another line and a spot, then another line parallel with a cross. A boy muttering "bitch, bitch, bitch," as though to a tune. A hand digging, burrowing beneath her waistband, drilling its way toward her crotch.

"Dude, get her fucking pants off, I'm almost done up here."

"There's, like, what the fuck—bicycle pants, I'll never get these fuckers off."

"You fucking give up too easy, dude."

"I can't let go've her fucking legs, she's like *bionic*, dude."

"I'll get her, go ahead, man, *rip* them, where's your knife?"

There's another voice that nobody's listening to, not even Ronnie it seems, until she realizes it's herself who hasn't shut up the whole time, *No . . . No . . . No . . . No . . .* biting the hand that periodically attempts to cover her mouth, *No . . . No . . . No . . .* heaving her entire torso right then left then back again despite the 150 pounds sitting on her head and another 150 on her knees, *No . . . No . . . No . . . No . . .* wrenching hands and arms free from a vice-grip and flailing not with fists but bared claws until he crushes her wrists together in one fist again, *No . . . No . . . No . . .* her throat growing more and more raw but the voice remaining strident, fueled more by feral dread than pain. Frightening enough to recognize it's herself she hears in abject, brute panic, even more horrifying to suddenly grasp there's another word she's yelling.

Mommy . . . Mommy . . .

Something familiar, as though she's cried like this before. But before the impulse is answered, her remaining senses come blasting back. The abrasive hard dirt and little pebbles and sticks scouring her back, skin of her arms twisted from front to back, the harsh sour smell of her own savage sweat, silvery bright taste of blood in her mouth, a car horn down on El Camino Real, tiny shout of the guy hawking papers at the traffic light. The voice becomes louder, but her own now obliterating everything else, and when at once, simultaneously, she is released, she's already, immediately on her feet as though she was a rat trap they'd been holding open, as though a *crack* when they release her and the trap snaps shut empty is the kind of detonation ending all other noise.

94

The long-haired migrant is beside her, holding a knife. The boys six feet away, a semi-circle, a stand-off, the migrant with a switch-blade, but there're three of them. The migrant's Mexican companions have not accompanied him into the bank's drive-through.

"What're you gonna do, dude, tell our parents?"

"Who'll believe a stinking homeless fucker like you?"

"No one'll even miss you if we kick your ass."

"*Gun!*"

Even before the boys' rubber soles slap asphalt, after they burst in three directions through the landscaping, Ronnie is instantaneously crouching, fingers in her ears but eyes up to locate where the game falls.

"Hey there," the ponytail guy is practically crooning, the first she hears his voice "it's okay, old man, it's over, they're gone now. I owe you one."

Her father, shotgun raised, stands amid the contents of the hand-cart that he'd had to empty in order to liberate the gun.

It's not until they're a mile east on La Costa Avenue—the four-lane road that crosses El Camino at the light, pushing uphill, above and parallel to a creek bed golf course—that Ronnie sorts through what she's been told by the ponytailed migrant whose name is Adrian. About a quarter mile ago the four men had turned off La Costa to cut through a residential tract. The canyon where they make their camp is that direction, over a hill developed with houses, just past an elementary school, an untouched hillside sloping down toward a dry rainwash arroyo. Ronnie and her father—now with no money, no bank card to access cash, no identification of any kind with which to obtain another bank card until she can get back to the safe deposit box downtown—are on their way toward a different place to camp, recommended by the ponytailed guy as safer because it's farther from work areas therefore not populated by worker camps. It's beside a creek, though the water might not be drinkable. He'd attached one of his water jugs to her hand-cart before he and his companions had crossed La Costa to make their way home. Just up ahead, he'd instructed, about a mile and a half, take the second left, downhill, it'll look like nothing but condos and apartments clustered around the end of one of the golf course fairways, but just keep going, there'll be a cul-de-sac where the road ends but there's a chained-off utility vehicle route that runs steep downhill—go past the no trespassing sign, down the hill to the creek. If the water's high it'll be flowing over the service road, but don't cross, take the trail to the right on this side of the creek. If you go left, you'll be on the golf course in less than a quarter mile, the creek cuts through the golf course, creating lawn-bordered ponds so that mallards, egrets, and great blue herons will be part of the golf resort's milieu. That's what he'd said, *milieu*.

Off the service road to the right, though—he'd said—as it progresses east there's a sheer, rocky ravine where the creek comes down. Actually it's in the midst of a housing development, but the houses are far above on the bluffs, with the creek way down below in the gorge, the sides of the canyon too steep to build on. The houses way up there look out over the golf course to the ocean, but right on the other side of their backyard fences, the natural canyon plunges almost straight down hill into the undeveloped ravine. Don't go too far into it, he'd said, you don't need to go far to feel it's like natural wilderness. Closer to the service road, the water is slower and spreads out in a pool with reeds and mud hens, towhees making nests underneath last season's fallen fennel with last year's dried grasses snarled in the stocks. Likewise, for people, crawl under the low laurel sumac bushes and it's a natural tent. Perfect camping place, he said, except too far from work and the bus to be practical for us. Meaning himself and his three friends and others like them.

She's still hearing her voice calling for her mother, a sound at once so utterly foreign and terrifyingly familiar.

The three Mexicans had reappeared immediately after the boys had fled, the sounds of skateboards and curses still clattering and hooting from the parking lot on the other side of the building. With plastic grocery sacks still dangling, one from each hand, the Mexicans had come from the dark drive-through entry lane, as though they'd been waiting there for their turn at the ATM. These're good guys, the ponytail explained, but they stay clear of those kids, there's been trouble, a lot of trouble, and, naturally, migrants like these guys can't go to the police. But *you* can, he'd said, do you want to call the police?

"No, I can't. My father. They'd take my father."

The tall ponytailed migrant didn't ask her why. The three Mexicans spoke in Spanish and he'd answered with much shorter sentences. "I just told them your father won't shoot," he'd said.

"The shotgun's not even loaded."

"You can imagine how they get jumpy about people with guns, but they're more leery of those kids than an old man with a shotgun." Some kids from around here, he'd explained, have made it a sport to harass migrant workers. Harass isn't even the word for it anymore, considering they've stolen food, money, watches, shoes, anything they can force a Latino to hand over. Plus there's scuttlebutt that they'd taken potshots, sniper-style, at men on their way to work in the flower fields; that they'd written vulgarities on people's bodies with ink that requires gasoline to wash off; that they'd driven past the roadside meeting places where contractors and landscapers pick-up daily workers, one kid hanging out the car window with a baseball bat, trying to get a crack at the closest head; that they've got some secret white-middleclass-kid club where they keep score of how many wetbacks they get, variable points earned for various infractions. Word's out to stick in groups of three, preferably four or more. There's even been farfetched hearsay of some rapes, of both men and women, with broomsticks or flashlights, one story had them attempting to castrate a worker they found waiting alone for a ride at the Home Depot—rumors, he said, which seem *somewhat* more credible now, although that last one was still a stretch.

Do the workers also scream for their extinct mothers, a sound suburban mockingbirds will mimic in calls to their mates, or does their fear of deportation keep them silent throughout?

At some point, while reloading the handcart, cleaning bits of gravel from a scrape on her father's elbow, or during the slow trudge up La Costa Avenue before the four men turned off—she could tell her father's pace was significantly delaying the migrants' usual trip home—the tall ponytailed guy, Adrian—she should remember to use his name—explained how he'd come to live and work with the Mexican migrants. He'd been a college student, probably ten years ago, doing field work on the native geology, flora and fauna in coastal scrub. Then he'd switched his major to cultural geography, a comparative study of the migrants and the nomadic indigenous people who'd populated this terrain hundreds of years ago. To really know something, you had to live it, not just watch it, he'd said. Hadn't gotten very far with the thesis, but had never left the life, he was one of them now.

When the ponytail had noticed no blankets in the handcart, just the one raincoat wrapped around the protruding barrel of the shotgun, he'd taken off his jacket and instructed his companions to do likewise, and had tied the bundle of four jackets to the side of the cart. She doesn't need to be told that it gets to below forty degrees out here at night, especially in the deep canyons, even lower next month, there'll be frost.

As they get nearer to the right turn downhill, the sidewalk levels off. Then at the bottom of the short hill, two level blocks of apartment or condo complexes, each with a gate into some kind of courtyard, sometimes a pool that's centered in the complex of doors like a fountain at the center of a mission's courtyard. There are still some empty lots between developments, green with thick new weed growth this time of year, taller anise and mustard at the property lines where the once-a-year tractor mower doesn't reach. And at the end of the street, a cul-de-sac circle of road, a for-sale sign on the last green, graded lot, and a cyclone fence with a chained-off opening big enough for a truck. From there, a cruder stretch of asphalt pours once again downhill, but at a steeper angle than would be suitable for any residential street. Their footsteps fall heavily as they make their way down into the gully, leaning backwards, the handcart now no longer being pulled but held back to keep it from pushing them downhill too quickly. The vegetation here has not been graded. Laurel sumac and lemonade berry bushes are thick and head-high.

As the ponytail had predicted, the creek runs over the pavement. The running water spreads out to about twenty feet across and several inches deep as it crosses the asphalt in a smooth liquid sheet. The service road acting partly as a dam, a small quiet pool of water has collected to the right, the shallow flow of water passing over the asphalt is like spillover on a tiny reservoir. On the other side of the creek, the service road makes a beeline straight up the opposite side of the gully to another housing tract up above.

The path off the road, running beside the creek east through the gully, is hard mud, not too slippery, with little litter, although if the creek had been higher in the past week or two, that would explain the absence of cans and papers. Dog footprints are pressed into the mud at creek's edge. Tall reeds circle the pool, a higher clump of green cattails near the center where a pair of mud hens glide silently, hardly creating a ripple. Ronnie stops. Dusk is quickly falling. She removes her rucksack, takes the hunting vest from her father's back and replaces it with one of the migrant's jackets. Her father moves away, several steps up the side of the gully then to the far side of a clump of lupine threaded with dry reeds from last year's wet season. There, she knows, he's peeing.

She'll need to do likewise, but doesn't until she's dragged the handcart and rucksack under the biggest laurel sumac, spread the raincoat over the hard dirt, helped her father to lie down and covered him with the remaining jackets. He sleeps almost immediately.

For this she didn't need instruction, she's always known the sumac bushes grow like tents, the thick gray-green leaves mostly on the outside. Underneath the branches there's a hollow shell, a fort, dark enough even grassy weeds won't grow. Standing outside, she can hear her father's slow, sleeping breath, but she can't see him. On this side, the bush's most recent growth reaches upright, each shoot supporting a Christmastree-shaped cluster of tiny colorless nodules—the flowers. When they turn to seed, they don't change shape but darken to rust then black-brown clumps of seeds, favorites of sparrow, bushtit, mockingbird, and phoebe. Not only drought-resistant but fire defiant as well. When wildfires blacken entire canyons and hills, the roots of the sumac remain intact, not reliant on foliage for nutrients, feeding on the carbon remains of other vegetation. With root systems already completely developed, they can rapidly restore themselves. Often the first signs of life on a blackened hill are the shoots of laurel sumac pushing through the sooty skeletons of their former bodies.

The silence of twilight is like the relief of a fading headache.

The ground is dark, the sky still slate. In the open, on a hillslope of sprouting wild oats, Ronnie lifts her T-shirt and sweatshirts; pushes down her canvas pants and jeans and spandex bicycle shorts, past her knees, to her ankles, frees one foot in order to spread her legs. Her pale body visible against the dusk, and she sees the letters, fat black ink on her skin, the *T C H* across her stomach and hips. And she feels, once again, the loops of the *B* circling her breasts, the dot of the *I* boring into her ribs. A brutal shudder, a silent shatter, something breaks, hot urine streams down her legs and tears down her cheeks, but no sound this time. Except a rustle of mice, hush of the creek, whisper of leaves. The mournful murmur of roosting dove, or an owl. The cry of a hawk. Or *is* that her voice again?

At what point did the earsplitting chaos start? Certainly not before our knees buckled to squat below the line of fire, the reflex so quick, so instinctive, impossible to say for sure which came first—the motion of our mother's gun being raised or the children hitting the dust at the sound or sight of game.

A mistake, an accident. The kestrel, smallest native falcon, doesn't have wings like fanned fingers. Its wings are pointed, like the dove. But such definite differences—without the dove's heavy-bodied silhouette, without the rhythmic wingbeat and whistle of feather. The kestrel can hover, rise like a helicopter, while the dove must take flight gradually like a bulky jet from a runway. Who could've made such a misjudgment?

Call it simultaneous—crouch down, knees hit the dust, fingers in ears, head up, the report from our mother's gun, our father's shout, and the screaming.

MOMMY—

SHUT UP, SHUT UP, WHY DID YOU—HOW COULD YOU—

QUIET, AL, HUSH UP, RONNIE—

MOMMY—

The vast, arid bottomland could hardly be touched, let alone filled, offered no resistance to our voices, just sucked the sound out of us and dispersed it. But whose voice cried for our mother? Chad, there and not there. Chad's red, wrenched face.

When did the noise end? Where was Chad?

The hawk was dead. Hooked bill flopped down against speckled breast. We dug, with bootheels, sticks, fingernails, the butts of shotguns. Suddenly the vast field existed only beneath our hands, the hard yellow earth, woody root of sage, a tiny snake who'd burrowed into sandstone. Where was Chad? Wasn't he here and there, always in the way, holding the dead hawk up by its wings—making it fly, dip and soar over our heads as we dug—and impersonating the CAW CAW of its cry?

Katherine Min

The Liberation of a Face

ONE DAY I STOPPED LOOKING IN THE MIRROR. I WAS TIRED OF
my face, tired of finding fault with it, of wishing it looked a different way or trying to make it look a certain way. It was always just
my face. Nothing could be done. So I stopped looking. And an odd
thing happened. My face went away. It disappeared. Or at least the
reflection of my face went away, the only means I had of regarding it.

Isn't it strange? That we can never look at our own faces without the aid of some object, a mirror or a lake or something shiny
to reflect it back for our own eyes to see? Eyes we can see out of,
but cannot see ourselves through. Without mirrors, without lakes,
we can only tell what we look like by what other people tell us. It's
like being blind.

At first, people greeted me similarly. They did not run away
screaming. It was apparent that they saw something still—some
apparatus of features in close approximation to eyes, a nose, a
mouth—that they could respond to. I looked in their eyes, at old

photographs and home movies, but all images of my face had been expunged. I was no longer visible to myself.

Once my face became unavailable to me, two things happened: I cared more about it; and caring for it became more difficult. I would wash extra carefully each morning, vigorously scrubbing with soap on a hot towel, then rinsing with warm water ten times; I brushed my teeth and flossed after every meal; I interrogated my face with my fingers constantly, vigilant against skin eruptions, overgrown brow or nose hairs, crust left in the corners of my eyes.

Putting makeup on became impossible. I couldn't trust myself to stay within the lines of my lips, my eyes. Blush I could still sweep on with a free hand, but I had no way of knowing whether I was wearing too much, whether one side was redder than the other. I could not tell whether the mascara was clumped or smudged, whether my eyebrows were plucked evenly, or if the concealer I normally wore to hide the dark hemispheres beneath my eyes, was concealing what was already concealed from me.

It was torturous not to be able to confirm a clean appearance, a tidiness of one's own features like a room well-swept. I did not like the idea that others could look at me while I could not; that I could see their faces but not my own. I realized that to recognize oneself each morning anew was a kind of exercise in existence. You get up and you see yourself in the mirror and you think, "Here I am." It was reassuring, this ritual, the familiarity of self, conjured and re-conjured like an auto-hypnotic spell. Without my face, I felt off-balance, tentative. I became obsessed by what I could not see.

I took to asking my lover to describe my face for me each day.

"You're beautiful," he would say, dismissively. As if that were the end of it.

"No, no," I'd protest. "Tell me truly what you see. In *detail!*"

And he would go over the checklist. Eyes brown with dark lashes. Sharp nose. Even teeth. Lower lip full, upper lip thin. Slight scar over the right eyebrow. Black hair to the shoulder.

I was not content with factual information, I wanted impressions, overall feelings.

"You look tired today," he'd say. Or, "Your eyes look sad." "Today your face is as fresh as a budding rose." "Your smile is like the flickering of a candle."

After we made love, he would run his thumb across my profile as though cutting with a blade. He would graze my forehead, the ridge of my nose, my mouth, my chin, all the time staring at my face as though it were something sacred to him, something rare. This became more exciting to me than the sex itself; this way he had of examining my face. Tenderness like exaltation. He took ownership through touch, through the authority of his gaze.

I began to live in his eyes, to live through them. To feel I could see what he saw: my own face like a thing separate from me. Or to put it differently, my face lived in his eyes. When he went away, it went away. I went away. I lost face. It began to be a problem.

"What do you see?" I'd say, greeting him at the door.

His own face would flush. "I see you," he'd say, thrilling me with his clarity.

"Anything different today?" I'd ask.

He would study me a moment. "No," he'd say, "it's looking much the same today."

"Nothing different at all?" I'd push him.

"Well . . ." He would look more closely. "Maybe a bit more desperate."

After a time, he grew tired of looking at me, of being the mirror.

"The problem with you," he said, "is you have a poor self-image."

"I have no self-image at all," I said.

"See what I mean?" he said, and left, swinging his portmanteau.

Without him, I was inconsolable. I did not like to go out. There was no one else I trusted with my face; I did not want strangers looking at it, desiring it, judging it, passing it by. I would peer out my curtains at the people walking in the streets and feel their indifference like a cold wind through the open window, and I was glad to stay inside, away from scrutiny.

Gradually I stopped caring what I looked like. What did it matter, if I had no one to tell me? I didn't wash for days. I threw my cosmetics out. I barely brushed my hair. On the occasions when I had to go out, to run an errand or to buy food, I noticed people shying away from me. Their own faces looked startled by mine, as though they were looking at a ghost. I did not bother to smile or to frown, or to evidence any facial expression at all. If I could not see, why should they?

In this way, I began to re-inhabit the world. I presented myself to it as I saw myself in it, a blank, a cipher, a nonentity. A faceless woman. I no longer expected any sort of reaction at all when people happened to look upon me; I began no longer to require one. And the strange thing was that I became happy. I saw the faces of others, their looks of suffering and boredom, of longing and displeasure. I saw also—mostly on children—looks of delight and curiosity, of sadness and rebellion. And I knew that their faces were my own, that I had access to all of these ways of looking by means of what I saw.

I sat in the park and sketched them. An old man sitting on a bench, wrinkled like a shar pei; a young girl sunbathing, pearls of sweat beading on her upper lip; a woman feeding pigeons, her expression of intense compassion; a businessman reading a newspaper with downcast mouth and eyes. I saw their faces like gifts offered up to me, like opened books. Their generosity astounded me. I found no face unlovely, none without interest or complication; the sheer variety moved me.

Sometimes I would dream my face at night, my features ardent, vivid. My eyes. My mouth. I would wake up smiling in the morning. Memory became my mirror. Private and nocturnal. My face floated in my unconscious like a balloon.

It was nothing I would share with anyone. I was shocked I ever had. It seemed too intimate, too crucial a thing. In dreams, my face was the face of my dreams.

I existed this way for many years. I was used to the way people treated me, comfortable with the non-recognition that stood in their eyes when they saw me, the passing over of someone not relevant to them, not fully registered. I, who for so many years, had craved the double take, the quickening intensity of a male gaze. I carried within me the memory of my beautiful face; I carried it like a secret fetish, like a relic. I knew what it was, what it had been. I was happy to have it hidden from public view.

And then one day, as I was hurrying down the street, I passed a shop window and caught a glimpse of my reflection. I stopped, stunned. I went back. There it was. My face in the glass. It was thinner than I'd remembered, rougher-complected, with deep creases at the corners of the mouth. The circles under the eyes had grown darker, more pronounced, and there was a general sinking-in of the cheeks, a hollowing of flesh. My hair, wildly knotted and standing out from my head, had gone completely gray. It was like looking at a ruin.

The memory of my face shattered then, like a mirror, each fragment a blade, a tiny sliver of cold, annihilating pain. I walked away in misery.

Mark Wisniewski

Pariahs

TODAY, AT WORK, A MEMO FROM PERSONNEL TOLD ME I'M ON probation. I don't cooperate, it said, and I have six months to apologize to B, who worked with me on The Project, for my lack of collegiality—and to file a document signed by her that states she's accepted my apology.

·◌·

It was The Summer of Love, and the alarm clock would ring, and my brother would rise from the other side of the room and wake me. He was in eighth grade, I in sixth, and I never wanted to leave bed to serve Mass. It wasn't because I was tired. I was, but who cared? It was because I hated the politics in that sacristy. Of course I didn't think of the dynamics there as politics then, but they were. You had this nun, Sister A, who minded the details—cassocks, candles, matches, altar wine, hosts, making sure our hair was combed and so forth—and the priests, Father Pastor and Father G. Sister A was holy. Father Pastor was holier. Father G, though, scared me more than both of them. He was tall, graying and lanky, and even at dawn he wore overwhelming amounts of cologne, this sour kind you'd taste on his thumb when he'd press it against your tongue with Communion. He had allergies, too, so he'd struggle with post-nasal drip, and he was cranky and concerned about his appearance, and he treated us altar boys as if we were slaves.

✑

I can't use B's name because I fear I'll get sued. Anyway, as long as I've known her, B has talked Causes at work, and her favorite Cause has to do with how my brother died, and because she stereotypes me as an evil, rock-hard guy who gets all the breaks and has no sympathy for victims, she despises me. They spread rumors about me, she and others at work.

✑

A year before my brother died, he lived in a compound in Arizona, with priests who'd been banished from parishes. I visited him once there, not so much because I wanted to, more so, I thought then, out of the obligation to family one feels near Thanksgiving. I suppose one could argue I wanted to, though, because I drove from New York to see him—and because, when I reached his area code and called him and he sounded standoffish, I invited myself over anyway.

✑

Five minutes before Mass, Father G would make an altar boy dress him. You'd have to open one of the vestment closets' fake-wood-grain doors and remove the vestment that boasted the color required that day. I don't know who made the rules about the colors—the Pope, the bishop, Father Pastor or Father G—but Father

G would mumble, for example, *The green one*, and expect you to open the right door. And whoever brought the vestments from the dry-cleaner would move them from closet to closet, so you'd never know which color was where. And when I'd open the wrong door, Father G would pinch my ear, and not in a kidding way, either—it would hurt. I would fight my impulse to yelp because the rules allowed whispering only; I wouldn't ask him to stop because he was cranky. I'd let him pinch and pray for patience.

·❧·

I feel hurt when I learn that yet another person at work misreads me as a tough guy, but, rather than tell them they've hurt me, I punish them by distancing myself and allowing them to proceed along not knowing that my brother died, or how.

·❧·

My brother didn't seem to mind Father G's pinching. Or maybe he knew more about the vestment colors than I—after all, he'd served Mass for two years before I'd begun—and he didn't get pinched. At least that's what I believed during The Summer of Love. Possibly, I think now, he was pinched all the time. I don't know. I was never there when he dressed Father G. There were two rooms in that sacristy, The Priest Room and The Altar Boy Room, and the steel door between them closed automatically, and Father G's rules said that The Priest Room allowed only one altar boy at a time.

·❧·

They say I'm sleeping with my boss, and that I slept with the significant other of a colleague on The Project. And that I threatened B physically, and that I'm bisexual, and that I mistakenly believe I'm not gay. They spread these rumors, I'm quite sure, because I haven't slept with any of them. Many of them, I've learned, have slept with one another—it's a game of sorts, I suppose, to fight the drudgery of our job—and it kills them that I avoid their happy hours and parties: they think I think I'm superior.

◌⁓

What I remember most clearly about Father G was a sermon he gave. My brother and I were serving that Mass, and my parents were out in the pews, and, because it was the last Mass of the morning, the church was standing room only. I don't remember what color Father G wore—my brother had dressed him—but the sermon, I remember, was about excellence. Actually it began as a discussion of the sin of sloth, but it was the word Excellent that made me listen. Father G. was shouting when he used that word, so loud feedback squeaked over the PA, and I remember one passage verbatim:

> If you're a diamond theif, you're a sinner for stealing, but at least be an *excellent* diamond theif! If you're a whore, you're a sinner for having intercourse outside the bounds of marriage, but for God's sake be an *excellent* whore!

I didn't know what a Whore was, but I believed I understood Father G's point. My brother and I were kneeling on opposite ends of the altar then, and I looked between the candles at him—and saw he was holding back tears. I didn't understand why. Maybe, I thought, it had to do with the definition of Whore. I thought to ask him why, but immediately after Mass he told me he hadn't been crying—and that he wanted to walk home alone.

◌⁓

I don't think I'm superior. I simply don't like people at work. Who wants to sleep with a backstabber? Plus I'm not physically attracted to them. Which isn't my fault. I mean, for one, most of these people are old. Yes, they were once hip, most of them, in fact, hippies, but now most of their Causes are as dated as The Summer of Love, and they can't handle the fact that they're dying.

After Father G's Whore sermon, my parents drove me home. At brunch, they were uncharacteristically quiet, especially since they'd just been to Mass. Then my mother said, Boys, you're father and I want to say something about the sermon today.

We're listening, I said.

We want you to know that we think it was wrong to say people should be excellent whores.

I glanced at my brother, who wasn't far from tears. Okay, I said.

Do you know, my father said, what a whore is?

My brother nodded quickly. My mother glanced at me.

George? my father asked. Do you?

I wanted to nod but didn't think I should lie. In a clear glass bowl between us, scrambled eggs were growing cold.

A whore, my mother said, is a woman who acts sexy for money.

Oh, I said.

That's not a perfect definition, my brother said.

Do you know what Sexy means, George? my father asked.

Sexy was one of those words that my gut, of late, had been teaching me. My mother had called Dean Martin Sexy. My father had said Goldie Hawn was too Sexy on *Laugh-In*.

It means, I said. Wearing little underwear. A sudden grin on my face surprised me.

My mother elbowed my father, who cleared his throat.

Sex isn't dirty, Son, he said.

Yes, it is, my brother said.

No, it isn't, my father said. Who told you it was?

No one, my brother said. I was glad they were talking to him until he bit his lower lip: again, he was near tears. It just is, he said.

No, it's not, my father said.

Love between a married man and woman, my mother said, can be glorious.

Fine, my brother said, and he threw his napkin at the eggs and rose and walked off to his room.

All we heard for awhile was my mother exhale. Then she, too, was silent: we were done talking about whores.

What is it with him? my father asked as if I were gone.

I don't know, she said. He gets edgy when we talk about us.

᷎ᵔᵕ

The Saturday after I learned about whores, I took a card table outside. I used it to sell lemonade, but no one was buying, so I moved
it to the back yard to make a fort. For its walls, I took comforters
from the house and particle board from the garage. I sat in it and
enjoyed how it kept out the sun. I ate half a tuna sandwich my
father had left in the refrigerator, then returned outside, where my
brother was in my fort—with SMB.

SMB had moved from Kentucky into his class. She wore sweet-
sour perfume and spoke quietly and had a gap between her teeth
that made you watch her lips shine. Hello, George, she said after I
poked my head past a comforter-wall. She and my brother were
facing me, their backs to the particle board. Can we, she asked me,
be alone?

For a minute, I said. Because this is my fort. After a minute, I
want it for me.

Five minutes, she said. She had a raised mole on the left side of
her neck, and I liked it and glanced away from it, then knew she
knew I liked her.

Three, I said.

Make it two, my brother said. It's too hot in here anyway. If
George wants his fort, he can have it.

Five, SMB said through her smile.

Okay, I said, and I pulled myself out and walked to the garage.
I began counting backwards from 300 but that bored me, so
I crawled to the particle board and eavesdropped.

Just once, SMB was saying.

No, my brother said.

Why not?

Because. Mine's not . . . clean.

No tongue is, SMB said. They're supposed to be coated. My sister's high school biology book says so.

Well, you won't like mine, my brother said. That's not the point,
Todd. The point is I want us to soul-kiss.

Their silence joined mine through the particle board. They're kissing? I thought.

What are you doing? my brother asked me: he was standing outside the comforter, glaring at me.

Waiting, I said.

Spying.

I didn't see anything. I was waiting to get in my fort.

He walked off and into the house. I was sure SMB would leave, but she didn't.

∾

I can handle dying. I think of it every day, probably because my only sibling died in his prime. When you don't talk about something like that, you think about it.

∾

SMB's perfume got to me—through the particle board. Just after it did, her voice said, George? in her considered, Kentucky way.

What, I said.

Come in here.

I wanted to be inside alone but wished she would stay with me too. Tell her to go, I thought, but after I raised the comforter, her forehead shone from summer-sweat, and there was that gap in her smile.

Come on, she said. I'm just fixing to leave.

I crawled inside and sat opposite her corner. Still, we were close. My brother had to have had a crush on her—that, I was sure, was why he'd left. Any guy, I told myself, would have a crush on her.

∾

I know my co-workers have invented stories about my sexuality because The Double Agent cornered me and told me so. Since then, The Double Agent tells me every rumor she hears, and we usually share a good laugh.

When we were altar boys, my brother and I were in what New Yorkers call Grammar School. In our part of the Midwest then, though, we called it Grade School. That's another reason they don't like me at work: I'm from the Midwest. I haven't been west of the Hudson for twelve years—in fact, friends I had there dislike me for having left—but my co-workers hold the Midwest against me.

·◇·

The sun was nearly up and we were almost late, but the sacristy was dark, and my brother yanked the door handle repeatedly until I said, It's locked.

How, he said, can that be?

They cancelled it, I said. Hardly anyone makes six o'clock anyway.

They don't *cancel* Mass, he said. Priests are like mailmen that way.

Says who?

Father G, he said—and the sacristy light went on, Sister A, inside, walking toward us, keys in hand. She unlocked the door, opened it enough to speak.

Go home, she whispered, eyes on Todd's.

Why? he asked, and she shrugged.

They cancelled it? I asked.

Father Pastor, she told him, said we should all go home.

An old woman, one of the three regulars for six o'clock Mass, appeared behind me. No Mass? she asked me.

Not today, Sister A said.

Why not? the woman asked.

Father G overslept, my brother said, and he tugged my sleeve, and I followed him.

For awhile we were just walking, and then we were walking home. That was strange, I said.

What, he said.

What just happened.

The guy overslept, my brother said. He's human, you know.

Yeah, but . . .

But what?

Why didn't he just wash his face and say Mass?

My brother kept walking. Half a step behind him, I kept glancing at the side of his head. He had to know I was glancing, but he kept on as if I weren't there. That was the thing about Todd as a big brother: he had his ideas and knew where he was going and rarely would tell me his plan. It wasn't that I didn't trust his leadership. It was only that, sometimes, I wished he'd talk. You know: we were *brothers*. Brothers were supposed to be close. Sometimes he would mime closeness, but never when I wanted him to. When I'd not know something, especially about adults, I seemed to disappear to him.

～⌀·

Father G's got a shiner, Paul C told me on the playground the following day. Paul C was the tallest kid in my class, a joker who scored *D*s unless he copied off me.

He does not, I said.

Does too.

You saw it?

No, he said. But my ma heard. From that lady who cooks in the rectory.

I was old enough to know about talk then—how, in that neighborhood, it usually wasn't true.

Cops brought him home drunk, Paul C said. He got drunk at a bar downtown and beaten up in an alley a block away. When the cops found him, he didn't remember where his car was, so they took his driver's license from his wallet and saw where he lived and brought him home.

The rectory, I thought, is a *home*. For me, that had been one of those facts you know but haven't realized. I pictured two policemen walking Father G into a kitchen, Father G having to explain himself to Father Pastor. I felt sorry for Father G but still scared.

I'll believe that story, I told Paul C, when I see the shiner.

You'll never see it, he said. He took a vacation. He's in Florida until the shiner disappears.

Says who? my brother said. A foot behind me, he was face-to-face with Paul C—actually, an inch or so shorter than Paul C.

Rectory cleaning lady, Paul C said.

And you believe her? my brother asked.

No, I said.

Yes, Paul C said.

You're being a gossip, my brother told him. Use common sense. Why would a priest drink in a bar?

Because bars, Paul C said, are where you buy whores.

He wasn't with a whore, my brother said.

How do you know? Paul C asked.

Because, my brother said.

Because why? Paul C said.

Because whores are dirty, my brother said. And Father G is clean.

Paul C fixed the aim of his eyes at my feet. He flattened an asphalt pebble with his sneaker toe. Todd's right, I thought, glad he was speaking his mind around me.

You don't get it, Paul C said. Father G wanted the whore *because* she was dirty. And because he was clean, he got drunk.

That's your theory, my brother said.

That's what I know, Paul C said.

It's *gossip* you *heard*, I said patiently, and Paul C. shrugged, then kicked the flat asphalt pebble toward the feet of three rope-skipping girls, including SMB, who saw us and gazed away from everyone. Todd and I are right, I thought, proud that we were on the same team. I turned around and watched him, ten feet away, facing the rectory, walking toward it. He's not *going* there, I told myself. He just happens to be walking toward it.

⟡

Maybe I hadn't wanted to visit my brother at that compound in Arizona as much I'd wanted to see the manner in which he lived.

116

Maybe I'd wanted to see that like I'd wanted to see Father G's shiner: to witness it and figure it out.

᳭

At the reception after my brother's funeral, I discovered how he'd died medically from my parents, who, during his final months, had tried to establish a dialogue with him, and, like me last I'd seen him—on that Thanksgiving in Arizona—had failed. Minutes after they told me this, I felt guilt for having abandoned him, and I sat away from everyone, refusing strangers' offers of food and drink. Priests were there, as well as plenty of folk who supported the Cause related to the medical reason my brother had died, and they talked among themselves, hugging, smiling and drinking. They view this as healing, I thought. They believe discussing the Cause can defeat evil. Their glances at me indicated they saw me as other than them, and several of them, I imagined, equated my solitude with coldness. If I continued to sit alone, I also realized, I was abandoning the opportunity to right my reputation, but I didn't care: my brother was gone, and, last I'd seen him, I'd left without shaking his hand.

᳭

On the playground that day, halfway between me and the rectory, my brother stopped walking away from me and Paul C and folded his arms against his chest. He stood like that, near the border between the girls' and boys' halves of the playground, head tilted, eyes apparently fixed. Praying? I wondered, because he was holier than me. He wasn't as holy as Father Pastor or Father G—but he knelt and prayed every night and morning while I, across the room, tried to sleep.

᳭

The Double Agent wants to sleep with me—she's made that clear—but she understands my choice to remain professional, or seems to. Despite their longstanding acquaintanceship, she dislikes B; she's made that more clear than anything. I used to think she knows nothing of my brother's death, but lately I've suspected otherwise. She asks me about siblings. She tells me about hers. She tries to know me more than anyone.

◦

Inside that compound, I felt like I'd felt in the sacristy with my brother and the priests and Sister A: everyone else, it seemed, knew something I didn't or didn't know something I did. My brother introduced me to his housemates, who had just finished eating; as I shook their hands, I felt misgiving in their grips—in one of them even shakiness. They're all Father G's, I told myself. In all of them, something went wrong enough that their superiors made them pariahs. There was no point in wondering what that something in each was, because I would, I sensed, be there for an hour at most—probably just enough time to become confused.

◦

In Paul C's presence on the playground while Todd stood facing the rectory, I didn't want Todd to be praying: that would have made him—and therefore me—too different. He's just staring, I told myself. At that tree stump in the rectory's garden.

◦

The other priests in that compound were polite enough, at times interested in the bland facts of my trip. My brother served me rewarmed turkey and potatoes and gravy, and he and they smoked and talked as I ate. I ate clumsily and self-consciously, and my brother appeared humored by the sight of my uneasiness, but only fleetingly, because the tentativeness I'd sensed in the other priests' handshakes felt as if it were spreading to all of us. After I finished my potatoes, I realized I hadn't shaken my brother's hand, and, as he brought me pumpkin pie, I wondered what particular wrongdoing had led him to the compound, then told myself not to wonder—because two impatient flicks of his wrist couldn't shake a dollop of Cool Whip soon enough onto my plate. I continued to eat as nonchalantly as I could, remembering how he and I had served Mass, and it struck me that perhaps he'd known more about Father G's disappearance than Sister A, Paul C or the rectory cleaning lady. It also hit me that the other priests at the table knew more about his—Todd's—reputation than I, and I couldn't stop thinking that, inside everyone in that compound, something appalling enough to keep secret had gone wrong. Maybe some had drunk to the point of rampant alcoholism, or had been caught with whores, or had made the wrong sermons to the wrong audiences, or had embezzled church funds, or had fondled young students or had engaged in affairs with parishioners—and my brother was one of them. Among themselves, I also realized, they might have shared Confession and forgiveness. Or maybe, because they were the bad boys of their order, they hadn't bothered with that. Maybe none of them knew more about my brother than I: maybe each, like me, was sharing Thanksgiving with strangers. Maybe my brother questioned their histories—and, perhaps, his own—as much as I.

·◊·

B was in the conference room when I was interviewed for my job, and the first time ours eyes met, she winked. My first thought was that she couldn't have done that, but today I remain certain she did. After I began working, I convinced myself to believe she'd meant it as a simple greeting. I now know it was her invitation to my co-workers' politics: an invitation to on-the-job sex.

·◊·

I'll never know why my brother's here, I decided as I ate that pumpkin pie, because asking him what had happened to him—on Thanksgiving, among those priests—would have rendered me more uncouth than anyone there. Anyway, I told myself, if I ask, he'll leave the table. I was angry that our brotherhood had led us to this deadlock of knowledge, and then, perhaps because I was among priests, I silently forgave him and me for whatever we'd done to conjure my anger. I wanted to tell him I'd forgiven him but didn't—because forgiveness without apology is rude enough to require apology itself.

◦◦

The Project, designed to raise money for B's favorite Cause, was an art contest for our fellow employees' children, and my task was to serve on a panel that judged the entries. During this panel's third meeting, called by B, we discussed criteria for awarding points to determine the winners, and I worried that my brother's death might lead me to favor unfairly entries that blatantly promoted the Cause, so I proposed that—because we were judging an art contest—we value artistic merit more than anything. The conference room fell silent, and B changed the subject to the issue of how we should divide the prize money, and the following day a memo from Personnel told me my appointment to The Project was the result of a word processing error, and that my attendance at future meetings was pointless.

◦◦

After we shared coffee and watched the second football game and the other priests rose to tell me goodbye, my brother walked me out the compound's front door and stopped us just outside it. Trusting that he, like me, was gazing over the desert to choose his words, I remembered how I'd joined SMB in my fort, then wanted to ask if he'd liked her and known I had done it, and, if so, whether his anger about that had led him to seek Father G's counsel, and if so, whether Father G had taken liberties beyond pinching his ear, and whether being victimized by those liberties had confused him yet led him into the seminary. Wild speculation, I thought. Still, I wanted to ask.

Well, he said. Anything else?

No, I said. I considered shaking his hand. Just everything.

I know what you mean. But you know? You can never talk about everything. Talking only makes everything bigger.

So what do we do?

I usually find it best just to leave.

Then how will we ever know each other?

We won't. But no one does, George. No one knows anyone. Thinking about each other makes people feel close.

I pointed behind us, at the compound's doorway. So you're just going to walk back in there?

No, he said. I'm going to stand here and watch you walk to your car and drive off. And think about you more than I would if you stayed.

·◌·

To get B to sign the statement to save my job, I could ask her to dinner and tell her that her favorite Cause was related to my brother's death: a revelation as personal as that might provide her impulse to like me. But then she'd only like a fraction of me that, combined with the rumors she's heard about me, would probably lead her to understand me less. After all, her favorite Cause, significant as it is, does nothing but explain my brother's death medically.

·◌·

Kiss me goodbye, SMB said as we sat in those corners of my fort. And I'll go and leave you alone.

I don't think I should, I said.

Why? she asked. I scare you?

No. Because Todd'll get mad.

He won't know.

He might hear. He'd probably hate me for just being here.

Why would he do that?

Because, I said. He likes you.

If he liked me, she said, he would've kissed me. At least he would've been nervous.

Why, I asked, would he be *nervous?*

Her finger ran up the particle board wall; her chewed nail glinted clear polish. Same reason you are, she said. When boys start to like girls, nervous is natural.

I might be nervous, I said. But I'm not scared.

Then kiss me.

Her perfume and mole made me want to nuzzle her neck.

You sure he wasn't nervous? I asked.

Positive. She pouted. I really don't think he likes girls. She clasped her hands in front of her face, a thumbnail bridging her gapped teeth. Anyway, she said. He left me here. And you want to kiss me. And kissing in secret feels best.

She's Sexy, I thought, and I knew right then that, for some words, perfect dictionary definitions are worthless. Crawling toward her, I felt myself abandon my brother—how he'd wake me in the morning and rush me to the sacristy and force me to comb my hair for Father G—and then we kissed and touched tongues, both hers and mine dirty, but attentive and careless and free.

Timothy Donnelly

Purgatory Chasm

The earth has done this to itself. It heaved its rock
pectoral as an animal will, a brute mating. It must have
known that it would suffer endlessly thereafter

as the sea, reverberating, raised one steely claw, a second
and another: water's slow, erosive ritual.
That brand of love. The ghosts of razor grasses

watch from precipice and crevice, seething under
and above, swept hypnotized, as we are, by the shock
and aftershock of each anticipated wave. A minute.

A millennium. It's hazy, but we're here:
a study in repetition, breathing drowsy as the brume
we're watching struggle to disperse, particle

by particle, dulled by the hauled-out act, the redundant
sea and earth. Hapless would-be gas!
It's bound by laws of physics, laws of habit, laws

and love, love, love, the heat is overwhelming, but it isn't
our affair. We've traveled southwards
from the city, so ill-at-ease en route; you held

a radiant lemonade, and I, the satisfactory radio
wired in my head: disjunctive music's drowning out.
Slaking still and still devout, we make a pair

in judgment, cast it everywhere but in; we both
approved of, once, the vista, but now it's harrowed out
The Sea Mist Inn, peopled the cliff with a pack

of naturalists. Wave on wave, this rite continues. Earth will not
recoil from sea, sea digs the deeper groove
we cut through others to inspect. A little closer.

Close. The rusted rail and sign suggest all
take precaution, be responsible. Shift in sediment
or squall can force the careless over easy—

and often does, we pray: the granting of the asked-for.
And look, I've grasped your hand. Spurred
by passion as before, I pull us near enough to drop

into the chasm, doubled over. An answer, an idea.
We want this want but turn, demure.
We are not alone. All the world is here.

Eamon Grennan

At a Turn in the Road

Lapis lazuli, gold and cochineal:
          you move through collapsed barns,
rafts of Canada geese on a stream the ice has run off,
          shaggy horses in a soaked field.

Low-tide moment, nothing grows, and you imagine
          being emptied out like this,
withered back from attachments
          like apple orchards in December:

the child striking sweet chords; the face across the table
          smiling at something the cat does;
the smell of what's cooking
          when you come in again from the cold.

Mingled Yarn

Cut to the bone, they kiss at the door. Lips
a little scaly, only the child's cry can bring them
together and running: she dances
heartbreak, sings whatever has no cure.

Silence is a fever of wishes, the knowledge
bodies carry, walls of the skull hung
with annunciations, still lifes in which his
own skin dangles, a nest the crows emptied.

By degrees, sycamore leaves crowd out the sky:
a mansion of green and blue, air speaking leaftongues.
How can feathers, airy bones, changes in the weather
turn his mind around, melt the ice in his mouth?

He is making what has to pass for prayer
to sea-sounds, the smell of salt, that dull thud
his own heart is in the shell of his chest, recalling
moon secrets, cauldron of sweet herbs, a simmering.

Yellow petalflakes from the old elm. Keeping
one eye on the shadow flashing its last
manifestoes over darkened glass, he's leaving
the child to school: Don't worry, he tells her, soon

you'll get used to it. Now, for certain minutes,
the air fills with what he thinks are flakes of light,
snow's last flitterings, the very air turned
on itself, teeth bared, and some unanswerable thing

chilling everything—though still, in the house
at morning, random flashes of sunlight will
ignite bedclothes, eyelids, three freesias in a vase:
sunfingers burning into their waxy yellows and

into five red speckled apples in a green dish
and into the white chairs' gilded edges and the
child's scattered books and her doll's blonde hair,
and into two black leather shoes, their dry tongues

out to catch a splash, a splash of it, this light.

Tully High Road, Dusk

A scream breaks the stillness
of the road I walk home on,
arms loaded with two blue
bags of groceries. Sheer joy,
it circles and circles, a bright
stone striking the still pool
dead center, riding out. A
girl between two boys, their
laughing voices. A bat is a
black flutter, flickering about
its business, gone. When we
swallow our fear, it seems,
we can invent a present tense
to part between us: bread is
broken, hands joined, although
the rest can be catastrophe—
to the vanishing point where
cicadas sing themselves to death
and the heart in your chest
has wings, you catch it, blind
and glimmering as it flies.

After-Image

Little glimmer of breasts. Someone
asleep behind them but only a moment.
Eyes open. Who flows in on the edge
of light? Meantime, the creature in the box
keeps scratching, though for the moment
it's a world of *nows* in every breath.
How to let go of this, except as the
crows do, rising abruptly and circling
and plunging into what happens,
night heads thrown back, a whole self
gathered into one high cry from that
small breast behind which lodges like
a kept secret the kept heart. Silence:
the grave neat and tidy for once; later
a glass of Powers in the bar, sitting
with absence. *Blue aster, yellow rattle,*
thyme, trefoil, seastrife, valerian, he says
to fill the gap, hearing the unleashed
whistle of an oystercatcher, ears a tunnel
of whispers and claspings, salt rumors,
depth charges to where light has winged
the skin of her wrist. *Deep breath now,*
she says, *now go on under.* Resting
on a bench beside the dead boy's willow,
he hears the ice crack, thump of a heart
turning on itself and stopping. Under
her tongue he imagined taking the
temperature of the soul, where it lurks
in some honeycomb corner, small and
final as a full stop. But to live in exile
from that breath, all those rowdy
instruments of joy dumbed at once,
their faces fleeing from the mirrorglass.

Birdshaped, this miniature bottle
blown to hold Roman perfume
had to be broken for use, perishable
and everlasting. And only this morning,
burning papers, he saw their words
as after-images on the ghost of ash, as
near to nothing as you could imagine
until a little gust ruffled suddenly
the remains, what remained of them,
and blew every last trace, maybe, away.

View from Renvyle

Low cloud exactly sliced.
Ridge of Mweelrea
visible in cloudveil.
Alignment: white rock
to white rock. System
and network. Things
in the glacial aftermath.
Hillforts and farms
drawing their lives
out of the heartsoil here.

Gravemarkers. Sacred space.
Little stones of children:
pink granite speaking
their hard sentence,
limboing the kiddies.
Hawthorn—regenerative
for a thousand years—
clouding over them.

Curlews pick the inlet:
high heartcries; hush.
Mountains of limestone
worn to simple hills.
One inch of bog
our right span. We
are a hair's thickness,
no more. The story
commonplace: no boats,
no night flight, only the
knowledge of *That was it.*

When you reach, she said,
the harbor called
Beyond Question, this is it.

Marilyn Hacker

Crepuscule with Muriel

Instead of a cup of tea, instead of a milk-
silk whelk of a cup, of a cup of nearly six-
o'clock teatime, cup of a stumbling block,
cup of an afternoon unredeemed by talk
cup of a cut brown loaf, of a slice, a lack
of butter, blueberry jam that's almost black,
instead of tannin seeping into the cracks
of a pot, the void of an hour seeps out, infects
the slit of a cut I haven't the wit to fix
with a surgeon's needle threaded with fine-gauge silk
as a key would thread the cylinder of a lock.
But no key threads the cylinder of the lock.
Late afternoon light, transitory, licks
the place of the absent cup with its rough tongue, flicks
itself out beneath the wheel's revolving spoke.
Taut thought's gone, with a blink of attention, slack,
a vision of "death and distance in the mix"
(she lost her words and how did she get them back
when the corridor of a day was a lurching deck?
The dream-life logic encodes in nervous tics
she translated to a syntax which connects
intense and unfashionable politics
with morning coffee, Hudson sunsets, sex;
then the short-circuit of the final stroke,
the end toward which all lines looped out, then broke.)
What a gaze out the window interjects:

on the south-east corner, a black Lab balks,
tugged as the light clicks green toward a late-day walk
by a plump brown girl in a purple anorak.
The Bronx-bound local comes rumbling up the tracks
out of the tunnel, over west Harlem blocks
whose windows gleam on the animal warmth of bricks
rouged by the fluvial light of six o'clock.

Alto Solo

Dear one, it's a while since you turned the lights out
on the porch: a decade of separate summers
passed and cast shed leaves on whatever river
carried our letters.

Merely out of habit, I sometimes tell you
when I've learned a word, made a friend, discovered
some small park where old men debate the headlines,
heard some good music

—it's like jazz, which, even at its most abstract
has the blues in it, has that long *saudade*
like a memory of what didn't happen
someplace that might be

inlaid with mosaics of recollection
which in fact's a street-corner of the utmost
ordinariness, though the late light steeps it
in such nostalgia

I can hear a saxophone in the background
wail an elegy for the revolution
as someone diminishes in the distance
and the film's over.

Now you know there won't be another love scene.
Do those shadows presage undreamt-of war years?
Twenty, thirty pass, and there's still a sound-track
behind the credits:

Cecil Taylor's complex riffs on the keyboard
which a prep-school blonde, seventeen, named Julie
sneaked me into the Blue Note for, because she
knew how to listen—

or it could be Janis packing the Fillmore
West with heartbreak, when I knew that I'd see her
playing pool again at Gino and Carlo's
some weekday midnight.

This is not about you at all: you could be
anybody who died too young, who went to
live in São Paolo or back to Warsaw
or just stopped calling

(Why did Alice Coltrane stop cutting records?
—think of Pharaoh Sanders being your sideman!—
Lapidary grief: was its consolation
all stone, all silence?)

Now it's morning, gray, and at last a storm came
after midnight, breaking the week-long dog-days.
Though I woke at three with a splitting headache,
I lay and listened

to the rain, forgave myself some omissions
as the rain forgave and erased some squalor
It was still too early for trucks and hoses.
A thud of papers

dropped outside the news-agent's metal shutters.
Am I glad we didn't last out the winter?
You, the street I made believe that I lived on,
have a new address.

Who I miss: the girl of a long-gone season
like my sturdy six-year-old in her OshKosh
overalls, attaining the age of reason
and senior Lego.

You've become—and I never would have wished it—
something like a metaphor of the passage
(time, a cobbled alley between two streets which
diverge, a tune that

re-emerges out of the permutations
rung on it by saxophone, bass and piano,
then takes one more plunge so its resolution's
all transformation).

Someone's always walking away; the music
changes key, the moving-men pack the boxes.
There the river goes with its bundled cargo:
unanswered letters.

Brian Henry

Gesture

Having lost her in her sleep beside you,
you twist the thought of the day

she spent without you as if the motion
could draw light to what you know
you cannot see, never will.

Something in her breath less rasp than heave
pulls you out of the self bearing down on your sleep:

you try to will her to touch
and when she does—an ankle across
your shin—the shock of what's inside you

grows into its own pain, that which gives
until the fear of giving is gone.

Andrew Hudgins

Mango

1

The slippery flesh slides underneath the knife.
　　Hold it firmly, slice off the sides
and score them precisely to the skin. Press it.
　　Tidy cubes of flesh pop up
and you may eat them gracefully.
　　Or snatch the soft fruit in your hand.
Devour it as juice streams down your arms.
　　Until it's broken on the teeth,
the fruit is neither nourishment nor joy,
　　until it's broken on the teeth
and lavished on the harsh, adoring tongue.

2

"Who cares how someone makes the bed?" I sneered
about my girlfriend's
　　　　　　poem, and I walked home,
where for four months I'd written and rewritten
—eleven
　　　　to forty lines, then down to eight,
in free verse,
　　　　blank,
　　　　　　and rhymed tetrameter—
a poem on how to eat a mango,

                              a poem
I'd versified from a cookbook. I'd never seen
a mango.
              It was a metaphor for art,
I said, how we consume the world's sweet flesh.

Night after night, the pale
                    poem waxed and waned
till I abandoned mangoes
                    and quit popping
imagined cubes of fruit from tough green skin.

Last week I read her vivid poem again—
starched cotton,
                    cool sheets to rumple and ignite
with meaning. It loves its subject and itself.
Goodbye
              to metaphor, I thought. Goodbye
to *like*. Goodbye
                    to *blank* is *not blank*. Goodbye
to *Is* harumping through a foreign film.
But trope returns us
                    to what it isn't—as kisses
return us
              to what our lips are pressed against.
Mango. Made bed. Movie. And now
                              this door.
I knock.
              My knuckles break. My fists are bloody.
I dream. I dream I enter and abide.

The Poet Asserteth Nothing

The poet asserteth nothing. This elegy's
the best damn poem I've ever written. The poet
asserteth nothing and therefore never lieth.
That's not what we called Sapphics back at Yale.
The poet asserteth nothing. Eight lines or eighty—
it's my damn poem and I say it's a sonnet.
The poet asserteth nothing and therefore
never lieth, Sir Philip Sidney wrote,
and drunk at parties, I cornered nervous friends
and badgered them. Did they think poets asserteth
nothing and therefore never lieth? I was sure
that I asserteth much and lieth plenty
in the old poetic way of knowing a truth's
a lie because it can't contain this world,
the next, the truths opposing it. No lies, no truth.
No truth, no beauty. The poet asserteth nothing
and therefore never lieth—both an assertion
and a lie, a beautiful and true, life-changing lie.

Lives and Stories

After workshop we drifted to the Union,
and argued. How would we transform our lives?
A's divorce, B's suicide attempt,
M's sleeping with N, O, and, strangely, P—
What angle would we take? What would it mean?
Simplify the action and complicate
the motivation, we learned in class. But young,
or young enough, we found
our motivations easily—ambition,
lust, rage: the obvious. We embraced
complication and kept entangling
our frantic lives—complicate! complicate—
as if we were sole authors of our stories,
as if, in those first drafts, we understood them.

But over time life simplifies itself
and soon you're happy sitting at a desk,
uncertain what you are remembering
or making up. And thus, in life, we move
from Hemingway to Henry James, from The Sun
Also Rises to The Golden Bowl,
which I have never finished. Too little action,
too many motivations—much like my own
dwindling happy life, in which I write
for all the old bad reasons, yes, and habit.
But less and less for the old rage, which I miss,
and more for the unreliable delights
of breathless Subject crooning his desire
to coquettish Object. Oh, her cold heart!
And how she teases him! I love them both,
And more and more I love
the work of doing what my masters did,
the masters whom I used to fear and envy

because they were my masters. How I miss them!
and how I fear and envy my new masters:
Monsieur le Sujet, Mademoiselle Objet
his ardent songs and her elusive twitter.

Cynthia Huntington

The Strange Insect

The lights have gone out in the hallway.
The boy who polishes the stairs has found
a strange insect—he wants me to see.
It clings to his rag and won't shake off.
It is black and long, like a widow, or a
sacred priest, has a yellow necklace and
yellow beads upon articulated leg joints,
has a tail eight inches long, three plumes
of a tail, black like ripped lace; is thin,
thin like a straw, like a wasp, thin as a
quill, is hanging on a piece of what was
once a shirt, appears to have no wings
and not to know day or night, to neither
look up nor to acknowledge our regard:
ancient, hieratical, the most mutant
butterfly, the wickedest jeweled queen.
The boy shakes the rag again, beats it
against the wall, and it drops, deigning,
into the dry fountain, grazes the brick,
drops further, lowering its banded legs
on to the blunted grass, drumming small,
horny feet in a cadence, beginning to speak
with its hands moving in air, a message
beat against the floor of patriarchy, ceiling
of the world's brain, speaking reason to
desire, order to confusion, state against
state, telling another version of the world.

River of Doubt

Rio da Divuda, Brazil 1914

The way down is all portage and jungle:
marshes, cataracts, rapids and rocks.
Weeks of hacking through vines with machetes,
downed trees and pines with thorns like spears,
fighting fever and septic rot, maggots in the flour,
boots rotting, weapons fouled, blood poisoned.
Then dysentery, malaria, rations low, one man
drowned, one man murdered, another gone mad.
And the fire ants, which make you forget the mosquitoes,
drawing blood, and the huge, venomous wasps
before which all dread of the fire ants vanishes.

Why map this river? Who cares where it goes?
Because a man is over fifty, because he has lost
an election and led his party into ruin, because
they would not give him troops to command
in the new war, he takes a party of men
into the worst jungle, and loses them there.
He takes his eldest son, who carries him out
when the wound on his leg flares and festers,
when the fever stews in his brain and he sings:
*In Xanadu did Kubla Khan a stately pleasure dome
decree . . . In Xanadu did Kubla Khan a stately
pleasure dome decree . . . In Xanadu . . .* over and over
in his delirium, begging to be left to die.

He takes his strength and his will to the river,
his outsized pride, his charm, his endless resume.
The river *so-what's* him. He shits, pisses,
bleeds in it, vomits bile. Courage, ambition,
memory, stamina, know-how—the river

takes it, the jungle has it, the world is vast
and measureless to man: he gives up hope.
Floats rapids and shallows. Fifteen hundred miles.
Arrives at last, after months, in a dirty village,
a savage place. Starved, stinking, unable to walk.
Baffled, they rename the river: Rio Roosevelt.

Sandra McPherson

The Mexican Acrobat

I stood on top of the linen cupboard where neither my cat nor I had stepped before. I promised him his turn if he could just wait, with supportive eyes, till after I'd hung the Mexican acrobat right under the cathedral ceiling. The acrobat has a way of boosting us high even when the painting rests on the bed. Over the little Mexican village storm clouds saturate with color paradoxes. The acrobat waves atop a pole on a man's head. Right outside, I found a crow feather to lift up a mantis with. Green aglow on black aflame. I "flew" her to the apex of a prickly rose. She was threatened
with play
by a paw.
Then paws raced October leaves down the middle of the street. A person in the morning love poetry class is going to see a young death. She says she doesn't want to miss any class. She likes the discussion, and the laughing. A tree burning from a Nazi v-1 resembles a person with the bark peeling off, wrote the painter Godderis. It is a farm outside Antwerp, where he took his paints and his family to feel safe. A bomb burns up seasons, which, as appointed as they are, nonetheless begin to look like freedom. Trumpet and drum: in *el campo*, to balance above the palm trees is one way to serve up a circus to the angry clouds.

Tom Sleigh

After a Long Illness

Ten thousand fathoms down: The self a Mindanoa trench, and in
     that trench
As from a porthole in a bathysphere, an observer, pure eyeball

Witnesses devils, demons, their confessions too intricate
To follow . . . cattle prods, bathtubs full of ice, a matchbook and
     a needle,

Will and heart debased, pleasure in terror mounting to
     exaltation:
Burn, burn, strip everything away, reduce it to increate nothing!

Then, brightening, like a bubble surfacing, expanding,
A water glass refracts sunlight across a tablecloth,

The light so clear as to be almost painful: Overself
Spying on self crying out in pain, pathetic, reduced to howling,

Mewing; then words inside of fever mutating into nonsense
     rhymes,
Never ending logorrhea, then an autism immune

To terror whispering in the dark: Out the window,
Tainted by scaly bark and snow melting from the gutter

Snow clouds massing over the city's flashing beacons
Boil into themselves: Open up your eyes, open them!

The couch burns away beneath the sleeping body,
Ash and magma harden round the head and neck,

Flow downward over torso, arms, legs
. . . Turn over now, turn over if you can, the fire's an illusion,

It's only what I'm seeing there on the table: Where are you,
     Ellen,
Who held that glass an hour or so ago, and left it there distilling

Afternoon light into this isolate clear shining
That is yours in your absence, that is your touch

Remembered on my sweating face haunted by
Your coming close, the room laboring in sleep.

The Fissure

Your power to make me feel that I am
     I and none other dims like lights going
Out room by room. Just to think of you can seem
     Ridiculous—a hopeless way of hoping
So when I wake from a nap into amnesia
     For a moment, I imagine you sleeping
Here beside me . . . at least till the abyss
     Opens next to my bed . . .
                          Your jeans faded
In the sun's mindless wash, by what slow degrees
     You were taken from me: Baffled
By your absence, who I was when
     I knew you now seems like some outpost isolated
And unreckonable from every known
     Landmark . . .
                    I never bothered to conceal
My need of you: I was Scott freezing in
     His tent, my stumbling quest of the Pole
Tireless, but absurd, your magnetic center always
     Moving, and finally, unreachable:
Between dots of photographs infinite space
     Seeps unstoppably: Flash of hair, an eye,
An otherworldly dahlia, a jigsaw puzzle piece,
     Two ghosts shredding into mist, all blurred by
Habit—for how many years did you exert
     Your influence like pressure undersea
That keeps giant crabs' armor from splitting at
     The seams?
                  Such armor! My beard a fortress
You saw right through, my green linen suit,
     Fraying now, my studied "fierceness"—
All because I was scared to be seen
     As you saw me: Your dog with muddy paws

Jumping up, too eager, addicted to the tone
      Of your low whistle, our pre-arranged sign
For the afterlife if a heaven
      Or hell would take us in . . .
                              Your seduction
Of this world, which was convinced you were
      Self-sufficient, took place not in a garden
But in your den of marijuana where
      You and your friend Susan stripped all pretensions
Bare: Such scams I practiced, eager
      To convince X I was worthy as Y to win
The prize honoring "the third most unknown
      Younger older poet never to have been
Recognized by the Pope, the Queen of Sweden,
      And Tony the counter man"—our Elvis
Look-alike who played Elvis's Christmas album
      All year through . . . To a pro like you, all this
Was amateur: Even with Death you were at ease,
      Making him put off his visit's purpose
With your repartee!
                        Now, just to get a glimpse
      Of you, I have to imagine you laughing,
Bemused, clinical, a virologist
      Tracing pathways ceaselessly mutating,
My memory's residue blown down the highway
      To Rt. 16 to potholed streets deadening
In warehouse parking lots next to sludgy
      Tidal flats raw and stinking in the sun: There,
In the haze the fissure opens, there, I
      Descend:
                        Without you to lead me from upper
Worlds of sodium vapor that lit the shore
      We walked along under your sign, Cancer,
I'm just a tourist gawking at your lower
      Zones of night, the submarine and souterrain
Of dream-sewage, rat tunnel, scum-bottomed harbor
      In which you plunged your own personal Damned,

Miming on the phone their need of you to listen,
        Your voice empathetic even as you yawned . . .
My shadow hugely slips and stumbles down
        Rubble, midnight construction lamps dimly
Haloing my head, my new-shaven
        Face still raw, my wobbly legs grazed by
Winged shadows swarming in the fumes
        Billowing from that fissure until our sweetly
Interchangeable *We I You* that contain
        And pour us out into the mouths of others
Seeps away into eternal frozen rain:

        At the world's bottom I see you hover
Like fog over polar seas, your presence
        Glinting in footprints across the glacier.
(Of course I don't see you, the image is
        Ripped off from the 1911 encyclopedia you
Would have loved to read if you still had eyes.)
        The flow of seconds is a floe
Of ice hardening round faces that peer
        Past each other into drifting snow.
How far down in the ice shelf they'd have to bore
        To find us, the block of ice we're frozen in
Moving with the ice pack toward open water.

Trees by Firelight

What shapes they make are shapes they hide from day.
As if seeing what we see by night would give
Us nightmares if we saw it clarified by day.
As if our world that they and we inhabit is
Really a world of shadowy forms suggestive
Of antlers flickering from our brows in the hiddenness
Of our own natures giving themselves away.

The human figures in the windows at the party
Next door, mammalian croonings, touchings, the current
Of courtship that plays across the dark the way fire
Plays across a log, do these figures know, or maybe
They don't know that just behind or in front a shadowy
Creeping adheres to their footsteps, inescapable
As the fire's shadows creeping across the wall?

Looming on the flame's far side is a void
Of tree shadows mimicking the beak of a bird
Pecking, then jabbing whenever the breeze
Lifts. The beak pecks into the dark a script
Like braille, but no matter how we try to turn
Ourselves or the darkness inside out, the dots
Are punched into the side of the paper we can't feel . . .

Now the flame abstracts another tree
To waves blowing up in exponential fury, the ship's
Prop not turning fast enough to breast the water wall
Driving the prow under, rupturing the hull, the cargo
Signaling from the deep . . . A month ago, two months now,
At my cousin's funeral I sat before the gas fire in the funeral home's
Parlor and listened to a man tell me business was booming:

His penis pumps and prostheses and sex toys
Were all the highest quality, and if ever I needed a dungeon
Or dungeon master/mistress trained in safe S & M,
"My dungeons are floor to ceiling mirrors, everything
Spotless, antiseptic; our people are all bonded,
We don't do anything with children or animals,
But we've got whatever else you and the missus want."

Once upon a time we slept out on the hard ground,
We were dreamless, artless, our minds blank as stone.
Against the other gods' wills, a god stole for us
Divine fire, they chained him to a cliff; a vulture
Swooped down each noon to eat his liver that grew
Back overnight while our fires kept us warm,
Our backs to the shadowy corners of the house.

Gary Soto

With Nature

The goats chewed in sunlight,
Their ancient beards touching the valley floor.
Shadows fidgeted over granite rocks and tree stumps.
Rabbits kicked themselves in the Manzanita,
And in the brush crickets rattled their thighs.
I wiped my brow and thought, This ain't me.
A week before a bud and I imagined that we might trek
Where John Muir trekked, his own beard sweeping
The valley floor. Namely, hike in the hills in early morning
And discover a hilly rise. From that vista,
We'd pronounce one philosophical thing or another,
Then carry happiness like water in our cupped palms—
Much of it spilling between our fingers,
But some of it coming back with us. But we found out
There was no water, no, indeed, only salt mines under our arms.
I slapped the soulless gnats from my face,
The little devils on wings. After an hour,
I said to my bud, This is the rise?
When we come to a steep climb. He licked his lips
And said, John Muir weighed only a hundred and thirty.
I said, Ben Franklin said God meant for men to drink beer.
My bud licked his lip. How so? he asked.
I bent my arm three times
And said, The elbow is like a hinge, brother.
I made a motion of my arm going to my face.
But there was no beer, no John or Ben, no answer of whether
This was the dusty rise from which happiness springs.

I sat down on a stump. Goats bleated down below,
Some of the older ones perched on granite rocks.
One slip, and their hooves would have sparked up a fire,
Sent up in smoke even the grass in their mouths.
I considered the goats and my hands,
Dry ravines. There was no happiness for me.
I was tired, used up. The wind brought me the smell of a dead jay
With its legs like spurs
And a bead of ants crawling away from the left eye,
Its juices long gone.

Mortgage

The dead man lay with a plum in his throat. His left hand
Held a pen, its vein of ink nearly gone.
His right hand gripped his mortgage papers.
Water dripped in the kitchen sink. But that was no clue,
Neither were the worn slippers on his feet.
The Detective tipped back his hat. He had seen the dead
In many posture and this fellow was nothing new.
He had seen the dead lodged in chimneys,
The adulterous dead caught in the outstroke of love making.
Drowned men sunk in rivers and buoyed up with their bellies full
Of moonlight and murky water. Yes,
After many years, the Detective understood the map of bloodstains
And the murdered starched by justified fear. That's how he saw
Those who succumbed on a wet Thursday. It was Thursday now,
Thought dry. A crime was involved. The Detective noted
Breathing on a window, a splotch the size of a baby's new born head.
But that evidence would fade soon. So would the last pinprick
Of red in the man's red cheek. The Detective knelt
And rolled the man's head back and forth—no, no was the answer.
He wrote this much in a notebook. He whittled away time,
Tapping his pencil his thigh. Time had stopped
For this man, age 48, on the floor. That his fingernails would continue
Was a given. But how he would claw his way out of the morgue,
Once he was fitted on a tray and rolled into darkness?
And what if they turned him onto his belly
And they dislodged the plum pit. It was an open and shut case
That he lived and died, and had signed on the line
At Dot.Com Savings and Loan. The wind whistled
When the door opened. The men with latex gloves were here,
Wiser by one more day: don't suck a plum pit
With a pen in one hand, a thirty-year mortgage in the other.

What's Left

I like your body, she said,
And I said, What part?

She told me to strip off my shirt,
Flag of defeat that hid my chest and belly,
Two collapsed empires dissipated into provinces.

She held up my arm, flaccid snake on an old trunk,
And narrowed her eyes,
The pinched mouth of a tailor with a needle in his teeth.

This is yum-yum, she said, and I asked, What part?
She smoothed the back of my arm near my shoulder,
Only visible to me when I look in the mirror,
Barely reachable when I soap my body.
I twisted my neck trying to see what she saw,
An unnamable anatomy, not like teeth or nose,
Chin or cheek bones riding the crest of noble beauty.

I touched the back of my arm,
Skin to graft on the burned part of my writing hand.
And I was burning then, the shame of having nothing left,
Just skin with the shrinking territory of a half-dollar,
A quarter, a dime, the diminishing value
Of an old man with shrubbery hanging from his nose.

Virgil Suárez

Ho Chi Minh in Havana

Plastered on walls by the sides of buildings,
        on stamps, posters hung from classroom ceilings,
everywhere the same picture of the Poet/Leader,
        his country torn into a bloody paper pulp.
My grandmother, still alive in 1969, the last year

of my Cuban childhood, despised him because
        she couldn't understand how such a poet
could lead his people, his country, into death.
        At school, though, we learned about the great
poet, white haired, wisdom-filled eyes. We drew

circles around his eyes. I believe all poets wore
        glasses with which to magnify their scribbles
into egrets and dragons. We painted horns
        on his forehead. When the teacher caught us,
she tore the paper and threw it away in the trash,

chastised us for not knowing how soon enough
        we would find ourselves in the deep jungle,
under the dark canopy of trees, a tiger's growl
        in our ears like the blasts of mortar rounds.
At home, my parents talked of leaving Cuba,

of better chances elsewhere, away from this talk
        of war, of constant revolution. My grandmother
smiled at us. She said there was nothing different

in the world. My parents disagreed in silence.
At night, I dreamt of half-egret, half-dragon poets

roaming the countryside, feeding in the dark
        of moonless nights, out of people's trash, growling
the discontentment of their lives, how some men
        will spend their lives in pursuit of one word, one
image, like this one of a tiger turning into mist.

Leaving

for Ha Jin

We all leave our countries with empty pockets,
the weight of broken nights in our hands,

the way anger storms crackle in our throats
from years of silence. A muted soft cry.

An ashen bird that refuses to fly out of the way
on the tarmac when the jet that takes us

so finally from our native country refuses
to move, save itself from the blast of useless

moments, a resurrected memory: a child clings
to his mother's coattails. A boy, like you,

like me, no more than eight years old, fingers
clawed into the hems of his pockets, afraid

like any other child who has not been told
that he will forget where he came from. Who

he is. How one fine day he will stop in a field
of tulips, steel himself against so much red,

and he will look up at the sky and see a river
of white froth where a plane has cut across

the sky. A deep silence rattles his bones, echoes
inside his body for an eternity, for what cannot

be prevented—an exile's daily lamentation
for all those about to leave, cross into emptiness.

El Santo Niño Chupatintas

We went to school together, shared
        lockers in gym. He called me *El Guapo*,
not because of my good looks, but
        because of my temper, my ability
to storm through this life, fist in mouth.

        I couldn't think of a name for him
until the day I caught him in a corner
        of the locker room, sucking on a marker,
one of those thick, permanent-ink black
        markers, and after he scribbled his name

on the walls, on the dented doors of so
        many lockers, he sucked on the tip,
closed his eyes after gazing at this work,
        then the name *Chupatintas* came to me
in a flash, the *El Santo Niño Chupatintas*.

        The ink drinker. How fitting, I thought,
and when he saw me staring at him, he smiled,
        dark lips, a row of blackened birds in his mouth,
a carload of words fluttering out his throat,
        this tunnel so many enter and never see light.

David Wagoner

High Steel

The path ahead of you is the upper serif
        Of an I-beam, a rigid girder
                Riveted, secure, as stable
As the earth and the next wind
        Will allow. But you don't quite
                Believe it, do you. You think you're here
To examine the view or the lofty poise
        Of the overhead crane, to visualize
                Fire escapes and curtain walls
Or to calculate how far you may be off
        The ground. Instead, you've decided you simply must
                Walk on a surface no more likely
To wobble under you
        Than a sidewalk. You're not inclined
                To stagger, are you? You're wearing shoes.
You're trailing no loose ends.
        So all that's required of you is (easy now)
                To put one shaky foot ahead
Of the other and to follow
        That terribly simple-seeming good example
                With the rest of you. You needn't depend
On anyone but yourself to cooperate
        In an act you've been performing for the bulk
                Of your life: conducting your leg bones
Under your torso without changing your mind
        Or your definition of progress.
                So why are you half crouching

There, flushed at the knees, your arches
  As depressed as your soles, holding
    Your semiprecious center of gravity
Too heavily or too lightly from one moment
  To the next? As a higher mammal
    Descended from those who first presumed
To take an upright posture and aimed themselves
  Forward and took a step in the right direction
    With only a second thought,
Why are you leaning backwards and hanging on
  And shutting your eyes against what's obviously
    Waiting dead ahead?

Owl

The crows, a stark black-and-blue whirling
      Murder of them, have treed an owl and are screeching
        At the tops of their sharp voices
And flat from the gut and the ends of their claws
      Against this outrage. They don't want him to be
        There or anywhere. They're proclaiming this evening
Death to all owls, and they're here to tell you
      Owl, owl, owl at the heart of their gyrations,
        Owl in *their* world, and they can hardly
Contain themselves to escalating spirals
      And feints and flaring attacks on the crown of a maple
        Where an owl has made itself
Manifest and motionless: some fly off
      At even louder tangents to other trees
        To scold them in advance for harboring
Future owls. They want to leave no doubt
      In any simple mind: they intend to go on
        Roosting and rousting and treating everything
As murderously as they please, while the owl waits,
      Speckled, shadowed, and still
        As tree bark. The sunlight thins. And now the crows
Are thinning out and heading two by twenty
      And finally three by one toward the rookery
        As the day fades, and the dusk, and the owl
Slowly and silently becomes
      A wide-winged soft-horned shape skimming from under
        The leaning branches and down across the orchard
And over the arch of the arbor by open mouths
      Of morning glories to catch in midair
        The first hummingbird moth of this long night.

Joshua Weiner

Song

FOR THOM GUNN

There is no east or west
in the wood you fear and seek,
stumbling past a gate of moss
and what you would not take.

No east. No west. No need
for given map or bell,
vehicle, screen or speed.
Forget the house, forget the hill,

And what you thought you had
(that Here that is no rest)
and make from it an aid
to form no east, no west.

Out of Range

Between one screen
Behind your dream

Another screen
The broken lamp

Beside her lip
Inside the needle

The whistle-stop
When you wake up

Between your plan
And how the song ends

Behind the lock
The mis-cut key

An opened door
Beneath the field

The ruddock reeks
A lurking skill

Between two noons
One grip one strap

You'll hear the speech
Of speech unheard

Before the storm
Above the hawk

You'll feel the rein
It will not slake

Cricket

Cricket says
you know cricket by my rubbing
and cricket knows you by a like tune,

vain lovers, playing games
of sweet moan to seal the hour.
Watch cricket

leap across your ugly tile floor
and play to your boot
as it misses once again.

I'm cricket, blacker than coffee
and tobacco juice, my song
more bitter, more buzz

if you'd only quit your typing
and shut up a minute.
Cricket says

your lips confuse the issue,
cricket's long antennae pick it all up,
cricket knows where cricket is.

Cricket burrows with forelegs,
chews your paper. Cricket says
stop straining for effect.

Cricket loves a napper in the grass.
Cricket is never wretched.
In a room of smoke

cricket can breathe.
Cricket sings outside
   your sealed room of stone.

Alan Williamson

Primrose Hill

Today the soft, usual fold of London sky,
threatening nothing.
Even to me, the dogs don't signify
danger or rage, a small one somersaulting

over the calm back of one slightly larger.
Paths crisscrossing toward a mild
summit, where you thought, *take the children sledding* . . .
A few things different, even in the weather,

you might have turned into any
of these women with half-grown children,
as I am any father
here with his grown daughter,

despite what you too knew, the steep
climb from minute to minute, day to day;
the insectile rush down across the mind;
and the various emptinesses, some rainbowy . . .

By your life- and
death-house I make my funny bow.
Then *with the word the time*, I'm quoting Shakespeare,
down toward Camden Town

where whole housefronts have been redone
as 60s bandit faces . . .
Effortful line, *the time will bring on summer,*
as if we had to help on

what happens anyway, *when briars shall*
have leaves as well as thorns (All's Well, the play
no one's quite easy with, because the characters
are allowed to be so bad before they're good).

How long ago you taught me
knowledge that did not save you,
how near the insect footprints across the mind
are to its spaces of columnar blue.

Susan Wood

Desire's Kimono

Whatever we do, the self
    goes on spinning desire
        from deep inside, the self

    a silkworm spinning out its various forms,
enough silk to fill the world's warehouse with yearning!
    And from that fabric, kimonos are made

        in all the forms desire can take.
    Here are the chaste and delicate wishes,
kimonos fragile as the one my friend found once,

        hanging on the back wall of an import shop, clinging
           there like a moth disguising itself
    as a shadow of pale winter light.

And here are the insistent longings, the ones which interest me
        most, though small desires, too, have their own designs on us.
           The large ones are fevered, swooning, burning

        from the inside out. Fabric of darkness, of liquid, fabric
of the body's secret grottos, spun into kimonos to clothe
    the favorite courtesan. Only she may wear them,

        the story says, and she may wear them only.
    Their colors are the red of painted lips, of menstrual blood,
black of hair unbound in ropes of ebony, black of night, deepest night

in which the lover comes. And on them is embroidered
      every attitude the body can devise, lovers shown
in every form and pose of love. Lip and tongue and breast.

A manual for pleasure. So that when she moves
      the lovers move, their bodies shifting
          with each rustle of the silk, limb to limb

and mouth to mouth, first one on top, then one
behind, below, kisses here and here and here.
      And seeing this, she is riven

      with desire and so enflamed
    that she is drenched with love
and must lie silent and unmoving on her silken bed

      or else she'll drown. Until at last her lover comes
          at midnight to her room and lights the lamp
      and takes down the kimono from her shoulders.

Each night they must enact this ritual. Possessed
      by beauty, her desire strung tight as invisible wires
          to bind her to the bed, she sees, closing her eyes,

      only their bodies mirroring the bodies
on the robe, feels in dreams his body moving over hers,
      silk crackling like the cracking open of a shell.

          And the lover, too, dreaming of beauty, dreams
      the falling open of desire, feels their bodies move
like rivers in their hands, the way love pools in the deepest lake.

      This is a story of pleasure and of pain. This is a story
          with no end. We wrap ourselves in longing
      and lie down. We rise. We begin again.

The Unthought

The unthought is the highest gift
that a thought can give.

Martin Heidegger

When the weight fell and took the tip of my finger—
the key pad, the plastic surgeon later called it—
everything went suddenly far away, the clank
of the machines, the grunts and groans
of other exercisers, like a picture on television
with the sound turned off, though the bright room hummed
somehow, beneath the surface. For a minute it didn't even hurt.
It wasn't much, just a small piece of me left behind
on the bloody floor, but I'd lost pieces
of myself before and those more essential to myself
—ovaries, uterus—not to mention the more metaphoric
losses, little shards of a broken heart, or the past
itself, which is all loss, its facts fading to dumb blankness.
It was the finger with which I gave the world
the finger, an irony not lost on me.
                             And later, someone would say
the most unique part of me was changed forever,
that my fingerprints would never be the same.
I could commit the perfect crime, they said.
And I thought of my friend's sister, whose fingers
                             all end at the knuckle—
But what were they anyway, those signs
of our uniqueness, those little whorls,
like snowflakes in which our selves appear?
Not selves, really,
but bodies, just something to tell one from another
until the world discovered DNA.
What is the self? It isn't at one's fingertips.

In the plastic surgeon's office, everywhere
I looked so many ways
to construct the self, but, really,
they were all the same.
                    In the waiting room, a brass Pegasus soared
over paintings of medieval princesses and mermaids,
and on a door a naked woman etched in glass let down her hair.
And the examining room hung with stalactites
like a cave, tables and chairs made out of rocks.
It was like being inside a fairy tale, and it was clever,
even, since what was desired was eternal youth,
though it was only my finger I wanted saved.
                    When the nurse came in, I saw
she'd stepped out of a painting I'd seen once
of Venice at Carnival, where everyone's disguised
as someone else. She had that look of fantasy—
golden hair below her waist, an alabaster face, and breasts
so large they had to hurt, but, really, she was the doctor's wife,
and I kept wondering if this was her fantasy, or his?

As for me, I was lost
in thought, imagining the self
as a kind of Venice, a maze
of intricate structures, solid and fragile at once.
First the shrouded, narrow Rio Terrà dei Assassini, the route
of murderers fleeing San Stéfano, pickpockets
hovering around us in their black cloaks like dark angels
in some Renaissance version of Hell.
                    Or palaces of evil and the nightmare
chambers of the soul, the torturers
at 3 AM, to which one passes on the Bridge of Sighs.
Then the sudden opening
                    into space and light and joy, birds wheeling
over San Marco while the orchestra at the Quadri
plays Cole Porter, and around the corner of the Piazzeta
the broad sweep of the lagoon.
                    Now the wide steps

of the Salute, its bridge of boats and candles, the Virgin
rising over the altar of the Frari in Titian's painting
or the reappearance of St. Mark's body, all containers
for the sacred. And the Ghetto Vecchio,
where the Serenissima herded its Jews, seat
                              of courage and despair.
The self has room for all of these and more.

Sometimes the self is
                    other people, revenants
moving through the frescoed rooms like wind
in the chestnuts, curtains billowing
at the windows, leaving behind
traces of themselves, like a fine coat of salt
from the Lido, or the bright shine of time, its fluid patina.

The object of desire is to be fulfilled.

                         And that moment when
something reminds you—the play of light
on water, the shadows vines make, or maybe
it's some half-forgotten music, say a Mozart sonata
heard from the window of a house he once visited—
and the longing for someone you've lost
suddenly turns you inside out,
the body laid open
                    and driven into itself at once.

I used to believe
                as one got older everything
became clearer, the self emerging
from the dark water, rising
to the surface, a limpid pool.
                    But it's not like that.
Every year the waters
get muddier, too many motor boats
cluttering the canal, and the street signs

seem more and more confusing. Who would have known
San Zanipolo was really Santi Giovanni e Paolo?
You know how easy it is to get lost.
                   Though that, too, can be a kind of happiness.

I've studied subjectivity. I know the unitary self
is an illusion. And yet sometimes
                            I believe
I can feel it, sitting somewhere
between my breast bone and my belly, not an organ
exactly, but a solid thing, fat
as a tome a child might sit on each night
to reach the table.
                   It's times like these I could swear
I've written it and I feel closer
       to death, to life.
But then the words begin
                      to waver and disappear
as though written in invisible ink,
       or water, and there's the shadow
of the unthought, a tiny figure
dressed in black—see it? there it is, just up ahead—
now vanishing inside Palazzo Labia,
now disappearing into the crowd outside San Stae.

David Ferry Talks
with Harry Thomas' Class
at Buckingham, Browne
and Nichols, March 7, 2000

BRANDON CODY: At what age did you decide to become a writer? What events led you to want to be a writer?

DAVID FERRY: I got started in graduate school. I guess it was having to write a Ph.D thesis, and enjoying the experience, that made me have ambitions to be a writer. I thought I was going to end up as a scholar, and I did become an author that way—I wrote a book about Wordsworth, which was a revision of my thesis. But I got interested in writing poems because I was reading a lot of poems. I think I do recall scraps of things, furtive scribblings of a few lines when I was in high school and college, but nothing that was evidence that put writing poems at the center of my interest. But I had begun to get more and more literary in

college, at Amherst, because I had a couple of really great teachers there, Reuben Brower and César Lombardi Barber. So I was
developing in that direction. But, as I've said, I didn't really
start to write poems until I was in graduate school. The first
poem I really worked on and finished was "The Embarkation for
Cythera." It got published in the *Kenyon Review*, then edited by
the poet John Crowe Ransom, one of my idols, and that was a
thrill. A very big thrill.

JUSTIN ELSWIT: I think you started out doing a lot of translations.
How did you move from being a translator to writing your own
stuff?

DF: It's the other way around, really. There's one translation in my
first book, a translation of a poem by Ronsard, a famous one—
"Quand vous serez bien vieille," and then in my second book—
and there's a long gap between my first book and my second
because—I don't know why—I wasn't writing very much and I
was doing a lot of other things as a teacher at Wellesley College—there were three translations, one of them an ode of
Horace, the only one I knew at that point. I don't even remember how I got into doing that one, but I did it. There was also
the translation of a poem by Jorge Guillén, a distinguished
Spanish poet, who was teaching at Wellesley, in exile from
Franco's Spain. And there was a short poem by Eugenio Mon-
tale. Then in the next book, *Dwelling Places: Poems and Translations*, the mix was about half and half, so in other words I was
moving in the direction of being a translator as well as a poet.
In my new book, *Of No Country I Know: New and Selected
Poems and Translations*, in the new part of it the mix is once
again about half and half. I've made an effort, both in this new
book and in *Dwelling Places* to make connections between the
poems and the translations. Friends began to help me by suggestions of poems to translate that they thought would go with the
poems I was working on and that would go with the general
character of the book I was working on. In most cases I tried to
be as faithful as possible in my translations, but some were more
free, shaped and somewhat changed to fit the purposes of the
book as I was conceiving of it.

During this last decade I've also produced some books that are purely translation: my rendering of the Gilgamesh epic, my translations of the Odes of Horace and the Eclogues of Virgil, and, just finished, the Epistles of Horace. I got interested in the Gilgamesh material through a friend, the Assyriologist William Moran and in the Horace material through another friend, the classicist Donald Carne-Ross. In both case I started out with a few passages or poems suggested by them and then I got hooked and did the whole kit and kaboodle.

ALISON ELLSWORTH: What about other people's writing draws you to do translation and to do responses? There are a number of poems in this collection that are responses—like Johnson on Pope and a number of others—and poems from your father's writings and your grandfather's.

DF: I think I'd say two or three things about that. I tend to be a hero-worshipper of some writers, and Dr. Johnson is one of them. So I was very interested in everything of his that I could find and when I had begun translating a little Latin I became aware of two or three translations that Johnson did of Horace, early in his career. He wrote the poem I called "The Lesson" in his old age. It's about parental love, telling how his father took him out and tried to teach him to swim, and how he wasn't good at it. It fit with some other poems in the book, like my poem "A Young Woman" and "Goodnight." So I responded to the Johnson poem out of admiration of him but also because it suited my bookmaking purposes.

As for using other people's writing—I guess you're referring to "After Spotsylvania Court House" and "Counterpart," two poems which derive from and quote from letters I found in my father's apartment after he died. Finding them was a useful accident. All I know of my great-grandfather and of any kind of connection with American history that I've got is through writing, through letters and through photographs (which are a kind of writing). My great-grandfather was a Methodist preacher who went down to Virginia after the bloody battle of Spotsylvania Court House, in 1864, and wrote letters home to his wife using a kind of nineteenth century idealist language—"It is a wonderful honor to be here and to do good"—that kind of whole-hearted language I found both admirable and endearing, and also naive in a way that didn't destroy my admiration of it. It was my link to a past that meant something to me, and the poem "Graveyard," about a photograph of my father was another sort of link. I also found that photograph in his apartment after his death. Links to the past, through writing. It's what you have left.

MICHAEL KENNEDY: I'm wondering why don't you write about your close family—your wife, your daughter, and your son—as you did about your great-grandfather?

DF: There's a poem in *Strangers*, "On a Sunday Morning," that's about my son. There's a poem in *Dwelling Places*, "A Young Woman," that's decidedly about my daughter. In fact, I wrote it because my daughter said to me, How come you never wrote a poem about me? And so I wrote the poem about her, and showed it to her, and it was only several days later that she came to realize that it *was* about her. The dedicatory poem in this new book, not a poem by me but a medieval poem adapted by me, is about our marriage. So's the poem "Aubade" in my first book and the poem "A Tomb at Tarquinia," in *Strangers*. But you're quite right that, compared to some other ways that I've written, there are relatively few such poems. I'm not sure of the answer to that, except that I think there are some ways in which it's easier to write when the writing is deflected into some other circumstance than the most immediately personal ones. It's eas-ier to write about the dead or to write about a great-grandfather because it's harder to formulate what's here and immediate, right up close. I do have intentions of writing more often in more per-sonal ways. But this is only one of my intentions.

As you know from reading my book, there's a lot of interest in photography in some of these poems. My son is a wonderful photojournalist and there have been times when I wanted to get into writing some direct responses to the work he's been doing, often in harrowing situations. But there's a kind of shyness on my part that enters into it: not wanting to scribble across the surface of his remarkable work.

ELIZABETH HOWIE: I was wondering why you go back to the Bible. For example, in the poem "The Proselyte" you use the phrase "unclean spirits." I was wondering, did you derive inspiration from the Bible? Is that the reason you go back to it?

DF: Certainly for the purpose of the poem you're referring to, that one passage from the New Testament has been very important for me, the anecdote about the wild man, crazy man, the very marginal character who was on the edge of the town and Jesus came upon him and the unclean spirits in him were crying, "Torment me not!" and Jesus called them out of his body and into the bodies of the Gadarene swine, who then rushed into the waters and were drowned. It's a very compelling story. When I was writing *Dwelling Places* and doing a lot of writing about street people I was also doing—I think I talked about this the last time I was here—a certain amount of reading about wild men, all the medieval and ancient writing and art about wild men—Nebuchadrezzar the king out eating grass, Enkidu the wild man in the Gilgamesh story I rendered. The connection between this kind of reading and the New Testament story came about that way. I don't think of myself as in general as strikingly more of a Biblical reader than most people, so it's more a matter of a particular raid into some useful material. On the other hand I guess I *am* influenced in a way by the strong Methodist-preacher-missionary strain in my father's family. I suppose the Bible gets into my head by that route, though not very systematically. Also, the context for some of my poems about street people is the supper program we help run at a church in Boston, so it's no surprise that a biblical vocabulary gets into those poems.

It's been more a question of what I've found compelling and useful for the purposes of some particular poem.

MICHAEL DOHERTY: Are there any other authors or poets who have inspired you to write or whom you want to model your writing after?

DF: I think my double answer to that would be that I can right away think of the American poets and the English poets of the now-past twentieth century whom I find myself admiring most, and that's a very clear, obvious list—Robert Frost, Wallace

Stevens—when I was an undergraduate I wrote my honor's thesis on Stevens, he and Frost were the first modern poets whose work really took hold of me—Thomas Hardy, Philip Larkin, Elizabeth Bishop, William Carlos Williams. The other side of the story, of course, is the worry of ending up sounding like an imitation of somebody you admire. It's almost like saying that my list of people I admire is my list of people I don't want to sound like. And I'm sure I end up, in an inferior way, sounding like some of them at various times.

Then I'd have to double back again and say there's another kind of answer to your question. Much as you want to find your own voice and differentiate yourself even from, and maybe especially from, the people you admire the most, poetry (and any other kind of writing) is made out of what's in your ear, your memories of what language sounds like in various situations. If you're writing in any form you've got in your ear the cadences you've heard in other people's use of that form, and so while trying to avoid sounding like somebody else you're at the same time using the way the English language has behaved rhythmically as you've heard it elsewhere. We don't make up anything in our language. It's all, in a sense, memory. It's, as Frost says, "things that live in the cave of the mouth," that were always there. You don't make it out of nothing. You make language out of language. It's both trying not to sound like other people and using ad hoc what's gotten into your ear.

KRISTIN TYMAN: How much time do you devote to writing or research in a week, and when you're writing, is there a certain place where you feel most comfortable?

DF: Yeah, in front the computer in my study. I work on writing some of most mornings, and one of the great things about doing more and more translating is that it gives you something to do on those days—and those are most days—when you don't have any ideas about you're doing with your own writing. Translating gives you something to do that's very useful because it puts into your ear useful pieces of language, useful cadences, useful habits of writing. So I work part of every morning in a kind of scrappy way. I have a piano right downstairs under where I work, so I go down and play the piano a lot and then I go back up and sit in front of the screen and try something else out. Sometimes I work like this all afternoon too, but often I don't because I have other stuff to do, chores, letters, prose obligations.

ALI GORSKI: I was wondering how you feel about revising poems—whether once you've published them you leave them in that form, or whether you think of revising them over the years.

DF: When I put together this new and selected volume, I looked very hard at my first book, and I revised it drastically. I left out a lot of it, and rewrote some of it. I kept all the poems in the two later books (*Strangers* and *Dwelling Places*) almost without change. There's one poem, "Caprimulgidae," that I'd been very unhappy with, it wasn't working, and I redid that one and now I feel better about it. There are a number of poems in my books that were changed between the time of their magazine publication and their inclusion in the books. After that I usually left them alone. But of course there are almost no poems where I couldn't think over and over again about some possible revision or another. There comes a time, though, when you say, let it be.

But it's hard for me to distinguish between the process of writing and the process of revising. One you get something down on paper, everything else feels like a revision of it.

CHRIS BILELLO: Is there any poetry that you write just for yourself, for your own benefit, that you don't publish?

DF: I have a number of things in notebooks that I'm hoping someday to finish. I'm such a slow writer and such a reviser that almost everything that I've gotten to the point where you could call it a poem has ended up in the book. I don't have a big supply of alternatives. I kind of wish I did, but I don't. Some of my poems I've worked on for twenty years, thirty years, I don't care. They're sort of sitting around and finally I get it done. But my notebook of other stuff is small.

JUSTIN ELSWIT: How would you describe the changes in both your writing style and the subject of your poems from when you started writing in graduate school to some of the new poems?

DF: The most important change for me took place right in the middle of that first book. It's a little hard to describe the change now because for the purposes of the new book, *Of No Country*

I Know, I changed the order of poems from *On the Way to the Island,* that first book. There they occurred more or less in what I could remember as the chronological order I wrote them in. The poems in the first half are a good deal more elaborate in texture than the poems later on, and they tend to be about situations that occur inside other works of art. "The Embarkation for Cythera," for example, the first poem I ever wrote, is based on a painting by Watteau, and another poem, "On the Way to the Island," is related to that one. They're very much more 'art' than most of the plainer poems later in the second half of that book. So, generally speaking, I took that turn rather early in my career. I think the poems in the second half of that book, as it was originally printed, are more like poems I've been doing ever since.

ANNA BACON: I think it's interesting that you've written in many different forms. You've done a sestina and sonnets and the *Gilgamesh* in couplets. I know that the sestina is difficult because you have to use the same words, and I was wondering if that poem was a struggle for you. Did you find that had to force it to incorporate the six words? Also, do you have a favorite form? And, finally, how do you choose the form that a poem is going to be in?

DF: The sestina is certainly not my favorite form. I hope never to write another one. I think that the last time I was here I quoted Richard Wilbur as saying that the sestina form is a horrid doily. In the case of "The Guest Ellen at the Supper for Street People," though, the poem keeps asking questions over and over, obsessively, and the lives of the people being looked at are the same over and over—"the quotidian," the dailyness, "of unending torment." I began to find that in the lines I was writing into the computer the same vocabulary tended to occur—words like "torment," "enchantment," "body," "voice," and so one, and a lot of them began to occur at the ends of lines (which always tend to be emphasized in one way or another), and all of a sudden—I have a note on the computer where I said to myself, what if this turned into a sestina?—and so I looked up the sestina form, because like everybody else I had trouble remembering what it was, and I began to reshape the poem in that direction, because in this instance the sestina form, obsessive and insistent and repetitive, seemed particularly appropriate. Often the form just seems like an academic exercise. There are very great sestinas, though. Elizabeth Bishop's poem called "Sestina" is one. Sir Philip Sidney's double sestina, "Ye Goatherd Gods," is another.

If I thought about what a favorite form for me is, I suppose the form I have found myself writing in most often, or more often than others, is unrhymed iambic pentameter, and often unrhymed iambic pentameter arranged in couplets. Because I learned from the Gilgamesh experience. I started trying to do that one in blank verse, that is to say, in uninterrupted paragraphs of unrhymed pentameter lines, and it was *very* heavy. I couldn't get it to go. But when I started putting it into couplets it sort of oxygenated the verse, aerated it. I could see what I was doing. I could get at it. The poem began to move. And so I've used the form quite a lot. A part of that is that one of the poets I most admire in the world is the eighteenth-century poet Alexander Pope, and I most admire him for the focus and intensity of the workmanship within a recognizably framed form, the so-called heroic couplet, the rhymed iambic pentameter couplet. Rhyming at that length is something I would shy away from doing systematically, but the idea of the couplet, the idea of a form that's plain, most like talk, and at the same time a highly, complexly, usable art form, was something I could really work with, and so I've used it pretty often.

JASON POKRANT: You seem to enjoy very much what you do. But looking back now, is there anything you regret or would change, whether it be in your style, form, or your profession entirely, or would you do everything the same if you could do it again?

DF: I would write a lot more. I don't know what I was doing about writing in the years between my first book and my second, and I very much regret that I didn't build up more of a stock of material in that period. I can't explain how that happened, or rather didn't happen, but it's something I regret. Naturally, I think probably I have the feeling that everybody has over work they've done, that there's a mixture of pleasure that you did something, inevitably combined with a feeling that, well, it could have been better. I don't know how I would particularize it further, but I bet you recognize that feeling about work. But it's mostly a quantitative matter. I wish I had done more poems of my own and there are a lot of other translations I would like to do—that I'll still do. But it would be nice to have even more of it done.

MICHAEL KENNEDY: Your poems seem to describe a picture so well, you seem always to be able to get a perfect picture into the reader's mind. How do you get a poem started? Do you sit at your computer and remember something that's happened in the past, or do you see something happen and try to turn it into a poem?

DF: Thank you. It varies a lot. Sometimes I have a line hanging around in my head, and just sort of getting that line onto the computer and fooling around with it gets something going. Very often it doesn't get something going, at least not that year. But it's still there in the computer. In the old days, before the computer, it was still there in a notebook. Sometimes I've written out something that I wanted to get said, in prose, and then worked from that prose to see what a viable way of getting it into lines that had some music in them was going to be. With *Dwelling Places*—well, really with the last three books, starting with *Strangers*—after a certain point in the writing of a book I began to see that it was going to turn into a *book*, with a certain character of its own, or a certain kind of prevailing subject matter. In the case of *Dwelling Places*, people who didn't have dwelling places and people who did. And that led to some governing ideas for poems, and led me to look, as I said earlier, for relevant things to translate.

I can't say I always start from the same kind of point, because I don't.

ALISON ELLSWORTH: When you last spoke with us you mentioned having been in the army. How did that affect your writing, if it did at all?

DF: Hardly at all, I think, except in the poem called "The Soldier." The army experience I had was extremely lucky. This was World War II. I was mainly stationed in England, well out of harm's

187

way. So, because of my luck, I didn't have the sort of war material that some other poets of that generation had. The effect of the army was minimal, at least as it relates to my poetry. Except that—I don't know exactly how this bore on the poetry or not—but because I was in the army between my freshman and sophomore years in college I came back, like a lot of people at that time, as a lot older sophomore than I would have been otherwise, and a somewhat different person. And that made me, I think, a more serious reader, and reading led to all the rest.

KRISTIN TYMAN: When you have a dry spell with your writing, do you ever get anxious or nervous?

DF: Very.

KRISTIN TYMAN: How do you cope?

DF: I don't. I just kvetch a lot. But, as I said earlier, translation is helpful. It gives me something to do. I'm translating the Epistles of Horace now, a big work. I'm getting near the end of it and I'm getting a little anxious, because I need another big translation project. I'm fooling around with some of the Satires of Horace, to see if that's what I'm going to want to do, and I'm fooling around with the first Georgic of Virgil. I don't know which I'm going to get into, the Horace or the Virgil, but I need one or the other, both because I love being a translator and also because translating helps with dry periods.

In fact, I can't really make a distinction that's all that clear between being a poet and being a translator. There's the big difference, of course, that Horace or Virgil had the original idea and that they're a lot better than me, so I admire them and fall in love with them. But once you've got the translation going it's like having a rough draft of a poem that you're working on, and your experience of the activity is remarkably the same. So translating gives you the illusions—and it's not entirely an illusion—that there isn't a dry period after all.

ALI GORSKI: Some of the poems that we've read take place in and around Cambridge. Has Cambridge had an impact on your poetry?

DF: It sure has, in those poems. I thought during one dry period that I might make a whole book of poems about Ellery Street, the street I live on. But I shied away from that, partly because I knew I probably couldn't do it. I just don't work that systematically and also I kind of hate ideas for a book, topics, that are *that* tightly defined But I did think about it, and there are several other poems, beside the one called "Ellery Street," that are about my immediate neighborhood.

Cambridge is extremely important to me because it has people I talk about poetry with a lot, and other translators and writers; it's got people like Harry in it, and Christopher Ricks, people I love to talk about these things with. There are other poets. It's a very good community for poets. There are lots of generous-minded people around. We do a lot of exchanging of things. So Cambridge is extremely important for me, and Boston as well.

ALISON ELLSWORTH: When you are translating, do you tend to try to emulate the style of the original writer of the poem, or do you tend to try to make the poem your own?

DF: I have a couple of ways of talking about that. Certainly I try to be as faithful as possible to the poem. Let me come back to that point in a second, after I confess that there are some poems where I've taken certain liberties in order to suit my purposes in making a book. Rilke's "Song of a Drunkard" is an example. He has his drunkard say:

> Es war nicht in mir. Es ging aus und ein.
> Da wollt ich es halten. Da hielt es der Wein.
> (Ich weiss nicht mehr, was es war.)
> Dann hielt er mir jenes und hielt mir dies,
> bis ich mich ganz auf ihn verliess.
> Ich Narr.

I translated the stanza as:

> I don't know what it was I wanted to hold onto.
> I kept losing it and I didn't know what it was
> Except I wanted to hold onto it. The drink kept it in,
> So at least for awhile I felt as if I had it,
> Whatever it was. But it was the drink that had it
> And held it and had hold of me too. Asshole.

"Ich Narr" is "I fool" or "I was a fool" or "I'm a fool," any one of which sounded awkward to me in my poem, and untrue to the voice I wanted for the poem as placed among other poems about street people in that section of my book. "Asshole" seemed to me what the voice would say. But it also seems to me to be true to the tone of Rilke's poem. At least I persuade myself that that's so. But I do acknowledge that from somebody's point of view—maybe Rilke's—I've taken a liberty in this case.

I do sincerely mean that as a translator I want to be as true as possible, as faithful as possible, to the poem I'm translating. But there are built-in limitations. One is the limitation of talent. I only translate great poems and of course I know I'm not good enough. (It's some comfort that I think nobody else is, either.) Then there are the differences of language. In translating Horace or Virgil I make no attempt to imitate the Latin meters systematically, because the whole system of Latin meter is so different from English meter, but I do try very hard to find some kind of equivalent for the tones of voice that I hear in the original; I try to respect and use and responsibly interpret the detailed narrative, the situations, the figures of speech I find there, and to use English meters that have some aspects of equivalence. This is true for most of the other translations I've done, from other languages. A translation can't carry the original bodily over the line. It's a form of reading, of interpretation, but my hope is that it's faithful reading, faithful interpretation.

Horace:
Translated from the Latin by David Ferry

from Epistle I.1

Listen to someone like me—
(What fighter in the dusty arena wouldn't
As soon be crowned with the wreath without the dust?)
Gold is worth more than silver, virtue's worth more
Than gold. Here is the way the moneymen talk,
Down by the Arch of Janus: "Citizens, listen,
Get money first, get virtue after that."
That's what you hear wherever you go these days.
"Suppose you have good sense, and eloquence,
You have good morals, your word can always be trusted.
So what? If, nevertheless, you're short of the money
It takes to buy a knighthood, you're just a pleb."
But children at their play have a song that goes:
"He who does right will be a king, all right."
Let this be our defense: not to have any
Wrongdoing on our conscience to worry over.
So tell me, which is better, the things they say
Down by the arch of Janus, or what the children
Sing and chant as they play their game in the street:
"He who does right will be a king, all right,"
The song that manly Camillus probably sang,
And manly Curius too, when they were kids?

Is it better advice you get from the one who says:
"Fair means or foul, get money if you can;
No matter how you get it, be sure you get it"—
All for a seat down front at some bad play?
Or better to listen to him whose advice prepares you
To stand up, a free man, defying arrogant Fortune?

What if the Roman people should ask me why,
Since I walk the same streets and under the same
Colonnades as they do, I'm not a lover
Of what they love, or hater of what they hate.
I'd give the answer the fox gave to the lion:
"I see those footprints. I see that those footprints all
Go into your den, and none come out again.
You're a monster with many heads, so why on earth
Do you think I'd be willing to go along with you?"

Epistle I.10

Dear Fuscus, I, a lover of the country,
Send greetings to you, a lover of the city.
It's true, we differ in this; in everything else
It's just as if we were twins, with brotherly hearts;
One shakes his head, the other one shakes his head;
One nods his head, the other one nods his head;
We're like a pair of good old turtledoves.

But you love the city, so you never leave it;
I love the country, so I go on praising
Brooks and groves and mossy rocks and such.
I feel I'm truly living, truly myself,
The minute I leave the city and everything
You city lovers lavish praises on.
I'm like that slave who ran away because
They fed him honey cakes and he longed for bread.

If we're supposed quote "to live in accordance with
The nature of things" unquote and therefore have to
Choose where best to do so, then, I ask you,
Is any place better for this than the blessed country?
Where are the winters milder? Tell me, where else
Could you with anything like such pleasure feel
The cooling breeze that calms the rabid Dog Star
And the raging Lion struck by the sun's fierce arrows?
Is there anywhere else where sleep is so untroubled?
Is the grass less fragrant or less shining than
Libyan mosaics? Is the water that does its best
To burst the leaden pipes in city streets

Purer than water that makes its murmuring way
Downhill in mountain streams? In your atria,
Among your elaborate columns, you've planted trees,
And houses with views of the fields are always praised.
Drive Nature out with a pitchfork, she'll come right back,
Victorious over your ignorant confident scorn.

The man who doesn't know the difference between
Wool dyed with Sidonian purple or just with dyes
From Aquinum isn't as badly off as the man
Who isn't able to tell the true from the false.
Change will upset the man who's always been lucky.
You hate to lose what you've always been pleased to have.
Avoid the grand: you can live in a little house
And still live better than kings and the friends of kings.

The stag was a better fighter than the horse
And often drove him out of their common pasture,
Until the horse, the loser, asked man's help
And acquiesced in taking the bit in his mouth.
But after his famous victory in this battle
He couldn't get the rider off his back
And he couldn't get the bit out of his mouth.
The man who's afraid to be poor and therefore gives
His liberty away, worth more than gold,
Will carry a master on his back and be
A slave forever, not knowing how to live
On just a little. If what he happens to have
Won't fit a man, it's as it is with a shoe:
Too big, it makes you stumble; too small, it pinches.

Aristius, you'll be wise if you live happy
With what you have. And if you see me set
On having more for myself than I ought to have,
Don't let me get away with it unreproved.

The money you have is either your master or slave.
The leash should be held by you, not by your money.
I'm writing out back of Vacuna's ancient shrine,
Happy in every way, except that you're not here.

Epistle I.20

My book, you look to me as if you're longing
To get yourself down to Janus and Vertumnus
And put yourself on sale, all pumiced and ready.
I know you hate the idea that modesty loves,
Of being locked away from people's gaze.
You want to be available to the many,
Not just the few. You weren't brought up that way.

But off you go, down where you're itching to go.
There's just one thing I want you to remember:
Once you're out there, there is no coming back.
"What have I done?" "What was I thinking of?"
That's what we'll hear you cry, your feelings hurt,
After your lover has had enough of you
And packs you off somewhere in a dusty closet.

But unless my disapproval of your behavior
Undoes my prophetic powers, here's what will happen:
You will be dear to Rome till your youth goes by.
Having been soiled by all those pawing hands,
You'll either lie in silence while the moths,
That cannot read, will feed on you, or else
You'll make your way to far-off Africa
Or be tied up and sent away to Spain.

Your guardian then, to whom you wouldn't listen,
Will have the last laugh, like the man whose donkey
Kept pulling against being pulled back from the very
Edge of a cliff, till finally the man
Lost patience and pushed the stupid thing right over.
Why save a creature that doesn't want to be saved?

And after all that you'll end up in a school
Far from any city, God knows where,
A babbling poor old man, trying to teach
Young boys in a little school their ABCs.

But when the day is nearly done, and people
Are sitting around you, taking the evening air,
Please tell them who I was: son of a freedman,
In humble circumstance, my wings too strong
For the nest I was born in. What your tale subtracts
Because of my birth may it add because of my merit—
The foremost men of Rome, in peace and war,
Were pleased with me and what I was able to do;
A little man, and prematurely gray,
A lover of the sun; easily angered,
But easily pacified. If anyone asks,
I was forty-four years old in that December
When Lollius chose Lepidus as his partner.

Satire I.7
*Et Tu, Brute?: A Frontier Anecdote**

All the drug store cowboys and barbershop loungers
Have heard the story of Perseus the halfbreed
And his revenge on King' Rupilius, the outlaw,
A poisonous bag of pus if there ever was one.
Persius, who was rich and had a thriving
Business at Chazomenae was involved
In a lawsuit with this guy. Persius was tough
And sure of himself, a loudmouth blusterer—
If he was a horse in a foulmouth race against
Barrus or Sisenna he'd win in a walk.

To get back to the "King." The case between them
Couldn't, of course, be settled. It's always like that
With people like that—heroes on the field,
Say, Hector and Achilles, eyeball to eyeball,
Locked together in mutual rage such that
Nothing but death could possibly separate them.
The reason this is so is that in each
The quality of courage is absolute.
With cowards or with an uneven pair it's different,
As when Diomedes encountered Lycian Glaucus
And Glaucus surrendered at once and gave him lots
Of very expensive presents.
                              The epic battle
Of Persius and the King' took place at the time
When Brutus himself was governor of Asia.
The King' and Persius, just as evenly matched
As Bacchius and Bithus the gladiators,
Sallied into court, a sight to behold.
The courtroom roared with laughter as Persius
Laid out his case. He lavished praise on Brutus
And all of Brutus's people. He, Brutus, was

"The sun shining on Asia," his followers were
"Beneficent health-bringing stars," all but the "King,"
Whom he compared to the pestilential Dog Star
Everyone hates. On and on he roared like a wild
Mountain torrent let loose in the spring.
And then it was the turn of the "King," who gave
As good as he got, against this flood of invective.
He was like some tough crazy old farmer who'd beat up
Whoever it was who dared to call him cuckoo,
And make him say Uncle.

                                                   But after the "King" got through,
Then Persius the Greek, thoroughly drenched
From having Rupilius' bottle of wop insult
Poured out all over him, cried out to Brutus,
"Brutus, for God's sake, you're famous for being good
At killing off kings, so please kill off this 'King.'"

It seems to me it's a job just made for you.

---

*After he participated in the assassination of Julius Caesar, Brutus became governor of the
Asian provinces.

Cesare Pavese:
Translated from the Italian by Geoffrey Brock

Sad Wine (II)

The hard thing's to sit without being noticed.
Everything else will come easy. Three sips
and the impulse returns to sit thinking alone.
Against the buzzing backdrop of noise
everything fades, and it's suddenly a miracle
to be born and to stare at a glass. And work
(a man who's alone can't not think of work)
becomes again the old fate that suffering's good
for focusing thought. And soon the eyes fix
on nothing particular, grieved, as if blind.

If this man gets up and goes home to sleep,
he'll look like a blind man who's lost. Anyone
could jump out of nowhere to brutally beat him.
A woman—beautiful, young—might appear,
and lie under a man in the street, and moan,
the way a woman once moaned under him.
But this man doesn't see. He heads home to sleep
and life becomes nothing but the buzzing of silence.

Undressing this man you'd find a body that's wasted
and, here and there, patches of fur. Who'd think,
to look at this man, that life once burned
in his lukewarm veins? No one would guess
that there was a woman, once, who gently touched

that body, who kissed that body, which shakes,
and wet it with tears, now that the man,
having come home to sleep, can't sleep, only moan.

Habits

On the avenue's asphalt the moon makes a lake
of silence; my friend is recalling the past.
In those days, for him, a chance meeting sufficed
and he wouldn't be lonely. Watching the moon,
he'd breathe the night in. But fresher the scent
of the woman he'd met, of the brief romance
on precarious stairs. The comfortable room
and the sudden desire to live there forever—
they'd fatten his heart. Then, in the moonlight,
with great dazed strides he'd go home, contented.

In those days he kept himself company well.
He'd wake in the morning and jump out of bed,
finding his body still there and his thoughts.
He used to like going for walks in the rain
or the sun, enjoying the spectacle of streets
and talking to people he met. He believed
he could start, if he wanted, a new line of work
with every new morning, till the end of his days.
And after a hard day, he'd sit there and smoke.
His most powerful pleasure was being alone.

My friend's gotten older, he'd like for his house
to mean more than it does, he'd like to go out
and stop on the street to look at the moon,
and on the way back encounter a woman,
submissive and calm, patiently waiting.
My friend's gotten older, he isn't enough
for himself anymore. Always the same passersby,
the same rain, the same sun, and morning's a desert.
There's no point in working. And walking in moonlight,
if no one's waiting, there's no point in that.

Creation

I'm alive and at daybreak I've startled the stars.
My companion continues to sleep unaware.
All companions are sleeping. The day is a clear one
and stands sharper before me than faces in water.

In the distance an old man is walking to work
or enjoying the morning. We aren't so different,
we both breathe the same faint glimmer of light
as we casually smoke, beguiling our hunger.
The old man, too, must have a body that's pure
and vital—he ought to stand naked facing the morning.

Life this morning flows out over water
and in sunlight: around us the innocent splendor
of water, and all the bodies will soon be uncovered.
There'll be a bright sun and the sharpness of sea air
and the harsh exhaustion that beats down in sunlight
and stillness. And my companion will be here—
a shared secret of bodies, each with its own voice.

There's no voice to break the silence of water
at dawn. And neither is anything moving
beneath this sky. There's only a star-melting warmth.
One shudders to feel the morning trembling
so virginally, as if none of us here were awake.

Originals © 1962 by Giulio Einaudi editore, Torino

Umberto Saba:
Translated from the Italian by Geoffrey Brock

A Memory

I cannot sleep. I see a street, some pines,
and in my heart the old anxieties gather.
We used to go there alone, to be together,
another boy and I.

It was Passover, the old folks' rites arcane
and slow. And if he doesn't care enough,
I thought, and if he doesn't come tomorrow?
Tomorrow he did not come: a new pain.
Spasms of grief that evening. Now I know
friendship wasn't what we had in our grove;
what we had was love—

the first. And such love then, and what a glow
of joy, between the hills and sea of Trieste.
But why, tonight, am I unable to rest,
when all that happened fifteen years ago?

Claire Malroux:
Translated from the French by Marilyn Hacker

Highs and Lows

January 30, evening

the hours dropping like a pleated curtain
on a standing statue
                    or one stretched out in
an ivied slumber. They felled the forest
laid the tree-trunks out in their burial dress
but the man on the roof of his brain is busy
raising the metal yard-arms
the exploit is within rocket-range

uselessly the mermaid thrashes
in her aquatic antique shop
dashes from coral to coral
all in silence, disillusioned
dreams of footprints on wet sand in the world's sun
the prince is not yet dead to the day
rocked by the shrieking of seabirds
and she will never be dead to the night

it's snowing on the rooftops
winter isn't over
leprous petals will glitter at the moon
on bloodied lips
a snowy night drops dawnless
                    a sheet
hours like a curtain

                    dreaming
that a giant purple lily rises from the sea
a fiery octopus
the earth its iridescences devoured
like a greedy or too-curious insect

a muted
    rumbling
        in the soul's crevices
on the sleeping city
    (and then another city awakens
    higher up, lower down)

it only takes an insect
    to endanger
        silence
but remember
    that after the sirens' commotion
latin will live on peacefully
    in the catacombs

a hymn of crickets
    breathing their music
        amidst the snowflakes

February 3, morning and evening

because it's Monday man takes up his tasks again
he pries the scales from his brain one by one
the dark parts are uncovered
patches of mildew shiver in the daylight
unwashed unshaven old crimes get up
stretch their numbed backs
processions of daydreams and recollections
flee through the interstices
ploughshares and goose-down litter the rubbish dump
birds soar above it with disdain
they, to cross the sea
need only replace their wing-feathers

hour when the sky turns from black ink to blue
what will you have written at the table where you cut your bread
what scrap will find its way
not toward the ear but toward the mouth the heart?
what flavor
stronger than garlic and honey?

the same day at nightfall
a pulse diminishing in the sky
its lantern
firefly, shooting star, perpetual zero
to the eye
blindly wide open
to the burst of signal-lights on landing

the octopus dances on the ocean floor
our ancestor our princess
                        her sapphire eye
among the blood-red veils of her tentacles
a circle of sky in the prehensile flesh
as if innocence had its paradise
twenty thousand leagues under us

as if another creation were possible
escaping the degradation
below the shimmering

sea   carnivore
devourer in joyous recklessness

don't allow the past
            to melt in the nets of the sun
which fossilizes, robotizes
however hungry we may be for freedom

bathe our barely-born bodies
in your sap

and you from the future
passing your finger's ray across the archaic script
out of some piety or encyclopedic impulse
                            don't forget
that the seaweed-hand has lovingly
followed the sun's quake in the long night
and hunted the wave down in the glacier
cloud among clouds

Charles Baudelaire:
Translated from the French by Kristin Hennessy

The Cries of an Icarus

from *Les Fleurs du Mal*

Lovers fulfilled by prostitutes' desires
Know sated satisfaction's warm fatigue,
Not so with me—my arms grow limp and worn
From sharing solely the embrace of clouds.

I have consumed the peerless cosmic spheres,
The orbs that blaze beyond the celestial rim,
Until my flame seared eyes can worship but
The shadowed memories of brilliant suns.

In vain, I sought infinity—to plumb
Its middle and devour its endless end.
Beneath a singeing gaze I cannot see,
My wings, which strive for suns, give way.

And scorched by my divine love for Beauty,
I'll never gain my most sublime desire
To claim as mine this dark abyss, which steals
Eternity and me, and is my tomb.

Robert Whittaker

Tolstoy's American Visitors: Memoirs of Personal Encounters, 1868–1909

TOLSTOY NOT ONLY RECEIVED HUNDREDS OF LETTERS FROM Americans—in all over 1800 from 1868 to 1910—but dozens of Americans visited him at his home in Moscow and estate at Yasnaya Polyana over this same period. He had become acquainted with many of these visitors through correspondence, but a significant number simply showed up at his doorstep, expecting to be received by the famous writer, who—they had heard—received all visitors. Meetings and conversations with American visitors not only enriched Tolstoy's understanding of American life and culture,

This is the fifth in a series of articles presenting Tolstoy's correspondence with Americans, based on material from the joint U.S.-Russian project "Tolstoy and His U.S. Correspondents" ("Tolstoy's American Mailbag: Selected Exchanges with His Occasional Correspondents," "Tolstoy's American Disciple: Letters to Ernest Howard Crosby, 1894–1906," "Tolbut contributed to his generally positive impression of Americans and their unusual, young country. Tolstoy seemed to believe that they were the most receptive to his ideas, since they eagerly translated his writings and responded with more letters than any other nation.[1] Not only did Tolstoy carry on a lively correspondence with Americans, but he received many American publications—periodicals, brochures, pamphlets, books—frequently representing minority, usually radical views. Thus, when Americans visited Tolstoy, they found in him a well-informed, lively conversationalist, as interested in the latest ideas from across the Atlantic as he was opinionated about and often critical of American values.

A study of Tolstoy's American correspondence would not be complete without a survey of memoirs of his actual meetings with Americans. Most of his American visitors wrote accounts of their conversations with Tolstoy—twenty different visitors published detailed descriptions of their meetings and conversations for an audience that was apparently eager for eyewitness accounts of the great novelist and moralist. These accounts provided an important forum for Tolstoy's ideas, even in those cases when his visitor remained skeptical and even argumentative.

The first American to visit Tolstoy was a member of the U.S. diplomatic legation in Russia. Eugene Schuyler (1840–1890), U.S. consul in Moscow from 1867 to 1876, was the first American to translate and publish Tolstoy in America—"Sebastopol Sketches" and "The Cossacks" appeared in 1869 and 1878[2]—and his letter of November 18 (30) 1868 is the earliest American letter to Tolstoy

stoy's American Translator: Letters to Isabel Hapgood, 1888–1903" and "Tolstoy's American Preachers: Letters on Religion and Ethics, 1886–1908" appeared in TriQuarterly 95, 98, 102 and 107–108). Begun in 1986 under the auspices of the International Research and Exchanges Board, the Association of Learned Societies, and the Academy of Sciences of the USSR, since 1991 this project has been sponsored by the Gorky Institute of World Literature of the Russian Academy of Sciences in Moscow. The project has received major and essential institutional support from the Tolstoy State Museum in Moscow, especially the staff of its Manuscript Division. Activities of the project in the U.S. have greatly benefited from the support of the staff of the Slavonic and Baltic Division of the Research Libraries of the New York Public Library. The director of the project for the Russian side is Dr. L. D. Gromova, the chief editor is N. P. Velikanova; the activities of the American side are coordinated by the author of this publication, who expresses his gratitude to the staff of the Tolstoy State Museum and its Manuscript Division and to the Gorky Institute for assistance in this research.

that survives.[3] In 1889 he published his memoir of a week spent twenty years earlier with Tolstoy and his family, in October 1868.[4] This is the only American account of a meeting with Tolstoy before his religious and spiritual "transformation" which began in the late 1870s, and as such it differs radically from all succeeding accounts. (Well aware of the changes that Tolstoy's views had undergone, Schuyler nonetheless did not attempt to compare the "old" with the "new" Tolstoy.) First of all his account differs in the absence of discussions on religion, morality, marriage, the church, government, non-resistance—topics that dominate all later accounts. Secondly, this Tolstoy is still very much the traditional Russian aristocrat, member of the landed gentry, avid hunter and sportsman. For example, Schuyler noted that Tolstoy was planting the whole estate in birch trees, which "in twenty years would yield a large and steady revenue. . . , and thus he would leave the estate to his children far more productive than he had himself inherited it."[5] True, Schuyler had been warned by Princess Olga, wife of Prince Vladimir F. Odoevsky and representing Moscow's best society, that he would find Tolstoy "very shy and very wild," which, although not borne out, suggests that she sensed something of the future Tolstoy in his earlier manner.[6] And thirdly, the discussion of literature focused upon Tolstoy's admiration for the English novel, and in French literature for Alexandre Dumas and Paul de Kock, whom he called the French Dickens.[7] Schuyler assisted Tolstoy in rearranging the books in his study, which naturally led to a variety of literary topics. They discussed *War and Peace*, which Tolstoy was still writing, especially questions of genre, historical style and veracity, his distrust of historians, and the objections of critics (which he had just addressed in an article seven months earlier[8]). Schuyler, who knew both authors and their work, devoted much space to an account of the relations between Turgenev and Tolstoy, the origins of their personal conflict, and their views of each other's novels.

Tolstoy's comments on two topics—the peasantry and music—anticipated the storm and protest to come in ten years. He noted that, although the peasants were religious, they respected and were more influenced by landowners that by the priests: "abolition of the priesthood would probably have no effect whatever on the morality of the peasantry." Although he supported it at first, Tolstoy believed that the emancipation of the serfs seven years earlier had come too soon, the result of "reasoning only by theoretical men, and not . . . through the demand of the people, or by the necessity of the case."[9] Explaining his theories of pedagogy, Tolstoy expressed views on literature and art that foreshadow his pronouncements twenty years later: "all we have done in poetry and music is false, exclusive, without meaning and without future, and insignificant in comparison with the needs and even with the productions of these arts of which we find specimens among the people." His conclusion is indistinguishable from his later declarations: "Pushkin and Beethoven please us not because they express absolute beauty, but because we are as depraved as they, and because they only flatter our abnormal irritability and our weakness."[10]

Schuyler knew well how Tolstoy's emphasis and views had changed since they first met, for he knew My Confession and the other works which document the change. However, at least in 1889, he still considered the change temporary. In extensive footnotes to his own account of Tolstoy's early life Schuyler provided passages from My Confession which describe his "new" understanding of these events. But Schuyler warned his readers: "we must remember that [My Confession] was written under the influence of a very strong religious emotion." In a postscript to his memoir Schuyler directly addressed these changes in Tolstoy:

> Judging from the past there has never seemed to me any reason to believe that the present phase of mystical religious enthusiasm, through which Count Tolstoy is now passing, would last for the whole of his life; or that he is permanently lost to literature.[11]

By way of confirmation he cited lengthy passages from a letter of the writer G. P. Danilevsky, who visited Yasnaya Polyana in 1886, and who found Tolstoy "not so different after all from what he once was." But Tolstoy was in fact very different, if not in essence, then certainly in emphasis. This was not a "phase of mystical religious enthusiasm": it was certainly not 'mystical,' and it was driven by emotions more desperate—even suicidal—than 'enthusiastic.' So subsequent visitors would confirm without exception.

The first American to visit the "new" Tolstoy was George Kennan (1845–1924), a journalist who wrote extensively on Russia and Siberia (and nicknamed "the elder" to distinguish him from his namesake and relative, the well-known twentieth-century diplomat.) Kennan met Tolstoy during his second visit to Russia, in 1886. An accomplished telegraph operator, Kennan had gone to Siberia in 1865 on a surveying expedition to find a telegraph cable route through Russia to Europe. When the project was abandoned after the successful laying of the transatlantic cable, Kennan wrote up his experiences, published them in a journalistic account, *Tent Life in Siberia*, and thus became an acknowledged authority on Russia.[12] In 1885 Kennan returned to Siberia as a professional journalist, now on assignment from a popular magazine, *The Century*, to report on the Russian system of penal colonies of exiles.[13] After a brief rest in London to regain his health, he returned to Russia and St. Petersburg in the spring of 1886, this time with his wife, to meet with prominent figures with whom he discussed his experiences in Siberia and verified his impressions. In May he left the capital and traveled south, continuing his interviews and meetings, and in June he visited Tolstoy at Yasnaya Polyana. Kennan, who had begun as a supporter of the Russian state and a defender of its policies, after his detailed study of the life of Russian exiles and convicts had become one of its severest critics.[14] He had promised a number of the exiles that he would visit Tolstoy and personally relate to him the details of their situations. Tolstoy's opposition to the government was already widely known, although the basis for his anti-government views—a doctrine of non-violent resistance to evil—was not a theory to which Russian revolutionaries could subscribe. Kennan's revised political assessment of Russia underlay his positive portrait of the Russian writer and thinker.

"A Visit to Count Tolstoi" described the Russian writer and thinker as eccentric, extreme, even childlike, but nonetheless logical, consistent and sincere.[15] Kennan's image of Tolstoy glowed with the journalist's affection and with generous humoring of ideals that seemed impossible to realize. The rustic setting described by Keenan became the standard introduction given by all visitors to Tolstoy's country estate. The informality of country life, Tolstoy's attire of simple, homespun cloth, and the pointed lack of upper-

The proper way to resist evil is to absolutely refuse to do evil either for one's self or for others."[17]

Kennan interspersed his accounts of Tolstoy's ideas with descriptions of his family, of lunch and dinner shared together, and of the good-natured informality which dominated conversations. Tolstoy described his own religious conversion and the response he received to My Confession and My Religion from Americans. In addition to sharing with Kennan details of his correspondence with American supporters, he took the opportunity to check with Kennan (whose Russian was excellent) the accuracy of a recently published translation of one of his tracts from French into English.[18] Tolstoy then described his impressions of America, especially of its most remarkable writers, among whom he numbered William Lloyd Garrison and Theodore Parker—the former for his teachings of non-resistance (rather than for his anti-slavery activities), and the latter for his "Discourse of Matters Pertaining to Religion," which he considered "the most remarkable effort of the American mind in that field."[19] Tolstoy criticized America for having "in two particulars proved false to her traditions. . . . In the persecution of the Chinese and the Mormons. . . . You are crushing the Mormons by oppressive legislation and you have forbidden Chinese immigration."[20] To the latter charge Kennan could find no reply to Tolstoy's refusal to consider the Chinese "aliens"—they were all "brothers" to him. As for the Mormons, Kennan ceded the question "by default."

Kennan's summary judgment of Tolstoy combines affection with tolerance. He found in his character and philosophy a peculiarity that "distinguishes Russian character as a whole"—a "childish faith in the practicality and the speedy realization of plans, hopes, and schemes which an American, under precisely similar circumstances, would regard as visionary and quixotic. . . . When this national trait is united, as it is in the Russian character, with a boundless capacity for self-sacrifice, it brings about results which, to the American mind, are simply bewildering and astonishing." He found this trait of "childishness" to be "no less apparent in the reasoning and the activity of the Nihilists than in the doctrines of and the eccentric practices of Count Tolstoi." Both Tolstoy and the revolutionaries ignored question of practicality: "The Russian seems to throw himself with a sort of noble, generous, but childish enthusiasm into the most thorny path of self-denial and self-sacrifice, if he can only see, or think that he sees, the shining walls of his ideal golden city at the end of it. He takes no account of difficulties, heeds not the suggestions of prudence, cares not for the natural laws which limit his powers, but presses on, with a sublime confidence that he can reach the ideal city because he can see it so plainly, and because it is such a desirable city to reach." In sum, Kennan saw in Tolstoy, as in the exiled revolutionaries he met in Siberia, and no less in the pilgrims who trudged towards holy shrines for personal salvation "this national characteristic—the disposition to seek desirable ends by inadequate and impractical methods."[21]

Kennan's portrait of Tolstoy created a public image of the Russian writer and philosopher in this positive, although affectionately qualified tone, in which he combined open admiration with tolerant incomprehension. Kennan considered this portrait sufficiently typical and instructive to serve with several other essays as an introduction to his series of articles on Siberia and the Russian exile system.[22] He continued to express his admiration of Tolstoy, and hoped to visit him again during a trip in 1901. Unfortunately, before they could meet, Kennan was arrested in St. Petersburg and deported as *persona non grata* from Russia, no doubt in response to his criticism of the government in his writings on the exile and prison system. Unable to write from fresh first-hand observations, Kennan nonetheless continued his support in print with a series of articles interpreting Tolstoy's activities.[23]

Kennan's respect was returned by Tolstoy, who praised the American's account of his visit and of the condition of Siberian exiles. He described Kennan as "a true gentleman and a man of his word," unlike some correspondent of a Russian newspaper who would write nonsense nineteen to the dozen.[24] Tolstoy closely followed Kennan's series on Siberia and reacted emotionally to the accounts: "I would be ashamed to be the czar in a government where there were no other means for my security than to exile thousands to Siberia, including sixteen-year-old girls."[25] The ultimate impact of

Kennan's account can be found in the later chapters of *Resurrection*, where Tolstoy provided a scathing description of the system of exile in Russia.[26]

Kennan's essentially positive view of Tolstoy, conditioned by his sympathy for the liberal and often revolutionary opposition to Russian internal policies, met with some tacit dissent from other commentators on Russia, one of the most qualified of whom was Isabel F. Hapgood (1851–1928). This redoubtable translator of Russian classic prose and energetic public supporter of Russian secular and religious culture spent several years in Russia (1887–1889), during which she developed a close relationship with Tolstoy and the many members of his family.[27] The nature of Hapgood's understanding of and sympathies with Russian internal politics, the aristocratic establishment and the monarchy developed in a direction quite opposite to Keenan's. This might explain why her understanding of Tolstoy and his family and her allegiance in the family conflicts occasioned by his moral philosophy produced a picture of Tolstoy in some ways markedly different from Kennan's.

Kennan's account of his visit to Tolstoy appeared but a few months before Hapgood's own departure for St. Petersburg. She wrote a letter of effusive praise to the journalist, which, given the subsequent differences in their views, takes on special interest. Hapgood wrote from Boston on June 14, 1887:

> I cannot forbear writing to tell you how intensely I have enjoyed your account of your visit to Count Tolstoi. Nothing could have so well set forth the full scope of his doctrines as the expressions which he used to you with regard to the extreme cases proposed by you for his consideration.
>
> I take the most intense interest in all he writes and does, having been inspired by his writings with that strong sentiment of personal regard which so few writers possess the art of conveying to their readers, and which you mention having immediately experienced on meeting him. Thousands of his friends in this country owe you a debt for your delightful article, which shows us the man so clearly, yet which is, if I may be permitted to refer to so tender a subject, a model of interviewing. I shall look for your future articles with impatience.
>
> You were very courteous to use my translation for your quo-

tation, when you could have translated the passage for yourself. This shows that you know who I am, and that I may venture to hope that my note of personal thanks for your article will not seem altogether an intrusion.[28]

Hapgood apparently was unaware that in a letter to Tolstoy written in December 1886 Kennan had praised Hapgood's translation of *Childhood, Boyhood and Youth*.[29]

Hapgood visited the Tolstoys in Moscow several times in December 1887 and January 1888, and then spent over a week at Yasnaya Polyana with the family in July of that year. She gave her impressions of these visits in two accounts, "Tolstoy at Home" first published in 1891, and "A Stroll in Moscow with Count Tolstoy," which appeared only in 1895.[30] The intervening years between her meetings with Tolstoy and the publication of her memoir witnessed a major evolution not only in Hapgood's views of the writer but also in her personal commitment to Russia and things Russian. First of all, Tolstoy's religious crisis and spiritual transformation in the early 1880s resulted in a family conflict over property: consistent with his thoroughgoing interpretation of Christ's teachings Tolstoy abjured all his rights to real and intellectual property. His wife, on the contrary, fought to defend these rights as the sole source of support for the family. In this family conflict, Hapgood took the side of Sofia Andreevna Tolstoy, even going so far as to urge the novelist to return to his former habits and writing. Eager to have the latest work of fiction by Tolstoy to translate, Hapgood received at last *The Kreutzer Sonata* early in 1890. She was appalled by the work—by its frankness and indecency—and because she could not agree with Tolstoy that such a work was necessary and would do good, she refused to translate it. Before even publishing her memoirs of their much earlier meeting, Hapgood publicly explained her refusal to translate *The Kreutzer Sonata*.[31] The first account of Hapgood's visit with Tolstoy, when it appeared the next year, reflected her personal allegiance in the family conflict over property and her differences with Tolstoy himself over the morality of sex and marriage.

"Count Tolstoy at Home" presented the writer as a rough field hand: "He looked even more weather-beaten in complexion than he had in Moscow during the winter, if that were possible. His broad shoulders seemed to preserve in their enhanced stoop a memory of recent toil. His manner, a combination of gentle simplicity, awkward half-conquered consciousness, and half-discarded polish, was as cordial as ever. His piercing gray-green-blue eyes had lost none of their almost saturnine and withal melancholy expression."[32] When Hapgood joined a conversation with Tolstoy and several peasants in the field, she was unpleasantly impressed by their lack of courtesy and elementary politeness, which seemingly resulted from the unorthodox behavior of their former landowner. An evening conversation on the non-resistance doctrines of Adin Ballou elicited only disdain from Hapgood: belittling Tolstoy's faith that the non-resistance movement will soon attract much attention, she commented that the sad fate of Ballou's Hopewell community "did not seem to shake his faith." Of Tolstoy's daughter, Masha (Maria), who followed her father's teachings, Hapgood commented: "She works for the peasants in various ways, and carries out her father's ideas in other matters as far as possible. Her Spartan (or Tolstoyan) treatment of herself may be of value in character-building, as mortification of the flesh is supposed to be in general. Practically, I think the relations between peasants and nobles render her sacrifices unavailing."[33]

Hapgood's descriptions of Tolstoy's interests and theories comprise a series of anecdotes, which show his impracticality and foolishness. Repeatedly she takes the opportunity to show him the error of his views, usually with liberal doses of sarcasm. As with the theories of Adin Ballou, so with his interest in the Mormons and why they were persecuted in America. Hapgood ascribed his inability to understand the problem with the Mormons to a lack of proper education on the subject. She noted sarcastically to Tolstoy: "the only argument in favor of them which can possibly be made is that their practice, not their preaching, offers the only solution of your own theory that all women should be married"—a reference to his view expressed at the end of his article "What Then Must We Do?" but radically changed since then to a position like that of the Shakers, i.e., celibacy.[34]

Hapgood did add a new observation about Tolstoy that, although opposed in sentiment to Kennan's conclusions, does share the point of view that there was something very Russian about Tolstoy's philosophy.

Those who have perused attentively his earlier works will have perceived that there is really very little that is absolutely new in these doctrines. They are so strictly the development of ideas which are an integral part of him, through heredity, environment, and personal bias, that the only surprise would be that he should not have ended in this way. Community of goods, mutual help, and kindred doctrines are the national birthright of every Russian, often bartered, it is true. But long residence in the country among the peasants who do not preach these doctrines, but simply practice them, naturally affected the thoughtful student of humanity though he was of a different rank. He began to announce his theories to the world, and found followers, as teachers of these views generally do,—a proof that they satisfy an instinct in the human breast. Solitary country life anywhere is productive of such views.[35]

There follows in Hapgood's account a lengthy description of the unsavory disciples who flocked to Tolstoy and of their foolish and, at times, even dangerous activities. Whatever the wellsprings of his moral philosophy, Hapgood found its application to be impractical, when not ridiculous. She enjoyed demolishing his faith in the essentially non-violent nature of the Russian peasant by citing his own play, *The Power of Darkness*. His abhorrence of luxury as sinful made no sense to Hapgood, and on the contrary, she faulted his vegetarian diet and punishing physical regimen as the cause of his frequent illnesses. Her final judgment of Tolstoy was that he was impressionable, often changed his opinions, and "his reading and meditation are fruitful of novelties, which he bravely submits to the judgment of the world without pausing to consider whether they coincide with his other utterances or not." His inconsistency, thus, was the measure of his sincerity. "That he does not always express his abstract ideas clearly is the inevitable result of the lack of philosophical training." Ultimately Tolstoy was an amateur, talented and enthusiastic, but not a serious moral philosopher.[36] This view, while not unsympathetic, nonetheless served to vitiate Tolstoy's moral teachings. By way of conclusion, Hapgood claimed that her account served to defend the home life and family of Tolstoy "against various misrepresentations and misconceptions . . . which are current." By this she apparently meant recent scandalous accounts of conflicts between Tolstoy and his wife over his new principles (some of which she could not accept and he would not compromise) and especially over property rights (she wanted to preserve copyright to his works which wanted to relinquish).[37]

This denigration of the "post-conversion" Tolstoy, however, did not prevent Hapgood from assisting the writer and his family with funds gathered from American donations to aid the starving peasants during the famine of 1892. During this humanitarian relief effort, Hapgood traded heavily upon Tolstoy's absolute reliability and trustworthiness, his knowledge of the peasants and their needs, and his ability to provide the most practical assistance at the least expense. By sending the several thousand dollars of contributions directly to Tolstoy and his wife, she avoided official government committees, both Western and Russian, a decision which avoided inefficiencies and even corruption, but also appeared somewhat inconsistent with her own political sympathies.

Hapgood's shorter account of earlier meetings in Moscow, "A Stroll in Moscow with Count Tolstoy," appeared in her *Russian Rambles* in 1895, well after their collaboration in assisting starving victims of the famine. Here Hapgood's persistent disagreements with Tolstoy over philanthropy and non-resistance seem shallow and uncharitable. Of his principle of how to help one's fellow man, she noted: "The count retreated to his former argument,—that one's personal labor is the only righteous thing which can be given to one's fellow man; and that the labor must be given unquestioningly when asked for." She dismissed his absolute refusal to resist evil violently with the comment that "perhaps Count Tolstoy had never been so unfortunate as to meet certain specimens of the human race which it has been my ill luck to observe."[38] The stroll through Moscow's streets appeared more remarkable for the attention attracted by Tolstoy's attire—a peasant's sheepskin coat and rough boots—than for his comments on urban poverty and the city's economic strata. In her concluding summary of Tolstoy's character and moral teaching Hapgood seems to address more a Russian than an American audience, for it was in the upper circles of St. Petersburg and Moscow society that Tolstoy's sanity was most often question. Her defense suffers somewhat from faint praise:

> I am aware that it has become customary of late to call Count Tolstoy "crazy," or "not quite right in the head," etc. The inevitable conclusion of any one who talks much with him is that he is nothing of the sort; but simply a man with a hobby, or an idea. His idea happens to be one which, granting that it ought to be adopted by everybody, is still one which is very difficult of adoption by anybody,—peculiarly difficulty in his own case. And it is an uncomfortable theory of self-denial which very few people like to have preached to them in any form. Add to this that his philosophical expositions of his theory lack the clearness which generally—not always—results from a course of strict preparatory training, and we have more than sufficient foundation for the reports of his mental aberration. On personal acquaintance he proves to be a remarkably earnest, thoroughly convinced, and winning man, although he does not deliberately do or say anything to attract one.

To this she added her own self-justification: "His very earnestness is provocative of argument." The effect of such an assessment by a respected, highly qualified observer of the Russian scene and of Russian literature and culture in particular cast serious shadows on the evolving image of Tolstoy.

A number of early American visitors to Tolstoy who met him during the late 1880s and early 1890s not only knew of his recent moral and philosophical writings but came specifically because of them. One of these visitors was Alice B. Stockham (1833–1912), a physician and publisher from Chicago, who had contacted Tolstoy to learn more of his theories of education and sent him a copy of her practical guide to childbearing and health, *Tokology: A Book for Every Woman*.[39] The work so impressed Tolstoy that he offered to have it translated and published in Russia, and Stockham traveled to Moscow to assist in this project. She met with Tolstoy for two days, October 2 and 3, 1889, at Yasnaya Polyana.[40] The impressions of her trip and memoir of meeting with Tolstoy she published in *Tolstoi. A Man of Peace,* an extended appreciation of Tolstoy and his ideas.[41]

Stockham contributed enthusiastic details to Tolstoy's image as a pioneer moralist and forward looking advocate of woman's rights. The same traits that amazed Keenan and enervated Hapgood seemed heroic to Stockham: "His avoidance of conventionality, his quick response to our thoughts, his eager, rushing sentences—real shoulder thrusts, made us know at once that we were in the presence of the world renowned writer, simple as a child, great as a lion."[42] His manner of dress and physical appearance likewise struck Stockham as not at all eccentric, but appropriate to his position: "Count Tolstoi has the appearance and bearing of a soldier. Stately and commanding, an imposing figure of massive proportions and majestic picturesqueness is fittingly crowned by a leonine head and the strong face of the enthusiastic man of mighty genius! Although dressed as a moujik, one feels he is of the nobility, that he is born to command."[43] Above all, Stockham accepted Tolstoy's religious views, his strict interpretation of Christ's teachings, and his moral principles. "One knows he has found the Christ, has clasped hands with God! He is in the world but not of it! His enthusiasm impresses one. His theories seemingly Utopian and unpractical, still carry a deep current of genuineness, not born of intellect, but rather the inspiration of one who has become conscious of the divine in his soul."[44] A practical, progressive woman, trained in science and medicine, Stockham found no inconsistency between Tolstoy's moral principles and his behavior. In this she is more sympathetic than Keenan to Tolstoy's ideals and more tolerant of his human failings than Hapgood.

Stockham deeply admired the Countess Sofia Andreevna and credited her with successfully adapting the household to her husband's needs. In contrast to Hapgood, she avoided any suggestion of conflict between the couple. Stockham saw the positive side of the relationship: "the infinite patience with which the Countess copies [Tolstoy's] various books bears witness to her devotion. . . . She has the entire control and management of the household, endeavoring to reconcile all material things to the rigid conditions demanded by the theories of her distinguished husband, the while maintaining some measure of comfort for herself and children. . . . She counts it her glory that in the very prime of his powers she has given him a quiet happiness, untroubled by storms, with a long series of domestic joys which have been afterward reflected in his works."[45] These observations appear amidst descriptions of everyday family concerns, of lively exchanges at meal times, and of visits to the peasants and a sick call, all of this presented as normal, healthy and spiritually strong. With her professional training and considerable intellect, Stockham no doubt could have found details that suggested discord and conflict. However, her temperament was strongly affirmative and she preferred to admire and elevate the Tolstoys rather than expose frailties.

The result is a sympathetic account of his principles presented not by a "believer" or follower of Tolstoy, but by a radical reformer who respected his sincerely held beliefs. She quoted him extensively on non-violent resistance to evil—"Tolstoi's conversation constantly reverted to the Christ's teaching of non-resistance"— echoing quotations cited by Keenan and Hapgood, and she noted that his counterpart in America, Adin Ballou, had begun preaching non-resistance in 1830. Occasionally she offered some of Tolstoy's stranger ideas without comment, such as his remark: "I can understand how pain is silenced by thought. I know this by experience; whenever I have an attack of pain, I put myself in the attitude of non-resistance and welcome it as a friend. . . . Oh, yes, all pain is a blessing!"[46] On the whole, however, she focused on the sensible and practical side of his moral principles, which she defined without difficulty. For example, she begins a striking analysis of his theory of non-resistance as follows:

Tolstoi, with many others, is coming to know that man, through realization of innate powers, creates his own defense. In this consciousness he is unharmed by deadly poisons or the venom of vipers. It is not only steel and armor to ward off attacks, but by its radiation is a constant protection; it is the white flame of love that consumes hatred, enmity and strife. Man in the full knowledge of his divine nature, is in possession of such a power

228

that none can covet his possessions, none can enter his gate with the thought of theft or murder.

Non-resistance was a real force for Tolstoy because "the divine radiance from such as Tolstoi would be so great that no thought of evil or violence could enter man's heart in his presence." She continued, "Tolstoi would say to Christians: prove your Christianity by your faith in man. Unbar your doors, not only beat your swords into plows and your spears into pruning hooks, but turn the locksmith's genius into the production of tokens of love and fidelity."[47] Stockham probably inferred more from Tolstoy's reading of Christ's teachings than he himself understood. Her enthusiasm suggests a degree of religious ecstasy that Tolstoy never expressed, and his moral principles remained more rational and unemotional than Stockham's interpretations of them.

Although her recollections of their conversations emphasized Tolstoy's "metaphysics" and especially the doctrine of non-resistance, he himself recalled in more detail their discussion of American religions. He wrote to a friend that "she supplemented in many ways my information on the American religious movement."[48] Stockham mentioned his interest in Lucy Mallory and her periodical *World's Advance-Thought and the Universal Republic*, which he had just begun receiving in 1888.[49] Stockham noted, "it did give me a thrill of pleasure too, when, in speaking of a paper on progressive thought received from Oregon, he said, 'I like these Western ideas, they seem to bring with them the freshness and breadth of your magnificent country!'"[50] Stockham recalled their discussion of American religions in the back of a horse cart as they were traveling to a court appearance concerning peasant loans. Tolstoy showed great interest in American "social conditions" and whether "any religious sect was declaring itself radically for peace." Of the Quakers he expressed "surprise that they were not numerically greater"; "he asked especially of Unitarians, Universalists, Christian Scientists, Swedenborgians and other new sects, and was astonished and regretful to learn that the doctrine of non-resistance was so far held to be of minor import."[51] Stockham reported no more of this conversation, but she apparently made a much deeper impression on Tolstoy than she realized, judging from his diary entry of the following morning. He saw in these sects evidence of "practical Christianity," which leads "to universal brotherhood, and the sign of all this is non-resistance."[52] Tolstoy apparently took more encouragement from her comments than Stockham intended to give.

At the time of Stockham's visit Tolstoy was working on *The Kreutzer Sonata*, the final draft of which he would finish the following spring. There is no indication from her account or Tolstoy's own notes that Stockham discussed the work with Tolstoy, nor is there any suggestion that they discussed her book *Tokology* or even the chapter on chastity in marriage. However, she discussed the reaction to this scandalous work, which appeared well before Stockham published her memoir of Tolstoy, and her comments on his ideas are interesting, since her *Tokology* contributed to the process of creating *The Kreutzer Sonata*. Stockham chided the reviewers of the novel: "a person gets from an artistic production what he puts into it; if that be true, of the reviewers of this work, ninety-nine one hundredths of them reflected sensuality and lust. . . . They forgot . . . that Tolstoi in his realistic pictures wades deep in degradation to pluck the lotus of virtue and spirituality." At the foundation of the work, Stockham believed, was Tolstoy's belief "that offspring should come only by the desire of the wife; that marriage should in no ways be a license; that man's obligation to respect a woman's slightest wish does not cease when he puts the wedding ring on her finger. With this thought he began a novel, as his daughter expressed it, in behalf of the rights of woman; to free her from man's domination in the marriage relation, that she might have complete control of the crowning function of her life, maternity." This emphasis, while not wholly unjustified by Tolstoy's final text, seems more consistent with Stockham's own writings in *Tokology* than with *Kreutzer Sonata*. In this same vein she defended Tolstoy's conclusion "that in the perfected life there should be no marriage at all."

Stockham provided a pointed rebuttal to Hapgood's assessment of Tolstoy in two respects. First, she emphasized the deep love and respect which the peasants showed towards Tolstoy, in contrast to the picture of careless inattention and the absence of elementary manners described by Hapgood. To her intimation that Tolstoy's idealization of the peasants and democratic treatment of them had undermined social discipline and standards, Stockham replied (without naming Hapgood): "It is almost impossible to estimate the influence for good which Lyeff Nikolaevitch exerts over the peasants with whom he comes in daily contact."[53] The second point of rebuttal concerns Tolstoy's inconsistency as a moral philosopher. "Tolstoi is honest, earnest, enthusiastic and indefatigable in his search for truth. That there are inconsistencies in his theories is true; these do but mark the epochs of his life. One will always find Tolstoi outdistancing Tolstoi. His very honesty and frankness lead him to proclaim truth as he sees it." This is not unlike Hapgood's point of view, which credited Tolstoy with not being a slave to consistency for its own sake. However, Stockham went considerably further in her praise:

> Tolstoi would be great in any country. Even in free America would he stand head and shoulders above other giants in proclaiming truth from his view point. In Russia, however, he is the one Vesuvius, the one mountain peak, rising in boldness and loneliness above a drear and barren plain. Only those acquainted with the limitations, the prison walls, of the forms and functions of the Greek Church can have a glimpse of the stoutness of heart demanded to protest in word and action against its caste and creed.[54]

Stockham attacked the Russian Orthodox Church, described the totalitarian control which it exerted over Russian spiritual and secular life, and hailed the heroic dissent of Tolstoy. She ended her memoir on the prophetic note that by denying Tolstoy the rituals of Orthodox burial, the Russian church had guaranteed his immortality.[55]

Following Stockham's visit in October 1889, Tolstoy received visits from two American journalists—professional travel writers in Russia on behalf of New York newspapers—each of whom wrote of his impressions and added to the accumulating interpretations of the Russian's personality and thought. On July 4, 1890, the popular travel writer Thomas Stevens (1855–?) visited Yasnaya Polyana on his way from Moscow to the Crimea by horseback—on mustangs.[56] Stevens' journey on behalf of the New York World was followed eight months later by a visit by James Creelman (1859–1915), a special correspondent for the *New York Herald*, who made the first of his two visits to Tolstoy in March 1891.[57]

Stevens' travels on horseback through Russia seemed less exotic than his excursion a few years earlier—around the world on a bicycle—and his travels the previous year to East Africa, of which Tolstoy had heard.[58] Tolstoy began his conversations with Stevens by discussing his "koumiss cure"—a diet of fermented mare's milk—and introducing him to the family of Bashkirs whom he had brought, together with their horses, from Samara to produce the koumiss (which Stevens reported as having tasted like buttermilk). Unlike Tolstoy's conversations with Hapgood and Stockham, but more like those with Keenan, his discussions with Stevens primarily concerned questions of politics and social questions. Tolstoy began by announcing that his future writings would be "on education rather than on purely social matters." He based his educational reforms on a simple principle—"the purity and perfection of the parents. In the shadow of paternal perfection the boys will attain perfection, and the purity and goodness of the mothers will be transmitted to the girls." However, he did not expand on his principles of family morality, recently expounded in *The Kreutzer Sonata*, or if he did, Stevens did not report them. Rather, they spoke of Siberia (without mentioning Kennan's work, which Tolstoy was reading in the serialized version at just this time) and of the state: "The government is altogether bad," Stevens quoted Tolstoy: "It is a monument to superstition and injustice." Tolstoy found government influence most pernicious on the youngest citizens: "The government sins most against the people in the matter of education. None of the concessions it makes are of any value. They are only makeshifts. Schools are in every village, but nothing is taught but 'nonsensical catechism' and the 'three Rs'."[59]

Talk of children and education led to conjectures about the future. Tolstoy had read the immensely popular utopian novel of Edward Bellamy, *Looking Backward* (which Hapgood had given him). It was a pleasant "fairy tale," he remarked of this story of a Boston Brahmin become Rip Van Winkle who, after a hundred years' sleep, awakened to a future communist society in 1990. "To be of value, the book should have shown how the results which are portrayed were to be arrived at," Tolstoy noted. Stevens pointed out, however, that Bellamy's utopia, at least in its external traits, was not unlike that which Tolstoy projected: "He condemned the author's judgment in presuming that such a state of society as he describes would be possible with human beings, possessed with the weaknesses and frailties of our kind. Only angels, he said, could exist under such conditions. Yet in the case of these same human beings, with the same weaknesses and frailties that would be the stumbling block in Bellamy's new social world, he advocated 'no government, no police, no prisons, no army, no church, no judiciary, no punishment for wrong doing'."[60]

Nonetheless, Tolstoy was enthusiastic about America and held a positive vision for its future. He felt that "of the governments of the present day . . . the United States government [was] a long way ahead." "The people of the United States have a 'natural government'—they govern themselves," unlike the French republic, for example. "A people who are simply living under a 'republican form of government,' because they think it better than any other, may possibly change their minds in time of some great public excitement and think that a king or an emperor would be better after all, but no such change is possible where the government is really and truly a government of the people—'natural government'."[61] Tolstoy expressed a bizarrely optimistic view of American wealth and the captains of industry who had created the "Gilded Age" at the end of the century:

> . . . the mission of the large American millionaires would be to hasten the climax, when the eyes of the people will be opened by the display of tremendous contrasts. The moral consciousness of the people needs a rude awakening, he thought, and only the development of abnormal contrasts in wealth and poverty is likely to bring the people to consider seriously the equal rights of all. Just as the undue development of the military will one day result in general disarmament, so, he believes, will the vast accumulations of the few and the poverty of the many open the

people's eyes to the fact that banks and government treasuries are robber's caves, in which is hoarded the money that has been taken from the people.

The Count, however, didn't think the equalization of property will be brought about by violence, but by a general moral awakening. Millionaires will become convinced that they have no right to the property that they now regard as their own, and will give it up; just as he would be willing to move off the family estate at Yasnaya Polyana. America, he thought, will one day set the example. England will follow; then Russia. The thinkers of Russia, he said, are already seriously studying the problem of doing away with the private ownership of land.[62]

In some small way, perhaps, the philanthropic movement that was about to begin in America would effect some equalization, if not to the extent Tolstoy hoped. Given such optimism, it is no wonder that Tolstoy found it hard to understand why pacifism, non-resistance and similar moral principles enjoyed so little popularity in America. For the present, however, until this moral awakening, he felt that the theories of Henry George provided the best solution for the problem of land ownership. "He declared George the greatest American citizen of the present time," although he could not understand the New Yorker's decision to enter politics. Tolstoy believed that "all forms of government are humbugs, that the whole machinery of law and lawyers, courts and judges, is a barbarity, and an excuse for setting one man above another, and enabling the privileged few to rob the many."[63] Significantly, Tolstoy agreed to a rare compromise: to grant government a right to limited violence with the single tax, which measure he would suggest on several occasions to the government over the next fifteen years. He believed that George's theories represented a step towards the elimination of private property, and that for Russia this was as important as the elimination of serfdom.[64]

Of Tolstoy's personal life Stevens commented laconically that "temperance finds in the great novelist an enthusiastic supporter." "Temperance" included not only alcohol, tobacco, and caffeine, but virtually all forms of self-indulgence, from romantic love to theater, dancing and music, romantic literature—"anything, in short, that excites the imagination to thoughts of love." Of the topics raised by *The Kreutzer Sonata*, Stevens commented that "his interest in the relations of the sexes seemed to me to be abnormal, almost morbid. Men and women, he insists, should love one another only as friends or as brothers and sisters."[65] And yet his family life "appeared to be altogether charming. Both wife and children fairly idolize the Count." Although the nieces took issue with him on certain principles, like romantic love, Stevens noted that although "these young people do not always fathom the Count, . . . they never doubt the wisdom of his actions or the goodness of his motives. Everything he does is right."[66] This tolerant understanding Stevens extended to the Countess, whom he credited with managing to keep the family and the estate from being squandered away by Tolstoy's refusal to resist any request for help.

Stevens' concluding judgment on Tolstoy was not unlike Kennan's, in that it saw in his extreme principles something peculiar to the character of Russia and the Russians. He observed, "Russia is a country where fantastic religious ideas seem to find a congenial soil. The dwarfing of the people's intellects in matters political is productive of curious expansions in other directions." One of these directions was that of the "queer religious idea," which for Stevens confirmed Tolstoy's national typicality.

On assignment to investigate the persecution of Jews in Russia, James Creelman was directed in March 1891 by the editor of the *New York Herald* to visit Tolstoy. His task was to determine whether the author really believed the ideas set forth in *The Kreutzer Sonata*, which was attracting attention at just that time.[67] Creelman titled his account "The Avatar of Count Tolstoy," by which he suggested the novelist's transformation into a deity on earth. He described him as "the god of Russian literature," whom he found "in the savagely bare house where his greatest novels were written." Creelman continued, "At the rough table on which *War and Peace* and *Anna Karenina* were penned, I sat for hours with Count Tolstoy, struggling against the force of his sweeping condemnations of marriage as it is and not as it ought to be. And then I came to know how the husband of a high-souled, loving woman and the father of thirteen children came to write that awful protest against married life in the nineteenth century." Of the Countess, he commented,

No man had a happier life, and no man owed more to marriage. But for the influence of this young wife, the pages of his greatest novels might have been spoiled by the brutalities which she persuaded him to abandon. These things the Count confessed with almost boyish frankness. And yet, so complex is human nature and the workings of the human mind, that no man in the whole range of literature has held bitterer views of the influence of women upon the higher nature of men. As I saw these two sitting together, after thirty years of unbroken love and sympathy, it was hard to believe that I was talking to the author of the *Kreutzer Sonata*.[68]

In order to explain the apparent paradox, Creelman gave an account of Tolstoy's spiritual transformation based largely on *My Confession*. "Then the avatar occurred. The soul of the romancist and poet died, and the soul of the reformer and prophet was born."[69]

Creelman recounted their conversation about *The Kreutzer Sonata:* "I never saw a more earnest countenance than that which he turned to me as he curled one leg up under him and clasped his muscular hands over his knee. It was all so simple and real—a man who had struggled out of conventionality, back into naturalness." Tolstoy opened the exchange with the explanation that "the story of the *Kreutzer Sonata* is simply a protest against animality and an appeal for the Christianity of Christ."[70] Creelman questioned, Tolstoy answered, and at each point the latter made the same point: the work addressed real people and practical problems, and to deny the actuality of these problems was self-delusion. Tolstoy concluded: "Marriage is the worst kind of selfishness, for it is double. There is no egotism like family egotism. In the selfishness of their life the husband and wife forget the love they owe to the rest of the world. Real love is simply the cohesive force of the spirit which draws the whole race together. That cohesive force I call God. God is simply love. This is what Christ tried to tell the world, but the churches have put another message in his mouth."[71] From here the conversation ranged over such topics as the nature of the soul, the true nature of Christ's teachings, and the conflict of good and evil. By way of conclusion, Tolstoy noted: "Modern Christians believe that human nature is evil, . . . but the Chinese believe that human nature is good. In this I am Chinese. When good and evil are brought together on equal ground, the good must prevail. That is a law of the universe."[72] At this point Tolstoy's young son, Vanya, stole into the room, and the conversation ended.

Creelman's image of Tolstoy is of a serious, thoughtful, giant of a man—both literally and figuratively. By way of providing the context for Tolstoy's "avatar" Creelman described the peasants of Yasnaya Polyana.[73] He gave a detailed account of his visit to peasant families with Tolstoy's daughter Maria and a visit to the peasant school. Later he continued this winter stroll with Tolstoy, during which they discussed America. After noting that "you newspaper writers are an irreverent tribe" (Creelman commented, "that statement being true, I made no reply"[74]), Tolstoy severely criticized Colonel Robert G. Ingersoll, who had written a series of articles on him and his latest work.[75] He was incensed at Ingersoll's pragmatism: "He argues that Christ's Sermon on the Mount is not practical when applied to our present industrialism. . . . He is an ignoramus. He talks as if industrialism were a law instead of a product of human activity which can be changed." Tolstoy was tempted to write a book to refute Ingersoll: "In my new work I intend to quote Thomas Jefferson's declaration that the least government is the best government. He might have gone a step forward, and said that no government at all is better still."[76] The stroll ended when Tolstoy greeted pilgrims on the road and invited them to his home to share dinner.

Creelman concluded his interpretation with a defense of Tolstoy's moral principles based on his personal observation:

Those who blame Tolstoy for his too literal Christianity should see his surroundings, and then they may comprehend the stages by which he arrived at his present point of view. He is honest and sane. Even in the harshest periods of his austere life he has seemed to be happy. No one familiar with the facts can doubt that, however erratic his course has been, he has aroused in the thinking people of Russia a partial sense of the social, industrial, and political iniquities against which his peasant life has been a standing protest. . . .

While we talked together that night Tolstoy told me that he

could never give up his idea that physical labor was a duty imposed upon every man, and that he would continue until his dying day to plough in the field, and to make shoes, no matter what society might say. . . .

Here, then, was the secret of Tolstoy's life—love and labor. He worked four hours every day with his pen, but he also did his stint of manual toil.[77]

Creelman concluded by comparing Tolstoy to Shakespeare or Goethe or Dante or Hugo or Thackeray—inviting the reader to imagine them "leading such a crusade in their declining years." The paradox of *The Kreutzer Sonata* remained unresolved, however. Creelman saw Tolstoy as the conscious beneficiary of a warm, supportive family life, yet an uncompromising critic of conjugal love and marriage. Behind the inconsistency he described a sincere, conscientious moral philosopher within whose personality the contradiction may perhaps be resolved, but whose solution remained inaccessible to Creelman. Nonetheless, the greatness and genuineness of this "god" remained obvious to the reporter.

The following year after Creelman's visit, in 1892, Tolstoy received a number of visitors interested in observing his work during the famine that was devastating the peasants in the lower Volga region. One of the most influential accounts in English appeared in *The Century*: Jonas Stadling (1847–1935), a Swedish journalist and travel writer, published a detailed description of Tolstoy's humanitarian work.[78] Stadling's account, which enthusiastically supported Tolstoy's activities against a background of harrowing details of disease and suffering, continued the anti-government tradition of reporting on Russia begun by Kennan in the same popular magazine. Two years earlier Stadling had written a book on native religions in Russia, which had been forbidden by the government censor, and a mutual antagonism characterized this trip, which began in February and continued into the summer of 1892.[79] The account begins with a description of the campaign against Tolstoy waged by the conservative press and certain aristocratic circles who insisted that there was in fact no famine and that Tolstoy was inciting a peasant rebellion. The foreign press reaction to this attack included false rumors that Tolstoy had been subjected to house arrest. In fact, initially, the Russian government denied the seriousness of the famine and forbade the publication of news accounts and especially photographs from the suffering regions. Stadling himself took a number of photographs, which are reproduced in his American article. He detailed the continued harassment of Tolstoy not only by the government but also by the church: the latter preached against him and his work by calling him the Antichrist and forbidding peasants from sending their children to his shelters, where they could be fed and housed. Stadling described the work of both Tolstoy and his wife to assist the peasants with private funds: in Moscow she received the bulk of the donated funds and made the purchases of food and fuel; Tolstoy himself worked among the starving peasants, setting up and supplying kitchens and dining halls, distributing fuel, and supplying feed and seed. On March 6 Stadling arrived in Klekotki, where he met with Tolstoy and his daughter Maria and his niece. He described the suffering of the peasants and the difficulties of assisting them, the menu served at the dining halls, the special shelters for children, and the attempts to provide work for the peasants and stables for their horses. For reasons that remain unclear, Stadling provided more information on the Countess Tolstoy and Maria than he did on Tolstoy, who was the driving force behind the work but did not appear in much detail in this account. The terrible suffering of the starving peasants and the heroic labor of the Tolstoys remain the principal theme of this account.

The only American to write a detailed account of his visit during the famine was neither a reporter nor a travel writer, but rather a businessman, banker and community activist from Philadelphia. Francis B. Reeves (1836–1922) accompanied a humanitarian shipload sent from America in May 1892 to help alleviate the suffering—the wheat and other grain had been donated by farmers from Iowa and Minnesota. Reeves had served on Philadelphia's committee to aid the starving peasants in Russia, which appointed him to supervise the delivery of foodstuffs on the MSS Conemaugh, one of two ships sent from Philadelphia (five ships were sent from America, each containing about 2800 tons of flour, grain, and other foodstuffs). Reeves visited St. Petersburg, Moscow, Kursk and

Tula Provinces, where he met Tolstoy in Begichevka. He was so impressed with Tolstoy's work and the needs of the peasants that he ordered an additional carload of grain to be sent to him. The two exchanged letters, but only in 1917 did Reeves write a memoir of his visit, *Russia Then and Now, 1892–1917*.[80]

In mid-May Reeves found himself spending a few days at the estate of Vladimir A. Bobrinskoy (1867–1921), a wealthy landowner in Tula Province who served as chairman of the Bogoroditsky District Red Cross. Reeves visited various peasants, shared their simple hospitality (for which he paid with digestive upset for several days after consuming at one home a cucumber and several hard boiled eggs), and then went to Orlovka to visit the chairman of the Red Cross in this district, who invited Tolstoy to dinner to meet his guests. Tolstoy arrived on horseback, much to the amazement of Reeves: "The Count came, like our Yankee Doodle, riding on a pony, a little black beauty, on which he sat with all the dignity of a First Regiment trooper."[81] He invited the party to visit him the next day, when Reeves then had an opportunity to talk with him. In answer to the question of what he was writing, Tolstoy responded that he was preparing a book whose title would perhaps be "The Kingdom of God Is in You": they were talking in English and he asked Reeves whether this was the correct text.[82] Rather than pursuing the ideas in this treatise on non-resistance, their conversation kept to the topic of the suffering peasantry. Tolstoy expressed the view that the sending of such generous aid was evidence of "the great progress of the Christian religion." He continued, "the time seems to have come when the Fatherhood of God and the brotherhood of man are being universally acknowledged."[83] Reeves then noticed an elderly pilgrim sitting in an adjoining room: Maria explained that her father had taken him in after he claimed to have had a vision of and message from God that he must spend his last days with Tolstoy. In response to the question as to what her father would do when they all return to Moscow, she answered that he would most likely take him with them. Upon parting, Tolstoy commented that it was too bad that Reeves had to depart Russia so soon. Reeves responded: "I dropped the American adage—'Time is money'." He then quoted Tolstoy's

response: "No, time is not money; that is placing too low an estimate on the value of time."[84] As a good omen, during this tragic
time of drought, Reeves recalled that, just as he left in an open
cart, the gathering clouds let loose a torrent of rain and soaked
him thoroughly. His optimistic tone and hope for positive change,
however, were only partially realized, for Tolstoy wrote him later,
in July 1892: "the harvest is very bad in our district, but happily
the space where the crops are failing is much smaller than it was
last year."[85]

Two years later Tolstoy received visits, in April and May 1894,
from two Americans of quite similar backgrounds, yet each with a
very different appreciation of Tolstoy's significance. Andrew Dickson White (1832–1918), a diplomat and educator—most promi-
nently as the first president of Cornell University—and Ernest
Howard Crosby (1856–1907), a young lawyer, lecturer, and author,
both had enjoyed the privileges of an upper-class family background, served in the New York State Legislature and early in their
careers held significant posts abroad, White as attaché in St.
Petersburg (1854–55) and Crosby as an international jurist at the
World Court in Cairo (1889–94). Politically, however, they occupied opposite positions—White held conservative, pro-government views, while Crosby became a radical social reformer. White
had returned to Russia as U.S. Minister (1892–94) and his visit
with Tolstoy began with official inquiries as to the state of the
peasants, in view of the official aid provided by the U.S. government during the famine. Tolstoy reported that their condition was
still deplorable, even hopeless.[86]

White inquired further of Tolstoy's opinion of the state of Russia. Tolstoy reported that he found Kennan's description of the
Siberian exiles "overdrawn at times, but substantially true." Tolstoy sympathized with the Jews, although he felt statements regarding their persecution were "somewhat exaggerated." He
expressed his surprise that certain highly placed government figures (White diplomatically omitted names) "could believe that
persecution and the forcible repression of thought would have any
permanent effect at the end of the nineteenth century."[87] White
and Tolstoy met over four days in March, walking together to visit

a museum, the Kremlin, an Old Believer church, and also meeting in each other's rooms.[88] During one of their later conversations, White pursued the problem of civil liberties and especially limitations on freedom of expression in Russia, about which Tolstoy had expressed himself quite strongly. Their conversation, as related by White, concluded with Tolstoy's dire prediction:

> I asked him how and when, in his opinion, a decided advance in Russian liberty and civilization would be made. He answered that he thought it would come soon, and with great power. On my expressing the opinion that such progress would be the result of a long evolutionary process, with a series of actions and reactions, as heretofore in Russian history, he dissented, and said that the change for the better would come soon, suddenly, and with great force.[89]

White made no comment on Tolstoy's foresight (his text was published in 1905, the year of the first, 'gradual' revolution in Russia). This sense of an impending cataclysm Tolstoy expressed with increasing frequency, and although ultimately correct, he generally seemed to expect these revolutionary social and political upheavals to come earlier than they did. Tolstoy was not only acutely aware the St. Petersburg government's antagonism towards him— it had just recently aborted his election to a learned society in Moscow—but he fully expected serious reprisals against him for his insistence on freely expressing himself and openly practicing his ideas. White reported of Tolstoy that "every morning, when he awoke, he wondered that he was not on his way to Siberia."[90]

Perhaps out of diplomatic tact, White wrote little about Tolstoy's moral, religious or economic views. However, his recollections of their visit to the Tretiakov Gallery, the principal collection of Russian art in Moscow, contain pointed observations of Tolstoy's tastes. White described Tolstoy's vivid interest in the religious paintings of N. N. Ge (sometimes spelled Gay or Gue, 1831–1894), especially the depiction of Christ and Pilate titled "What is truth?" and the Crucifixion.[91] Tolstoy appreciated the vividly realistic manner and total lack of idealization—"this spectacle of the young Galilean peasant, with unattractive features, sordid garb, poverty-stricken companions, and repulsive surroundings, tortured to death for preaching the 'kingdom of God' to the poor and downtrodden, seemed to hold him fast." White commented, "sympathy with the peasant class, and a yearning to enter into their cares and sorrows, form the real groundwork of his life."[92] White agreed with Tolstoy in rating landscape painting infinitely below religious and historical painting. He noted that Tolstoy was particularly attracted to paintings that showed sympathy with the poor, even with criminals (namely paintings of the arrest of a nihilist and the return of an exile).

Although Tolstoy's major treatise on aesthetics, *What Is Art?*, appeared four years after their meeting, White included comments on it, perhaps because he agreed with its basic principles and values. Certainly what he described of their experiences in the Tretiakov Gallery was consistent with the aesthetic and moral principles Tolstoy later expounded in *What Is Art?*. White noted of Tolstoy that he was "one of the most sincere and devoted men alive, a man of great genius and, at the same time, of very deep sympathy with his fellow creatures. Out of this character of his come his theories of art and literature; and, despite their faults, they seem to me more profound and far-reaching than any put forth by any other man in our time. There is in them, for the current cant regarding art and literature, a sound, sturdy, hearty contempt which braces and strengthens one who reads or listens to him."[93] White indulged his own disgust "with the whole *fin-de-siècle* business"—impressionism, sensationalism, naturalism, and all that "ministers to sensual pleasure." He remarked on Tolstoy's "love for art which has a sense, not only of its power, but of its obligations, which puts itself at the service of great and worthy ideas, which appeals to men as men," and he concluded: "in this he is one of the best teachers of his time and of future times."[94] This is high praise indeed from a man who considered himself an authority on and defender of education.

A number of times their conversation touched on American life and letters, and here White found Tolstoy's information strikingly limited and his views idiosyncratic. White was confused by Tolstoy's qualification of his respect for the Quakers by the fact that they believed in private property: property for Tolstoy implied the violence that potentially would be needed to defend property rights; White did not accept (or understand) this implication since he viewed force as military, not as police (which Tolstoy considered a domestic form of unacceptable violence). They discussed Frederick Evans, with whom Tolstoy had recently been in correspondence,[95] but again White believed his ideas were not at all like the Shakers: "the Shaker his imagination had developed was as different from a Lebanon Shaker as an eagle from a duck, and his notion of their influence on American society was comical."[96] Although White does not explain what eagle-like qualities Tolstoy saw in these duck-like communities, no doubt different perceptions of the Shaker's agricultural, communal life, their Christian ethics, and belief in celibacy produced the disagreement. Tolstoy was also deeply interested in the Mormons, particularly their good reputation for chastity. Some of their books had interested him, and although Tolstoy found much deception in their belief, he "said that on the whole he preferred a religion which professed to have dug its sacred books out of the earth to one which pretended that they were let down from heaven."[97] White judged Tolstoy's knowledge of American literature to be incomplete, even gathered at random: Tolstoy especially liked Emerson, Hawthorne, Whittier, admired Theodore Parker greatly, and revered the character and work of William Lloyd Garrison. Of contemporary writers he knew some of Howells's novels, liked them,[98] but said that "literature in the United States at present seems to be in the lowest trough of the sea between high waves." From several other sources it is clear that Tolstoy considered the literature of the 1840s and especially that of the Transcendentalists to have been the earlier high; exactly what would constitute the following high was not clear. Tolstoy astounded White with his answer to the question of who was foremost in the whole range of American literature, who was the greatest of American writers when he named Adin Ballou. White had neither the slightest expectation of this answer nor the least explanation.[99]

Like his predecessors who both deeply admired Tolstoy and profoundly disagreed with some of his ideas, White attempted to explain how such a paradox could exist. He believed it resulted from two circumstances: Tolstoy's isolation and the Russian environment. Tolstoy had briefly traveled to Europe, had spent only a few years in St. Petersburg, and the rest of his life he lived in Moscow and in the interior of Russia. For White this accounted for some of his chief defects: of the many distinguished men he had met, Tolstoy seemed to him "most in need of that enlargement of view and healthful modification of opinion which come from meeting men and comparing views with them in different lands and under different conditions." White observed that "this need is all the greater because in Russia there is no opportunity to discuss really important questions."[100] As a result, Tolstoy's opinions "have been developed without modification by any rational interchange of thought with other men. Under such circumstances any man, no matter how noble or gifted, having given birth to striking ideas, coddles and pets them until they become the full-grown, spoiled children of his brain. He can at last see neither spot nor blemish in them, and comes virtually to believe himself infallible." This isolation, White believed, was responsible for the "sundry ghastly creeds, doctrines, and sects—religious, social, political, and philosophic—[which] have been developed in Russia."[101] As examples he cited nihilism, the divinity of the Russian monarch, a return to barbarism in science, literature and art, and a deep pessimism in the theory of life and duty.

The evolution of Tolstoy's ideas, White believed, was mainly determined by his Russian environment. Russia, in White's view, was still emerging from the middle ages, life was disheartening, nature was depressing, the population was either given over to pleasure (the nobility) or sunk in fetishism (the peasantry); the poetry and music were in a minor key; and old oppressions lingered on. Great men regularly appeared in Russia to astound Europe, and they all had "some well-defined purpose" or "one high aim" that allowed "rigidly excluding sight or thought of the ocean of sorrow about him."[102] However, if "a strong genius in Russia throws himself into philanthropic speculations of an abstract sort," then chaos could result, like Kropotkin's "wild revolt, not only against the whole system of his own country, but against civilization itself, and finally the adoption of the theory and practice of anarchism. . . ." Or in the case of the statesman and theologian Pobedonostsev, it produced "medieval methods . . . to fetter all free thought and to crush out all forms of Christianity except the Russo-Greek creed and ritual."

> Or, if he be a man of the highest genius in literature, like Tolstoi, whose native kindliness holds him back from the extremes of nihilism, he may rear a fabric heaven-high, in which truths, errors, and paradoxes are piled up together until we have a new Tower of Babel. Then we may see this man of genius denouncing all science and commending what he calls "faith"; urging a return to a state of nature, which is simply Rousseau modified by misreadings of the New Testament; repudiating marriage, yet himself most happily married and the father of sixteen children;[103] holding that Aeschylus and Dante and Shakespeare were not great in literature, and making Adin Ballou a literary idol; holding that Michelangelo and Raphael were not great in sculpture and painting, yet insisting on the greatness of sundry unknown artists who have painted brutally; . . . loathing science—that organized knowledge which has done more than all else to bring us out of medieval cruelty into a better world—and extolling a "faith" which has always been the most effective pretext for bloodshed and oppression.[104]

White found so many of Tolstoy's principles to be worthy of ridicule, and he clearly enjoyed displaying them as such, and yet the personal impression he gathered was not in the least ridiculous, but that of a sincere, profound and genuine man of genius. In the end White could only conclude that Tolstoy's "paradoxes will be forgotten; but his devoted life, his noble thoughts, and his lofty ideals" will give life and light for centuries to come. Exactly what thoughts and ideals would survive the momentary paradoxes remained undefined.

Ernest Howard Crosby, perhaps Tolstoy's most articulate disciple in America, saw only the ideals and none of the paradoxes.[105] His visit to Tolstoy—just two months after White's— was a pilgrimage to the author of My Religion, which had redirected Crosby's life from that of statesman-politician to pacifist, reformer, and advocate of the oppressed. For two days in mid-May 1894[106] Crosby visited with Tolstoy at Yasnaya Polyana, where they discussed philosophical and theological question, literature, social problems and economic theory. In his memoirs of the visit Crosby provided a number of new details on Tolstoy's interest in and information about America.[107] In the summer the mail arrived at Yasnaya Polyana after eleven in the evening, and the family would stay up late reading. Letters, newspapers, books from all over the world, but mostly from America predominated in Tolstoy's "midnight mail." Crosby observed that he had recently received the works of Henry George and letters from advocates of the single tax, and the Mormons and other "peculiar people," as Crosby called them, were also sending their literature. A number of his observations coincided with those of White: for example, Tolstoy's daughter expressed what her father had commented about fearing arrest, namely that with "the appearance of each book they are in doubt for a time as to whether they will be sent to Siberia or not"; Tolstoy expressed his deep admiration not only for Henry George, but also for Felix Adler (1851–1933), the educator, social reformer, and founder of the Ethical Culture Society.[108] However, the purpose of Crosby's visit and the attitude and tone of his memoirs, so different from White's, exclude the possibility of any probing analysis of Tolstoy's views. For as Crosby wrote, "Some of my friends had prophesied that my admiration for the Count would fade away when I saw him actually living as he preached. But the result was quite the reverse. . . . I had met one of the most sincere, earnest, yes, and one of the sanest men on earth."[109]

Nonetheless, his perceptions, however uncritical, provide new, valuable first-hand information about Tolstoy's life and views. His analysis of the Tolstoy family relationships confirm more positive views, like those of Stockham. Crosby wrote, "The wonder to me is not that there should not be entire agreement among [Tolstoy and his wife and children], but that he has influenced them as much as he has. Madame Tolstoï seemed to me to agree on the whole with her husband's theories, but she thought that he was in advance of his times, and she would not consent to educating the children as peasants. The count, like a good non-resistant, gracefully yielded."[110] Enchanted by the countryside, the family setting and by Tolstoy himself, Crosby was disinclined to emphasize dissention.

Crosby questioned Tolstoy on a number of his principles, first and foremost non-resistance. He quoted Tolstoy as remarking that "people always ask me what I would do if I saw a man murdering a child. As a matter of fact, I have lived sixty-five years without witnessing such a scene, but I see the misery caused by legalized violence every day of my life."[111] In response to Crosby's observation that Americans, because they looked upon their country as free, would not appreciate the anti-government principles put forth in *The Kingdom of God Is Within You*, Tolstoy claimed that it "was the result of ignorance" because they "did not see how the government oppressed them in preserving an unjust state of society." By way of assent, Crosby expressed his abhorrence at the numerous lynchings in America. In a remarkably extreme expression of his stand against legal execution, which he described many years later in *I Cannot Be Silent* (1908), Tolstoy responded to Crosby's observation that "as far as he was concerned, he preferred lynching to capital punishment under the form of law."[112]

Their discussion of the nature of God and of whom one loves first, one's neighbor or God, yielded no clear conclusion, save that Tolstoy expressed his admiration of Matthew Arnold's definition of God ("that within us not ourselves which makes for righteousness"). Of the immortality of the soul and the divinity of Christ, Tolstoy stated that "true life is in its essence eternal" and that "it was a great mistake to represent Jesus as absolute God," for this makes "his example impossible to follow." These answers might not satisfy a metaphysicist, but Crosby found them clear and concise. A number of their subjects elaborated, albeit tacitly, on topics that dominate Tolstoy fiction. They discussed with Tolstoy's daughters the concept of death and attempted to convince Crosby that there was nothing to fear, especially physically, for it is "only as if you had to cross the Atlantic, and were obliged to go through with the sea-sickness." Tolstoy added that "it was a good practice to have death constantly in our minds." On the topic of the woman question, Crosby reported Tolstoy to have said:

Women's duties are domestic, . . . but man has been in the wrong from time immemorial in forcing her to keep her place. Set her free, and she will come back and do voluntarily, and as an equal, the same work which she used to do as a slave and a drudge.[113]

These comments reflect quite faithfully the idea behind Tolstoy's earlier work, notably *Family Happiness* (1859), but are less progressive than his position recently expressed in *Kreutzer Sonata*.

Tolstoy's views of American literature and culture, as reported by Crosby, while consistent with previous accounts, appear in a new light when colored by the latter's personal enthusiasms. For example, Crosby found it difficult to accept that Tolstoy "could not make out" Whitman's poetry and felt that there must be a "secret affinity" between the two. Later Crosby heard that Tolstoy was reading the essays of Edward Carpenter (1844–1929) "with delight"—which seemed to confirm his expectation, since he considered the British social reformer to be "simply Whitman in prose."[114] The American author of whom Tolstoy spoke in highest terms to Crosby was Henry George. He explained, "I like his works especially for the strong Christian feeling running through them," and for this reason he could not understand why George was willing to be a candidate for mayor of New York (two years later, in 1896).

Upon parting, Tolstoy advised Crosby to become acquainted with Henry George, to say exactly what he thought (not because it was good to be truthful, but in order more effectively to improve his own behavior by opening all inconsistencies to public scrutiny), and to remember the proverb "where there is a will, there is a way."[115] Crosby not only met Henry George, but he became an avid advocate of his theories, including the single tax. As to the corrective potential of complete openness, it is difficult to say whether Crosby found the advice useful, for unlike his mentor, he rarely reflected upon his own behavior. Tolstoy's final piece of advice, however, Crosby took in the full Tolstoyan sense of pursuing an idea with total dedication, irrespective of the consequences, especially in public opinion and social acceptance. Crosby confounded his relatives with his social conscience and activism, his pacifism and anti-imperialism, and his attempt to institute land rent reforms—anathema to a family much of whose income came from valuable Broadway properties in Manhattan.

A third American to visit Tolstoy in 1894 was the Rabbi Joseph Krauskopf of Philadelphia, who spent a day at Yasnaya Polyana in July, but only spoke of this visit publicly and published his memoirs after Tolstoy's death.[116] The purpose of his trip to Russia was to propose a plan to resettle persecuted Jews to unoccupied lands in the interior of the empire, where they would be "colonized on farms, and be maintained, until self-supporting, by their coreligionists of other parts of the world."[117] This was the final year of the reign of the anti-Semitic Alexander III, and the so-called "Temporary Rules," already in effect for two years, forbade Jews to live outside towns and forced them into business and other professions. Given the general persecution of Jews and in view of this recent legislation, it was not surprising that Krauskopf gained permission to enter Russia only after considerable pressure was exerted by the U.S. government, and that he achieved little in his interviews with prominent Russian officials. However, his meeting with Tolstoy produced remarkable results. Krauskopf credited Andrew White with making the visit to Tolstoy possible, principally by writing a letter of introduction.[118] He was as mesmerized by Tolstoy as Crosby had been: "From the moment I first gazed upon him he held me captive, and, by a strange psychic power, he has held me enthralled ever since." His rapture exceeded even Crosby's:

> I had often wondered how a Moses, an Isaiah, a Jeremiah, a Socrates, looked and talked, denounced and dreamed, the moment I saw Tolstoy I knew. One hour's talk with him seemed equal to a whole university course in political and social science; one walk with him on his estate stored up in the listener more knowledge of moral philosophy than could be crowded into a year's seminary instruction. Great as was the power of his pen, immeasurably greater was the power of his living word. In some mysterious way the flow of his speech seemed to exercise an hypnotic spell upon the speaker as much as upon the listener. The speaker seemed at times translated into a superhuman

being, seemed inspired, seemed to speak words not his own, as one of the ancient prophets of Israel must have spoken when he said the words: "Thus saith the Lord," while the listener seemed scarcely capable of thought or speech, felt his being almost lose its identity and become merged with that of the speaker.

. . . He had never learned the art of concealing his thoughts and emotions. His face and voice were as a mirror that revealed with microscopic exactness his innermost self. What he felt moved to speak he spoke; what he felt urged to do he did; he never stopped to consider whether it will please or displease, whether it will bring praise or censure upon him. Like a piece of living, weather-beaten New England granite he looked in his homespun crash blouse, his jean trousers girded at the waist with a rope, his coarse woolen shirt open at the neck, his well-worn bast shoes. He seemed, indeed, a composite of the looks and traits and thoughts that characterized the Puritans in the early history of the New England states.[119]

Krauskopf expressed his reverence for Tolstoy in a manner and to a degree no other American visitor exceeded. This no doubt explains the extraordinary impact Tolstoy subsequently had on the Philadelphia rabbi.

As might be expected, a number of Krauskopf's observations confirm those of Crosby and White. Tolstoy had just received a copy of his essay "Christianity and Patriotism," which had been published in English, nonsensically mutilated (with black ink) by the Russian censor in the London *Standard*.[120] Tolstoy expressed his amusement at the stupidity of the censor, but also his apprehension of government retaliation. When asked how he had escaped arrest, exile or imprisonment, Tolstoy responded: "I am not yet sure that I shall not end my days in Siberia. That I have escaped thus far is due to the government's sensitiveness of the world's opinion. It knows of the hold my publications have gained for me on civilized people. It fears the cry of outrage that would be raised at the banishment or imprisonment of a man as old as I."[121] This quotation—the fullest on this topic in any of the memoirs—strikes a genuinely Tolstoyan note at the end, with its typical, unexpected self-deprecation.

Although Krauskopf related little of their conversations on religion and morality, he did include an exchange on the nature of Jesus. In answer to Tolstoy's question regarding his belief about Jesus, he replied that he considered "the Rabbi of Nazareth as one of the greatest of Israel's teachers and leaders and reformers, not as a divine being who lived and taught humanly but as a human being who lived and taught divinely." Tolstoy responded, "Such is my belief," and continued with the observation that the Jews of Russia would not share Krauskopf's belief, since "they have been made to suffer so much in his name that it would be little short of a miracle if they loved him. Mohamed was more honest, he gave to people the choice between the Koran and the sword. Christians profess love, and practice hatred."[122] As he had with Stevens, Tolstoy blamed improper education for many of the ills of society. He objected to compulsory education, and to Krauskopf's observation that without it some parents would never send their children to school, Tolstoy replied: "What of it? The children would probably be no less moral and no less happy than those of highest education. . . . I have found more honor and honesty, more fear of the Lord and more true happiness, among the unlettered than among the lettered. . . . The world lives by the love of God and not by the primer or the multiplication table." Of the schooling received by Jesus and the other prophets, Tolstoy responded that their spiritual and moral powers came not from schooling but from the heart: "God puts more education into the human heart than man has ever been able to put into the head." Finally, of the benefits St. Paul received from Greek schools of his day, Tolstoy noted, "the schools made of Paul a theologian, and Christianity would have been better without the theology of Paul."[123]

Tolstoy commented at some length on America, beginning with his gratitude to Philadelphia and to Reeves for the generous donation of foodstuffs during the famine. His detailed knowledge surprised Krauskopf, who was equally struck by Tolstoy's stern criticism:

Your country has interested me even more than mine. I have lost hope in mine; all my hope was, at one time, centered in yours. But yours is a disappointment as much as mine. You call yourselves a Republic; you are worse than an autocracy. I say worse because you are ruled by gold, and gold is more conscienceless, and therefore more tyrannical than any human tyrant. Your intentions are good; your execution is lamentable. Were yours the free and representative government you pretend to have, you would not allow it to be controlled by the money powers and their hirelings, the bosses and machines, as you do."[124]

Six years later, in his letter to Americans published in 1900, he named these "hirelings" and "bosses"—Gould, Rockefeller, and Carnegie.[125] The solution, Tolstoy explained, was to return to an agricultural mode of life, in which life was simple and ideals high, where politics was more akin to religion and less a matter of barter and sale. The urbanization of America, the destruction of villages and farms, the transformation of farmers into factory hands had resulted in lust for luxury and corruption. Krauskopf summarized: "We forget that our greatness lay in the pursuit of husbandry, and we seek our salvation in commerce and industries." Indeed, he even understood Tolstoy to have prophesied a class war in America, where "our rich become degenerates, our poor become desperates, and in the struggle to come the desperate will rise up and slay the degenerate."[126] Tolstoy spoke at length of the appalling contrast between the very rich and the very poor in American and European cities, and he held that this contrast would never have been so great had the poor remained farmers and not congregated in the cities, which have allowed their enslavement by industries and commerce.

Tolstoy recommended to Krauskopf his own *What To Do?* (1886), written in response to the poverty he encountered several years earlier in Moscow, and which he described as "an appeal for pity for the submerged, for justice for the wronged, for liberation of the oppressed and persecuted, and for the application of the only remedy—a return to the simple life and labor on the soil." Even more pointedly Tolstoy suggested that the problem of poverty and persecution of the Jews might be solved in much the same way:

Your plan to lead your people back to the soil, . . . back to the occupation which your fathers followed with honor in Palestinian lands, is of some encouragement to me. It shows that the light is dawning. It is the only solution of the Jewish problem. Persecution, refusal of the right to own or to till the soil, exclusion from the artisan guilds, made traders of the Jew. And the world hates the trader. Make bread-producers of your people, and the world will honor those who give it bread to [eat].[127]

By way of illustrating this solution, Tolstoy cited the few Jewish agricultural colonies that had been allowed in the Russian steppes since early in the century: "They are as successful farmers as are the best." However, given the current attitude of the government, Tolstoy saw little chance for any such a Jewish colonization scheme in Russia at that time.

If not in Russia, then why not in America? Tolstoy presented a plan that would allow her to avoid the problems now faced in Russia and throughout Europe:

What are you, Americans, doing to prevent a Jewish problem in your own country? How long before the evils that are harrowing your people in the old world may be harrowing them in the new? Your people are crowding into your large cities by the thousands and tens of thousands. You have built up Ghettoes worse than those of Europe. There is excuse for it in Russia; there is no excuse for it in the United States. Yours is the right to own land and the best of it, and to till as much of it as you please. Granted that ages of enforced abstention from agricultural labor have weaned the elder generation from a love of country life and farm labor, why may not a love for it be instilled in the young? Lead your young people to the country and to the farm. Start agricultural schools for them. Teach them to exchange the yardstick for the hoe, the peddler's pack for the seed-bag, and you will solve the problem while it may yet be solved. You will see the lands tilled by them overflow, as of old, with milk and honey. You will see them give of their plenty to the people of the land, and receive in return goodly profit and esteem. And once again there will arise from among Jewish husbandmen prophets, lawgivers, inspired bards and teachers to whom the civilized world will do homage.[128]

Tolstoy continued to speak on the topic at length, and ultimately he convinced Krauskopf to begin such a movement to the land by establishing an agricultural school for Jewish young people in America. When he returned to the U.S. and to Philadelphia, he founded, in 1896, the National Farm School, near Doylestown, the county seat of Bucks County, Pennsylvania. Krauskopf was himself astounded: "I had gone to Russia to see the Czar, and I saw a greater man instead. I had gone with a plan for colonizing Russian Jews in Russia, and I returned with a plan for teaching agriculture chiefly to Russian Jewish lads in the United States."[129] The National Farm School, which began with the land of a local farmer, rapidly expanded in size and enrollment, and exists to this day under the name of Delaware Valley College.

Krauskopf's remarkable memoir ends on a minor key: he wrote several times to Tolstoy, sent him reports of his travels and the new agricultural school, but never received any response. He supposed that, as a *persona non grata* in Russia, his mail had been censored; in fact, three of his letters did reach Tolstoy, who read them and marked the envelopes "no answer."[130] Why Tolstoy did not acknowledge the letters is not clear, although he rarely answered but a very few of those who wrote him.

Two years later Tolstoy received another visit from an American who was equally committed to solving problems of urban poverty. Jane Addams visited Tolstoy at Yasnaya Polyana in July, 1896, with the "hope of finding a clue to the tangled affairs of city poverty."[131] She turned to Tolstoy, whose works she had assiduously read since first coming upon My *Religion,* "not as to a seer—his message is much too confused and contradictory for that—but as to a man who has had the ability to lift his life to the level of his conscience, to translate his theories into action."[132] Addams looked to him for practical suggestions, and like Krauskopf, she found herself instructed by him on the reasons for urban poverty. At first he disconcerted her by commenting that her dress with its "monstrous" sleeves should doubtless prove a "barrier to the people." Then, when he found that she was personally supported by a farm far from Chicago, he disconcerted her again: "So you are an absentee landlord? Do you think you will help the people more by adding yourself to the crowded city than you would by tilling your own soil?"[133] Addams attentively took in his sermons on the benefit of personal labor and working the soil "because Tolstoy had made the one supreme personal effort, one might almost say the one frantic personal effort to put himself into right relations with the humblest people, with the men who tilled the soil. . . ." However, she experienced some frustration, especially with his position on non-resistance. She wrote, "it seemed to me that he made too great a distinction between the use of physical force and that moral energy which can override another's differences and scruples with equal ruthlessness." Perhaps this expressed a sense of victimization after her own confrontations with Tolstoy's dogmatic preaching. She expressed other misgivings about his teaching:

> Was Tolstoy more logical than life warrants? Could the wrongs of life be reduced to the terms of unrequited labor and all be made right if each person performed the amount necessary to satisfy his own wants? Was it not always easy to put up a strong case if one took the naturalistic view of life? But what about the historic view, the inevitable shadings and modifications which life itself brings to its own interpretation?[134]

This reluctance, upon reflection, to accept Tolstoy's simple answers reveals her own practical experience at Hull House struggling with the effects of urban poverty. She could not ignore the fact that "exigent and unremitting labor grants the poor no leisure. . . ." Her modest attempt to apply Tolstoy's philosophy to her own life—to save her soul by working two hours every morning in the bakery at Hull House—failed in the face of "actual and pressing human wants."

The twentieth century brought a new category of American visitors to Tolstoy—politicians. The archetype of American chauvinistic nationalism, Albert J. Beveridge (1862–1927) visited Tolstoy in June, 1901, as part of a trip to Russia, Siberia and the Far East to study the encroachment of the Russian Empire into the Pacific region and China.[135] A U.S. Senator from Indiana (1900–1912), Beveridge was one of the most outspoken proponents of American imperialism in Cuba and the Philippines, as expressed in his wildly popular campaign speech "The March of the Flag" (1898) which proposed annexing the Philippines, and in his essay "America's Destiny" (1900) which proclaimed with religious zeal that America "will not renounce our part in the mission of our race, trustee, under God, of the civilization of the world." Tolstoy received no American visitor more antagonistic to his ideals of non-resistance, anti-imperialism and pacifism, and consequently Beveridge's attempt to discredit Tolstoy are not surprising.

Beveridge's account of their conversations repeats much the same criticism of American life and culture that Tolstoy had expressed to previous visitors—that America had become wholly materialistic; that with the sole exception of Henry George, her present writers could not compare with Whittier, Emerson, or Paine; and that attempts to civilize the Philippines were a mistake—if the natives "are happier in their nakedness and beneath their palm trees, let them remain so."[136] Beveridge devoted equal detail to Tolstoy's criticism of Russian politics, economic advances, and her expansion into Manchuria and China (matters of particular concern to the Senator). However, in a footnote to these comments, Beveridge offered an explanatory comment so grossly misinformed as to call into question just how much he understood of Russian political reality: "Notwithstanding Tolstoï's antagonism to all government by force, it is said that the Czar is very fond of him, and that Tolstoï is the ardent personal friend of the Czar."

Beveridge described Tolstoy's views as a "protest against everything in the existing order, including religion" and called him "the Autocrat of Protest in Russia." Most important, he claimed that he was not popular, particularly among those who favored reform and improvement in Russian government. He quoted Tolstoy's critics: "He is erratic, impossible, impracticable, and thus delays by unwise insistence upon fanatic propositions any real practical advice"; "his power among extremists is due to the fact that because of his outspokenness and radicalism his name has become the flag of revolt"; "Tolstoï is jealous of Christ—it will end with him trying to establish a religion of his own." Of the Russian masses Beveridge observed that, "so far as his name has penetrated into the homes of the Russian peasantry, it stands for some vague good, without any definite notions of what that good is." By way of conclusion, he noted that "it is certain that the influence of Tolstoï upon Russian thought and opinion is not yet so great as it is upon the thought and opinion of non-Russian nations, and especially the American people."[137] Beveridge had principally canvassed the political elite and influential commercial circles of Russia, who returned Tolstoy's contempt in equal portion. More remarkable is his acknowledgment of Tolstoy's impact on American thought and opinion.

The pro-government position Beveridge expressed in his memoir account followed the tradition of Hapgood, even to the extent of praising the heroic efforts and achievements of the Countess Tolstoy. He dismissed her husband's moral scruples as the eccentricities of the nineteenth century's greatest artist : "Tolstoï himself is no exception to those weaknesses which genius everywhere, in some form or other, displays—a negligence of his affairs, which, if some person did not attend to them for him, would soon starve him out, and an almost abnormal dissatisfaction with his own work." Indeed, had the Countess not copied out his works, they would never have been published; furthermore, she "personally manages his still considerable holdings" and "sees to the income from the literary product of her famous husband's amazing mind." In short, "keeping in the background, doing her work with patience and in silence, the wife of Tolstoï is not only his helpmeet, in the marital sense of that term, not only his amanuensis, his financier, his comforter; she is his very preserver."[138] In the conflict over property, material comfort and civilized refinement that divided the Tolstoys, Beveridge clearly supported the conservative side.

No American politician presented greater contrast to Beveridge than Tolstoy's visitor and soon to be friend, William Jennings Bryan (1860–1925), who journeyed to Yasnaya Polyana two years after the Senator, in December 1903.[139] In contrast to Beveridge, who left no trace of his visit—no comment of his visit in Tolstoy's letters or diary—Bryan greatly pleased him, and they began a correspondence that continued until 1909. Such was the American's positive impact that this Russian non-resistor, who was opposed to all forms of government activity, expressed his support for Bryan's candidacy in the U.S. presidential campaign of 1908. In his account of meeting Tolstoy, Bryan explained Tolstoy's religious principles and Christian ideals with sympathetic understanding and did not balk at the absolute idealism that had bothered previous, otherwise receptive Americans. Bryan fully agreed with Tolstoy's anti-militarism and even shared his enthusiasm for Henry George and the single tax, but understandably qualified his support for the total rejection of all government.

An American traveler, author and public lecturer, Peter MacQueen (1865–1924), who visited Yasnaya Polyana the same month, June, 1901, described Tolstoy's criticism of American life, culture and politics in a special report which covered the same topics that Beveridge discussed. However, MacQueen's trip was a "pilgrimage" to the "apostle of divine faith and a divine law," to a "remarkable man who stands almost alone in the midst of surrounding darkness."[140] Tolstoy spoke out most vehemently against American action in the Philippines (which had just ended) and against all military activity.[141] The power of commerce and finance disturbed him no less than the preparations for war:

> It is a pity you think you need any battleships. After the Pleiad of writers America produced in the Civil War you can now only show as your most brilliant brain Carnegie the millionaire. . . . You had Thoreau, Ballou, Emerson, Longfellow, Whittier and Walt Whitman. It was your Homeric Age. Then rose the Achilles among statesmen, Abraham Lincoln. All these were a giant constellation. Your war-fever is over, but gold has you now. The great men are your millionaires.[142]

These remarks echo Tolstoy's comments to Krauskopf and his Address to Americans, noted above. Despite this impatience, he felt a personal affection for Americans: "I like the Americans, so reasonable, so sane, so easy to get along with."

Of Russia's future Tolstoy expressed expectations of revolutionary change similar to those he had described to Andrew White seven years earlier. "A change must come here. When it comes it will be very thorough. The Slav is the most radical of all the races. He will not do anything by halves." Tolstoy continued, however, with an expression of some hope: "Russia is young, strong, fresh. There is plenty of land here. We could manage the single tax better than you could in America."[143] MacQueen had noted copies of Henry George's works on Tolstoy's shelf in his room: the Russian's deep respect for the American journalist and reformer had continued unabated in the eleven years since he first acknowledged his admiration of his theories to Stevens. However, now he had an explanation of why George's impact had been so limited: "the press in every country is held by gold."[144]

The celebration of Tolstoy's eightieth birthday in 1908 focused the world's attention on his achievements, brought a large number of journalists to interview him, and caused the Russian government considerable discomfort. Among those present was an American journalist representing the *New York Times*, Herman Bernstein (1876–1935). In addition to work as a journalist in New York, the Russian born Bernstein wrote poetry and stories, and translated a number of Russian writers into English—Leonid Andreyev, Gorky, Chekhov, Turgenev, and Tolstoy as well. He first wrote to Tolstoy in 1902 to send him a copy of his work, *In the Gates of Israel*. Two years later he sent a copy of his translation of Tolstoy's "Garrison and Non-Resistance"[145] and one of his own stories. Although he received no answer, Bernstein continued writing Tolstoy and sent him another work, *Contrite Hearts*, on the Jews of Russia. In a letter of March 1906 he wrote to apologize to Tolstoy for incorrectly attributing to him article he translated (received with this false information from a cousin in Russia), "To the Tsar and His Advisors."[146] Finally, he received a response to letters written in May and June 1908 asking permission to visit Tolstoy.[147]

Bernstein arrived on July 8 (June 25) at Yasnaya Polyana after attending a meeting of representatives of the press in St. Petersburg. During this first congress of the Russian press there was a movement to honor Tolstoy on August 28—his birthday—by making a unanimous call for the end of executions and the abolishment of death sentences (the government threatened to shut down the congress if the discussion continued). Tolstoy, on the other hand, was delighted at the thought: "Yes, an appeal by the press for the abolition of executions in Russia would please me better than any other honor."[148] Just that month his outraged objection to the execution of revolutionaries and to capital punishment—"I Cannot Be Silent!"—had been published abroad and had appeared (partially and illegally) in Russia. On the future of Russia and violent change, Tolstoy now seemed less optimistic: "One of the most horrible superstitions, more harmful than all religious superstitions—one which has caused rivers of blood—is that very strange superstition which sprang from the use of violence, and which makes people believe that a small number of men can now establish the social life of the whole community." The revolutionaries, who dedicated themselves to assassination, were no better than Stolypin (Minister of the Interior and President of the Council of Ministers), who hanged them by the hundreds: neither revolutionary violence nor government violence could improve the life of the people.[149] Nonetheless, Tolstoy remained hopeful in the long run. He placed his hope in religion: "All religions are based on love, but Christianity is based on the highest form of love." To this Bernstein responded, "in life as well as in theory?" Tolstoy replied: "Meanwhile only in theory. But the world is growing ever more perfect. It cannot become perfect unless our inner religious consciousness is directed toward this highest form of love. With the highest form of love as our law, we will be perfect."[150]

Bernstein asked Tolstoy about his views on the Jewish question. Tolstoy responded at some length, however abstractly:

> Most of the things ascribed to me as my expressions on this question are exaggerated. To me all questions are solved by my religious view of life. All people are alike. Therefore there can be no such thing as a Jewish question. It is as if you asked me about the Russian question, the German question, or the Japanese questions. There is no Jewish question, no Polish question, no Russian question—all people are brethren. It is very sad and painful if we must make an effort to realize this. If there are any bad traits in the Russian Jew, they were called forth by the horrible persecutions to which we have subjected them. How do I account for the anti-Jewish feeling in Russia? We often dislike more those whom we harm than those who harm us. This is exactly true of the attitude of the Russians toward the Jews.[151]

This answer says more about Tolstoy than it does about the Jewish question, which he had earlier acknowledged and certainly could have analyzed in considerable concrete detail. However, he preferred to ignore the situation by consigning it to what should not exist in the true scheme of things. He repeated his position later and in simpler terms: "I do not believe in these various national and political questions."[152]

The largest part of Tolstoy's conversations with Bernstein were devoted to Henry George and the single tax: "the leaders of the revolutionary movement, as well as the Government officials, are not doing the only thing that would pacify the people at once. And the only thing that would pacify the people now is the introduction of the system of Henry George."[153] He described his own proposal to the government and the Duma that George's system be adopted in Russia, as well as his understanding of the reasons why his suggestions were ignored.

> Henry George's idea, which changes the entire system in the life of nations in favor of the oppressed, voiceless majority, and to the detriment of the ruling minority, is so undeniably convincing, and, above all, so simple, that it is impossible not to understand it, and, understanding it, it is impossible not to make an effort to introduce it into practice, and therefore the only means against this idea is to pervert it and pass it in silence.[154]

Tolstoy fervently believed that this idea would survive all attempts to smother or ignore it. The time was right to introduce it in Russia: "in Russia there is a revolution, the serious basis of which is the rejection by the whole people, by the real people, of the ownership of land." Nine-tenths of the Russian population were tillers of the soil, and George's idea "expresses what in Russia had been regarded as right by the entire Russian people." By applying this idea "during this period of reconstruction of social conditions," what Tolstoy believed was a wrongly and criminally directed revolution would be "crowned by a great act of righteousness."[155]

Concluding his conversation with Bernstein, Tolstoy expressed his feelings as he neared the end of life:

> Yes—yes, I am growing old and weak. My end is nearing rapidly. But the older I grow the happier I am. You cannot understand

it. When I was as young as you I did not understand it. Yes, the older I grow the happier I am.[156]

The gradual shift from anger and protest to a positive vision of man's destiny perhaps lay at the root of this increasing sense of joy. It is a remarkable comment from a man who would leave home two years later in frustration and despair at his personal life. The conflicts with his wife over changes to the text of his will, her hysterics and paranoia over his trusted disciple Chertkov, and finally her intriguing to get at his diaries, all of which climaxed in 1910, ultimately deprived him of all peace of mind and drove him from his home in October.

The last American to meet with Tolstoy before his death in November 1910 was the son of Henry George. No more appropriate visitor could have come from America than Henry George, Jr., who visited Yasnaya Polyana in June 1909 (just a year after Bernstein), and for whom the journey was a pilgrimage, "a visit to a holy man," "to meet for the first time the man of greatest moral influence in Russia, and perhaps in all north Europe."[157] Tolstoy himself felt such heightened anticipation of this visit that he wrote a special short article on the significance of Henry George and eagerly gave a copy to the son.[158] George quoted several paragraphs from the article as "showing the vigor and hope of this wonderful old man's mind." The passages follow quite closely the ideas Tolstoy had expressed to Bernstein. The land question in Russia, he believed, "will and must be solved in one way alone: by the recognition of the equal right of every man to live upon and to be nourished by the land on which he was born—that same principle which is so invincibly proved by the teachings of Henry George." Tolstoy continued:

I think so because the thought of the equal right of all men to the soil, notwithstanding all the efforts of the 'educated' and learned people to drive that thought by all kinds of schemes of expropriation and the destruction of village communes from the minds of the Russian people, nevertheless lives in the minds of the Russian people today, and sooner or later—I believe that soon—it must be fully realized.[159]

The attraction of this idea was that it would bring people back to the soil, that it promised to reestablish the agrarian-based life style and economy that Tolstoy believed was necessary to man's salvation, as an individual and as a community, and that it would satisfy what he felt was a basic need in the Russian character—to work the soil. Later in their conversations Tolstoy once again expressed his sense of historical optimism about Russia: he found the present times reminiscent of the conditions in the 1860s, when America was freeing the slaves and Russia its serfs—"now we face industrial slavery, and that will be destroyed, too."[160]

Tolstoy expressed his views on American politics, especially his admiration for William Jennings Bryan. He showed George a letter just received from Bryan which included both President Roosevelt's attack on Tolstoy and Bryan's response in The Commoner.[161] He had no direct comment on Roosevelt's attack on his principles of non-resistance and pacifism, but rather expressed his complete indifference to politics. He shared with the son his persistent question about Henry George's involvement in politics, "I take no interest in [politics], and I cannot understand why your father risked his life in them." The son responded, "to bring his ideas into practical discussion," but to this Tolstoy gave no response.[162]

Tolstoy was not in good health, he had to rest for much of the afternoon, and therefore George spent considerable time with Tolstoy's family and commented on their conversations and family relations in some detail. His observations coincide with those of previous American visitors, especially those who saw expressions of Tolstoy's ideas in the activities of his wife and children. Now a new family member appeared in the American's memoirs—his youngest daughter Alexandra (1884–1979), who by this time had become his chief confidant and secretary. The visit culminated in a treat which Tolstoy had enthusiastically promised George: the famous musician and perhaps finest balalaika player in Russia, Boris Troyanovsky, gave a two-hour concert dominated by works of Tchaikovsky and other classical masters. Tolstoy greatly enjoyed this presentation, and perhaps his objections to music (expressed by the hero of The Kreutzer Sonata), if they still existed, were mollified by this performance on the Russian national folk instrument.

George ended his memoir with an account of his parting with Tolstoy:

> And at the head of the stairway he stopped and took my hand, saying simply: "This is the last time I shall meet you. I shall see your father soon. Is there any commission you would have me take to him?"
>
> For a moment I was lost in wonder at his meaning. But his eyes were quietly waiting for an answer.
>
> "Tell my father that I am doing the work."
>
> He nodded assent, and I left him.[163]

This mystical, even sentimental closing would not deserve special comment, were it not the words of a man who had expressed in no uncertain terms his disbelief in any afterlife, any life after death, or any miraculous future existence like heaven or paradise. Tolstoy by nature was unlikely to say something just to humor the person he was talking with, nor is there any indication that Henry George, Jr., embellished their last conversation. Nothing in Tolstoy's other writings or remarks at this time suggests a change in his strictly rational approach to life after death. Perhaps, in the end, he had been overwhelmed by the presence of the son of the one American whom he not only admired, but whose writings he accepted without qualification. Tolstoy had always wanted to meet Henry George, who died suddenly in 1897, and finally upon meeting his son, he may simply have yielded to the hope of visiting at last with one of the greatest Americans he had ever known.

Endnotes

1   Letter to V. Chertkov, January 15, 1890, in Tolstoy, *Polnoe sobranie sochinenii* (Jubilee edition), v. 64, pp. 153–154. Hereafter abbreviated *PSS*. The American traveler Thomas Stevens remarked on this special sympathy when he visited Tolstoy in 1890 and ascribed it to the fact that America was the first of the English-speaking countries to translate, read and appreciate his works (*Through Russia on a Mustang* [New York: Cassell, 1891], p. 103); this same view was expressed by the English journalist, William Stead, in his *The Truth about Russia* (London: Cassell, 1888), see pp. 399, 405.

2   "Sevastopol in May, 1855." *Hours at Home*. 1869 Feb; 8(4):328–336. Pts. I–V. "Sevastopol in May, 1855. (Continued.)." *Hours at Home*. 1869 Mar; 8(5): 416–422. Pts. VI–X. "Sevastopol in May, 1855. (Continued.)." *Hours at Home*. 1869 Apr; 8(6):526–531. Parts XI–XV. *The Cossacks: A Tale of the Caucasus in 1852*. (New York: C. Scribner's Sons, 1878).

3   This letter is in the L.N. Tolstoy State Museum in Moscow (hereafter abbreviated GMT), no. Ts 239 9, and is dated both Old Style (Julian) and New Style (Gregorian, which in the nineteenth century was 12 days later, and in the twentieth, 13).

4   "Count Tolstoi Twenty Years Ago." *Scribner's Magazine*. 1889 Jun; 5:537–552; 6:732–747. Republished as a chapter with the same title in his collected memoirs, *Selected Essays. With a Memoir by Evelyn Schuyler Schaeffer*. New York: Charles Scribner's Sons, 1901, pp. 205–300.

5   *Selected Essays*, p. 217.

6   Ibid., p. 213. The terms she used were *très farouche et très sauvage*.

7   Ibid., p. 236.

8   Tolstoy's "*Neskol'ko slov po povodu knigi 'Voina i mir'*" (A few words apropos of the book 'War and Peace') had appeared in March in the journal *Russkii arkhiv*.

9   Ibid., pp. 278, 279.

10   Ibid., p. 290.

11   Ibid., p. 294.

12   London and New York, 1871, and republished several times, most recently in Salt Lake City, 1986.

13   The results of his investigations appeared in the magazine in 25 installments, from May 1888 to October 1891: Siberia and the Exile System (May 1888); Plains and Prisons of Western Siberia (June 1888); The Steppes of the Irtish (July 1888); My Meeting with the Political Exiles (Aug. 1888); Exile by Administrative Process (Sept. 1888); The Tomsk Forwarding Prison (Oct. 1888); Political Exiles and Common Convicts at Tomsk (Nov. 1888); Open Letter: A Question of Judgment (Nov. 1888); Life on the Great Siberian Road (Dec. 1888); The Life of Administrative Exiles (Jan. 1889); Exiles at Irkutsk (Feb. 1889); The Grand Lama of the Trans-Baikal (March 1889); The Russian Police (April 1889); A Ride Through the Trans-Baikal (May 1889); The Convict Mines of Kara (June 1889); The Free Command at the Mines of Kara (July 1889); State Criminals at

the Kara Mines (Aug. 1889); The History of the Kara Political Prison (Sept. 1889); In East Siberian Silver Mines (Oct. 1889); Adventures in Eastern Siberia (Nov. 1889); The Latest Siberian Tragedy (April 1890); Blacked Out (May 1890); A Winter Journey Through Siberia (Sept. 1891); My Last Days in Siberia (Oct. 1891); Mr. Kennan's Reply to Certain Criticisms (Oct. 1891).

14 For an account of the transformation of Kennan's views, see "George Kennan and the Russian Empire: How America's Conscience Became an Enemy of Tsarism," by Helen Hundley (*Kennan Institute Occasional Papers*, #277, 2000).

15 *Century Magazine*. 1887 Jun; 34 [n. s. 12]:252–265.

16 Ibid., p. 258.

17 Ibid., p. 259.

18 Kennan did not identify the author of one particular letter which Tolstoy showed him, however it is clear from the context that the letter was that of a Mennonite, J.H. Mussed, written 24 April 1886, to whom Tolstoy responded in May 1886. Mussed described the effect of *My Religion*—the edition that Tolstoy received in June and checked with Kennan: *My Religion*. Revised edition, translated by Huntington Smith, New York: T.Y. Crowell and Co., 1885. Tolstoy's response to Mussed included a quotation from William Lloyd Garrison, whom he also discussed with Kennan.

19 This volume has not survived in Tolstoy's library at Yasnaya Polyana, and therefore it is not clear which edition he had, from the first of 1842 (C.C. Little and J. Brown, Boston) through fifth edition (1870) or a London edition (Trubner & Co., 1881).

20 "A Visit to Count Tolstoi," p. 263.

21 Ibid, p. 264.

22 See the editorial remarks appended to Kennan, "Russian Provincial Prisons." *The Century*. 35: 397 (January 1888).

23 "Tolstoi and the Russian Censors." *Outlook*. 1901 Nov 16; 69(11):694–695. "Count Tolstoy and the Dorpat University." *Outlook*. 1903 Nov 7; 75(11):525–526. "Count Tolstoi and the First Russian Duma." *Outlook*. 1909 Sep 18; 93:123–127. "Count Tolstoy and the Russian Government." *Outlook*. 1910 Dec 3; 96:769–771.

24 See the memoirs of I.I. Yanzhul'. *Vospominaniia I.I. Yanzhula o perezhitom i vidennom v 1864–1909 gg.* Vol. 2 (St. Petersburg, 1911), p. 19.

25 *PSS* 50: 5.

26 On Kennan and Tolstoy, see E.P. Melamed "Lev Tolstoi i Dzhordzh Kennan (po novym materialam)." [Leo Tolstoy and George Kennan (from new materials)]. *Russkaia literature*. 1981; no. 3: 153–157.

27 This relationship is the subject of the third article in the current series, "Tolstoy's American Translator" (*TriQuarterly* 102).

28 Library of Congress, Manuscript Division, Kennan MS, Box 1.

29 Letter to Tolstoy of December 21, 1886, *Literaturnoe nasledstvo*. Vol. 75, book 1, p. 418.

30 "Tolstoy at home." *Atlantic Monthly*. 1891 Nov; 68:596–620, 659–699. Republished in Hapgood's collected memoirs, *Russian Rambles* (Boston: Houghton, Mif-

flin, 1895), 134–147. "A Stroll in Moscow with Count Tolstoy." *Russian Rambles*, pp. 148–202.

31 "Tolstoi's 'The Kreutzer Sonata.'" *Nation*. 1890 Apr 7; 50:313–315.

32 *Russian Rambles*, p. 158.

33 Ibid., p. 164.

34 Ibid., p. 173.

35 Ibid., p. 179.

36 Ibid., p. 201.

37 See, for example, Madame L.T. Dovidoff. "Count Leon Tolstoi." *Cosmopolitan*. 1891 Apr; 12:719–724.

38 *Russian Rambles*, pp. 136–137.

39 On Tolstoy's letters to Stockham, see "Tolstoy's American Preachers: Letters on Religion and Ethics, 1886–1908" (*TriQuarterly* 107–108: 578–580).

40 October 14 and 15 (n. s.). N.N. Gusev. *Letopis' zhizni i tvorchestva L.N. Tolstogo 1828–1890*. Moscow: GIKhL, 1958, p. 734.

41 The 84 page monograph was published by Stockham's own publishing house and appeared together with an essay by H. Havelock Ellis (1859–1939) entitled "Tolstoi. The New Spirit." (*Tolstoi. A Man of Peace by Alice B. Stockham, M.D. The New Spirit by H. Havelock Ellis*. Chicago: Alice B. Stockman & Co., 1900). The appearance of this essay on Tolstoy by the British essayist and pioneer writer on sexual behavior together with Stockham's essay testifies to her broad connections and innovative spirit.

42 *Tolstoi. A Man of Peace*, p. 19.

43 Ibid., p. 24.

44 Ibid., pp. 24–25.

45 Ibid., pp. 28–29.

46 Ibid., p. 20.

47 Ibid., pp. 40–41.

48 Letter to I.D. Rugin, October 15, 1889. *PSS* 64:314.

49 On Mallory and her correspondence with Tolstoy, see "Tolstoy's American Preachers," loc. cit., pp. 593–597.

50 *Tolstoi. A Man of Peace*, p. 35.

51 Ibid., p. 49.

52 Diary entry for October 15 (N.S.), 1889. *PSS* 50:153.

53 *Tolstoi. A Man of Peace*, p. 55.

54 Ibid., p. 79.

55 Ibid., p. 84.

56 The account of his journey, *Through Russia on a Mustang* (New York: Cassell Publishing Co., 1891) devoted a chapter to this visit, "With Count Tolstoï" (pp. 92–115). The visit was also noted in Tolstoy's diary, June 22–23 (O.S.), see Gusev, p. 761.

57 "Visit to Tolstoy." *Harper's Weekly*. 1892 Apr 16; 36:380. Expanded in two chapters, "The Avatar of Count Tolstoy" and "Tolstoy and His People" in Creelman's

On the Great Highway: the Wanderings and Adventures of a Special Correspondent. (Boston: Lothrop Publishing Co., 1901). Pp. 120–140; 141–156.

58 See Stevens' *Around the World on a Bicycle*, 2 vols. (New York: C. Scribner's Sons, 1887–88) and his *Scouting for Stanley in East Africa* (New York: Cassell Publishing Company, 1890). Tolstoy requested a copy of the latter volume, which Stevens sent him, and which is presently in the Yasnaya Polyana library.

59 *Through Russia on a Mustang*, pp. 96–98 passim.

60 Ibid., pp. 99, 113.

61 Ibid., pp. 99–100.

62 Ibid., pp. 106–107.

63 Ibid., p. 105.

64 Tolstoy's letter to his wife of 22 February 1885 (*PSS*, vol. 83, no. 300).

65 *Through Russia*, pp. 109–110.

66 Ibid., p. 114.

67 The work appeared in three different American editions in 1890. Hapgood's article appeared in April 1890 (see footnote 31), and the work was banned from the U.S. mails in August—"*Kreutzer Sonata*: Transmission through Mail Prohibited." *New York Times*. 1890 Aug 1: 8 (col. 4); 2 (col. 2). Creelman's account appeared a year after his visit, in April 1892. He was sent by James Gordon Bennett (1841–1918), proprietor of the *New York Herald*, who had financed the Stanley expedition to Africa to find Livingston, about which Stevens had written and which so interested Tolstoy.

68 "The Avatar of Count Tolstoy," *On the Great Highway*, pp. 121–123 passim.

69 Ibid., p. 125.

70 Ibid., p. 130.

71 Ibid., pp. 136–137.

72 Ibid., pp. 139–140.

73 In the next chapter of *On the Great Highway*, titled "Tolstoy and his People."

74 Tolstoy later suffered considerable embarrassment at the hands of Creelman himself. In his account of his second visit, on June 24–26, 1903 (published in the *New York World/NY Sunday World*. [New York; 1903 Aug.] and as an article "Our youth gone, our ideals base—Tolstoi" in *North American* [Philadelphia; 1903 Aug 8]) Creelman cited Tolstoy's derogatory comments on the intelligence of the president of the University of Chicago, William R. Harper. For details of this contretemps, see "Tolstoy's American Preachers," loc. cit., pp. 609–610.

75 "Christianity and woman's love. Colonel Ingersoll on Count Tolstoy." *Review of Reviews*. 1890; 2:343. "Tolstoi and 'The Kreutzer Sonata' [excerpts]." *Essays in Criticism*. 1890; 17:580–581. "Tolstoi's Kreutzer Sonata." *North American Review*. 1890 Sep; 151:289–295. "Tolstoi and Wannamaker." *North American Review*. 1890 Sep; 151:298–99.

76 *On the Great Highway*, pp. 144–145.

77 Ibid., pp. 152–154 passim.

78 "With Tolstoi in the Russian Famine." *Century Magazine*. 1893 Jun; 46 [n. s.

24]:249–263. A fuller account appeared a few years later: *In the Land of Tolstoi.
Experiences of Famine and Misrule in Russia*. William Reason, Translator. (New
York: Thomas Whittaker, 1897), 286 pages.

79 Apparently Stadling's work on shamanism was the book forbidden by the censorship in Russia. See his *Shamanismen i norra Asien; nagra drag ur shamanvasendets
utveckling bland naturfolken i Sibirien, af J. Stadling. Med inledande forord af professor Nathan Soderblom om makten och sjalen*. Stockholm, Cederquists grafiska
aktiebolag, 1912. (*Populara etnologiska skrifter*. 7).

80 *Russia Then and Now, 1892–1917. My Mission to Russia during the Famine of
1891–1892 with Data Bearing upon Russia of Today*. (New York: G.P. Putnam's
Sons, 1917). The work was completed before the events of February and October
in Russia, and there is no mention of revolution or even a suggestion of the possibility.

81 *Russia Than and Now*, pp. 67–68.

82 The English text was published (in 1894) as *The Kingdom of God Is Within You.*

83 *Russia Then and Now*, p. 69.

84 Ibid., p. 70.

85 A photograph of this letter is reproduced in *Russia Then and Now*, between pp.
70–71.

86 *Autobiography of Andrew Dickson White*. Vol. 2 (New York: The Century Co.,
1905), p. 74.

87 Ibid., p. 77.

88 During this period Tolstoy did not write entries in his diary, however the daily
journal of White has survived. It indicates that the two met four days in a row in
Moscow, from Saturday, March 24 (n. s.) through Tuesday, the 27th—of the
eight days White spent in Moscow (March 23–30). (I am most grateful to Professor Patricia Carden of Cornell University, who provided me copies of pertinent
pages of White's journal, which is preserved in the Cornell University Archive.)

89 *Autobiography*, p. 94.

90 Ibid., p. 78.

91 Of the first of these see Tolstoy's correspondence with Isabel Hapgood several
years earlier, in 1890 ("Tolstoy's American Translator," loc. cit., p. 23–25).

92 *Autobiography*, p. 79.

93 Ibid., p. 96.

94 Ibid., p. 97.

95 See "Tolstoy's American Preachers," loc. cit., pp. 590–593.

96 *Autobiography*, p. 75.

97 Ibid., p. 87.

98 It is not clear, however, whether Tolstoy was aware of the impact his own writings had made on Howells.

99 *Autobiography*, pp. 82, 83.

100 Ibid., p. 84.

101 Ibid., p. 85.

102 Here White named Suvorov, Mendeleev, Nesselrode, Miliutin, Khilkoff, DeWitte, among others—only one or two of whose names are familiar today to anyone but Russian historians.

103 White is mistaken: at the time there were nine children in the Tolstoy family. Thirteen children were born from 1863 to 1888, of whom eight survived into adulthood (three lived less than a year, over the period 1872 to 1875, and two died at four and seven years: Alexsei, 1881–1886, and Ivan [Vanya], 1888–1895).

104 Ibid., pp. 98–100 passim.

105 For a description and analysis of their correspondence, see "Tolstoy's American Disciple" (*TriQuarterly* 98).

106 The visit took place around May 12 (24 n. s.), 1894, see N.N. Gusev. *Letopis' zhizni i tvorchestva L'va Nikolaevicha Tolstogo. 1891–1910*. Moscow: GIKhL, 1960, p. 132.

107 "Two Days With Count Tolstoy." *Progressive Review*. 1897; 2:407–22. "Count Tolstoï at Home. As Seen by a Well-Known American." *Leslie's Weekly*. 1898; 87:374.

108 "Two Days," pp. 415, 419.

109 Ibid., p. 422.

110 "Count Tolstoï at Home."

111 "Two Days," p. 417.

112 Ibid.

113 Ibid., p. 420.

114 Ibid., p. 418. Carpenter, indeed, was deeply influenced by Whitman. Crosby later wrote a short work on Carpenter, *Edward Carpenter: Poet and Prophet*. 2nd ed. London: A.C. Fifield, 1905. Reprinted, Folcroft, Pa.: Folcroft Library Editions, 1974. 51 p.

115 Ibid., p. 421. Tolstoy remarked in his own diary account of their meeting that Crosby's question as to what he should do surprised him greatly. See "Tolstoy's American Disciple," loc. cit., pp. 212–213.

116 "My Visit to Tolstoy." *Five Discourses by Rabbi Joseph Krauskopf, D.D.* Philadelphia, 1911. These discourses were delivered at the Temple Keneseth Israel in Philadelphia in weekly lectures, December 11, 1910, through January 8, 1911.

117 "My Visit to Tolstoy," p. 1.

118 Citing White's recommendation, Krauskopf wrote to request an interview with Tolstoy on July 16 (4), 1894 (GTM, Ts 224 88).

119 "My Visit to Tolstoy," pp. 3–4.

120 See Gusev, 1890–1910, p. 132.

121 "My Visit to Tolstoy," p. 9.

122 Ibid., p. 8.

123 Ibid., pp. 12, 13.

124 Ibid., pp. 13–14.

125 See "Tolstoy's American Preachers," loc. cit., pp. 562, 616. To the original draft of the letter and original list of names, Tolstoy later added Admiral Dewey.

126 "My Visit to Tolstoy," p. 14–15.

127 Ibid., p. 19.

128 Ibid., pp. 21–22.

129 Ibid., p. 22.

130 Tolstoy received letters from Krauskopf dated August 4, 1894, August 11, 1897, and September 4, 1901 (GMT Ts 224 88).

131 On Jane Addams visit, see "Tolstoy's American Disciple," loc. cit., pp. 221–222.

132 "Tolstoyism." In Twenty Years at Hull-House, with Autobiographical Note. New York: Macmillan, 1912, p. 268.

133 Ibid., p. 272.

134 Ibid., p. 276.

135 Beveridge's account of his journey, The Russian Advance. (New York: Harper & Brothers Publishers, 1904) contains memoirs of his meeting with Tolstoy in a final chapter, "Three Russians of World Fame."

136 The Russian Advance, p. 432.

137 Ibid., pp. 436, 437.

138 Ibid., pp. 434–435.

139 For an account of Bryan's visit and his relationship with Tolstoy, see "Tolstoy's American Preachers," loc. cit., pp. 609–615.

140 MacQueen published virtually identical accounts in two articles: "Russia's Gray Giant Talks for 'The National.'" National Magazine. 1901; 14:579–584. "Tolstoi on America. A Frank Criticism by Count Tolstoi of America and England." Frank Leslie's Popular Monthly. Oct 1901; 52(610):610–614.

141 "Russia's Gray Giant . . . ," p. 584. Tolstoy specifically noted his agreement with Ernest Crosby that the capture of the insurrection leader Emilio Aguinaldo was wrong.

142 Ibid.

143 Ibid., p. 583.

144 Ibid., p. 584.

145 Published in the Independent. 1904 Apr 21; 56:881–883.

146 Ernest Crosby assisted in clarifying the confusion caused by this article (see "Tolstoy's American Disciple," loc. cit., pp. 242, 250).

147 Twelve letters written by Bernstein, 1902–1919, are in GMT (Bl. 206 57, 77 152/58, 78 180/46, 2 80, 2 81).

148 "Leo Tolstoy," the first chapter in With Master Minds. Interviews by Herman Bernstein. (New York: Universal Series Publishing Co., 1913), p. 11.

149 Ibid., pp. 11, 12.

150 Ibid., pp. 23–24.

151 Ibid., pp. 20–21.

152 Ibid., p. 22.

153 Ibid., p. 13.

154 Ibid., p. 14.

155 Ibid.

156 Ibid., p. 23.

157 "Tolstoy in the Twilight," *World's Work.* 1909 Oct; 18:12144. George wrote of his visit in two other articles as well: "My farewell to Count Tolstoy (A visit to the home of the great Russian reformer; The veneration of the Russians; Mrs. Tolstoy)." *New York World.* 1909 Nov 19. "A visit to Tolstoy." *World's Work.* 1910 Feb; 15:251–261.

158 Tolstoy began the article upon receiving a telegram (on May 20 [June 2]) from Henry George, Jr., announcing that he would arrive three days hence. The article appeared on May 27 (June 9) in *Sankt-Peterburgskie vedomosti* (No. 130) with the title *"Po povodu priezda syna Genri Dzhordzha"* (apropos of the visit of Henry George's son) in *PSS* 38:70–71.

159 "Tolstoy in the Twilight," p. 12147.

160 Ibid., p. 12153.

161 Bryan wrote to Tolstoy on May 27, 1909 (GMT Bp 2 1579). Theodore R. Roosevelt, "Tolstoy: an estimate." *Outlook.* 1909 May 15; 92:103–108. "Feeble Folk" *The Commoner* (Lincoln, Neb.) May 21, 1909. Vol. 9, no. 19, p. 1.

162 "Tolstoy in the Twilight," p. 12149.

163 Ibid., p. 12154.

Sandra M. Gilbert

Yahrzeit

PARIS. FEBRUARY 10, 2000. NEARLY MIDNIGHT. NEARLY FEBRU-
ary 11, the ninth anniversary of Elliot's death. Tomorrow David
and I are leaving for a month in Bogliasco, just outside Genoa,
where I have a residency at a rather grand villa that's been converted into a study center for artists and scholars, so I dash off a
last e-mail to my kids back in the States, giving them our itinerary
for the next three days, then add: "It seems very odd & sad to be
starting on this journey on Feb. 11, but even if it's an inauspicious
day perhaps it's not inappropriate, since I'm going to this place to
work on my elegy book, now renamed 'Death's Door,' I think."

We're going to drive slowly to the Mediterranean coast, through
Bourgogne, Switzerland, and northern Italy, spending a night each
in Dijon, Montreux, and Torino, not just so we can see some sights
along the way but because I'm worried that I might fall asleep at
the wheel, overcome by a fog of mourning and melancholia. What
if, even though I'm distracted by beautiful vineyards and glittering
Alps, I have what's called an "anniversary reaction" and get nar-

coleptic from grief? That's happened to me before. Many times, especially in the first months after Elliot died, I'd pass out in my chair, as if not only I myself but the world were sinking into sleep, poisoned by misery. When Keats wrote, "My heart aches and a drowsy numbness pains/My sense, as if of hemlock I had drunk," he wasn't suffering bereavement, unless it was anticipatory grief for his own rapidly approaching death, yet the narcoleptic feeling he records in "Ode to a Nightingale" is one I sometimes associate with mourning: body and soul not wanting to stay awake, not wanting to be conscious. Clearly that's no state in which to be at the wheel, especially not in the Alps! So we have to go slowly, since David will do most of the driving, and I don't want him to have to keep at it eight hours a day.

David and I have been together for nearly seven years now, and he's always kind about the impulses to mourn that still master me from time to time. He understands quite well, I think, that one can love and grieve for the dead person who shaped the past even while loving and living with a new person who's central in the present. But as in some sense a "hard" scientist—a mathematician who theorizes games and economic strategies—he has trouble understanding what I guess he considers my excessively mystical (perhaps even sentimental) tendency to brood on the chronological milestones that mark my personal narrative of loss and sorrow. So I won't remind him of "the anniversary," although he knows perfectly well the meaning February 11 has for me: over the years we have, after all, spent six such days together, with me usually planning a good part of each one well in advance.

But perhaps David's right to be skeptical about my bitter tenderness toward "the anniversary," the anxious reverence with which, each year, I tremulously meet and meditate on this date. Why, after all, *isn't* this day a day like any other?

Mah nishtanah halailah hazeh,
Mikol haleilot? Mikol haleilot?

Sheb'chol haleilot, anu ochlin,
Chameits umatsah, chameits umatsah,
Halaylah hazeh, halaylah hazeh kulo matsa.
Halahlah hazeh, halaylah hazeh kulo matsa.

Why is this night different from other nights?
Why this night? Why this night?

On other nights we eat leavened bread,
Leavened bread and cakes,
But on this night, this night we eat matzoh,
On this night, this night we eat matzoh.

How is this day different from other days? And *"why is this night different from other nights?"* There was always an ironic edge in Elliot's voice when now and then, as a joke about something or someone, he used to intone those words with which the Jewish passover ceremony—the ritual family seder—begins. *On other nights*, Jewish parents tell their children, *we eat leavened bread. But on this night*, they say at the first evening meal of the seven-day feast that memorializes the journey of their ancestors across the Sinai, *we eat unleavened bread—matzoh—the raw stuff of affliction that we snatched from the ovens just before our desperate flight out of Egypt, the flat bread we baked in the harsh sun of the desert. And on this night we eat bitter herbs, to remind us of the bitterness of our slavery and suffering in Egypt.*

Is commemoration—and in particular the commemoration of suffering—a specifically Jewish theme? Certainly anniversaries of death, desperation, and disaster are built into ceremonies I came to know quite well through Elliot, relentlessly secular though his Judaism was. Every winter, for example, on the anniversary of his father's death a *Yahrzeit* card (and sometimes, in the early days, a candle) would arrive in our mailbox, courtesy of the Riverside Funeral Chapel that had arranged Harry Gilbert's burial in 1970. At first I wasn't sure what this signified—Yahrzeit? *What is that?* I asked my husband—but after a while the ritual remembrance of ending, the commemoration of the *deathday*, began to seem as obvious and plausible as the annual celebration of beginning, the commemoration of the *birthday*, with which we're so culturally familiar.

The *Yahrzeit*—literally, in Yiddish, the "year-time"—writes one chronicler of Jewish customs, "is the yearly anniversary of the death of a father, mother, relative or member of one's extended family. . . . There is a universal Jewish custom to light a special candle which burns for at least twenty-four hours on the day of the *Yahrzeit*. This is an act of respect for the deceased." And, too, on the day of the *Yahrzeit* the recital of the *Kaddish,* the ancient Hebrew prayer for the dead, "can cause the soul to rise to higher levels in Gan Eden"—the Hebrew paradise—while "When a person leads the prayer in the synagogue on the *Yahrzeit*, it can elevate the soul even more than the Kaddish." Moreover, the *Yahrzeit* "is a time of judgment for the deceased. Therefore, charity or any good deeds which are done on behalf of the departed can help him or her pass judgment and even be elevated. Some people have the custom to fast on the *Yahrzeit*"—and this also "brings atonement" to the dead.

Is the marking of *Yahrzeit* intended, then, to soothe the dead, to ease their passage from our world toward the other, mysterious realm into which we imagine they must travel? Some accounts of Jewish mourning practices suggest as much. For the first week after a death, the bereaved "sit" *Shiva* (which means "seven") in their home, concentrating for seven severely focused days on their loss while sharing their grief and their memories of the dead one with visitors from the community. Notes one commentator, the *Shiva* candle, "*symbolic of the soul of the deceased*" [emphasis added], is "lit immediately on returning from the cemetery" to mark the beginning of this period during which all must "sit low as a symbol of 'being brought low' in grief," there must be "no 'luxurious' bathing or cutting hair" since "these are signs of vanity," mirrors must be covered "for the same reason as not bathing," "sexual relations are forbidden"—as is almost any other "business as usual"—and "wherever possible" services are held in the household. On the morning of the seventh day, however, the ceremonial *Shiva* candle "is blown out in silence" and the mourners go for "a walk around the block," not just "as a way of taking a first step back into the world" but also "*to escort the soul out of the house, indicating that they are going to be all right.*"

Yet still the Jewish soul would seem to be in transition from here to there, from "our" place to another one, for the seven-day period of *Shiva* is followed by a second period of mourning called *Shelo-*

shim, meaning thirty, during which mourners avoid festive events and say Kaddish as often as possible, preferably at daily services, as if, again, to speed the departing spirit on its way to "Gan Eden." And interestingly, some "follow the custom of not visiting the grave until after *Sheloshim*" (though others only wait until "after the Shiva period") as if, in a sense, the dead person had not at first quite settled into the tomb.

For those who have lost the most intimate relatives, moreover, there is yet another eleven-month period of grief during which Kaddish must be recited, which rounds out to a year the time of *Avelut*, or mourning. During this period—or quite often at its conclusion, on the first anniversary of the death or funeral of anyone close—a *matzevah*, a tombstone or marker, is "placed on the grave and dedicated in a ceremony called 'unveiling' [during which a] cloth is removed from the stone in the presence of the immediate family and friends. . . . The top of the stone often has the Hebrew letters pay and nun standing for 'Here lies buried' [while] on the bottom are five Hebrew letters, *tuf, nun, tzadi, bet, hay*, meaning 'May his [her] soul be bound up in the bond of life eternal.'"

Now the dead one is in and of the earth—and, it is hoped, has found some sort of rest there as well as in the bonds of a "life eternal" that is not just of the earth but, somehow, beyond or *without* the earth. And now, too, or so this sequence of ceremonial practices might seem to imply, the living can free themselves from their anxieties about the fate of the wandering soul, the spirit cast into darkness that had been for a time so helplessly dependent on the prayers of survivors for aid on its mysterious journey.

Still, as the anthropologist Nigel Barley has written, in almost every culture around the world it is thought to be "above all the dead that feel desperate grief and loneliness." Thus, that we who are still alive must perform certain obligatory tasks so as to care for them also seems to be a powerful, nearly universal human belief. The Chinese "feed" their dead with paper food, supply them with paper houses and paper automobiles, while the ancient Egyptians housed them in solider, grander mansions, elaborately furnished with the equipment of quotidian life. And from Africa to Oceania and Asia, other peoples offer quite substantial nourishment to the "departed," a term that in itself reminds us of the equally wide-spread impulse to imagine death as a journey which might well require literal as well as spiritual provisions. "Have you built your ship of death, O have you?" asked D. H. Lawrence, anticipating his own death in a late poem that drew on Etruscan as well as Egyptian iconography. "O build your ship of death, for you will need it."

> O build your ship of death, your little ark
> and furnish it with food, with little cakes, and wine
> for the dark flight down oblivion.

Yet surely the jobs we do for the dead are also jobs we do for ourselves—to reassure ourselves of our own worthiness, to ensure that others will take care of *us* when we are "gone" on the same journey, and perhaps most important of all to keep ourselves in *touch* with our vanished travelers, and even, in a way, in *view* of them. Is the *Yahrzeit*, then, another way of staying connected to the dead, of imagining that we might pierce the cloud of unknowing that separates us from them? Does one feel, on "the anniversary," the nearness of the dead, as on All Soul's Day, when the veils or walls between "us" and "them" are thought most permeable?

I have always planned what I do on February 11 so carefully, hour by hour, because each hour evokes all too vividly the events of February 11, 1991, events I can't help recalling throughout the day, just as in a larger liturgical context Catholics trace the Stations of the Cross on the walls of churches. Maybe, like the Stations of the Cross, the sad plot of February 11, 1991 exists for me in a kind of eternal present that has to be ceaselessly reenacted with every annual recurrence of the fateful date: 6 AM, now an orderly had arrived—has again arrived!—to take Elliot down to the surgery suite; 6:15 AM, now Elliot is once more saying goodbye to me and the girls; 7:00 AM, now they're wheeling him again into the operating room and now, at 7:30 AM they once more, as in my mind they do every year, cut into his body and now, at 11:15 the surgery is over and someone is moving him into the corridor and now, yet again, again, it's 3:30 in the afternoon and he's alone in the recovery room, *now* he must be starting to bleed internally (though no one realizes)—and now it's 6:30 in the evening and

279

he's beginning to die (a nurse has noticed this and called for help), and now it's 7:30, the sky has gone dark, he's dying (though *we* don't know it, for the girls and I are innocently waiting in the hospital lobby), and now, at 8:15, he *has* died, *now* he's dead.

Do I secretly believe, then, that if I recall and rehearse each of these events, hour by hour, I can somehow change them, alter the configuration of the day through an act of remembrance so clear and fierce that it will revise the story of the death itself? 3:30 in the afternoon: he's alone in the recovery room, starting to bleed internally—*but someone notices!* 6:30 in the evening, he's *not* beginning to die—the doctors and nurses are hovering at his bedside, transfusing him with clean new blood! 8:15 PM, the girls and I are in his room, hugging him in the yellow glow of a lamp that beats back the shadows beyond the tall window, we're congratulating him on his narrow escape from death, celebrating his survival!

Yet surely such revisionary hopes don't shape the "drowsy numbness" that "pains my sense" throughout the anniversary day. On the contrary. Recurring annually, February 11 bespeaks finality. The gloom of the *Yahrzeit* reminds us (just in case we needed a reminder) of the reality of the death it commemorates. The card that came in the mail each winter, announcing yet again that Harry Gilbert had in fact died in January, 1970, was a thick, white square of cardboard, a kind of *slab* of cardboard, edged in black. The card told us that we should light a candle for the soul of Harry Gilbert, wayfaring alone in some cryptic distance, because there was now no way we could bring him back to us; the tiny signal of the candle, said the card, was the only communication possible between us and my husband's father—and a frail, chancy one at that. The card told us how inexorable, how irreversible were the events of the day that had killed Harry Gilbert. And in this sense the *Yahrzeit* card was like—metaphorically, indeed, the Yahrzeit card *was*—the stone that marked the grave of Harry Gilbert.

Maybe it's no coincidence, then, that according to Jewish custom the gravestone itself must be "unveiled" by or at the first *Yahrzeit*. And the concept, as well as the moment, of "unveiling" is surely significant. We want the veil between us and the dead to be lifted, we yearn toward the beings (and what we hope is the *being*) "beyond the veil." Yet what is unveiled and revealed on the grave, at the first *Yahrzeit*, is the enigmatic factuality of the stone itself, the crypt that symbolizes the materiality of death. The very moment we look at the stone is, arguably, *the* moment of recognition (or re-cognition) when we know or re-learn what has happened: here is the name of the dead one, the collection of ciphers that remains to remind us that he *was* and is no more; here— indelible, ineradicable—are the dates of his life, these numbers telling when it began and these telling not just when but *that* it has ended.

In the beautiful, wistfully autumnal "Medlars and Sorb Apples," written some years before his "Ship of Death," Lawrence announces the theme of the journeying soul that he was so poignantly to elaborate in the later work. Meditating on the "exquisite odour of leave-taking" and the pilgrimage of Orpheus down "the winding, leaf-clogged, silent lanes of hell," he celebrates what he calls the "Intoxication of final loneliness" that is or should be experienced by

> *Each soul departing with its own isolation,*
> *Strangest of all strange companions,*
> *And best.*

Yet the loneliness of the departed soul, as it continues "down the strange lanes of hell, more and more intensely alone" on the other side of the silence that divides it from the living, must of course be matched by the loneliness of the living, forced to acquiesce in their irrevocable separation from the dead. This separation, this ontological loneliness, is what the stone quite literally re-presents to us, for in recording (and thus re-membering or re-evoking) the date of loss the stone becomes a signifier of loss and thus, in a way, an incarnation of the *Yahrzeit* whose recurrence tells us, over and over again, that to go on living is to go on living with loss.

And doesn't the word "grave" itself express the congruence between loss or separation and the *writing* of loss that the gravestone preserves? My dictionary tells me that "grave" meaning an "excavation for the interment of a corpse; burial place," and "grave" meaning to "sculpt or carve; engrave," to "stamp or impress deeply; fix permanently, as words or ideas" both derive from the Indo-European root "*ghrebh*," meaning to "dig, bury, scratch." In western culture, at least, the inscriptions on stone that mark the hollows where we bury our dead strikingly parallel the very trenches or hollows en-graved—inscribed—in the earth where the urns and coffins of the dead are actually interred. And if to inter is to engrave, then perhaps to engrave is to inter. Thus the dates engraved or inscribed on the *Yahrzeit* card, or on the stone whose herald it is, manifest the crypt or grave of the dead one, the hollow beyond or outside time in which he is hidden away from us, forever inaccessible to the living, hard as we may struggle to rend the veils that divide us from him.

Poets have, of course, repeatedly brooded on graves and their engraving—not a surprising point, given the connection between the mystery of death and the mastery of language that is as implicit in the philological history of "*ghrebh*" as it is in the story of Orpheus's journey to Hades. And the "epitaph" or "inscription on a tomb" (from the Greek *epi-taphos*, literally writing *epi*—over—the *taphos*—tomb) is a time-honored poetic genre. Tennyson's *In Memoriam*, however, must have a special place among meditations on what I want to call "the epitaphic moment"—the moment, perhaps, when a mourner fully recognizes the reality of loss. This elegiac sequence—not really a single poem but a series of related verses—was produced by Tennyson in the course of more than fifteen years, during which he struggled to come to terms with (and find terms for) his grief over the unexpected death of his beloved friend Arthur Hallam. Indeed, the structure of the poem, with its reiteration of Christmases past and passing, emphasizes the enmeshing of what we now call "grief-work" in the turnings of the year, while the poet's self-consciousness about the problems of memory and memorializing is obviously implicit in the title of the work. But maybe, in connection with epitaphs and anniversaries, it's most interesting that *In Memoriam* focuses at key points on the torment of the veil that separates us from the dead and on the haunting enigma of the stone that both certifies and symbolizes the lost friend's death.

"Behind the veil": the almost too well-known phrase, so often used, was originally Tennyson's. "O for thy voice to soothe and bless!" he cries out to Hallam in section 56, after lamenting humanity's entrapment in evolutionary processes dominated by "Nature, red in tooth and claw," but then concedes that his yearning for communication beyond the grave is as hopeless as his wish for "redress" of what seems to him at this point the cosmic injustice that condemns living things to die:

> O life as futile, then, as frail!
>   O for thy voice to soothe and bless!
>   What hope of answer, or redress?
> Behind the veil, behind the veil.

Eleven verses later, though, in section 67, the poet confesses to a strange, recurrent epiphany—a nighttime vision of the "commemorative marker on the wall of the church above the vault" in which Hallam was buried.

> When on my bed the moonlight falls,
>   I know that in thy place of rest
>   By that broad water of the west,
> There comes a glory on the walls;
>
> Thy marble bright in dark appears,
>   As slowly steals a silver flame
>   Along the letters of thy name,
> And o'er the number of thy years.
>
> The mystic glory swims away;
>   From off my bed the moonlight dies;
>   And closing eaves of wearied eyes
> I sleep till dusk is dipt in gray:
>
> And then I know the mist is drawn
>   A lucid veil from coast to coast,
>   And in the dark church like a ghost
> Thy tablet glimmers to the dawn.

Why does a "silver flame"—a "mystic glory"—here light the very stone that signifies loss? And why is the mist that's later, with the gray of dawn, drawn "from coast to coast," a "lucid veil"? (In what sense, anyway, is the mist "drawn" from coast to coast—drawn as in "sketched" or drawn as in "pulled"? And if "pulled," pulled open or pulled closed?) At the least, I suppose, the poet finds some comfort in the factuality of history: although Hallam *is* no more, the "mystic glory" of Hallam *was*, as the silvery tablet testifies in the tenuous moonlight of memory. After all, terrible as the epitaphic moment may be, with its reiterated, Poe-like assertion that the lost beloved will "Nevermore" return, fate might deal even more hardly with the bereaved if there were *no epitaph*, leaving behind what Whitman called "the terrible doubt of appearances," specifically the doubt whether who and what "was" really *was*. Perhaps, then, though the veil of mist that's drawn (open or closed) from coast to coast at the end of this section is profoundly ambiguous, it gains its oxymoronic lucidity from the "mystic glory" buried in the vault of the past to whose reality the tablet bears glimmering witness.

At the same time, however, I have to confess that my own puzzlement at the "mystic glory" is rooted in skepticism, specifically in a feeling (maybe a very anti-Victorian, very agnostic and "postmodern" feeling) that there's something inauthentic, something false about all this talk of glory. Sorrow and pity are what we mostly feel today when we contemplate the dead; glory, especially "mystic glory," is alien to us, isn't it? And didn't Tennyson himself confess that he *hadn't in fact viewed his friend's memorial tablet when he wrote these lines?* "I myself did not see Clevedon [Hallam's burial place] till years after the burial of A.H.H.," the poet noted, adding that after visiting Clevedon he substituted the somewhat pessimistic phrase "dark church" for the more devoutly Christian term "chancel" (meaning the space around an altar) that he'd used in his original draft of this passage. Maybe the lines "in the chancel like a ghost/Thy tablet glimmers to the dawn" would have attributed almost a priestly role to the spectral Hallam, hovering before the altar near which his body lay, while a glimmering "in the dark church" is more akin to a glimmering—a fading in and a fading out—in a darkness of theological mystery we twenty-first century readers can find more congenial, though hardly more comforting.

By the end of *In Memoriam*, in any case, the past whose reality is re-presented in letters engraved on tablets like the one that Tennyson at least *seems* to see in section 67 becomes the stony foundation on which the present can move forward into the future. The sequence that began with the death of the friend who had been engaged to the poet's sister Emily ends with the wedding of the poet's sister Cecelia, here pictured standing at the altar,

> *Now waiting to be made a wife,*
> *Her feet, my darling, on the dead;*
> *Their pensive tablets round her head,*
> *And the most living words of life*
>
> *Breathed in her ear.*

Standing above a vault like the one in which Hallam is buried, the bride is surrounded by "tablets" like the one that commemorates him: the dead are below and around the living, as the newlyweds move forward into a future that, as Tennyson reminds us (significantly through an allusion to the ceremonial *inscription* of their nuptials), must include their own deaths. "Now sign your names," he admonishes the happy pair,

> *. . . which shall be read,*
> *Mute symbols of a joyful morn,*
> *By village eyes as yet unborn;*
> *The names are signed. . . .*

And as the wedding bells begin

> *. . . the clash and clang that tells*
> *The joy to every wandering breeze;*
> *The blind wall rocks, and on the trees*
> *The dead leaf trembles to the bells.*

"The blind wall rocks. . . . The dead leaf trembles. . . .": we know that Tennyson is going to will a happier ending to this poem, just as he had fantasized a "chancel" rather than a "dark church." *In Memoriam* concludes with a vision of a new child conceived on the bridal couple's wedding night—a child "No longer half-akin to brute" but like "the man, [Hallam] that with me trod/This planet . . . a noble type"—and this vision itself culminates in the poet's assertion that the newly conceived child will "live in God" as Hallam did and does, heralding the "one far-off divine event,/To which the whole creation moves." And yet—the blindness of the wall, the tremor of the dead leaf! Though Tennyson claims that on this joyous wedding day even "the grave is bright for me," his own rhetoric betrays him for a moment here. The "lucid veil" has become a "blind wall," the "mystic glory" of the dead man no more than a "dead leaf," as if, at least temporarily, the real, unvisionary stones that signify death and loss had closed around the "dark church" in which the poet momentarily finds himself, sealing him off from his hope of reunion and communion with the dead man just as they seal the dead away from him.

Tennyson's descendants are still more grim about the epitaphic moment that is entombed in the bleakness of the *Yahrzeit*. Here's Robert Frost, writing "In a Disused Graveyard," a poem that appeared in 1923, some three quarters of a century after Tennyson published *In Memoriam*:

> *The living come with grassy tread*
> *To read the gravestones on the hill;*
> *The graveyard draws the living still,*
> *But never any more the dead.*

> *The verses in it say and say:*
> *'The ones who living come today*
> *To read the stones and go away*
> *Tomorrow dead will come to stay.'*

> *So sure of death the marble's rhyme,*
> *Yet can't help marking all the time*
> *How no one dead will seem to come.*
> *What is it men are shrinking from?*

> *It would be easy to be clever*
> *And tell the stones: Men hate to die*
> *And have stopped dying now forever.*
> *I think they would believe the lie.*

The gravestones, Frost declares flatly, are markers of irrevocability. Not only will "no one dead" come back from beyond the wall erected by "the marble's rhyme," no one dead will even "*seem* to come" just as this poet won't even *seem* to see a "mystic glory" in the "lucid mists" of moonlit nights.

Perhaps the graveyard Frost describes is literally "disused," then, because it's too full of death and the dead to offer space to more corpses, but metaphorically it's "disused" because, as he ironically notes, not even the dead to whom it's dedicated will "come" (back) to it. Yet there will be more and more dead bodies to populate (and not come back to) *other* cemeteries, since only (or maybe not even) a stone would believe the second (lying) half of the claim that "Men hate to die/And have stopped dying now forever." In Frost's view, human will (we hate to die, yearn *not* to die) and human fate (we can't stop dying, and can't stop dying *forever*) are hopelessly at odds, issuing in a harsh conundrum to which the "disused" graveyard mutely testifies.

Hard and bitter though it may be, however, to cope with the eternal disappearance—the intransigent *absence*—of the dead, wouldn't it be worse to imagine them somehow *present* within their death? Isn't there some comfort in reflecting that "the graveyard draws the living still,/But never any more the dead?" Certainly, if we construe Frost's line differently, we can find some consolation in believing that the dead have journeyed away from death, into that better place most cultures construct for them through myth and ritual. "Peace, peace! he is not dead, he doth not sleep—," exults Shelley, declaring that his "Adonais" "hath awakened from the dream of life." Yet what if Keats has awakened into the reality of death?

Perhaps, as we gaze at the grave in which we want to believe the dead are *not*, we can't keep from thinking that they are *not* not there! Perhaps we fear that the dead aren't just figuratively speaking "beyond the veil" but literally trapped behind the "blind wall" that seals them away from us. And what if our horror at the imperviousness of that wall is really a displacement of the deepest horror we feel, a horror at the stony imperviousness of the dead body itself, behind which the soul of the one we love may be trapped, unable to escape or speak or cry for help? What if the dead body itself *is* "the veil" beyond which the dead somehow still *are?*

I suspect that this ultimate horror—sometimes clearly formulated, sometimes not quite conscious—shapes countless poems that focus on what I've been calling the "epitaphic moment," as if the contemplation of the tomb were really a way of meditating on the sheer terror evoked by the dead body itself. And maybe the old, old fear of living burial (intended or accidental) really masks a fear related to this terror—the fear that *any* burial is a form of "burial alive."

Apparently ironic and resigned, Thomas Hardy's "Rain on a Grave" seems to me to record at least a tentative confrontation with this fear, as the poet meditates on what his buried wife is presumably not (but by implication *might be* and therefore maybe *is*) feeling:

> Clouds spout upon her
> > Their waters amain
> > In ruthless disdain,—
> Her who but lately
> > Had shivered with pain
> As at touch of dishonour
> If there had lit on her
> So coldly, so straightly
> > Such arrows of rain:
>
> One who to shelter
> > Her delicate head
> Would quicken and quicken
> > Each tentative tread
> If drops chanced to pelt her
> > That summertime spills
> > In dust-paven rills
> When thunder-clouds thicken
> > And birds close their bills.

How alive, and how fearfully vulnerable, the dead woman becomes in the course of these lines that begin so matter-of-factly! "Clouds spout upon her"—upon *her* who had so disliked the rain, who had felt so "dishonored" and so urgently sought shelter if "arrows of rain" had dared to insult her "delicate head"! And she is helpless, now, to "quicken and quicken" her "tentative tread," helpless because (although she may still suffer the dishonor of the rain) she is not among the quick but among the dead.

This last thought of his lost Emma's helplessness is so dreadful to Hardy that he suddenly casts about for a remedy—something, anything, to do to make things better:

> Would that I lay there
>   And she were housed here!
> Or better, together
> Were folded away there
> Exposed to one weather
> We both,—who would stray there
> When sunny the day there,
>   Or evening was clear
>   At the prime of the year.

If living husband and dead wife could just, *at least*, be "folded away" together, even if they were both exposed to the pitiless rain—if they who once had strayed together through sunny days and clear evenings could now weather the awful climate of death together—the two might perhaps shelter or anyway solace each other.

But as it is, Hardy can only turn at the poem's end to what seems here like a cold comfort, even though it's a traditional one.

> Soon will be growing
>   Green blades from her mound,
> And daisies be showing
>   Like stars on the ground,
> Till she form part of them—
> Ay—the sweet heart of them.
>   Loved beyond measure
>   With a child's pleasure
>   All her life's round.

"Soon will be growing/Green blades from her mound": the thought of the biological processes through which death (re)generates life fails to comfort here because the curious animation the writer attributes to his wife's body makes the thought of such a transformation distinctly unpleasant. What must the shivering Emma, with her "delicate head" have to go through in order to "form part" of a constellation of daisies? How ironic that she, who loved such flowers with an innocent, childlike pleasure throughout her lifetime should now have fallen into a state where she will become no more than the "sweet heart"—and maybe the unwilling, dishonored *sweetheart*—of the inanimate!

I remember that when the rains came in March 1991, and the drought that had settled over California that winter suddenly ended, I was almost distraught. I'd often of course read Hardy's *Poems of 1912*, the brief elegiac verses in which he mourns his first wife Emma—modern British lit. is, after all, one of my professional "fields"—but I certainly hadn't "read" "Rain on a Grave" as I do now. At first, in fact, I'm not sure I knew what was bothering me about the tumultuous sheets of water that began to spill from the sky just a few weeks after Elliot died. Then, one night I dreamed that he complained to me in sorrowful tones about what he had to endure: "Sem, it's so cold here," he whispered in my sleep. And I understood my anxieties. He was *out in the storm!* And how could I have left him on the western slope of a chilly California hillside where "arrows of rain" could torment him! He was a man who hated the wet, the cold; on nasty days, he wore galoshes, a tweed hat, a heavy parka. . . . Mad as it may seem, I think I really believed he was suffering through the weather just as Hardy seems to imagine Emma is suffering. And perhaps, I feared, I was to blame for his woe, perhaps I shouldn't have "left him" out there!

"Full fathom five thy father lies," begins Ariel's famous song from *The Tempest*:

> *Of his bones are coral made;*
> *Those are pearls that were his eyes:*
> *Nothing of him that doth fade,*
> *But doth suffer a sea change*
> *Into something rich and strange.*

Ah, but to the one who mourns, the sea change that the beloved must undergo seems terrible. What if he *feels* his bones turning to coral, his eyes becoming pearls? Think of how the dead must suffer in being made "rich and strange"! As for "the buried life" of those bodies more prosaically planted in graveyards on damp and chilly hillsides, many a poet has reflected anxiously on that sad condition. Writing to her husband a year or so after his death, Edna St. Vincent Millay asked what may be a representative question:

> Ah, cannot the curled shoots of the larkspur that you loved so,
> Cannot the spiny poppy that no winter kills
> Instruct you how to return through the thawing ground and the thin
> > snow
> Into this April sun that is driving the mist between the hills? . . .
>
> [But] I fear that not a root in all this heaving sea
> Of land, has nudged you where you lie, has found
> Patience and time to direct you, numb and stupid as you still must be
> From your first winter underground.

Maybe I had a trace memory of this Millay poem—or maybe I was just remembering my dream of Elliot's plaintive "it so cold here"—when I noticed one day in May, some fifteen months after his death, that "On the Surface" the "oaks are pollinating, sexual and yellow," then realized with rue, with horror, that

> . . . down there this new
> warmth hasn't trickled through
>
> to you
> and it's so dull, I know,
>
> and I suspect
> nothing touches what's inside the silent
>
> boxes, nothing creeps into the heaviness
> that covers all of you
>
> except the bulbs, the dreadful bulbs exploding
> everywhere and rising
>
> toward the surface
> through this season's placid grass.

But the gloom of the anniversary may have a special connection to this morbid, physical dread that the epitaphic moment some-times evokes. For if the dead one is entombed in the *Yahrzeit*—or anyway the *Yahrzeit* annually recalls and as it were "engraves" in memory the interment of the dead one—then that anniversary time is not just a time for speaking to the spirit of the dead that's journeying (we hope) away from the desolation of the material and onward into a "better place" behind the veil but also a time for addressing the *body* of the dead in the "resting place" where it's helplessly immobilized.

In "R. Alcona to J. Brenzaida," a dramatic monologue Emily Bronte wrote so her fictive heroine "Rosina Alcona" might utter her loyal grief for her dead beloved, "Julius Brenzaida," the author of *Wuthering Heights* specifically linked the inexorable recurrence of anniversary after anniversary of the "deathday" that severed the lovers with fears (like Hardy's, Millay's—and my own) of the tor-ments weather might bring to the dead:

> *Cold in the earth, and the deep snow piled above thee!*
> *Far, far removed, cold in the dreary grave!*
> *Have I forgot, my Only Love, to love thee,*
> *Severed at last by Time's all-wearing wave?* . . .
>
> *Cold in the earth, and fifteen wild Decembers*
> *From those brown hills have melted into spring—*
> *Faithful indeed is the spirit that remembers*
> *After such years of change and suffering!*

Like Hardy's dead wife (or Millay's husband and my own), Julius Brenzaida seems almost to have been imagined animate and wake-ful in this poem, as he endures the terrible passage of "fifteen wild Decembers." For though the phrase "such years of change and suf-fering" overtly refers to the transformations experienced by the survivor, Rosina, who faithfully remembers her dead lover despite the forces that have reshaped her life, the reader shudders to con-template (and half fears Bronte may be contemplating) the "change and suffering" that the dead Julius has undergone, trapped in his grave on a wintry hillside.

And *can* "Time's all-wearing wave" sever us from the dead? Bronte's emphasis on the ever-increasing interval, the sheer duration, that separates Rosina from Julius reminds us that what is buried in the grave isn't just the body of the beloved but the body of the past itself that the lovers shared. Judith Wright's "Rosina Alcona to Julius Brenzaida," a moving revision of Bronte's powerful poem, brilliantly surfaces the notion that, as T. S. Eliot brooded in "Burnt Norton," "Time present and time past" coexist, and that "both [are] perhaps present in time future." To survive into mid- or late-life, Wright observes, is to witness the ways in which the past is interred in the present, for

> Living long is containing
> archaean levels,
> buried yet living.

To dramatize this point, she recounts a moment of epiphany when, driving along "the new freeway . . . rushing forward," she suddenly catches sight of "the old wooden pub/stranded at the crossways" where she and her dead lover once

> in an absolute present
> drank laughing
> in a day still living,
> still laughing, still permanent.

At that moment, as "Present crossed past/synchronized, at the junction," the poet insists, "Three faces met"—the "vivid" living face of her lover as he once was, his corpse's "face of dead marble," and her own, so that as the past rises from its grave,

> Holding the steering-wheel
> my hands freeze. Out of my eyes
> jump these undryable tears
> from artesian pressures,
> from the strata that cover you,
> the silt-sift of time.

And here, as if to parallel the momentary resurrection of dead love, Wright invokes "dead Emily"—the writer whose love song of "R. Alcona to J. Brenzaida" this twentieth-century poet is also, as it were, resurrecting:

Have I forgot, my only Love, to love thee,
Severed at last by time's all-wearing wave?. . .

The pure poem rises
in lovely tranquillity . . .
from the soil of the past,
as the lost face rises
and the tears return.

But if any moment of memory can resurrect the past in which we lived with, instead of without, the one whose absence we now lament, how much more compelling is the regular, mournfully recurring *Yahrzeit*, with its reminder not only of the other we have lost but the *self* we have lost or buried in the irretrievable past. Marking anniversary after anniversary—key moments at weekly or monthly as well as yearly intervals—Donald Hall's poignant *Without* struggles to revive and revitalize at least the shadow of the person he himself had been even at the disease-haunted end of his married past while ruefully tracing a lonely pilgrimage forward into grief at the death of his wife, Jane Kenyon. As he notes in "Independence Day Letter" that "I undertake another day/twelve weeks after the Tuesday/we learned that you would die," Hall's funereal language ("I *undertake* another day") emphasizes the irony of "Independence" while his perpetual evocation and re-evocation of the events leading up to his wife's death dramatizes his continued inhabitation of the time when he lived *with*, rather than *without*, the dead woman.

Yet over and over again the past keeps dying in Hall's elegies; over and over again, Jane Kenyon is buried; over and over again, the poet studies the marker on her grave, as if repeatedly straining to decipher its meaning. In "Independence Day Letter," he confesses that

. . . I go to bed early, reading
The Man Without Qualities
with insufficient attention
because I keep watching you die.
Tomorrow I will wake at five

to the tenth Wednesday
after the Wednesday we buried you.

Not too many Wednesdays later, in "Midsummer Letter," he is still dwelling on and, as it were, in the interstices of the calendar, as he observes that

The polished black granite
cemented over your head
reflects the full moon of August
four months from the day
your chest went still.

And in "Midwinter Letter" he surfaces one of the imperatives that shape these poems.

Remembered happiness is agony;
so is remembered agony.
I live in a present compelled
by anniversaries and objects.

For the mourner compelled by the "remembered agony" incarnate in "anniversaries and the objects," however, there are two key moments around which the calendar of grief is organized, as the *Yahrzeit* ritual itself suggests: the moment of burial that the first *Yahrzeit* commemorates and the moment of death commemorated in each later *Yahrzeit*. Although he isn't Jewish and doesn't allude to Jewish procedures for mourning, Hall's poems are certainly shaped by his inescapable awareness of the (endless) moment of death and of the (unending) fact of burial. In "Letter from Washington"—significantly undated—the poet confesses that during a professional meeting with "distinguished patrons/and administrators/of the arts," he was really "elsewhere," in the eternal present (and eternal presence) of his wife's never-ending dying:

in that room I never leave
where I sit beside you listening
to your altered breathing,
three quick inhalations

and a pause. I keep my body
before your large wide-open eyes
that do not blink or waver
in case they might finally see
—sitting beside you, attentive—
the one who will close them.

And in the carefully dated "Midsummer Letter"—the poem set "four months from the day/your chest went still" that follows "Letter from Washington"—Hall's mind "enter[s]/the coffin,/where even the white" of the Indian salwar kameez in which his wife chose to be buried paradoxically evokes the "absolute blackness" of the absence on which he perpetually focuses and to which, in poem after poem, he strives to speak. Again, then, in "Midwinter Letter," he hikes to his wife's grave through snow "a foot deep, but stiff," so "I sank down only a little," and finally in "Letter after a Year" he explains the relief he felt at being sustained by the hard snow, confessing that

All winter
when ice and snow kept me away
I worried that you missed me.
"Perkins! Where the hell
are you?"

"Perkins! Where the hell/are you?" The voice from beyond the grave is uncannily colloquial, cranky, wifely: the dead woman addresses her husband by his pet name, frets at *his* absence, and nags as if the two were safely, still, alive together. But if the wife is in fact (as we know) "beyond the grave"—"behind the veil!"— does this mean the husband, too, is somehow "beyond the grave," spiritually if not physically incorporated into the mysterious other world where his beloved has now so dreadfully settled? An eerie line from "Letter in Autumn"—a poem recording the "first October of your death"—fleetingly implies as much:

I sleep where we lived and died
in the painted Victorian bed

under the tiny lights
you strung on the headboard
when you brought me home
from the hospital four years ago.
The lights still burned last April
early on a Saturday morning
while you died.

That the couple "died" in "the painted Victorian bed" is no doubt in one sense a sexual fact, alluding to the "little deaths" of orgasms achieved throughout what other poems in Hall's sequence testify was an erotically joyous marriage. Yet the deliberate repetition of "died" at the end of this passage—"while *you* died"—underlines the double meaning of the phrase "where *we* lived and died." When the wife died, the coupledness of the couple died; thus, when the couple-as-couple died, the husband at least symbolically died too. And now, just as Hardy longed to be "folded away" with his dead wife, "Exposed to one weather/We both," Hall yearns to be literally as well as figuratively assimilated into the natural setting in which *his* wife is lodged. There in the New England graveyard, he enviously notes, the trees, seemingly indifferent to the griefs of autumn, "go on burning/without ravage of loss or disorder," go on, that is, in an oblivious fullness of being without the pain of knowing how much they are (in his title word) *without*. Declares the poet:

I wish you were that birch
rising from the clump behind you,
and I the gray oak alongside.

How inevitable it is, this wanting to join the beloved in death, this wild or wistful sense of death's plausibility, especially at those times—"All Soul's Day," the *Yahrzeit*—when the door of otherness seems to open and the lost voice speaks, sometimes crossly ("Perkins! Where the hell/are you?"), sometimes woefully ("Sem, it's so cold here"). Perhaps, then, the metaphorical death the mourner dies with every glance at the beloved's gravestone, every recurrence of the deathday or funeral time, inevitably evokes the "time future" that is as implicit in "time present" as is "time past"—the time when the mourner too will be not just figuratively but literally at death's door.

The epitaph has of course traditionally been as much a *memento mori* for its reader as it is a reminder of the one whose death and burial it confirms. And this is especially true when the spirit of the dead seems to speak from beyond the grave in an icy prosopopoeia—a speech of absence attributed to the departed by poet or stonecarver (or perhaps planned in advance by the one who was to die). "Look on my works, ye mighty, and despair," pronounces the ghost of Shelley's "Ozymandias," once a "king of kings." "Cast a cold eye, on life, on death/Horseman, pass by!" commands William Butler Yeats, on the tombstone that he asked to have planted "Under Ben Bulben." More ironically, "Life is a jest; and all things show it./I thought so once; but now I know it," declares the Restoration playwright John Gay, author of the scathingly cynical *Beggar's Opera*, while more plaintively (but perhaps most persuasively) one "Master Elginbrod" inscribes a public prayer on his stone:

Here lie I, Master Elginbrod.
Have mercy on my soul, O God,
As I would have if I were God
And thou wert Master Elginbrod.

How desperately the dead seem to want to instruct us—or even God—from beyond the grave!

Such instructive epitaphs, however, record the terms of a generalized fate rather than a specific, individual destiny; they're addressed to all who fear the *Dies Irae, Dies Illa* of death and judgment—which is to say, they're addressed to *all*. But to the husband or wife, lover or child, sibling or parent of a singular, much-loved dead person, the tombstone speaks with greater particularity, unveiling the mystery of "time future." And sometimes the loving mourner struggles, himself or herself, to unveil that mystery. In 1641, for instance, Lady Catherine Dyer caused the following epitaph to be engraved on the monument she erected to her husband, Sir William Dyer, in Colmworth Church, Bedfordshire:

My dearest dust, could not thy hasty day
Afford thy drowzy patience leave to stay
One hower longer: so that we might either
Sate up, or gone to bedd together?
But since thy finisht labor hath possest
Thy weary limbs with early rest,
Enjoy it sweetly: and thy widdowe bride
Shall soone repose her by thy slumbering side.
Whose business, now, is only to prepare
My nightly dress, and call to prayre:
Mine eyes wax heavy and ye day growes old.
The dew falls thick, my beloved growes cold.
Draw, draw ye closed curtaynes: and make room:
My dear, my dearest dust; I come, I come.

By turns erotic and rueful, gently chiding and delicately resigned, Dyer's epitaph is also—isn't it?—subtly chilling: "Mine eyes wax heavy and ye day growes old./The dew falls thick, my beloved growes cold." Physically cold in death, the husband grows emotionally colder as he journeys away from his wife into death's forgetfulness; and as the day of her life draws to its end, the "widdowe bride" prepares for the only consummation she can now imagine— a (re)union with what is now, though dear, no more than "dust."

Our contemporaries are perhaps even fiercer in their transcriptions of the individual, mortal truths learned through incursions and recursions of the epitaphic moment. In *The Father*—a series of passionate elegies for her father, who comes, in the course of the collection, to represent the flesh that is "father" to all of us— Sharon Olds records a graveside education in the sheer materiality of death. "One Year," for instance, examines the literal revelations displayed above, beside, and below the stone unveiled at the *Yahrzeit*:

When I got to his marker, I sat on it,
like sitting on the edge of someone's bed
and I rubbed the smooth, speckled granite.
I took some tears from my jaw and neck
and started to wash a corner of his stone. . . .

Ants ran down into the grooves of his name
and dates, down into the oval track of the
first name's O, middle name's O,
the short O of the last name,
and down into the hyphen between
his birth and death—little trough of his life . . .
I saw the speedwell on the ground with its horns,
the coiled ferns, copper-beech blossoms, each
petal like that disc of matter which
swayed, on the last day, on his tongue. . . .
Then I lay down on my father's grave.
The sun shone down on me, the powerful
ants walked on me. When I woke,
my cheek was crumbly, yellowish
with a mustard plaster of earth. Only
at the last minute did I think of his body
actually under me, the can of
bone, ash, soft as a goosedown
pillow that bursts in bed with the lovers.
When I kissed his stone it was not enough,
when I licked it my tongue went dry a moment, I
ate his dust, I tasted my dirt host.

Intensely detailed, Olds's communion with the eucharist of earth—the "dirt host" that *is* her father and in which her father is embedded—is relatively serene, as the poet wills herself to come to terms with the meaning of her own impending termination as well as her father's. In "The Swimmer," for example, the poem that follows "One Year," she celebrates the oblivion she finds when she "throw[s]" herself "like a sperm" into the sea, insisting that then

I am like those elements my father turned into,
smoke, bone, salt. It is one of
the only things I like to do
anymore, get down inside the horizon
and feel what his new life is like, how
clean, how blank, how griefless, how without error—
the trance of matter.

Yet for every poem that is a least ostensibly "griefless" or even (like those by Hall, Hardy, Dyer) sadly desirous in its contemplation of the epitaphic moment in which each mourner must inexorably become the one who is mourned rather than the one who mourns, there are notable others that explore the *"timor mortis"* whose perturbations have preoccupied poets for centuries. Detached from the specifics of grief, Michael Fried's "A Block of Ice" is almost surrealistically scary in the purity of dread it dramatizes:

I stamp my foot and a black wave races across the field,
I close my eyes and white stones spring up that I must avoid,
My hand in the freezing water gropes for but fails to find a block of ice
On which to sign my name and the date and hour of my death.

But Ted Hughes's "The Stone" is subtler in its examination of the historicity that groups deaths together, forthrightly linking one inscription to another in what we might think of as an epitaphic chain. The gravestone (that will literally or figuratively bind his name to another's—presumably a wife's), writes Hughes,

Has not yet been cut.
It is too heavy already
For consideration. Its edges
Are so super-real, already,
And at this distance,
They cut real cuts in the unreal
Stuff of just thinking. So I leave it.
Somewhere it is.
Soon it will come.
I shall not carry it. With horrible life
It will transport its face, with sure strength,
To sit over mine, wherever I look,
Instead of hers.
It will even have across its brow
Her name.

When my children and I were ordering the stone that was to mark my husband's grave, we were given the option of inscribing my name, too, as well as my date of birth, on the polished granite.

Some people make that choice, said the solicitous representative of the Sunset View Cemetery, in El Cerrito, California, to save time and money "later." The kids were, I think, appalled at such an "option." And I? I was frightened and, I guess, somewhat taken aback by the certainties implicit in the gesture: not, obviously, the certainty that I'd some day die but, say, the certainty that we could foresee if not when, *where* and *how* I'd die (somewhere safely within reach of the Sunset View Cemetery, not in a plane crash, a shipwreck or a distant jungle or, or—). And maybe we were even bemused by the implied certainty that California wouldn't be ripped apart by the earthquake ("the big one"!) everyone fears, the certainty the Sunset View Cemetery itself wouldn't tumble into the Pacific. So we said "No thank you" to the man who was taking our order for Elliot's stone, "No thank you, *just leave a space.*"

And there's a dark space on the stone, a blank to be filled in—a blank I see every time I visit my husband's grave. Wrote T. S. Eliot,

> *Time present and time past*
> *Are both perhaps present in time future*
> *And time future contained in time past,*

His metaphysical musings seem, now, suddenly to mean that in some sense time past and time future are both implicit in the annual, mournful recurrence of the *Yahrzeit.* Thus if this day of suffering bread and bitter herbs is, like the first night of Passover, a time when I reenact "remembered agony," it's also a time where a premonition of my own future is buried—a day on which, willingly or unwillingly, I have to say "My dear, my dearest dust, I come, I come."

Gary Adelman

Naming Beckett's Unnamable

THIS ESSAY POSES THE PROBLEM, WHO IS THE TITLE CHARACTER
in *The Unnamable*, the third novel in Samuel Beckett's celebrated
trilogy? Beckett wrote the novels in French in the late 1940s, *Molloy* and *Malone Dies* appearing in 1951, *The Unnamable* in 1953,
and translated them himself into English in the mid-1950s.

In the first section of the essay I explore the voice of *The Unnamable*. In the second, I offer three frames of reference for contemplating its identity. The first frame, that the text enacts an explo-
ration of the origins of artistic creation, belongs to the critical
literature on *The Unnamable*. In the second frame, the Unnamable
represents the conscience of an ethical person, striving for an
impossibly elusive justice. Here I follow Anthony Uhlmann on
Levinas, Derrida, and *The Unnamable*. The third frame is my own
idea based on a continuous impression about the work and the
spiritual excitement to which it gives rise. I explore the connection between the text and oral testimonies of survivors of the

Holocaust, making use of Maurice Blanchot's *The Writing of the Disaster* to draw out the suggestive correspondences. As interpretations, my three approaches parallel and reinforce each other.

1

The Unnamable, a confessional monologue like the other novels in the trilogy, consists entirely of the narrator's speculations about his "situation." Where the voice comes from must be inferred. Facts are impossible to ascertain. The strongest impression is of a voice emanating from a presence, a demi-urge; it has been selected, its turn come round perhaps, to be born human, to undergo the passage. It refuses to cooperate. It does not want existence, and it/his courage enlists our admiration. He bears a faint resemblance, which he himself notes, to Prometheus. But where is he? Alone, in darkness, riveted in a fixed position. Is he in a pit? A dungeon? Does the space he inhabits have a shape? He speculates, and one speculation gives rise to another. He is being acted upon by a delegation of socializers—sadists—preparing and training him for existence. But how does he know what he knows about life? How is it he has what seem to be memories? Had he a prior existence? And who is he whom he calls himself? Can there be an "I," a self, that is not the construct of human shaping? This is desperate business, and there is nothing concrete, evidentiary, to go on. Can there be an "I," a me, a pre-existent self prior to socialization, prelinguistic? If so, how can he get back to that self?

All his inquiries about who he is, and where, and why, and the conjectures and suppositions and stories they give rise to, constitute his force of arms, so to say, against the necessity of existing. It is what keeps him going and what keeps at bay the dreadful suspicion that he is speaking from dictation, that the personae of his stories are decoys tempting his acquiescence to the life process.

He combats despair with seemingly endless "perhapses," suppositions about his situation in which escape is possible. One of his favorite constructions, which he returns to for fortitude, postulates a master with an agenda opposite to that of the master's delegates, a persecutorial junta determined to give him existence. The master wants something from him, some perception of his situation, some word or words before releasing him; so he must go on in the hope of coming up with that something unbeknownst to him that will satisfy the master "before I can be let loose, alone, in the unthinkable unspeakable, where I have not ceased to be, where they will not let me be" (*The Unnamable* 335). His implacable aversion to being given a life generates parodies about life's triviality and awfulness, and gives meaning to his resistance. We are persuaded that his resistance is wise, which is one source of the novel's enthralling effect.

The narrator begins with the surmise that there is an "I" unshaped by life. But it is only surmise. In any case, he cannot reinhabit that time. Therefore, "It" would be more appropriate than I. "It, say it, not knowing what" (291). True, he speaks, but about what, whom— him? But presuming he has a presence, an "I," how differentiate his being from the constructs foisted upon it by others and by himself? Is there a rock-bottom, authentic, naked, palpitating, conscious "I" with its own sound? What sound? How sound it? The very voicing of words, language, vastly distances him from this pre-linguistic self, if it exists at all. He refuses to cooperate, he does not want existence; but does not the ceaseless monologue prove he already exists? And why has he been put in such a situation? He is angry, he feels he has been had. He speaks on and on to get at the nub of himself while speaking at the same time prevents him from getting at the nub. What is necessary to find the core self, which in any case living will extinguish? "Perhaps in the end I shall smother in a throng. Incessant comings and goings, the crush and bustle of a bargain sale" (292). He wonders if he is a final recrudescence of consciousness, a vanishing presence still responding to intimations of a core self. Wherever he is—and the question "where?" generates continuous speculation—it is preferable to the losing of self in life's repulsive clownishness.

Some of his speculations float off undeveloped, to be jettisoned; yet, for the moment, they fuel his will to protest. His only fuel is speculation.

Perhaps the "I" he is in search of is the "he" condemned to the opaque void he inhabits and perhaps always inhabited. He thinks of Lucifer punished for protesting creation; but why, he wonders, does he emulate creation, making up stories, representing life, babbling ideas that are not his own? Can such knowledge be innate, or has it all "been rammed down my gullet" (298)? Fellow feeling, love, a moral sense—he snorts at these travesties. Despite his deep suspicion of his personae, he chooses to speculate that his creative drive expresses an obscure need to find and reveal his true self, a frenzy to speak in order to achieve silence—the invisible retreat; speaking, endless speaking, fictionalizing, creating, in the hope of hitting upon the magic word, the open door, to his core self; that through misdirection and lies he may chance upon the truth that will free him from his torment.

Torment, physical torment: "my body incapable of the smallest movement" (300–301). His eyes are incapable of closing, "but must remain forever fixed and staring on the narrow space before them. . . . They must be as red as live coals" (301). So he perseveres; he must go on in order to end. "[T]o end would be wonderful, no matter who I am, no matter where I am" (302).

Dread arises at the prospect of some ghastly recurrence, the process endlessly repeating itself, his refusal scripted. The question, what drives him and towards what, when he creates, that is, orders experience by speaking, cuts to the heart of his situation. Dread compels him to return to it repeatedly. What if he were being driven to speak "in obedience to the unintelligible terms of an incomprehensible damnation" (308)? His attention ought instead to be fixed on the "feeble murmur" of the essential self, barely audible because of the noise he was making. He speculates that it might be better if he were simply to keep on saying, "babababa" than drone on with suppositions and stories that tempt him away from his essential self (308). For the "he" in the stories he tells, the persona-narrator, Mahood, speaks with his voice, with a voice woven into his, testifying for him, living in his stead, "preventing me from saying who I was, what I was" (309). Why does he do it, then? Out of compulsion? A new speculation emerges:

Yes, I have a pensum to discharge, before I can be free. . . . I was given a pensum, at birth perhaps, as a punishment for having

been born perhaps, or for no particular reason, because they dislike me (310).

How did it come about, this inner need to speak, that is, to
become complicit in his socialization, education, existence? Ah,
the sadists molding him, Basil, the most hateful, had made him
feel an inner need to expiate his recalcitrance. He creates Mahood,
Basil internalized, in order to discharge the pensum and "obtain
his [master's] forgiveness" (311).

He has found a loophole through a fairy tale: he speaks in order
to please his master! But what is it that his master wants to hear?
"Let the man explain himself and have done with it. It's none of
my business to ask him questions, even if I knew how to reach
him. . . . assuming he exists and, existing, hears me" (313).

He provides other speculations: he posits a junta of masters dif-
fering in their opinions of what they want from him; and then
wonders why they do not just wash their hands of him; and further
speculates that it is all a lie, that he invented the whole "business
of a labour to accomplish, before I can end, of words to say, a truth
to recover . . . in the hope it would console me, help me to go on"
(314). He contradicts each speculation and then contradicts the
contradiction, on and on, running to stay in place.

But he is resilient. He tries the old pathways again, seeking new
avenues of speculation, which is his only way of challenging futility. So, prodding at the motive of his creative drive, he speculates
that his persona, Mahood, is a decoy, a lure, and a usurper cozen-
ing him into being a living human specimen. "Then they uncorked
the champagne. One of us at last! Green with anguish! A real little terrestrial!" (316). Well, then, he decides mockingly, a story to
tempt him towards conformity, a story to give satisfaction to his
teachers, a story about the "me" they would have him admit to
being.

"In a word I was returning to the fold" (317). In the new story,
he, Mahood, the one-legged wanderer on crutches, arrives at what
appears more like a concentration camp than a home: a "vast yard
or campus, surrounded by high walls, its surface an amalgam of dirt
and ashes" (317); the family house "windowless, but well furnished

with loopholes" (317); all his kith and kin "with their eyes glued to the slits" (318) watching at night "[w]ith the help of a search-light" (318). They spot him and cheer. And then they all die, "the whole ten or eleven of them, carried off by sausage-poisoning" (318).

The idea of ties, liability to pain, of being schooled, made delicately susceptible to suffering in a world licking its chops, a Schopenhauerian world, or better yet, Hitlerian, a world of catastrophe—"this circus where it is enough to breathe to qualify for asphyxiation"—goads the Unnamable into several different accounts of his homecoming (323). Was he repelled, turned back "by the noise of their agony, then by the smell of their corpses" and "wafts of decomposition" (321, 322)? No, he reasons, the truth more likely is that he did not turn aside and vomit, beating a retreat from the stench and groans. He entered the building.

[A]nd there completed my rounds, stamping under foot the unrecognizable remains of my family, here a face, there a stomach, as the case might be, and sinking into them with the ends of my crutches, both coming and going. To say I did so with satisfaction would be stretching the truth. For my feeling was rather one of annoyance at having to flounder in such muck (323).

The point of this extravaganza is to stick it to his teachers. "Do they consider me so plastered with their rubbish that I can never extricate myself, never make a gesture but their cast must come to life" (325)? But the more likely truth is that "[t]hey've blown me up with their voices, like a balloon," and that there is no escaping speaking the way they intend him to speak, "that is to say about them, even with execration and disbelief" (325, 326).

He decides to tell another one of Mahood's stories. Why? "To heighten my disgust," he says, i.e., disgust for them, his tormenters, or disgust at playing into their hands (326). But he also speculates, "Perhaps I'll find traces of myself" (325).

Mahood II is a strangely heroic version of the narrator's situation: an impish little fellow sans arms and legs, housed in a deep glass jar, so very brave under the circumstances, his jar festooned with Chinese lanterns and the menu of the restaurant across the

street. He hangs as an advertisement. In part it is a joke, an entertainment, an escape from self, and how the tale keeps him going,
imagining this Mahood thinking away the day, earning an income,
maintaining a relationship with the proprietress of the chophouse,
who changes his straw once a week; a competent social unit be-
stowing his benison on the proprietress's family in the way of fer-
tilizer for their kitchen garden during the growing season, nothing
but a puckish grin on his face when his mouth had been visible,
before having been throttled by a cement collar.

Inevitably the narrator's distrust and fear of his creative drive
kills it. He returns to himself, his mood brittle and volatile. He is
being sported with. His creative urge has been instilled in him by
the enforcers, and serves their ends, not his. He must hold out
against their influence, refusing life "until they have abandoned
me as inutilizable." Then the master will "give me quittance" (331).
Or, the more desperate version of the fairy tale: it is only by pleasing his persecutors, i.e., giving vent to his creative drive, and perhaps in portraying "how to succeed at last" in being human, that
he may please his master. According to this theory, he must lose
himself, "behave as if he were not," by creating fictional self-repre-
sentations, thereby taking on existence, and believe in the lie,
before being allowed to go silent (334). He must deny his intrinsic
self with conviction in order to receive his master's praise. Here,
the creative urge is an angling for mercy. "The essential is to go on
squirming forever at the end of the line" (338).

A sudden playful mood leads him back to Mahood II. He enters
his persona, recalling times before the collar had stifled him. A
fatalistic tone slips in: if only he could die. But how does he know
that he himself is an autonomous being, alive? Immediately the
narrator expresses his predicament as Mahood II, the bottle dweller,
who is suddenly aware that nobody takes notice of him, not even
those who stop to study the menu attached to his jar. How could
this be? "The flies vouch for me, if you like, but how far? Would
they not settle with equal appetite on a lump of cowshit?" (341).

The game afoot is how to prove he exists. The narrator's loophole is his fairy tale—pleasing his master, proving to be one of the
"chosen shits" of "a sporting God" (338). His existence is based on

that of his master; as for the little rascal in the jar, he finds proof of his substantiality in the proprietress's attention to him. "Would she rid me of my paltry excrements every Sunday, make me a nest at the approach of winter, protect me from the snow, change my sawdust, rub salt into my scalp, I hope I'm not forgetting anything, if I were not there?" (343). Why, she must love him!

The novel's form—of constant contradiction, modification, and counter speculation, or more precisely, of hopeful constructions negated in reiterated variations—creates the illusion of perpetual motion, a going round and round in endlessly circling interpretations of the narrator's situation. Three affirmative constructions give rise to numerous negations:

1) The Unnamable narrator speaks in order to catch a trace of his essential self, his intrinsic "I" trying to emerge, but the characters he has created, his various personae, the Murphys, Molloys, Malones, and Mahoods, reveal to him nothing about himself, and he continues to doubt that he has an independent existence.

2) He speaks to put an end to things, to come upon a formula, a phrase, that will free him from the necessity to speak. But his stories—representations of himself "in the midst of men, the light of day"—are told under compulsion, as part of his socialization (297). He is a mere puppet speaking from dictation whose existence is the enactment of an unintelligible damnation. He is trapped in a circuit, endlessly repeating himself, damned like the Sybil, condemned in a jar to an undying existence.

3) He speaks either to prove himself intractable and "inutilizable" or to display obedience to his socializers—losing himself in his personae, adapting to life, showing conviction—in either case in order to please his master and receive quittance. But the master remains distant, his purpose hidden, his torturers adept.

The fairy tale of a loophole, a spur to his ongoing monologue, is repeatedly exploded by two additional powerful negations: he speaks merely to console himself; he suffers merely to amuse his torturers.

Worm, a shadowy persona little more than a name, emerges as an occasion for describing the sadism of the socializers, the life-shapers. In some accounts, Worm is the embryo of the speaker:

There he is now with breath in his nostrils, it only remains for him to suffocate. . . . A head has grown out of his ear, the better to enrage him. . . . It's a transformer in which sound is turned, without the help of reason, to rage and terror. . . . The rascal, he's getting humanized, he's going to lose if he doesn't watch out, if he doesn't take care, and with what could he take care, with what could he form the faintest conception of the condition they are decoying him into, with their ears, their eyes, their tears and a brainpan where anything may happen (355–356, 360).

Worm's continuous persecution (birthing) elicits this and other anti-creation stories.

"The dirty pack of fake maniacs" (368) are expertly trained in what they do, till Worm is violated, had, sufficiently throttled: "[t]hen the blaze, the capture and the paean" (366). Then "diapers bepissed and the first long trousers" (378). But they won't catch the narrator.

The pace quickens, injecting a note of panic in the breathless protest. But safe in the labyrinth of speculation, he can still joke about the awfulness of life, and even parody his own aversion for it. The human specimen: "sight failing, chronic gripes, light diet, shit well tolerated, hearing failing, heart irregular, sweet-tempered, smell failing, heavy sleeper, no erections, would you like some more. . . . yes, I was right, no doubt about it this time, it's you all over" (377).

Abjuration: "[S]ome people are lucky, born of a wet dream and dead before morning" (379–380).

But suddenly, the climax: a disabling and mortal acknowledgement is made, it would seem, admitting the futility of his protest. It could well serve as the culmination of the spectacle, signifying capitulation, if it did not occur thirty or so pages from the end—if *The Unnamable* ended in defeat:

[N]o need of a mouth, the words are everywhere, inside me, outside me . . . impossible to stop them, impossible to stop, I'm in words, made of words, others' words, what others, the place too, the air, the walls, the floor, the ceiling, all words, the whole world is here with me, I'm the air, the walls, the walled-in one, everything yields, opens, ebbs, flows, like flakes, I'm all these flakes, meeting, mingling, falling asunder, wherever I go I find me, leave me, go towards me, come from me, nothing ever but me, a particle of me, retrieved, lost, gone astray, I'm all these words, all these strangers, this dust of words . . . and nothing else, yes, something else, that I'm something quite different, a quite different thing, a wordless thing in an empty place, a hard shut dry cold black place, where nothing stirs, nothing speaks, and that I listen, and that I seek, like a caged beast born of caged beasts born of caged beasts born of caged beasts born in a cage and dead in a cage, born and then dead, born in a cage and then dead in a cage, in a word like a beast, in one of their words, like such a beast, and that I seek, like such a beast, with my little strength, such a beast (386–387).

Since he has no identity, if he speaks, it must be ventriloquism. If he can be said to have an identity, it is trapped in an inescapable circuit. And his hope of an end to his torment? Of course, the hope is fiction, too. There is no escaping existence.

A mind in search of a way out of its own circularity becomes frantic. Is the speaker "I," or do I speak from dictation? How do I know what I know? Can life be understood only from words? Why cannot this voice go silent? What can be said of the real silence? Where am I?

Enormous prison, like a hundred thousand cathedrals . . . and in it, somewhere, perhaps, riveted, tiny, the prisoner . . . it will be unending . . . wait somewhere else, for your turn to go again . . . it's a circuit, a long circuit . . . it's a lie . . . all lies (409–411).

On and on goes the mind, accelerating, touching all the nodal points. From where did he get his stories? "[I]t's such an old habit, I do it without heeding" (413). Or, they are expressions of his fortitude to go on. Or, the life-shapers have taught him to internalize their lessons. Or, they are born out of a need to find traces of himself, the time that exists before the voice. "I'm waiting for me there." Or, "all words, there's nothing else" (414). And on and on.

The narrative consists of the reiterated variations of these speculations and counter speculations, while within the work nothing
progresses (unless it be a breathlessness and tone of urgency and
desperation). Perhaps the book is a portrayal about how a mind
copes with inevitability. The inevitability is death, inverted in the
novel so that life becomes inevitable, while the labor of denial, the
pathetic strategies to which one clings for solace, remain the same.
The inversion, in which life takes on the repugnance usually reserved for death, broadens the satire on human existence. The
novel, then, may seem to explore and give fullness to Camus's
statement that the only question worth answering is whether or
not to commit suicide. Is the Unnamable heroic, Promethean, the
indomitable human spirit? Or does he represent the abjectness, the
mean grubbiness, of the desire to live?

The portrayal needs to be a long piece because the reader must
be made to endure this emotional state in time. The only dimension is time. There is no progression and no three-dimensional
world. It all exists in a point. Could the book be a kind of formal
design, a structure of prisms and refractions? One struggles to say
what the novel suggests as an abstract composition.

In a "manifesto" on art, "Three Dialogues,"[1] which Beckett
wrote in December 1949 when struggling with the final part of *The
Unnamable*, he says that the true artist must turn away from "the
plane of the feasible" in disgust, "weary of its puny exploits, weary
of pretending to be able, of being able, of doing a little better the
same old thing, of going a little further along a dreary road" (*Disjecta* 139). The only stance, he goes on to say, is "that there is
nothing to express, nothing with which to express, nothing from
which to express, no power to express, no desire to express, together with the obligation to express" (139). He dismisses the idea
that he is calling for a minimalist art, stripped, abstract, expressive
of the void, or inner emptiness. No, Beckett says: the artist must
turn away from anything and everything "doomed to become occasion" for expression, including his predicament, which "is expressive of the impossibility to express" (144, 143). "Art loves leaps"

("L'art adore les sauts," *Disjecta* 128), he says, and notes in his letter to Axel Kaun, "[o]r is literature alone to remain behind in the
old lazy ways that have been so long ago abandonded by music and
painting? . . . An assault against words in the name of beauty"
(*Disjecta* 172, 173).

The main points of Beckett's aesthetic are these: Objective unity
is an illusion. Efforts to create coherent artistic form are deadening
falsifications. The essence of the object is resistance to representation. The artist moreover is torn by a need to disparage his desire
for order and structure and to disrupt it altogether. Art can only
represent the instability of the subject and the indeterminacy of
the object. A new art form is needed, one which of necessity must
always be a failure both as objective representation and as subjective expression. The artist either strives for the new or is an anti-
quarian.

Perhaps *The Unnamable* can be discussed only as a series of formal manipulations. Perhaps its effect is like that of a Rorschach
blot, "unintentionally provocative; not a created object but a creative one, or better still, no object at all but a concatenation of
possibilities, limited by nothing but the mind's capacity to endow
shape with meaning" (States 6). Perhaps it is the shape of the
unheard hysteria that is the mental landscape of *Waiting for Godot*.
Beckett wrote the play as a "relaxation" before embarking on *The
Unnamable*. Perhaps the novel is the abstract music of a frenzied
collapsing of that small, private stock of ideas, the permutations of
which always protected one from an engulfing sense of nothingness.

Within the broad critique of the human condition that, one
might argue, is the chief aim of the novel, Beckett also searches for
the source of artistic creation. Whomever the man is who is doing
the talking, says Maurice Blanchot in his 1959 essay "Where Now?
Who Now?," it is not Beckett, "but the necessity that has displaced
him," making "him a nameless being," "masked . . . by a porous
and agonizing 'I'" at "the empty, actuated site where the summons
of the work reverberates." What is enacted, Blanchot suggests, is
"the fundamental exaction of the work" experienced at the search
for its point of departure. It cannot be authored in the sense of

managed, controlled, a product of the familiar, "the commodity of an available reality." The searching must be done stripped of most attributes of the world and involves a falling "out of the world," a "hovering between being and nothingness," where the self dissolves into its new creation. So the novel is an enactment of the process by which the author makes himself available as mediator to the unspoken (144, 147).

Andrew K. Kennedy adds "that what is being projected here is the writer's consciousness caught in a verbal no-man's land. . . . [a]t an imagined mid-point, somewhere between the discarded and not yet created personae" (141). Knowledge of the world is continuously being inflicted upon the speaking "I" by an external agency, deputies of some higher authority that would control, dictate the new genesis, interfering with the quasi-magical incantation that will allow the artist to be silent, dissolving into his character.

> [Y]ou must say words, as long as there are any, until they find me, until they say me, strange pain, strange sin, you must go on, perhaps it's done already, perhaps they have said me already, perhaps they have carried me to the threshold of my story, before the door that opens on my story, that would surprise me, if it opens, it will be I, it will be the silence, where I am, I don't know, I'll never know, in the silence you don't know, you must go on, I can't go on, I'll go on. (*The Unnamable* 414).

In Anthony Uhlmann's philosophical study of Beckett's trilogy (1999), the Unnamable's resistance against the it/they attempting to absorb him is "one of extraordinary power" (184). At issue is his identity. But how prevail in his struggle to preserve it—how escape the labyrinth of language that is not his, and that in no way constitutes him? Uhlmann suggests that the Unnamable's desperate struggle exemplifies a striving for justice.

He develops his discussion in counterpoint with works of philosophy by Emmanuel Levinas and Jacques Derrida, underscoring the resonances, the philosophical ways of thinking, that shed light on the novel.[2] Beckett inverts Levinas, for whom language is a link between the ego and others and is primarily aligned with justice. Injustice arises from the efforts of the ego to reappropriate the

315

other into its totality. In *The Unnamable*, the other moves to appropriate the "I," or ego, "by playing it with its language and hauling
it into the light of its day" (161). So, in Beckett, language is aligned
with injustice, and the Unnamable is in the impossible situation of
being enveloped in a closed system of injustice and violence, and
striving for freedom.

What constitutes striving? Derrida suggests, says Uhlmann, ethical awareness, i.e., responsibility for the hospitality of the world
the newly born enter, and for keeping the lessons of history alive.
It is a struggle against immurement in "the (fixed) presence of the
present," which Derrida suggests is the worst form of injustice
(182). Derrida's phrase is close to the Russian *poshlost*, living a life
without consequences or contexts. In Uhlmann's view, the Unnamable's resistance "is resistance to [Derrida's] entire discourse of self-
presence" (184), a dynamic picture of ethical striving for the impossibility of justice to which the alternative is spiritual death.

It seems possible that Beckett's Unnamable narrator merged in
his mind with the idea of the Jew survivor of the Holocaust. There
are striking correspondences throughout the narrative: in the
laments, which evoke concentration camps, annihilation camps;
in the narrator's torments and fate, laced with the imagery of pits,
fires, furnaces, ashes, and the implements of torture, and in the
sadistic adeptness of his persecutors. The suggestive material is
extensive, and had to have been drawn from Beckett's familiarity
with and closeness to the German atrocities. Beckett spent the
years 1942 to 1945 in Roussillon, a village in the southwest of
Vichy France, living among Jews from all over Europe who had
fled there and who were trying to survive the war. Initially, he was
mistaken for a Jew. His biographer, James Knowlson, believes
Beckett saw film footage in 1947 about the liberation of Bergen-
Belsen, Dachau, and Auschwitz, and that in the same year he read
two remarkable memoirs describing life in Mauthausen (Knowlson
344). The idea of the Jew behind the Unnamable is sustained by
the narrator's "anonymity," "loss of self," "loss of all sovereignty,"
"utter uprootedness," "radical alienation" (terms from Blanchot's
The Writing of the Disaster).[3] He, too, has been worn down past the
nub to the point where all values have been exterminated, surviv-

ing in nihilistic desolation, where all objective order has been given up. He, too, is waiting, "awaiting a misfortune which is not still to come, but which has always already come upon [him]," a knowledge that impoverishes all experience (Blanchot, *Disaster* 18, 21).

Both the Unnamable narrator and the Jew survivor of the death camps have the double consciousness of different kinds of knowledge, which interact and intersect continuously. The distinction, in Blanchot's terms, is between "knowledge of the disaster," the reflection of a person in the secure present, a value-oriented and judgment-based remembering which seeks to reassure, to mediate, and to skirt the subversive experience of the devastation; and "knowledge as disaster," the unmediated experience of the devastation, which assaults the very integrity of the self. The Unnamable narrator exists at the site of anguished experience where the disaster is taking place. But for the survivor, the disaster is present as an absence. It is the "un-story" (Blanchot's term) in the Mahood stories (28).

Surviving in the normal world, through creating personae, means in Blanchot's words:

> [Y]ou are dead already, in an immemorial past, of a death which was not yours, which you have thus neither known nor lived, but under the threat of which you believe you are called upon to live; you await it henceforth in the future, constructing a future to make it possible at last—possible as something that will take place and will belong to the realm of experience. (65)

Through the lens of Blanchot, in *The Unnamable*, the "pensum," the need to go on, to exist, to create a self adapted for life in the normal world, expresses an inner need to pay off a debt for not having died. Death is the "un-story" in the Mahood stories, death invading the space of survival, "absence in its vivacity," "[making] the real impossible and desire undesirable" (Blanchot, *Disaster* 51, 66)—relentlessly reducing the personae, stripping away their humanity in a progression from one-legged Mahood I to limbless Mahood II to shadowy Worm. Both Mahoods are dying of deaths they have not lived or known.

The Unnamable narrator depends on and suspects his personae, needing to enact his death through them, but distrusting their commerce with life. The voices glide into one another, merge, and become double voiced. Mahood I suggests that some human bonds are inviolable while simultaneously mocking such an idea. Mahood II maintains a measure of humanity while simultaneously excluding himself from the cosmic order, giving a terrible poignancy to his ludicrous parody of imposing a meaningful sequence on the details of his life.

The Unnamable character, in the hell of deep memory, keeps himself going by creating personae through whom he enacts his death, a totally paradoxical killing of the self by the self in order to keep the self alive. Death is due; it is an atonement. Wrapping his death in the mythology of life is a part of the atonement; for the exposing of lies, the mocking of life, the parody, condemns existence and maintains the austere imaginative space within which the Unnamable atones for continuing an existence in which his death is due. He suffers from survivor guilt.

There is no closure. The demand for closure would be a demand for moral meaning. Similarly, the staples of fiction—plot, description, symbol, dialogue, scene, a sense of character—imply consequence and are discarded. There are no lessons, there is no consoling future. Life is disaster.

Hence, the Unnamable narrator speaks from "the absolute passiveness of total abjection" (Blanchot, *Disaster* 15). Between life and death, that is where he is, crushed, a destroyed man—a mussulman (in the concentration camps, one who gives up). The voice is the interior life of the mussulman, who is neither living nor dead, refusing, resisting both life and death.

His consciousness is at a remove from the reality of the camp. His former life seems a dream; he does not believe in it, or that the he in it, if it is a memory, is he. He cannot be sure he has a self, an "I," apart from the master. He longs for a former time, but a time out of the world, a time in which he existed in the peace and silence of a restful mind. Clinging to that keeps him going, though the end must be a given, his fate in the hands of the master.

His eyes, mental eyes, are never shut; but there is no light in them. He would not see the world they would wrest him into. The voice of his thought is continuous, a soundless, incessant noise. It is his universe's element, his world's oxygen, a realm between nothingness, oblivion, and the master's domain, where his agents, whom he can no longer see or hear, would inflict upon him the horror of life.

Why then not simply oblivion? Why does he lie to himself, tease himself about escape, "quittance," from this realm between nothingness and horror to another "unthinkable unspeakable" existence? He cannot answer this question. He dreads and evades it, and spins round and round it. He knows that his ceaseless thinking is madness, yet believes that his madness is a kind of vigilance and refusal. Blanchot says that a mute protest rises out of the crushed victim's refusal to be blamed for the crimes of his persecutors, and also out of his tormented need to be held accountable, to "answer for the impossibility of being responsible." His continued existence is a bond of "friendship for that which has passed leaving no trace" (*Disaster* 25, 27).

So he protests, keeping that other world at a remove, enclosed within his thoughts, railing at his persecutors and resisting his own oblivion. He can even laugh, not at the life of the camp, known, felt, seen suggestively through the glaze of his retraction, sometimes almost starkly seen, as in, "the distant gleams of piteous fires biding their hour to promote us to ashes" (*The Unnamable* 306). His laughter is turned rather on the former world, the once normal world, serving to buoy him like a life preserver leaking air: the cynical cracks about human nature, black retellings of the story of creation, wisecracks about the overrated human emotions, grotesqueries concerning the ties that bind, mad cacklings about the average human specimen, and on and on, though he may be merely a rat treading water in a tall pail, encouraged, wagered on, a sporting event; kept going by the dumb, elementary force of life.

Perhaps his Mahood tales arise on the insistent tide of this force, stories about a former life in a former world, but sardonically afflicted by his knowledge of the world as it is. He would laugh if the question of his continuing were not desperate, and if laughter, the feeling of freedom in its burst and expansiveness, did not instantly petrify under the scrutiny of the master grasping him by the chin with a hand like a cement collar.

What did the master want of him—oblivion? Life? If they were the only alternatives, if the other, the possibility of "quittance," of being "let loose, alone, in the unthinkable unspeakable," was a lie, he could not goad himself to take another step (*The Unnamable* 335). But, "impossible to find out, that's where you're buggered," and "[t]he best is not to decide anything, in this connexion, in advance. . . . Time will tell," and so forth, and so on, and inevitably "slipping, though not yet at the last extremity, towards the resorts of fable" (*The Unnamable* 412, 292, 308).

In this way he keeps at bay the absurdity of his hope of quittance. He blows bubbles and then bursts them, taking a modicum of strength from his jaunty moods, before blowing them again, and bursting them again, when with bitter jocularity he tells it as it is, sucking it up, breasting forward: "You've been sufficiently assassinated, sufficiently suicided, to be able now to stand on your own feet, like a big boy," and "They can't do everything. They put you on the right road, led you by the hand to the very brink of the precipice, now it's up to you, with an unassisted last step, to show them your gratitude" though the whole production is nothing more than a moribund's dreadful subterranean activity (*The Unnamable* 333).

Bibliography

Beckett, Samuel. *Disjecta: Miscellaneous Writings and a Dramatic Fragment*. Ed. Ruby Cohn. London: John Calder, 1983.

———. *Three Novels: Molloy, Malone Dies, The Unnamable*. New York: Grove Press, Inc., 1958.

Barale, Michèle Aina and Rubin Rabinovitz. *A Kwic Concordance to Samuel Beckett's Trilogy: Molloy, Malone Dies, and The Unnamable*. Two volumes. New York: Garland Publishing Inc., 1988.

Begam, Richard. *Samuel Beckett and the End of Modernity*. Stanford, CA: Stanford University Press, 1996.

Bersani, Leo and Ulysse Dutoit. *Arts of Impoverishment: Beckett, Rothko, Resnais*. Cambridge: Harvard University Press, 1993.

Blanchot, Maurice. "Where Now? Who Now?" in *On Beckett: Essays and Criticism*. Ed. S. E. Gontarski. New York: Grove Press, 1986: 141–149.

———. *The Writing of the Disaster*. Trans. Ann Smock. Lincoln: University of Nebraska Press, 1986.

Henning, Sylvie Debevec. *Beckett's Critical Complicity: Carnival, Contestation, and Tradition*. Lexington: University Press of Kentucky, 1988.

Kennedy, Andrew K. *Samuel Beckett*. Cambridge: Cambridge University Press, 1989.

Knowlson, James. *Damned to Fame: The Life of Samuel Beckett*. New York: Simon and Schuster, 1996.

Murphy, P. J., Werner Huber, Rolf Breuer, and Konrad Schoell. *Critique of Beckett Criticism: A Guide to Research in English, French, and German*. Columbia, SC: Camden House, Inc., 1994.

States, Bert O. *The Shape of Paradox: An Essay on Waiting for Godot*. Berkeley, CA: University of California Press, 1978.

Thiher, Allen. "Wittgenstein, Heidegger, the Unnamable, and Some Thoughts on the Status of Voice in Fiction" in *Samuel Beckett: Humanistic Perspectives*. Eds. Morris Beja, S. E. Gontarski, and Pierre Astier. Columbus: Ohio University Press, 1983.

Uhlmann, Anthony. *Beckett and Poststructuralism*. Cambridge: Cambridge University Press, 1999.

Endnotes

1 With the exception of his monograph on Proust, Beckett's discursive writings on art have been collected in *Disjecta*. The volume contains his early essay on *Finnegan's Wake*, book reviews of 1935–36, his letter to Axel Kaun (the "German Letter of 1937"), and essays on painters, which he wrote between 1938 and 1957. "Three Dialogues" is the best known of his aesthetic statements, a serio-comic testing or playing out of his ideas in a parody of a Socratic dialogue.

2 Uhlmann orbits around the problem of justice, comparing the manner in which it is treated in *The Unnamable*, Levinas's *Totality and Infinity* and Derrida's "Violence and Metaphysics," "Force of Law," and *Spectres de Marx*. The trend in Beckett criticism is to treat *The Unnamable* as a central text for seeing how post-modern theoretical concerns have become the very stuff of fiction.

3 To my knowledge, Blanchot himself did not connect his writing on *The Unnamable* (1959) with his writing on the Holocaust (1986).

B. H. Fairchild

Rave On

> . . . wild to be wreckage forever.
>
> *James Dickey, "Cherrylog Road"*

Rumbling over caliche with a busted muffler,
radio blasting Buddy Holly over Baptist wheat fields,
Travis screaming out *behold, I come like a thief*
at jackrabbits skittering beneath our headlights,
the Messiah coming to Kansas in a flat-head Ford
with bad plates, the whole high plains holding its breath,
night is fast upon us, lo, in these the days of our youth,
and we were hell to pay, or thought we were. Boredom
grows thick as maize in Kansas, heavy as drill pipe
littering the racks of oil rigs where in summer boys
roustabout or work on combine crews north as far
as Canada. The ones left back in town begin
to die, dragging main street shit-faced on 3.2 beer
and banging on the whorehouse door in Garden City
where the ancient madame laughed and turned us down
since we were only boys and she knew our fathers.
We sat out front spitting Red Man and scanned a landscape
flat as Dresden: me, Mike Luckinbill, Billy Heinz,
and Travis Doyle, who once said, *I don't want to die*
before I'm dead. We had eaten all the life
there was in Seward County but hungry still, hauled ass
to old Arkalon, the ghost town on the Cimarron
that lay in half-shadow and a scattering of starlight,

323

and its stillness was a kind of death, the last breath
of whatever in our lives was ending. We had drunk there
and tossed our bottles at the walls and pissed great arcs
into the Kansas earth where the dust groweth hard
and the clods cleave fast together, yea, where night yawns
above the river in its long, dark dream, above
haggard branches of mesquite, chicken hawks scudding
into the tree line, and moon-glitter on caliche
like the silver plates of Coronado's treasure
buried all these years, but the absence of treasure,
absence of whatever would return the world
to the strangeness that as children we embraced
and recognized as *life*. Rave on.
                              Cars are cheap
at Roman's Salvage strewn along the fence out back
where cattle graze and chew rotting fabric from the seats.
Twenty bucks for spare parts and a night in the garage
could make them run as far as death and stupidity
required—on Johnson Road where two miles of low shoulders
and no fence line would take you up to sixty, say,
and when you flipped the wheel clockwise, you were there
rolling in the belly of the whale, belly of hell,
and your soul fainteth within you for we had seen it done
by big Ed Ravenscroft who said you would go in a boy
and come out a man, and so we headed back through town
where the marquee of the Plaza flashed *Creature from
the Black Lagoon* in storefront windows and the Snack Shack
where we had spent our lives was shutting down and we
sang *rave on, it's a crazy feeling* out into the night
that loomed now like a darkened church, and sang loud
and louder still for we were sore afraid.
                              Coming up
out of the long tunnel of cottonwoods that opens onto
Johnson Road, Travis with his foot stuck deep into the *soul*
of that old Ford *come on, Bubba, come on* beating
the dash with his fist, hair flaming back in the wind
and eyes lit up by some fire in his head that I

had never seen, and Mike, iron Mike, sitting tall
in back with Billy, who would pick a fight with anything
that moved but now hunched over mumbling something
like a prayer, as the Ford lurched on spitting
and coughing but then smoothing out suddenly fast
and the fence line quitting so it was open field, then,
then, I think, we were butt-deep in regret and a rush
of remembering whatever we would leave behind—
Samantha Dobbins smelling like fresh laundry,
light from the movie spilling down her long blonde hair,
trout leaping all silver and pink from Black Bear Creek,
the hand of my mother, I confess, passing gentle
across my face at night when I was a child—oh, yes,
it was all good now and too late, too late, trees blurring
past and Travis wild, popping the wheel, oh too late
too late

        and the waters pass over us the air thick
as mud slams against our chests though turning now
the car in its slow turning seems almost graceful
the frame in agony like some huge animal groaning
and when the wheels leave the ground the engine cuts loose
with a wail thin and ragged as a bandsaw cutting tin
and we are drowning breathless heads jammed against
our knees and it's a thick swirling purple nightmare
we cannot wake up from for the world is turning too
and I hear Billy screaming and then the whomp
sick crunch of glass and metal whomp *again back window*
popping loose and glass exploding someone crying out
tink tink of iron on iron overhead and then at last
it's over and the quiet comes

                        Oh so quiet. Somewhere
the creak and grind of a pumping unit. Crickets.
The tall grass sifting the wind in a mass of whispers
that I know I'll be hearing when I die. And so
we crawled trembling from doors and windows borne out
of rage and boredom into weed-choked fields barren
as Golgotha. Blood raked the side of Travis's face

grinning rapt, ecstatic, Mike's arm was hanging down
like a broken curtain rod, Billy kneeled, stunned,
listening as we all did to the rustling silence
and the spinning wheels in their sad, manic song
as the Ford's high beams hurled their crossed poles of light
forever out into the deep and future darkness. *Rave on.*

I survived. We all did. And then came the long surrender,
the long, slow drifting down like young hawks riding on
the purest, thinnest air, the very palm of God
holding them aloft so close to something hidden there,
and then the letting go, the fluttering descent, claws
spread wide against the world, and we become, at last,
our fathers. And do not know ourselves and therefore
no longer know each other. Mike Luckinbill ran a Texaco
in town for years. Billy Heinz survived a cruel divorce,
remarried, then took to drink. But finally last week
I found this house in Arizona where the brothers
take new names and keep a vow of silence and make
a quiet place for any weary, or lost, passenger
of earth whose unquiet life has brought him there,
and so, after vespers, I sat across the table
from men who had not surrendered to the world,
and one of them looked at me and looked into me,
and I am telling you there was a *fire in his head*
and his eyes were coming fast down a caliche road,
and I knew this man, and his name was Travis Doyle.

Allen Grossman

Not All Wanderers Are Lost
(A leafy elegy)

1

"Hey YOU! What's the joke?"—In a crowded photograph
A boy is grinning, and looking up, and to his left!
"Wipe that grin off your face, kiddo! This is
The Day of the Dead and over all are shadows."
The boy thought about it for a long time
And in the fluent course of time he grew

To be a beautiful youth. *Then* he answered me.
"Sad old man, do not weep for this philosopher.
Do not even remember him. *Remember, instead,*
What he remembered—THE LUMINOUS BODY
OF TRUTH: A great golden head never shorn,
A white bosom not feminine but promising

Abundant sweetness, a genital to be stroked
And sucked and received with gratitude
And all the rest." "But at the end of the day,"
I replied. "At *the end*, when the sky darkens
And night and the shadows are over all,
Will there be no thought-storm, no fulgurous

Lightning as I turn my face to the wall?"
"No. Only *susurrus* of rain on salt pond,
On garden, and on the forest floor: leaf
Over leaf, leaf over leaf, leaf over leaf,
Oak over beech and over oak the pine,
And over all the shadows?"—Then, the beautiful

Youth, *still* grinning ("SO, kid, what IS the joke?"),
Lines out a song called "Benefits of Rain"
And everybody in the photo, living and dead,
Joins the chorus, first one and then another one.
They sing in turn. But when each song is done
They sing it all, together, again.

2

—I have found these moments before my death
Which may yet be many or few, in any case
A long school room. There is, for example, a
River in Babylonia called the Over-
Flowing River. . . . *Remember, old man,*
What I remember. Do not remember me.

Then, the smirking boy calls out another verse:
"Rain was before all things. In the beginning,
Rain was equivalent to the resurrection
When all the dead stand up, as in a picture,
And from the heavens pour down memories,
Destroying everything, dragging down the hills

Where many keep the room they were born in
And now die. Deep calls to Deep in the voice
Of cataracts! And the dead cry their cry, *'Remember*
What I remember. Do not remember me.'"
—It is true, as I now remember, even jewels
Benefit from the rain, as do the fields,

The sown and the unsown and the blue thistle.
"Ocean water is water that eats water.
The ocean is *insatiable* of rain.
The entire Name-Of-God is not enough.
Before religion was God. Before God
Was holiness. Before holiness was

The sound of waters disappearing under waters:
Land's End—and, then, *Lyoness, Lyoness, Lyoness.*"
In the photo, all the dead sing it—*Ly-o-ness.*
The sound of their song is as rain is far out,
Rain falling into open ocean at first light,
The true light, without color, making things clear:

3

In the beginning, the frozen minute of Creation's
Photographic flash, lightning-like, portending rain,
Grandpa Harry (up front in the picture), a *Jewish* farmer
(What a laugh!), crushes something, I don't know what,
In his right hand. And *there* stands Harry-the-farmer's
Deaf daughter Dorothy who tutored Tuesday Weld

And died in the bath (of a massive heart attack)
In Sri Lanka on a California teacher's pension.
And next to Dorothy, Aunt Rose, *con de la famille,*
Who devoured one blossom each morning for breakfast,
Smiles to remember what she remembers: how
Her CEO fiancé was conked in an ill-considered

Jibe and drowned off Sirmione, April 1937.
Dear God! Remember what Rose remembers.
Do not remember her. And there in the back row
Is our Uncle Leo, an Anne Arbor junk man
Who still remembers the lost, billion dollar
Locomotives he found (Leo, dream on!) rusting

In Wisconsin corn fields (ca.'42). And Bess his hairy-
Chested wife who tormented her male children
Until at last they ate their dinners off the floor
With the other kitchen filth and died young:
Merton (life-insurance) *dead* (cross him off);
Mickey (auto-sales) *dead* (cross *him* off);

And another whose name I can't remember.
Also Uncle Raymond, bus driver, thick as a post
(Married to a narrow person with a wan smile,
Daughter of the whirlwind traffic of contingency)
Who once stopped for me and said, jamming his clutch
With an enormous boot: "You're on the wrong bus, boy."

4

So THAT'S the joke, kiddo? *"Not all wanderers
Are lost."* And who is rabbi? *"He to whom
The people come.* Remember what I remember:
A girl's body of light, as smooth as glass—
Diana, her genital a star.
Remember what I remember. Do not remember me.

I am the gazing ball wherein does congregate
All the light there is. And I am the philosopher
Who saw the naked goddess plain (O body of truth!).
I am rememberer of the garden oak.
In its mysterious well. I am the peonie that harbors
In its ear the ant, the worm, the water drop.

I am acquainted with the shouting tiger lily
(I will tell you *everything* it says),
The whispering baby breath, the pansy low,
And in its season the silencing snow
That fills the well where the oak stands, and stills
The garden and the tongues of all its fires.

At the bottom of the garden, in the waste
Where the paths end, grow the RESISTER WEEDS,
Makers of the poet's mind (*"remember what I remember"*)—
Square root of two. O woe. There the *body* learns
Something about the body:—WHAT EVER IN THAT
WASTE IS ROOTED, THAT THING IT CANNOT MOVE.

To this place the death-animals of Diana
Followed me. Where is she NOW? Take ship,
Heavy with lights, so burdened that the phosphorescent
Ocean paints the deck, leaf over leaf, gold over green.
Land ho! There shines Diana's star on Lesbos.
There sleeps the goddess with her gruesome animal.

5

—A man or woman without religion is mad.
His children are mad, and also her children
Eat filth and die. RIGHT HERE (*sparagmos*)
In the waste places among RESISTER WEED
The philosopher turns his face to the wall
At the moment of death. The philosopher remembers

(Himself he does not know) what God remembered
In the beginning. The God, before religion,
Wept for himself, alone, among the sanctities.
Then the God forgot himself: "LET THE LIGHT BE."
The Lord, Our God, taught us how to do things
With tears. Then the great God forgot himself.

(THE GOD IS THE SELF THAT FORGETS ITSELF.)
Then the God forgot himself and remembered LIGHT,
LIGHT that has heaped up in the Roman paths
Of Lyoness, under water, time out of mind,
Light that has no colors, *no rainbow at its heart*
Under 40 fathoms. The shallow sea is

A hard crossing to the rats and the one palm tree
Of the Scilly Isles. This is the Day of the Dead.
But the poet is still laboring (night falls in the room)
As the light fails, still laboring in a room
At this leafy elegy. But now it's done.
NOT ALL WANDERERS ARE LOST. NOT EVEN YOU.

America is the greatest poem, as Whitman said.
In fact, America *is only* a poem. Old man,
Here's another joke: the God is many.
But—Hear, O Israel!—THE LIGHT IS ONE.
Now. Shall I tell you my *best* joke? It's a douzer."
—Give me a break, kid. I've heard 'em all.

Mark Irwin

The Way Things Are

FOR GEORGE MOORE

The violent wonders that contain us. The day
purpling toward cloud—then sun—till the trees
seem defenses against blue and you forget, content
in the now's drizzling lens. Perhaps when we have
nothing to say, when everything is changeless
but changing like waves, perhaps it's then we are
happy, wanting and discussing nothing, as the moment
ripens and goes on till a child asks you a question
you can't answer and suddenly you remember

one day you'll die. So you get lost in the now, the way
bees rumble their gold chariots through clover
for every bored kid around the pool. And perhaps that's how
some poems come to be, when the days stall
in heat and one is forced to push years into the tedious
hour's piece of paper timed to go off fifty years later
in a library filled with sleep, or in a classroom

locked in rhyme. Perhaps that's why
we delay in order to hurry, creating so many
miniature dramas while the ordinary yawns, and as we
rush toward that tree whose lessening green
gives way to white flowers, already a wild yellow

catches up like shadow, and you arrive out
of breath, dumbfounded at leaves the color of

blood at your feet. Looking back does not help
for the view that was green, voluminous, and sunstruck
seems wobbly and out of focus in a snow
that dreams of our bones and what sugary moments
remain. "I'll take one of those, and one of those,
extra fruit on the side." And why not—that's
what a child does, mouth open like a fish

facing upstream, devouring each moment's
food, or walking in a field, pausing to inspect
glossy things—strawberry, honeysuckle, bee—forgetting
the ouches with wows while opening, marveling,
unfencing the world. The history of a child
is now: Kool-aid, blood, and flowers, ponds
swarming with frogs, firedogs, and fish.

~

It all drifts into the far, the spaces,
while something else like wind arrives, flutters
at our lips, then passes, the undetermined
it that graces being, that white house occasionally
glimpsed which seems to have no walls, yet surrounds
our joys and sorrows. And though we tell ourselves
to make it last, it hovers then vanishes

as our words hover and vanish around what they
name. I say, "The *raspberries* bled in the sun,"
and the barbed word continues to wound
with its music. I step through its rivers, cross its
shadowy, sunlit caves till I'm delivered back
to the knee-high field where the tiny heart still sounds.
I want the word that makes us linger, the laddering hesitancy
that holds for any of it to matter fully, for any of its

shivering to continue. There's the dream
of the house, and then the building, living,
savoring—and there's the leaving and remembering
till all that remains is a picture of the house that's
gone. Now memory becomes a glass of water
containing the light of all surrounding things,
and we drink the water to remember—glad to be here,

glad as the catalpa's green leaves. To make things
last we push them into the far:—Reyes and I
felling trees in a picture taken by a friend.
See, we are tiny and will live forever.
Death is close-up and tall. Push it away
with music, poems, laughter, and the sounds
of kids playing by a river. The river lusts

for their laughter, rains with their sun
voices. The river will move them far
and safely into the light. The light that
is the outside we lean to, the light that longs
for us to ripen, the light that graces being,
so that by giving we seem to open time and in
its slow air we linger. Watch the August

bees wrestle gold in purple thistle, watch
them dumb to hours drinking sun from anthers.
Watch them become the sun that is the flower,
all the flowers, fuses to which the bees
are fire, moments moving, both undoing
and doing what's been done, both mirroring
and making. Their fires measure exactly
what they are, what we occasionally

found in song and—while singing—
discovered that the very end of the world
is language, a place once seemingly true
but when we returned to our rooms the words

grew tired, bored, and dusty, elegant
in the shade of things, while all around us
youth leaned lustfully toward that star we call

the sun. We wanted something true
but the truth was something only seen
while looking back, as in a ruined
house we find a truth in splinters and in
rot, the finish and the start. And though vision
is a kind of truth, its time's not yet, and we come
to sadly realize that each moment of our lives

is true but that the whole escapes us. Yet we go
on hurrying, moving to some where through the way
things are, and often, when we get there
we realize there's nothing to do, for the time
like a great sea has not yet, or already
occurred, and we are there alone, standing
beneath clouds, waiting for the moment
to begin, waiting to be caught up to.

Campbell McGrath

The Florida Poem

Let me start by saying this
about Florida.
About the history of Florida, the proud beginnings
of Florida, proud and noble begin-
ings/genesis/roots/traditions, about the
histo—about the mythic identity
of Florida, its sun-loving soul, its vital essence,
vegetable essence,
its profound and mythic something,
it's something.
Let me start
again: organ swell, diapason,
incant the appropriate invocation.
Hear me now, o Floridian muse!
Sing through me, o native goddess, o sacred orange
blossom nymph, o Weeki Wachee naiad,
o Minnie, o Daisy,
o dappled condominium queen,
o dryad of the fairway and practice green, o
my, oh my, o one more
try. Flo-
ri-
da. Florrr
rrrida!
Florida: it's here!
Florida: it's here and it's for sale!
Florida: it's neat, in a weird way!

Florida: Fuckin' Fantastic!
This would be my official suggestion for a new state motto,
certainly not something the Legislature
is likely to consider
an appropriate means of promoting
our fabulous natural resources and dynamic
growth potential. Their idea of useful
is another ladle of lard from the old coffee can
of boosterism and bacon fat,
something like—Florida:
shelter your profits in the sunshine state!
Florida: wreak your retiree havoc here!
Florida: just come on down
and exploit it!
Ah, but I digress. The point
was to buy into Florida, not to sell it again,
and anyway when it comes to sloganeering
I'm no match for the marketers
and technocrats and mousketeer aparatchiks
industriously zoning and rezoning the commonwealth,
though I still believe the perfect tag-line is waiting
to be coined, the perfect come on
for a place whose history begins and ends
with a sales pitch,
a shill, a wink and a nudge
and a can of green paint to valorize the scrublands
and scorched savannas peddled to unwary out-of-towners,
beginning with Ponce de León himself,
who sold an expedition of greed and self-gratification
as a mystical quest for a Fountain of Youth which,
had it existed, would by now
have been hijacked as symbolic centerpiece
for some cookie-cutter cluster
of master-planned contemporary custom home communities
and then bled dry with the vanishing aquifers
until the riddled earth itself surrendered
and every beloved one of those

houses and lap pools and riding mowers and mortgage balloons
vanished into the maw of the newly-rechristened
Sinkhole of Youth. Luckily,
this tragic scenario was averted by the Calusa,
who recognized at a glance the vehicle of their annihilation
and so dispatched unhappy Ponce with an arrow
dipped in manchineel sap,
and by the unfortunate fact that there was no miraculous
resuscitative font but merely the false
promise of loot to lure
the conquistadors into this land of illusions,
though I myself have more than once
been enticed to swim in the icy oasis of DeLeon Springs,
and have eaten at the remarkable restaurant
reputedly housed in an old Spanish mill
where they grind still the wheat
to mix the batter you pool and flip on a griddle
in the middle of your very own table.
Pancakes!
Pancakes and alligators and paddleboats and ruins
of vanished conquerors vanquished
in their turn. It's one of my favorite places in the state,
not merely for the flapjacks and historical ironies
but for the chaste fact of its beauty,
its palmettos and live oaks and the liquid upwelling
of subterranean rivers that have underlain this peninsula
for millennia, waters we are even now
exhausting but which endure,
which yet remain to nourish and sustain us,
a consolation
which must become the fountain
for any communal future we might dare imagine,
source and wellspring of the hope
and courage it will take
to fight for the preservation of what is good
against the diverse and relentless forces of destruction
loosed upon this flower-drunk relic

of the original garden,
mere vestige perhaps
of the trackless cornucopia of the Calusa,
but at least it is a vestige
of paradise.
Now this, in all fairness, is not
a purely local issue
in the way that, say, alligators scarfing pet poodles is.
Paradisal vestiges could serve as synonym
for reality as we know it,
a working definition of the human condition,
shorthand for the universality of our postlapsarian inheritance,
the ways in which the world we inhabit
survives as an embodiment of previous and equally viable
worlds, civilizations, epochs, reigns,
as even the galactic clouds where stars are conceived
like Moorish idols in a crucible of swan-light
riven by gestures of radiant indigo
themselves refract the luminous matter of some previous
inchoate and irrecoverable dawn.
I refer, of course, to the past, the sunken treasure fleet
of time gone, lost realm of anchor chains
fixed in coral, pearls returned
to the forge of their origin, cannons and amphorae
that beckon us not so much for what they are or were
as for what they represent, as His Excellency
Juan Ponce de León
represents the beginning
of the end
for a regime with roots
descending unbroken twelve thousand years
to the Pleistocene, a mosaic
of indigenous cultures ripped from the walls
by the wind of European arrival
in scarce two centuries. And then the walls demolished.
And the temple razed and burned.
Not that Ponce in any literal way discovered the place,

not even euphemistically, not even Eurocentrically,
it being known to Cuban slavers a dozen years
before he made landfall,
April 2nd, 1513,
prior to which moment he had been famous primarily
for his rapacious and impecunious service
as Royal Governor of Puerto Rico,
which *Isla del Encanto* he had Most Fittingly
Conquered and Enslaved in the name of his Majesty,
and of Our Lord, Jesus Christus,
and we would certainly no longer remember him
except for the business about the Fountain of Youth,
and his nominal status as founder of Florida,
and the lingering controversy as to why he named it as he did.
Well, for one thing it sounds better in Spanish,
elegant and florid, peaks and valleys,
a far cry from that flat, Americanized dogbite: Flrda.
Also it was Easter, *Pascua Florída*,
when the land bloomed
heavy with flowers and Catholic piety
and so the name was struck like a two-faced doubloon,
duly minted, sealed, bestowed,
and stuck: *La Florída*.
Island of Flowers.
The Beflowered Land.
Flowervania.
It doesn't really translate
but you'd know it by the odor of jasmine
and rain-drenched earth, fat worms in warm puddles,
fronds and petals in riotous abandon,
a continent of elastic green fecundity looming
floral and renascent. And after De León another fifty years
of Spaniards shipwrecked on the rock of the unreal,
noble adventurers eighty-sixed at the hands of intransigent nature
or the primitive, soon to vanish *indios*—
Pánfilo de Narváez, Tristán de Luna y Arellano,
so read their sandy and melodious epitaphs,

most famously that of Hernando de Soto, "the never-
conquered cavalier," veteran of the egg-scrambling *entrada*
that fried the Incas up in one big
genocidal omelet, mighty De Soto whose watchword
was gold—*Where is the gold? Where are
the mountains?*—who marched north with 500 soldiers
through swamps and plains and forests, north
the length of a state with a heart like a giant stalk of celery,
mocked by the clouds that are the actual mountains
of this place, no more than a rumor
of rain on the horizon,
a horizon of expectations no literal horizon could meet,
burning the villages of the Indians who fled
at word of his approach, palm-thatched huts
and cypress palisades and plantings
of squash and pumpkins trampled by the horses,
fields of green corn in flames,
screams of the dazed or captured peoples,
a people not hard to see as not people,
daughter of the *cacique*
thrown to the wardogs and torn asunder,
others impaled on spikes,
others burned alive,
the *cacique* himself with nose cut off, and ears,
by Sword of mine own Hand, for his Impertinence,
for Refusal to Tell the Location of the Gold most surely Abounding
in That Land, or the next kingdom north, or the next
beyond that—Ocale, Potano, Napituca
where he massacred hundreds for like misbehavior,
Iniahica now Tallahassee, then north again
beyond the state line and the bounds of this poem—*where
is the gold?*—north as far as Carolina
and west almost to Texas, dying at last
of fever and despair near the banks of the Mississippi
he is wrongly said to have discovered,
his corpse dispatched to the great river's mercy
under cover of darkness so as to keep hidden from the enemies

surrounding his starving and diminished army—
tribes already incubating
the germs
that would extinguish Mississippian
civilization—the fact
of his mortality.
He was no god, De Soto.
He was ours
and we cannot disclaim him.
So we must seek to understand his desire
to sow devastation as the staple
crop of the republic. Was he insane?
Or just being sensible?
Equipped as for war one does not arrive uninvited
in the land of another folk simply
to bake cupcakes. In this regard the Indians were nothing
but grain crushed in the mill of his merciless errand,
the gears of profit, yes,
of alienated desire, greed beyond limitation,
but that machine could not function without the grease
of human industry, the oil of human nature,
the psychology that drives armies of men
across a blood-engirdled globe
even now. And these Indians, however easily romanticized,
were similarly human, familiar with power and avarice,
plagued by incessant warfare,
only their systems were simpler and less efficient,
they had evolved no complex structures
or technologies of destruction,
they created no lasting monuments, built no highways
of nail salons and auto parts discount stores,
fashioned no industrial parks beyond sand mounds and shell middens
and so their ten-thousand-year tenure has been erased
with barely a ripple in the sawgrass
to betray it. So much
for the Calusa. So much for the Appalachee,
the Tequesta, the Jororo, the Aís.

So much for the Spanish.
They founded Saint Augustine and later Pensacola,
evicted the French, enslaved the locals,
their missions subsisted for a hundred years
among the Timucua before disease and exhaustion
ravaged the converted and the depredations of colonial tribes
and proto-Americans extirpated the rest.
Next the English took a turn, the Spanish once more,
the English again—Florida danced at heel
like a dog with many masters,
like a lady finger soaked in brine, pretty to look at
but who would deign to banquet
on sodden cookies when the grand buffet of colonialism
groaned with bullion and silver plate?—
until at last Andrew Jackson bought the whole place
for five million dollars and a solemn promise
to relinquish all future American
claims to Texas.
Hmm.
By the time the deal was done
it was 1821. A new
century, a new society, a new destiny
shivering the tracks like a clamorous locomotive,
whirling dynamo of energy and change!
Actually, not much happened in Florida in the 19th Century.
It drifted along, balmily somnolent,
a backwater of boll weevils and palmetto cowboys,
hardly less a colony for davening
to a new set of stars
and stripes. The town of Cowford
was renamed Jacksonville, to honor Old Hickory
and in udder disregard
for the sentiments of the cows.
Steamships appeared, opening the interior to navigation
and thereby requiring the removal of the last, unwelcome indigenes,
so came the Seminole Wars, forty years
of episodic guerrilla campaigns that made of the U.S. Army

a laughing stock for its cowardice, sloth and ineptitude,
culminating in the infamous capture of Osceola
under flag of truce,
a lowpoint in our military annals,
to say the least. And then
the big tamale,
the Civil War, Florida
on the wrong side, per usual,
mandarin in its certitude
of chattel ownership and the patent inhumanity
of its African constituency. Little drama
at the siege of Pensacola, the battle of Olustee;
Florida had no Shiloh, no Gettysburg or Appomattox,
no Valley Forge, no Alamo
except the rental cars,
no Plymouth Rock or Liberty Bell or even Monticello—
Florida is bereft of mythic infrastructure,
symbolically impoverished,
its hallowed grounds are golf courses,
its great cathedrals malls and themeparks,
its founding fathers rank profiteers,
its poets and sages the hucksters and boosters
who banged the drums of development at any price.
Not from the head of Zeus
but of Henry Flagler
have we sprung. "That Government
will be most highly esteemed
that gives the greatest protection
to individual and industrial enterprises at the least cost
to the taxpayers," said Governor George F. Drew,
an unusually frank equation for corporate entitlement
at the expense of civic need, no huge surprise
in a state whose political legacy
is the legislative equivalent of Osceola's ambush,
a daisy-chain scissored from sweetheart bills and broken treaties
in the image of old Jim Crow
crowned with paper shackles riding a piebald mule.

What the Governor meant was
come and get it,
tear it
down, rip it up,
mill it for lumber, boil it for turpentine,
orchard it for oranges or pit-mine it for phosphates,
shoot it for hides or skins or quills
or fun, can it for soup,
pack it, ship it, fish it to the verge
of fishlessness, suck
the candy
from this cane as best you can
before the sugar runs dry,
a mindset of witless and exploitative destruction
embraced not only by gilded tycoons
but by hunters and gatherers of every stripe,
as witness those original tourists riding paddlewheel steamers
up primordial rivers in an orgy of gunfire at whatever
moved and much that did not,
or the entrepreneurial collectors who scoured the Everglades
for the colorful shells of tree snails, each
island-like hammock of mahogany and gumbolimbo
harboring a uniquely patterned sub-species,
and after finding some dozen or hundred
they would torch to barren rock each irreplaceable islet,
each evolutionarily distinctive micro-environment,
thereby assuring the extinction of that type
and maximizing the value
of their specimens. Which brings us
stumbling into the streamlined stage-lights of modernity
with its attendant surfeit of the all-but-miraculous,
sound and fury befitting a century of marvels
and yet for all the hubbub not much
really happened in the last one hundred years either.
Not much has ever happened in Florida, to tell the truth.
Another way of conceiving our history
would be to admit up front

that from De León's very first sand-cast heel-print
to the final toe-touch of Neil Armstrong's silver space-age booties
bound from Cape Canaveral for a sea of lunar dust
not a single human footfall within these soggy confines
could dare assert any claim to lasting, world-historical import.
Another way of conceiving this poem would be
to acknowledge that all of this—
16, 17, 18, 19,
even our lovingly-eulogized 20th Century—
comprises five hundred years of humid inconsequence,
prologue to a long-deferred moment of reckoning,
an invoice of accountability come due at last,
now that it is no longer possible
to erase what has come before us and begin anew,
now that the ruined orchard rejects our claim of usufruct,
now that fifteen million must drink from one spigot
and Florida's crucible of self-definition
is at hand,
its coming out party, its *quinces*,
the dawning
of its Immortal Metal Age,
though who but an alchemist would dare predict
whether Gold or Lead it shall be? O
the future, the future,
the future,
o!
Frankly,
it scares the hell out of me.
Yes, I know that our very weaknesses might
become a source of unsuspected strength,
that a lack of iconic identity allows us the chance
to fashion unfettered a society of diverse and fluid beauty
unlike any ever known, of course,
after all I'm an optimist,
a romantic, a believer but also
a skeptic and so
fated to perform the calculus of the probable

and weep at our stupidity
carried forward through the steam tables and logarithms
of a new millennium, where already the ocean
at whose hem we kneel in oiled worship
rises to consume us incrementally,
to reclaim a rebel province for the holy empire of salt,
and even if Florida does not believe in history
it cannot help but believe
in the tide, and the tide for its part is
a compelling historian. And yet, all it takes
is a day at the beach
to witness the sociohistorical slate scrubbed clean
and scribbled anew
by the beautiful coquinas, to watch
the laws of hydraulics rendered moot by the munificent
tranquillity of their variegated colonies
thriving amid the chaos of wave-break and overwash.
All it takes is a *cafécito* in the Miami airport,
five minutes at the brushed aluminum lunch counter
to realize that an entire hemisphere of human possibility
is wobbling toward us
upon an axis whose orbit no astral mathematics
could possibly model. All it takes is a summer afternoon
floating the pellucid Ichetucknee River
to plumb the dragon fly's eye
of its fluvial essence
and recognize how much has been lost since William Bartram's day
and yet how much of such elemental loveliness
is left. One immersion is all you need
to be born into such faith,
one brushstroke to be watermarked,
indelibly graven—one glance
towards that pool of azure light through the trees ahead—
nomad opal drenched in nectar!—
to understand that the Fountain of Youth does exist, it always has,
our chronic myopia must be reckoned a token
of the years lost deciphering Ye Olde Spanish Maps,

because they too could never find what swam
before their eyes, and like them we have been blinded
by larcenous intentions, by the vanity of mastery,
by our fear at being labeled traffickers
in utopian fantasies,
though it is not in actuality some fairy tale
geyser of childish enchantment or escape from the real
but a reservoir of the profound,
an oasis of the sacred,
an emblem of solace and renewal
in a difficult world. A simple leap is enough
to know the invigoration of that embrace, visceral opulence
of an element so clear each grain of sand
sings forth, each bordering leaf of oak or heliconia,
each minnow or sunfish in the mineral wicker-work,
one jump, one plunge
toward the crevice of rifted limestone
wherefrom the earth pours forth
its liquid gift,
glorying in the acids and sunlight of motion
as you stretch to reach the ungraspable,
striving forward,
borne back, held suspended
within its invisible pulse—austere, enigmatic, elastic—
like the votive force of time we push against
and are scoured and scourged
and washed clean by, what it's like
to be alive, how
it flows, not from past to present or present to future
but from source to vanishing, from source
to vanishing to source,
which would be an even better way
of conceiving this poem, to reverse its polarity,
invert the pyramid of chronology
and retreat from the saw-buzz of highrise cranes
constructing the moment, draw back
toward the silted and the half-dim, past Spanish moss

and dangling chads, Apollo in flames,
past Arthur Godfrey's ukulele,
past railroad tycoons and the Green Cross Republic,
slaves and zealots and buccaneers,
past the Calusa and the Creek moving south
to supplant them, past the Okeechobee mound-builders,
past the Weeden Island people,
the unnamed people,
past the Hopewellian and the Archaic
to the fringe of the Holocene when they came,
in the hoar weather of early spring,
across Beringia and down coast or canyon
or glaciated sluice-way into the open plains of the continent,
human beings, clans and bands of paleo-Indians
trailing the great herds through the dying winter of the megafaunal
        age,
crossing somehow the mountains and steppes and rivers,
finding their way to the brine tide of the gulf,
continental shelf rich with shellfish,
sharks and rays in the shallows, sea turtles
over-turned and butchered and eaten among the dunes,
following the coastline as it bent
to the east and southward
toward this terminal, scallop-backed cul-de-sac,
higher and drier then, arid peninsula
of grasslands and brushy savannas that meant
good hunting of glyptodonts, ground sloths, giant tortoises,
peccary and jaguar, horse and condor,
mastodons and camelids and bison, varieties of horned stock
unknown to us these millennia past
gathered at muddy pools and waterholes,
a place beyond which there was no further passage,
a place where some would turn again
to the north, some double-back west and away, gone,
a place where, after hesitating,
after testing the air for what they most depended on,
some few among them

moved cautiously forward and so became
the first of our kind to enter
into Florida,
and stooped at the edge
of a spring among rushes and tall sedge,
touching knee to muddy verge
to cup a palm
and find that it was fresh and thus
a livable land,
a place of mutable possibility, tabula rasa,
a place in which to fashion
from the mortar of water and sunshine
a life, now
as on that day so long ago,
that unmarked and immemorial day,
the first day
of our existence,
today.

C. Dale Young

Triptych at the Edge of Sight

I

Whip of sea-grass covering the dune
or the child's kite blown from her hands:
on what should the eye train itself?

Lash of sea-grass, sting of bristle
and sand thrown into action
late in the afternoon on a beach.

Above the trash dotting the seaside,
the cloud-gatherer takes his place and extends
his arms above a landscape filled with failure.

II

There is light and there is dark,
the trees ringing the field and something stirring
at the edge of sight. Someone stirs at the edge of sight.

Do your hands underestimate the weight of air
or the weight of the body as it acquiesces,
a pawn in the hands of a Prince, a Borgia?

A falcon's shadow slips over the shoulder,
and the field flattens as the great wingspan
rushes ahead into the dark grove.

III

Color, color everywhere: striped yellow awnings,
domes of white marble reminiscent of churches,
campaniles somehow redder than their bricks.

It was the season of Titian, the *Assumption*.
There were Madonnas at every turn, but they
were only women wearing too many pearls.

In a gallery not too far from here, a Bonifazio:
the steps of a Palazzo given more attention
than the woman's face done in chiaroscuro.

IV

A football in the chair. A bee bumbling
at the window. Tangerine blossoms on the grass.
The hair on your legs flat as if combed.

Your yellow towel crumpled beside you.
You had fallen asleep while it was my turn
to shower. The heat moved

through the house, slowly. You were
wheezing in your sleep, damp and uncovered—
afternoon was changing its name.

V

Rumble of the streetcar and the quickening
sound of the fog-horn signaling danger
and the clicking of the radiator coils and

the windowpanes crackling and the man
coming home from work and the opening
of a door and the anxious bark of a dog

on the street and the refrigerator kicking in
and the static in my ear as I grind my teeth
as I wake myself up.

VI

The steps, cut into the cliffside's creases,
were hidden by a canopy of gnarled branches,
and the darkness of the trail was speckled

by filtered sunlight, the path ending
at a bluff. There, the cloud-gatherer
swept his hands across his chest and turned.

Strange shadows, we stood on the path and watched.
The ocean kept up its noise. There was someone
at the edge of sight. There was footfall retreating.

VII

The again unused wedding dress—white light
spun into fiber and gowned in a stagnating
envelope of air under a clear, plastic wrap—

is protected from dust, from the body's remnants
loosed from our towels and bed sheets,
our flakes of skin and body hair.

What tricks the mind constructs—
let the wedding dress remain as is
lacking the nostalgia of garments worn.

VIII

A dying palm tree hung its tattered fronds
above our heads. The polished, noontime glare
surrounded everything; even branches

black with the city's soot seemed young again.
Who can deny the hopefulness of Spring?
At water's edge, a small armada of crabs

began to mine the sand, to no avail:
a broken bottle of gin, a rumpled shirt,
the memory of something almost evil.

IX

We had gone so far, down past the ferns
dead and swaying in the shadow of a breeze,
down into a land half swamp, half ocean floor.

Fancying ourselves modern Greeks, we had descended
into the earth—not to point out souls like Anchises,
but to point out lichens, mosses, molds, those classics

seldom studied anymore—but our sense of direction
was terrible, and we had not summoned Virgil
or Edith Hamilton to guide us out of that other world.

X

The wind picks up. The sky darkens.
The surfers' dark outlines shift among waves.
I carry nothing. I seek everything.

Your hands are what I remember most,
the way, when you gestured, your fingers
passed through the air in a singular motion.

The cloud-gatherer extends his hands,
his chest opening as he lifts the imaginary
toward me, I who have never been generous.

XI

The rowboat is white, is empty and white,
the white greyed with age, and no one
can remember the man who rowed,

or the dark figure that shouted directions
that time and time again had steered the boat
toward a moon come to rest against black water.

There is no sky. There is only cloud.
The water begins, and the water ends.
The boat, the boat is empty. It does not move.

XII

It is Winter there but the sun remains aloof
(sated with control of the islands),
a tropical Machiavelli wearing golden ribbons,

the Right Honorable Duke of Light
who has no rebuke for the landed gentry,
for their sprawling cane fields.

Unfaithful ally, the sea
gives those people nothing but salt,
copper-green seaweed for meals.

XIII

Why haven't you come? The trees
with their flaking bark still black from the rain
bend in the wind, their leaves chattering.

A lone jogger cuts across the path
after an owl makes itself known.
There is light and there is dark.

There is water and the threat of water.
Why haven't you come? The moon drips
from leaf to air to ground and is gone.

XIV

There were trees ringing the field.
Grasses and weeds crowned with white
and yellow petals flanked us

as you pinned my arms, your breasts
dangling above my face as I squirmed
in mock-resistance. A bird's shriek

and its shadow passed over your shoulder.
There was something stirring at the edge
of sight. Our breathing quickened.

XV

The so-called fish-wife in my paintings,
always seen from the back with a bundle
of fish hanging over her shoulder,

the skin bluish-green, the hair like seaweed,
the orange belt made of fish and the nets
worn as a skirt, the shells worn in the hair.

Is there any question now about whom
I used as my model? Her arms blue but green,
slender, muscular, the hands always out of sight.

XVI

If there are no gods, then why does the pond
demand so much attention? Year after year,
it swallows our reflections, our faces older each visit.

I say the pond is a god, its almost circular body
the half ring of eternity. I say the pond is where
it all began, the sudden stir surprising the air

with the explosion of a cell into many cells.
Out in the field, the pond watches over us.
It sees everything we have done here.

XVII

I have no use for titanium white, its tint
whiter than the canvas itself and able to negate
so much and so quickly. In the dark studio,

in an attic of sorts, I watched you reading,
you who felt that painting was a sort of negation,
a fear of the world that required one to make

a new world. It was so dark. Maybe I believed
that the streaks of titanium white would brighten
the room. But it was much too dark. Too dark.

XVIII

But this is nothing new; you like to lie,
to save yourself the slow embarrassment
that always lingers longer than you'd like.

And what you found irrelevant is now
discussed with urgency: the sand, the angels,
the way they vanish at the edge of the grove.

The angels? Yes, the angels, camera-shy
and all, are bothersome and ignorant,
you say, their unfurled wings unladylike.

XIX

There is light and there is dark,
the man's face and the man's face in water.
His eyes were pools of grief, bottomless

and dangerous. Who could resist him?
When his lips touched mine, I could not
rise to the surface of such grief; I sank.

Can anyone return from such sadness?
My arms grew limp. I became like water:
calm, silent, capable of unthinkable stillness.

XX

Someone stirred at the edge of sight.
In the field, your body pressing mine flat,
your lips on my neck, something stirred

at the edge of sight. Water swallows every
image, holds it briefly before a fish
disturbs the very center of it.

There is water and the threat of water.
There is a cell invading another cell.
There is an explosion. There are many cells.

XXI

Because Spain flickered in the hearts of men,
the ceiling was littered with coats of arms,
heraldic lions, banners billowing . . .

An aged Henry James once sat under this barrage
of color, no doubt annoyed—Spain more imperial
in the original. Here, Ponce de León knights the air

with a lance, the etched birds scattering,
the painted clouds parting: O ceilings vaulted with light,
canonize us with the subtle glow of angels.

XXII

Did you hear the cry of the falcon?
The fourth call, made for a response
and different from the warning note that precedes

the attack or the cry that signals *storm, storm?*
At the edge of the park, atop the dunes,
the cloud-gatherer spirals his hands.

For a moment, he is the maelstrom of birds
spiraling above the windmill,
continuously moving to evade attack.

XXIII

Someone at City Hall had scaled down our
solar system—a foot of 8th Avenue the equivalent
of what had to be a ridiculous number of miles,

light years maybe—and installed stakes along
the road, each bearing the name of a planet.
Saturn, Uranus, Neptune, Pluto, and then the hill

lifting the road to remind us of gravity, something
that could be felt as well as measured. I had no idea
that Distance, too, could be felt, the way it could hurt.

XXIV

If a child is a compilation of genes,
the amalgam of our traits, our actions,
is it not also the inheritor of our faults?

Of course, questions like these are answers
in and of themselves. The wind turned
and my eyes stung from the salty air.

How could such a child survive
carrying so many faults? It was a gift
for two who had never learned to be generous.

XXV

Mother of tears, Mother of the grey-blue stone,
pray for us sinners. I have come to the edge
of a bluff, the Pacific crashing below me.

I have come with an old grief that is heavy
but refuses to sink. Holy Mother, Star of the Sea
who guides the ships across straits and shallows,

I have come without help or guidance.
The ocean keeps up its terrible din.
There is no one at the edge of sight.

XXVI

You must be still. You must move as if
through water. Your feet must be an anchor,
your hands both graceful and terrible.

You must become water. You must absorb force.
Let yourself ripple each attack to stillness.
Whatever happens cannot be erased.

Let your surfaces reflect and distort.
Be still and move only with purpose.
You must be calm but capable of great force.

XXVII

I think of you when I least expect to do so.
There, above the Pacific, the surf challenging
the rocky coast with deceptions, the wind turned.

Sometimes, early in the morning, I believe
you are the one lying next to me in bed,
your hands clenching the sheets under your chin.

I who have painted only precious landscapes
failed to capture those hands on canvas.
Memory, do not fail me. Let me try again.

Carolyn Alessio

Casualidades

On the street near the bus stop a group of teenaged boys stood in a circle, sharpening their rusted machetes. Berta pulled her market bag closer as she walked toward the bus. The *ladrones,* the thieves, weren't likely to rob anyone until payday—two days off—but Berta moved with caution. Three rotting onions knocked together inside her bag, next to a vial of medicine. She always carried old onions with her medicine because the people in her village were nosey and if they tried to look into her bag they would smell the odor and stay away.

This morning she had taken off work to go to the hospital on the hill for a checkup. She had not had a seizure for two weeks, but the medicine gave her gas, a constant rumbling that pained and embarrassed her. A week ago she had stopped taking the full dosage.

The faded green bus started uphill, groaning and halting. Berta looked in vain for an empty seat. The bus driver shifted gears jerkily, and Berta nearly stumbled. As she reached for the bar above to steady herself, a woman in an embroidered smock pulled her basket of chicks onto her lap and gestured at the empty seat next to her. Berta smiled and sat down.

At the sewing cooperative where she worked, none of the women wanted to sit by Berta anymore. Her seizures had increased in the past year, and the women had begun to treat Berta like someone they thought the priest should exorcise. She took to working alone, hunched over in a dim corner of the cinderblock building, but even that didn't work. Two weeks ago she had been cutting out striped *jaspe* fabric for a vest when the strange singing rose up inside her, the low song without words that always heralded her attacks. She tried to muffle the sounds, to quiet her trembling hands, but the rumbling notes escaped from her mouth and her fingers shook, releasing the scissors. They landed a foot away from her nearest coworker, Esperanza, but Esperanza screamed anyway. Later, when Berta opened her eyes, the women stood around her in a circle and the gringo boss told her that she needed medical attention.

A man sitting near the front of the bus stood up, pulled out a package of colored pencils, and began to call out their virtues. Berta shifted in her seat near the back, next to the woman with the basket of squirming, squeaking chicks. She wondered if they could smell her onions. The vendor walked down the aisle. In a clear plastic case he held a rainbow spread of pencils: red, light blue, green, yellow, and an orange that nearly matched the pair of vinyl shoes Berta wore, a purchase that had cost her a month's wages. "Good prices, a bargain," the vendor said, strolling up and down the aisle. Neither Berta nor the woman next to her looked as he passed, but inside Berta's head she had begun to draw, starting with a red pencil for the clay along the road, then moving upward, shading in the sky as it looked at daybreak, a blue-gray haze that covered the mountains and the inactive volcanoes. This was her view from the roof of her mother's house as Berta fed the roosters in the early morning. The bus lurched and Berta felt a nip from a chick at her elbow.

The seizures always began with singing, a low thrumming that started below her breastbone and traveled upward, swirling in gritty circles around her throat and emerging from Berta's mouth in syllables that many villagers thought were too low for a woman. Sometimes they started at work, but mostly the attacks happened at home, the strange song catching her as she leaned over the *pila* to wash a glass sticky with rice drink, or tend the fire for tortillas that her mother had started but forgotten to watch.

Berta's house was made of cinderblock and sheets of thin wood that darkened in the rain and shuddered during the windy season. She was twenty-nine and lived with her mother. Every other woman of her age in the village had a man and children; some even had grandchildren. Sometimes Berta babysat for her neighbors' children, not minding even when they rubbed their grimy hands in her long hair, but lately their mothers had been worried about the evil eye she might carry, and they asked Berta not to stare too long at their babies.

Berta had never been on a date and she rarely looked in the mirror. Mornings when she pulled her glossy long hair into a barrette, she remembered what her mother said once when Berta asked if she were pretty: "M'*hija,* you have beautiful hair."

Gray letters arched over the steel gate, announcing "El Hospital Mental Público de Guatemala." Berta had disembarked from the bus a mile before and walked uphill, muddying her lovely shoes as she trudged past a long shallow garbage pit whose odors mixed with the day's heavy humidity and clung to her skin. She approached the guard, who slouched against the bumper of a military truck. He stood up, crushed out a cigarette, and asked for her identification.

Berta reached into her bag for her medical card, the one that her gringo boss had gotten for her when he drove her there for her initial consultation. The guard glanced at the green cardboard pass, grunted, and motioned with his gun to the path beyond the gate.

The grounds were a maze of low, squat buildings connected by dilapidated paths. The grass looked tired, yellow-brown in patches. Berta stepped over snarls of dirt and roots.

A man with a ragged beard approached her, and began to ask for money in a high staccato voice. Berta shook her head no, but he persisted, calling her pretty, complimenting her hair. Berta's head hurt.

"Por favor," the man said to Berta, "just a few *quetzales*." Berta sucked in her breath: she had never understood why her country's currency was named after the nearly extinct national bird.

The man reached for her arm, with a grip that was surprisingly tight.

Berta remembered her father before he left the family, on nights when his boss hadn't paid the workers their due at the coffee plantation. Drunk, he raced around the house, ripping laundry off the line, sometimes throwing pots into the street.

"Listen," she hissed now, turning around. *"No hablo español,"* she said, trying to sound nasal like the gringo boss at the sewing cooperative. "Speek Ing-lish."

The man loosened his grip, stood back and studied her. *"Gringa?"* he said, his heavy-lidded eyes widening.

"Sí." The laughter rose in her like odorless gas as she turned to look for the big building with the high padlocked gates.

The doctor didn't call her name during the first hour she waited, nor the second. When he finally got to her, Berta's back was stiff from leaning so long against the damp wall, and the doctor didn't even say her full name—Berta Francisca Torneo de Monterosso, but simply, Señorita Torneo. Her face burned as she got up to follow; everyone seemed to know just by looking at her that she was still Miss, Señorita.

The examining room was divided by a torn, faded curtain. Berta hesitated at the edge, noting the fabric's uneven cut, when the doctor waved her in.

The doctor spoke slowly and his lower lip was punctuated with dark indentations, like bruises on mangoes past their time. Berta wondered if he were nervous. He looked up from her file and said, "This is too early for your follow-up appointment."

Hands in her lap, Berta told him about the medicine's side effects. She tried to explain how she could not stand rumbling with gas out in public; making a rude sound at Mass just before the

366

offertory, at work when she and the other women presented their wares to a traveling missionary group. Nearly whispering, she mentioned she had lowered her dosage, and had suffered a flare-up at work.

The doctor said, "Do you want the seizures to return?"

She shook her head. Outside an ice cream truck played a jangly, carnivalesque tune.

"Señorita," he said, "I could switch you to another medicine but you'd have different problems. Sleep too much, thirsty all the time. With all epilepsy medications," he said, sweeping his long thin arm across the desk, "there are *casualidades*."

Chances of side effects. She looked down at her market bag and the odor of old onions rose to her eyes.

A woman with matted hair pushed into the examining room, yelling that she had lost her son, and pulling at the dirty rags wrapped around her wrists.

The doctor glanced at her. "Suleni," he said quietly, standing up, "They need you down at lunch."

The woman stared, pulled at her wrists. "My son is missing," she said. "He doesn't know I've moved."

The doctor went to her, placed his hands gently on her shoulders. "Let's find a nurse," he said, leading her toward the doorway. "We'll be right back," he said without turning to look at Berta.

A moment later he returned. He did not sit down, but reached for Berta's file from the desk. "Well," he said, turning back to Berta, "you will try the medicine a bit longer?"

She stared at the barred window for a moment, at the dingy walls. She imagined her shiny long hair matted, and putrid rags wound around her wrists. The doctor looked at her and she nodded.

Berta reached for her market bag and stood, moving toward the door. The doctor's voice stopped her: "Before you leave, let's see you take your noon-time dosage."

The pills left a bitter white paste on her tongue. Berta stopped on the street near the bus stop to splurge and buy a Coke, but even as she sucked the sweet soda through the straw in the plastic bag, she could not rinse the sourness from her mouth.

On the ride home she dozed a little, leaning up against the window that rattled and shook as the bus plodded forward. The metal clasp of her crooked barrette pushed into her scalp so finally she sat up. At one of the stops a group of schoolchildren in uniforms got on, waking Berta with their laughing and talking. Judging from their pressed uniforms she guessed they lived in the village two bus stops beyond hers, a cleaner place where there were no sewage ditches and the dogs did not howl all night for food.

The children unwrapped bright red suckers and tiny taffy squares. Dry wind blew in from the windows and Berta remembered playing in the wind as a child, pretending as her skirt billowed out that she was a flower.

The bus pulled into the last leg of Berta's journey. One-room cinderblock houses and wooden shacks pressed up against the sides of the road, their doors only feet from the sewage ditch.

Berta straightened her blouse, and wondered if, when she returned to work, the other women would ask her where she had been. Maybe she could slip into the corner, and they would be too busy to notice as they stitched tiny brown-faced dolls onto barrettes to ship up North to the States.

A sharp pounding shook the bus as it pulled near the sewing cooperative. The bus slowed and everyone turned around to look. Two young men had climbed on the back, yelling and beating at the windows.

The stooped, gray-haired driver stopped the bus and stood up. He pulled a tiny knife from his pocket, stepped off the bus, and went around to the back. Berta heard shouts and curse words. Inside the bus she saw other passengers pulling their bags closer. She did not have to be told they had been stopped by *ladrones*.

Finally the driver returned to the front, but he was followed by a young man waving a machete. Berta recognized the tall *ladrón* with the unusual green eyes.

"Don't worry yourselves," the bus driver called out to the passengers, but the *ladrón* stamped on the floor with a ragged boot and pushed him back to his seat.

Another young man with a machete entered from the side, also carrying the bus driver's tiny knife. A schoolchild began to cry.

"Pass up your money," the green-eyed *ladrón* called, slightly slurring his words. Everybody began to dig in their pockets and purses. Berta heard muttering. Payday at the factories and fincas was not for two more days—most villagers were down to bus fare and enough for a few eggs. She thought the *ladrones* must be desperate, drunk or high on sniffing glue bought at the shoemaker's shop. Berta looked in her bag: two onions and a vial of medicine. She swept her hand beneath them, found a single *quetzal* note. She handed it to one of the *ladrones* as he passed down the aisle, scraping his machete along the floor. The bus driver slouched in his seat, holding his face in his hands.

Nobody had much more to offer than Berta: single *quetzal* notes were pressed into the ladrones' hands, some loose change. Even the schoolchildren with the nice uniforms only had enough for another bus fare or two: they had spent most of it on candy.

The *ladrones* counted the money at the front of the bus, cursing every time a handful of loose change appeared. Berta estimated that at most they would have enough for an evening or two of beer, the regular kind with the rooster's head on the label. They counted the money again, then the green-eyed one muttered something. They talked back and forth a little, conferring, and spitting in the aisle.

Outside the bus, people from the neighborhood were beginning to gather. Berta thought she saw Esperanza from the cooperative, the woman she had scared with her scissors. Nobody ever called the police in their village, because the police were scared of the *ladrones*, too. It was hard to enforce law in their village, and revenge only came rarely, usually in the form of a midnight beating in the garbage dump.

The *ladrones* stared at them and paced, walking up and down the aisles and panning the passengers with their too-wide pupils. Finally the green-eyed *ladrón* turned to the passengers and said, "Pass up your shoes."

Nobody spoke. Many of them had been robbed before, of bus fare, jewelry and even food, but Berta had never heard of this. She looked down at her own, orange vinyl shoes. Until she was twelve she had gone barefoot, like most of the other young women in the village. After that she had worn plastic beach thongs, the cheapest kind at the market. But a month ago, she had treated herself to these beautiful durable shoes, after finishing a shipment 34 purses, 12 vests, and 25 barrettes. She still knew the numbers. The *ladrones* began with the schoolchildren, urging them to hurry as they passed up their dark-soled loafers. One child even passed up his socks.

Berta looked around. The adults with no shoes looked the most frightened. One woman had pulled several mangoes out of her bag as if to offer them in compensation. The others with shoes were taking them off, slipping their feet from plastic beach thongs, and unlacing boots in clumsy hurried movements. The muscular ladrón paced the aisles. His machete looked like it had once been used on a plantation.

Berta removed her shoes, stroking the smooth orange vinyl. The muscular *ladrón* hissed at everyone to hurry up. In the front of the bus the green-eyed *ladrón* was piling shoes into the T-shirts he and the other one had stripped off, makeshift knapsacks. Berta held her shoes for a moment longer in her lap, cradling them, then she slipped one into her bag. The other she slid beneath her shirt, hoping that in the commotion she wouldn't be noticed. The vinyl felt nice against her chest and she crossed her arms to camouflage.

The bare-chested *ladrones* now had full knapsacks. Outside the bus more villagers lined up, talking and wringing their hands. Berta thought she saw the priest, a friend of her mother's. She hated her town, herself, for always backing away from danger.

Everybody on the bus had bare feet now. The shirtless *ladrones* walked along, grabbing some shoes and purses that had not been handed up. The green-eyed *ladrón* stopped at Berta's seat. "Pass it," he said, staring at the bag on her lap. "Señorita," he said, grabbing her wrist, "Pass it here."

"Only vegetables," she began, but he emptied it. Three mottled onions fell out and a medicine vial, then the thud of one orange shoe. The *ladrón* let the onions roll down the aisle in off-white rotations, but he stooped to pick up the shoe. Normally the drugs might have interested him, Berta thought, but now everybody was watching. He held the single shoe in his hand, gripping it by its muddy sole.

The other passengers turned around to stare at her, but Berta was used to this. She knew how to be a spectacle.

The shoe dangled in front of her head. "Your other shoe," the green-eyed *ladrón* said. His assistant walked toward them. "Hey crazy lady," the muscular *ladrón* said, a glimmer of recognition crossing his broad face, "give us the shoe."

Berta shook her head. Inside her blouse, the vinyl felt cool against her clammy skin. "Now," the green-eyed *ladrón* said.

"It's mine," Berta said, clutching the shoe to her chest, "*Mío.*"

The muscular *ladrón* moved forward, but the green-eyed *ladrón* waved him off. She could tell he thought he had a way with women. "Señorita," he said, in a voice that reminded her of her visit to the doctor, "your shoe, please."

Berta shook her head. He was so close she could smell the perspiration on his chest. He reached for a lock of her hair, not pulling as hard as she expected.

The bus was quiet. The green-eyed *ladrón* worked a strand of her shiny hair in his fingers, then muttered something to the muscular *ladrón* behind him. The muscular *ladrón* laughed, and Berta spit in the green-eyed *ladrón's* face.

Now he yanked her by the hair, pulling her down the aisle to an empty seat at the front of the bus. He tugged so hard her barrette snapped open and the orange shoe fell out from under her shirt. The muscular *ladrón* lunged for it, but the green-eyed *ladrón* shoved Berta to the floor, a handful of her hair still caught in his fist. Her head smarted and her hands felt numb. Outside the bus people had begun to shout. Breathing hard, the green-eyed *ladrón* laid her hair out straight on the seat. As he positioned his machete to cut her hair, Berta opened her mouth and began to sing.

Kevin Casey

The Coffin

Stoner and his brother drove to the town where they had lived as children to make arrangements for their mother's funeral. The odd thing was that their mother was still alive but she was very old and growing increasingly vague and feeble in a nursing home, her mind fixed on aspects of the past rather than on a future that contained little other than her own funeral. The logic of this was that arrangements had to be made.

They drove along a broad new motorway that avoided most of the places that Stoner had expected to see, proceeding in a dull, straight line past the back of cramped housing estates with graffiti scribbled walls and factories protected by tall meshed wire fences and muddy patches that had almost certainly been intended as green areas. Then, suddenly, after a roundabout, they turned onto a narrow and familiar road and there were deep ditches and fields abandoning morning mists and cracked old gateposts with rutted avenues leading towards farm houses hidden by trees. Stoner felt, suddenly, that he was going home, that he was entering into his

memories in some elusively designated way. His childhood beck-
oned to him with an odd and ambiguous allure.

He wished that he could feel more deeply about his mother's predicament. She occupied a lost and baffled world and often appeared
to be frightened when the diminishing sum of her consciousness
failed to disguise the long gaps in her powers of recall. Pity was
inadequate and the occasional irritation that he felt was probably
unforgivable. He had noticed, before, that he was often capable of
shameful emotional superficiality. His response could be like a definition of democracy that he had come across somewhere; always
under threat and always insufficient. His brother, who was driving
with characteristic expertise, spoke about the concerns that he had
for her happiness and Stoner agreed, looking out at the green fields
and the opalescent sky, but privately experienced some anger that
she no longer had the strength and determination that he seemed
to remember from his boyhood. Her diminished state was like a
considered rejection not only of the present but of his memories of
the past. He stared out of the window at the approaching world
that had once defined the totality of his experience and felt that
something important had been lost.

The graveyard was close to the town. They parked on a pathway,
near to a house in which a schoolfriend of Stoner had once lived.
It was easy to find the plot where their father was buried. It was
close to the gate and marked by a granite headstone. The stone,
although a little weather-stained with a filigree of gray-green,
moth-like mould, was in good condition and the marble chippings
that covered the grave had battened down all but the most persistent of weeds. His mother would be buried in the adjoining plot.

Stoner went down on his knees, as if in an act of devotion, and
pulled up an elongated and sticky weed with fibrous, acidic-
smelling roots. He eased out one or two others, much smaller and
less offensive. His brother sprayed the headstone with a chemical
that would help to clear the mould. It hissed against the granite
like a sudden outbreak of rain. Stoner attempted to say a prayer
but found that he had lost faith in the words. This saddened him.
Some trickles of the chemical were trapped in the dark, carved letters of his father's name.

They drove into the town and had lunch in a hotel that had

changed very little since his childhood. The waitress spoke with the flattened accent of the region. Stoner wondered if he had known her parents. There was something about her intrusive friendliness, her inquisitorial manner, that suggested this as a possibility. She certainly reminded him of someone.

His brother had never really liked the town or spoken about it with any retrospective warmth but the memories that they shared, although inconsistent, were generally reassuring. They had felt constriction but no real unhappiness. Their parents moved unambiguously through the past.

After lunch, they parked outside the undertaker's house. He was a small man with a persuasive and comforting manner, evolved from years of addressing the bereaved. He said how wise they were to make decisions now. Far too many people left everything to the very last minute. It was such a mistake. He asked them for the date of their father's death then found, in a stout and tattered ledger, the details of the funeral; the price of the coffin, the quality of the brass, the size of the car assigned to the principal mourners.

"That's my father's handwriting," he said cheerfully, rocking back and forward on his heels. He had assumed a more avuncular manner as if he could relax now that some formalities had been got out of the way. "He died just a few months after that himself."

The room in which they were sitting contained a large, old rolltop desk, some high backed chairs and a table on which there were some glasses, a half filled bottle of whiskey and an unopened bottle of gin.

"Wont you have a small drop?" the undertaker asked, looking from one to the other in a gesture of jocular persuasiveness.

They said no. A shaft of harsh afternoon sunlight pierced through the glass of the dusty window and, from the distance, there were sounds of children playing with a ball.

Stoner's brother, who was accustomed to bringing business meetings to order, said, "Well I suppose we should make some decisions."

"If you think so," the undertaker said as if this were a surprise to him. They went into another room, an extension to the back of the house, narrow and windowless, with a musty smell and there were coffins there, presented like items of furniture in a store. Some

374

had impressive carvings on the lids, others had elaborate brass plates and handles, and others were decorated with intricate purple silk ribbons.

"American oak," the undertaker said, tapping one of the coffins. "A wonderful wood. Just look at that beautiful grain." He stroked the coffin with stubby, nicotine-stained fingers. Stoner looked into it, surprised at how small and contained an area was revealed. Could a body really fit in there? Was this where it all ended? They selected a simple coffin with a silver plate.

"You've both made an excellent decision. I really mean that! I'll bring it up to the city whenever it's needed."

They drove home, more constrained with each other, listening to music on the car radio. It was as if they were embarrassed about the transaction or as if there was nothing important left to say. When they arrived at his brother's house, they relaxed a little and agreed that it had been a worthwhile journey. Then Stoner got into his own car and drove to the nursing home, a long, low building placed well back from the road with large windows looking out towards an expanse of sea. As he walked down a corridor towards his mother's room he assumed that she had a visitor as he could hear her talking animatedly but she was alone, lying in her narrow bed, talking to herself. "We must go up there," she said. "It will be a big climb and we'll have to be careful but it will be worth it."

She was intent on this idea, her face shadowed by concentration and didn't seem to notice his arrival in her room. He thought, as he had so often thought before, that the business of growing old was terrible, something to be resisted for as long as possible, something to be feared. He was saddened that he would grow old in the presence of his daughters. They would witness the initial signs of decay, suspect indignities, notice the onset of infirmities, as he had once noticed the small glories of their ascent to womanhood.

He sat down beside the bed and took her hand. The fingers were cold, the flesh loose about the bones like an ill-fitting glove.

"Hello," he said, "how are you today?" willing her to respond. She stared at him and then smiled.

"I'm not so bad really," she said. She held his hand tightly. "I could be worse."

Then, suddenly and unexpectedly, she laughed. He found that he was laughing as well. They laughed together and separately at some unknown and unshared joke, laughed loudly and inordinately, laughed until they both had tears in their eyes.

Refugees

THERE WERE REFUGEES IN THE CITY THAT YEAR, SAD PEOPLE FROM some distant country, seeking political asylum. They dressed inappropriately for the weather and for the local sense of style. They looked like gypsies. Perhaps they were gypsies. They combined the flamboyant and the drab in an oddly confusing manner, the women in peacock costumes, the men in dark, tight, inexpensive suits.

They begged on the streets, aggressively, the women displaying their babies like trophies and hissing some mysterious message in a language that was not understood. The men stayed in the background, except for a few who had musical abilities and played accordions and trumpets on the streets. Their music had a haunted quality, thin and mysterious. It seemed to have its origins in another time, echoing some lost inheritance, plaintive notes raised in ineffectual protest. Stoner sometimes stood and listened to it, attempting to comprehend its meaning and to gain some insight into the tensions in the country that this music had failed to resolve. It was the music of the dispossessed. It confronted failure and then evaded the implications of this with a flourish of false gaiety, a bravado pretense that it was the music itself that mattered.

The amount of antagonism that these people provoked was surprising. It was out of proportion to any possible reason. Stoner read reports of verbal and physical attacks; businessmen shouting abusively, out of the windows of cars, at women begging at crossroads; children ganging up on smaller numbers of children; men being refused drinks in bars. It was difficult to believe that such a small group of unimportant people could provoke such outrage.

Stoner's daughters and most of their friends shared this negative view.

"What are they doing here anyway?"

"They're seeking asylum. They were being persecuted in their own country."

"I've heard that they're just here for the money, that they're nothing but economic refugees."

"I'm sure that some of them are and they won't be allowed to stay."

"Nobody likes them. Everyone comments on it. They're so aggressive."

"They're just trying to adapt to a new way of life. They're country people who suddenly find themselves in a city."

Stoner knew that he was saying the things that he wanted to believe yet he wondered if there wasn't some intolerance, some suppressed racism hiding behind the articulation of his ideas. A woman had approached him on a street that he particularly liked, looking for money, her dark eyes intent on the force of her quest, her voice almost hysterical and he had felt angry and a little flustered as he handed over some change. And there had been a sexual dimension to this transaction, something that had compromised them both in the false act of giving and taking. It embarrassed him to remember the incident. He remembered that he had not been able to look at her after he had taken the change from his pocket, that he had placed it on her shaking palm and turned away as if towards a previous order that held no conflict as dubious as this. It was an unpleasant memory. He knew that the common attitude towards the refugees was not only wrong but dangerous yet behind this perception was the shameful secret of his own emotional discomfort at their presence. He would be relieved if they were somewhere else where they would not remind him of disconcerting truths about himself.

Every second or third Saturday he would take a bus into the city and visit a number of bookshops. He was a collector, on a modest scale, concentrating on the works of ten or twelve contemporary writers. He liked the atmosphere of these second-hand bookshops, the faint feeling of mustiness. The suspension of urgency, the prospect of surprise. He often recognized other customers, intent on pursuits of their own, looking for a book or books that would finally complete a collection and fulfill some obscure attempt at achieving order, volume after volume, each complete with a dust jacket, arranged neatly on a shelf, like people waiting patiently in a queue.

On this particular Saturday, he found nothing that was relevant to his collection. There was another shop, in which he could have looked, but he was suddenly bored by the close focus of his search, the triviality that lay behind the precision of the obsession. He went to a nearby bar and ordered a glass of red wine, a Merlot that he had come across recently and particularly liked. The bar had literary associations and there were tourists at the counter, talking loudly to each other and drinking the local beer. Some carried copies of the book in which there were references to the bar. They would bring it home and in all probability, give up reading it after the first few pages. Stoner listened to their conversation for a while, complaints about hotels and the inadequacy of local transport, their anger at political events at home. He felt isolated in their company; he shared none of their concerns.

He left the bar and heard music coming from a nearby street. He went there and found that a small crowd had gathered around a man playing an accordion. The man was short and stout and middle-aged. The jacket of his dark suit was tightly buttoned. There was a comic contrast between the disillusioned expression on his face, which was emphasized by a drooping, gray moustache, and the gaiety of the music that he was playing. His fingers moved swiftly along the keys, producing chords that uncharacteristically suggested energetic dancing and laughter and success yet he stared sadly at some point above the heads of his listeners as if he were in fear of them. His accordion was the most elaborately decorated that Stoner had ever seen with gold and silver stars and rainbows fixed to the side of the keyboard and painted on the bellows. It was strange to stand on this familiar street and hear sounds that came from somewhere else played by someone who seemed so unhappy to be there.

He was about to move away when a man stepped forward and began to dance. For a few seconds he appeared to be displaying real skill then it was evident that he was moving aimlessly, even drunkenly, not always in time to the music. He attempted a twirl and almost fell but some of the people were amused and started to clap as if they were watching an adept performance. The musician looked uneasy as the man moved closer to him in a manner that suggested aggression rather than enjoyment. He was certainly local and almost certainly drunk; encouraged by the clapping, he uncovered some well of anger in himself and began to shout at the musician, single words that were hardly coherent, but which conveyed their meaning through their tone, as he continued his meaningless dance, like an inexpertly controlled puppet. The musician took some steps backward; his fingers faltered over a few notes, then he regained control. People were laughing. There was certainly something humorous about the threatening dance performed to music that continued as if nothing had changed, a counterpoint of celebration and anger. Other people joined the crowd; the occasion was becoming an event. The larger audience encouraged the man to increase the pace of his performance, lurching from one side of the street to the other, his arms in the air, his fingers moving, as if using castanets, his face red and bloated from the considerable effort.

Stoner watched the musician and wondered what he could be thinking.

Would he assume that this kind of incongruity was a normal part of life in this country? Did he already regret that he had left home and crossed borders to arrive at so strange a place? There was no way of guessing at the reality of his previous life, the day to day happenings that had occupied and formed him. He was a man without a comprehensible past, existing only on this street at this time, playing an accordion as if fulfilling some improbable destiny.

The dancer stumbled, regained his balance, then stumbled again, knocking against the musician. Both men fell backwards, the accordion detaching from its straps and landing on the street with a sad sound of breakage and then a prolonged and anguished groan as the bellows emptied of air. Both men lay sprawled on the street, their legs intertwined in what looked like some unusual ritual of intimacy. A few people laughed.

As both men got to their feet, the musician looked anxiously for his accordion as if he were searching for a lost child. He picked up a piece of the broken keyboard and held it against his cheek. It was as if he were seeking contact with some part of his past and his face was made ugly by grief. There was an uneasy silence then people began to leave. Stoner looked around and wished that he had never been a part of the crowd. They wanted to pretend that nothing very important had happened. They were habituated to caution. They did not even realize that by their silence they had given the musician a history.

David Evanier

Danny and Me

I

ON SABBATH NIGHT, THEY GATHER FOR PRAYERS AND DINNER.
I am the volunteer staffer. No one knows the Hebrew prayers, so
the black attendant, Gaylord, his arms folded, emotionally sings
"The Lord's Prayer." As he sings, the group stares out into space.

Buddy, about forty-five, struts like a peacock in his purple shirt,
and wears a large and bushy orange, purple, and chartreuse rabbit's
foot key ring on the right side of his pants. He likes to act like the
big shot, and calls out to the men in wheelchairs, "Hey, how ya
doin', old man?" and winks to the rest of us.

"Black people are the best," Buddy says to Gaylord. "I never feel
fear among blacks. Such a sweet black nurse my uncle had, so kind
to him. My uncle got robbed, and he shot at them, but he shot at
the cops too. So the cops shot his ankle off. His leg was amputated.

"I bought him a bottle of Scotch. And I went to Barracini's for a three-pound box of sour candies. I gave them my order. I say, Look at me. I want my order, and I want it now. And I told the sweet black nurse: give him one. If he wants more, you give him a little bit at a time. You take a little ashtray, and you fill that up by his bed. And you fill up a shot glass with a little water, take a little Scotch, and an ice cube. Then hide it from him because he wants more. I tell my uncle, you want to take a walk? I'll wheel you in your room, I'll wash you around, get you dressed. Then I'll dress you up warm, put you in a wheelchair, put his artificial leg on."

"I would like some cookies, Joseph," an etherized voice wafts up to me. It is Leah, whose body is twisted and whose head circles around constantly. I get the cookies for Leah. "I said I want some cookies, but I didn't say I want them now. When I'm done with dinner I would like some cookies please—"

"Here they are—"

"You're not listening. I would like three cookies please, when I am done with dinner. Please get me three cookies on a plate when I am done with my dinner."

"Okay—"

"What kind of cookies do you have?"

"Pecan and oatmeal."

"Pecan, please. Three cookies, when I am done with my dinner. My father will be picking me up at eight o'clock. Could you take me downstairs at 7:45?"

"Not eight o'clock?"

"My father will be picking me up at eight o'clock. Please listen. My father will be picking me up at eight o'clock. We will go downstairs at 7:45 and wait for him. Will you take me downstairs at 7:45 please? I would like my cookies now."

Danny Stein is one of the people I've volunteered to counsel. An obese young man in his twenties with a sharp, whining, robotic voice, he is slumped in his chair. Seated across from him, Michelle, a pretty young girl, his former girlfriend, is staring at him.

"Hi, Danny," I say.

"I'm so glad I don't have to speak to Michelle anymore. She was always bothering and disobeying me. She was just impossible to deal with," Danny responds.

"Danny, she'll hear you."

"No, she won't," Danny says. "She's deaf as a doorpost."

This is true. Michelle keeps staring, a little smile on her face.

At 7:45 an arm grips mine in a hammerlock. It is Leah. I suggest we wait in front of the house. "We will sit in the lobby and look through the window for my father. My father will be here at eight o'clock. We will sit behind the glass and wait for my father." I tell Danny I will see him on Wednesday, and take Leah downstairs.

When her father arrives, I wave goodnight to Leah and I go home.

II

The next morning, I take a beaming Julius Goldberg on a tour of Hollywood. Julius is 30, very fat, bursting out of an orange shirt and red suspenders. He has a bright red yarmulke on his head, which keeps falling off. Early mornings, before I meet him, he takes buses back and forth across the city to pass the time.

Julius usually walks slowly, but now he darts excitedly down Hollywood Boulevard. He heads directly for the booth with bus schedules and takes forty of them. He spies more booths at the Hollywood Roosevelt hotel, swoops down, and takes a pile of free coupons. He picks up the phones at booths to see if anyone is on the other end, and checks for coins. He plays "peekaboo" with me. He peers through slats to watch construction crews and checks out the baseball caps and T-shirts at the schlock shops along the boulevard. "I'm having a wonderful time," he says with a warm smile. Suddenly he hugs me. I hug back. "And a left to the right and a right to the left and a left to the right," Julius shouts. "There's only one Julius and there's only one Joseph. Julius! That's my name and that's the game."

Since Danny is no longer dating Michelle, I have arranged for Julius to go out with her on a date. But Julius didn't know what to say to her, and told me that Michelle kept calling her mother on the phone and saying, "Julius isn't talking." Today I give Julius a list of questions he can ask Michelle on their next date: "Do you like to walk on the beach? What are your favorite foods? Who is your favorite movie star?"

Today Julius talks to the leaves and barks back at barking dogs. He says he wants to go to Australia "to see the ostriches, kangaroos, and hyenas." He takes leaves off trees, pretending to chew them, and playfully says "Yummy" to me. Gazing at flowers, he mischievously asks me: "What shall I have for dessert? Maybe a cheeseburger or a knuckle sandwich." Wrapping paper rustles in the wind as we walk and he says, "The wrapping paper is following us down the street."

When we get back to his house, Julius' fragile father is waiting for us. Mr. Goldberg is despondent about his son's condition, and I have suggested that Julius watch a video of Mr. Goldberg's Holocaust testimony.

The three of us sit in Julius' bedroom watching. On the screen Mr. Goldberg talks of Hungary in 1944: of watching his younger brother being cruelly beaten every day; of seeing his sister relinquish her one-year old baby to a capo because she is being sent to the gas chambers. On screen, he cries.

I feel a hand on mine, and a body shaking. Julius is revving up to one of his trademark hale and hearty laughs, which he usually emits every three or four minutes, no matter what we are talking about, sometimes followed by a high five. I put my finger to my lips to shush him.

He is silent the rest of the time: about an hour and a half. He fidgets, yawns, and scratches his fingers. But Julius is listening.

At the end, we all stand up, the three of us. Julius is not laughing, or smiling.

His father turns and looks at his son in surprise.

III

At three o'clock Danny, my prize client, is waiting for me. "I still have my problem with pretty women, Joseph," he shouts at me. "I'm like a buzzing bee among a lot of flowers." The people around us try to look casual.

Danny has a tortured look. Everything about him is slightly off: as he walks, he holds his left hand up in the air.

Danny is a surprise kisser. He kisses beautiful women, strangers, whom he cannot resist on the hand. "But I'm not the only one with problems, Joseph. Today I was walking with my friend, Michael, and we saw a pretty girl. Michael walked into a store window and broke his nose. He had to go to the hospital." Danny smiles. "And Michael has a tragic past. His girlfriend drowned in the bathtub."

He has gotten into trouble with the police and been warned that if it happens again, he may go to jail.

"I had a little trouble this morning myself," Danny reports. "Judy, this girl at work. But I only stared at her and said certain things."

"What happened?"

"Well . . . she triggered my urges. She was wearing a pink sweater with a black brasseire under it. I got carried away again. But I've solved the problem. When I see her next time, I'm going to cover my eyes with my hands.

"Or I'll just have to talk about good things. Not about things that will scare her. I'll just strike up a good conversation and not concentrate on her clothes and body. Just concentrate on appropriate eye contact. Rather than stare, I'll move my eyes around the way my therapist told me to." Danny demonstrates how he will move his eyes "toward his head" rather than toward the girl. "And my therapist told me to move my hands up and down while I walk. This is my relaxed mode." I don't see much improvement. Danny still looks a little weird. "I just get so anxious when I'm around a woman. I don't know how to act appropriately with her. And I do stupid things because I don't care about life. But once I meet the girl of my dreams, hopefully my life will begin spinning in another direction."

Danny knows how his autism affects people and what he's missing by a few inches: normal friends and a decent social life, the ability to fit in and be accepted, and above all, a relationship with a beautiful girl who does not have a disability. It's like a hungry man looking through the window of a restaurant at a banquet. He joins college clubs and watches the other students sit far away from him and even quit the clubs to get away from him.

"It may have something to do with the way I see my eyes, Joseph," he says. "I think I have what's called evil eyes. So I see things differently from anyone else."

"What are evil eyes?" I say, even though I know what he means.

"I use my eyes for evil looks."

"But you're not evil, Danny."

"I know. I stare because I'm afraid of saying anything to a pretty girl. That's why I do it."

"What would you say to them if you could?"

"I would try to say hi to them."

Danny pauses for a moment. "I think it may also have something to do with balls and pillows too."

"What do you mean?

"Somehow I see women like pillows instead of human beings. Someone to hug and kiss and lie on and all that stuff. I even bite my pillows. When I was with Michelle as boyfriend and girlfriend, I bit her sweater and squealed.

"Eleven years ago, on June 12, 1988, a Wednesday, at two PM, my mom was driving and she got *very upset* on the freeway because of all the cars. And I'd been so nice to her that day: I'd taken her dogs out for her and they'd done potty and poo-poo. But she got *very upset* with me, Joseph. And I squealed at her. And I've begun squealing at pretty girls a lot again. They don't hear me. I do it from a distance.

"The laws have gotten tougher because there are a lot of women that have been raped by a lot of nasty men. And a lot of children kidnapped by a lot of crazy men. It's not like the old days anymore when men were allowed to kiss women on their hands. Those days are gone."

We sit in Baskin-Robbins and Danny finishes his double ice cream cone. "And then there was the mall last night."

"What about it?"

"Well, there were these female piano players."

Danny pauses. "Same old stuff. Anyway, I could have gone further with Judy. I could have taken my pants down and placed my penis on her hand. I didn't do that."

I say goodbye to Danny. I have a date tonight.

I am seated in my car, locked in Maria's garage. The garage door is shut, and will not open. I took too long getting my car, and the garage door shut on me. I look for a way of getting out. I feel utterly alone and lost, the history of my failed relationships with women cascading through my head.

Maria is a hooker. I have been seeing her for four months. I have fallen for her, even though she is moist with semen and wine, saturated with it in that darkness of hers. She has a kind of crazy, lyrical, elegaic sentimentality.

She is dark and Italian and thirty-three. She has beautiful large breasts, with hard dark nipples, big brown eyes, and a voice with music, childhood and womanhood in it. I always wanted an Italian girl. My whole life. An Italian girl in black stockings to marry and have kids with.

I met her in a room of sage and chimes and bells. Her mother was in the hospital dying of leukemia. Maria was vulnerable. We stood on her terrace in early February sipping wine. "Don't you go falling in love with me," she said. "Joseph, do you know what I'm going to do up here when the weather gets warm? I'm gonna get some trees and some Chinese lanterns. I can have my kerosene lamps out here. It will be beautiful. I love fixing the place up. I love having friends over and making things really nice for them and having parties, but I can't do that right now. Joseph, are you Jewish?"

"Uh huh."

"Because over in Jersey and New York, my Mom said her first love was a Jewish boy, Morty. A candystore boy. Her grandfather wouldn't let her see Morty unless she screwed him first. That was his trip."

Her puppy, J.J., barked.

"What are you doing, you busybody? He has such a manly bark."

Later she said, "I'm on a death trip. I left home at sixteen and went to Chicago. I've been through a paper shredder. I ate out of garbage cans. I was afraid for so much of my life. I've done nine porn films. I've fucked men as a way of getting rid of them."

When we made love and she came, she said, "Oh God. I didn't think I was so open."

Afterwards, she did somersaults with J.J. on the floor.

At the door she said of the two of us, "We're like twins."

Waving, she said, "Please don't ever laugh at me or try to change me."

On the day her mother died, she called me from her car after the funeral. "I won't be able to work for three or four days. Joseph, I brought heather for my mother. It was her favorite flower. To honor her as my mother and as a woman. I should be home in a couple of hours."

I fantasized about the day I would help her move out of that apartment, carrying boxes, moving decisively. And in bed, thinking all night of the wedding with her in a white gown, even a priest, who gave a fuck? And the two of us in bed and our kids crawling in with us calling us Mommy and Daddy.

For four months I have struggled. All these strangers, paying her. At the end of our sessions, she walks around the room with the phone, answering her messages, whispering, purring and laughing. She complained that my messages on her machine are too long. "That one about Celine and Gogol took up half my tape," Maria said. "Joseph, you're in my head all the time. I put my energy into you and I lose my concentration in other areas where I have to survive. This business can be pretty horrendous. A guy made me be a dog today."

I have pleaded with her that we see each other outside the apartment, that we walk on the beach, see a movie, go to dinner, or even breakfast (the only free time she said she had). I had never been with her outside that apartment. When I walked the Venice beach or on the green UCLA campus and looked at the mountains and the trees, I thought of her, stuck in that room day and night.

She was afraid of leaving that apartment and that structure. "A guy in the gym was talking to me while I was riding the bike. I know what he wants! But I was nice to him. Otherwise when I leave the gym I might find my car smashed or dented or defaced." She laughed. "Well, I guess I had a crazy father."

But tonight I finally took her out. There was a chink in her armor. She was busted this week and she has to move. She may need me.

In the restaurant tonight, she was a new Maria. I knew this mood of hers, and my hopes sank. Having been busted, she was on a new quest to change her life. In addition to seeing her psychic and her healer, now she would go into Reichian therapy and also learn Tantra on top of it.

She said the therapy groups met on each floor of a large building. "As I walk by, I hear people from every floor crying out 'No, no, no, no!'" She seemed to find this thrilling. And then there was Tantra, a refined form of massage, legitimate, spiritual, classy. She would even get a license. I wanted to ask her if she would not have to jerk guys off anymore, but she'd hate the question.

Maria put on a serious look and said she was thinking of my marriage proposal. I knew it was bullshit. When the wine came, she hooked arms with me and I drank out of her glass and she drank out of mine. I wondered who taught her that.

Back in the apartment, I stroked her face and gently kissed her, and this time she opened her mouth at last and kissed back and I kissed her and kissed her gently and held her.

"I'm turning off the phones," she said, as if that was a permanent move. She paused. "But I do have one call I'll have to make later."

Afterwards, she was on the phone in the corner, whispering and laughing.

In the garage, I sit in the car. I wedge my way out of the structure and call Maria on the intercom in front of the building. Her line is busy for a long time. She finally answers. "My car is locked in. Buzz me out."

"I was buzzing you," she said impatiently. "I never heard of anybody taking so long to get out of a garage."

V

The next day, Danny and I walk on the beach, looking at the girls in bikinis.

We pass a pretty girl that I would die for.

Danny says "Hi" to her, and she smiles.

He turns to me. "See how appropriate I was, Joseph?" he asks.

Greg Johnson

Sticky Kisses

ONE KISS HAD STAYED WITH THOM SADLER THROUGHOUT HIS LIFE.

After three decades he could still recall the greasy surprise as he touched two fingers to his cheek—then the sight of them blood-smeared, a bright vivid red—then the stale heavy smell as of spoiled berries as he brought them to his nose.

Later he'd raced into the house, into his room. His cheek flaming, burning. Stopped breathless in front of the mirror where the smeared lipstick reminded him less of blood than war paint, his pale small-boy's face taking on a cockeyed glamour since the other cheek was white, untouched, giving him an unbalanced look. He turned sideways to see himself in profile, his glance cutting sharply to the right until his eyes ached. No, not war paint, and not even a kiss any longer, just a smeary red stain that wasn't anything but itself. Opening his palm he'd rubbed savagely at the kiss, the paint, the mark, whatever it was, then rushed into the bathroom and used a soap and washcloth until his skin stung. His cheek felt aflame for the rest of the evening, but the kiss was gone.

. . .

That day, his birthday, had begun as the most exciting of his life. this was the first time he'd had a real party, one to which he'd been allowed to invite his friends. There were eighteen children in his kindergarten class, which was run by the nuns at Sacred Heart but taught by a lay teacher, Mrs. Simpson, a sweet, pink-faced woman with upswept blond hair. For weeks he'd been pestering his class-mates with reminders about the party. His other birthday celebra-tions attended only by family members now seemed to him baby-ish, something he'd left behind. Now he'd started school. Now he had friends, and they were coming to his party.

When he and his mother talked about the plans for his birthday (which he loved doing, darting mothlike around the kitchen while his mother tried to work) she would use the phrase *your friends* as though repeating a kind of mantra. He'd never thought about this word before. Two or three boys in the neighborhood had been his "little friends" (but somehow they did not count, and in fact he hadn't invited them to the party) but now there was a whole roomful, boys and girls, from school. All shapes and sizes. Even a black boy. Even a girl from Korea. All these were his "friends." (What about Abby, though? He played more with his sister than with anyone. But no, she was his sister, a word he didn't like because that's what the nuns were called, and Abby was nothing like the nuns; and because a fat third-grader had shoved him one morning at recess, calling him "little sister," and Thom had fallen facefirst into the sandy mound of dirt near the merry-go-round. Still, he couldn't say "my friend Abby." She was his *sister*, a fact that would never change.) In the days before his party that new word lived in his imagination, became palpable in his mind's eye and ear, a solid, welcome shape on his tongue: *friend*. He tasted the word, heard its rich, full tones, even shut his eyes and saw the let-ters that had burned into his thinking in their unbreakable, changeless order.

Because his parents and Abby and even sometimes Verna read to him, and because Mrs. Simpson wrote words on the blackboard in kindergarten class, he already knew how to read, though not as well as his family bragged he did. To him, the words he did know were still new and exciting, like the faces or smells or colors of certain people. For him, their maid's name *Verna* was a rich brown word, like her skin, the same color as the battered antique rolltop desk, inherited from Thom's great-grandfather, where his mother sat to write the bills. He thought *Abby* was a sweet, girlish word, and once when they were talking about words in kindergarten class Mrs. Simpson had pointed out that his sister's name had the same letters as "baby" and said that was an *anagram*—which was a word he didn't like, since it sounded mean and fussy, though he remembered it. He'd told Abby that her name had the same letters as "baby" but he supposed because she was older than Thom and in third grade she didn't seem to like it. Soon she'd figured out that his name had the same words as "moth" and for a few days called him "Thom the Moth," and of course he fought back by chanting "Abby the Baby" and quickly enough by mutual unspoken consent they'd dropped the game.

But he kept thinking about names, about words. His mother's name was *Lucille,* which sounded like breaking glass, and his father's was *George,* which made him think of a big comfortable dusty room. But as his birthday party approached he thought mostly about *friend* and how it was a solid, good word, full of ordinary letters that you used a lot. He'd told Mrs. Simpson about the party his mother was planning and that she'd called the other mothers to invite his "friends," and something about the careful way he'd said the words made her smile. That day, she'd written the date of his upcoming birthday on the blackboard—*May 1, 1970*—and said in other countries this was called "May Day" and it was a very special occasion. He liked the ring of "May Day," too, because it sounded important and he liked words that rhymed. The day she wrote his birthday on the board was only the middle of April and he felt the day would never come. He imagined the next two weeks as a sprawling desert of time across which he must crawl, going to sleep at night, waking in the morning, dressing and undressing, eating and drinking, going to kindergarten and coming home, doing all this patiently, impatiently, for days and days before his birthday and the party would finally happen. All this depressed him, so to distract himself he thought about words, and pestered his mother about the party and what they would do, what they would eat, what would happen, all to make the time pass more quickly.

His mother insisted they were going to have an old-fashioned birthday. They were going to have a big homemade chocolate cake (she hated those flat, white ones you got from the bakery) and six big blue candles that matched the color of Thom's eyes. They were going to play games like pin-the-tail-on-the-donkey. She'd dug an old watercolor of a donkey, folded in quarters, out from a dusty box in the tool shed and said it was the same one they'd used at her own parties when she was a little girl. The tail was missing, though, so Abby had made a new one out of brown construction paper, and the color wasn't even close to the faded brown of the original donkey, but Thom said he didn't care. It's just a game, he said, trying to sound nonchalant though his excitement made his voice squeak. He was thrilled by the idea of all his friends playing games at his party. His mother said they were also going to play "go fishing," which meant each child in turn would be handed a cane fishing pole with a string on the end, which would be lowered behind a tarp stretched across the swing set in the back yard. On the other side of the tarp his father would crouch, invisible, and each time a new child "went fishing" Mr. Sadler would attach a party favor to the end of the line with a clothes pin. And they would play musical chairs out on the patio, with his father playing his harmonica, and whoever was the last one sitting would win another favor. Then around 5:15—his mother had written all this out, planning how long each event would take—his friends would don their paper hats and sing "Happy Birthday" and Thom would make his wish and blow out the candles and then, at long last, he would get to open all his gifts and they'd all eat ice cream and cake and Thom and all his friends would be happy, happy.

Beyond that moment, Thom hadn't given a thought.

On the morning of the party Thom was behaving, his father grumbled, as though he'd had ten cups of coffee, racing around the house, double-checking that everything was there for the games, asking his father if he was sure it wasn't going to rain (his father pointed up at the cloudless sky, not saying a word), asking his mother if they should call his friends and remind them (no, his mother insisted, that wouldn't be polite; of course they would remember), asking Verna if she'd remembered to make the punch, had his mother bought enough ice cream, did they have enough party favors? "Yes, child!" she'd cried, shaking her head. Verna worked for the Sadlers from eight until noon, and Thom caught her watching the clock; though Thom's mother had offered double her hourly wage to "work the party" Verna had claimed to have business in town; she'd slapped her man's felt hat over her black sour-smelling curls and left at twelve on the dot. So Thom ran to his room and tried to pass the time playing with the microscope-and-slide set his Grandmother Allan had sent him from Philadelphia; it had arrived two days early but his mother let him open it, and by now he was tired of looking at pieces of sugar and salt under the microscope, he was ready for his friends to arrive, he was ready for his party. When his mother phoned each of his class-mates' mothers, she'd told them it would begin at four and end at six, and by 3:30 Thom was so frantic and darting from room to room so often, and so aimlessly, and asking so many questions he'd already asked that his mother ordered him to sit at the kitchen table and eat a cookie and drink a glass of milk.

"And take some deep breaths," she said, rolling her eyes.

He wasn't hungry or thirsty but he obeyed. To make the last half hour pass he thought about *cookie*, a word that sounded sweet and crumbly just like it really was, and *milk*, a word that sounded white and cold just like it really was, but he was tired of thinking about words and when he heard the doorbell ring at ten till four, of course he dropped the milk and the glass shattered on the kitchen tiles, occasioning a deep groan from his mother—"Why couldn't Verna have stayed this one afternoon?" she muttered—and half the milk had splashed onto his shirt and shorts so he'd had to run up and change, and by the time he got to the den, sixteen of his friends were there. (Two of them never showed, a fact that later, whenever he thought about it, made his chest ache.) The mothers had conferred, and four of them had volunteered to car pool. The four cars had arrived in unison, like a funeral procession, each dis-gorging four children, and at six o'clock four different cars would arrive to pick them up again.

It was a perfect Saturday, a sunny May afternoon. His birthday. When he came into the kitchen, though, suddenly dragging his feet out of shyness when he saw the brightly chattering kids, the breakfast-room table piled with gifts, his sense of time shifted abruptly and the party careened along from the first moment his friend Danny saw him and shrieked "HAPPY BIRTHDAY!" and all the kids began swarming around him like bees, the boys punching his arm, the girls trying to kiss him, Thom giggling and fidgeting all the while, the back of his head tingling with nearly unbearable excitement, pleasure.

Happy birthday! Happy birthday! The words came at him like tossed flowers through the rest of the party even as his mother seized control, informing the children of the "activities" she had planned and shepherding them along, first into the den for pin-the-tail-on-the-donkey, where Thom's parents handed out cloth napkins to use as blindfolds, summoning them one at a time ("in alphabetical order," Thom's mother insisted) to approach the wrinkled, melancholy-looking donkey profile tacked against a giant bulletin board, which Thom's father had brought home from his office just for this purpose. One by one, they approached blindfolded and tried to pin the tail (actually, thumbtack the tail) in the right place. The other children watching in silence for the first couple of tries; laughing uproariously when Susie Blanchard pinned the tail onto the donkey's rear hoof; shrieking with delight when Tim Daniels pinned it directly onto the animal's exposed, balefully staring eye (several of the children grabbed their own eyes, crying "ouch, I can't see!" "oooh, where am I!"); but even as Thom's mother determinedly made her way through the alphabet (consulting a handwritten list of the children's names, which she held crumpled in the same hand that normally gripped a wadded Kleenex) the children began to lose interest in watching, preferring instead to don their blindfolds and walk into walls, into each other, laughing and shoving, deliberately falling on the floor, so that Thom's mother announced anxiously (Thom's father and Abby had observed all this from the den sofa, smiling) that they should go outside for the next "activity" and even Luther Washington and Amy Zins, who hadn't yet had their way with the donkey, didn't seem to mind. So Mrs. Sadler corralled them all into the backyard, where Thom's father had already affixed an electric-blue tarp to the swing set against which an impossibly long cane pole was leaning, prompting Kenny Martindale to shout, "Hey, Thom, is that the switch your dad uses on you?" More shrieks of laughter from the children. "Yeah, Thom's got to have his birthday spanking!" one of them yelled. "Yay, Thom's going to get his birthday spanking, yay, yay!" the others cried.

"And now," Thom's mother announced, gesturing her husband behind the tarp, "it's time to play Go Fish!"

So it went, one game after another just as Thom's mother had planned, each child getting party favors and strawberry punch and cookies just as Thom's mother had planned, and before he was even quite ready she'd brought the huge five-layer cake out onto the picnic table, its six big blue candles lighted, *Happy Birthday, Thom* written across the chocolate icing in pale-blue script, and Mrs. Sadler and Abby lugged the brightly wrapped packages out from the kitchen. Everyone donned their cone-shaped metallic-blue hats and sang the birthday song that again made Thom feel bashful, with his parents and sister and all the children watching him while they sang (he felt an odd lunge in his stomach when they got to the verse "Hap-py *Birth*-day dear Tho-om") but soon enough it was over and Thom was summoned to make a wish and blow out the candles. The other children were giggling and shouting and shoving, but they receded in Thom's awareness as he approached the cake, trying to remember what he'd decided to wish for, but again his scalp was tingling, his head was spinning, he couldn't feel the ground underneath him as he neared the gigantic cake with its six candles lighted just for him. He couldn't remember, he could not remember, so he closed his eyes and pretended to wish and opened his mouth and pursed his lips—he'd practiced this, lying in bed last night—and blew.

Then the chaos of cake and ice cream (Mrs. Sadler and Abby apportioning the pieces onto paper plates, Mr. Sadler scooping the French vanilla and handing off to the next waiting child), and one by one Thom opened the presents, always remembering to stare at the tag and say thanks to the person who'd brought it, always remembering to look surprised and pleased even if it was something he already had (a Batman coloring book, a kaleidoscope from Toys R Us), and as he opened the presents Abby and his mother methodically gathered the torn wrappings and folded them neatly into a garbage bag, his mother setting aside the store-bought bows for the box where she stored her Christmas ribbons. Before Thom had absorbed what had happened, and certainly before he was quite ready, it was six o'clock. The four mothers assigned to pick up the children arrived promptly: the sixteen children, shirttails and hair bows askew, mouths smeared with chocolate, cried "Happy Birthday!" a few more times as the six adults (talking forgettable grown-up chatter over the noise) coaxed them out the front door and down the sidewalk.

Thom, his vision still throbbing with the bright shrieking flame-like colors and the frantic happy cries and dizzying motion of the party, stared at the front door, which had closed a final time. His parents and sister stood with him in the suddenly hushed foyer, like actors stranded on an unfamiliar, poorly lit stage.

His mother said, "Whew!" His father gave a gentle laugh, but Abby was staring at the door, too, her face a bit long, forlorn.

No one looked at Thom.

They spent the rest of the afternoon out back, Thom and Abby going through his gifts, playing briefly with the good ones and making fun of the bad ones (there was a cheap balsa-wood air-plane: "That must have set the Vaughns back at least ninety-nine cents," Thom's mother laughed), and around six o'clock his parents, once they'd cleared away the plates and cups and napkins, and once Thom's mother had finished tidying up the kitchen—had settled into their metal lounge chairs, his mother lighting one Kool after another, occasionally giving out an exhausted sigh, both his parents sipping leftover strawberry punch spiked with vodka. As he sipped the concoction Thom's father made a face—"This is too damned sweet, Loo, why don't you make me a real drink?"—but since Thom's mother seemed unwilling to move, he finished the punch, then poured them both more vodka, and added more punch from the plastic pitcher they normally used for sweet tea. He drank that one, too. When they finished playing with the gifts Abby went inside and made two more plates of ice cream and cake for her and Thom—"Honey, you'll ruin your appetite for dinner," their mother complained, but it was a vague, automatic remark that even the obedient Abby ignored—and as their parents sipped their punches Thom and Abby sat side by side on top of the picnic table, their feet planted on the bench, and ate their cake and ice cream.

To Thom, everything felt different. Already when he thought about the party he could not remember much of it, or else he remembered the parts he hadn't liked (the boring half-hour when the kids had lined up to go fishing; the embarrassing moment when everyone stared at him, singing the birthday song) instead of the parts that had excited him. He remembered there were moments when his eyes squinched shut with pleasure, when his sides ached from laughing, when surprising things happened that made him blink his eyes, but . . . what were they? He could remember the last couple of weeks as he looked forward to the party, his chest aching, his head reeling, but then the party had come, gone. So quickly. He had pestered his mother and Verna with questions, he'd lain awake sleepless with longing, imagining the huge lighted birthday cake and the glossy, mysterious packages, he'd practiced blowing out the candles (afraid somehow that he would embarrass himself, that the candles wouldn't go out: but they had, they had), he'd worried that his friends would forget to come or get the day wrong or that it would rain or that his Grandma Sadler (who'd just gotten home from the hospital, after a gall bladder operation) would die and his parents would cancel the party altogether, but after all that fretting and wondering and thinking and dreaming and looking forward, looking *forward*, the party itself had glittered a moment and then passed, exactly like a candle so carefully lighted but then extinguished in one breath. Even as he sat beside his sister eating leftover ice cream and cake (which he'd forgotten to taste during the party, and which now that he was full seemed doughy and wet, and sickly-sweet) everything was returning to normal, the afternoon was darkening, soon his mother would return to kitchen and start dinner, an ordinary dinner, and Thom would merely be a year older and nothing would have changed except now there was nothing to look forward to; nothing to think about at night; no reason to count the days, wish they would hurry past; no reason to think about much of anything, one way or another.

It didn't seem fair.

Yet the afternoon waned and dusk started falling and no one seemed ready for the day to end. His parents sat on their patio chairs, gazing out into the woods behind the house, chatting idly. Thom's father had kept pouring little dabs of the vodka in his glass, then refilling it with punch—he'd stopped complaining the drink was too sweet—and though his mother had stopped drinking, she kept lighting cigarettes one after another, her smoke fading upwards into the darkening air in a way Thom liked to watch, his eyes straining to separate the thinning smoke from the delusive blue-gray sky spreading above the roof of their house and visible in chinks through the trees, the stilled oak and magnolia leaves. After finishing their ice cream and cake Thom and Abby had stayed at the picnic table, slapping at flies and mosquitoes, massaging their itchy bare legs, passing Thom's opened gifts back and forth for inspection and reinspection, until finally Abby got tired of the mosquito bites and went inside to do homework. So Thom took the balsa-wood plane Danny Vaughn had given him and, abruptly filled with energy, started running up and down the stretch of grass in front of the patio, before his vaguely smiling parents, making airplane noises—"rrrhmmmm, ssssstt!"—and occasionally stopping to send the plane into the air for brief unsuccessful flights.

"Be sure you don't send it over the fence!" his mother called. "I'm not in the mood to go next door to the Hendersons and fetch a cheap little airplane."

His father laughed, briefly. "Humph."

". . . So, why *was* she crying?" his mother said.

Thom picked up the airplane from where it had crashed nose first into the azalea bush near the fence; he pretended to examine it, adjust the wing piece, but really he was eavesdropping. Halfway through pin-the-tail-on-the-donkey the little Korean girl, Rita Kim, had plopped onto the den sofa, on the end opposite Mr. Sadler and Abby. Her face had crumpled and she'd raised both hands to hide herself. Thom had glimpsed this from the sides of his eyes but had decided not to pay attention. Fortunately Rita Kim was one of those noiseless criers; she would hang her head and her shoulders would shake, her face cupped in both hands, but that was all. She had cried in school the past two days, too, and some of the children had started calling her "crybaby," but Thom had not. Neither had he consoled her. It was too close to his birthday and he didn't want to think about someone crying and spoiling his party. Today Abby had gone over and put her arm around Rita's shoulders and they'd whispered for a few minutes, and the next time Thom noticed Rita she was happily fishing in the backyard, giving her shut-eyed grin as she hauled in a tiny Miss America doll wrapped in plastic.

Thom's father shrugged. "Her dog died, Abby said. A few days ago. Little girl can't stop thinking about it."

"Aww. Poor thing," Thom's mother said.

So Rita Kim's dog had died. What kind was it? How old was it? Why did it die? Thom had many questions but he kept fiddling with the plane, his head bowed. He didn't want to hear his mother's answers. Last Christmas he'd asked for a puppy and that was exactly why his mother said no. Something would happen to the dog. It would get sick. It would get run over. It would die, and break Thom's heart. Dogs and cats, Thom's father had explained, gently, don't live as long as we do.

Thom had trouble standing still—he had so much energy left over from the party, from all the ice cream and cake!—but he wanted to hear what his parents were saying. So he started running again with the plane, making soft noises to himself, staying within a few feet of the patio where his mother and father had become lumpy blue-gray blurs in the dusk. The only lights were the soft glowing yellow rectangles from the house, and the occasional flash of the fireflies that had invaded the yard, winking on and off, here and there, unpredictably, and at the patio table the bright crimson glow, every few seconds, of his mother's cigarette as she smoked.

"Well, it happens," his father said flatly. Thom heard the chink of his glass against the glass-topped table.

"What happens?"

"Dogs die. That's what."

Again his father gave that brief mirthless laugh. Humph. Thom zoomed back and forth with the plane. *Rrrrhmmmm. Sssstt.* The fire-flies winked on and off.

"Oh, isn't that nice," his mother said.

A brief silence during which Thom listened hard and then his father said, "Well, it's the goddamn truth. None of us gets out of this alive."

Thom wished Abby hadn't gone inside. They could get a Miracle Whip jar and catch fireflies like they did last summer, punching holes in the lid with an ice pick so the bugs could breathe. But already it was getting too dark for that.

"And that's nice, too," his mother said. Her voice sounded damp, unhappy. "Why would you say such a thing?"

His father's glass clinked against the table.

"Why," his mother said. "Why would you?"

Thom began running around in the grass, directionless. Feeling dizzy, he stopped a few feet from his mother, lifted the plane, aimed, and threw it with all his strength. In the faint glow of moon-washed sky he glimpsed the plane sailing over the fence into the Hendersons' yard.

A scraping of chair legs against the concrete patio.

"Thom?" his mother said. "What are you doing?"

Thom turned and ran to his mother; up close, he could see her face looking tired, confused, frightened. Her eyes still moist. But her cheeks were dry, so impulsively he kissed them, first one and then the other. Then he laughed. But his mother didn't laugh. He felt the vague unhappy push of her palms against his shoulders.

"Stop being silly, Thom. Your mouth is all sticky from the ice cream."

She pressed one hand against her glass, then rubbed at her cheek with her wet palm; she dried it with the napkin.

Thom's father stayed silent.

Quickly Thom retreated back into the yard, far enough that his parents could not see him. They'd started collecting their glasses, the pitcher, the ashtray. "I'm getting eaten alive out here," his mother said, to no one in particular. But as she neared the back door she stopped and called out, "Thom?"

He didn't answer.

"Thom?" Her voice sounded wobbly, uncertain. "Happy birthday, honey . . ."

His father had gone inside.

"*Thom . . . ?*"

He didn't answer.

That's when she came at him, her large, blurry face floating toward him, dreamlike through the dark, her moist red lips shaped for a kiss, parted slightly. Just in time he turned his head and the kiss landed on his cheek not his lips but it was a messy kiss. A wet, greasy kiss. A sticky kiss. His cheek tingled, the skin along his arms and neck seemed to crawl. The sweetish fruity odor of her breath filled his nostrils. "Happy birthday, honey," she muttered again, vaguely, but he didn't answer or kiss her back—he'd done that, hadn't he?—nor did he glance in her direction. He sensed her quick retreat, the absence of warmth. He let out his breath, relieved.

She'd stopped a few yards away. She cleared her throat. "Now don't stay out much longer, you hear? And be sure to bring your presents inside."

He knew that in a few seconds she would turn on the backyard floodlights, so he could see to collect the gifts. He dreaded the moment when this would happen.

He stood quietly in the yard, his ankles itching from the mosquito bites. They were eating him alive. None of us gets out of this alive. Happy birthday, honey. He didn't yet know that words, even good strong words like *friends*, would never again have as much power to thrill, enliven, console him. He saw the reddish aureole of his mother's hair at the kitchen window; she was washing dishes, just as she had washed away his kiss. She hadn't thought about the floodlights, after all, or about him. That was one good thing.

Around him the fireflies were winking on and off; on and off. As if lighting his path to the future.

He longed to race inside the house and wash his face, but first he waited there in the yard until the darkness was complete and the fireflies had vanished. He turned from the house toward the invisible black woods, and when he waved his hand before his face Thom could see nothing. He wasn't even there.

Joe Meno

Bustle in the Window

One part of her quarter-horse was found down by the well, spilling out its brains across the little green fjord and we all knew what it meant, we all thought we knew what it meant without one more cough of that poor ol' horse's breath over its cold and still pink-hewn teeth and lips.

Marry-me.

Jesus. What kinda' a maniac would do something like that? Jimmy Cussler. Jimmy Cussler, I do believe.

Winny put her hand across her thin and gentle brow, turning her face away. It was all right there. The answer was right there at the end of her nervous white lips, stitched in tight along her perfect white teeth. It wasn't any kind of protective distress I was feeling for her. She had dug her own grave, lying down with a fellah like that. Jimmy Cussler. What the hell was my sister thinking anyway?

"What's it mean, Pops?" my mom asked, shaking her big white head. We all stood over the damn thing, shaking our heads like a bunch of ignorants. The poor ol' horse gave one more puff of last breath and then, like the emptiness of sound you feel when a clock winds down, we all knew that horse was gone and dead. My dad shook his head, pulling on his chin, closing his fist.

"It means there's a goddamn lunatic running about. I guess it's a sign that someone's awful displeased with someone or some body."

I don't care much for it myself. That kinda' carrying on. It seems like a goddamn waste of time. When a fellah falls for a girl, it just seems that it would be better off to come and knock on the front door and declare it so than sitting in the dark, creeping and stirring and pining and shooting off in desperation for her. I sit in the dark for my own reasons, I guess. I'm sixteen and too old to be kept up in the damn house all night. I've got a girl in town, goddamnit. Lucky fellah I am, finding a girl to fall for me like Loess. Her parents are heavy-sleepers and we can meet most nights at the edge of my folks' property and have a real time snapping at each other's underpants. She has a car and all, if I didn't mention it. Her parents bought it for her when she was sixteen. It's some kind of Japanese sport coupe. It's got reclining seats, if you know what I mean. What I mean is the seats go way back and usually it's the passenger seat where I take to sitting and then the prettiest girl in the world, Loess Labrise, climbs right on top and starts giggling and there I am, the luckiest goddamn goof in the world in all of my glory. Hell, between you and me, I wouldn't know what to do if things ran afoul, if she got sick of me or her parents found out, or even worse, say I knocked her up. What would a no-good son of a dumb-ass dairy farmer do? Skip town, I guess. This fellah a year older than me, Darrel Summs, got a girl pregnant last year and so he went off and joined the goddamn Navy. At least that's what he told everybody. The damn fool ended up just leaving the state, getting a job over in Tennessee. The worst of it, the poor baby was born blind 'cause Darrel and the girl, Elizabeth Jenns, a real dopey-looking gal with a soft broad can, both of them had a dose of the clap. I don't know. It seems like a pretty meaching thing to do, running away on a girl. But what else can a dumb fellah do if he's a victim of perfidy like that? I don't know. It's something I think about, sitting out on my roof in the dark late at night. That and the fact I've been having trouble sleeping. I keep dreaming about chickens getting their head pulled off and the like. It's downright creepy. I see the veins and the red tendons and the small little head popping right off. It's goddamn unsettling if you ask me. If I sit out on the roof until it's late and the sky is just about to turn from black to blue and I'm really tired, for some reason, I have a better chance of not having those kind of goosey dreams. Sitting on the roof also late at night lets a fellah hear what kind of magic his older sister's beaus are trying to spin. From the edge of my roof, I can hear any poor guy getting himself all worked up, cooing and whispering and smiling, hoping it is a small wish keeping Winny's sweater buttoned and her skirt from being raised past a pair of thighs that have already surrendered any sense of restraint or decency.

Shit. If you wanna know, the real reason I sit on that roof is I started smoking this summer, well, Loess smokes so I joined in, anyway, the roof is only place I can light up without getting caught. I'm only a laid back kind of smoker now, which means I don't know more than shit about it, and if coughing like a damn fool in front of your sweet-assed best girl with a nice car doesn't make you feel silly, I don't know what will. Regardless, sitting on that roof, smoking, lets a fellah hear all kinds of things. The least of which, like a night about five weeks ago, usually begins just like this.

"Hold my hand," I heard my sister tell him. She's eighteen and what the fellahs are known to call "easy." Not easy, but hell, what I learned about sex is from what I heard from hearing her name tossed around like a flimsy pair of silky underdrawers from fellah to fellah in the gym locker room at school. She wasn't a whore or nothing, just indecisive if you know what I mean. "Hold my hand, Jimmy, go on, don't be shy, Jimmy."

Jimmy is Jimmy Jackass, whose real name is Jimmy Cussler who once broke a goddamn rotten egg on my head at the beginning of gym period my freshman year. He's three years older than me and something of a real goddamn Neanderthal. He's built like the side of a goddamn brick shithouse and solid and angular with a face that could plow dry fields. Not a pretty boy, but from the way you hear the fellah talk, he's gotten a load of trim or outright taken it in the backseat of his old man's '68 Impala. Jimmy Cussler is what I would call a no-good fucker, not on account of the egg in gym period thing, but it's rumored that he deflowered Cheryl Hayby, the nicest, prettiest gal in my grade. This was the girl, who in grammar school, used to pass out Valentines to everyone in class on Valentine's Day. Savage. That's what he is. A goddamn savage.

"Did you ever look at the stars?" my sister asked ol' Jimmy. Oh, hell, when Winny goes into that one, you know there's bound to be trouble. Asking a fellah if he ever notices the stars is like leaving your top button unbuttoned, it's a kind of distraction, not any kind of useful question, really.

"You get more beautiful every time I see you," he mumbled, and for a goon like ol' Jimmy, something like that seems pretty goddamn sincere. From on top of the roof, right outside my bedroom window there, I get a clear sight of the barn and the long dusty yard and the pasture and hills tumbling at the ends of my feet. Right along the other side of the barn, propped up on a pile of soft, fresh sedum, was my sister and ol' Jimmy. The moon was high and nearly every star in the sky was twinkling and burning a hole in the big blue blanket of that lonely wide sky. This was about two days after my pretty Loess got caught sneaking out. Two days since I felt her climb on top of me and wiggle her pert little breasts right in my face. (Twixt you and me, Billy, her folks had no idea where she was going when they caught her. She was sitting in the car and like a crazy high school girl, sat there for an extra moment, listening to the end of "Roxanne" by the Police.) From my spot outside my window there, I could see directly along the edge of the barn and the two then one then two different shapes those lusty kids kept making. I could see my sister heft herself right on top of Jimmy Cussler, kissing his neck playfully. Jesus. A goddamn thing like that will make you sick. There was the smooching and kissing and tickling and pinching and giggling and then quiet, a kind of quiet that takes the breath right off your shiny teeth. Shit. There was nothing but the quiet firmament of crickets chirping in the air and awful goddamn displeasure of not having someone to kiss burning upon my own lips. I put out my smoke and started pulling myself back inside my room when I heard my sister starting to cry.

Shit. Shit. My face got all red and I scooted back on down the tiles, cutting up my palms good, trying to be quiet. I was sure that moron had done her wrong somehow. It was a safe bet with a big goon like that.

Jimmy Cussler. What a goddamn savage. With those dark green eyes and thick crop of red hair, I shoulda' known better leaving her alone out there with him. I had my feet over the side of the roof and was feeling around for the edge of the trellis there when I looked down and saw Jimmy Cussler standing there holding poor dumb Winny in his arms and her shaking and mumbling and him letting her bury her face all in his chest. It was a moment that made me feel stupid as hell. It was a moment, in light of all my tumblings around with Loess in the front seat of her very own foreign car, left me feeling shocked dumb and sore and confused. I climbed back up the roof and into my room and laid there all night just wondering if love ever fell upon me like that if I would have the courage or common sense to either hold it in quiet or just get up and move away as quick as I could please. Carrying on crying like that. What kind of crazy woman trick was that? I didn't know. I didn't want to know. I crawled inside my room and shut my window tight. God forbid if Loess ever started crying like that. What do you do? What the hell can you do when a gal just starts bawling out of the blue like that?

The next night, I couldn't sleep again, and I was smoking and sure as hell caught more of the same goddamn thing.

"Kiss me," I heard Jimmy mumble. "Kiss me, Winny." And then she leaned over and put her small hand along his chin and brought him right in and gave it to him, a softly-lipped kiss that made him draw himself in even closer, clutching at her blouse like it was the last holy thing on all of earth keeping him from losing the long and uncomfortable battle with all of time-less-ness and gravity. Then she did it. She started crying again and I hung my head over the side of the roof and Jimmy had his hands up in the air, just as confused as me.

"*Why not?*" he kept asking. "*Why not?!*"

"*Because,*" she mumbled. "*I'm not ready. You can't rush a thing like that. It's up to providence. It's providence now, Jimmy.*"

Well, hell. I didn't know what it was all about or what the hell to make of it.

The next afternoon is when my dad found Winny's horse all busted up, as a sign of Jimmy Cussler's own anger and love and confusion, I guess. It had been down in the south field grazing sometime that morning and when Pops couldn't catch sight of it down by the two-boughs, he walked on down there and saw its neck all twisted-up and its neck wrung and ribs battered in and its wide black eye still soft and calm and blinking. Then right there in its soft white gut was a huge red welt along a spot that looked like it had been beaten with a baseball bat. Seeing something like that makes you hate just about everybody. Especially the fool that had done it. Especially the fool that had done it and made your older sister cry, all right.

"Who would kill a poor horse like that?" my mom kept asking. "What's wrong with people? What's wrong with people today?"

Winny only stood there shaking her head. She knew it. She knew right then. And I thought I knew. I thought I knew what it all meant but I didn't. It was just another goddamn thing. Like when you draw a picture of a pussy as a triangle and think that's all there is to it. Or that aisle in the grocery store full of all kinds of mysterious feminine things. You think you know what it means when really you don't even have the faintest idea.

"Winny, you OK?" I asked her, trying to rattle her a little bit.

"Of course, she's not OK," my mom frowned, slapping my shoulder. "How would you feel if you found somehow had killed your horse?" And I thought, heck, I'd feel fine, because I never did get a damn horse like my older sister when she turned fourteen. I got a new suit. A goddamn new suit because my uncle decided to hang himself two days before my birthday and I didn't have anything to wear to the funeral and money was tight and it was decided by the powers that be that me having a nice brown suit for old Uncle Hank's wake was more important than having a horse to raise. Shit. Getting a brown suit for your birthday? What's an unlucky thing like that supposed to even mean?

I looked over at Winny and squinted, nodding my head.

In that light, she looked like a woman, standing there. There was the sun across her broad white face and the wind curling her hair up out from her back and her face looked calm and serious and slow and grave. She looked at the horse's hollowed neck with all the seriousness of staring right at death but seeing something else. That soft dis-composure had nothing to do with that old horse of hers. She never did ride the thing since she was about seventeen and discovered boys were built for pretty much the same thing. But in that light, in the coolness of that afternoon and quiet dullness of that summer shade, it struck me that my sister, Winny, looked a lot older than eighteen and full of some kind of hardness and weight. Her fingers held the top-most button of her shirt, fiddling with it, turning it in place.

I looked at the horse and shook my head. But I didn't hear it. I looked down and saw its big dead gray eyes and couldn't hear what was winding up through its broken lungs and ribs.

Marry me.

That's what that poor dead horse was saying.

Marry me, Winny.

I couldn't see it. I was too dumb or too young to hear it in that poor horsey's empty neigh. I looked over to my sister there and saw her turn and watched as her long red hair whipped around and along her back, still fiddling with the top button there in place. It's a moment I always think of when I think of my sister. Standing there all alone, on the edge of some grave decision, holding the top-most button in place. Then the image in my head fades right away. Then it is only the sound of her voice, then not even that and a blur of someone at the end of the hall, behind a closed door, all alone and singing, "I go out walking, after midnight . . ." nothing like poor ol' Patsy Cline at all, but just as sweet.

In that moment, there, those small fingers held that round button tight and then that night, that night sure as any other pregnant teenage girl in flight, my sister was gone. The back bedroom window where her room was had been left open and blue and wide and when my mom came in to check on her that night, the window shade was flapping against the sill there and the bed was empty and some of her clothes were gone and so was her small yellow suitcase and the window was propped open, cold and wide and rushing with air inside.

"She's gone," my mother whispered. "She didn't even say goodbye. She didn't even have the heart to say goodbye or goodnight."

Looking at it now, I guess I can see why she did it. My mom and dad can't. They don't seem to understand why'd she'd run away with a fellah, carrying his kid, most probably, the baby of a fellah that would kill a horse with his own two meaty hands like that. But I see it. It was a show of love in all that dirt and blood and his last hope to change her mind. He killed that poor creature to show her that he'd do anything, anything at all, to get her to run away with him and take up their lousy love and be his half-lucky, unblushing bride. Love is a gruesome thing, I guess, sometimes. Looking at it like that, it's something I wouldn't wish on anybody, not even my worse enemy, not someone I hated my whole damn life. Looking at it now, it all seems startling. It all seems more startling to me now than just un-kind.

Leslie Pietrzyk

Slumber Party, 1975

Since it was June, two months after my mother killed herself, I was hoping that my friends would decide I was "fine." Or
their mothers would decide. Or someone would give the signal to
get back to talking to me as if I were a normal person—which I
was. (Well, except for having a mother who'd killed herself by playing chicken with a train. No one knew why. No note, no nothing.
Just, suddenly, no mother—to go along with no father. Just my
brother Will and crazy Aunt Aggy, the "adult" in "charge.")

School had been hard. It was way too easy for everyone to stare
down at the floor when I passed in the hallway. Or hunch over
lunch trays when I walked down the main aisle of the cafeteria.
Ugh.

I was hoping summer wouldn't be like that. The first week was
easy enough: I weeded the whole garden, baked five dozen brown-
ies for the bake sale to raise money for my brother's baseball team,
politely listened to a Fuller Brush sales pitch from a sweaty man
who looked like Santa Claus, and replaced all the spices in the

spice cupboard—all useful, important things. So it was the second week, the week after that frenzy of activity, when I realized the summer was going to stretch out longer than usual. You would think that a long summer would be a good thing, but not like this, not long this way. I used to love summers because Mama and I would take on projects—like making strawberry jam and molding sand candles and writing a murder mystery set in our small town in Iowa and learning how to waltz, foxtrot, and tango and reading all the books in the library about a particular subject like wolves or Florence Nightingale or Alaska. We'd already planned our projects for this summer—it was something she'd liked to talk about on snowy days—and this was the summer we were supposed to learn to play croquet like experts and look up all the National Geographics at the library as far back as they went and make curry. She was always worrying that each summer was going to be the last, that suddenly I'd be too grown up to "play with your mother," as she said, "instead you'll be going out with boys and sneaking cigarettes and every little thing I do will immensely annoy you." I'd laugh and deny it, and she'd say, "No, really," and she'd say it in such a way that I'd stop laughing and realize that she was right.

My brother Will and I lived with Aunt Aggy who was far too busy to worry much about me because she'd decided to work through her grief over my mother's death by learning to paint. (When she said it that way, it almost made sense.) She wore a beret and refused to wash the paint off her hands because she said that's how you could tell a true artist, by the rainbow of colors under her fingernails. It was hard to think that if Leonardo da Vinci's hands were clean no one would've known he was an artist, but Aunt Aggy seemed so certain she was right that it was useless to argue.

It wasn't like my brother Will was much help, either. He was batting .456 and everyone thought that couldn't possibly last the season, but I thought maybe it would. Every time Will was up to bat, he seemed to become someone else—a taller, bigger, stronger version of himself, a stranger. I sat behind home plate, and I could see the opposing pitchers realizing the same thing: my brother wasn't going to stay a boy forever; maybe he wasn't even a boy anymore.

Will's arm was a rocket, and no one was able to steal second base when he was catching, not even that really fast kid from Kalona we'd all been hearing about. But going to baseball games and practices were about the only times I saw Will these days because his new friend Joe Fry had gotten him a job working for his brother-in-law who managed the movie theatre. Will was busy "tearing tickets and mopping kids' barf," as he put it, "a real glamour job." But it was: he was the first to scope out who was dating, who was broken up, who was arguing over what in the lobby. He got to wear a necktie and look important, and he could eat as much popcorn as he wanted for free. He called previews "trailers" and he even got to put the letters up on the marquee on Thursdays when the movie changed.

I was getting scared that the summer wasn't going to shape into much of anything and that my only option was going to be learning to paint with Aunt Aggy, so what a relief when my second-best friend Linda Johnson called to invite me last-minute to a surprise slumber party for Becky Mann. Even though Linda was my second-best friend—and had been since we were in fifth grade—she was one of the absolute worst when it came to head-ducking and lunch tray hunching at school. If I tried to talk to her, she'd say, "Oh, um, hi, um . . . Alice," like she'd forgotten my name and who I was or she'd give me a wide smile that looked carved across her face like a jack o'lantern. Her family was so perfect—father, mother, two boys, two girls, a dog, and a cat. Linda was the oldest kid and we all just knew she'd end up Homecoming Queen when we were seniors; that had been clear since seventh grade. Her father was mayor, and her mother was the president of the PTA. One brother played the violin like someone you'd hear in a real orchestra, and her sister had won the state spelling bee and a free trip to Washington, DC. So I could sort of understand why Linda didn't want to talk to someone like me, someone whose mother had killed herself. I probably wouldn't talk to someone like me either. I mean, look what I had in MY family: no father, a mother who parked her car on the train tracks, and an aunt about ready to fall apart at any minute. Still, as long as we had baseball-hero Will, we weren't an entire family of crazies.

So I was happy to hear about the party for Becky Mann even though it was the next night. "Only it's not a surprise anymore," Linda said. "Becky found out, and she asked if you were invited. I told her I didn't invite you because we didn't know if you were still in mourning or what."

"I was never IN mourning," I said.

"You know, because your mother died."

Like I'd forgotten. Still, I wanted to go to the party so I smiled which made my voice sound smiley and said, "I'm glad you called."

"Well, in *Gone With the Wind*, Scarlett wasn't supposed to go to the ball," she said. "You know, because she was in mourning."

"I'm not in mourning," I repeated. It was impossible to shake an idea out of Linda's head.

"So you're all better now?" she asked.

"I'm fine."

"And how's Will?" she asked.

"Fine," I said. She loved to talk about how cute he was, and if you really pushed her hard on it, she'd admit that she'd already picked out names for their four children. When Linda really got on my nerves (which Becky and I agreed happened on a too-regular basis), I'd casually mention that Will had told me he'd never, ever, under any circumstance whatsoever date a girl who was shorter than five-four (Linda was five-three and a half) or that Will preferred brunettes (Linda was as blonde as they come). Something about Linda just made me want to say those things to her—even though she was my second-best friend.

"I saw him with Joe Fry the other night."

My heart pumped a little bit extra whenever I saw Joe or thought about him or someone said his name. Becky was the only one who knew this about me.

I twisted the phone cord in my hand, said, "Yeah, Will and Joe are hanging out together. They're both playing baseball."

"Well, everyone knows what Joe's like," Linda said. "Your brother should be careful."

"What do you mean, everyone knows what Joe's like?" I said.

"You know," she said. "Wild. Crazy."

I twisted the phone cord harder, let it snap free. When I didn't say anything, Linda said, "The kind of guy who gets girls pregnant."

"Who did he get pregnant?"

There was a silence, then Linda said, "No one yet. But people say it's only a matter of time. And they'll start thinking Will's that way, too."

I listened to myself breathe, in, out, then slowed it down, innnnn, ooooout.

Linda said, "Look, I'm just trying to help. You don't want people gossiping about your family more than they already do."

I wanted to be mad, but Linda was right. People did gossip about us, and I knew that I'd gossip about us if I were someone else. For a brief moment I thought about what if I went to a Saturday night movie with Joe and everyone saw him buy us a box of popcorn to share and watched me follow him to seats in the far back corner where it was extra-dark and what people would say about all that. They'd say, "Ever since that crazy mother of hers killed herself, those kids have run wild." They'd say, "She'll get herself in real trouble—only a matter of time."

Mama used to say, "What's gossip anyway? Empty air blowing out of empty people."

Even though it was useless to try to change Linda's opinion, I said, "Joe's not that bad."

"If that's the kind of girl you are, he's not so bad," she said. I could just about hear her tossing her head, flipping all that blonde hair and it falling back into perfect place. You had to wonder how different things might be for her if she didn't have that hair. "Anyway," she said. "Come over at seven-thirty," and even though she'd been mean and was a gossip and didn't know as much as she thought she did, I was still happy she'd invited me to her party. It meant I was part of the real world again. It meant maybe my summer was going to work out fine.

⌒

Including me, there were six girls at the slumber party: me, Linda, Becky, Pam Hansen (whose father owned the Square Meal Cafe;

he wrote a letter a week to the *Des Moines Register* claiming that he fried up the best pork tenderloins in the state and that a reporter should come check them out; no one ever did, and finally he canceled his newspaper subscription in protest and offered a ten percent discount at the cafe to anyone who canceled their subscription), Denise Peterson (the shortest girl in our class—she was only 4'10"; her mother was taller than her father, and everyone said that's how come he was always roaring way too fast down First Avenue on that ridiculous motorcycle that would probably be the death of him some day), and Lily Flowers (all her sisters had flower names too: Iris, Rose, Violet; everyone always said thank God there were no boys in the family because obviously her mother was a little crazy on the topic of flower names).

Linda's mother had made snacks that looked straight out of a *Family Circle* article titled "Time for a Teen Party"—hot dog chunks wrapped in refrigerator crescent roll dough, polka-dotted with circles of green olive and pimento slices; cottontail bunny canned pears (dyed pink with food color), with cottage cheese tails, slivered almond ears, cinnamon red-hot candy eyes, nestled on individual lettuce leaves with criss-crossed carrot and celery sticks as garnish; a watermelon that had been carved out in the shape of a whale filled with little balls of watermelon, honeydew, and cantaloupe. Everything was perfectly perfect. There were paper plates that matched the paper cups that matched the napkins that matched the paper tablecloth that coordinated with the fanned-out tissue paper watermelon centerpieces and the pink and green twisted streamers Scotch-taped from the corners of the basement ceiling and strung throughout the room. In fact, Mrs. Johnson took several pictures of the whole set-up before she let us even pick up a paper plate, making Linda shift the candlesticks to several different locations as she snapped photos, finally deciding to leave them where they'd started, in the middle of the table.

"Mom, will you scram already?" Linda said, but Mrs. Johnson just smiled and started taking close-ups of the food.

We were down in the basement, but it wasn't like my basement which was crammed with old boxes and cobwebs and had an ice-cold cement floor. Mr. Johnson had refinished this basement himself, putting up wood paneling to cover the brick walls, laying down floor tiles that matched up exactly right, moving down the old living room set with the brand new pillows Mrs. Johnson had sewn, setting in ceiling tiles that were supposed to be soundproof (and they were, sort of—all we could hear were footsteps when people upstairs walked through the kitchen), arranging big carpet remnants they'd gotten a good deal on from the biggest furniture store in Cedar Rapids when they'd bought the new living room set. It was the perfect place to have a slumber party: there was a private bathroom (that Mr. Johnson had built himself, with only a little bit of help from a plumber) and a separate door leading outside to the backyard in case we needed to sneak out and tee-pee someone's house. You could always hear if an adult was walking through the kitchen, about to come downstairs. There was even an extension phone so we could make crank hang-up calls without worrying that anyone would catch us. It was the perfect basement, almost as if Mr. Johnson had designed it with slumber parties in mind.

Mrs. Johnson snapped another picture and looked at the back of the camera to see how much film was left. "How about one of all you girls?" and she lined us up behind the card table of food. "Say cheese," she said, smiling brightly.

"Chee-eese," we droned. The flashcube went off, and I blinked away the purple dots that seemed to fill the room.

"These are the best days of your lives," Mrs. Johnson said.

Linda turned her head so her mother couldn't see and rolled her eyes.

"You don't believe me, but it's true," Mrs. Johnson said.

"Mo-om," Linda said, horrified. The rest of us stood silently. It could've been anyone's mother being so embarrassing. (Okay, anyone's except mine.)

"Things only get more complicated," Mrs. Johnson said. I shifted my weight from foot to foot. Was that true?

"You'll see," Mrs. Johnson said, almost as if she were talking to me, though she was looking at her camera, not at any of us. Linda opened her mouth, but before she could say anything, Mrs. Johnson spoke again, using a totally different voice, her usual bright, cheerful chirp: "Yes, Linda, I'm going," and she smiled in sort of the forced, "say cheese" way we'd smiled for the photo, then she headed up the stairs.

We looked at Linda. She flipped back her hair, shook her head. "Let's eat," she said, taking the top paper plate off the stack. "She'll be back for cake, but then she'll be gone for good." A sudden silence felt wedged into the room; everyone turned to stare at me. Linda said, "Oh, sorry, Alice. I didn't mean it that way."

My face was as pink as the bunny rabbit pears. Everyone turned to stare at me. I took a paper plate, pulled a bunny rabbit pear off the tray and set it on my plate even though I didn't really like canned pears.

Becky said, "Maybe these are the best days of our lives. I've heard people say that."

Linda said, "She's just crabby because she's got her period. She's always crabby that time of month. Ugh."

So we ate and talked about that time of the month and decided Lily had the ultimate embarrassing story: her boyfriend Doug Flinn was in her living room talking to her parents, picking her up for the Homecoming Dance, and she looked perfect as she entered the room (she was wearing a green silky dress that we all remembered took her a month to pick out). She reached the bottom of the stairs, and Doug stood up and held out a corsage box, and Buster, the family dog, ran over and stuck his nose right in her crotch and kept at it even though she pushed him away, and all her mother and father did was laugh and one of them even TOOK A PIC-TURE. Pam's story was second worst: she got her period while she was out in the fields detasseling corn last summer and she didn't have any "stuff" and she was too embarrassed to ask anyone for napkins from their lunchbags, so by the end of the day she was rip-ping corn leaves right off the stalks and wadding them in her underwear.

That led to a discussion of pioneer women and how come Laura Ingalls Wilder books never talked about that sort of thing or going to the bathroom when there were details about every other aspect of pioneer life which led into whether Laura really loved Almanzo or she just felt she had to get married which led into a discussion of who we would marry if we had to get married right this minute. Linda instantly said Will (of course) and sucked up by saying how fabulous it would be to have me as a sister-in-law. Becky said Mr. Miller, our chemistry teacher she'd been in love with for the whole year. Denise said Mark Flanagan (the boy she'd dated for so long that they were finishing each other's sentences and they couldn't stand next to each other without their arms wrapped around each other's waist). Lily said Doug Flinn (who'd dumped her two months ago). Pam said John Travolta which got us arguing about whether to accept that or not since obviously a TV star like John Travolta wasn't ever going to come to Iowa to meet her, let alone marry her. She argued back saying obviously Becky was not going to marry our chemistry teacher (which made Becky very, very sad) and that if Doug Flinn even thought a pinch about marrying Lily, why'd he dump her so he could date Lynn Mason (which made Lily cry), so we decided to accept Pam's answer before she found a way to make the rest of us cry.

Then it was my turn. "No one," I said. Becky knew about Joe Fry, but that didn't mean I wanted the whole world to know—which was what happened if you told anything to Linda, the gossip.

"You have to pick," Pam said.

"It's like someone is standing there saying you HAVE to get married," Lily said.

"Sure you're not thinking about someone?" Becky said.

I gave her a narrow-eyed glare which meant "I don't need your help."

"Come on," Linda said. "We all told."

Mama had always talked about James Dean, so I said, "James Dean."

"Who's he?" Linda said.

"A movie star," Pam said. "But he's dead."

Everyone stared at me. Again. I felt like something on a slide under a microscope in biology class.

Linda said, "You can't marry a dead man."

"I know that," I said.

"I mean, don't you get it?" Pam said. "He's dead. He doesn't count."

There was a moment of silence. All I could think about was not crying. Then Becky said, "My mother said she used to be wild about James Dean."

Linda flipped her hair. "Alice, you're weird."

"We bared our souls," Denise said. "You didn't tell us anything."

"It's not like saying Mark Flanagan was baring your soul," I said. "You've been dating him practically since kindergarten. We're all so SHOCKED you chose him."

"Alice is holding out on us," Pam said. "I say . . . tickle her!" and she lunged at me and started tickling my stomach, getting me to giggle and gasp and roll around, nearly knocking into the card table of food. Lily and Denise piled on so I was being tickled from all sides and I could barely breathe, and I started tickling back and we were all a big jumble of flailing limbs and giggles.

"No, no!" Linda shouted, banging her sandal on the floor. "Stop!" and we eased up, gasping for air, holding our stomachs. "I know how we'll get the truth," Linda said. She stood up, started stacking everyone's dirty paper plates and cups.

"Please not Truth or Dare," Becky said. "Last time I was crowing like a rooster in my bra and panties while Linda took pictures."

"This is better than dumb old Truth or Dare," and Linda lowered her voice into a spooky whisper: "Way better." She shoved the stack of used paper plates into a garbage can with a decoupage rose on the side (made by Mrs. Johnson) and flipped off the overhead lights. Shadows appeared on the wall, cast by the lamp in the far corner and the candles on the card table. It felt like the moment in a scary movie where the axe murderer comes tiptoeing down the stairs, so when the door at the top of the stairs opened and Mrs. Johnson's voice called out, we all jumped. "Honey!" she called. "Are you girls ready for cake and ice cream?"

Linda turned the lights back on, got that oh-so-annoyed look on her face. "Now?" Then she murmured to us, "Let's just get it over with. Then she'll leave us alone." She shouted, "Okay!"

There was a flurry of footsteps tapping across the kitchen floor— the refrigerator door whooshing open, silverware clinking.

Linda said, "She's such a pain."

"My mother doesn't even let me have parties because she says the noise makes her head pound for a week," Pam said.

Denise said, "My mother would do something like make fish sticks and tater tots for us to eat and complain about how much work she'd done."

Lily said, "My mother doesn't let anyone wear shoes in the house. In fact—"

Becky interrupted, "Stop it," and everyone gave me the exotic-zoo-animal-in-a-cage stare again. I closed my eyes and saw Mama's face, so I quickly opened them.

I said, "My mother was a pain, too."

Becky said, "Of course she wasn't."

"Yes, she was," I said. "She could be a big whopping pain."

"Oh, Alice," Becky said. "Never say bad things about someone who's passed away."

"It's not right," Lily said.

I said, "She was just like your mothers: weird, nagging, annoying, a pain." No one said anything, but they didn't have to because I knew exactly what each of them was thinking: Not EXACTLY like my mother because MY mother didn't go and kill herself.

"Cake!" Mrs. Johnson called, and her footsteps thumped the uncarpeted stairs. She reached the bottom of the stairs carrying a large silver tray with an angel food cake coated in creamy pink peaks of whipped cream, sprinkled with slivered almonds. Individual slices of Neapolitan ice cream surrounded the cake like striped bricks. Sixteen burning candles flickered as Mrs. Johnson walked towards us, that bright smile on her face. A camera dangled from a strap off her wrist. She set the tray on the card table. "I already took pictures upstairs, so we can start singing!" She led us in "Happy Birthday" then said, "Make a wish!" Becky puckered up to blow and the flashcube went off several times as Becky blew out every last candle with one long breath. Tiny columns of smoke rose and twisted off the candles. Linda asked, "What'd you wish for?" and Becky said, "It won't come true if I tell," but she had that dreamy, Mr. Miller look on her face, so we all knew.

Mrs. Johnson cut big pieces of cake for us; and we oohed and ahhed when we saw that she'd hollowed out the inside of the cake, filling it with more whipped cream stuff—chocolate. "Isn't this lovely?" she said as she slid pieces of cake and ice cream onto the little dessert paper plates that matched the big dinner paper plates.

We all agreed that the cake was lovely—and delicious!—and that all the food had been lovely—and delicious!—and that, yes, so far the party was lovely!

Mrs. Johnson sliced a tiny sliver of cake for herself and sat down on the sofa, crossed her legs neatly at the ankles. Her back was straight. I thought for sure Linda would say something, but she just sighed so heavily that her bangs flew up off her face. Mrs. Johnson said, "So, what are you girls talking about?"

Linda said, "Nothing."

"I find that hard to believe," Mrs. Johnson said. "You were talking about boys, weren't you?" No one nodded, and Linda's face turned bright red. "You don't have to tell me; I know ALL about slumber parties." She finished her cake and scraped the side of her plastic fork along the paper plate to get the rest of the whipped cream smears. Then she licked the fork, leaving it in her mouth an extra moment or two before saying, "All you do is talk about boys at your age."

Linda groaned then turned it into a cough.

"Well, what do you talk about at your bridge parties?" Pam asked.

Mrs. Johnson laughed. "I suppose we still talk about boys—but now they're our husbands."

"And gossip," Becky said.

"I suppose there's a tiny bit of gossip that sneaks in here and there, try as we do to keep away from that sort of thing," Mrs. Johnson said.

Mama hadn't gone to many bridge parties—sometimes ladies invited her, but she made excuses. I told her that Mrs. Johnson and Mrs. Mann thought it was strange that she wouldn't go—I'd overheard them talking once at Becky's house, wondering what Mama did with herself all day long, deciding she was stuck-up, thinking she was too good to play cards—and Mama had only said, "Most women are the bridge party type, and a precious few aren't." Then she peered closely at my face and said, "I'm still not sure which you are, Alice," and Aunt Aggy shouted from the other room, "Bridge parties!" and I was only twelve, so what was I supposed to think? All my friends' mothers loved their bridge parties; Mrs. Mann was even teaching Becky how to play bridge, and Becky tried to teach me, but she wasn't that good herself so I couldn't get the hang of it (though Becky and I agreed that we really liked the word "trump"). Why couldn't Mama just play cards with them once in a while? Was she really stuck-up?

Linda grabbed her mother's empty paper plate, stuffed it in the garbage can. "Done?" she asked. "Aren't you going back upstairs?"

"Of course I'm going back upstairs, Linda," Mrs. Johnson said as she stood up. "What kind of mother wrecks her daughter's slumber party by hanging around? How can you talk about boys and gossip about everyone who's not here?" She laughed and glanced at us like we were supposed to laugh too, but none of us did. She was standing, but she hadn't taken a step, and I had a feeling she really didn't want to go, that if Linda wasn't rushing around, noisily stacking up serving trays and grabbing everyone's paper plates, Mrs. Johnson would keep on sitting right there on that couch with us for a good long while and maybe never go back to her upstairs that was as perfect as her downstairs.

But that was silly. Why would she want to talk about boys with us?

Mrs. Johnson smiled so broadly it must've hurt her face. "Alice, dear, would you mind helping me carry a few things?" and she said it so smoothly that I was picking up the cake tray and following her up the stairs before I realized why she'd asked me to help her.

"So, Alice," Mrs. Johnson said in that terribly sympathetic voice I was learning to hate because it was a bad combination of pity, sympathy, and nosiness. "How are you doing? Really?"

"Fine," I said, and she didn't say anything except, "That's good," for a minute or two as we got to the top of the stairs and into the kitchen. I was hoping that would be the end of it. I put the cake tray on the counter and turned to head back downstairs, but she handed me the stack of serving trays and bowls she'd been carrying. I glanced around, but there was no room for it on the counter, so I stood there holding it.

She reached for a box of toothpicks from a cupboard and started jabbing them in the top of the leftover cake. Then she draped Saran Wrap over the cake without wrecking the frosting.

Mrs. Johnson said, "We were all simply shocked that a person could do such a thing. What was your mother thinking? Leaving you and your brother alone in the world the way she did. Who would do that sort of thing? That's what we all asked ourselves, who on earth would do such a thing?"

My teeth clenched together. Part of me wanted to slap the perfect smile right off Mrs. Johnson forever, but part of me secretly agreed with her. How could my mother leave us alone in the world? What WAS she thinking? Who WOULD do such a thing?

She put the cake in the refrigerator and then took the tray out of my hands and set it in the sink, started running water over everything. "I love my new garbage disposal," she said. "Mr. Johnson put it in for my birthday." She flipped a switch on the wall and a grinding noise filled up the silence. When she turned off the disposal, she asked, "How are things at home?"

"Fine," I said.

"I want you to tell me if that aunt of yours isn't taking good care of you. Mr. Johnson can speak to some people and get things arranged in a more satisfactory way." She turned off the water, looked at the dishes in the sink. "Washing dishes sure is easier now with this nice disposal." She tipped the dirty water out of the top bowl, then flipped the disposal switch, let it grind.

I spoke over the noise: "Everything's fine. Aunt Aggy is fine."

"This thing could take a hand right off," she said. "You probably wouldn't even feel it." Then she flipped off the switch and said, "We were really just so shocked. We couldn't stop talking about it, wondering why." She touched my arm. Her fingers were surprisingly cold. "Your mother never was like the rest of us, was she?" Mrs. Johnson paused for a second—was I supposed to answer that question? Then she went on: "One thing I've been happy about is that all my children fit in. Everything is so much simpler that way."

She was right about that. Look at her perfect family.

"And I want you to know that I tried with your mother, I really did." Mrs. Johnson reached under the sink and pulled out a pair of yellow rubber gloves. "I invited her to our bridge parties, I begged her to join the PTA Bake Sale Committee; plenty of times I told her that no one gave it a second thought that she didn't have a husband. It was like she deliberately didn't want to be part of anything. She didn't care. For example, I remember one time calling her up to tell her that people were going around saying that she took walks alone out in that old graveyard off the county road late at night, and do you know what she said to me? She said, 'So?' Just like that. I said, 'No, people are really going around saying and thinking all sorts of bad things,' and again, she just said, 'So?' Well, whatever can you do with someone like that? Someone who doesn't care if they fit in or not." She grabbed a dried up sponge from the counter, ran water over it, wrung it, soaked it, wrung it. "How can someone be like that?"

She paused like it was a real question that I could answer. I shook my head, shrugged one shoulder.

Mrs. Johnson drew in a deep breath, said, "If there's one thing I've learned in this life, Alice, it's that the only way to get through life is to fit in. It's as simple as that."

Here—finally!—was an adult who knew how the world worked. An adult NOT like my mother who went off and killed herself. An adult NOT like Aunt Aggy who'd decided she was some sort of genius artist after skimming a how-to-paint book from the library.

Mrs. Johnson continued, "Your mother was a woman with a lot of secrets. That's what happens when someone doesn't fit in, they have secrets. And look at what happens when someone has secrets." There was a pause, and then she quickly added, "Of course, your mother wasn't like the rest of us. She was crazy." Mrs. Johnson reached over and gave me a stiff-armed sort of hug, making sure not to touch me with the rubber gloves. Up close she smelled like a mixture of skin lotion and hair spray. "But you, you're not crazy, are you?" she said. "You know how to fit in. You're lucky that way," and it seemed strange to hear myself called "lucky" by one of the luckiest women in town.

I shut my eyes, scrunched up my face so I wouldn't cry.

"Alice!" Linda called from the basement. "We need you!"

Mrs. Johnson let go of our hug and I quick opened my eyes. I could've hugged her longer, forever. Was it so awful to wish she was my mother? Maybe that's what she meant when she said Mr. Johnson could speak to people; maybe she wanted to adopt me and fit me into her perfect family.

"Remember what I said." She smiled, not the big bright, say cheese smile, but a little tiny smile that made her look wise or knowing or sad or something that was hard to figure out exactly.

She flipped on the garbage disposal, and I headed down the stairs. Linda was waiting at the bottom. "Jeez, what took so long?" she asked.

Ugh. She didn't even know how much she should appreciate her own mother.

Linda said, "We're ready to start."

"Start what?" I asked. The overhead lights were off again, and my eyes had to adjust to the shadowed dimness from the bright kitchen.

Becky said, "Linda has a Ouija Board."

Denise said, "She secretly bought it herself from the Sears catalog."

"My mother would kill me if she knew," Linda said. "She thinks it's bad luck to mess with ghosts."

"Maybe she's right," I said.

"Oh, Alice, don't be such an old lady," Pam said.

"It's just for fun," Denise said.

"Anyway, we're all doing it," Linda said, "at least one question each," and she grabbed my arm and yanked me over to where the others sat cross-legged in a circle on the carpet. The Ouija board was in the middle, printed with all the letters of the alphabet and the numbers from zero to nine, the words YES and NO in opposite corners, and centered across the bottom the word GOODBYE. Lily was sliding the plastic pointer back and forth to the letters of her name, her thumb smack in the middle of the round glassy "eye." It was hard to believe that spirits would come from wherever spirits are to spell out the future for us through this crummy little piece of plastic.

Becky said, "I heard about some girls who were doing a Ouija board at a slumber party and they accidentally called up evil spirits instead of good ones. The pointer was zig-zagging all over the board, spelling out horrible words, and then my cousin's friend's sister's friend started screaming and trying to strangle one of the other girls. The dad had to come and pull her off. To this very day, she's still in the hospital, and they tie her arms to her bed with rope every single night, and some people say she's possessed by the devil."

There was a brief silence as we all thought that over. Lily took her hand off the pointer. It sat there, unmoving, on the letter *E* and we all stared at it. Linda pushed it over to the letter *G*.

Denise said, "Well, there were two girls asking the Ouija board normal dumb questions like what boys liked them, and suddenly the cats in the room ran howling under the sofa. Then the sky turned yellow and purple and there was really horrible thunder and lightning and wind blowing rain sideways and hail the size of baseballs, and the roof blew clean off the house and no one ever found even a shingle. Of course, one of the girls was a minister's daughter, so maybe that's why."

Another silence. I thought about Linda's father having to put another perfect roof on their house.

Finally Pam said, "The Sears catalog wouldn't sell Ouija boards if girls were really strangling each other and roofs were blowing off houses."

"I suppose not," Becky said.

Linda said, "Let's have Alice call to the spirit world since her mother's dead."

Everyone stared at me for the nine billionth time. I looked down at the Ouija board, at the tiny reflection of the candles on the card table in the pointer's round eye. Was it real? Could you really get your questions answered? Could I reach my mother? The writing on the box said "For amusement purposes only."

Finally, Becky spoke. "Linda!" She sounded just like a mother who's had just about enough.

"What?" Linda said. "We want good spirits, don't we? You're supposed to call up a dead person, and all I've got is a grandmother I never even knew. How helpful will she be?"

"Alice doesn't want to," Becky said, still using that fed-up mother voice.

I said, "Yes, I do," before realizing that I did.

Nobody said anything, not even Linda, who looked down at the floor. She abruptly flicked a crumb across the room with her thumb and forefinger. Then she folded her arms across her chest.

"Maybe you shouldn't," Lily said.

It was so quiet I heard Becky's watch ticking. There were a couple footsteps in the kitchen, then nothing, just the quick tick-tick of Becky's watch.

Linda unfolded her arms and stretched out her hands to each side like a priest doing Our Father. She didn't sound very sure of herself as she said, "Everyone hold hands or it won't work." I was sitting between Linda and Becky and I grabbed their hands; Becky's was sweaty and Linda's was as cool as her mother's had been. When we were all holding hands, Linda whispered, "Go ahead, Alice."

I whispered back, "What am I supposed to say?"

She spoke in her normal voice. "Just say something like we want the guidance of some good spirits to help us as we seek to understand the secrets of life and the human heart."

"Don't forget to say 'good' spirits," Lily said.

"Don't we only want one spirit?" Pam asked. "We don't want more than one, do we?"

"Shut up everyone," Linda said, definitely back to her normal, bossy self. "Let her get in the mood. Close your eyes, Alice. Really concentrate."

"We should all close our eyes," Denise said, and everyone did. I looked around the circle at them. The whole thing was ridiculous—like Mama would even play by Ouija board rules anyway. Mama was definitely a blow-the-roof-off-the-house kind of player.

Linda whispered, "Any time now, Alice."

So I spoke slowly: "Spirit world, come to us. Good spirits find us here in Linda's basement. Help us in our quest to see the secrets of the world revealed, our mission to understand the human heart and the secrets it holds. Good spirits, we beg your assistance. Answer our questions . . . questions of the mind, the heart." I paused and listened to everyone breathing. Then I opened my eyes. Might as well make it good. "Send us a sign of your presence," and I let my voice drop lower, almost a whisper. "Tell us you're in the room." As I'd been talking, I was inching one leg sort of sideways and backwards, towards a card table chair I planned to knock over, but the door at the top of the stairs slammed shut, and everyone screamed and opened their eyes. No one let go of anyone's hand; Becky clutched mine even tighter.

A moment later, Linda said, "That was probably my mother."

"Probably," Pam said.

"I'm sure," Linda said.

"How come we didn't hear footsteps in the kitchen?" I asked. No one answered.

Becky said, "We shouldn't be doing this."

Denise said, "Too late."

"Go on, Alice," Linda whispered.

I let go of Linda's and Becky's hands and balanced my forefingers on the plastic pointer, one on each side of the glass eye. "Is there a spirit in the room?" I asked in a hushed voice.

Everyone stared but nothing happened. Then the pointer slowly slid towards the word YES. I whispered, "I swear I'm not moving it." I pulled the pointer back to the center of the board. "Are you a good spirit?"

Lily held her breath, and Becky bit her lip. Again, the pointer wasn't moving at all, then it slid bit by bit over to YES, and everyone started calling out questions: "Ask if Doug Flinn still likes me"; "Find out the initials of the man I'm going to marry"; "See whether Mr. Miller thinks I'm cute." Linda's voice rose above all the rest: "No, no. Start with Alice. Who is Alice going to marry?"

"I'm not asking that," I said.

"Then I will," and she nudged my fingers off the pointer, and put on her own. "Who is Alice going to marry?" she whispered. I crossed my arms. The whole thing was stupid. Didn't they know that I'd been guiding the pointer? It was just a game, something "for amusement purposes only." Like my mother was going to perform tricks at a slumber party.

"Look," Becky said. "J."

Sure enough, the pointer had moved to the letter *J*—which of course was a coincidence—but then it went to *O* and then to *E*.

"Stop it," I said, and I pushed Linda's fingers off the pointer.

"Whose initials are J.O.E.?" Denise said.

Linda said, "Dummy—it's Joe, the name Joe. Like Joe Fry."

Pam laughed. "Alice Fry."

"I think he's cute," Becky said.

"He's scary," Lily said.

"He's not scary," I said.

Linda shook back her hair. "You know what I heard about Joe Fry?" She leaned in as she spoke: "I heard that he plays poker for money with a bunch of men every Thursday night, and here's the reason they let him in: he invites guys from school into the game, and they lose their money because the men worked out a way to cheat, and Joe gets a cut."

"Don't be such a gossip, Linda," Becky said.

But Linda continued: "That's not all. AND there were some university students up in Iowa City who were making a porno movie and wanted Joe Fry to be in it, and he was, and the movie played at a dirty movie theater in California."

"That's not true," I said.

Linda grabbed back the Ouija pointer. "Was Joe Fry in a porno movie?" and the pointer quickly slid to YES.

"You pushed it," I said.

"Did not," Linda said.

Becky pulled the pointer away from Linda and said, "My turn. Will I marry Mr. Miller?" What a surprise that the pointer zipped straight to YES before she even got the words out.

Denise said, "It doesn't count if you ask the question AND work the spirit guide." She pushed the pointer back to me. "Alice should do it."

"Why me?" I said. No one looked at me—they stared at the floor, at the ceiling, at the walls. "Because my mother is dead?" I asked. No one spoke. I went on: "Do you actually believe she's here—that my dead mother is HERE in this room? That she's a spirit you can call up like we've got her telephone number or something?" Still, no one spoke. "Oh, brother. It's just a stupid game."

Suddenly the bulb in the lamp flashed and fizzled out, leaving behind only the flickering light of the candles on the card table. Linda whispered, "Let's ask something serious."

"No!" Becky said sharply.

"Ask," I said, placing my fingers on the pointer.

"Let's play Truth or Dare instead," Lily said.

"Ask," I said.

Linda smiled, the candlelight making it look like the smile I'd seen on her mother, the sad, wise, knowing smile I couldn't figure out. So I looked straight at her. Anyone would think she was beautiful, perfect. "You have a question, don't you?"

Linda's voice started normal but the last work was a ragged whisper. "Is my mother happy?"

"Of course she is," I said. I was the one with the mother who killed herself; that should've been MY question.

But Linda shook her head, and we watched the pointer as it slid partway to YES then partway to NO then stopped on the letter T.

"What does that mean?" Linda asked, same uncertain whisper.

"It means this is stupid," Pam said. "Let's play Truth or Dare or make crank phone calls."

"Why'd you ask that?" Becky asked Linda.

Linda shrugged and flipped her hair. "Why not?" she said. Her voice was clear and smooth, back to the way it usually was, like cold water washing up over sand. "Alice, you go," she said.

"I don't have any questions," I said. Of course my head was spinning with questions.

"You guys are getting creepy," Lily said, and she flopped backwards on the floor, reached for a pillow off the couch and put it over her head.

Linda said, "Okay, I have another question. Is Alice's mother the good spirit in the room?" Lily pushed the pillow off her face and sat up; everyone leaned forward.

My fingers rested on the pointer, and I held my breath as it slid to YES. Talk about NOT fitting in.

"It's just a stupid game," Pam said.

"It's not like your mother is actually in the room," Denise said. "I mean, actually with us." She looked around; everyone looked around. The corners of the room seemed awfully dark, like they could hide anything.

"How do we know?" I said. "Maybe she is. Maybe she's talking to us—maybe she talks to me every day now. Maybe she's a voice that just won't shut up."

"Alice!" Becky said. "You're being crazy."

"Maybe I AM crazy," I said. "My mother was crazy, wasn't she?"

The pointer quickly slid to NO.

"I'm scared," Lily said.

Linda said, "Oh, brother, Lily. Don't you know Alice is moving the pointer herself to get the answers she wants? Of course her mother was crazy. You know the way people talked about her."

"Leave Alice alone," Becky said.

"I'm fine," I said.

"You are not," Becky said. "Why do you keep saying that?"

Linda said, "If she says she's fine, she's fine."

"Hey, stop it," Pam said. She was looking at the picture on the cover of the box. "We're all supposed to have our fingers on the pointer, not just Alice." She set one finger on the pointer. Her nail was bitten way down.

Lily whispered, "Do you really think your mother is here, Alice?"

I closed my eyes. Where was my mother? Where was she? I shouldn't have to ask that question, because I should know where she was; she should be at home, reading a magazine or cooking up a big pot of beef stew, listening to Dotty Ray's Homemaker Hour on the radio.

Linda said, "It's not her mother. It's just a game."

"What about the lightbulb?" Denise asked. "And the door slamming?"

"Coincidence," Linda said. You'd think she'd been thinking it was a joke all along. I wanted to be that assured, that perfect. You just knew that if her mother were dead, she'd stay dead and not show up at some dumb slumber party.

"But what about what the board said?" Lily asked.

"Okay," Linda said. "Everyone put their fingers on the pointer and then we'll ask the same question and you'll see that Alice was pushing it." Everyone leaned in and set a finger on the pointer, and Linda started to speak, but I interrupted:

"Is Linda's mother happy?" I asked.

"Not that!" Linda said.

"Too late," Becky said, and the pointer started sliding, and even after Linda snatched her finger away, it went partway to YES, then partway to NO, then settled on the letter *T*, same as it had before.

"Oh my God," Lily said under her breath.

"Alice pushed it," Linda said.

The thing was, I hadn't pushed, not even a tiny bit. But Linda was staring up at the ceiling, blinking hard, about to cry, and of course it was a ridiculous question; there was no way her mother WASN'T happy, so I said, "You're right, I pushed it."

"Well, what are you trying to prove?" Linda demanded.

"Look," Becky said. "All we're doing is fighting. Pam's right, we should just go make phone calls or play Truth or Dare."

"I'm not trying to prove anything," I said. "I told you I was sorry."

"You think this proves your dead mother is right here in this room, don't you?" Linda said, each word coming out faster and louder. "Well, she isn't—she's DEAD. And that's too bad for you, but she's never coming back, never, ever, ever."

Maybe my mouth dropped open a bit, and for sure I felt that air was suddenly sucked up backwards from my stomach out of my lungs or something twisted like that, but I managed to say, "I know that," like someone had just said something simple like, It's raining. And at that moment I thought that no matter how perfect Linda was in every other part of her life, she could never be my second-best friend again after this night. But all I did was smile and say it again: "I know that."

Denise spoke suddenly. "Ask a question only your mother would know the answer to, Alice."

There was a silence. It was a good idea. Then we'd know. We'd know for sure. I'd finally know something.

Denise said, "And keep your finger off. Then we'll know if your mother is really, truly here."

"She's dead," I said, a too-calm voice I didn't even recognize as mine. "How could she be here?"

"No one thinks she's really here except you," Linda said. Her voice was just as calm as mine, but each word was like a separate slice of a knife. I heard Becky's watch ticking again. Someone's stomach gurgled. Linda said, "Ask."

I took a deep breath then whispered, "I can't." I was trying very hard not to cry.

"I'll do it," Linda said. "Why'd you park your car on the train tracks? Why'd you kill yourself?"

Everyone gasped, and Linda looked suddenly surprised, as if those weren't the words she wanted to say at all. But she couldn't unsay them. And, really, perfect Linda didn't even realize that she'd been the only one to dare ask the first reasonable question, the only question there was, the only question. I closed my eyes, so I didn't see everything that happened next, only heard it: Becky yelled, "That's enough," as she stood up and stomped over to the light switch, flipping on the overhead lights, making the inside of my eyelids suddenly go from black to orange. Someone threw a pillow that missed her but knocked into the card table. Linda screamed, "The candles!"; someone ran to the bathroom and ran the faucet, and I felt a few splashes of water on my back. There were quick footsteps on the floor above us, the door opened, and Mrs. Johnson asked, "What's going on down there?"; Linda called, "Everything's fine!" More footsteps, Pam saying, "Sorry," and Becky saying, "Told you this was a bad idea." I opened my eyes, and I didn't look at the mess around me but at the Ouija board, and I put one finger on the pointer and waited and waited and waited for it to move while behind me everyone fussed and called each other stupid and discussed how long it would take Linda's mother to find the wax spots on the carpet and sofa and if there was any way to remove wax stains. I remembered Mama getting wax out of tablecloths by putting ice cubes on then scraping the wax, but I didn't tell them that. I just let them talk away, let their voices fill up the sudden silence, waiting, waiting, still waiting for the pointer to slide, to tell me anything, even if it was just something as simple as the word GOODBYE.

436

An hour later, with the mess cleaned up, the Ouija board back in the box, the box stuffed way at the bottom of a garbage bag up in the garage, the furniture and pillows rearranged slightly to cover up the wax stains, and Mrs. Johnson safely out of the kitchen, we finished our list of people to crank call. Lily begged and begged until we agreed to put Doug Flinn at the top of the list.

"What should we say to him?" Becky was running her finger along the names in the phone book, looking up his number, since Lily had claimed she'd forgotten his phone number (even though she'd changed her school locker to match it at the time).

"Tell him he's a jerk," Lily said.

Linda said, "You can't just call someone up and say 'Hi, you're a jerk.'"

Pam said, "Tell his parents you saw him drunk at a party last week. You don't want him to get into trouble, but you thought they should know. You're 'concerned.'" She did finger quotes around the word "concerned."

We pondered that for a moment then decided it was exactly right: revenge masked as concern. Besides, Pam actually DID see him drinking beer at a party last winter.

"Who's going to talk?" Linda said.

"Not me," Lily said. "They know my voice."

"And his sister is in my sister's Girl Scout troop, so they've called our house tons of times," Becky said. "They might know my voice."

"I'll do it," I said.

Linda said, "You ARE the best. You never crack up."

"Remember that time we called the principal and Alice made her voice sound like an old lady and accused him of running over her pet poodle?" Denise said.

"That was hilarious!" Pam said, and we ran through a number of great moments in crank phone calls, before getting down to the serious business of practicing what I was going to say and outlining every possible eventuality—what if he answered? what if the sister answered? what if the parents asked who was calling? what if they asked which party? what if they said that Doug had been visiting his sick grandmother the night in question?—until we started getting silly, saying things that no one else would think were even remotely funny but that set us laughing hysterically, like, "What if the dog answers the phone?" and "What if his mother answers the phone with a mouthful of peanut butter and she can't talk?"

Finally, Lily pushed me over to the phone, and as I picked up the receiver, I said, "Okay, give me a minute to stop laughing," which we all thought was very, very funny (even though it wasn't), and I stood with the phone against my ear, watching everyone laugh, feeling very, very normal and very, very much like I fit in just fine in spite of my dead mother, but then I heard whispering on the phone: "I missed your voice," and then a man spoke, "Me too," and there was a pause and all I heard was breathing which made me think maybe it wasn't real, but then the man said, "She and the kids are visiting her sister for the weekend. Come over," and the whisper said, "I can't," dragging out the word "can't" into a word of immense longing and desire, and the man said, "Meet me. Just for a minute," and the whisper said, "I can't," and the man said, "One minute," and it was really very, very romantic except that the next whisper was, "My daughter's slumber party . . ." and I slammed down the phone.

Becky noticed I'd hung up the phone and said, "What's wrong, Alice?"

I started fake-coughing. "Tickle in my throat," and Denise ran to get a cup of water. After I slowly drank that and did a few lingering, very realistic sounding coughs, I took in a deep breath and picked up the phone again. Dial tone. She must've heard me slam down the phone.

"You look funny," Linda said to me.

"Beauty is only skin deep," I said. "Ha, ha." And we weren't as silly as before, because no one laughed, and Linda said, "That's not what I meant."

"What's the number?" I asked, and the call went off perfectly (no one's mouth was filled with peanut butter, no dogs were involved). The other calls went well, too, to the principal, Mr. Miller, a couple other boys from school. No one suggested calling Joe Fry—

438

what a relief. But every time I picked up the phone or sat near anyone else who did, I heard that whisper in my mind, that longing, that desire, that secret life I'd glimpsed. Linda kept telling me I looked funny, and I kept making stupid jokes, and finally she stopped saying anything, but she didn't stop watching me.

Finally, at four in the morning we spread out our sleeping bags. As usual, Becky was the first to fall asleep, and Pam snuck upstairs and hid her bra in the freezer. Then Denise dropped off, and Pam hid HER bra in the freezer. Then Pam fell asleep, but we were too lazy to take her bra upstairs, so instead Lily stretched it across a lampshade and made big breasts with wadded-up socks. Then Lily fell asleep—wearing her bra.

"Are you awake, Alice?" Linda said for the sixth time in a row. Linda's voice sounded different in the dark; it didn't make sense that it did, but it did. It was something we'd all talked about at the many slumber parties we'd been to together over all the years, how Linda's voice sounded different in the dark—how it was impossible to believe, but there it was. We even made a tape once—in the dark and the next morning, saying the exact same sentences, and everyone could tell which was which.

I was on my back, staring up at the ceiling, barely awake, but for the sixth time, I said, "Yes," and then she didn't say anything more. I was thinking that maybe she wanted to apologize for what had happened with the Ouija board, but I wasn't in the mood even for that. (Besides, if she apologized, I'd have to apologize, too.) I was thinking about her mother whispering on the phone to a strange man, her mother getting in her powder blue station wagon and driving somewhere to meet the strange man, just like the girls at school who wore lipstick and smoked in the bathroom.

A moment later, Linda said, "Alice, are you awake?"

"What is it, Linda?" I rolled over, propped myself up on one elbow so I'd actually LOOK awake. "What?"

Linda said, "Do you believe what the Ouija board said?"

"It didn't say much of anything," I said.

"About my mother," she said.

There were all sorts of ways of explaining that whisper. Wrong number. Crossed connection. A joke.

Linda went on, "I'm just so afraid that something's not right." Then she said, "You saw the Ouija board. I know you didn't push it the second time."

I said, "Linda, you have the most perfect family in town."

A moment later, she said, "I know," but she didn't sound at all happy about it.

Then she didn't say anything else, so finally I whispered, "Linda, are you awake?" and she wasn't. So I rolled onto my back stared at the dark ceiling tiles. It was stupid to think you could find answers in a Ouija board; it was something you bought from the Sears catalog, for God's sake.

Mama always used to say, "Some questions don't have answers," and we'd get in a big discussion. "Well, most questions DO," I'd say. "Like, what is two plus two? It's four. See? Not five sometimes, not three on alternate Sundays. Four. Just plain four no matter how you cut it." The fight never ended, just sort of fizzled off.

I knew it wasn't the same as asking what is two plus two, but I couldn't help but whisper my question: "Why did you kill yourself?" I asked. "Why did you leave me?"

Becky mumbled and rolled over. She talked in her sleep all the time, nonsense words mostly, but every now and then a full sentence like, "Are dinosaurs white meat like chicken or red meat like beef?" She never believed us when we told her what she'd said.

I sighed and flipped over onto my stomach. She wasn't going to answer. Why did I keep asking? I pounded my pillow; there was no cool spot left on it.

Becky suddenly sat up. "What? What's wrong?"

"Never mind," I said. "Sorry." I couldn't tell if she was awake or not. In the past, she'd had whole conversations that she claimed not to remember.

She said, "You're not tired?"

"I can't sleep," I said. "By the way, Pam put your bra in the freezer."

Becky said, "I'm sure your mother didn't mean to."

"Yes, she did, Becky," I spit the words out. I was tired of her always being so nice and perfect, so hyper-understanding and trying to protect me. That was about as bad as the way Linda was.

Why couldn't anyone treat me like a normal person? "How can you not 'mean' to park your car on a train track when there's a train coming? How is that not meaning to?"

Becky said, "Leaving you. She forgot that part." She flopped back down, rolled over, and her breathing slowed until I knew she was asleep and that she wouldn't remember any of this conversation.

A short time later, I heard footsteps through the ceiling above, the kind of tiptoes you make when you don't want anyone to hear you. It was a long night for someone else, too. I imagined Mrs. Johnson pouring out a cup of coffee, sitting alone in the dark, maybe staring down at the floor, as if by staring hard enough and long enough, she could see right through it, down to where all of us girls lay, with our uncomplicated lives, sleeping, dreaming our untroubled dreams.

Just as I lay staring up at the ceiling, unable to see through those perfect ceiling tiles that Mr. Johnson had placed himself.

I fell asleep at dawn, still waiting to hear those footsteps go back across the kitchen. I dreamed of nothing.

·◇·

Before leaving the next morning, I thanked Mrs. Johnson for the lovely party. There were dark purple circles under her eyes. Mrs. Johnson said, "Alice, everything is going to be fine." She smiled at me, then added, "As long as you fit in." She didn't look like someone who had ever stayed up all night, who whispered desire and longing into a telephone. "If there's a secret to having a happy life, that's it," she said.

"I'll remember that," I said.

We were standing in the perfect living room, looking out the window. Will was late to pick me up—as usual. Everyone else's mother had already come. I sort of poked at my rolled up sleeping bag with one foot. "My brother should be here soon," I said.

"I don't know where Linda went," Mrs. Johnson said.

Outside, the kind of big fluffy clouds I liked filled up patches of the blue sky. I could never remember what they were called, though I remember having to memorize the types of clouds in grade school. "Will is always late," I said.

"It's okay," Mrs. Johnson said, and she set her hand on my shoulder. "Everything will be fine."

Part of me wanted to say, "I heard you on the phone last night," but I wasn't sure why. Maybe because here was someone else who really knew what it was like to have a secret you can't tell. But I was afraid that if I said anything—even one word—she'd pull her hand off my shoulder. And I sort of thought I didn't need to tell her that I'd heard her, that she knew.

Will pulled into the driveway, honked the horn like I was the one keeping him waiting.

"There he is," I said.

Mrs. Johnson nodded, but neither of us moved right away. Then she took her hand off my shoulder, tucked her arms across her chest. I picked up my sleeping bag and the grocery sack with my clothes and started walking to the front door. Will honked again. Mrs. Johnson followed, held the door open for me as I walked outside, down the front porch stairs to the front walk.

She said, "Wait." I stopped, turned back to look at her. She stood in the doorway; I had to squint into the sun to see her. She said, "I just don't think you can understand what it's like."

I dropped my sleeping bag onto the ground, put one hand above my eyes to shield them from the sun as I looked at her. I wasn't sure what she was talking about exactly, but I nodded anyway.

Linda came up behind her, leaned her head out the door, gave Will a big cheerful wave and smile. Mrs. Johnson set one hand on Linda's shoulder. Linda flipped her hair back (for Will's benefit) and shrugged her shoulder, shaking off her mother's hand as if it were nothing, as if there wouldn't ever be a time when it might not be there. Maybe that should've made me mad, but actually it didn't. Actually, it sort of cheered me up.

~

For the rest of the summer, one of the things I did was watch Mrs. Johnson, and I waited for Aunt Aggy to come home with some piece of gossip about her and the man who wasn't her husband. But there was nothing, just Mrs. Johnson acting the way she always did, and just Linda acting the way she always did.

Another thing I did was get a book out of the library and learn how to play bridge from it.

And the last thing I did was one night when everyone in the house was asleep make a secret promise—one of those dark of the night promises that you know you're going to keep—that whatever I was going to end up being or doing, I for sure wasn't going to be a bridge party kind of woman.

The Universal Daughter

THE WEEK BEFORE HER FATHER KILLED HIMSELF HEIDI LEFT town. For a festival celebrating Ernest Hemingway—not just the writer Hemingway but the deep-sea fisherman, storyteller, the all around sexy dude. There would be workshops, contests, drinking in bars. Her acting coach, on whom she had a small crush, had gone the year before.

"That's a dumb idea," said Val, her younger sister, beside her at the dinner table. Val had a decent husband and a bright four-year-old son, and thought you could be in control of your life. You got what you wanted, if you had the guts to admit you wanted it. Val shook half of a packet of Sweet'N Low into her decaf. "If Chicago's a furnace in July, how do you think it'll be in Key West?"

"What about Daddy?" Heather, her older sister, mouthed the words, carefully not looking at their father at the end of the long table, who sat forking up the last of the apple pie from the pie tin. Heather, a pediatrician, thought people who didn't take charge of their lives were either lazy or stupid.

Heidi smiled. "He has rotten table manners."

It was Friday night at their parents' high-rise condo. Called the "New York," it offered from living and dining room a dazzling view of Lake Michigan. The sun had set though. Chandelier light drifted down on coffee stains and pie crumbs. Their father, a former professor of twentieth century American literature, currently CEO of a company whose products had 80% brand name recognition, wiped his mouth with his hand and told their mother to take off her blouse. His voice, casual, resonant, echoed off the dining room walls. "I want to see your breasts. Give us a little peek, Bea."

"Honey, please," said their mother, pale-eyed, slim, ladylike, sometimes mistaken for their father's mother.

"*The stain of love is upon the world! Yellow, yellow, yellow* . . . William Carlos Williams," he said smiling.

"Daddy," cried Heather, "stop it."

Val was shaking her head.

Their father gave the short, round, rolling Ho! of an evil Saint Nick. Gareth, the four-year-old, repeated the utterance, which made Granddad turn to him. "She stinks in the sack, I'm telling you. And two of the girls I wouldn't pay a buck for. But Auntie Heidi—now there's a sweet ass!"

Gareth produced the musical fake laugh of a somewhat older child, but his mother's mouth opened in shock, and Heather looked as if she wanted to cry. Heidi turned away from her father, stashing his remark in a side pocket of her brain. Then, later that evening as she loaded the dishwasher, Heather asked her, please, to rinse the plates first, and to help her take their dad to the neurologist. She'd already made the appointment.

"Take?" Heidi scraped chicken bones into the plastic garbage bag, as she had been doing, then set the plate on the rack. "No one takes Daddy anyplace."

Heather removed Heidi's plate, rinsed, then reloaded it. "Wouldn't you say he's been acting inappropriate lately? On the verge of sleazy?"

"He's always had that element!"

Her sister rolled her eyes. "There's something wrong with his memory. Yesterday he asked me how my tennis was going."

"So?"

"I don't play tennis. You're the one who plays tennis." An outraged sob roughened her voice. "If you could look past your own nose for once!"

"Heather, he was *kidding* you."

Heidi glanced back into the dining room through the haze that had been covering things lately. Their father was holding their mother's hand. He said something to Val, which, from her face, appeared to be authentically amusing. Six months ago at the JUF dinner in his honor for twenty years of increasing generosity, his speech had been clever, moving in spots. People had rushed up to shake his hand. Some had hugged him. Heidi was charmed as always—slightly in awe of her father and secretly proud of her place in his life as—both her sisters would agree—the most beloved daughter.

"He's sixty years old," she said, feeling the lameness. "You lose a little at sixty." At some point, she half-felt, she would start worrying about her father. A year or so ago, over the phone, he had said to her, "Things are closing in on me," but he hadn't explained and hadn't repeated the complaint. Whatever he was going through was still vague enough, and benign enough, for her to wave it away like cigarette smoke. Saying goodnight, she kissed his cheek. Kissed him twice, meaning it. He held her arm.

"What?" she said.

"I believe in the green light." He scanned her face as if trying to place her. "Like Jay Gatsby. There are still some things commensurate with our capacity for wonder."

"Yes," she cried. "Of course there are!" Behind him the wall of windows gave on a blackness thick and heavy as wool.

"I always liked that line."

In his voice was something furious and lost. It didn't jibe, though with her view of heaven and earth, and soon wafted away. She patted his hand. "You have an amazing memory!" She gave her mother a quick, firm hug. "Be good, people. I'll call you when I get there."

"Yeah right," said Heather, on her way out as well.

Her father laughed his old laugh, rich and merry. "Break a few hearts."

446

On the plane she felt euphoric almost, seated beside a friendly, balding corporate art director off to visit his still more ancient mother. Her father's behavior was at worst eccentric, almost to be expected from someone with that much power and money. And five miles up over marvelously regular squares of green and ocher farmland Heidi saw herself ascending toward the glory that had always haloed her father's being. She held her tennis racquet against her stomach, unzipping and rezipping the leather case. So what if up to this time there was little evidence of her ascent—she wasn't Meryl Streep or Demi Moore or even Steffi Graf. But it was because she had too many gifts, was good at too many different things, which, five miles up in the thin blue air, was basically a plus, no? She told her seatmate, Harry, about her two irritating competent sisters—one a doctor, the other married to a doctor— the stream of their lives already channeled into routines and minor accomplishments. Waitress work gave Heidi time for tennis, which kept her sane, and acting, her career goal. In her acting class she was the star pupil, with a real flair for comedy—her coach had said. "But sometimes I wonder," she confided, "will I ever make it if I haven't by now?" She was twenty-eight. The middle sister, she'd have been ignored if she hadn't worked at being the dynamic sister, but now, it seemed sometimes, she was becoming the flaky sister.

"You'll do just fine! I have a feeling about that!" Harry smiled warmly.

He gave her his last name (Borsteen), and his phone number in Miami, and told her to call if she needed anything. She thanked him, not surprised. Men her father's age often showed a fatherly concern for her. At times she felt like a universal daughter. A daughter-principle. The ur-Daughter. She put her racquet on the floor by her feet, lowered her tray table and began tinkering with the monologue she planned to present in the Festival storytelling contest, a comic rendering of her rejection of a recent boyfriend's proposal of marriage.

On the ground her good feeling maintained itself, but against odds, it seemed. She'd hoped to play tennis in between Festival events, but the air outside the terminal was so hot that sweat gathered in the dip over her upper lip. The carpet in her motel room felt damp to the soles of her feet. A spot below her anklebone began to itch. On medium, the air-conditioner made no perceptible change in the temperature of the room, and on high it clanged. But when she called her parents and got the machine, something loosened inside her. They were out at a restaurant. At a play. At the home of one of their many friends. She left her cheery voice: "We didn't crash! It's hot as hell! I love you, guys!"

The mood lasted through the night, and got her to her workshop close to on time. The instructor, Joanne True, who seemed smart despite her Southern accent and the broad Hemingway face on the front of her T-shirt, was still introducing. Heidi seated herself beside a tan fortyish woman with ashy streaks in her dark hair and a blue-jean mini-skirt. The woman had a library copy of Hemingway's *A Moveable Feast* set conspicuously on the table in front of her but Heidi forgave her. Heidi felt warmly toward everyone around the conference table, especially the loud-voiced man her father's age who ran triathlons and the shy, pretty high school girl smiling behind her stack of Xeroxes. In the Festival brochure that lay in front of each participant Heidi checked out the upcoming events. There was the Hemingway Trivia Contest, the Hemingway Arm Wrestling Contest, the Hemingway Fish-Off and the Hemingway Look-Alike Contest. A photo showed three rows of large-framed men, all broad-faced and grizzle-bearded like fifty-something Ernest Hemingways. Silly but you know? A half goofball, half glam *moveable feast!*

The high school girl passed out what she called her memoir and began to read. She had smoked pot, had a minor car accident, found Jesus. There was applause. Joanne's questions sidestepped evaluation. Heidi liked the hostess rhythms of Joanne's voice.

The aging triathlete, whose father had a fatal heart attack at forty-nine, described his first 5K. Joanne pointed out an effective paragraph. The group made approving comments. Under their attention, the man became even more expansive. He was a diabetic. He wrote five pages every morning, then ran three miles or biked or swam. A crazy life, but it was his.

The man had clean-shaven cheeks, a thick, white half-circle of beard. Impressed by his vitality, Heidi was trying to decide if he was older or younger than her father when a latecomer walked in. He didn't look at Heidi or anyone; still voices subsided. The discussion ceased, shoulders straightened, faces went neutral and alert. The uninvited guest. A white-haired woman sat up very straight in her chair. Joanne cleared her throat.

The man took a seat at a corner of the table just beyond the edge of the group. There was something deliberate in his movements but not at all restrained or apologetic, as if he were conscious of, and at the same time indifferent to, being looked at. His clean, tight white T-shirt revealed the small hard muscles of his arms and shoulders. He could be any age—thirty, sixty. Handsome, ugly? He had a red bandanna over graying blond sideburns, a narrow, faintly lined face. Although she knew she'd never met him before, he looked strangely familiar. Then it dawned on her. He was *bad* Ernest Hemingway, the snotty, cocky, frightened man who'd worked all his life, her father had said, to prove himself. This Hemingway traded insults with Gertrude Stein, put down multiple wives and F. Scott Fitzgerald (Scottie). Heidi imagined him in this conference room, gazing about with the same pained disdain as the man in the bandanna. She tried not to stare as he took a pen out of his pocket and began working on what looked like his own manuscript, his absorption putting up little jagged points all around him. Not at all tall or broad, he had large, muscled hands. Heidi wondered what his story would be about. Carving a block of granite? Strangling a woman? She mulled the varied textures of silence. One kind felt judgmental, another shy, a third friendly, loving even. How could that be?

Still, the discomfort he'd brought into the room soon fell below the level of the detectable. People with long pieces summarized, then read two or three pages. Applause followed each reading. As the three hours drew to a close everyone had presented their manuscripts except Heidi, the woman in the mini-skirt and the man in the bandanna, who so far had said nothing at all. "Mine's short," the woman said, smiling apologetically.

"I just have notes," Heidi said. "I'm not really a writer, I'm an actor. Well, trying to be."

The man in the bandanna made no comment, though Heidi thought she saw him rolling his eyes. His eyes looked different from each other, one blue, one smoky gray, though it could have been the angle.

The woman stood up, hands shaking on her manuscript. She was thin on top with heavy legs. Her name was Robyn with a "y," she said in a loud, brilliant voice. She was having domestic problems, she wasn't usually this nervous. When she went home she was going to get divorced.

Heidi tried to listen, but the piece was hard to follow. Robyn had been either gravely ill or in unrequited love, or both. In the end she had sex but Heidi couldn't figure out whether it was a good thing for her, or a bad thing. Her writing felt slightly inaccurate, as if translated. At her conclusion a little pool of silence spread out and out, till Joanne said, "Well, that's intriguing."

"It's so, well, *personal*," said someone else.

Heidi skimmed her copy of the manuscript.

"This is definitely complex," said the instructor. "So before we give our responses let's figure out what's being attempted here. What's it about?" Robyn smiled nervously. People shifted in their seats. Silence slapped at Heidi like waves on the beach. After a moment the high school girl raised her hand.

"Love and death?"

"A well-respected American theme," said Joanne, smiling like a proud parent. Robyn gazed downward but nodded to herself.

"Or," Heidi said, breathless with her own daring, "sex and death!"

The murmured concurrence seemed general. Joanne was advising Robyn that, by adding concrete details to the final scene, she'd include the reader more fully in her pain and joy, when a slap rang out. A rolled up manuscript had whacked the edge of the table. Heads turned toward the man in the bandanna. He stared back mockingly.

"What *about* sex and death? Sex is like death? Sex causes death? Sex triumphs over death?" His voice was soft and nasal, not quite contemptuous, like a pirate on the brink of weary of his trade. "I'm confused. Is fucking a religious experience or a shortcut to hell? Or is this too personal?"

"It's ambiguous," someone murmured.

"She leaves it up to the reader," said the high school girl. "That's why I like it."

Joanne nodded at the room in general, apparently delighted by this turn of the discussion. Robyn sat behind her tight smile. The pirate released the coil of manuscript. It sprang open on the table. "Crap."

His face looked almost tranquil now, and his large hands rested in his lap. Still, his ejaculation buzzed around the room. Joanne said, "You know, we try to be sensitive to each other."

Heidi stared coldly at the man, seconding Joanne. She saw him with what she imagined to be her sister Heather's eyes, as a guy to steer clear of. She turned to Robyn with words to fortify her and put the nasty man in a small and unimportant place, but Robyn had already gathered her things and was on her way out the door.

"Oh," said Joanne, looking at her watch. "Well, I guess that about does it?" She glanced at the pirate, who gazed back with mocking blankness.

Disbanding, everyone but the pirate moved down the long hall toward the stairs. There was a little hum of upset. "That was so *unnecessary*," said the high school student. The opinion was seconded by the white-haired woman, who belonged to a Great Books discussion group whose members were, invariably, courteous to each other.

Heidi followed them down, bonded to them by dint of their mutual enemy. She mimicked Joanne's courteous lilt. "He thinks very well of himself." People laughed. Her liking for them grew. In the lobby, before they could go their separate ways, she called out, "Hey, I need a tennis partner. Does anyone want to hit with me?"

There were friendly demurrals. One man had brought a racquet but he wasn't about to get a stroke running around in one hundred degrees. She was about to suggest an indoor court, if they could find one, when footsteps descending the stairs proved to be those of the pirate. He walked over to her as if they'd agreed to meet. "It's cooler outside in the early morning. Are you any good?"

On the other side of the net, the pirate, whose name was Armour —first or last, he didn't say—popped the can with a deft first finger. She reached out for her share of the balls, but he took all three like fuzzy yellow eggs in the palm of his hand. She had never seen, it seemed to her, a hand so large. The morning air was surely as hot as noon. Even the breeze felt warm on the back of her neck. "Ready?" he said.

She smiled, drying her racquet hand on the side of her shorts. "For the slaughter, you mean? For my demise?" She spun her racquet in the cylinder of her hand. The racquet was a birthday gift from her father, lighter than her old one, better balanced. She wasn't balanced though. Last night she'd called her parents and again got no answer. Although her tone was as breezy as before— "Out on the town again, kiddies?"—she included the motel phone number and hung up in slight disarray, as if she'd just misplaced her hairbrush. She felt dizzy now, in fact, and spoke to orient herself. "Balmy out!"

Armour made no comment. He seemed immune to the heat. Below his red bandanna his forehead looked like powdery clay. She continued her patter, trying for the laugh that would set her at ease. "Does 'warm up' seem redundant to you?"

There was no change in his expression. Perhaps he hadn't understood. It was a dumb joke. He said, "You want to start the game now?"

"God, no! Let's hit for a while."

She proceeded to her end of the court. It was past eight, but the sun beat on her shoulders, her neck, the top of her head through the eye of her visor, and although they hadn't started to play yet, the leather grip of her racquet was already damp in her hand. She squatted, rose stiffly. When the ball came over the net would she be able to run?

When the ball in fact came over the net, low and hard, no patty cake, she was gifted with the power of movement. The air was hotter than anything in memory, and she clambered through it as through heavy mist, but her new racquet had a yen for the fresh, new ball—it lusted, withdrawing, pulling back, twisting the screw of the tension, then sprong-whop!—and all she had to do was step, hold, left foot up, right back, back with the arm, shift, swing, sprong! The ball skimmed the net as if sucked down on the other side. In tournaments she had never played this well, or on the air-conditioned, windless, sunless indoor courts of her club at home. She found the time and the poise now to lengthen her strokes, driving the ball deeper and deeper, angling it—her father would be proud—and though the moisture in the air coated her skin thick as mud, when the ball came she was ready, for the sake of the tire-less, merciless man on the other side of the court—she had to get there and she got there, she ran, stopped, pulled back. When her breath came easily up from the bottom of her lungs, and her arms felt strong as iron, she caught the next ball on the face of her rac-quet. "So, Monsieur Armour, are you ready for zat zere *game?*"

"Any time you are."

She tossed her racquet in the air, higher than she had to. "Up or down, for Master of the Universe? Mistress!"

"You serve."

His flat voice weighed on her. Not only wouldn't he let her amuse him, he seemed to deride her very impulse to amuse, as if it were a personality defect.

She was pleased, though, with the way her serve came in. No harder than usual, it was more consistent, with a confusing little swerve to the left. He blooped the first two. She exulted. This was for Robyn and for all womankind, not to mention her own under-utilized gifts roiling behind her waitress bib.

Then he figured out her spin. No matter what she put on her serve it came back low and hard. The rhythm changed. She main-tained her quickness, her judgment, but his had compounded. She lost four points in a row. It was as if during warm up he'd been hus-tling, bringing her best game out into the light of day while con-cealing his, which assailed her now in strokes it was all she could do to meet. His serve came so fast she had no time for a backswing. By the time she managed to get her racquet on the ball the score was forty-love.

"Time out!" She took a breath, stretched. Mind over matter, said her father, who acknowledged neither fatigue nor another person's superiority. Her racquet was a log in her hand, sweat seeped under her visor, pooled in the sockets of her eyes, but she planted herself. The serve bounced high as before, but she had her racquet back and managed an overhead.

The ball rose, but so languorously he had time almost to stroll to the net. She watched from behind the baseline, shifting her weight from foot to foot. He stood tranquil as the Buddha as the ball slowed, then stopped for that nano-sec at the top of its arc. She bent her knees, steadied her racquet. His arm slanted back. His racquet head dropped, then rose toward the ball with a steady mindfulness, almost elegant. There was a moaning sprong. Then without having given the faintest sign of its proximity the ball was behind her.

Who was this masked man? His after-image towered over her like a building, like the muscular tail of a dragon, collapsing to rise again with such grace it made her eyes ache.

They continued the set, but though she focused her breath as her father had told her, exhaling thoughts of each finished point, there was no contest. She won occasionally but it felt accidental, the result of a momentary lapse of his attention. When it was over she advanced to the net with her hand out. "Good game, Mr. Sampras. You're a terrific player."

He nodded, ducking out from under her compliment. "How old are you?"

She told him, trying not to stare at his face, still dry almost and barely flushed. She reminded herself that men with their height and strength had the advantage at sports. Apart from tennis she had many graces and talents. Not to mention, she was a *nice person*. The late morning sun beat down from the sky and rose up around her from the asphalt of the court but she smiled, said with her usual lightness, "You're not even breathing hard. Are you an android?"

As usual he let her joke fall into the void of meaningless chatter. "You played better than I expected."

"Really? Why did you want to play me then? You wanted to slam someone into the absolute *ground?*" Her voice was shrill. He seemed taken aback. But she couldn't stop though her legs were shaking.

"Are you some kind of sleazebag? Really, if you thought I'd be so lousy, what did you set this up for?"

"Obviously, to fuck you."

She gave a small shriek.

He laughed. "That's what men want, right?"

"God! What's the point of this?" Her high voice careened on, strangely sure of itself. "There's nothing about you I like, and I'm sure it's vice versa." She looked him right in his mismatched eyes, she wasn't afraid of him. "And, not that you asked, but since you think you're so much better than everyone, and this couldn't possibly bother you, I'll tell you the truth. You're a jackass. You're a jerk with no feelings and nothing upstairs so you have to take it out on helpless women, so just get out of here!" She shook the weakness out of her legs and set off for her motel, jauntily swinging her racquet.

At the first stoplight he was at her side with no sign of having hurried. A cigarette hung from his lip. The color of his eyes matched now, it seemed, but one of them looked slightly larger than the other. "Excuse me, miss, but have you heard of irony?"

"I'll scream!"

"Go ahead, it's a free country." He fished out his pack of cigarettes, offered her; she ignored him. He took a drag, stepped neatly upon the butt. "Have I laid a hand on you? Have I touched you in any way? Have I offered to take you back to my room and rub you all over with hot fragrant oil? You have very soft-looking skin."

She tried to stare him down. His lips looked purple, as if he'd been in the pool too long. His hands were large enough to meet around her waist. She thought of the pads of his long fingers at the waistband of her cut-offs. Sweat rolled in drops down the sides of her sports bra.

"Why don't you tell me," he said, "what the ingenue act's all about? You're almost thirty years old and you act like a teenager."

"I do not."

She stepped onto the street. Still, his voice, oddly gently now, drifted past her eyelids; for a moment she was squeezing back tears. There was something bad wrong with her that couldn't be fixed, that certain people like this crazy man saw bright and clear. "Why are you doing this?"

"Doing what?"

"Back off! Get away from me!"

"The light's green."

Down the block a pair of men in business suits were strolling toward them. She hurried across the street so fast Armour would have had to trot to keep up.

All afternoon she was frantically social. She enthused over the dreadlocks of the girl who sold her a pair of sunglasses and learned it took eight hours to do it up like that. "Maybe I'll try it," she said gaily.

With a woman on the beach she had an earnest conversation about estrogen replacement therapy. When the time came, she told the woman, she would definitely go for it.

At dinner she met the bearded triathlete, who, it turned out, had a room in her motel. He moved to her table, showed her a photo of his "family," three Weimaraners—Marilyn, Ursula and Raquel. "What beauties!" She admired their noble heads, bright eyes, sturdy gray bodies. "I can't have dogs in my apartment," she confided, "but I've decided. When I get home I'm getting one."

"Good for you," said the triathlete, whose name was Bill Williams. "You're going to move?"

"I'll sneak him in. The landlord's a noodle. Besides, a dog can't be worse than what I've had up there."

Bill Williams snorted. "You can be trouble, I see."

She started laughing hysterically.

At the storytelling she had a microphone but her voice sounded feeble compared to the guy who came before her. Behind her rose the outside wall of a building; in front the ocean lapped against the breakwater. She felt small and meek. "This is about Noah, my ex-boyfriend, who was so good to me I broke up with him." There were scattered laughs but she had to fight for the crowd's attention.

456

As her coach had taught her, she lowered her voice, brought the mike closer to her mouth, as if she were speaking words of love. "Noah would have been a dream son-in-law. He was an attorney. He played the violin in the Northbrook Symphony. He played beautiful tennis. He made chicken soup when I was sick. He filled our apartment with the smell of chicken soup."

She breathed into the silence that meant close attention, then went on, detailing Noah's virtues, her own insensitivity. It was all true. She was high on truth, on self-revelation. She looked like a sexy virgin in her black tank top and white stretch jeans. But as she neared the end of the story—the moment at a Chinese restaurant when she opened two fortune cookies that said, respectively, "It is a bad day to refuse an offer," and "Will you marry me?"—her voice broke. She'd never performed the story before, she'd just written it out, and now, though she recalled what she'd felt at the restaurant table—pity for Noah and mild disgust with herself—it was obviously not funny. Why had she thought it would be funny? The faces of the audience grew expectant, their interest heightened by her silence. Bill, her buddy, sat smiling up at her from a folding chair in the front row. She said, high and emphatic like a valley girl, "Go-od! Do you think Mom was right?"

There was no sound but the wind, the plash of waves, the toot of a boat too far away to see. She maintained an amused face but knew the story had bombed. That happened sometimes—an audience identified with the wrong person or idea. Comedy turned tragic or mean. "Oh well. I guess you had to be there."

Someone chuckled. It didn't catch, though.

"I'm sorry. You caught me. Avoiding intimacy again. I should have told you the truth. Noah wasn't the man for me. I wanted Ernest Hemingway."

She hadn't paused long enough. It took a moment for people to understand what she'd said. Then Bill's laugh boomed out, followed by a wave of laughter with some staying power. She raised a hand for quiet.

"I still do! Come on, admit it, isn't that what we came down for? We either want to be Hemingway or to fuck Hemingway!"

This was bawdier than was her wont, but the laugh rose. It held her in its arms, lifted her up into the air over the heads of these laughing people, who wanted to go on laughing, who wanted her to make them laugh forever and ever. "Thanks very much! You're great, I love you! Hey, and if you see Ernest around here, tell him I'm looking for him."

She made the next round. She exulted, walking with Bill down brightly lit Duval Street. "That was a riot! I am high! You know, you remind me of someone. What did you say your name was? Bill Williams? Bill W. Williams?"

He smiled tolerantly. He said she reminded him of his daughter.

"Which one? Demi Moore or Sharon Stone?"

"That's great!" he said. "That's what Ann Marie would have said."

She laughed, took his arm. "I was great, wasn't I? I think there's hope for me. Is there hope for me? Do I have comic talent?" She wagged a finger at him. "I thought you didn't have children. You have Marilyn, Ursula, and Cher."

"Raquel."

"Just testing!" Holding his arm she walked, buoyant on her internal laughter. He was the string holding her to earth.

"I have my dogs," he said. "I also have a son and a daughter. I have an ex-wife. Two ex-wives, that is. I left a few things out, is all. For the rhythm. You're an actress, honey, you know where I'm coming from. I'm not a writer, either, I'm here to win the Aficionado Award."

She stared. He smiled as if he'd received a compliment.

"You get Aficionado points for all your events. One point for the writing group. That's a gyp, by the way, you get four for the Bell Regatta, just to enter." He scratched the skin under his beard reflectively.

"I'm just taking this in," she said. "You don't get up early in the morning to write?" She could tell she was being theatrical, but she truly felt dizzy. "You lied to us?"

"I get up to go fishing. I'm a genius at catching fish. The Fish-Off tomorrow will earn me five points, I'll bet you, for the biggest. I get ten for looking like Papa. Did you like my story? Ann Marie whipped it up. But I read a lot. I bet I've read as much as some of your college professors." He spread his arms. "Do I look like the Old Man? I won the Look-Alike six years ago. Last year I crowned the winner. Previous winners get ten points. Everyone, even if they shave or go bald."

She examined him. With his ruddy cheeks, grizzled beard and neat, jovial paunch he looked like the would-be Papas in the conference brochure. His face could have appeared on Joanne True's T-shirt. "Do you really run? Are you a real diabetic? Are you standing in front of me?"

"I hope you're not pissed. My ex hated anything that wasn't straight out in front of her. You have a sense of humor."

She smoothed the hairs over her arms, increased her walking speed.

"I was in the army," he went on. "I put in twenty years and got my pension, enough to live on if I don't spend too much. I read a book by Frank Conroy, what do you call it? And that guy who writes the spy novels, Le Carre? I read the biography of William Butler Yeats, now he was an oddball! You know, he didn't really write his best poems, a spirit wrote for him? But it was great stuff. 'This is no country for old men.' You can say that again!" He stopped in front of a clothing store window display featuring parrot-colored shirts and sun dresses. He wanted to buy a dress for his daughter, and for her too. "You're such a sweet little girl. You wouldn't take my money and leave me to rot on this godforsaken island."

She squeezed his hand but couldn't look at him. His skin gave off a watery, helpless light, disturbingly familiar though she couldn't remember where she'd seen it before. She kissed his cheek. "I'm dead on my feet. No, please, no need to walk me."

Back at the hotel the desk clerk gave her two memo-slips. In the first, from Heather, two boxes were checked—Please Call. Urgent. The second read, *The light is out,* signed Scottie. She looked at the clerk, who shrugged. "He made me read it back to him."

In her room she sat down on one of the queen-size beds and

dialed her parents' condo. Her mother answered. It was ninety degrees in Chicago at ten PM, could you believe it, she'd had the air conditioner running nonstop. In the background was Ted Koppel. For dinner she'd cut up a banana into some cottage cheese. The daughter of the woman who lived across from their old house had just had a mastectomy. "Julie Karpfinger, in her last year of law school. Younger than you, Heidi! Isn't that sad. You used to play with her older sister. Do you remember Julie Karpfinger?"

"That's horrible, Mom. Poor Julie." Her voice was sprightly though, an attitude she planned to maintain with her parents on her own deathbed. She described the storytelling contest, her confusion and miraculous recovery. "I wish I had a recording. To play in my old age. Just kidding. Now tell me the truth, where have you two been, lately? Hey, and could I say hello to Daddy?"

Dad was in bed. Her mother began to speak even more rapidly. Her days were so hectic. She was exhausted. She'd made a fruit salad for the symphony board ladies. The melon was unbelievably sweet.

Heidi called Heather.

Heather's first response was a contained, furious snort like the *whooss* of an igniting match. Heidi held the receiver out from her ear, waiting for Heather to gather herself sufficiently to yell at her. "I don't know how you do it," Heather said at last. "You leave, and all hell breaks loose, with the rest of us to pick up the pieces. How do you choreograph that?"

"I talked to Mom," she said mildly. "She didn't mention any—"

"Oh Mom! She's protecting you! That's what we do, your family, we protect you!"

Small in the ear piece, Heather's voice rose up and up, a pure, thin ray of hatred beaming from the city of Chicago all the way to Key West. Heidi's gaze moved from the blank TV screen to the dresser mirror, locked door, curtained window, framed prints over the beds of ships sailing on, respectively, sun- and moonlit seas. "From what?" she whispered.

At two AM the shops along Duval were bright as the gems of a fluorescent necklace but the street was near empty. A small black dog

460

trotted, tail up, blithely purposeful. A car raced after nothing that could be seen.

The Green Parrot—according to the brochure, Hemingway's old hangout—was crowded, though. An assortment of men in various stages of relaxation watched Heidi thread her way to the bar. But the glances didn't linger, perhaps because of what she'd worn, a white blouse, loose cotton slacks, a blazer of Heather's. As Heather, who made the right common sense choices, who infused a room with purposefulness, she could hide out from the merrymakers.

She ordered a Bloody Mary, Heather's drink, brought it over to a sparsely populated corner where a narrow shelf lined the wall. Behind her, men of drunken good will were telling each other unremarkable lies. She sat down on a stool, placed her purse on the stool beside her, sipped. In the protection of her loose clothing she was starting to feel the feeling she wanted to have for the rest of her life—an unassailable indifference—when a fingertip skated across the back of her neck.

At first she didn't recognize the man to whom the finger belonged—gloomy, narrow-jawed, maybe fifteen years older than she. Not tall. But leaning toward her, he seemed to press on her, enclose her in a space with limited air. "Are you going to run away from me?"

It was Armour without the bandanna.

She sat stiffly, a foot hooked on a rung of her stool, the other wagging. Part of her wanted to exit the bar, but by putting the act into words he'd turned it anticlimactic. She looked past him, noticing out the corner of her eye that while he had thick hair over his ears his forehead was balding. "I might," she said. "After I finish this drink."

Almost daintily he set his glass on the shelf beside her glass, then gazed at her purse till she took it off the stool. He sat down beside her. "I'm really not an asshole through and through, you know. My problem is I say what I mean, unlike most of the blow-hards here."

"Right," she said, "you're probably the only honest person on the island."

She dared a glance into his eyes, one of which still looked slightly different from the other. Then a new spirit entered into her. Her voice came low, mock sweet: "This place can make you crazy, all these aging frat boys." She smiled gracious as Joanne True, a faintly Southern lilt in her voice. What would she say next? She set her purse on her lap, folded her hands on it. "With all these *lightweights*, y'all must be feeling kind of lonely."

He smiled back, concluding, perhaps, that she was too simple-minded to be sarcastic, or else it didn't matter to him. "That pear-shaped babe yesterday, do you think she ever fucked? Seriously. 'Then he was inside me, outside and inside me, and all there was in me was the darkness of him'!"

I kind of like that, Heidi wanted to say. She said with her trace of drawl, "You have an outstanding memory. Do you think it's the salt water? Hey, are you one of the Boston Armours? Are you my knight in shining armour?" She hugged her purse. "Are you—" she started giggling before the words came out "—an Armour Star Frank?"

He didn't smile, but it didn't matter now. She sent him to the bar for another drink. She felt *Hemingwayesque*. Was there such a word as Hemingwayesque? As he returned with their glasses, a young woman walked in, with a bony, intelligent face and the kind of smoothly angled haircut that falls back in place after a toss of the head. The woman halted before a man old enough to be her father and kissed him on the lips. Heidi leaned toward Armour, her chin on the hand whose elbow rested her purse. "No one should write about fucking who hasn't a great deal of varied personal experience, hmmmm?"

Silent, he gazed downward, depressed, maybe. For a minute she felt sorry for him. But then she thought of Robyn, and of her shameful defeat at tennis, and besides, she was enjoying herself. "Would you show me a story of yours, Mr. Armour? I'm not a writer, but I have great respect for writers. I feel nostalgia for college. I read *The Sun Also Rises* in college in American Lit. I wanted to live in Paris in the Twenties. I admire creativity. In my field, if you're creative it's within strict limits." She took a swig of her drink, then sat up straight on her stool and leveled her gaze at him. "Don't you ever ask questions? Do you think it gives someone too much power over you to ask them something?"

"What would you like me to ask you?"

"You know, there are some basic social skills you seem to lack." She laughed merrily. "Aren't you wondering how I earn a living?"

He opened his eyes wider but the look was opaque.

"Poor," she said. "I'm an attorney. But I'll give you another chance. Ask me if I enjoy the practice of law."

"This is getting racy."

She smiled, one who knew how the uninitiated felt about the American legal system. "I despise real estate. Torts are fun." She rattled off words her ex-boyfriend had used. "I do a divorce now and then, for my close friends. That can be nasty, though I admit to a perverse fascination. It's a small town. We have to entertain our- selves somehow. Come on, ask me something."

"Where do you live?"

"Ithaca, New York!" It was where Noah had gone to school. "Beautiful place. Gorges and waterfalls."

"There's a college there."

"Two colleges."

"Which did you go to?"

"Now you're cooking! I went to Cornell. Nice campus but the suicide capital of the academic world. It's true. It's in the college guides. Depression at Cornell University. It rains a lot. Students jump off the suspension bridges."

"My father shot himself."

She set her drink down. She'd opened her mouth to elaborate on her fictional autobiography but his remark—its baldness—blocked her windpipe. She coughed, took a gulp of air.

He smiled. Was this the first time he smiled? She tried to remember.

"It's a family tradition," he said. "My great uncle did it too. Blew his brains out. The big death. Even better than the little death, or so it is said. That's my link with Ernest."

She closed her eyes, wanting to say something honestly kind, but the words in her head were snapping ferociously at each other. Her hand, the one that held the cold glass, was shaking. She placed it between her thighs. "That must have been *hard*."

"Oh, I don't know. Kind of expands the options."

He had resumed his cocky look but now she couldn't rush away. She told him about her own father, who'd been arrested yesterday for peeing in the marble lobby of an office building. Heather had said. A woman had screamed, and he turned, spraying her feet. He owned the building, he told the woman—and he did—so he could pee in it or on it, he could burn it down if he wanted. Heidi opened her purse, clicked it shut. This was the same man who'd written a book on modernism, then took the hardware store his wife had inherited and tuned it into an import business that offered shares on the New York Stock Exchange. He owned property in Chicago, New York, and Tel Aviv. He dined with the heads of small foreign countries, received their telegraphed congratulations on the marriage of his daughter, birth of his grandson, on his and his wife's thirty-fifth wedding anniversary. He was good at everything, even tennis—was seeded in the Midwest in the over-fifty division. Yes, he was occasionally unfaithful, but out of the overflow of his charisma, and he was good to his daughters, especially to her. He taught her to play tennis so well she led her high school to a state championship and got into college on a tennis scholarship. He took her to plays, her alone, because she was going to be an actress. She rolled her eyes. Tears, mildly bothersome, were running down her cheeks. The neurologist thought he had Pick's Disease, a flamboyant relative of Alzheimer's, which, over time would erode his memory and his judgment so that not only would he forget how to drive a car, he'd dangle his prick out over Lake Shore Drive from the window of his condominium. "They're looking for a caretaker. They're trying out some drugs on him. But probably he'll be a zombie. A sleazy zombie. I'm trying to present this humorously."

He didn't smile, even compassionately. He leaned toward her, ran a finger across the line of her mouth. "I know what you want." He held her jaw in his hand so tight she couldn't open her mouth. She gazed at him, her eyes wide as for an optometrical exam. "You want to feel something real for once in your life. You want an experience so deep you'll remember it even with Pick's Disease." She continued to gaze at him, transfixed by the pale luster of his eyes, one of which looked bluish to her and the other green brown, as his fingertips descending from her mouth to her chin, her neck, pressed till she gasped and for a moment after. The slope of his forehead rose high and smooth like a wise man's. "Pleasure at its peak is a lot like pain, have you noticed that? We use the same words: Sharp. Keen. Burning. Exquisite. How about throbbing? Throbbing pain, throbbing delight. At the extremes they merge like East and West. Do you know what I'm talking about?"

She bobbed her head fast. "Like the left wing and the right wing. Though of course at the extremes they're both terrorists." She tried to follow the thought but came up on blank, a clearing. Her mouth burned but her teeth were chattering. "This is a very weird discussion." She tried to smile, to make it ordinary.

"I guess I'm a weird person," he said. "But then so are you." His broad hand slid down the white cotton front of her blouse, then with an upward motion squeezed her breast. She felt sick with pleasure. It occurred to her that he might have a glass eye. She looked but couldn't tell. She was panting a little. He said, "Did you really go to Cornell? I didn't know they offered women's athletic scholarships."

"I went to the U of I at Champaign. I majored in theater." She had too much saliva. She wiped her mouth with the back of her hand. "I work at an Italian restaurant in Chicago called Signorini Linguini."

He cupped the base of her head, kissed her eyebrow. "Let's go back to one of our rooms and make the earth move."

As they turned down the road that led to her motel he stopped to light a cigarette. From on high came an audible click. The street lamps winked out. The pinwheel heads of palm trees emerged black upon the dying black of the sky. Out of a convenience store whose fluorescent whiteness was dimming in the rising dawn walked Bill W. Williams, fishing pole in hand.

Heidi pretended not to see him. But Bill waved, rushed up, launching at Armour—his good buddy like all men up and at 'em at five in the morning—a long appreciation of certain brands of Cuban cigars. Not that Bill smoked anymore. He used to smoke but he quit six years ago, stopped the day he heard his high school best friend was dead of lung cancer. He lit up once in the guy's honor and never again, not in six years, and frankly now he couldn't stand the smell. His voice was loud in the empty dawn. Armour listened, blowing smoke. Heidi stood leaning against his sinewy arm.

Armour's presence and the oddity of the encounter held her till the first shadow of morning drifted up the concrete road. Then tears of frustration sprang to her eyes. Bill opened his wallet to a photo of Ann Marie posed with an armful of books by some university's red brick gate. "You must be proud of her," Armour said.

Heidi whispered into his sleeve, "Don't be snotty. Let's go, I'm tired!" He said something about delayed gratification.

She wasn't tired though. She hated Armour for lighting up again. Hated herself for standing there like a lost child when she had a key to a door she could open and lock shut behind her. But wanting had swelled the bottom of her belly. She felt like a balloon stretched to the slightest waft from the dry-muscled man beside her—to whatever he had in mind, a caress, a pinch. Her arms and legs were trembling.

The sun was rising, a fat tangerine, from the sea at the end of the street, when another man approached, big-shouldered, big-bellied, Bill's age. Like Bill he carried a fishing pole. He too had a beard, though it was darker and shorter than Bill's. He clapped a hand on Bill's shoulder, kidding him about something. Another man appeared, who could have been their brother, and another, and another—heavyset with broad, smiling bearded faces like athletic Saint Nicks. "Who's the angel? Say, is that the pretty college girl you've been bragging about?"

Bill introduced her to Barney, Irv, Murphy, and Ted, all of whom maintained the belief, despite her denial, that she was Bill's daughter. They beamed down at her, weathered skin rosy in the rise of the sun—blustery, good-hearted. "You coming with us, doll? Hey, anybody got an extra rod?" To Armour: "You too, muchacho, long as you keep your mitts off her!"

The group laughed. Someone handed her a fishing pole. Armour finished his smoke, stomped the butt, squeezed her shoulder.

"Ready? Ciao, gentlemen. Remember, if you can haul it in, it's probably too small." He took the pole out of her hand, tossed it at Bill.

But the group was enlarging—eight, now ten, twelve hale, bearded men in Festival T-shirts, a mass of Papa Hemingways. Armour turned sideways, holding her hand as if he were leading her through water. "If you don't mind," he said to the man in front of him, who replied:

"So what's up, Frank? You're coming with?"

"Sorry, man. Prior engagement."

A second man laughed. "His name isn't Frank."

"Charles, then," said the first man, noticeably heavier than the others, a short, fat Ernest Hemingway. "You know, Charles," he said to Armour, "if I didn't know you so well, I'd have to ask your intentions with this here young lady." He winked at Heidi.

"Don't mess," the second man said. "Shit, the prostate goes, turns you into an old lady." He smiled at Heidi, as if this was somehow for her entertainment, then he turned again to his friend. "What makes you think *Charles?* Does he look like the Prince of Wales?"

"How about *Luigi?*" said the fat Hemingway. He sang, "'When the moon hits your eye like a big-a pizza pie, that's amore . . .'"

"*Charles,*" said the other.

"Come on! Don't you know Eye-talian when you hear it? Ciao! Bella! Right, Luigi? Come-a with us catch-a some fish-a?"

"Christ," said Armour. "Would you move please?"

The two men seemed not to hear him, so involved were they in their facetious argument. They started playfully shoving each other. She thought it was playful. Armour's annoyance mounted, though, as, arm over her shoulder, he turned to find another point of exit. Then Bill, who'd been watching the scene, cleared a path with his poles through the thicket of fishermen. "Fuck the assholes," Bill said. And to his buddies, "Boat's leaving without us."

Armour transferred his hold to her hand and led her through the breach, but she planted her feet, watching the Look Alikes heading down to the water. Bill stood, his fishing poles rising from the ground to his fists to the crown of his head like a pair of staffs.

"You're welcome to come along. To fish or not to fish, that is the question."

"Armour," she said, "let's go with them! Try something different. It'll be fun."

Armour let go of her hand. His glance brushed her face but she was fixed on Bill, a head taller than Armour and twice as wide. His face was round like the sun and fierce as the Power that kicked Satan out of heaven. The sunlit edges of his hair glowed iridescent.

One day, maybe, Bill would shoot himself between his grizzled eyebrows, leaving some woman a gaudy mess of brain and bone. But now he made his way toward the prospective glory of the Fish-Off. She smiled an apology at Armour, then trotted after the older man. He was her papa, sleazy, fierce, angelic—saving her one last time from everything in the world.

Mark Winegardner

That's True of Everybody

THERE WAS ONCE AN EARNEST MAN WHO, IN HIS LATE THIRTIES, had a heart attack, remarried, bought a high-end personal computer, left his job as a statehouse reporter and, despite a lack of talent, was admitted to a creative-writing program at a big, concrete university in one of those rectangular states, where he wrote the longest master's thesis in school history. He'd been a good statehouse reporter. The man's name was Phil Workman; his thesis was a 773-page autobiographical novel called *Legal Adulthood*. No one on his committee read beyond page nineteen.

The tenured professors of literature loved Phil Workman. He reminded them of themselves when they were his age, though some of them were in fact younger than he was. The writing professors liked Phil Workman personally—Workman was nothing if not likable—but his lack of talent made them embarrassed to talk to him. They rarely returned his phone calls. Their comments on his stories always contained the phrase *this has potential*, which everyone knows no one ever means.

But the professors of literature controlled the hiring of part-time faculty, so when Workman received his terminal degree, they hired him to teach four sections of freshman composition each semester, beginning that fall and continuing for the rest of his life. One hundred thirty-four people had applied for this punishing job, including another recent graduate of the writing program, Hayley Roarke, who'd already sold a story to a national magazine. The tenured professors of literature found out how much Roarke was paid for that story, a story read by more people than would ever read all of their opaque, fraudulent books and articles put together and, behind her back, began calling her Jane Grisham. Everyone knows that money ruins artists.

Workman felt badly for Roarke, whom he considered a friend. He took her to lunch, paid, tried to console her. She thanked him, said she felt better, wondered if not getting this job might somehow be for the best. Of course it was: she was hired the following year to teach two creative writing classes per semester at a much better school for far more money. Tenure-track job. Workman wrote her a note of sincere congratulations. A year later her first novel came out, to choruses of praise. Workman read it and thought it was glib. He didn't tell this to anyone, for fear it would make him look small.

Workman's second wife Amanda read all his work and encouraged him without fail. It's good, she'd say. The characters seem so . . . real. She knew this was what he wanted to hear a blessing, since it was all she could think to say. Amanda, once a cardiac nurse (they'd met after Workman's coronary), now worked at a plague hospice in the nearest city big enough to have one. She'd taken only one literature class in college, taught by a bearded foreigner of inscrutable accent, who told the class one could not prove *War and Peace* is in any way a better text than the menu in the faculty dining room. Amanda had never been in the faculty dining room, though she knew this wasn't the point. The man wiggled his fingers in the air when he said better. He did the same when he said "real." When she spoke of the realism in her husband's stories, she kept her hands at her sides, balled into fists.

For a year after they'd married and moved to the college town,

Amanda couldn't find a job, even at the health center. Finally she faced facts; she'd have to commute. A week later she was hired at the hospice, which wasn't as depressing as people seemed to think, nowhere near as depressing as those department parties to which Phil kept dragging her (even after she had her own friends at work, with whom they almost never did things as a couple). At the hospice she saw people at their best: noble, honest, caring, and sensitive—qualities in short supply at those parties.

Which, to be fair, were not all alike. The professors of literature *gave* parties, featuring wine, fancy finger-foods, people dressed in shabby clothes that had never been in fashion, odd references to Frenchmen Amanda never heard of, chitchat about films and mean-spirited gossip about department members not in attendance. At these, Phil Workman would be warmly drawn into any conversation he came near, as if he were a favorite performing child. In contrast, the writers *threw* parties, featuring beer, loud off-color jokes, people dressed in clothes from the same three mail-order catalogs, male visiting writers preying upon starstruck lovelies of both genders, chitchat about movies, and mean-spirited gossip about department members not in attendance. At these, the Workmans tended to get quarantined in some corner with a gloomy teaching assistant and someone's stray wife.

At both types of party, these professors—people who aren't asked to dress like grown-ups, arrive at work promptly, or labor during the summer—bitched endlessly about their jobs. Amanda's wasted, rheumy-eyed patients used less vehemence to complain about the injustice of their disease.

Except for one untenured poet—a poseur, though not a bad poet, who wrote in bars, museums or, she claimed, across the nude backs of her lovers—all the writers at the university wrote at home. Workman used to write at home, too, but he kept finding himself paying bills, doing laundry, or painting the trim of his rented house. He certainly couldn't write in his office at school, which he shared with other members of the part-timers' ghetto, a parade of exhausted mothers and fey young men with goatees. So he got a studio: a small windowless room with a toilet and no phone, above a package store, six blocks from campus. He began to write there, laboring on his new novel, *Amicable Divorce*, which was based on his first marriage. He wore a red chamois shirt as he wrote, for luck. When he someday gave readings from his books, he'd wear a coat and tie but bring this shirt along, hold it up, and tell a droll story on himself.

More often than not, though, he spent his time in the studio grading freshman themes. He was a rigorous grader, the last man alive who believed that C meant average. He typed his comments, which were often as long as the papers themselves. His students, in their evaluations, often wrote that Mr. *Workman was the best prof I've had so far* but that they wouldn't recommend his course *because its* [sic] *hard, unless your* [sic] *really motivated.*

One fall, four years into this pattern, he had enrolled in his eight AM class a young woman of indeterminate age named Clio Takamira, who dressed in leggings and men's flannel shirts, had long black hair and an unnerving way of holding eye contact too long. She'd been working for the university for years (as a bookstore clerk and aerobics teacher) before beginning to take classes part-time. Her first paper broke Workman's heart. He'd assigned them to write about either a time they hadn't wanted to cry but had, or a time they had wanted to cry but couldn't. Clio's essay took place last Christmas break, organized around three sexual liaisons: with her clumsy boyfriend, a student from one of her classes who'd then blurted a marriage proposal and scared her into dumping him; with her heretofore platonic lesbian friend Ulysses, a tryst on New Year's Eve which Workman found innocent and poetically rendered; and with her deaf stepbrother Lyle, the day before he left to join the Navy, as they gave in to a lust that had stirred in each of them, repressed, since they met six years earlier. The paper ended with Clio letting Lyle come in her mouth something, he signed, no girl had ever let him do. She swallowed, he smoothed her hair, their eyes met, and she gave him the sign for *I love you*, then signed, *but we can't do this anymore*. It was a moment more tender than Phil Workman would have imagined possible. It was the best student paper he had ever read. It made *him* cry.

He gave her a C. In the days of the plague, a C had become what an F used to be.

Workman had never before given a student a low grade on an A paper because he stood humbled before her talent, though he would not have put it quite that way. To him, it was just a strange whim. His comment, scrawled in red ink on the last page, was "This has potential. See me."

For two days, until that class convened again, Workman was haunted by what he'd done. He sat around watching talk shows and was short to Amanda. She asked if something was wrong. He said no. She feared he was angry because she couldn't become pregnant, which had recently been confirmed. He said that wasn't it. She was afraid he knew about the affair (her first) that, for reasons she could not explain, she'd discretely begun to have with a famous visiting poet named Murtaugh, whom she'd met at a writers' party. She of course couldn't ask. Workman, in fact, had no suspicions at all. Well, she guessed, are you going through a bad time with the novel?

No, he lied. The novel's going fine.

"Great." What if it *is* the affair? "Can't wait to read it."

In truth, the novel was literally marooned on an island (Hilton Head, where he and his ex-wife vacationed). It was going so badly, and his chances of selling his first novel seemed so remote, that Workman began wondering about that which so many people, behind his back, were certain: maybe he didn't have what it took to write fiction. But this was not the source of his woe.

Monday morning, the day he was to hand back the papers, Phil Workman almost changed the grade. But he'd written the C in pen and couldn't think how to transform it into another letter, how he'd explain the scribble or white-out. So he stuck to his guns. Clio Takamira, however, cut class that day. Wednesday, too.

Friday morning she was there. She came up after class, with a note from the health center that confirmed she'd had the flu. She asked if he had her paper. He did. He gave it to her, his every muscle tensed. She flipped to the page with the grade, started walking away, then glanced back at him. She returned to the lectern where he was packing his things, smiling like she knew something. He could smell her shampoo: Helicon, the same kind his ex used. The room filled up with the members of an interpersonal communications class—whatever that is.

"I thought," she said, "that maybe I fucked up."

Workman, that rare writer who did not swear in class, winced.

"That I failed to follow instruction," she said. "I'm no good at that. I mean, I don't even *have* a stepbrother, though I dated a deaf guy once. I guess that's why you want to see me?"

"I don't want to see you," he blurted.

She frowned, looked down at his comment, back at him, shrugged and walked away.

For the rest of the term, Clio would come to see him during office hours. She sat close, each of them hunched over her rough drafts. Her explanatory paper, "How To Fuck Up Your Life," described how her father quit his job in Silicon Valley and opened a sushi bar in a Midwestern city that had never elected an Asian-American to public office. Workman—blind to the paper's accidental, oblique commentary on his life—gave it the A it deserved, for which Clio didn't seem grateful or even pleased. Her persuasive paper argued that the university should adopt an ambitious, formal mentoring program; big A. Her critical essay, after a brief unit of poetry, discussed not the assigned poems but a chapbook of vitriolic haikus which Clio's mother, a WASP starchild now living in one of those Western cities where hippies go to die, had written in the throes of her divorce from Clio's father. Workman gave it an A+, the first of his career, which, hopelessly impaired by lust, he had no idea whether it deserved.

For years, Workman had been inviting classes to his home at the hour of their final, to hand in their term papers. He provided salsa, chips and soda; if they brought beer, fine, but he of course didn't supply his mostly underage students with alcohol. Clio's class, though, he invited to his studio. He iced down cheap, flavorless beer in a trash can and told his students, so packed into that room he could smell their hormones secrete, that he hoped they wouldn't drink unless they were of age. Amazingly, the only ones who did were the boys with bill-backwards ballcaps and Workman, who kept trying not to look at Clio. An hour later, the papers were collected, the beer and all but three students gone: one boy, a B student who was disk-jockeying the Motown tapes Workman played as he wrote; one girl, a chunky A student with designs on the boy; and Clio Takamira, who suggested they order some pizza—that is, if it was okay with Phil. Everyone looked up. It was the first time she'd ever called him anything but Mr. Workman. "Fine," he said. It was a food his doctor recommended he avoid.

Workman went down to the package store to call for pizza. The pizza came and was eaten. In a windowless room time passes in fits and starts; Workman was startled to glance at his watch and see it was ten o'clock. Amanda would have expected him two hours ago.

Finally, Clio spilled half a jar of salsa on herself. With rank immodesty she pulled off her leggings and stood in the middle of Workman's studio in a stained flannel shirt and lace panties. Her legs were dark and magnificent. Wars have been fought over less. "Do you have a towel," she said, "or a hairdryer?"

The boy, repeating himself on the tape player and drunk now, gave Workman a look.

"Sorry," Workman said. Then he remembered he had his gym bag with him. Oh, wait. As Workman got the towel and dryer, the other girl saw how this was going and, while everyone watched Clio, stuck her tongue in the boy's ear.

Moments later, Clio and Workman were alone.

Taking shampoo from his bag, she spot-cleaned the shirt and washed out her leggings in the toilet. "This was a great class."

"Thanks," he said. He sat across the room from her, at his desk. He pulled out the Motown tape and replaced it with Mozart.

"There's something I've been wanting to ask you." She rolled her leggings up in the towel.

"Wait," said Workman, pulse racing. "Not yet." Thinking quickly, he slipped her term paper from the stack. It was about the changing role of women in Japan. He'd seen an early draft of it, which, even at that stage, was good enough to be an A.

"What do you mean, not yet?"

"One second." He affixed an A to her paper, recorded it in his grade book and on the grade sheet he'd hand to the registrar. "There." She was no longer a student in his class. He sat down on the floor beside her. "Ask me."

"Do you think I have what it takes to become a writer?"

That's the question? His heart sank. "Yes," he said. "I do."

She squealed. Actually squealed. "Really?"

He nodded. But he couldn't let it go. He placed a hand on her breast.

She spun toward him, eyes flashing. "Phil!"

He recoiled. "I'm sorry." This was not like him. He stood up and walked across the room. "Oh, God. I'm so sorry."

"I didn't know you felt that way about me." She radiated honesty.

"I didn't know either." He seemed earnest, too.

She rose, graceful as an opening flower. "I'm in your class next semester," she said. "I requested your section."

"I don't know what I was thinking."

"Like hell you don't." She was no child. She drew near.

"You have to decide," he whispered as her face came inches from his, "whether you want to be my student or my lover." His throat was dry. He had not been this frightened since his heart attack. "You can't be both."

She smiled. "I'll drop." She kissed the hell out of him. "Recommend another teacher."

Moments later, she had him in her mouth. He came that way, reciprocated, and then, after erection problems that he blamed on having not worn a condom for years and that she handled with grace and leniency, he was inside her. It wasn't until the ninth or tenth thrust that it felt real to him. The condom was from a box he'd bought that day. Premeditation; first-degree adultery. They rolled around all night on the floor of his study, sex so crudely passionate that Workman remembered why some people call it "humping." Clio Takamira (who found the sex mildly disappointing) wrapped herself in Workman's red shirt and, near the dawn they could not see, admitted she'd made up everything in that first paper. This only made her more attractive to him.

The next morning, Workman dropped off Clio, still wearing his shirt, two discrete blocks from her apartment. When he got home Amanda had just left, the bathroom still damp and fragrant. She'd left him a note: *This is the man I married,* it read. *A guy who stays up all night writing, like you used to. "Amicable" will be the book that makes you. Keep it up. Love, A.*

It cut right through him; he vowed to end things with Clio.

Give Amanda the benefit of the doubt for that disingenuous note: she was as guilt-ridden as her husband.

At the very moment Phil had been received into Clio Takamira's mouth, Amanda was emerging from a hotel shower in the city where she worked, having taken the afternoon off to fuck a colleague of her husband's. Through a crack in the door, she saw Murtaugh, spread-eagle on the badly stained bed, staring at his reflection in the sliding glass door to the balcony. He was such a good lover that, between orgasms, you felt creepy, thinking about all the women he'd been with to get that way.

And it hit her: this was a man whose success her husband would cut off a limb to obtain. She fucked the man Workman thought he wanted to be. Was *that* why she'd fucked him? She'd ascribed it, variously, to loneliness, to the pressures of her job, to turning forty, or to the basic human need for reckless adventure. But now she feared it was that other thing. Worse, her husband, whose work could not find a publisher, was a much better *person* than this National-Book-Award-winning lout whose ejaculate she'd just washed from her hair.

From the bathroom phone, she called home. Phil wasn't there. She assumed that he was at the studio, writing. When bedeviled by the fear of getting caught, one does not imagine the shoe on the other foot. So to speak. Earlier, Amanda had left a lame message on the machine about working late, and now she added another, this one complaining about a nurse who'd called in sick. She made a kissing noise into the receiver, got ready as fast as she could and told Murtaugh it was over. He sat up, furrowed his brow but, with unctuous sensitivity, said he understood (*there are more where you came from,* he thought).

From a gas station on her way home, Amanda left another message, another weak lie proffered in a voice pinched with shame. She got home near midnight, ecstatic he wasn't there, that he hadn't played those messages, all of which sounded like they came from a woman who was fucking someone she shouldn't be. She reset the machine, took another shower and went to bed.

Days later, in the neutral turf of the nearly abandoned student union, Workman made a clean break of it with Clio. She looked down at the Formica top of their booth and said she understood. She said she had underestimated the guilt she'd feel sleeping with a married man. She accepted his recommendation for another comp teacher, along with his advice that she take a creative writing class (Fate, who as you know is one perverse bastard, will summon her to Murtaugh's poetry workshop). As they parted, Workman turned to watch those perfect legs walk out of his life, and it occurred to him that she still had his lucky shirt, and that there would be no easy way to ask for it back.

Then a strange and terrible thing happened. On a snowy New Year's Day, Phil Workman woke up, cooked a pancake breakfast for Amanda, made ardent love to her, then ate lunch, went to the studio to work on his novel and instead wrote a wonderful story.

It was about a sad, beautiful woman named Chloe Nakamura, who enrolls in an acting class taught by the burned-out unnamed narrator. The other students are themselves so manifestly clueless that none seem even to notice that she is a natural. She is that student who comes along once in a teacher s career, the one to which you'll always compare all the others.

And he wrecks it. He fucks her.

After that, everything's poisoned. Chloe doesn't know and now can't ever know if any of the encouraging things he told her were true. Even the narrator wonders. He traded the chance to change both of their miserable lives for a few capable fucks.

But there's a twist. Chloe steals the red taffeta dress the acting teacher wore during an off-off-Broadway show in which he'd received decent notices, wears it to a movie audition and wins the role of the repressed lead's slutty, wisecracking friend. Delirious, she rushes to break the news to the narrator and, on a whim, still in his dress, proposes marriage. He hears himself accept. They drop everything in their lives and get married in Las Vegas, on the way out to Hollywood, both on a wild, impulsive, exhilarating ride neither knows whether to trust. The story ends on the set of the movie, with Chloe wowing the everybody and the narrator standing in the wings, alone: unsure how he got there or what he feels, sure only *that* he feels.

Plot summary cannot do the story justice. For once, Workman's sentences were not curiously dead in the middle. For once, Workman's rhythms rose and fell like music. For once, Workman's symbols and metaphors just sort of happened.

He titled it "Midlife Crisis." Even if a blind squirrel finds the odd acorn, the nut still won't bestow vision.

Somewhere during the writing process, Workman's watch stopped. When he finished, he imagined it was the next morning. He hit *Print* and went down to the package store, which, oddly, was locked. Outside it was dark. Two feet of snow had fallen. It seemed like the end of the world. But it was just the middle of the next night. He had been writing for forty hours straight.

That spring, Hayley Roarke, on tour for her second book, a collection of stories, returned to campus to give a reading. Workman picked her up at the airport; they shook hands warmly. He'd already read the book, which he liked, and he told her so. In Workman's presence, Hayley felt disconcerted by her success. She changed the subject to ask about old friends and, as a courtesy, his work. He began talking about his novel, then mentioned that strange, uncharacteristic story which had come out of nowhere. She asked to read it. On Hayley's way back to the airport (having become the rare prophet who lives to gain honor in her native land), Workman gave her a copy of the story, which she read on the plane. To her surprise and relief, she loved it. She sent it to the editor at the big magazine which now published most of her stories. *He* loved it, bought it for a princely sum, deleted the last paragraph and changed the title to "Taffeta."

On the strength of that story Workman got an agent, a woman whose phone manner included vowels so cartoonishly elongated that he pictured her as the human incarnation of an old housecat. She asked to see *Legal Adulthood*. Her young assistant, an underemployed Ivy Leaguer, became the only person other than Amanda ever to read it. "It's a well-made old-fashioned novel," said the agent, who hadn't so much as touched the thing. It took Workman a while to realize this wasn't a compliment.

But, ever eager to please, he accepted this verdict. That summer, he abandoned *Amicable Divorce* and, in the quiet of his study, wrote three new stories, leaden variations on "Taffeta" which the assistant dutifully sent out to commercial magazines, where they were tersely rejected.

When the issue of the magazine that contained "Taffeta" finally hit the newsstands, Amanda put together a party, which was poorly attended. The tenured professors of literature grew cold to Workman. The writers who admired the story but seemed to see it as a fluke were as nice and distant as ever. His students read other sorts of magazines. In no time at all, a new issue of the magazine hit the stands, and the world kept spinning. To a starving man a single bite is worse than nothing.

Meanwhile, though neither Phil nor Amanda had the least suspicion of the other's indiscretion, they like so many couples after debasing stints of adultery fell in love all over again, an actual courtship, full of flowers, candlelight dinners and inventive, guilt-free lovemaking. They became reacquainted, engaged anew in each other's bodies, habits, lives, and dreams.

The year after "Taffeta," one of the writing professors sold a baseball novel to the film production company of an actor who'd won a mantel full of statuettes playing louts who contract diseases or suffer crippling injuries and are thereby redeemed. In the novel, the hero suffers from herpes and tendinitis; in the film script, this was changed to cancer and, relying on the magic of digital photography, a severed arm. But the writer had received enough money to laugh at these changes, and to resign his teaching job, which Workman decided to apply for.

He prepared his *curriculum vita* sodden with committee work and conferences attended and sought letters of recommendation. Having been so long at the same school, Workman was forced to ask the writing professors to write letters to themselves on his behalf and, worse, to ask the professors of literature to send letters to their nemeses. He was so likable no one had the nerve to refuse, but his superficially positive letters were, in the context of the fulsome prose of several hundred such letters, encoded with negatives. *Diligent*, for example, which means *untalented; drone-like. Mature*, which means *dull. He is a dedicated teacher*, which means *I've never seen him teach, but he seems to spend a lot of time grading papers.* Worst of all, *earnest*, which means *earnest.*

Hayley Roarke had applied for the job, too. Where he was called diligent, she was *vastly talented.* In place of mature, she was *wise beyond her years. In the classroom she is passionate, inspiring and sensitive—a born teacher*, which means *she may be an easy grader, but students love her, recommend her and flock to her classes.* No one called her earnest.

After he submitted his application, Workman began to wonder if it was what he really wanted. You need to get out of that place, I think, said Amanda, though she wondered if that was just her own baggage she was trying to leave behind. She was cutting his hair, something each of them found sexy. "Maybe apply to other schools," she said. "Or go back to journalism."

Workman flinched, causing her to jab him with the scissors.

"Sorry," she said. "But what's wrong with journalism?"

"Nothing's wrong with it," he said. "It's just that fiction . . ."

But he could not finish that sentence.

"You're the sort of person," she said, "who values only the things that don't come easily."

"That's true of everybody," he said.

"The opposite," she said, "is true of everybody."

He of course did not get the job, though he was sincerely pleased his friend Hayley, hired at the associate level, was back in town. He had, after Amanda's suggestion, applied for what few other jobs there were, and actually got an offer, from a small, barely accredited college in a faraway harbor town. Workman accepted. Then, the week he and Amanda were going to fly to that town to look for a house, the president of the university, an effete pederast whose own *vita* included more co-authors than pages published, read "Taffeta," professed to be horrified by its sexual content, and ordered the department to hire someone else. "It's for the best," Amanda said, consoling her husband. "Who'd want to teach at a place like that?"

"Me," Workman said. But he knew she was right.

That fall, every Wednesday, a day he did not teach, Phil Workman drove to the city along with Amanda, just to spend some extra time with her. He worked in a small back office, coming out every once in a while to watch Amanda work. After a while, he started talking to those victims of the plague, learning about their lives, listening to their fears, marveling at their unnerving acceptance of fate. That heart attack he'd survived had given him the reprieve none of these people would get. One day, on the drive over, he came up with an idea for an oral history of sorts, a book where these plague victims told stories about the lives they would lead, the truncated dreams they would reassemble, if a miraculous cure were suddenly found.

Amanda, as she heard him describe this, felt a warmth spread over her, and she began to cry.

Weeks later, he sent a proposal for the book to his agent, who sold it immediately, for more money than Workman could have made in ten years of teaching. He quit his job. He and Amanda moved to the city, where they bought a house on a hill and began to look into adopting a child.

In the age of the plague, tales no longer end happily ever after. Where happy endings once frolicked, now we see ironies, post-ironies, ellipses. If you re lucky and a bit old-fashioned, maybe a moral victory.

And so it came to pass that, one bright day, two years into his research on his book, months from its projected completion, there appeared in the women's ward of the hospice a frail, far-gone woman of indeterminate age. Workman who introduced himself to all new patients, to see if they d be willing to participate did not recognize her until he saw the name on the chart.

"I have it," said Clio Takamira. "I have the plague."

Workman stood dumbly in the light that streamed into her room. What could he say? *I don't have it?* This was true (some time ago he'd had himself tested), but not the thing to say, yet.

"I know why you're here," she said to her old teacher. "They told me about the book." She smiled. "Don't feel uncomfortable, okay?"

He nodded. He wanted to ask her if she'd ever read "Taffeta," but he was struck mute.

"I doubt if you have it," she said. "I know who I got it from, the plague, and it was after."

He nodded again, still thunderstruck.

"Please," she said. "Smile." She got up from her bed, went to her closet, and produced his old red chamois shirt. "Here," she said. "I believe this is yours."

He told her to keep it, please.

"Fine," she said. She shrugged it on over her blouse. "Sit down, okay? And cheer up. Let me tell you my story," she said.

He sat down. The room was spinning. For the first time in years he feared for his bad heart.

"You can give me eternal life. My story," she said, "will be the best one you ever write."

He looked at her. She was smiling, beatific. What Workman thought was, *Easy for you to say, you fucking muse bitch.* He considered slapping her. He didn't say what he thought and he didn't do what he wanted to. He was, finally, the sort of man who didn't want to do what he wanted to do. All he did was nod. All he could say was, "I'll try."

Rafael Campo

Poem for My Familiar

She's sniffing out the garden's rancid truths,
beneath the garbage cans, along the roots

arthritically attaching oaks to earth—
she means to do her business, back and forth

not nervously so much as in pursuit
of some unnamed perfection. Reddish coat

and barrel chest, the sleek embodiment
of what? Not loyalty so much as want,

not pleasure but the wish to please. Her piss
pools darkly; sudden wind makes the oaks hiss.

She trots off, proud of her obedience
(our countless warnings adding up to sense)

and in her I catch something of myself,
that eagerness with which I sought relief

pretending there was nothing wrong with us.
You call to me, your voice too serious

for scolding dawdlers on a summer day,
and Ruby charges by. I think I'll stay

behind, but soon think better of it. Still,
although I love you, it's unbearable

to watch you growing distant. Ruby yelps,
but somehow all her playfulness won't help:

like her, I want to beg forgiveness for
my mute mistakes, my urgent need for more.

Wensday Carlton

Fear of Summer

She dreamt death through July. The days burst
at one hundred and five, walls spitting heat at fans
and each night she was shot in the head—
robbed or kidnapped but always killed
before she woke. Diluted by sweat,
she searched the closets, expected
to find someone waiting for her,
sitting on the floor by her remains.
She stared at her wrists in the morning, wondered
if death was trying to talk her into something.

She drove through a fat, unhealthy wind
and cried because summer had always held her
alone in its throat. One year she'd given up
on days entirely, lived only in the night
when the heat's grip lessened. Then she could sit
by the river while locusts squawked, and beetles
fell into her hair, and the water lapped blackly
at the dock. She waited with all the dark
things until they left, hating light;
then she went inside to sleep.

One day in August, she rolled over
and death said he loved her. *It's not enough,*
she answered, and he didn't argue, only
reminded her what living would always mean.

When she left her house, she looked at the sky
glowing like a plate, as though safety
were tangible, blue and offered to the world.

Girls at Clear Lake City

We drive to Clear Lake, by the rocks that aren't rocks,
but crashed slabs of concrete in the water.
We get drunk there most Friday nights, wait until
we feel blurred and pretty before we decide
who to kiss, whose car to get in and maybe
take off our white shirts and tight shorts and see
how much we care about what happens next.

At the liquor store we wait for someone
old enough to buy bad wine, maybe sad
enough to think we mean it when we smile.
We make lists of all the stupid lines guys think
we believe: *Can I turn off the light, it hurts
my eyes; he's such a bastard, let's go for a walk
and talk about it; I've never believed
those stories about you* . . . Although
it doesn't matter what they say,
we're the ones who want an excuse.

There are houses where parents are never
home, where we smoke pot laced with opium
and lie on the floor for hours, hugging
each other to remember how our arms feel,
laughing at how soft the world has become.
In one of those houses we fuck someone
for the first time, but don't tell him
it's the first time. The next day
isn't much different, except now
there's less of a reason to say no.

The town isn't ugly, just flat and shaped
around a lake with fake rocks, parking lots
in front of shut-down buildings, houses

laid out hopefully with geraniums
around the mailbox. Our mothers
are right when they say we don't care
about anything but ourselves. We get
pregnant or jailed or sick or better . . .

Maybe some of us leave, dumbly looking
for a place that won't be home. But most of us
stay and don't look at the town anymore . . .
And when we look at each other, we still see
girls slender and sturdy as weeds . . .

Madonna and Child

After Seeing Lotto's *Annunciation*

So many paintings show her young and calm—
so obviously good, the baby doing
something to her breast, her face more than radiant . . .
Nothing like this hooded girl, turning her back
on the angel, who offers her a flower
in consolation; on God pointing
furiously at her, his red robe
matching her own—her eyes stubborn
and pleading to whoever else can see her.
She's like anyone willing to try to outrun fate . . .

Proof for what I've suspected: she didn't want
this divine child, she's afraid, even angry
that she has no choice. How could she love
a prophesied son, made almost without her?
She must have recognized that such a person
is doomed—as are all of those chosen by God.

Although her hands, palms out and close to her chest,
indicate what we already know
about existence—that our desires
are the least of it, that wherever she flees,
she'll still have a son who thinks about her,
even as he asks others to believe in him,
as he lives the way he must . . .
Maybe he falls asleep missing her,
but not really, as though missing something
that he doesn't know . . .

Geri Doran

Self-Portrait As Miranda

My story begins at sea, in the bitter liquid.
If not, it would begin in Florida, along 1-95
in the circular drive of a circular, lime-green motel.
But I have selected the sea, and you must

trust me on this. Truly terrible stories
begin in navigational error, a slight misreading
of the sight that sets the crew in a maelstrom.
Perhaps in another story it would be a man

standing at the door, surprised that he's knocked,
that you have, in turn, answered. He wishes
now that he had lingered in that drive, paused
before resuming the course toward your door.

As the crew, in desperate but unspoken straits,
wishes belatedly for a drag on the anchor.
Frequently, we are thus carried along.
Frequently, *de profundis*, we struggle ashore

to find ourselves, if not stranded, then beached.
We are inclined to be grateful for land.
Survivors of shipwreck cast two shadows:
the outline of interrupted light, and an aura, thirst

to drown again. Perhaps, in the unwritten story,
the man at the door looks thirsty. You sense

he has come to repair himself at the dry dock
of your flesh. There is nothing else to do.

Your home is an island of white sand
and he wades in from the shoals of the walkway
asking for fresh water. So you give him berth.
This much Miranda herself could explain:

how Ferdinand come shimmering from the sea
appeared no less a rescuer than she,
with his handful of kelp and the pretty words
of a man desperate for sanctuary.

Ferdinand missed that she was shipwrecked
too. Miranda had the shadowy thirst.
You know the rest of the story.
They're happy, then it ends in the bitter sea.

Steve Fay

Illness

Suddenly the things-to-do list
does not matter. Instead, your knees
tremble, you time and measure
your excretions, throbbing your way
from the medicine cabinet. You ride
the daybed hourly into troubled dreams:
steamboats missed at strange landings,
arguments about beans and prunes.

Your eyes totter toward the one
window shade you haven't drawn,
the picture of hollyhocks thriving
in the feverish sun. Scarlet corollas.
Fuzzy stamens that powder the
hummingbird's head. Only a few
buds at the top of the stalk left
to open and die. You see that this

is how the end may come. You'll think
it's only one more virus, one more
bug, but it will be the last one.
Riding on that final conveyor
the ripened seed rides back to earth,
you will toss aside the life you planned
like an invisible, dried bouquet.

Jesse Lee Kercheval

I Open Your Death Like a Book

I shall not die twice, Father, but I'll make you do it.

Pick up the scissors and cut your shirt away,
cutting into skin, pink as a burn,
then chest, that cave of shade striped gray,

until I find your heart, shy girl in corsets,
sad blue satchel,
only beating pow-wow now and then.

That's the beauty and the pity.
Your heart a crooked time-clock like your father's,
a box bomb strapped into your chest.

Now a change of venue. Put your clothes on, Father, please.

I put you in a hammock.
Me, your blue-eyed infant, beside you on the floor.
I was born to be there watching

when no one else was looking.
To see your arm go crooked,
see you fall asleep and not wake up.

To hear in flocking crows,
the wings of seraphim. In thunder,
your heart, that angel, bursting.

But children grow bored waiting even for disaster.
Get big, go to college,
send a postcard now and then.

What's a girl to do with a father
who is always dying, but make you into poems,
eat you like a deer I raised by hand?

Think of death, then, as an open season.

In the world outside, apples are falling,
people dying every day. Now in the house
where I grew up, a window darkens,

you pick up the phone to call me,
dial long distance. And answering,
I hear you die two hundred miles away.

Rose Red

Just back from the laundromat, Mother, soul and socks both clean,
I am feeling rather blessed, drinking wine from far Provence, sitting
in my wicker chair on cushions bright as schools of feeding fish.
For dinner I ate nothing but young food—scrambled eggs, small round
potatoes, the kind they call red bliss. How long have I been waiting
for this new life? Free, at last, from history, that hallucination,
from the sandy pit of grief. I sink into the tufted cushions of my life
and become again the child who watched you set the table every night
for dinner until she was old enough to help. Beyond the kitchen
window, a rose, red faced, dyes the clouds pink as skin, blushing throat
to ankle. Behind the clouds, the universe, bones and moving stars.
I hear an owl and know it's you. I hear a mouse inside the walls
and know it's you. I close my eyes. I see a bridge. I walk across it.

This Is a Kind of Haunting

Past dark, I go find your house,

the road all moondust
and starlight from Italian movies.

Be at home. Step to the door.

your silhouette a simple gray,
hair like fine white stitches

Listen—everything is moving.

The pine trees whip the air,
the wisteria is moaning.

Recognize your name when I call it.

Call mine back. Like a weed,
I blow into your garden.

Dream of the Red Palace

It is night, and we are leaving this world,

the board games in their boxes, the latch on the garden gate
that never fails to stick. Leaving history: J.F.K.'s rocking chairs,
the peanuts, Cracker Jacks. Like the Amish, like a silent film,
we will stand outside of time.

No more roots, those deep cuts. No more stones, bare white,
bone level to catch our long pink toes. In sleep, we burn, and
become as angels. This the bargain we keep: If I do not wake,
you will not die.

It is night, and we are leaving this world.

Timothy Liu

Passing through the Enchanted Circle

    Blanketed under sage-gray skies, the afternoon steeped
in mountains brindled with piñon
        and pine as the horizon thins to mottled foothills
            where the road bends—the aspen-
thickened canyon igniting spring's late fires, a hawk
shifting his weight from one wing
        to the other beside a cliff shorn away by gusts
            that swept across those lava-
                blackened mesas thunderstruck as we slept—
            arms in corpse position, a wasp
ensnared in the static nest of a widow's hair splayed
across her pillow, her hands
        immobilized in a dreamscape full of clouds shifting
            shape, all of America starved
        for the desert's brutal modesty stripping our wants
to the simplest forms—skull
        and arrowhead governed by the same unspoken laws.

Harriet Melrose

By Design

Nuclear snow coats
walls and floors
corners of cupboards
opaques the windows
gutted to studs
the roof
a tear-off
nineteenth-century shakes
rolled asphalt
and tiles now dust
and rot coating flower beds and lawn
space-suited men   haul asbestos
three months of contractor grunts
"uh huh   ok ok   yuh yuh"
the man's huge
and like a boulder   no waist
to hold up pants   as he bends to check a flange   I wince
when he's on rungs
or balancing thin plywood across joists
to blow torch copper risers
he yells a few
real words at his crew   ". . . not the plumb bob
the laser
watch the headers"
steps into my kitchen
through a zippered plastic seal
The Ghost of Eden on my table

". . . the edginess, coldness, *The Whirlpool* . . ."

                                            flashing from *his* lips

      what's surprising?

             that a worker in a trade with words

                              like *egress   jalousie   fascia*

                loves poetry's language?

     bullnose   mullion   mansard

                how they dance

                        acanthus   wainscot   screed

                               sounds to tickle ears

   to sip slowly like latte

                to play on the tongue

        swallow whole like kumquats and figs

              names like ice

          sheathing the heart

         seep out of the weep holes

Joseph Millar

Waking Up after Reading Proust

Maybe the heart decides while we sleep
what to remember
and the lights of a coal truck
sweeping our walls at midnight
will revisit us as an angel's face
we have already known.

Last week our son trod the dusty stage
of the living room carpet, secretly proud
in Egyptian dress, an elfin scribe to the Pharaoh,
his mother's bracelets jangling
on thin forearms as he held up the reed pen
fashioned from wire and thread, the hieroglyphs for "water,"
and the map copied out on shirt cardboard
to describe the Nile at flood.

I wondered if April's hennaed dusk
would leave its soft stain in his memory
as he reckoned the scribe's tasks on pale fingers:
keeping track of taxes and marriages, births, deaths,
and bushels of wheat; charting the arable land
of the kingdom, mapping the boundaries that disappear
under the river each spring.

Everything I wanted then was close at hand:
the juice glass glowing like a lamp behind him,
the smell of onions deepening over the stove,

dark violin phrases twisting from the radio into the air.
I remembered the resinous shadows under the lid
of the cedar chest where my grandmother kept
the toys: the cowboy hat, the wooden sword,
the chipped hull of the plaster sailboat; and the winter light
ebbing away through the elms on Montgomery Avenue.

And maybe the brown pond gleaming
like an amniotic veil
under the arbor at Swann's estate
leads down to that darker ocean Jung says belongs
to everyone. Over the deep-sea fracture zones
where the gods jostle and shove,
its tides keep bearing the fragments up
into more peaceful water:

hawthorn cluster and village steeple,
the madeleine soaked in lime-blossom tea,
all shining with mud and phosphorous
on the dream's brief shoreline,
before the waves close over us again.

Edward Nobles

To Shield the Silent Face

It is very quiet under this hat.
Why are you in my bedroom, Father?
The earwig has brought a message.

And now the house is crying
and the unexpected caresses
of a lake's breeze move quietly

through numberless needles. A scream
of wind and the impatient command
to be silent. I will be silent. Outside

the night window, the magical light
of a firefly dies. And the curled carcass
of a spider guards the only door.

Empty Home

Your hands shake. Are you not well?
The storm rages just outside the window.
The wind rattles the broken glass

while in our bed a strange kind of love rages,
one that excludes both you and I. But is you
as another, and another as himself.

I grip the broken pane and,
with that bite of glass on glass,
pull the pieces in. The wind

chills the veins of blood,
quietly. The snow
collects in a ring upon the dust.

This abandoned house can be a home
for the wind and all its children: the breezes,
the eddies, the blustery gusts.

One must have guts
to bare the weather, to bare
one's teeth in a defiant snarl.

I punch another pane
to illustrate how something becomes nothing
and then something else again

as the cold wind breeds roughly
with this house,
which is not well.

D. *Nurkse*

At Mount Sinai

As I waited for the doctor
I realized nothing was wrong with me,
just a voice whispering the words
triage, a few sleepless nights,
a change in the weather, great winds
visible in the crests of trees
I could glimpse through a vent
at the far end of the corridor,
the immense power of dreams
unchecked by waking. . . .

And I prepared to apologize
for presuming on his time—perhaps
the apology itself would waste
a minute marked for a real patient—
but he arrived from nowhere,
took my hand, and spoke
calmly, consolingly, as to a child,
yes, yes, he'd seen the tests,
in fact he had them on his person,
somewhere in his calfskin briefcase—

and I watched his lips, avid for a pause,
so I could whisper: *it's all a mistake.*

The Corridor

Glint of carnauba wax,
door after door with little numbers,
sometimes a digit missing,
and from within, such cries,
though the gunfire was television.

I was gliding with great momentum,
at certain turns I glimpsed
the shadow of my wheels,
and always the voice at my shoulder
—surprisingly like the voice in my mind
despite its faint Island accent—
soothed me: *courage,*
press on, don't let up,

but I wasn't up,
I never resisted,
it seemed that little trick
of growing old and suffering
had worked, the great halls
with their bodies on gurneys
and twitching gauges
dropped away like husks—

why did I woo you through suffering
when you would have come
at the crook of my finger—

and my door closed behind me,
many complicated maneuvers
in which I struggled and surrendered
in a single breath,
and here I am. This bed.

This chart facing away.
The radio loves me,
the clock advances
when no one is looking,
the endless footstep recedes
—how can it always recede—,
at midnight a voice murmurs
with great tenderness, *courage*,
to someone new who must also be
I, you, and a cry
woven into constant music.

Maureen Seaton

Eating Florida

Sailors died whirling while I funneled in the west wing, thunder
         of hospital noise,
lightning of nurses throwing doors back at five AM to take my
         mother's blood.

I dreamed pterodactyls at the window. There's a world out here,
         they bantered
with the slapstick of pelicans, turning away, pushing off.

Snook and grouper fell sick simultaneously, lavender sores gleamed.
Anglers drowned in sudden holes, coolers tied to their legs with
         hemp.

Mangroves mysteriously walked away.

When the moon sliced Gemini a woman jumped from the top of
         a nearby building
although there was a husband sleeping and there were children
         dreaming behind her.

And the earth feigned forgiveness below, and the sea lapped gently.

The stealing by raccoons of green turtle eggs,
the eating by panthers of ratty-coated raccoons,
the shooting by humans of tawny panthers,
a woman's bones devoured until one rib disappeared.

During her last rites the communion wafer stuck to the roof of
          her mouth
while her cracked lips smacked.

I thought: The ocean invented that sound.

For the fishes who died here,
for their breath that creates fog,
for the ulcers on the fishes' eyes,
for the fishermen giving up,
for the need to believe it won't be me,
it won't be me,
it won't be my daughters.

Even Godzilla, who rises from Atlantis in an ecstasy of fire,
          stomping sunbathers, fracturing
boardwalks, even he looks bewildered, cancer blackening his tongue,

eat-and-run gleam in his eye.

Dean Shavit

Woman Washing an Apple

There's a woman in an office breakroom washing
an apple. It's a big Red Delicious, and it's shining,

unlike her Chinese face, brow furrowed, cheeks white.
She's turning it, from dimpled bottom to pit of stem,

again and again in the sink too small somehow to contain
such labor. There's a woman bent over the stainless

sink next to the water cooler, making a cage of her
hands under the faucet and scratching the peel

of a softball-sized apple with worn fingernails.
There's a woman holding a ripe fruit, rinsing off

an unscented encomium or unseen spray, thinking
this is good for her, knowing this is no good for her,

that filth can soil the purest things, and filth's the grit
that gums up hinges, collecting nacre, the pearl of death.

There's a woman washing an apple, now holding
still, one hand in the running water, one hand cupping

its not-yet-ready-to-eat weight, a window-shaped
gleam on its tender cheek, a portal given scope

and depth by the scrape of brush or knife on canvas,
in which a tree waves inadvertent arms in a clement

breeze, and forks its knobby roots in an ever-denser-
tendril-mesh, scouring the imaginary soil for food.

Reginald Shepherd

Apollo Steps
in Daphne's Footprints

Everywhere one turns
a god, someone turning into one
(cedar, cypress, sandalwood
camphor tree, cinnamon, juniper)
green as new time ripening
on the vine, hunting shoots
down into bloom, relays
and intermittencies

I made her, break her down
to twig stripped clean, a girl
-shaped slip of driftwood, mandrake
root that makes a fatal sound

She's made of some aromatic wood
(common myrtle, eucalyptus) and
I'm running after trees, tripping
over brambles, creepers and fragrant
underbrush, magnolia or japonica
(sperm smell over everything). One branch
just out of reach, sweet smelling leaves
some kindling, good for burning through
October to the season's
other side, smoke for the bees

Tracking the scent of lack
through rills and branches, freshets
streaming over pebbles (scent of
no, not at all, overpowering
odor of negation), I lost the trail

(she's moving further
into verblessness, the roots
of meaning: true aloe, not
these bracts of sassafras
and cassia: bees swathe
her in hum, leave the honey
behind, beetles pollinate her)

and ran into a tree (I am
the hunted?), stayed there
centuries (fox to the wolves
that tear summer in half?)
a light seen through
dense crowns: *Laurus nobilis*
sweet bay, bay laurel, noon's
lush lingua, sexual lexicon

A pocketful of fame in the hand
crushed leaves staining the air
I place this chaplet on my brow
(a crown of wintergreen)
and I am the sun

Ryan G. Van Cleave

The Danaides

My father used to read to me their dark tale—
the fifty dew-eyed daughters of Danaus who knew
how to listen for water in the earth, the blurp

and whisper of dark springs so far underground.
When Danaus begged them to marry his uncle's
scaled offspring—their own hideous, yellow-clawed cousins—

the daughters did, swallowing spring water scented
with hibiscus and lotus blossoms, the flowers of forgetting.
But months later, when he asked all fifty to behead

their husbands for crimes done to the Great Horse Stars,
the out-bound ocean, his own unconsecrated flesh,
they obeyed, all except Hypermnestra, who knew love

beyond that of her father's caliginous greed, his petty fingers
that dipped into the city's golden coffers one too many times.
Sometimes I imagine that I have forty-nine siblings, and I am the one

who chooses the unsturdy docks of love over the simple,
ever-sure ship of blind parental obedience. The part I like best
is justice, how it crashes in like a creaking shrimp boat,

its catch, these forty-nine thinning-haired women who are caged
in boxes of ocean ooze, black as the obsidian knives that cut
forty-nine throats during sleep. Now these women labor endlessly

in Hell, trying Sisyphus-like to fill a giant pot with holes in the
        bottom.
My father no longer reads stories because he says he doesn't believe
in fairy tales or myths that speak of some clearly delineated justice

in the world. *Some things just aren't so black and white,*
he admitted once over *café con leche* and a blueberry torte
in the new kitchen of my new house in a new neighborhood

that, like him, has faith only in under-earth sprinkler systems,
morning papers, and sunshine on car wash days. I offer him
another pastry which he doesn't want. Always his reluctance

to take advantage of what's there, a wine-maker using fingers
and toes when the press stands untouched. Together we fumble
through growing silence like minnows bumping blind into aquarium
        walls.

Charles Harper Webb

Helpless

The word is a lead blanket on my son,
who can't roll over yet, or feed himself,
or grasp the frog-rattle I bring—who can't
control his sphincters, or clean up his mess,

or comprehend how he came to be
in this room, shadowed by a blue turtle lamp
in his crib under a Winnie the Pooh mobile
on which his eyes can't focus well enough to see.

I hate the sound of *helpless*—and the fact
of needing help, but lacking it. "Bound
and helpless, he was forced to watch as soldiers
raped his wife." "He struggled, helpless,

in the big croc's jaws." I can't forget
when Dana Creech, whom I called "Creech Owl,"
sat on me and rubbed dirt in my face—
when Dad pronounced, "You're grounded

for a week. One word, and it's a month"—
when the IRS agent sneered, "disallowed."
"Don't act so helpless," my wife says
when I protest I have no notion how to stop

the toilet's leak or assemble the baby's
chest of drawers—that I'm incapable

of changing diapers (weak stomach),
or interpreting infant cries. My dad was worse

than a baby after his stroke—bigger,
uglier, less mobile, and no growing out of it.
Each time I looked at him—a groaning
corpse, pre-curled to fit a funeral urn—

I heard Neil Young moan his song:
"Helpless, helpless, heh-*eh*-elp-less."
Each syllable wormed into my bones
and made me shiver, helpless to suppress a chill.

I don't remember what the song's about.
Old Neil is helpless against drugs, helpless
to stop war, helpless to avert an audit,
or most likely, helpless in love—a scary thing:

wanting someone so much you're helpless
not to come when she calls, even if you leave your wife
in bed, your son lolling in his crib. Helpless
not to love her, even if she's with another man.

Helpless not to forgive, not to respond
when she sits so you see turquoise panties,
you see nipples through her shirt. It's terrifying,
but good too, the helplessness of giving up

volition, letting whatever has caught you
rush you along like a doll in a flash flood,
having to go where the water takes you,
the drug takes you, the love takes you, but not

unwilling or *hopeless*—a word often paired
with helpless, but not the same. The flood
may dash you against granite walls, bashing
and grinding you to splinters, but it could

also set you down in a jade meadow,
spring sun rising, mountain bluebirds warbling.
You could give a desperate cry, and a goddess,
her breasts full of milk, could come.

Incarnate

My father believes he was Anton Chekhov in a former life;
my mother says he does sometimes wake up nights reciting
Uncle Vanya's lines, or occasional Russian phrases like
"ryha bec t h ko ha moe orobe"
which means *the moon hangs low above my head.*
I can't help but think that doing great things
at an earlier time in history
as someone completely different is *not* such an honor.
My father says honor is not what he's after,
but "the knowledge that people can inform each other
across time and space" until he actually convinces himself
the fact he shares a birthday with Chekhov,
has the same chin, the same habit of whisking
his hair back off his face when angry or excited, means
he can take credit for another man's words
written decades before he was born.
He thinks his own human failings
should be more easily forgiven
in light of his prior achievements.
After crashing the Buick into the side of the house, he said
he'd been composing a story silently to himself,
and did not notice he was driving backwards.
I try to listen when he tells me how
simultaneously harsh and joyful was his life "back then,"
how hypnosis has allowed him to access the vision of the man he
                    once was,
though whenever I question him further, he cannot remember

even one detail about his experiences
as a doctor—the illnesses he treated, how many people died
in his care, the first time he told a woman
her husband had fought
well into the last hour of his life.
My father says being a doctor was only a means to make money,
and hardly related to those "great Godly words"
that just poured out of him.
At night he relaxes on the porch with vodka and the paper,
smug in the delusion that he proved himself once
with "all those damn stories, and a couple of plays thrown into
                    the mix,"
and with that he lets out one harrowing, operatic belch,
crosses his arms and falls asleep.

The Ledge

Morning light migrates into the room
as he draws the white curtains.
Outside, the day is slowly succeeding,
opening out across the land
until the night is shrunk down
to the head of a pin.
He stands at the window
looking down into the garden
as though to find his own face
on the underside of each leaf on each tree
like a secret pact, a forlorn displacement of judgment.
He is the only one who knows
how beautiful he is right then,
how his face is nuanced, held
in the advancing light across his cheek.
He is the only one who can decide
whether or not to continue standing at the open window
with the breeze chasing itself through his hair,
and his hands on the railing,
and his toes in those soft leather shoes.
He is the only witness to his sadness,
the endless excavations of his heart—
which path to abandon—
which direction to take.
He is the only one who can talk himself out
of this "fantasy of leaving"—how he thinks
he might fly, how he suppresses
his own human wishes to abandon himself.
He is the only man
to disparage his life at that moment,
to step up onto the ledge
and know the end
is the beginning of simplicity.

Dean Young

How I Get My Ideas

Sometimes you just have to wait
15 seconds then beat the prevailing nuance
from the air. If that doesn't work,
try to remember how many times
you've wakened in the body of an animal,
two arms, two legs, willowy antennae.
Try thinking what it would be like
to never see your dearest again.
Stroke her gloves, sniff his overcoat.
If that's a no-go, call Joe
who's never home but keeps changing
the melody of his message.
Cactus at night emit their own light,
the river flows under the sea.
Dear face I always recognize but never
know, everything has a purpose
from which it must be freed,
maybe with crowbars, maybe the gentlest breeze.
Always turn in the direction of the skid.
If it's raining, use the rain
to lash the window-panes or,
in a calmer mode, deepen the new greens
nearly to a violet. I can't live
without violet although it's red
I most often resort to.
Sometimes people become angelic when they cry,
sometimes only ravaged.

Technically, Mary still owes me a letter,
her last was just porcupine quills and tears,
tears that left a whitish residue
on black construction paper.
Sometimes I look at used art books in Moe's
just to see women without their clothes.
How can someone so rich,
who can have fish whenever he wants,
go to baseball games,
still feel such desperation?
I'm afraid I must insist
on desperation. By the fourth week
the embryo has nearly turned itself
inside out. If that doesn't help,
you'll just have to wait which
may involve sleeping which may involve
dreaming and sometimes dreaming works.
Father, why have you returned,
dirt on your morning vest?
You can not control your laughter.
You can not control your love.
You know not to hit the breaks on ice
but do anyway. You bend the nail
but keep hammering because
hammering makes the world.

John T. Lysaker

White Dawns, Black Noons, Twilit Days: Charles Simic's Poems Before Poetry

> "The problem with true history and great literature
> is that they wallow in ambiguities, unresolved issues,
> nuances, and baffling contradictions. Let's not kid
> ourselves."
>
> Charles Simic, The Unemployed Fortune Teller
> (Simic, 1994:38–39)

IT IS 1907. A POEM OPENING THE SECOND PART OF RILKE'S
New Poems, concludes: "Du mußt dein Leben ändern," that is, "You
must change your life." And yet it is not Rilke who speaks this
line, nor a solitary aesthete marveling beneath an archaic torso of
Apollo, nor the torso itself, mysteriously animate. Rather, the im-
perative arises when the speaker engages a torso which ". . . glüht

noch wie Kandelaber,/in dem sein Schauen, nur zurückgeschraubt,/sich hält und glänzt," which ". . . glows like a candelabra,/in which its gazing, just twisted back, holds fast and shines." Engaged, the speaker is struck, even lit: *". . . denn da ist keine Stelle,/die dich nich sieht. Du mußt dein Leben ändern,"* or one could say: ". . . for there is no point,/which does not see you. You must change your life" (Rilke, 1955–66:577, lines 3–5 & 13–14).

It is 1989, practically yesterday compared to the distance which separates us from a day in 1907, a day itself some two thousand and five hundred days away from the onset of World War One. Charles Simic writes, introducing the poetry of Aleksander Ristovic:

> At times one comes across a poet who strikes one as being absolutely original. There's something genuinely different about him or her, a something that one has never quite encountered in all the poets one has read before. 'I will never look at the world in quite the same way,' one realizes at once, and that's what happens. From that day on, one feels deeply and fatefully changed by the experience of that reading (Simic, 1990c:113).

Simic's tale resonates with Rilke's and countless others. Struck while engaging a work of art, one proceeds differently. One comports oneself differently. One has changed one's life.

In directing us towards the radically transformative power of the work of art, Rilke and Simic enter a field of belief shared by Heidegger who insists that a work of art can:

> . . . transport us out of the realm of the ordinary. To submit to this displacement means: to transform accustomed relations to world and earth and henceforth bring an end to all familiar activities and assessing, knowing and looking, in order to linger within the truth occurring in the work (Heidegger, 1950:52–3).

A remarkable event, one we cannot do justice to here. For the moment, suffice it to say that occasionally works of art retune us such that accustomed habits of action and belief prove idle, appear inappropriate to the truth which has emerged in the work. And thus we begin to change our lives.

Around the work of art, or more specifically, around the poem, a group of names is gathering: Heidegger, Rilke, Simic. To what end? In the least, I want to explain why Heidegger insists: "Poetry—no game; a relationship with it—not some playful, forgetful, self-improving diversion, but an awakening and pulling together of the most proper essence of the exceptional and solitary through which a human being goes back into the ground of its existence" (Heidegger, 1980:8).[1] I want to explore why Joseph Brodsky seems so right to claim, introducing Aleksander Kushner: "Yet I do consider it my duty to warn you that an encounter with poetry in its pure form is pregnant with far reaching consequences, that this volume is not where it will all end for you" (Kushner, 1991:ix). Again, a work of art, it is proposed, can permeate us such that, perhaps slowly, it redirects our lives. But why should we think this? Why should Heidegger say of Hölderlin's work: "This poetry demands a metamorphosis in our manner of thinking and experiencing, one regarding the whole of being" (Heidegger, 1984:205). Perhaps this is what poetry seeks. Perhaps poems offer truths, and thus demand, if only implicitly, that we live accordingly. Perhaps Celan is right to suggest, responding in 1958 to a prize from the city of Bremen: "The poem may be, because it is a manifestation of language and thus dialogical by nature, a letter in a bottle sent with the faith— certainly not always full of hope—that it might sometime and somewhere wash ashore, perhaps on the land of the heart" (Celan, 1986:196). If so, what does it mean to wash ashore the land of the heart? What does it mean to take the poem to heart, to allow it to change one's life?[2]

And yet, I have begun with strokes broad beyond my wishes, for my concern is less with poetry *überhaupt* than with a remarkable contemporary: Charles Simic. To be more precise, my hope is not only to convince you that poetry can change your life, nor simply to explain what one welcomes when one allows poetry to do so, but to explore the work of Charles Simic, to show how his poetry would change your life if you were to guide it ashore, welcoming it into the land of your heart. And to that end, I must initially employ the ear of Martin Heidegger, for his way with poems makes evident, I shall argue, how deeply the fingers of poetry are able to dig, how far reaching their import is for one able to listen well.[3]

Heidegger and Simic? They strike me as natural interlocutors, although little has been written on their ties.[4] Given their preoccupation with the poetic word, Heidegger's texts open paths into a variety of authors and traditions, including those lying outside the German circles he read within.[5] And given his preoccupation with Heidegger, Simic's texts ask to be read along Heideggerian lines by readers able to re-trace Heidegger's hermeneutic path.[6] In what follows, I will read Simic's texts in a Heideggerian manner, and argue that his work embodies a threefold attunement. First, his work draws us to the utmost ontological limits of whatever sense can be had by mortal beings. Second, he nevertheless manages to take seriously the force of history in the labor of human production, particularly when it assumes totalitarian forms. And third, he never loses sight of the way in which these overarching dramas impact upon individual plights, that is, his work is able to remind us that on ontological and historical stages, creatures still feed, fight, flee, fuck, and die. Such attunements are not mere glosses on the human condition, however. Rather, or so I will argue, they come to us from originary regions, and thus have the power, at least potentially, to orient the full range of our comportment towards ourselves, one another, the world, even being itself.

POETIC DWELLING

"They arrive inside
The object at evening.
There's no one to meet them."

—Charles Simic, "Explorers" (Simic, 1971:66, lines 1–3)

Among Heidegger's claims on behalf of poetry, these are among the starkest.

Poetry is founding, the effectual grounding of what endures. The poet is the grounder of being. What we call the real in the everyday is, in the end, unreal (Heidegger, 1980:33).

Poetry is founding through the word and within the word. What is founded so? What endures. But can what endures be founded? Is it not always already what is present at hand? No! Even what endures must be brought to stand against what would tear it away;

the simple must be wrested from entanglement, the measure must be set before the measureless. That which carries and reigns through beings as a whole must come into the open. Being must be thrown open so that a being appears (Heidegger, 1971:41).

The saying of the poet is a founding not only in the sense of a free giving, but also, and at the same time, in the sense of the firm grounding of human existence . . . (Heidegger, 1971:41).

Several points are at play. First, poetry is a founding. Second, this founding grounds Being. Third, grounding Being brings it into the open which, and this is the fourth point, allows beings to appear. Fifth, poetry works ". . . through the word and within the word." Sixth, the grounding which poetry effects takes precedence over the so-called 'real.' And seventh, poetic founding provides human beings with a ground.

While we cannot work our way through every tangle in this thicket, certain points can be clarified. At base, poetic founding, in terms of its relationship with Being and humanity, concerns a measure.

. . . Poetry is the founding naming of being and the founding naming of the essence of all things—not any old saying, but that through which everything, what we discuss and debate in common language, first steps into the open. Therefore poetry never takes up language as some raw material ready at hand, but rather, poetry itself first enables language. Poetry is the originary language (*Ursprache*) . . . (Heidegger, 1971:41).

According to this passage, the measure which poetry provides assumes the form of an *Ursprache*, that "through which everything . . . first steps into the open." But what is an *Ursprache*? Initially, one can read it along the lines of Kant's notion of *Sinnlichkeit*, "sensibility." For Kant, time and space are not themselves things in the world, but the condition of the possibility of things appearing either in consciousness or in the world, that is, they are, respectively, the *forms* of inner and outer sense. They thus provide a skeletal horizon or arena of disclosure within which thoughts and things appear. Analogously, Heidegger's *Ursprache* involves tropes, which mark and overdetermine all beings in the moment of their disclosure.[7] In order for some thing to be present, the argument runs, it must appear in relation to the *Ursprache*, just as with Kant, thoughts and things become sensible only against the horizonal backdrop of time and space.

At this point, an example might help. In the 1950s, Heidegger often invokes "the fourfold," *das Geviert*, a figure comprised of Hölderlinian tropes.[8] At its root, the fourfold demarcates a horizon of disclosure, that is, beings are disclosed upon the earth, beneath the sky, among mortals, and in the wake of divine presence or absence. It thus provides a frame of reference within which beings come to presence such that they are open to determination.[9] For examples, Heidegger often appeals to pastoral figures such as a jug, a bridge, and a hut, showing how the place they inhabit itself belongs to beings as a whole, and how they and the whole to which they belong bear the impress of the fourfold.[10] One never encounters just a jug, bridge, or hut in the later essays, but jugs, bridges, and huts within the play of the four: earth, sky, divinities, and mortals.

In order to fathom poetic measures, we need not rely on Heidegger's noble-peasant imagery, however, for Heidegger is referring to all instances of "building" in these contexts.[11] Take an office park. It is commonplace to speak of how the office park establishes certain relationships among employees, employers, and members of the community as well as between the business conducted there and the surrounding "developed" and "undeveloped" environs. In short, the office park opens something of a small "world" in and around the physical and social spaces it occupies. Such a "world" does not emerge *ex nihilo*, however, but arises within a network of relations it both adopts and refracts. Now, an *Ursprache* engages and determines the *Wesen* or essence of beings (i.e., how they enter into and persist through disclosure), and thus it involves the furthest reaches of significance, a final network of relations surrounding the emergence of all "worlds."[12] Thus while an office park does establish various relations, these relations are themselves suffused with meta-relations concerning the nature of the earth, human being, the sacred and profane, etc. And an *Ursprache* like the four-fold is, according to Heidegger, a source of these suffusions.[13]

By tying poetic founding to an *Ursprache*, we can see how it is the founding naming of the "essence" of all things. In rewriting Kant's transcendental aesthetic, the *Ursprache* contextualizes how each being comes to be the particular being it is, e.g., as a house upon the earth, a coyote beneath the sky, a poet among mortals, etc. If this analogy is helpful, it means that the *Ursprache* does not name things one by one. Rather, it figures how things come to be the beings they are. One might say, it founds how a world worlds, not the particularities of that world. As Heidegger writes, the figurative authority of the *Ursprache* ". . . never means that language, in any old meaning picked up at will, immediately and definitively supplies us with the transparent essence of the matter like some object ready to be used" (Heidegger, 1954:184). Instead, again recalling the fourfold, it overdetermines with an earthliness and mortality particular beings.[14]

Given the nearly limitless range of its determinations, one can see how an *Ursprache* takes priority over the language of the every-day and even enables it in a certain sense. Rather than giving each word a meaning, an *Ursprache* determines the nature of language in an almost metatheoretical fashion. Insofar as words, sentences, and even grammars are written, spoken, or thought, they are events that take place within a constellation of forces. Keeping to our example of the fourfold, even if we believe that language is prima-rily a product of human subjectivity (something Heidegger denies), we are still setting language within the range of mortals who dwell upon the earth and beneath the sky. With regard to any language as *a language*, therefore, one can and in fact must speak of some *Ursprache* that determines the nature of the syntactical and seman-tic events which characterize it.

Understanding the *Ursprache* as something of a metalanguage, or better, as a language of essence, one establishing a horizon of sig-nificance for all disclosures, also allows us to see why Heidegger believes that poetry can be a ". . . grounding of human existence." Put concisely, an *Ursprache* provides human beings with their furthest points of reference. As we live our lives, an *Ursprache* allows us to find a place within the whole, e.g., as mortals (hence not gods) upon the earth and beneath the sky. Or, if some other *Ursprache* were to hold sway, say Trakl's instead of Hölderlin's, we might view ourselves, in the most fundamental way, as strangers irreversibly cast along a leprous path of slow destruction and madness. Or, to appeal to Rilke, we might see ourselves as erotically obsessed lovers who need to release ourselves into an open through the non-desirous productions of beautiful particulars. In short, an *Ursprache*, Heidegger believes, can provide us with some sense for our place within and alongside beings as a whole.

But how does an *Ursprache* "throw-open" Being? Our answer to this question hinges upon how we understand poetic naming. In later texts, Heidegger treats the production of an *Ursprache* as an instance of building. (Heidegger, 1954:183) The question concerning poetic naming can be taken, therefore, to concern how poetic building comes to pass, and thus an analysis of poetic building will clarify how poetic naming, "through and within the word," 'throws open' being.

In order to come to terms with poetic building, we also need to understand Heidegger's notion of dwelling, for each determination invokes the other. In "Building, Dwelling, Thinking," Heidegger asserts that dwelling marks the fundamental character of human beings, it is ". . . the way in which mortals are upon the earth." (Heidegger, 1954:142) Also: "Dwelling . . . is the fundamental relation of being according to which mortals are." (Heidegger, 1954:155) In short, "dwelling" names the way in which human beings undergo relations with themselves, the world, as well as being itself. It names our fundamental relation to the horizon of disclosure wherein beings appear, are determined, match or contradict our beliefs about them, etc. Dwelling is thus a matter of our *Wesen*, of how we come to be the beings we are.

Why is dwelling essential to the production of poetic names? For all its originality and power, an *Ursprache* is still an event within language. If it works "through and within the word," an *Ursprache* must come to word. One thus has to ask about the conditions of its emergence, and that brings us back to the question of the dwelling-site within which poetic determinations first arise. Is this to suggest then that the question of poetic building is really a question of how poets dwell, of how they come to be the beings they are? No, for it is not as if we could speak of dwelling apart from building. The two are essentially reciprocal events. On the one hand, dwelling involves our standing within a horizon of disclosure, what Heidegger at one point terms the "dimension" (Heidegger, 1954:189). And yet, disclosures take place only when the dimension has been "measured" or "surveyed" (ibid). We could say, the dimension unfolds only in virtue of its being measured, that is, we dwell only in relation to some measure.[15] But then, there can be no measuring-building unless there already is dwelling, unless a horizon of disclosure were already there to be built upon and within. The two are thus equiprimordial. Said otherwise, no dimension is pure, but always already measured-out. And yet, neither is there an instance of Ur-building apart from the opening of some dimension. Such projects would lack a site in and upon which to build.

Tracking the play between building and dwelling unlocks poetry's relationship to Being. Note first that the equiprimordiality of poetic measures and the dimensions they survey recalls a similarly intimate pair from "The Origin of the Work of Art." While explaining how truth takes place in the *work* of art, i.e., how beings and Being are unconcealed in the *work* of art, Heidegger claims that disclosure only occurs through a double event which shares a single essence: the event of a *Lichtung der Offenheit and an Einrichtung in das Offene*, a "clearing of openness" and an "arranging across the open" (Heidegger, 1950:48). While an open of disclosure must have been cleared in order for arrangements to be made, one cannot speak of an open of disclosure except in relation to arrangements which figure that open. As with building and dwelling, one requires the other.

If we set the measuring of the *Ursprache* into the play of *Lichtung* and *Einrichtung*, clearing and arranging, we access the way in which Being is "thrown open" in an *Ursprache*. It isn't that originary poetic names attach some name to "Being," e.g., Cosmos, Brahman, Emptiness, etc. Rather, they allow Being to come to presence as the clearing of an open, that is, they allow the "truth of being," the clearing, to be manifest. Recall that Heidegger believes that the *Ursprache* is ". . . that through which everything first steps into the open" (Heidegger, 1971:43). What we are claiming now is that the *Ursprache* is also that through which the opening of the open is disclosed, even "thrown open." Why "thrown open"? As the event which enables presence, the clearing of the open lags behind what comes to presence and falls away into concealment. In an *Ursprache*, however, the event of clearing, what withdraws behind that which comes to presence, is admitted into the open, that is, the lid of presence is "thrown open" so that the event of presencing also appears, albeit as what withdraws in the event of presencing.

One would like to know, of course, how poetry manages to allow the clearing of the open to presence, and how this disclosure contributes to the work of poetic founding. Let us begin with a *via negativa*. An *Ursprache* cannot name, straight-away, the event of clearing, thus bringing it within our reach. Proceeding in this way would conceal the clearing which enables that very figuration or "arranging," thus robbing the *Ursprache* of its originariness. And yet, an *Ursprache* must nevertheless account for the clearing-arranging event of disclosure which marks its own origins. Otherwise, the dwelling space it purportedly opens and arranges would be circumscribed by whatever forces open and arrange its own coming into being. In other words, it would no longer be a founding event. Therefore, if a body of poetry is to provide an *Ursprache*, it must do so alongside of and through an Ur-poem, a self-figuring poem of poetry.[16] In other words, as it opens and arranges a world or dimension wherein humans might dwell, it must also open and arrange the world of its own dwelling.

Now one might think it preposterous that a poem's self-relation could address questions concerning the very meaning of human existence. But suppose that what we are calling an Ur-poem, were read as a dramatization of the birth of sense or meaning itself? What if the Ur-poem portrayed, even performed, the emergence of the abundance of sense which makes up our world? Would it not then figure for us the very sense of what is? Not, of course, one being at a time, but in coming to terms with how sense itself

534

emerges, it would enable us to hear and see and think in each and every sense or meaning a genesis tale, a poem of origins to accompany every experience, every memory, even every flash of presence. And if an Ur-poetry provided us with such a far reaching sensibility, would it not then change our lives, and most dramatically? Would it not overdetermine whatever could be said to be, whether it *was* an index finger, a chestnut, starlight, or a poem? But let us not continue to consider this matter so abstractly. Rather, we should engage the matter within the context of a particular *Ursprache*, Charles Simic's.[17]

THE WHITES OF ALL EYES

"My lifelong subject, despite appearances to the contrary, was always an unknown woman who made me forget my name every time we bumped into one another on the street."

—Charles Simic, *Orphan Factory* (Simic, 1997:115)

Before beginning our engagement with Simic, it bears notice that his work explicitly engages Heidegger. As he explains in an interview from 1978:

I've always felt that inside each of us there is a profound anonymity. Sometimes I think that when you go deep inside, you meet everyone else on a sort of common ground—or you meet nobody. But whatever you meet, it is not yours though you enclose it. We are the container, and this nothingness is what we enclose. This is where Heidegger is very interesting to me (Simic, 1985:62).

And in another interview from 1991:

Already Hölderlin asked the question: "And what are poets good for in a destitute time?" And Heidegger replies: "In the age of the world's night, the abyss of the world must be experienced by those who reach into the abyss." I continue to believe that poetry says more about the psychic life of an age than any other art. Poetry is a place where all the fundamental questions are asked about the human condition (Weigel, 1996:210).

One is thus not unduly violent in bringing Heideggerian themes

535

into Simic's work. But where to begin? Because it recoils into the origins of sense, Simic's long poem *White*, an elusive lyric sequence consisting of three parts and totaling 245 lines holds the key to his *Ursprache*.[18] When all is counted, one sees that the first two parts of *White* are comprised of ten segments, each involving five, two-line pairs. The last, entitled "What the White had to Say," contains two twenty-line soliloquies. More interesting, however, is the fact that *White* opens with a speaker preparing to begin again, and without presuppositions, even virginally.

> Out of poverty
> To begin again
>
> With the color of the bride
> And that of blindness, (lines 1–4)

But he is unsure of how to proceed, and thus seeks to:

> Touch what I can
> Of the quick,
>
> Speak and then wait,
> As if this light
>
> Will continue to linger
> On the threshold. (lines 5–10)

Note how empty this beginning is. As the next line proclaims:

> All that is near,
> I know longer give it a name. (lines 11–12)

White thus begins by not beginning, opening instead with paralysis.

This paralyzing poverty is peculiar. First, it appears self-imposed, stemming from a refusal to name what is near, most familiar. Second, it is tied to a desire to begin again, freshly, as if existing names had failed or dimmed. I take it, therefore, that the speaker's poverty ultimately concerns his poetizing, his ability to name what surrounds him, even what is near, and that includes the work of poetry itself. If this is right, then *White* opens by confessing that its poetizing has floundered, that as poetry, it no longer knows how to conduct itself or even what it is. The fact that it continues on for several hundred lines is thus odd. Are these lines "poetry"? Perhaps they involve something prior to what we would normally call "poetry," something less certain, a kind of Ur-poetry which seeks less the essence or even flash of things than the rim of poetry itself, the site from which "poetry" commences.[19] That is how I hear *White*, as an Ur-poetry struggling to find itself at its origin, carrying out the task Simic announces in "Composition." "In the beginning, always, a myth of origins of the poetic act. A longing to lower oneself one notch below language, to touch the bottom—that place of 'original action and desire,' to recover our mute existence, to recreate what is unspoken and enduring in words of the poem . . ." (Simic, 1985:110).[20]

What remains of part one is a journey, a pilgrimage towards a place from which to begin, again. More precisely, the speaker seeks a bride who might enable him to visit the stars.

> *Enough glow to kneel by and ask*
> *To be tied to its tail*
>
> *When it goes marrying*
> *Its cousins the stars.* (lines 17–20)

And one finds the same thought in the fifth segment of the first part.

> *That your gaze*
> *Be merciful,*
>
> *Sister, bride*
> *Of my first hopeless insomnia.*
>
> *Kind nurse, show me*
> *The place of salves.*
>
> *Teach me the song*
> *That makes a man raise*
>
> *His glass at dusk*
> *Until a star dances in it.* (lines 41–50)

What is occurring here? How might we regard the betrothed, the honeymoon stars? Since the speaker hopes that the bride will bring song, she seems muselike, a giver of words which aim to bring stars to the glass of whomever sings them. This is thus a bride whose dowry includes the poetic word.[21]

But what of the stars that the speaker would summon and journey towards on the wings of his bride? In "Reading Philosophy at Night," Simic claims:

> Both poetry and philosophy, for instance, are concerned with Being. What is a lyric poem, one might say, but the recreation of the experience of Being. In both cases, that need to get it down to its essentials, to say the unsayable and let the truth of Being shine through (Simic, 1990c:60).

And in "Assembly Required," he asserts:

> Every poetic image asks why is there something rather than nothing, as it renews our astonishment that things exist (Simic, 1997:96).

Finally, in "Poetry is the Present," he suggests:

> The poets, so we believe, remind the philosophers, again and again, of the world's baffling presence (Simic, 1994:55).

In other words, I take the shimmering stars to be the shimmering of Being, of the world in its presencing, of all that is there and not nothing, for that is what poetry seeks, according to Simic—to reach into the heavens and sing the "baffling presence of the world" within a raised glass or word.

But the speaker's journey results in naught. Along the way, he remarks:

> There are words I need.
> They are not near men.
>
> I went searching.
> Is this a deathmarch?
>
> You bend me, bend me
> Oh toward what flower!

Little known vowel,
Noose big for us all. (lines 53–60)

Despair strikes. He fears that this "O," perhaps the "O" of a mouth opening to speak, will prove his hangman. And things do not improve as the first part ends. When he presses his fingertips against the white page, he hears only a "holy nothing" "blindfolding itself." (line 93) The speaker thus finds himself back at the beginning with his poverty, hoping to 'begin again with the color of the bride and that of blindness.'

In part two, the speaker redirects his search. No longer an itinerant pilgrim, he turns inward, ascetically, and prepares for the White should she arrive. In a mocking self-interrogation the speaker describes how he will prepare himself as a sacrificial meal, offering to ". . . roast on my heart's dark side" until ". . . the half-moons on my fingernails set," that is, until the death after death when our finger nails finally cease growing (lines 102&108).[22]

The next segment makes evident, however, that this is far from a labor of self-mastery, underscoring the poverty of the speaker's situation.

Well, you can't call me a wrestler
If my own dead weight has me pinned down.

Well, you can't call me a cook
If the pot's got me under cover. (lines 111–114)

Nor are the efforts at self-sacrifice entirely successful.

Nor can you call me a saint,
If I didn't err, there wouldn't be these smudges. (lines 119–120)

In other words, the speaker's ascetic self-erasure is incomplete—smudges remain, darkening the White.

Amid this intensifying poverty, some insights do seem to flash, however. Segment four opens with discovery. "This is breath, only breath" (line 131). "This"? Poetizing itself is implied, for song and speech are, in a sense, only breath. The nature of breath eludes the speaker, however, who confesses:

But when I shout,
Its true name sticks in my throat. (lines 135–136)

But things couldn't be otherwise, for one cannot speak the name of breath, only presuppose it. What then?

White—let me step aside
So that the future may see you,

For when this sheet is blown away.
What else is left

But to set the food on the table
To cut oneself as slice of bread? (lines 145–150)

The White, with its poetic word, appears to have forsaken the speaker at his altar of self-abnegation, and thus he pursues this abnegation to an extreme, renouncing even his desire for the White, opting instead for the banality of a life without a White upon which to name the world in its baffling presence.

But perhaps this was what was required all along, for in the wake of his apostasy, fate strikes in segment six (lines 151–160). A "true-blue Orphan" encounters an "obscure widow" in the "unknown year" of an "algebraic century" on an "indeterminate street corner." Note the radical indeterminacy here. Given the speaker's poverty, his world is nearly formless, his century one of variables awaiting determination. But fate pushes through this limbo, and the orphaned speaker is given:

A tiny sugar cube

In the hand so wizened
All the lines said: fate. (lines 158–160)

While sugar is sweet, the widow's hand is sweeter, initiating the wedding ceremony that is segment seven.

Do you take this line
Stretching to infinity?

I take this chipped tooth
On which to cut it in half.

Do you take this circle
Bounded by a single curved line?

I take this breath
That it cannot capture.

Then you may kiss the spot
Where her bridal train last rustled. (lines 161–170)

Note that the speaker does not simply accept the vows. Twice he is offered the hand of infinity, what I take to be the infinite lines of fate which converge in the wizened hand of the "obscure widow." The first time he responds with a chipped tooth, cutting in half the fateful line. He later refuses the infinite and perfect loop of the circle (i.e., the wedding ring) in favor of breath, recalling the breath of speech and song uncovered in segment four. What does this suggest? In each instance, I find an affirmation of mortality over and against whatever the infinite would offer. If you recall the spinning Fates of Greek mythology (Clotho, Lachesis, and Atropos), you'll also recall that a snip of their lines results in death, and this seems to be what the speaker embraces in place of the infinite line being offered (with its implicit promises of "lineage" and "destiny"). Likewise, he elects to remain with the breath that he breathes and which carries whatever song he, as a mortal human being, might sing, whatever name he might shout. But such a choice renders this an odd marriage. While it is implied that the couple has been pronounced "married," the speaker is only invited to ". . . kiss the spot/Where her bridal train last rustled," that is, insofar as he remains mortal, he remains wedded to the wake of the White's gait, grasping after her sublime hem.

Despite the irony which consummates his nuptials, the speaker achieves some repose. Recalling Stevens's "The Snow Man," he welcomes Winter and the way in which it turns our planet into a grave.[23]

Winter can come now,
The earth narrow to a ditch—(lines 171–172)

And the poetic word is granted, albeit in a form appropriate to one who has refused to renounce mortality.

The snow can fall . . .
What other perennials would you plant,

. . . For those remote, finely honed bees
The December stars? (lines 175–180)

It would seem, then, that the speaker receives the poetic word, thus abating his poverty. But if this is so, it is only for a moment. The snow of this breath which he refused to abandon will melt, disappear.

And yet, despite this repose, the journey has taken its toll. The ninth segment opens with an odd line: "Had to get through me elsewhere" (line 181). Syntactically, the subject is ambiguous. Who or what 'had to get through'? In the self-effacing efforts of the earlier segments, was the speaker trying to work through himself such that he might finally leave himself behind and engage the White? Such is the logic of asceticism. Perhaps the subject is thus "I." But then, lines of fate also run through us on their way to elsewhere. By definition, fate scorns our autonomy, leaving us at the mercy of its motions. Is the subject then "It" or "They"? But a choice seems artificial. After segment six, the speaker is so thoroughly in the grasp of fate that "fate" no longer lies outside him. Regardless, whatever pushes through moves relentlessly, ant-like: "Gravedigger ants," "Village-idiot ants" (lines 189–90). He thus moans:

Woe to the bone

That stood in their way. (lines 182–183)

But "woe" is not his only affliction. In fact, the repose of the eighth segment wanes in segment ten, which begins, "This is the last summoning," as if the speaker seeks more than the ". . . the spot/ Where her bridal train last rustled," as if words of snow, despite their evident and unique, crystalline whiteness were insufficient. Moreover, the speaker invokes the dead letter office of his fear, confesses his doubt, bemoans his insomnia (lines 192, 195, 196, 199).[24] Part two then finishes "Solitude—as in the beginning," perhaps annulling whatever had been brought together in the nuptials of segment seven (line 192).

But *White* is not yet at a close. A third part remains, entitled "What the White Had to Say." One might think that this marks the final desperate summons "successful," and the former efforts, the opening pilgrimage and the labor of ascetic self-effacement, failures. But the White bears curious tidings of her ways and days. First, she asserts her radical anteriority to whatever demands might be made upon her, claiming that she has ". . . gone through everyone already" and ". . . thought of you before you thought of me" (lines 206–07). Moreover, she insists, most radically, ". . . I am nearer to you than your breath" (215). In other words, whatever articulations we might employ to name or represent the White, she stands before them, enabling breath, thinking us before we think her. Open your mouth, exhale, let words sound forth—the White is already there. Note how this recoils on the notion of a summons; the breath which calls out has overlooked the fact that what it seeks is always already there.

Though always already there, the White is far from placid. It runs through us, like a bullet:

> Because I am the bullet
> That has baptized each of your senses,
> Poems are made of our lusty wedding nights,
> The joy of words as they are written. (lines 225–228)

Speeding like a bullet, the White has already come and gone by the time poems are born, by the time words are written. Moreover, the White is already there baptizing by the time one's senses feel the impress of *aisthesis*—the emptiness of a sky, the age of an oak, the mute life of a mannequin, the unnerving independence of a numb finger. One is always too late for the White. But words are nevertheless written, poems nevertheless born. And yet, one should not expect to write with the White in tow. Rather, the birth of poems testifies to her having already been there, to consummated vows, as does the presence of what is. But this coition eludes our gaze, precedes our voice. By the time we turn to express our affection, all that remains is ". . . the spot/Where her bridal train last rustled" (lines 169–70).

Through "What the White had to Say," we are realizing that the speaker is not given insight into the grounds of his voice despite the fact that the White appears to address him. That bed remains unfathomable. All one apprehends are searing joys of inspiration, the impress of presence.

> Each one of you still keeps a blood-stained handkerchief
> In which to swaddle me, but it stays empty
> And even the wind won't remain in it long.
> Cleverly you've invented name after name for me,
> Mixed the riddles, garbled the proverbs,
> Shook your loaded dice in a tin cup,
> But I do not answer to your curses . . . (lines 208–214)

Note again her insistent anteriority: she is quicker than the wind which is already too quick for our hankies. How then capture her? We can't: ". . . the most beautiful riddle has no answer" (line 231). Instead, one is left with and in the wake of her train, with traces of blood, poems, stark presences.

To insist upon the anteriority of the White is not to substantialize it, however, as if it hovered above poets and things as a transcendental ground or condition of the possibility of meaning, poetry, or sense. The White, like Heidegger's clearing, locates herself in the everyday.

> One sun shines on us both through a crack in the roof.
> A spoon brings me through the window at dawn.
> A plate shows me off to the four walls . . . (lines 216–218)

In other words, the White moves in the shine of things, that is, they carry it, testify to its having been there. As one lifts a spoon or sets a plate, the White, flying through the roots of all commerce, is reflected around and about. And ubiquitously:

> Steadily, patiently I lift your arms.
> I arrange them in the posture of someone drowning,
> And yet the sea in which you are sinking,
> And even this night above it, is myself. (lines 221–224)

In still other words, the White moves through the fabric of sense which animates all things.

Anterior, searing, ubiquitous, mundane, the White reminds the speaker of her fatedness.

> *Take a letter: From cloud to onion.*
> *Say: There was never any real choice.* (lines 235–36)

But then there couldn't be, for choices come too late within this drama. Choices move with breath and the White moves just prior to those inhalations, leaving the whole marvel of sense suspended in emptiness.

> *I am the emptiness that tucks you in like a mockingbird's*
> *   nest,*
> *The fingernail that scratched on your sleep's blackboard.*
> (lines 232–234)

Again, ubiquity. White provides an empty nest for our squawks, and, given the ambiguity of "sleep's blackboard," it seems to both spell out our dreams (or poems) and call us into the waking world. And Simic's use of "emptiness" underscores that here lies the "most beautiful riddle [that] has no answer." Out of the emptiness comes the poetic word, like scratches in the night. Push past those scratches, however, and only emptiness remains. As Simic says in 1972:

> Poetry is an orphan of silence. The words never quite equal the experience behind them. We are always at the beginning, eternal apprentices, thrown back again and again into that condition. (Simic, 1985:5)

White's speaker was right, therefore, to muse: "A zero burped by a bigger zero—" (line 193).[25]

As a poem of poetry, an Ur-poem, *White* unveils a stark drama. Poetic words come like scratches in the night, but if one seeks the chicken foot dragging down sleep's blackboard, one will only find a riddled emptiness. I take it that this is why the poem closes with the White saying:

> . . . *That milk tooth*
> *You left under the pillow, it's grinning.* (lines 244–45)

It's grinning because one cannot summon this muse like the tooth fairy; she remains anterior to such antics. I suppose it is also grinning because in the end, the tooth remains 'white,' and thus the summoner has overlooked the fact that the White was already there, whispering: "I thought of you long before you thought of [or summoned] me." But these ironies may elude the speaker, and thus the White worries at the close of her second soliloquy that the speaker has yet to really understand her ubiquity, her mundaneness, and above all, her anteriority.

> *Street-organ full of blue notes,*
> *I am the monkey dancing to you grinding—*
> *And still you are afraid—and so,*
> *It's as if we had not budged from the beginning.* (lines 239–242)

What a wonderfully helpless conclusion. One cannot summon the poetic word from its ground; it comes when it will, like fate, and refuses to attest to its origin, even though the blood we find come morning lets us know that our wedding night was lusty indeed. And yet, Simic refuses to render the White otherworldly. Instead, it is there among and alongside every letter and thing, elusive, riddlesome.[26]

For all its self-conscious concern with poetry, I think we do *White* a disservice if we limit the range of its Ur-musings to that field of meaning we have come to call "poetry," even given poetry's manifold forms and voices. While *White* no doubt pursues the origin of the poetic word and even poetic inspiration and imagination, it also engages much broader questions concerning the birth of sense per se. I find this to be most poignantly evident in the following lines from "What the White had to Say."

> *Because I am the bullet*
> *That has baptized each one of your senses,*
> *Poems are made of our lusty wedding nights.* (lines 225–27)

Here the "bullet" testifies to the ways in which events of disclosure rip through our senses. After all, we do not summon experience, it washes over us, or rather, strikes us, laying claim to our attention. And I have already suggested that this passage sets the anteriority of the White before the *aisthesis* which initiates the experience of the poet and inspires the poet's work, e.g., in the guise of a startling vista, an event of love or loss, the ring of two consonants, the patter of a marvelous phrase. But we can push farther than this and claim that the White is here asserting her ability to wash over each of the senses, i.e., taste, touch, sight, smell, and hearing. And yet, neither reading captures the radical sense lurking in the White's claim on "each one of your [or even our] senses."

Etymologically, to "baptize" means 'to dip,' from the Greek *baptizein*. Into what does the White dip "each one of your senses"? Into the ". . . emptiness that tucks you in like a mockingbird's/ nest" (lines 323–33). That is, the White baptizes "each one of your senses" into the "profound anonymity" and "nothingness" that Simic senses inside us, what he regards as our "common ground" to recall some lines from the interview with Rick Jackson and Michael Panori (Simic, 1985:62). But note that Simic does not limit this anonymity to the ground of poetic inspiration or language, but marks it as the "common ground" that lurks "inside each of us." One thus has reason to believe that the White lays claim to more than the sense of the poem, although most certainly to the sense of the poem. Second, as a "ground," common or otherwise, this "profound anonymity" lies at our root, and thus is tethered to the full range of our foliage, that is, to "each one of [our] senses," hearing in "sense" the very figure of sense itself. In other words, I hear in the White's claim to "each one of our senses" a claim upon whatever we might suppose to have sense, to be-there before us, to be present, to be disclosed as something *that is* rather than nothing.

On my reading, then, *White's* Ur-poem poetizes not only the origin of the poem, but the origin of whatever can be said to be, to have sense, and in a remarkably reflexive way, that is, through poetizing what comes to pass before its own emergence into sense. As an Ur-poem, *White* is thus also an *Ursprache*, dramatizing how beings come to presence. But recall, an *Ursprache* does not name beings one by one. Rather, it baptizes their sense in its sense of sense, thus recasting whatever can be said to be there within the ranges it opens. One can thus see how *White* reaches into the 'abyss of the world' that Simic seeks, following Heidegger. It reaches beyond what is present and fingers the rim of presencing itself. And this is how *White*, to recall Heidegger himself, ". . . demands a metamorphosis in our manner of thinking and experiencing, one regarding the whole of being" (Heidegger, 1984:205). Rather than effecting transformations at the level of particular things, say poetry, *White* transforms our sense of sense, thus bearing upon 'the whole of being.' It is thus with good reason that I began this engagement of Simic's work with a long reading of *White*, for in dramatizing the originary moments of sense itself, its silences punctuate all of Simic's work, that is, to hear a Simic poem is also to hear the White out of which it has emerged and upon which it has been written. In a very real way, then, *White* is part and parcel of every Simic poem, and any attempt to engage his *Ursprache* must trace out the journeys it enacts.

For all the radicality at play in *White*, Simic routinely invokes the philosophy of (un)consciousness in his prose accounts of the origins of poetry, at times sounding more Husserlian than Heideggerian.[27] Particularly in interviews and essays from the 1970s, he writes as if the origin of the poetic word lay within the poet's psyche, buried beneath the structures and temporality of consciousness. If this were so, then the origin of poetry would not be, as *White* seems to suggest, a radical, fateful silence, but the hidden percolation of human subjectivity. True, unconscious or preconscious eruptions may be mysterious, but they are not truly "orphans of silence." Instead, their silences are mere lacunae within a much theorized and explored discourse of the psyche, one common to surrealism and psychoanalysis.

In his conversation with Rick Jackson and Michael Panori, Simic says in response to their questions concerning 'the poem's space':

> I'm one of those who believes that there is something that precedes language. The usual view is that there is some kind of equivalence between thought and language, that if you can't verbalize it you can't think it. I've always felt that there is a *state*

that precedes verbalization, a complexity of *experience* that consists of things not yet brought to consciousness, not yet existing as language, but as some sort of inner pressure. Any verbal act includes a selection, a conceptualization, a narrowing down (Simic, 1985:61—emphases added). [28]

Likewise, in "The Partial Explanation," he writes:

This is, indeed, the crucial event. The instant when that slumbering, almost anonymous content [here a phrase which initiated a poem—"a long time since the waiter took my order"—JTL] becomes audible, when its *privacy* is abolished and it translates itself into language (Simic, 1985:102—emphasis added).

Simic here refers his explanations, partial as they might be, to three fundamental tropes of subjectivity: experience, states, and privacy. And one can understand why. The language of the poem is in some sense written by the poet and not any old bystander. Likewise, poets have to work on that language, refine it, revise it, and thus it is in some sense their affair. Intuitively, then, one can understand why Simic would believe that the language of the poem appears mysteriously within the receptive confines of consciousness.

Despite its intuitive appeal, Heidegger resists locating the origin of poetry within subjective orbits. In his 1941–42 course on Hölderlin's *Andenken*, he states: "The poetizing word names that which comes over the poet and transposes him into an affiliation which he has not created but can only follow" (Heidegger, 1982:7). And in the 1942 course on *Der Ister*: "The poetic is never conceived through the poet, but conversely, the poet is to be conceived *only* out of the *Wesen*/essence of poetry" (Heidegger, 1984:149). Finally, in "Das Gedicht," from 1968: "The poet has not invented that which is his poetry's ownmost. It is allotted him. He joins himself to [its] direction and follows [its] call" (Heidegger, 1971:183).

At stake in Heidegger's remarks, and Simic's apparent distance from them, is the question of the origin of poetry and ultimately, of "sense" itself. Heidegger is driven away from subjective tropes because he finds them insufficiently originary. As he argues in an early Marburg lecture from 1925, a phenomenology which focuses upon acts of consciousness (and here it matters not if they are conscious, unconscious, or preconscious), forgoes any interrogation of the being or sense of those cognitive events.[29] Instead, they are taken as primitives, thus foreclosing questions concerning their own coming to be. Second, a poetry which delimits its figurations within such theoretical tropes forgoes all claims to the originary and allows its musing to be circumscribed by the conceptual frame instituted by the adopted theory, hence the appearance of terms like privacy, experience, state, and consciousness in Simic's prose. Simic's reliance on the tropes of subjectivity thus counteracts the logic of his belief that: "The poem is the place where origins are allowed to think" (Simic, 1985:112). In assuming that something like the human subject lurks at the origin of the poem, Simic precludes his poetry from thinking the origin at all.[30] Instead, his thought, at least in his prose reflections, is forced by its initial assumptions to return again and again to the supposed originariness of the pre-linguistic, simple psyche. I would thus prefer that he follow Heidegger here, and leave Husserl's subjectivism behind.[31]

Simic might be loathe to forego the philosophy of consciousness, however. Repeatedly, he insists that lyric poetry has political import precisely because it expresses the view of one over and against the reign of many. As he writes in "The Minotaur Loves His Labyrinth": "The individual is the measurer, the world is what is measured, and the language of poetry is the measure. There! Now you can hang me by my tongue" (Simic, 1994:107). And in "The Flute Player in the Pit": "Lyric poets perpetuate the oldest values on earth. They assert the individual's experience against that of the tribe" (Simic, 1994:4). But one need not invoke the philosophy of consciousness in order to claim that lyric poetry defends the singularity of presencing. By keeping to the phenomenological orientation invoked above, lyric poetry, simply by attending to things as they show themselves from themselves, remains opposed to totalizing tribal schemes. In other words, even as an orphan of radical silence, lyric poetry could remain a defender of the mortal singularity of presencing, and refuse, with the speaker of *White*, to marry into an infinite line.[32] In fact, by making evident the silence that underwrites presence itself, an *Ursprache* like Simic's would underscore that presence is not the consequence of some metaphysical ground, not an instance of a universal type, but a singular sense born out of apparent, even readily apparent, nothingness.[33]

SLAUGHTER-BENCHES AND WRITERS' TABLES

"The street of many concealed felonies
So pretty in the morning sunlight."

—Charles Simic, "The Big Coverup"

For all its force, *White* does not exhaust Simic's *Ursprache*. In "Fried Sausage," we find:

> This is how I see it. There are three ways to think about the world. You can think about the Cosmos (as the Greeks did), you can think about History (as the Hebrews did), and since the eighteenth century you can think about Nature. . . . I myself fancy the cosmic angle. The brain-chilling infinities and silences of modern astronomy and Pascalian thought impress me deeply, except that I'm also a child of History. I've seen tanks, piles of corpses, and people strung from lampposts with my own eyes. (Simic, 1994:20)[34]

The mouth of Simic's Ur-poetry is thus at least two sided. On the one hand, Simic can write in response to Joseph Cornell's eerie boxes: "Cosmogenies are soap bubbles. . . . A soap bubble has no content. After it has burst, there's nothing left of it" (Simic, 1992:54). And with the other, he can insist, as he does while introducing the work of Ale? Debeljak: "The poet who is not sensitive to the enormity and complexity of our historical and intellectual predicament is not worth reading" (Simic, 1994:119).

But how does a poem testify to the force of history? And how does Simic's work understand the history it has inherited? Consider "Empire of Dreams" from *Classic Ballroom Dances* (Simic, 1980:17).

On the first page of my dreambook
It's always evening

In an occupied country.
Hour before the curfew.
A small provincial city.
The houses all dark.
The store-fronts gutted.

I am on a street corner
Where I shouldn't be.
Alone and coatless
I have gone out to look
For a black dog who answers to my whistle.
I have a kind of halloween mask
Which I am afraid to put on.

"Empire of Dreams," like *White*, opens before the moment of writing, or rather, it doubles back upon its own inscriptions and asks: what is already there? This is thus another originary poem, one which explores the moment before poetry is written. Here, however, the speaker encounters something more than an elusive White. Instead of a dimly lit threshold, the speaker finds on the first page of a dreambook, the "dream" a classic image of the poem, an occupied country, a pending curfew, and a city in ruins.

In its recoil, "Empire of Dreams" returns to a point before the poem's commencement and finds a history already in play. More specifically, the speaker finds a fiercely authoritarian setting. The curfew suggests that soon the allotted time for dreaming and poetizing will end, that is, forces have come to regulate what a poet might write. That such a fate is not simply the stuff of nightmares should go without saying. Not only are poets killed (e.g., Lorca, Mandelstam), imprisoned, and exiled, but the lines of totalitarianism can be found right on the page, as is evident in the second part Akhmatova's *Poem Without A Hero*. Stanza ten begins with three lines of ellipses followed by: "And the decades file by,/Tortures, exiles and deaths . . . I can't sing/In the midst of this horror" (Akhmatova, 1992:569). Stanzas Eleven and Twelve follow, composed only of ellipses, which maintain the graphic form of the previous stanzas. How are we to regard this "can't," this inability? The ellipses signify elisions, for Akhmatova did not believe that she would be permitted to publicly address the atrocities of the show trials and purges. Completed stanzas do exist, however, and thus we know what Akhmatova wanted to sing. Stanza Eleven, for example, speaks of "How we lived in unconscious fear,/How we raised children for the executioner,/For the prison and for the torture chamber" (Akhmatova, 1992:582). But such a song had no place in the public text of *Poem Without A Hero*. Instead, one had to make do with the punctuated presence of totalitarian rule.

But then, I think that "Empire of Dreams" imagines a fate more sinister than censorship. Its dreambook is open, but before a word is even written occupation is there. As the short, clipped sentences suggest, these are hushed tones, remarks hurried by fear. Why all this stealth? This open page is a street corner where the speaker shouldn't be, that is, to open the dreambook is already to brook insubordination. In this empire, even to broach the possibility of poetry is to violate existing rules. Moreover, it is to expose oneself, 'alone and coatless' in an evening of occupation. But the speaker has risked these violations and gone out. To write? Not yet. First, s/he seeks a ". . . a black dog who answers to my whistle." The image is cryptic, but suggests a few things. On the one hand, the dog may offer protection on these streets, as though one is less likely to suffer harm with a quasi-familiar at one's side. On the other hand, the dog, more accustomed to skulking about after hours, may be able to lead the less adept speaker through the mazes of road blocks and guard posts, thus enabling him or her to record with greater precision what remains of the life of this city.[35] Under occupation, perhaps the best muse is a street wise cur.

The poem closes with an unnerving image. Whistling for a black dog, alone and coatless, curfew time drawing in, the speaker carries a Halloween mask. Not yet writing, the speaker holds a mask in his or her hand. Why? To elude detection? To participate in a secret festival of the dead? We cannot be sure. What is more palpable, however, is the speaker's fear. Why is s/he afraid? Before a word has even been written, can one don a mask? If so, what will one write? According to Simic, ". . . the poet is driven to tell the truth" (Simic, 1994:2). Under times of occupation, and the present is anything but a time of autonomy, poetic or otherwise, must the writer risk the distortion of a mask in order to pass through the censors of the day? If so, can the truth be told, whether it concerns 'the world's baffling presence' or the slings and arrows of a fate, which does more than 'scratch on sleep's blackboard'? From out of the darkness that surrounds "Empire of Dreams," a question emerges. To what degree is poetry, a poetry, which would tell the truth, presently possible? Might not the weight of historical forces over-power the poem at the outset, before words can be written on the first page of a dream book, its page no doubt white?

At stake in this question concerning history's force in the lan-guage of the poem is the originary power Heidegger attributes to poetry. Does poetry always have the power to fashion an *Ursprache* and bathe presence itself in its sense of sense? In "Poem Without A Title," from *Dismantling the Silence*, a poem which again calls to mind Akhmatova's *Poem Without A Hero*, Simic best addresses this question.

> I say to the lead
> Why did you let yourself
> Be cast into a bullet?
> Have you forgotten the alchemists?
> Have you given up hope
> Of turning into gold?
>
> Nobody answers.
> Lead. Bullet. With names
> Such as these
> The sleep is deep and long. (Simic, 1971:62)

This is a startling poem. First, it too begins at the beginning, addressing the lead of a pencil, what enables a poem to be written upon the white pages of a dreambook. Second, it struggles with the history that lead has led—war, assassination, domestic tragedy, and the shame ridden glory of defense. And it interrogates, presses, tries to awaken promises now dormant. But it fails. "Nobody answers." Instead, lead has become the bullet, and it cannot be reminded of times when its future was less certain, less grim, when it could lay upon an alchemist's table and dream of being gold. Hence, this is a "Poem Without a Title," for it never becomes a poem. The speaker fails to take the lead of the pencil into the region of the poem where the possibility of new names is somehow preserved, where the possibility of new figurations lurks.

According to Simic, then, poetry can fail, and the outset.[36] It can find its Ur-pretensions rebuffed by the weight of historical forces. What does this tell us about the pretensions of an *Ursprache*? I think the claim must be that poetry is always a site of contestation among historical forces, that just atop the silence located and exhibited in *White* a din rattles and rages such that Ur-poetry not only must reflexively return to its origins, but engage its historical inheritance as well, and win from it the right to speak with its own voice.[37] If this is so, then an *Ursprache*, if it is to be truly originary, must always address at least two facets of its nature: its ontological rims and the historical fabric out of which it tries to cut itself.[38]

But one should beware of taking "history" too abstractly, for Simic is more specifically concerned with the force of particular histories, totalitarianism first of all. And yet, despite its palpability, Simic's fear of authoritarian rule is hauntingly elusive. What forms will the censor take? How will the poem police find their way into the first pages of our dream books? I think we might gain better access to Simic's understanding of totalitarianism if we return to his insistence that the singularity of lyric poetry is staunchly political. In "Elegy in A Spider's Web," he writes: "The lyric poet is almost by definition a traitor to his own people. He is the stranger who speaks the harsh truth that only individual lives are unique and therefore sacred" (Simic, 1994b:38). Now, this declaration that individual lives are sacred descries any who would willingly sacrifice individuals to some systemic religious, political, or philosophical end. But this cannot be all, for "Empire of Dreams" claims that the secret police not only can compel conscription in some (un)holy war, but that they have the power to work their way into our thoughts and dreams, such that, without our knowing it, our first person might not be ours. If this is so, then the war that lyric poetry fights against totalitarianism involves more than affirmations and defenses of the value of individuals.

Two questions are in play. First, what understanding of totalitarianism is appropriate to the fears which manifest themselves in poems like "Empire of Dreams"? Second, how does Simic's work confront those fears, that is, how does it resist totalitarianism? In order to appreciate the depths of Simic's fear, we need to come to terms with the kind of totalitarianism that moves across the pages of dream books with the speed of neural transmissions. To this end, consider Jean-Luc Nancy's and Phillipe Lacoue-Labarthe's analyses of "new totalitarianism."[39] In contrast to "classical totalitarianism," which seeks to subordinate particularities to some transcendental end, e.g., the drive of reason in history or the destiny of a *Volk*, new totalitarianism obliterates transcendence altogether, and subjects every moment of presencing to a coercive logic always already attempting to totalize the range of its extension. The difference is decisive. Whereas appeals to transcendence in classical totalitarianism allow one, if only formally, to test their legitimacy, thus opening regimes to normative spheres which lie outside the naked power they wield, new totalitarianism denies the existence of an "outside" (or of alterity) altogether.

According to Arendt:

> The fundamental reason for the superiority of totalitarian propaganda over the propaganda of other parties and movements is that its content, for the members of the movement at any rate, is no longer an objective issue about which people may have opinions, but has become as real and untouchable an element in their lives as the rules of arithmetic. The organization of the entire texture of life according to an ideology can be fully carried out only under a totalitarian regime. In Nazi Germany, questioning the validity of racism and anti-Semitism when nothing mattered but race origin . . . was like questioning the existence of the world. (Arendt, 1958:363)

On the surface, this kind of self-evidence, one which protected Nazi racial theories from scrutiny, gives us an example of new totalitarianism at work. But certain facets of Arendt's account suggest that Nazism, at least on this analysis, failed to employ the wholesale immanence of new totalitarian politics. First, new totalitarian proclamations are not "propaganda." "Propaganda" connotes "lying," and this is precisely what does not occur under the conditions of new totalitarianism. Whereas Stalin routinely rewrote Russian history to suit his needs, new totalitarianism, under the supposed rigors of neo-positivist methodologies, purports to traffic in the real. In fact, I would even hesitate to refer to new totalitarian ideologies as "theories." "Theory" suggests a qualification at odds with the kind of purported necessity that organizes new totalitarian regimes. Established along positivist lines, they trade in facts, ever committed to a no-nonsense realism. As such, their "theories" are limited to inductive predications and thus, as the positivists would have it, they are practically devoid of theoretical content, content one might call into question or, in either a dialectical or deconstructive fashion, explore as the trace of an unacknowledged origin. As Adorno and Horkheimer would say: "Factuality is confirmed, cognition is restricted to its repetition, thought proceeds towards empty tautology. The more that this thought-machinery subjects a being to itself, the more blindly it contents itself with its reproduction" (Horkheimer, 1987:49).

Second, there is an ambiguity in Arendt's account. It isn't clear whether Germans refrained from questioning National Socialist racism because they took it to be true or considered it idle to oppose it. If the latter was the case, then what remained self-evident was not the truth of Nazi ideology but the fact that disagreement was pointless. Under conditions of new totalitarianism, however, reigning ideologies do not appeal to a cynical reality principle, stick in hand, but present themselves as reality itself. One has to reason to suppose, therefore, that forces like the secret police might prove anachronistic in a new totalitarian regime. In the face of what we take to be reality, we would police ourselves.

Because they speak from the standpoint of reality itself, new totalitarian regimes not only are able to perpetrate their occlusions and oppressions outside the official channels of recognition, but they are able to reduce Simic's dreambook to just that: mere dream, mere fancy. They are thus able to deny that poetry has access to what Simic insists the lyric can articulate: the truth in its singularity and radical indeterminacy, i.e., the world in its baffling presence. Under conditions of new totalitarianism, nothing is baffling, only inconvenient, only a set back for the prediction of the

557

day. One is thus denied even a peek past the walls erected as the demands of reality itself, although one can always daydream.

If it is proper to read Simic through analyses of "new totalitarianism," then poems like *White* assume political significance. Where new totalitarianism would erect walls of a *real* governed by necessity, those attentive to the White which underwrites all articulations hear only the winds of contingency. In other words, *White* makes plain that no system is ever compete unto itself, for those who attend to the origins of the sense it pretends to make, or rather, represent, will always find beneath totalitarian ground cover a white tooth grinning. To live in a world figured by Simic's *Ursprache* is thus to live in a world opposed to totalitarianism from the "ground" up. This may be why totalitarian regimes would keep us from the street corners where poems and poets convene. The threat is not simply posed by poems of agitation and protest, though so-called "committed" work may offer some measure of resistance. Rather, the challenge issues forth from that originary corner itself, its whiteness barely visible beneath the yellowing rubble. As the poet opens the white pages of his or her dreambook, thus exposing the indeterminate, silent origin lying at the bounds and grounds of sense, the closing dome of totalitarian rule is punctured, its claims to necessity thwarted by a sense of sense which refuses to render itself transparent to those who would transcribe the laws of the real. On the corner where poet and poetry meet, therefore, in that dream, *possibility*, in its most originary sense, is both preserved and exposed.

Besides interrupting the totalizing pretensions of totalitarian rule, Simic's *Ursprache* also returns us to the bursts of presence flailing beneath the thick canopies of what purports to be real. That is, it not only spans silent, white reaches of irrepressible possibility, but receives along those reaches whatever sense flashes: thumb, fern, lover, fir, and all that has yet to be named. Simic's *Ursprache*, beginning with *White*, thus cuts against the grain of totalitarianism in two ways: 1) by belying the totalizing pretensions of all tribal systems, and 2) by awakening us to the utter singularity of what the tribe would normalize, streamline, spit polish, and douse with its no-nonsense realism.[40]

Now, one should not exaggerate the import of an Ur-poetry's power to almost formally expose and thus transgress the limits of totalitarian systems of signification and incarceration. After all, rigorous, determinate negations of totalitarian rhetoric will neither topple walls nor halt the cruel swiftness of unconverted lead. But I would caution against underestimating the force of an event in language which can claim to address each and every instance of sense. True, the weave of Ur-poetry is not kevlar. Moreover, and this was apparent in *White*, the street corner where poem and poet meet can often point towards exile, that is, the possibilities which stir curbside may remain promissory, almost empty. One should know, then, that the street corner where poem and poet meet may lie on "Dream Avenue."

> *Monumental, millennial decrepitude,*
> *As tragedy requires. A broad*
> *Avenue with trash unswept,*
> *A few solitary speck-sized figures*
> *Going about their business*
> *In a world already smudged by a schoolboy's eraser.*
>
> *You've no idea what city this is,*
> *What country? It could be a dream,*
> *But is it yours? You're nothing*
> *But a vague sense of loss,*
> *A piercing, heart wrenching dread*
> *On an avenue with no name*
>
> *With a few figures conveniently small*
> *And blurred who in any case*
> *Have their backs to you*
> *As they look elsewhere, beyond*
> *The long row of gray buildings and their many windows,*
> *Some of which appear broken.* (Simic, 1994b:7)

Through its richness, a richness I will not treat with due respect, a central line runs through this poem. There are times when "All that is near . . ." (to recall *White*), disperses, leaving only a ". . . vague sense of loss . . ." along a *via negativa* of diminution, decay, abandonment, etc. To reach beyond what reigns as the *real* is therefore neither without risk nor a universal catalyst for reconstruction. In fact, one may grow bewildered, lose one's way, and in turning around and around, find only ". . . a few figures conveniently small/And blurred in any case/. . . their backs to you/As they look elsewhere . . ."

And yet, recall Rilke's "Archaic Torso of Apollo" from the second volume of his *New Poems*. It closes: ". . . for there is no point,/ which does not see you. You must change your life." My claim is that an *Ursprache* has that power. There is no nook or seam of sense in which to elude its reach. It lays claim, as Heidegger says, to the breadth of being. And if that claim insistently draws its readers back behind the ever thickening curtain of new totalitarianism, as is the case with Simic's *Ursprache*, then it will do so wherever its sense of sense washes ashore. Now, one may doubt others' ability to receive or engage such a claim, but one will have similar doubts with regard to any event in language. Such a risk is unavoid-able for those who stuff letters into bottles and hurl them towards the shorelines of the heart. However, if one's letter has the power to reach the ends of the cosmos, and in the most thorough way, I do not think that one can even begin to calculate where "it will all end" with Ur-poetry, even along "Dream Avenue."

Through questions concerning the force of history in the language of the poem, including the threats of totalitarianism, we are thickening Simic's *Ursprache*. Beside fateful, bursts of presence that fly out of a silent whiteness eluding signification, one finds historically bound, socio-political forces threatening to normalize or silence those bursts of presence. And yet, even as his work follows out these supervening narratives, fingering their limits, uncovering their seams, white threads frayed, Simic's corpus also accompanies those singular beings which bound through the cosmos and its histories. More precisely, Simic's poetry remains attuned to the fragility and even pain of what I called bursts of sense or events of presence, although I also could have termed them "lives."

Consider "History," from *Unending Blues*:[41]

> Men and women with kick-me signs on their
> backs.

Let's suppose he was sad and she was upset.
They got over it. The spring day bore a semblance
    to what they hoped.
Then came History. He was arrested and shot.

Do they speak in heroic couplets as he's dragged
    away looking over his shoulder?
A few words for that park statue with pigeons
    on it?
More likely she wipes her eyes and nose with a
    sleeve,
Asks for a stiff drink, takes her place in the
    breadline.

Then the children die of hunger, one by one.
Of course, there are too many cases for
    anyone to be underlining them with a red
    pencil.
Plus, the propensity of widows to flaunt their
    widowhood:
Coarse pubic hair, much bitten breasts.

History loves to see women cry, she whispers.
Their death makes Art, he shouts, naked.
How pretty are the coffins and instruments of
    torture
In the Museum on the day of free admission to
    the public! (Simic, 1986:15)

In order to gauge the force of this facet of Simic's *Ursprache*, we need to work our way into this scene. A couple quarrels. Perhaps he is drifting, incommunicado. The indulgence of it may be what angers her. But they "get over it." And between their own desires and the budding eroticism of Spring, what is and what is hoped for seem closer to one another. Something rare, no doubt, a time when time present is not only bound by the weight of time past, but, clock hand to our cheek, it pushes us towards a budding future.

Particularly in his more recent works, Simic draws our attention to moments when eros propels us towards something more than we had thought possible, or, more humbly, into moments of intense, ecstatic respite.[42] I want to consider one such poem, "Crazy About Her Shrimp," from A *Wedding in Hell* in order to see what might be at stake in these opening lines of "History." As I do so, keep in mind, however, that an Ur-poem plays over an entire corpus, and thus as we read "Crazy About Her Shrimp" into "History," so too must we read "History" back into "Crazy About Her Shrimp," that is, do not believe, for a minute, that the lovers of "Crazy About Her Shrimp" are somehow exempt from the fate unfolding in "History."

"Crazy About Her Shrimp" reads:

We don't even take time
To come up for air.
We keep our mouths full and busy
Eating bread and cheese
And smooching in between.

No sooner have we made love
Than we are back in the kitchen.
While I chop the hot peppers,
She wiggles her ass
And stirs the shrimp on the stove.

How good the wine tastes
That has run red
Out of a laughing mouth!
Down her chin
And onto her naked tits.

"I'm getting fat," she says,
Turning this way and that way
Before the mirror.
"I'm crazy about her shrimp!"
I shout to the gods above. (Simic, 1994b:40)

The drive of the poem is hard and plain: love, sex, they breed play, drive the everyday away, set us dancing in a kitchen, naked, and compel our voices (at least we males) to testify towards a heaven we might otherwise think sealed, deaf, uncaring.[43] As "History" opens, then, we should see eros assembling a day into something which bears a semblance to what we hope for: nakedness, laughter, pulls of pleasure, or even just the knowledge that this moment is one well shared. But: "Then came History." The man, nameless, is arrested, dragged away, shot. The children die, one by one. No one takes special notice. There have been so many, after all. And the wife? The mother? Also nameless, she 'flaunts her widowhood' as widows are wont to do, her "Coarse pubic hair, much bitten breasts"—the marks of one forced to barter with all that history has left her.

"Then came History." One might regard this as a personification: "History as ghastly visitor." But the poem does not present us with some character or figure named "History." Instead, the poem attends to the foreground and wake of History's arrival: mending love, promise, disaster. This poem thus refuses to turn history into an object and "History" into an instance of speculative inquiry. The refusal is instructive, for it suggests that one encounters "History," the ostensible subject of this poem, by turning one's gaze, with acumen and courage, into the paths it cuts through lives and hearts and hands. In contradistinction to Hegel's philosophical history, it thus seems that Simic is unwilling to find in this ". . . slaughter bench upon which the happiness of nations, the wisdom of states, and the virtues of individuals are sacrificed . . ." any supervening narrative, dialectical or otherwise (Hegel, 1988:24).

"Then came history." What is so unnerving about this line is its sudden arrival within a narrative just beginning to show promise. It is as if, like coastal weather, history can gather and strike without warning. And yet, this suddenness is accompanied by a matter of fact tone, suggesting that history may be unpredictable in its movements, but reliable with regard to the fact that it will arrive. When history strikes, therefore, we both have and do not have the right to be surprised. "A silent killer will come," we are told, "and no one will be prepared, and yet, one should have known. Such things happen all that time, after all. History is always in the wings." Benjamin has suggested that: "The tradition of the oppressed teaches us that the 'state of emergency' in which we live is not the exception but the rule. We must attain to a conception of history that is in keeping with this insight" (Benjamin, 1968:257). On my reading, Simic's *Ursprache* contributes to such a conception, and in an originary way, that is, it sets the threat of historical violence right at the rim of the White out of which all sense emerges.

But note how Simic also drapes the cruelty of history in dark comic plays of slapstick and sarcasm. "Men and women with kick-me signs on their/backs." There I am, there you are, loosening knots, stirring with Spring. "Then came History," sneaking up behind us. Does the crowd giggle? Perhaps I say, turning into my fate—Oh History . . . you're killing me, baby, just killing me. I read Simic's comic insistence in two ways. First, the apparent senseless-ness of history (and sense itself), seems to constantly farce what-ever narratives we wrap ourselves in.[44] As we account for ourselves and our fates, History sneaks up behind us, and as the sign requests, kicks. In other words, the arrival of sense is often marked with a wicked sense of timing—just killing me, baby. Second, humor defines in part what Heidegger would call the *Grundstimmung* of Simic's *Ursprache*, that is, the "fundamental attunement" charac-teristic of a poem's comportment towards what it poetizes.[45] Know-ing there is no answering the question "why me?" Simic's poetry quiets that desperation with a paradoxically knowing laugh of incredulity: ". . . she wipes her eyes and nose with a/sleeve/Asks for a stiff drink, takes her place in the/breadline."

One shouldn't overplay the stoic elements of Simic's comic bent, however. If it softens the blows of fate, it does without denying that fate nonetheless rains blows upon us, blows which sting, pul-verize, even annihilate. Simic's humor is thus far from jolly. Rather, it is cold, leathered, and profoundly sorrowful. I am thus tempted to say of Simic what Benjamin has written of Proust: "His style is comedy, not humor; his laughter does not toss the world up but flings it down—at the risk that it will be smashed to pieces, which will then make him burst into tears" (Benjamin, 1968:207). And my temptation is only strengthened when I read Simic telling Stanley Plumly and Wayne Dodd in 1972:

> Humor. Why humor? I guess when you think of classical com-edy, humor seems to be a temporary interruption of harmony. The audience knows better. I think in the twentieth century humor has become ontological. It's a permanent disruption, it's a world view, a philosophy of life" (Simic, 1985:19).

Simic's humor is thus not only not simply stoic, but its contrary, bent on undermining the utter matter of factness with which history's goon squads patrol our lives. As he writes in the more recent "Cut the Comedy." "It is impossible to imagine a Christian or fascist theory of humor. Like poetry, humor is subversive" (Simic, 1997:41).

Another aspect of "History" bears notice at this juncture. Beneath its humor, or rather, resounding along with it, a confession unfolds. Art cannot rescue those broken in and by history. Heroic couplets cannot accompany those who have been dragged off to die, or if they do, they will die all the same. And if history loves to see women cry, the realization fails to bring solace. In this instance, no amount of truth will set you free. And these limits apply to those who, like myself, risk aesthetizing disaster by engaging those works which document it. "How pretty are the coffins . . ." In other words, "History" denies that any narrative logic can account for the lost. Thus Simic's *Ursprache* not only presses one into history's wake, attesting to all that is lost within the ways and days of singular beings, but it also attempts to present misfortune in the integrity of its unredeemability, if one can speak of such a thing.

The farcical, often crippling force of historical fate so apparent in Simic's work doubles the silence documented in *White*. There, a white tooth grins, ironically, at a speaker who had sought what has always already arrived and persists only in traces. Within the folds of history, however, the grinning white tooth mocks those who ask: 'Why?' The point is not lost on Simic, whose *The World Doesn't End* begins precisely in that realization.

> *My mother was a braid of black smoke.*
> *She bore me swaddled over the burning cities.*
> *The sky was a vast and windy place for a child*
> to play.
> *We met others who were just like us.*
> *They were trying to put on their overcoats with*
> *arms made of smoke.*
> *The high heavens were full of little shrunken*
> *deaf ears instead of stars.* (Simic, 1989:3)

Note how far away this poem is from the stars sought and praised in *White*. Here they have turned into "little shrunken deaf ears." When the poet raises a glass, therefore, a poetic word in which to capture the shimmering stars, it may be that only an awful silence rings in its crystal bowl as coffins are arranged in the wake of yet another air-raid.[46]

IV. REPRISE

For asking, why is there something
Rather than nothing?
The schoolmaster sends the little punk
To see the Principal.

—Charles Simic, "The Childhood of Parmenides"
(Simic, 1982:18, lines 1–4)

Simic writes of Aleš Debeljak's work: "My sense while reading Debeljak is that this is what pondering one's life feels like in this waning century" (Simic, 1994:119). This is the sense I have reading Simic as I ponder the sense of sense. I find there an *Ursprache* that overdetermines the world around us, drawing it into registers well attuned to the fates and violences that swirl through the mundane and extraordinary alike. Again, the force of an *Ursprache* is not the force of a summoning. Its power is not one which fathoms the essential traits of things. Rather, it figures the "sense" of what can be said to be-there, of what is disclosed as something and not nothing. And with Simic, sense is figured in a threefold way.

On the one hand, Simic's *Ursprache* pushes us to the rim of sense itself, to the white limit upon which sense is scratched, fatefully, so that it shimmers around us, peering out of white shadows. His work pushes us to the white limit, which has always already baptized all our senses. "Take a letter: From cloud to onion," or from the sensible to sense itself, and "Say: There never was any choice." To move within Simic's *Ursprache* is thus to see shining in all things, e.g., thoughts, sentences, poems, twigs, trees, and seas, the emptiness of this White which cradles even as it sears us with bullet-like swiftness. To move within Simic's *Ursprache* is thus move ever towards a silent origin that cannot be cracked. As he writes at the end of *The World Doesn't End*:

MY SECRET IDENTITY IS

The room is empty,
  And the window open. (Simic, 1989:74)

Push inside us, inside sense itself, and regardless of one's reflexivity, one will find, ad infinitum, an empty room leading elsewhere. The origin of sense cannot be apprehended, although its traces are everywhere.

But Simic's *Ursprache* bears the marks of another hand as well, one callused and burned. That is, this *Ursprache* is far from univocal, but twists back and forth among registers. If Simic hears empty wind in his sleep, he also hears soldiers pounding at doors, nooses tightening, boots marching, and men and women turning their backs on other men and women being carted away. Simic's *Ursprache* thus not only drags each moment of presence back to the White out of which it was burped, a zero following another zero, but it also pulls back the sleeves of things, including the implements of writing itself, and calls our attention to the scars and scrapes that history has left upon them, to the threats which loom under tables and behind doors. It thus reminds us that those presences which hearken towards the White are not simple instantiations of some cosmological drama, traces lighting up the sky, fireworks gleaming. Rather, those fireworks are friends, neighbors, and enemies too, and when they burn, they burn. As Simic writes in "War," a poem from *Hotel Insomnia*:

> *The trembling finger of a woman*
> *Goes down the list of casualties*
> *On the evening of the first snow.*
>
> *The house is cold and the list is long.*
> *All our names are included.* (Simic, 1992b:26)

I cannot help but hear in "first snow" the White of the origin, although here I find an additional thought: as one wakes to ice paned windows, recall that casualties, including ourselves, have been etched there.

But the point isn't only that mortal things die on White days and nights, often unjustly, even without reason. Rather, the point is also that mortal beings, as orphans of silence, are born into seemingly endless contestations. Consider the revised version of "Spoon" (Simic, 1990b:35).

> An old spoon,
> Chewed,
> Licked clean,
>
> Polished back
> To its evil-eyed
> Glow,
>
> Eying you now
> From the table,
> Ready to scratch
> Today's date
> And your name
> On the bare wall.

First, note how human fragility is underscored. One (the poem addresses "you," the reader) finds oneself thrown into a barren situation: a table, a spoon. Now, a spoon is a tool, but this one looks back, evil-eyed.[47] In this house, then, surrounded by alien presences, we are far from masters. More concretely, the alien spoon is old, ready to scratch. But what? Perhaps it knows the day of our death, a day which may come soon given history's habit of stopping by unannounced. Or perhaps the spoon might scratch "On the bare wall" some forgotten lesson, some runes once legible upon its now worn surface.[48] Or perhaps this readiness to scratch simply attests to the way in which an exile or prisoner (the earlier version notes a "prison wall," not just a "bare wall"), must make sense of his or her sentence with whatever is at hand, even though instruments may have, as this spoon does, a life of their own, and a malevolent one at that.

Read generally, "Spoon" allegorically presents the fate of those who would record their time, fashion a name for themselves, or even author their own sentence. They must make do with what they have. More importantly, what they have may involve peril, and not just at the level of events to which they must respond. Even the implements of writing may be hostile, instantiating, therefore, a struggle within a struggle. "Spoon" thus crystallizes another central motif at work within Simic's *Ursprache*. Writing itself, these scratches of a spoon, the poems it might etch, are more than white whistles in the dark, although they are surely that. They are also multi-leveled struggles to make sense in a hostile world. Yes, beings suffer, but as they do, they also fight to scratch sense into the walls of a world lacking just that.

Few risk Simic's triple attunement: a) empty, white heavens, b) contesting histories, totalitarian violence, and c) the struggle of our embers to stay lit between mortal time's closing thumb and forefinger. Perhaps most recoil in the ironies which afflict one so attuned, for it is a strange thing to rage at an empty sky, history's soup preparing to boil:

> From inside the pot on the stove someone
> threatens the stars with a wooden spoon.
> Otherwise, cloudless calm. The shepherd's
> hour. (Simic, 1989:69)

Whereas the stars are courted in *White*, here, in *The World Doesn't End*, Simic scolds them, and yet, without self-righteousness or the didactic mania of the prophet. Running through Simic's *Ursprache* is thus a perpetual openness to the tensions which coil when one combines ontological sensitivity, historical perspicuity, and moral outrage within the truth telling and world figuring promise of the poetic word. No wonder Simic is forced, at times, to throw up his hands. "What a mess! I believe in images as vehicles of transcendence, but I don't believe in God!" (Simic, 1990c:92).[49] But then what else is one to do? As Simic notes: "The death of God, you may say, is no big deal if everybody behaves well, but once the slaughter of the innocent starts, how do you catch any sleep at night?" (Simic, 1997:75).

This willingness to venture towards the vanguard of what currently passes for ontological, historical-political, and moral consciousness, and this willingness to embody, without sanctimony, the tensions which arise at the edges of that foreground, that is what marks Simic as the kind of poet Heidegger termed " a poet in a time of need," a title he reserved for Hölderlin. Creeping about the double silences of a twilight blanketed in white smoke, Simic's *Ursprache* enables us to attend equally to: a) the fateful whiteness of a luck which gives him the poetic word and opens his work (and its readers) to sense itself, b) the black booted march of a history that could easily crush even our passing snowflakes of illumination, and c) cries of desire and despair in the grayness that lies in between. Such power is remarkable beyond my esteem. Where else can one witness being itself, thrown open, such that the presenc-ing of presence, even in its withdrawal, rings whitely through its silences? And where else will one also be drawn back from what truly are the furthest reaches of the cosmos into the realization that poetry is, to turn again to *White:*

> A song in prison
> And for prisoners,
>
> Made of what the condemned
> Have hidden from their jailers. (lines 141–144)

And then, where else will the cries of the erotically lit and/or his-torically broken still echo in the barbed wire mobile swinging above our empty cradle? If it still makes sense to turn to poets in times of need and distress (and I think it does, having tried to out-line what such a turn involves), I would have us turn to Simic. Let us hope that no one comes and takes away his spoon.

Bibliography

Akhmatova, Anna. *The Complete Poems of Anna Akhmatova*. Boston: Zephyr Press, 1992.

Arendt, Hannah. *The Origins of Totalitarianism*. Cleveland: The World Publishing Company, 1958.

Benjamin, Walter. *Illuminations*. New York: Schocken Books, 1968.

Bóve, Paul. *Destructive Poetics*. New York: Columbia University Press, 1980.

Celan, Paul. *Gesammelte Werke in fünf Bänden: Dritter Band*. Frankfurt am Main: Suhrkamp Verlag, 1983.

Fóti, Véronique. *Heidegger and the Poets: Poesis, Techne, Sophia*. Atlantic Highlands: Humanities Press International, Inc., 1992.

Hart, Kevin. "Writing Things: Literary Property in Heidegger and Simic." *New Literary History* (fall, 1989): 199–214.

Hegel, G. W. F. *Introduction to the Philosophy of History*. Indianapolis: Hackett Publishing Co., 1988.

Heidegger, Martin. *Holzwege*. Frankfurt am Main: Vittorio Klostermann, 1950.

———. *Vortraege und Aufsaetze*. Pfullingen: Verlag Günther Neske, 1954.

———. *Unterwegs zur Sprache*. Pfullingen: Verlag Günther Neske, 1959.

———. *Erläuterungen zu Hölderlins Dichtung*. Frankfurt am Main: Klostermann, 1971.

———. *Prolegomena zur Geschichte des Zeitbegriffs*. Frankfurt am Main: Klostermann, 1979.

———. *Hölderlins Hymnen »Germanien« und »Der Rhein«*. Frankfurt am Main: Klostermann, 1980.

———. *Hölderlins Hymne »Andenken«*. Frankfurt am Main: Klostermann, 1982.

———. *Hölderlins Hymne »Der Ister«*. Frankfurt am Main: Klostermann, 1984.

Horkheimer, Max. *Gesammelte Schriften Band 5: ›Dialectic der Aufklärung‹ und Schriften 1940–1950*. Frankfurt am Main: Fischer Verlag GmbH, 1987.

Jackson, Richard. "Charles Simic and Mark Strand: The Presence of Absence." *Contemporary Literature*, Vol. XXI, No. 1 (1980): 136–145.

Koch, Kenneth. "The Language of Poetry." *New York Review of Books*, Vol. XLV, No. 8 (May 14, 1998): 44–47.

Kushner, Alexander. *Apollo in the Snow: Selected Poems*. Translated by Paul Graves and Carol Ueland with an Introduction by Joseph Brodsky. New York: Farrar, Straus and Giroux, 1991.

Lacoue-Labarthe, Phillipe and Jean Luc-Nancy. *Retreating the Political*. London: Routledge, 1997.

McClatchy, J.D. "Figures in the Landscape." *Poetry*, Vol. CXXXVIII, No. 4 (July 1981): 231–241.

Milosz, Czeslaw. *The Witness of Poetry*. Cambridge: Harvard University Press, 1983.

Muratori, Fred. "Review of *White: A New Version*." *Northwest Review 22*, No. 3 (1984): 121–125.

Nancy, Jean-Luc. *The Inoperative Community*. Minneapolis: University of Minnesota Press, 1991.

———. *The Experience of Freedom*. Stanford: Stanford University Press, 1993.

Orlich, Ileana A. "The Poet on A Roll: Charles Simic's 'The Tomb of Stéphane Mallarmé'." *The Centennial Review*, Vol. XXXVI, No. 2 (spring 1992): 413–428.

Rainer Maria Rilke. *Sämtliche Werke in Zwölf Bänden: Band 2*. Frankfurt: Insel Verlag, 1955–66.

Simic, Charles. *What the Grass Says*. San Francisco: Kayak, 1967.

———. *Dismantling The Silence*. New York: Braziller, 1971.

———. *Return to Place Lit by a Glass of Milk*. New York: Braziller, 1974.

———. *Charon's Cosmology*. New York: Braziller, 1977.

———. *Classic Ballroom Dances*. New York: Braziller, 1980.

———. *Austerities*. New York: Braziller, 1982.

———. *Weather Forecast for Utopia and Other Vicinities*. Barrytown, New York, 1983.

———. *The Uncertain Certainty*. Ann Arbor: The University of Michigan Press, 1985.

———. *Unending Blues*. San Diego: Harcourt Brace, 1986.

———. *The World Doesn't End*. San Diego: Harcourt Brace, 1989.

———. *The Book of Gods and Devils*. San Diego: Harcourt Brace, 1990.

———. *Selected Poems, 1963–1983: Revised and Expanded*. New York: Braziller, 1990b.

———. *Wonderful Worlds, Silent Truths*. Ann Arbor: The University of Michigan Press, 1990c.

———. *Dime Store Alchemy: The Art of Joseph Cornell*. Hopewell, New Jersey: Ecco Press, 1992.

———. *Hotel Insomnia*. San Diego: Harcourt Brace, 1992b.

———. *The Unemployed Fortune Teller*. Ann Arbor: The University of Michigan Press, 1994.

———. *A Wedding in Hell*. New York: Harcourt Brace, 1994b.

———. *Walking the Black Cat*. New York: Harcourt Brace, 1996.

———. *Orphan Factory*. Ann Arbor: The University of Michigan Press, 1997.

———. *Selected Early Poems*. New York: Braziller, 1999.

Stevens, Wallace. *The Palm at the End of the Mind*. New York: Random House, 1971.

Weigel, Bruce. *Charles Simic: Essays on the Poetry*. Ann Arbor: The University of Michigan Press, 1996.

Endnotes

1 Two years later, Heidegger will repeat his assertion in "Hölderlin and the Essence of Poetry" (Heidegger, 1971:35). All translations are my own, unless otherwise noted.

2 I must stress, at the outset, that my question here is not psychological. I am not interested in addressing questions concerning the power of so-called aesthetic experience over the perceptions or personalities of subjects. Rather, I want to explore the nature of what one accepts when one says yes to a work of art which claims "you must change your life."

3 This is not to say that Heidegger would be able to appreciate all that comes to pass within Simic's work. But I will forego any detailed discussions of where Simic's work might elude Heidegger's ear in the interest of focusing upon Simic's accomplishments.

4 As far as I know, Kevin Hart is the only one who has expressly compared the two. Although more a treatment of Simic's work than a reading of Heidegger's, I found his essay helpful (Hart, 1992).

5 Few read Heidegger in this way, exceptions being Véronique Fóti, who reads Heidegger and Celan together, suggesting that Heidegger lacks ears for Celan's poetics of mourning, loss, and response, and Paul Bové, who reads Heideggerian concerns into Whitman, Stevens, and Olson (Bóve, 1980; Fóti, 1992:78–110). Perhaps many, like Robert Bernasconi, believe that Heidegger's work with poetry is inextricably bound to his nationalism, as if only *German* poets could found human dwelling. I am unconvinced, however, that Heidegger's account of poetic building and dwelling *requires* a German poet. True, he treats the trope *Vaterland* as signifying *das Seyn selbst* in 1934 (Heidegger, 1980:121). But as the lecture unfolds, it is unclear whether this renders *Seyn* German or opens '*Vaterland*' to the ungroundable event of its own formation. I think both emphases are at work here, and thus it seems mistaken to seek the 'real' Heidegger. A more fruitful tack involves bringing those elements of Heidegger's thought which escape and even counteract nationalism into new arenas while noting that his dialogue with the poets was in fact infected with the Greco-German mania that Bernasconi documents (Bernasconi, 1993:135–148).

6 References to Heidegger can be found throughout Simic's prose, e.g., Simic, 1985:62,118; 1990c:63–66,68,104,106; 1994:102–103; and Weigel, 1996:210. Richard Jackson has employed Heidegger in a review of Simic and Strand, but he does so without seriously engaging Heidegger, invoking, without distinction, thinkers whose differences are as great as their similarities, e.g., Heidegger, Lacan, Derrida, and Foucault (Jackson, 1980:136–145).

7 Heidegger would insist that we not equate an *Ursprache* with the contours of transcendental subjectivity, however, and thus the analogy with Kant has its limits. Rather, the *Ursprache* is truly *ursprünglich*, "originary," and thus not the production of some primal Ur-agency.

8   That Heidegger takes the fourfold from Hölderlin is evident from the 1951 address, "Poetically Man Dwells," where he draws the figure's four elements from a reading of Hölderlin's late, cryptic poem *"In lieblicher Bläue"* (Heidegger, 1954:181–198).

9   Now, it isn't the case that without the fourfold, significance would be lacking. According to Heidegger, other constellations currently provide alternative *Ursprachen*, most notably, modern technology with its "standing-reserve," a horizon of disclosure which organizes things along elemental and sub-atomic lines, or, more specifically, in terms of constitutive parts believed to be useful.

10 These examples are taken from "The Thing," "Poetically Man Dwells," and "Building, Dwelling, Thinking," respectively (Heidegger,1954:157–180,181–198, 139–158).

11 Shortly, we will explore what Heidegger means by *bauen*, "building." For now, let us not equate building with human production, but regard all instances of human production as parasitic upon building.

12 It is important to recall that Heidegger does not understand *Wesen*, "essence," as a series of traits that outline the necessary and sufficient conditions for some *x*, for example, a poem. Instead, Heidegger treats *Wesen* as the substantive form of the verb to be. When Heidegger speaks of essence, therefore, one should think of how a being comes to presence, of those factors that enable its presencing and thus are archaic in an almost literal sense.

13 Heidegger thus writes of the fourfold in "Building, Dwelling, Thinking": "From the fourfold, building takes over measures for all traversing and every measuring-out of the spaces that in each case are furnished through the founded sites" (Heidegger, 1954:153). In other words, poetic measures not only wrap the whole in their economies of presence, but overdetermine emergent sites of human activity and belief as well. This is not to say, however, that an *Ursprache* only engages human activities. After all, disclosures of non-human events/things (e.g., roses, three-toed sloths, and asteroids) are themselves bound to economies of presence, for example, the "natural world," "space," etc. They are manifest, therefore, already within an *Ursprache*, or, to use the language of *Being and Time*, they are disclosed already within a world.

14 We should add here that Heidegger denies independent existence to the fourfold, as if hovered above beings and granted them shape. Rather, the two are bound to one another. The fourfold presences through beings even while beings presence within the fourfold. We shall have more to say about the reciprocity between an *Ursprache* and the beings it founds.

15 When Heidegger claims that dwelling requires building, he has in mind the kind of building which only poetry brings about. "But dwelling happens only if poetizing takes-place and comes to pass, and indeed in the way of . . . the measure-taking for all measuring. This measure-taking is itself the most proper, not a bare gauging with ready-made yard-sticks for the preparation of maps. Likewise, poetizing is not building in the sense of raising and fitting buildings. Rather, poetiz-

574

ing, as the most proper appraisal of the dimension of dwelling, is inceptual building. Before anything else, poetizing admits the dwelling of human beings into its *Wesen*. Poetizing is the originary allowance-of-dwelling" (Heidegger, 1954:196).

16 I think this is why Heidegger insists, when reading Rilke, that a poet in a time of need must poetize the *Wesen*, the essence of poetry, claiming that: "Where that happens, one can assume that there lies a poetic way that sends itself into the fate of the world-age" (Heidegger, 1950:268).

17 For a more thorough reckoning with Heidegger's understanding of how poetic building engages Being, and how that engagement drives poetic dwelling, see my "Heidegger's Absolute Music, or, What Are Poets For When the End of Metaphysics is at Hand?" (*Research in Phenomenology*, Vol. XXX [2000]: 180–210).

18 *White* has a complex editorial history. First published in 1972, adorned by Simic's own illustrations and a handful of typographical errors, it was revised and reissued in 1980 sans artwork (Simic, 1972; Simic, 1980). While the 1980 version was reprinted in *Selected Poems: 1963–1983*, yet a third version has recently appeared in *Selected Early Poems* (Simic, 1990b; Simic, 1999). Because each version is different to the point of having a character all its own, I think that, despite certain repetitions, each should be regarded as an individual poem and not dissolved into a series of textual variants. Presuming the singularity of each, I have decided to focus upon the second *White*, leaving for future labor a careful comparison of the three.

19 As Fred Muratori muses in a review of *White: A New Version*: "Why would this particular poem, already published, continue to obsess its author for so long? Perhaps because *White* confronts . . . the creation of poetry itself . . ." (Muratori, 1984:122).

20 Although he isn't speaking of *White*, I share Richard Howard's appreciation for Simic's 'originality': "When we speak of writing as *original*, as I am bound and determined to do in speaking of Charles Simic's writing . . . , we mean that it has to do with something very old, not something very new—it has to do with origins, beginnings, sources" (Simic, 1971:xii). And it is my respect for this kind of originality which leaves me distraught when a poet of Kenneth Koch's caliber claims, insipidly: "Ordinary language is of course where the language of poetry comes from. It has the words, the usages, the sounds that a poem takes up and makes its own. It constitutes, along with thoughts and feelings, what may be called the raw materials of poetry" (Koch, 1998:45). I take it that tropes like "ordinary language," "thoughts," and "feelings" mark the points from where poets like Simic and philosophers like Heidegger begin to reflect.

21 Later, the speaker repeats his request for words, and even terms the bride a vowel (lines 53&59). And still later, the speaker seeks her again with "Five ears of my fingertips/Against the white page," as if one must first hear her if one is to fill a page with words (lines 93–4).

22 Peter Schmidt claims that the speaker is here engaged in an imaginary dialogue with the White (Weigel, 1996:28). Perhaps, but I don't know how we would

determine whether that were so. What seems certain, however, is that the speaker is preparing himself as a sacrificial meal for his bride to be, hence the mocking use of "sweetheart" and "loverboy" in his questions (lines 103&105).

23   Recall that it was in virtue of having a mind of winter, of renunciation, that the listener in Stevens's poem, being "nothing himself," is able to behold "Nothing that is not there and the nothing that is" (Stevens, 1971:54, lines 13–15).

24   In poems from *Hotel Insomnia* and *A Wedding in Hell*, insomnia invokes the posture of waiting for a something or someone that may never arrive (Simic, 1992b:2; Simic, 1994b:29). Likewise, "Dead Letter Office" from *Charon's Cosmology* depicts a "Dream penitentiary/Without doors or windows," an impregnable repository for lost greetings, wishes, and solicitations (Simic, 1977:29, lines 5–6).

25   Other, equally vacuous images of the White were thus more appropriate than the speaker had imagined, e.g., the vowel 'O' and the "holy nothing" (lines 59–60 & 96). Incidentally, Simic returns to the idea of writing as "A zero burped by/ Another zero . . ." in "Figuring," from *Weather Forecast for Utopia* (Simic, 1990b:177–78, lines 1–2).

26   Of the riddle, Simic says in reference to the work of Vasko Popa: "In the riddle the word truly becomes *mythos*, becomes the place of origins" (Simic, 1985:94).

27   In "A Clear and Open Place," Simic writes: "The experience of consciousness, however, precedes thinking; thinking derives from it. For Husserl, for example, the living present is the ultimate, universal and absolute form of transcendental experience" (Simic, 1985:109). This is somewhat odd given that Simic elsewhere claims that part of Heidegger's appeal is precisely his attack on subjectivism (Simic, 1990c:63).

28   This view is not limited to the 1970s, however. In a more recent essay, "Poetry and Experience," he writes: "The experience of being eludes language. We need imagination because the presentness of the present moment cannot be worded except through poetic image. Consciousness is mute" (Simic, 1997:39).

29   One can find this critique in the third chapter, §§ 10–13, of the "Preliminary Part" of the lecture course entitled *Prolegomena zur Geschichte des Zeitbegriffs* (Heidegger, 1979).

30   Simic seems better off in an aphorism from *Wonderful World, Silent Truth*: "A metaphysics without a self and without a God! Is that what you want Simic?" (Simic, 1990c:94).

31   Interestingly, I am asking Simic to do precisely the opposite of what Helen Vendler has requested. She is uncomfortable with his references to the spectral and metaphysical, because she views poems as one facet of ordinary human activity. "Poems, like all human fabrications, from straw huts to theology, are made to our measure and by our measure, and are not above or beyond us. We do not need to ascribe more to art than we ascribe to unaided human powers elsewhere" (Weigel, 1996:131). In a certain way, I agree. Poems, like straw huts, emerge out of the scene of human dwelling, and thus partake of all that is in force within that dimension. And yet, Vendler takes the dimension of human dwelling to be some-

thing that "empirical critics," folks who evidently eschew the metaphysical and spectral, are best suited to explore. With this commitment, I couldn't agree less, assuming that her empiricism is anything like the empiricism which occasionally recrudesces in philosophical circles. Empiricism routinely appeals to something like "experience" in order to explain matters or settle disputes, e.g., to sensory experience or experience under the controlled conditions of revisionist scientific inquiry. In debates about originary matters, however, (i.e., any matter having to do with the nature of some *x*), such appeals are specious, for it is precisely the nature of experience which marks the initial point of inquiry, and this has been the case at least since Kant. But then I don't think Simic needs to be reminded of the limits of empiricism. That "experience" itself is part and parcel of the riddle seems quite evident to him.

32 This is not to say that Heidegger himself understood the task of an *Ursprache* to involve a defense of the singularity of presencing. In fact, his persistent invocation of the *Volk*, in "The Origin of the Work of Art" for example, suggests that he was more interested in the singularity of a people than any given person or event of presence (Heidegger, 1950:63). However, there is nothing about the notion of the *Ursprache* which compels us to believe that it addresses itself to a "people." That seems rather to be the result of Heidegger's provincial (and Hegelian) obsession with an ethically seamless state. One can thus speak of Simic's *Ursprache*, release it from the confines of a philosophy of consciousness, and still applaud and account for his concern with singular presencing.

33 One finds precisely this line of argument in the work of Jean-Luc Nancy, most notably in *The Inoperative Community* and *The Experience of Freedom*. For a discussion of the kind of politics which arises out of this perspective, one which owes much to Heidegger but does not share his affection for the totalized state, see my essay "On What Is to Be Done With What Is Always Already Arriving" (*Studies in Practical Philosophy*, Vol. 1, No. 1 [1999]: 86–113).

34 Simic finds the "Nature" of much contemporary literature too pastoral a trope to take seriously. When he does take Nature seriously, I think he is drawn to its inarticulate stoniness, not its supposed rhapsodic harmonies. In an interview from 1980, he says: "A stone is the uttermost limit; there's nothing beyond stone. . . . Stone is so alien to us, distant from us, any attempt to speak across that distance is interesting." (Simic, 1985:52–3) One should also consult "Stone" and "Stone Inside a Stone" from *Dismantling the Silence*, as well as the fifteenth poem of Part 1 in *The World Doesn't End*. (Simic, 1971:59–61; 1989:17)

35 One sees Simic's concern with this kind of reporting in "The Flute Player in the Pit": ". . . one wishes to say something about the age in which one lives. Every age has its injustices and immense sufferings, and ours is scarcely an exception. There's the history of human vileness to contend with and there are fresh instances of it every day to think about. One can think about it all one wants, but making sense of it is another matter" (Simic, 1994:2).

36 I would thus suggest that while "Poem Without A Title" does recall Akhmatova's

relentless poem of witness, *Poem Without A Hero*, it also broaches a fate where poetry is not simply repressed, but almost impossible, that is, unable to twist free of a history and language which conspires to return it, almost immediately, to the fate it would condemn and transform.

37   Interestingly, Simic believes that Heidegger fails to appreciate how history contests itself within the language of the poem. In "Notes on Poetry and Philosophy," he writes: "Mallarmé thought there were two kinds of language: *parole brute*, which names things, and *parole essentielle*, which distances us from things. One serves representation and the other the allusive, fictive world of poetry. He's wrong. It's not that clear cut. If anything, it is both. Poetry is impure. I don't think Heidegger understands this either" (Simic, 1990b:68). Some scholars, notably Véronique Fóti, agree with Simic's assessment of Heidegger. In Chapters Four and Seven of her *Heidegger and the Poets*, she argues that Heidegger loses the contestations and singularities of ontic history within his "onto-history," an account of how the West has figured Being since the Greeks. In a way, she is right. For example, Heidegger often hears in Rilke the tropes of Descartes, Pascal, and Nietzsche (Heidegger, 1950:301–02 & 398 and 1982b:235). But this is not to say that Heidegger has no ear for how the language of the poem is a site of historical contestation. Rather, it proves that his readings are very much attuned to such contestations. In the case of Rilke, however, he believes that the history of modernity is too strong for Rilke's language of the heart, open, angels, lovers, Orpheus, etc., that despite Rilke's efforts, his work remains trapped within modernity's orbit. Not that I agree with Heidegger's reading, but it seems wrong to say that he exempts the language of the poem from the wheels of history. In fact, the Epilogue to "The Origin of the Work of Art" takes very seriously the question of art's ability to disclose truth in the present age (Heidegger, 1950:65). Is this to say that Simic and Fóti are wrong to be troubled by Heidegger's sense for the role history plays within the language of the poem? No, but I do think that the issue here concerns a full-flown theory of history, a debate about where and how the real contestations of history take place. And while that is a real debate, and one that Simic's *Ursprache* initiates despite its obvious sympathies with Heidegger, I cannot pursue it here. For Simic's relation to Mallarmé, see his "The Tomb of Stéphane Mallarmé," and Ileana Orlich. "The Poet on a Roll: Charles Simic's 'The Tomb of Stéphane Mallarmé'" (Simic, 1980:61–2 & Orlich, 1992)

38   Concerns over historical contestation lie at the heart of Adorno's aesthetics. For discussions of such matters, see my: "Between Impotence and Illusion: Adorno's Art of Theory and Practice," co-authored with Michael Sullivan (*New German Critique*, No. 57, Fall 1992: 87–122), and the forthcoming "Binding the Beautiful: Art as Criticism in Adorno and Dewey" (*Journal of Speculative Philosophy*, Vol. 12, No. 4 [1998]: 233–244).

39   One can find a basic analysis of "new totalitarianism" in their "The 'Retreat' of the Political" (Lacoue-Labarthe & Nancy, 1997:126–28).

40   Before long, it will be time to gather, distinguish, and evaluate the various responses

to our century of disaster. Given the range of work associated with the poetics of witness, e.g., Akhmatova, Celan, Forché, Milosz, the various ways in which theoreticians have explored the work of memory, counter-memory, and mourning, e.g., Benjamin, Blanchot, Foucault, and then responses like Simic's which bear witness from the recesses of oblique angels but strike at totalitarianism nevertheless, one should not suppose that a univocal front exists. In fact, significant differences separate several of these figures, differences which may prove incompatible. For example, throughout his Norton Lectures, Milosz maintains a longing for the creation of a "great human family," something unimaginable in the work of Simic or Nancy, whatever their own differences (Milosz, 1983:31&15). A comparative yet argumentative study might prove useful, therefore, for those who would carry this work into the next century. Unfortunately, I cannot take this matter up here.

41 Simic has written several poems either entitled "History" or having "History" in the title, for example: Simic, 1982:13; 1983:20; 1992b:42; 1994b:55–6.

42 In *Walking the Black Cat*, Simic explicitly sets the power of eros within the historical landscape it no doubt remains oblivious to while passion pulses and pants are cast aside. "Shadow Publishing Company" opens with a couple strolling in a world of their own. It closes: "Lying there, closing one's eyes in revery,/A figment among figments/Living one of their blessed moments/Without recognizing the century,/Only the scent of the lilacs on the pillow" (Simic, 1996: 11–12, lines 26–30).

43 The poem is complicated by the fact that the woman is not opened up to heaven by the event, but to a mirror which convicts her of failing to maintain an ideal of sorts, and a sinister one at that. I cannot address this matter here, however.

44 These farcical elements are complemented by Simic's often remarked upon debt to surrealism. The images in Simic's poems seem to stare at us from the most unusual places: storefronts, street corners, tree limbs, mannequins, aunts, silverware, etc. But then, this is how history unfolds: through chance meetings, uncanny coincidences, and unfortunate cases of right time right place for disaster. J. D. McClatchy fails to appreciate this in his review of *Classic Ballroom Dances*. He complains of what he calls the ". . . drabbest kind of automatic writing," and hopes that in the future, Simic will pursue "fresher" paths (McClatchy, 1981:235). But this is to suppose that Simic's "surrealism" (McClatchy employs the term), were some abstract technique rather than a formal aspect of his relentless attempt to expose the truth of our cosmological and historical predicament.

45 One finds this language of the *Grundstimmung* in the first Hölderlin lecture course (Heidegger, 1980).

46 I think one would be hard pressed to find a similar attunement to suffering in the thought of Heidegger, although I cannot argue the point here. In order to pursue the claim, one would have to consider the remarks on *dike* in the Anaximander fragment, the remarks on how to regard a fallen *Geschlecht* in the reading of Trakl, and the rhetoric of "essential sacrifice" in "The Origin of the Work of Art" (Heidegger, 1950:317–168; 1959:37–82; 1950:1–72).

579

47 In the earlier version from *Dismantling the Silence*, the speaker suggests that this spoon has in fact eaten him or her and become a living thing in its own right (Simic, 1971:54, lines 5–9).

48 Simic tells a similar tale in "Knife," writing of "crooked letters" and "mysterious writings," signs which lead a "We" under the earth through dimly lit corridors of geological time (Simic, 1990b:36, lines 15&16).

49 One can find a similar remark in "Charles the Obscure" (Simic, 1997:19). These disavowals retract Simic's faithful testament in 1972: "But then I don't mind admitting that I believe in God" (Simic, 1985:6).

I would like to thank Garrett Hongo for his comments on an earlier draft, Rebecca Szekely for introducing me to the work of Charles Simic, and the many students with whom I've studied Simic's poems. I would also like to dedicate this essay to Dallas Mayberry in memory of the five years (1991–1996) we spent filling the Nashville airwaves with puns, pranks, and most importantly, poems.

Timothy Liu

Looking West

What are those magpies doing over there
picking up crusts I've scattered in the field
only to stack them neatly by that well
filled up with cement? All of it
done without a thought as a black ant
paddles in the toilet bowl, mesmerizing
the cat. So many books I'll never read—
a dusty weight making the bookshelves sag.

and Giroux. His collection *Of No Country I Know: New and Selected Poems* (University of Chicago Press, 1999) won the 2000 Lenore Marshall Prize of the Academy of American Poets and the *Nation* magazine and the 2000 Rebekah Johnson Bobbitt National Prize for Poetry of the Library of Congress. **Tess Gallagher**'s most recent books are the essay collection, *Soul Barnacles* (University of Michigan Press, 2000), her story collection, *At the Owl Woman Saloon* (Simon & Schuster, 1999), *Portable Kisses* (1996) and *My Black Horse: New and Selected Poems* both by Bloodaxe/Dufour Editions. Her current project is *The Courtship Stories with Josie Gray*. **Sandra M. Gilbert**'s most recent publications include *Kissing the Bread: New and Selected Poems 1969–1999* (Norton, 2000) and *Interventions of Farewell: A Book of Elegies* (Norton, 2001). She is working on a book titled *Death's Door*. **Gail Godwin**'s most recent books are *Evensong* (Random House, 1999) and *Heart: A Personal Journey through Its Myth and Meanings* (William Morrow & Co., 2001). **Eamon Grennan**'s most recent collection is *Relations: New and Selected Poems* (Graywolf Press, 1998). His volume of translations, *Leopardi: Selected Poems*, won the PEN Award for Poetry in Translation. A collection of his essays, *Facing the Music: Irish Poetry in the Twentieth Century*, was published in 1999 by Creighton University Press. **Allen Grossman**'s most recent book of poetry is *How to Do Nice Things with Tears* (New Directions, 2001). He is also the author of *The Long Schoolroom: Lessons in the Bitter Logic of Poetic Principle* (University of Michigan Press, 1997). **Marilyn Hacker** is the author of nine books, including *Presentation Piece*, which received the National Book Award in 1975, *Winter Numbers*, which received a Lambda Literary Award and

the Lenore Marshall Award of the *Nation* and the Academy of American Poets, both in 1995. Her most recent book is *Squares and Courtyards* (Norton, 2000). She has been editor of the *Kenyon Review*. She is director of the MA program in English literature and creative writing at City College in New York. **Kristin Hennessy** lives in Paris, France. This is her first published translation. **Brian Henry**'s first book of poetry, *Astronaut* (Arc, 2000), was a finalist for the Forward Prize in England. He is an editor of *Verse* and recently founded Verse Press. He teaches at the University of Georgia. **Andrew Hudgins** is a Distinguished Research Professor and professor of English at the University of Cincinnati. His most recent books are *Babylon in a Jar* (Houghton Mifflin, 1998) and *The Glass Anvil* (University of Michigan Press, 1997). **Cynthia Huntington**'s most recent book is *The Salt House* (University Press of New England, 1999). She directs the program in creative writing at Dartmouth College. **Mark Irwin**'s poems have appeared in *APR*, the *Atlantic*, *Antaeus*, the *Nation*, the *Paris Review* and *New England Review*, among others. His fourth collection, *White City* (BOA Editions, 2000). He teaches at the University of Colorado at Boulder. **Greg Johnson** is the author of three volumes of stories in addition to the books *Pagan Babies* (Dutton, 1993) and *Invisible Writer: A Biography of Joyce Carol Oates* (Dutton, 1988). His new novel, *Among the Living*, will be published this year. He teaches in the graduate writing program at Kennesaw State University. **Jesse Lee Kercheval** is the author of a poetry collection, *World as Dictionary* (Carnegie Mellon University Press, 1999), as well as four books of prose, including *Space* (Algonquin/Penguin, 1999), a memoir about growing up

Council grant and the Pushcart prize. She currently is an artist-in-residence at Columbia College Chicago. **Dean Shavit** is a computer consultant and editor of the online literary journal *Valence*. He received his MA in creative writing from the University of Illinois Chicago. **Reginald Shepherd**'s third book is *Wrong* (University of Pittsburgh Press, 1999). He teaches at Cornell University. **Tom Sleigh**'s books of poetry include *After One* (Houghton Mifflin, 1983), *Waking* (University of Chicago Press, 1990), *The Chain* (University of Chicago Press, 1996) and *The Dreamhouse* (University of Chicago Press, 1999). His translation of Euripides' *Herakles* has recently been published by the University of Oxford Press. **Sharon Solwitz**'s story collection *Blood and Milk* (Sarabande, 1997) won the Carl Sandburg and Society of Midland Authors awards and was runner up for the National Jewish Book Award. She teaches creative writing at Purdue University. **Gary Soto** is the author of thirty books for young people and adults, including *Living Up the Street, Junior College, Nickel and Dime* and *Chato's Kitchen*. His most recent novel is *Poetry Lover*. His novel *Buried Onions* has been adapted for a feature film to be released in the summer of 2002. **Virgil Suárez** teaches at Florida State University. He is the author of fifteen books of poetry and prose, including *Palm Crows*, due out this year from University of Arizona Press. **Ryan G. Van Cleave** is a freelance photojournalist originally from Chicago. He is the editor of *Sundog: The Southeast Review* and serves as coordinator for the annual "World's Best Short Short Story" competition. His recent books are *Say Hello* (Pecan Grove Press, 2000) and the anthology *American Diaspora: Poetry of Exile* (University of Iowa Press, 2001).

David Wagoner's most recent book, *Traveling Light: Collected and New Poems* (University of Illinois Press, 1999), won the William Stafford Memorial Award from Pacific Northwest Booksellers. He edits *Poetry Northwest* for the University of Washington. **Charles Harper Webb**'s most recent book, *Liver* (University of Wisconsin Press, 1999), won the Felix Pollak Prize. He also received the S.F. Morse Poetry Prize, the Kate Tuffs Discovery Award and a Whiting Writers award. He teaches at California State University at Long Beach. **Joshua Weiner** is the author of the poetry collection *The World's Room* (Chicago, 2001). He teaches at Northwestern University. **Robert Whittaker** is coeditor of Russian editions of the correspondence between Leo Tolstoy and Americans and of the letters of the nineteenth-century poet and critic Apollon Grigoriev (Nauka, 1999), and is the author of a biography of Grigoriev, *Russia's Last Romantic* (Edwin Mellen Press, 1999). **Alan Williamson**'s most recent book of poems is *Res Publica* (University of Chicago Press, 1998). He teaches at the University of California Davis. **Mark Winegardner** is the author of five books, most recently *Crooked River Burning* (Harcourt Brace, 2001). His stories have appeared in *Double Take*, *Playboy*, *GQ*, and *Esquire*. **Mark Wisniewski**'s first novel, *Confessions of a Polish Used Car Salesman* (Hijinx Press, 1997), is in its second printing. A Pushcart Prize winner, he has published more than 80 stories in magazines such as the *Virginia Quarterly Review*, the *Yale Review* and the *Missouri Review*. He teaches a fiction writing correspondence course for the University of California Berkeley. **Eve Wood**'s poems have appeared in the *New Republic, Poetry, Antioch Review, Alaska Quarterly Review, Best American Poetry,*

1997 and other journals. She wrote the chapbook *Paper Frankenstein* (Beyond Baroque Press, 1998) and *Correspondence*, which was published last year in Europe. She is the recipient of a Jacob Javits Fellowship in creative writing and a Brody Grant from the California Community Foundation. **Susan Wood** is the author of two books of poems, *Bazaar* and *Campo Santo*, which was a Lamont selection of the Academy of American Poets. She teaches at Rice University. **C. Dale Young**

is a physician at the University of California at San Francisco. His poems have appeared in the *Paris Review, Ploughshares, Poetry* and elsewhere. His first collection of poetry, *The Day Underneath the Day*, was published by TriQuarterly Books in the spring of 2001. **Dean Young**'s books include *First-Course in Turbulence* (University of Pittsburgh Press, 1999) and *Strike Anywhere* (University Press of Colorado, 1995), which won the Colorado Poetry Prize.

Prairie Schooner
has a long tradition of
publishing the best
contemporary writing
available.
As *Literary Magazine
Review* says, "Prairie
Schooner rolls along,
avoiding the quagmires
of fads and schisms,
steadfastly defining the
American idiom."

We're old but
we're not stuffy.

NOTRE DAME

REVIEW

A FIRST-CLASS LITERARY
magazine

The Notre Dame Review is an independent magazine of contemporary American and international fiction, poetry, and criticism. Each issue takes on big issues, showcasing celebrated authors like Nobel laureates Seamus Heaney and Czeslaw Milosz as well as new voices. If you want to be engaged with contemporary literature, this is the magazine for you.

recent contributors

Susan Bergman
Robert Hahn
Richard Elman
Eavan Boland
Seamus Heaney
Robert Hass
Richard Burns
David Wojahn
Robert Creeley
Paul Muldoon
Ed Falco
John Peck
Michael Martone
Charles Simic
and an interview with
National Poet Laureate,
Robert Pinsky

subscriptions
(two issues/year)
$15 (Individuals)
$20 (Institutions)
$8 (Single copy)

Send check or money order
to: The Notre Dame Review
The Creative Writing Program
Dept. of English
University of Notre Dame
Notre Dame, IN 46556

or visit us at
http://www.nd.edu/~ndr/review.htm

Subscriptions

Three issues per year. **Individuals:** one year $24; two years $44; life $600. **Institutions:** one year $36; two years $68. **Overseas:** $5 per year additional. Price of back issues varies. Sample copies $5. Address correspondence and subscriptions to *TriQuarterly*, Northwestern University, 2020 Ridge Ave., Evanston, IL 60208-4302. Phone (847) 491-7614.

Submissions

The editors invite submissions of fiction, poetry and literary essays, which must be postmarked between October 1 and March 31; manuscripts postmarked between April 1 and September 30 will not be read. No manuscripts will be returned unless accompanied by a stamped, self-addressed envelope. All manuscripts accepted for publication become the property of *TriQuarterly*, unless otherwise indicated.

Reprints

Reprints of issues 1–15 of *TriQuarterly* are available in full format from Kraus Reprint Company, Route 100, Millwood, NY 10546, and all issues in microfilm from University Microfilms International, 300 North Zeeb Road, Ann Arbor, MI 48106.

Indexing

TriQuarterly is indexed in the Humanities Index (H.W. Wilson Co.), the American Humanities Index (Whitson Publishing Co.), Historical Abstracts, MLA, EBSCO Publishing (Peabody, MA) and Information Access Co. (Foster City, CA).

Distributors

Our national distributors to retail trade are Ingram Periodicals (La Vergne, TN); B. DeBoer (Nutley, NJ); Ubiquity (Brooklyn, NY); Armadillo (Los Angeles, CA).

Publication of *TriQuarterly* is made possible in part by the donors of gifts and grants to the magazine. For their recent and continuing support, we are very pleased to thank the Illinois Arts Council, the Lannan Foundation, the National Endowment for the Arts, the Sara Lee Foundation, the Wendling Foundation and individual donors.